THE BOOKS OF ALEXANDREA

THE BOOKS OF ALEXANDREA

Book 3: The Library

JH NADLER

ISBN 978-1-7370098-7-0
Library of Congress Control Number: 2023914979

Cover design | Jason Nadler
Cover photo of the Author | Laura Nadler
Illuminated Letters | William Morris, public domain

Printed in United States of America

Published by WorkingCat, Inc
Wading River, NY 11792

Visit **jhnadler.com**

For Laura
My navigator and my true North.

Chapter Ninety-Nine

lex gasped as her ears popped. A moment before, she was in the Library—close enough to Jeremiah to feel his body heat—and then she wasn't.

The sudden, jarring change reeled her senses, throwing each one in another direction. She raised her arm to defend her eyes from the battery of blinding daylight.

Recollections of Jeremiah's memory lingered like ghosts seared in her eyes. It haunted her. Watching the young Jeremiah murder the beautiful woman was a startling recollection on its own, but the lie it told seemed not in the deed but the scope. Who was she? Did killing her give Jeremiah all his powers, or something more? Why had he seemed concerned that she had seen such things that he intentionally avoided touching her again?

As her eyes adjusted from the heavy darkness of the Library, her surroundings offered her no clue as to where she was.

The tall wall of windows to her right was brighter than she'd seen in hours. Glare burned her eyes from the highly polished, dark stained wood plank floor. A plush white throw-rug anchored a steel and glass contraption that served as a coffee table, sitting before a sleek white leather sectional. Beyond the window, New York City sprawled in panoramic beauty, a view much wider and significantly higher than she saw from Susan's apartment. A fire gently burned in a sleek chrome fireplace mounted into the wall to one side. Behind her, a narrow kitchen and dining room enjoyed the continuation of the view. A cocktail shaker lay askew on a square white towel beside a martini glass, the chilled, clear liquid frosting the outside.

Beside her, Abby hunkered. She looked frightened by the way she clung to her book; her jeans and muscle shirt clashing with the cool elegance of the apartment.

And then Alex remembered in all painful details, asking—no, demanding—that Abby break her oath by reading from Jeremiah's Book. To send them here: To kill Matthew.

Her brain was still catching up; whether it was an effect of the spell or a result of instantly transporting between locations, she was still shedding expectations of her former location. Rose. Heather. The Book Club. They'd been devastated; Betty and Donna were dead. Colette and Lydia taken to the Farm to be tortured, probably turned into Books—those human-like golems who were completely loyal to Jeremiah. Heather…. Just thinking of her aunt was like forever falling into a lonely abyss. She'd swallowed Heather's coin—had it shoved down her throat. She knew Heather now with the intimacy of the self. Leaving Heather an empty husk, a zombie, a fate foreshadowed by her brother—Alex's father—Peter.

They were all gone. Gone from sight. Left with Jeremiah. Abandoned. Probably all dead if they were lucky, suffering inhuman torture if they weren't. Alex would likely never learn what happened to them. Would never see any of them again.

Alex cursed her predicament. To save them she had to leave them. In leaving them, she sealed their fates. She cursed her weakness, vowing never to leave those she loved to Jeremiah—if, that is, she ever had the opportunity again. Although he would—had—killed them, it was her who had left them. To leave them, she lost her Familiar. Giving Abby back her freedom was not the triumph Alex had anticipated. She felt their bond break the moment Abby read Jeremiah's Book. Like learning a once close childhood friend had died tragically, Alex's sense of loss was both great and distant. She suspected that for Abby, that wouldn't be true at all.

Alex cursed herself. She'd lost. Jeremiah had beaten her. Left her no one. Looking into Abby's eyes, Alex saw the truth that made her regret her every decision. He may have left her Abby, but she lost her herself.

Chapter One Hundred

"Swanky digs," Abby whispered. "Where are we?"

The answer gave Alex chills. *This is where Matthew lives.* "Get behind me, Abby," Alex warned.

"Why?" Abby looked for whatever Alex warned her about. Nothing was there; yet.

Alex huffed at Abby's non-compliance. They were in danger and she felt more responsible for Abby than ever. "Abby, get behind me: we're at Matthew's." Alex fretted his surprise attack. It seemed impending and unavoidable.

"Where?" Abby looked around again. As though Matthew's name cleared the fog of confusion from Abby's brain, panic bloomed across her face. Her Book thudded to the floor, the pages springing open briefly as it bounced on its spine and fell, closed. Abby followed, dropping to her knees with a sob.

Alex's chest thudded ferociously; Abby's clatter startling her into believing the attack had begun.

"All of this," Abby whimpered, "he told me about all of this."

"Who?"

Their eyes met. Alex's sharp with inquiry, Abby's wide and soft with apology. "Peter. Your father described this place to me once."

"He was here." Alex stated, not sure she whether she meant it as a question.

"He never said it was *Matthew's* apartment."

Alex couldn't understand if Abby felt betrayed. That Peter worked with Matthew was something she grudgingly accepted. She couldn't escape the fact that they now stood in this sleek apartment while Jeremiah probably slaughtered Rose and the others. She struggled to take a full breath, so heavy was the weight of that notion. *They're okay*, she lied to herself over and over. At this point, only a lie could sustain her. They went to the Library because of Matthew: Their deaths were his fault.

Alex turned slowly, looking for doors and rooms where Matthew might be lurking. *Does he know we're here?* She wanted to leave, to get Abby to safety. A small part of her looked forward to Matthew's appearance. She thought of how she would confront him, the accusations she'd hurl with her spells.

Abby shivered. "Peter worked with *him*, here."

Alex wanted to know more, but her guard was up. They should be searching for him and not waiting for him to wander in. "Abby," she hissed, "get behind me. Now."

Abby meekly placed herself as directed.

"Matthew?"

Abby cringed, shushing her.

Alex scanned the doorways leading from the room. "Better he knows we're here than comes out and startles." She thought about their encounter in Oblivion when he told her how to get to the Library. There was something almost civilized about it. Now she understood how he set his trap with deception. *Will he be surprised or is he expecting me?* She doubted Matthew was cunning enough to anticipate anything like this.

"Matthew? It's Alex. Jeremiah sent me. Are you home? We should talk."

There was movement from behind the door, past the kitchen. The sound of someone putting something away—or taking something out.

"Did you hear me? Matthew? It's Alexandrea. Come out."

The door handle slowly tipped down. It held there.

"I'm opening the door, Alex," the door muffled Matthew's voice. "I have my Book, but it's closed."

Alex couldn't help but laugh. It was like telling her the safety was engaged on his gun: He was still armed.

The door crept open. Matthew's face craned around it as he peered, his neck crooked and twisted.

He crossed the threshold into the kitchen; paused. Behind him, Alex caught a glimpse of his office, the furnishings from a more ornate and elegant time.

"Jeremiah sent you? You came from the Library?"

He worked with Peter. Alex took a chance. "He killed Heather."

Matthew's momentary expression confirmed Alex had made the right call. He handled the news as though it had been a fifty-pound sack she tossed to him without warning. It nearly sent him reeling.

Matthew grit his back teeth. "Tell me what happened," he said as though searching for clues.

"No."

Matthew looked hurt by her refusal. "You don't get to tell me what to do, Matthew. You told me I would save Billy by going there."

Matthew steeled himself.

"If you won't talk, then neither will I."

Behind her, Abby was unsuccessfully muffling her sobs. She wiped tears like her eyes produced them inconveniently.

Alex's doubletake took her eyes from Matthew, but he didn't take advantage of her distraction. Like her, Abby's outburst came as a surprise. As Matthew said, "What happened to her," Alex asked, "What's wrong, Abby?" Before the words came out, Alex knew.

The question burst the dam holding Abby's emotions. Abby wailed, tears spilling down her cheeks as she dropped to her knees. "I'm so empty, Alex. It's all gone. My love is all gone. I thought I could bear it, but the emptiness hurts and it keeps getting bigger and bigger. I can't endure it, Alex." She took a quaking breath and glared at Alex. "You have to help me."

As Alex asked, "What do you need me to do?" Matthew asked, "What did you do?"

Abby's voice was small when she replied, "Please give it back. Or kill me."

"What happened to your Familiar?" There was panic in Matthew's voice.

"Please." Abby clasped her hands as she scrambled on her knees, clutching fistfuls of Alex's shirt to beg, "Ask me to take the oath. Please, I need to feel the love again."

Alex didn't know what to say. Matthew stood beside her, agog. "You let her break her oath?"

"Alex made me do it!"

Matthew looked between them. He gasped. "Why would you do that?" He pointed at Abby. "What is the point of having a Familiar if you release her?" He looked up at the ceiling, pulling on the salt and pepper tufts of hair over his ears. "What do we do now? He never said anything like this would happen."

Alex turned from Abby, feeling callous as she freed her shirt from Abby's covetous clutch. "See what you've done," she accused Matthew. "Heather and Abby. Betty and Donna. Colette and Lydia and Marta."

Matthew shook her accusation away. "There are always casualties in war. But this? You don't know what you've done, Alex."

For a moment, Alex felt on the defensive. His accusation demanded justification. She started to speak but held herself. She understood what the oath did to Abby. It was slavery where both parties could believe they weren't complicit.

As much as she wanted to help, Alex wouldn't let Abby's crisis derail her purpose. "Matthew," she aggressed a step towards him. "I'm giving you one chance to explain yourself. Explain it all to me: Why you really sent me to the Library. How you're going to beat Jeremiah. Everything." She glanced back at Abby. "And why setting her free could possibly be wrong."

Matthew looked off balance; Alex's sudden step forward had him on his heels and her barrage of demands tipped him. With a hand pressed to the wall, he stabilized himself. "That's a tall order," he began.

"You're stalling."

He looked slapped. He stood before her like a sulking child, his face suppressing his frustration behind reddening cheeks. "You've seen his power," he said after another moment. "Don't you agree, it must be taken from him?"

Alex nodded.

"Alex," Abby interrupted, "I'm sorry. I don't know what came over me."

Alex tried not to take her eyes off Matthew. She hoped by ignoring Abby, her former Familiar would understand she had picked a hell of a time to fall apart.

"Most people go through life not realizing their dreams are real, so to speak. That we go to this place, where imagination takes the place of magic. Magic is still real there."

"So what?"

"It wasn't always like that, Alex." He used his hands to delineate two boxes. "Here and there. Once they were the same."

Alex squinted.

"It's not just taking magic away from him, Alexandrea. It's restoring the balance of everything."

"And once I take all the Books, you'll take the magic from me to do that?"

Matthew looked away from her, as though her gaze was too intense for him. "I've told you we're on the same side. When will you believe me?"

Alex thought about Jeremiah jamming Heather's coin down her throat. About the agony as her body was twisted back from fire. About all the people she lost. While Matthew luxuriated in safety. His lofty plan never involved putting himself at risk. "When you tell me the truth."

"I haven't?"

"You told me if I didn't go to the Library that Billy would die."

"That was the truth. If you didn't go, he would."

Alex's head exploded in a chorus of chattering whispers. "You lied to me. You knew there was nothing else that would get me to go."

Matthew grinned and looked complacently at Abby. "I've told her since the beginning that I needed her to empty the Library. All I did was motivate her." His tone changed when he added, "He still may die."

Alex wanted to scratch his eyes out. She wanted him to hurt. Still, Matthew always presented her with an odd formality. It held her at bay as though there would be a right time to claw his face and to do so preemptively would be gauche.

"Heather," she whispered. "Betty. Donna. Colette. Lydia. Marta."

Matthew motioned to the kitchen. "Why don't we sit. I was making myself a martini. I can make two more." He backed up a step, as though unwilling to yet turn his back on her. "It will help calm your nerves. You need to relax."

"Heather. Betty. Donna. Colette. Lydia. Marta. Heather. Betty. Donna. Colette. Lydia. Marta." She closed her eyes to picture them as she whispered their names, repeating them like a chant.

"Something you want to tell me?"

"They're dead because of you."

Matthew looked unimpressed. He walked to the kitchen, his rubber-soled slippers gripping the shiny floor, each step peeling like a sticker.

The emptiness that opened in Alex's chest felt vast enough to suck this reality into it. *Why would he care? They're just another knuckle to break with his little hammer.*

Matthew made his way to the kitchen. Stepping behind the peninsula, he pulled a bottle of gin out of ice hidden beneath the counter. His motions were slow and serene. Alex couldn't decipher what her gut was trying to tell her to do. She was so tired. Tired of fighting battles she'd never win. Tired of the manipulations and humiliations. Jeremiah let her think she was powerful and then proved her power meant nothing. Matthew possessed none of Jeremiah's arrogance, yet, without so much as a spell, Matthew had cornered and disarmed her.

She watched as Matthew watched her, his crooked neck making him arch his back awkwardly. Suddenly, Abby rushed forward to take a stool. Matthew leapt back, perceiving Abby's act as the start of an attack. He tried to place the bottle down, fumbling to summon his Book. The bottle exploded on the tile floor. Alex held her breath. She didn't want to overreact. But she also didn't want to be the one casting the second spell. This felt like a duel; a flinch would make them both draw their weapons.

Matthew blanched, grabbing at the peninsula, the broken bottle crunching under his backpedaling footsteps as he crashed backwards into the stove. His eyes widened as Alex forged forward, a fury.

Matthew appeared his Book. Alex snapped her arms out to her sides. A blooming arc of glowing plasma crackled as it leapt between her fingertips, sizzling the air.

Matthew again backed into the stove, trying to distance himself from the blinding material as it swayed magnetically in the air, undulating side to side as though balanced with will alone.

Alex had never produced so much power before. This wasn't lightning, this was matter, glowing ferociously. Unlike lightning, it wouldn't fly from her fingertips. This she'd have to guide. This she'd wield willfully. She edged forward, the blinding light casting hard reliefs of Matthew against the wall, finding amusement at his expression as he realized he'd lost and there was no returning from this.

Abby screamed.

Alex cursed the distraction, knowing Matthew's only chance was to exploit it. The quick flash of her eyes became a captured stare as Abby disappeared into darkness.

Without a second thought, her plasma discarded to the floor like a splash of molten steel as she leapt to catch Abby's wrist. As wet fire whipped across the floor, sizzling the air, Abby's momentum was already too great to stop, and darkness consumed Alex's entire world.

"Not Alex," were the last words—spoken by Matthew—she heard.

Chapter One Hundred and One

Alex floated in darkness.

I've been here before. Too recently. This was her third visit to Oblivion. The vast, endless emptiness, the sense of being in constant spinning freefall still elicited its own kind of terror.

"Abby?"

Where is she? She hadn't released Abby's wrist, but only saw her own hand, curled in an empty grasp. Reaching with her other hand, she heard an "Oomph," smacking Abby's face.

"I'm here. I feel you holding my wrist. And smacking my face. Why can't I see you?"

Alex pulled Abby closer. Alex's fingertips confirmed they faced one another. "Do you see anything?"

"Just myself. Is this what Marta went through?"

Alex understood the fear in Abby's voice. Alex muttered, "I never flipped my coin dark. That's how I get out."

"Can't you just flip it now?"

Abby had a point. *If I get out, can I take Abby?*

The last time I was here.... As though summoned by her thought, the field appeared. The field Matthew created when he told her to go to the Library to save Billy. *That turned out well.*

The field established a sense of up and down. Vertiginous sensations vanished. As though flying were second nature, Alex stretched towards the ground.

The field drifted closer. Abby asked, "Is that a house?"

Their feet landed on dark ground just before the lawn. "There you are," Abby said before gesturing at the house. Alex remembered Matthew wasn't visible until something connected them, as the dark ground now did with her and Abby. The ground; a fantasy they both believed in enough to stand upon.

Stretching out before them, the green grass of a gently sloping hillside led to a house. Sort of. *The house wasn't here before.* Possible explanations terrorized and thrilled Alex. Perhaps Matthew had returned. Perhaps someone else was here.

The house was little more than a lopsided yellow square, fenestrated with several lopsided blue windows and a red door. A red-roof triangle resting above it. Curls of gray smoke hung frozen in the air, ascending from a red square chimney. Above it, a tight yellow spiral with radial arms floated in a patch of hastily scribbled blue.

"It's like a child's drawing."

Alex nodded. It was eerily like a child's drawing. Yet there it was, as real as any house she'd ever seen, however flawed and childishly rendered. She stepped; the grass cracked underfoot.

Startled, Alex knelt. Unlike Matthew's creation, this lawn was a collection of thousands and thousands of unique blades of grass, as though drawn with crayon; elongated green triangles, stiff and firm and sharp enough to draw blood from her inquisitive fingertips.

"Who did this?" She put her fingertips in her mouth. She told Abby about the lawn Matthew made, showing her the dots of blood on her fingertips.

Abby asked the question Alex was thinking, "Who made the house?"

"Answer unclear."

Abby took a loud breath, "I'm sorry, Alex." Alex let her eyes ask, *For what?* "I can't help it. It just hits me, one minute I'm fine and the next, all I feel is absolute emptiness."

Alex didn't respond; forcing her eyes to linger on Abby's face. Abby needed her, but she hadn't had the ability to be there for her. Grieving felt indulgent amidst such dangers. And not just for Heather. She might never discover what befell Rose and the others. But Abby needed her now. Needed her to listen and to understand. Alex put aside her pain and concerns and bade Abby explain.

"Being your Familiar gave me something and it's gone. Every little thing I did for you gave me that feeling, and now nothing does," she sobbed. "It's overwhelming." She hiccupped, "I'd rather die than not get it back."

Now? Just the thought felt callous. So did wanting to tell Abby she was overreacting. "Abby," Alex rubbed the others' shoulder. Heather's memories showed her the truth: Being a Familiar made Abby her slave. "I can't imagine how you're hurting. And I don't know how to make it better. I still need you. I need you to be strong if we're going to get out of here."

In a piteous, child-like voice, Abby said, "You could ask me to take the oath again."

The thought horrified Alex. "Never, Abby. It made you my slave."

"It made me happy."

"No." The word felt final and cruel. She embraced Abby. "Let's get out of here and we'll work to make you better. I love you so much and you've always been there for me. Once we're out, I'll do whatever I can."

"It's not working, Alex."

"What?"

"You're trying to hug me to make me happy, like you did to Heather. It doesn't work; not anymore. Never again. I used to feel that any time you asked me for something. Pure bliss. Now it's gone."

Alex lowered her arms. "I'm sorry, Abby. I don't know what else to say."

Abby smeared tears across her cheeks. "If you can't ask now, then tell me you'll think about it."

"What good would that do?"

"It would give me hope."

Abby sobbed in the extended silence.

Alex bit her lip to hold back her first response. "I'll think about it."

Abby's face brightened. "Really?"

Alex lied, "After we're out of here, I'll give it a lot of thought."

Her face brightened more. "A lot?"

Alex nodded.

Abby shook her fists in the air. "I'm gonna be your Familiar again! I know it! You won't regret it. We'll be so happy together, you and me."

Alex rubbed her eyes, trying to hide her tears. "We will be happy, won't we?"

Abby grinned like a naughty child promising to be good the night before Christmas.

Alex didn't know what else to say. She'd lied enough, and lying to Abby, especially, made her miserable. She needed a minute to let the choking guilt and the pain subside.

The last radial arms of the crayon sun disappeared unexpectedly below the distant lawn, as though it had dropped. It was rapidly replaced with a green "C": the moon. The ambient light was unchanged, however, whether the sun or the moon claimed the sky.

Abby's expectant eyes bore into Alex. The longer she waited, the deeper she feared Abby's stare would penetrate. *Is she wrong? After everything she's done for me, is it wrong to not honor her one request? She's an adult. This is what she wants.*

Abby beamed. A promise was all it took, for now. She took Alex's hand. "Let's check out the house."

They circumscribed the dangerous lawn, their view of the house never changing, as though its never blinking face followed them. Whatever created it—friend or foe—was likely inside. At this scale the rough edges and uneven lines reminiscent of a child's drawing gave the bright colors a sinister undertone.

Closer to the house, Alex pointed out blue scribbles on the lawn. "Look, steppingstones."

With trepidation, Alex stood on the first one. She'd seen enough movies to expect poison darts or some deadly or ridiculous booby-trap. The first one took her weight without sinking or clicking or starting some timer of doom. They were haphazardly spaced and sized and shaped, but they led to the front door. "Come on," she waved to Abby as she hopped to the next.

Abby followed a steppingstone behind her.

The yellow sun leapt into the sky as if sprung there, hiding the moon. *Someone has no concept of time*. Alex hopped to the next stone.

Closer, the hand-drawn detail revealed the outline of each shape—the wall, the roof, the door, the windows—were uneven, the lines intersecting and overlapping at the corners. Haphazardly scribbled color filled the interior incompletely. Everything about it reminded Alex of a child's crayon drawing.

Reaching the front door, standing on a blue square large enough for them both, the house had texture that resembled wax crayons laid down on the texture of paper, with skips and curls and an unevenness that suggesting whoever drew it pressed too firmly. With caution, she touched the wall. It was coarse and solid. If she ever imagined encountering a crayon house, this would be how she expected it to feel and smell.

"It's amazing," Abby pried a small piece from of wall and studied the waxy yellow curl. "How is it here?" She motioned like she was drawing in the air. "When I was little, I had a book about a kid who could draw reality with a crayon. Do you think it's like that?"

In the small gaps between the chunks of wax wall, Alex saw the rest of the field, as though this was but an inch thick façade and nothing more. "I don't know," she said absently. She rested her hand against the red door. Color aside, there was nothing different about the door than the house. A yellow line delineated the doorframe and a red line the door. Jarring scribbles colored them each in. *Does it open*? She didn't see hinges but pushed anyway. *This is ludicrous. I can see right through it.*

The door slowly opened, swinging inward.

Neither had anything to say. Although the door showed through to the field, the doorway revealed an interior. "I think this is what gob-smacked means," Alex said.

"Should we go in? I vote no."

Alex wasn't sure what she thought. Her brain struggled with the optical illusion of an entire house within this thin wall. What was before them was in such a state of chaos she wasn't sure what she'd stumbled upon. A tremendous foyer with a grand staircase faced them. The walls were a collection of doors. A second-floor landing circumscribed the room at its middle, twice as high as Alex could reach. This was no child's drawing; this was an actual, solid interior with straight, level, and plumb lines. To one side of the staircase, an immense pillow fort, complete with suspended flashlights, covered a ridiculously large couch. Sheets tied to the stair rails made the tarp-roof, and oversized, square, brown pillows with large tan fleurs-de-lees, the walls.

To the right of that, a sandcastle was half-collapsed on a pile of golden sand. A yellow shovel and red bucket lay half-buried beside it. A red sailboat with a white sail bobbed in a small pond complete with croaking frogs.

Alex's eyes felt bombarded. Everywhere she looked she saw another vignette. A tire hung from a knotted rope. A slide spiraled from the second floor. A mud puddle surrounded by hand and footprints; mud-cakes stacked beside it. Swings. Crawling tunnels. A campfire and a teepee—*a campfire*—inside the house. It was like a collection of childhood memories. *But whose?*

Alex took Abby by the wrist. They stepped inside, closing the door behind them.

Outside, the air had a waxy crayon smell from the house and field. Inside, however, smelled of fire, of mud, of beach, of the sweet burnt smell of roasted marshmallows. It was alive with creaking ropes and rotating tire swings and croaking frogs.

Wistfully, Abby said, "I can't decide if its adorable or creepy."

Alex voted for creepy. *Who lives here?* The steppingstones didn't shoot poison darts, but this was feeling more and more like a trap. This place was so unknowable—so bizarre—that Alex felt unprepared for anything that might happen. Curiosity battled caution in her brain. She wanted to explore, hoping who—or what—ever lived here was friendly and kind, to meet them and learn how they created something to insanely amazing. And yet, she worried that this was the crayon version of a gingerbread house where the witch waited for hungry children. *Witches aren't like that.* She thought of Heather's version, recalling both Rose's explanation and Heather's distant memory of telling it to her young daughter.

"Halt! Who goes there?"

Alex spun, her heart banging against her ribcage. The shouting voice was a false baritone, like a woman impersonating a man. It was familiar; a hint of an accent; but Alex couldn't put her finger on it....

Side-stepping down the stairs, a tall, very thin person wrapped head to toe in aluminum foil armor—helmet, gauntlets, and all—carrying a cardboard sword, called out to them, "Who dares enter my kingdom?" The foil knight flailed the sword in a threatening circle above their heads. "Speak or I will cut off your heads!"

"Where the hell are we, Alex? What's going on?"

"No idea," was all Alex could say.

The tall person, crinkling in foil, finished stomping down the stairs. "Are you friend or foe?"

Alex had seen some crazy, amazing things recently, but she kept wanting to give her head a knock to dislodge the tumor causing these hallucinations.

"Has someone cut out your tongues? Speak!"

Alex figured she'd best play along and said to the cardboard knight, "My name is Alexandrea. Alexandrea Hawthorne. But call me Alex."

The crinkling knight lowered its sword. "Alex. I know that name." The Knight reeled back, "Alex? It's really you?"

The voice gave Alex chills. "Marta? You're alive!"

Marta peeled her foil helmet off and dropped it to the ground with her sword. She tore off her gauntlets and embraced Alex. From over Alex's shoulder, Marta said, "Good to see you, too, Abby."

Alex said, "We all thought you died."

Marta made a face. "I thought I died, too. I floated in darkness for the longest time. I lost my token—I mean coin. It just floated away."

"Matthew ate it."

"Ate it?" Marta looked like she suffered heartburn from the thought.

"It does things. Revitalizes the eater. Gives them the memories of the person."

Abby made a noise.

"You sound like you speak from experience," Marta said.

Alex couldn't look Marta in the eyes, "Heather."

Marta gasped. "Did Matthew make you do it?"

Abby laughed.

"What's so funny?"

"Marta," Alex explained, "there's worse people than Matthew. He's called Jeremiah. We lost tonight. He destroyed the Book Club."

"Book Club," Marta said, her face sobering as realization dawned. "They're all dead?"

"Heather, Donna, Betty, yes. Colette and Lydia are missing. Taken and probably dead by now. We had to leave them behind. With him, so who knows if they're okay."

Marta collapsed on the stairs. "I can't believe it. All of them?"

"It's horrible," Alex confessed.

Marta nodded. "How are you here?"

Alex sat beside Marta. Abby joined them, sitting between their feet. Alex told Marta the abridged history of what happened since her disappearance. Beginning with the Library. How she rescued Rose and got magic. Billy jumping off Picnic Rock with Matthew. Meeting George, all burned up and learned about Jeremiah. The fight in the field. Sara and Rose and the Book. Lesedi and Banhi and Kholwa and Yeswhere on The Between. Going to the door in the city. The labyrinth. Burning the Books. Jeremiah and Book and all that happened in the Library. Arriving at Matthew's apartment and falling into Oblivion.

Marta's face was slack. "How are you alive?"

Alex had no answer. *Luck? Sheer will? Part of Jeremiah's plan for her?* "How aren't you, you know, a zombie like my dad was? What is this place?"

Marta looked around as though she'd never seen it before. "It's his head."

Alex was confused. "Who's *he*?"

Marta spoke slowly, as though deep in thought. "I'm trying to process things I have in my mind. I haven't had to put my experience in words before."

"Okay," Alex said. *I can't wait to hear this.*

"Heather told me about what your father did, untwining you. How much do you know about that?"

Alex witnessed the event from inside Sara. "I'd say I know enough to follow whatever you're about to tell me."

"It's so complicated," Marta clutched her head. "The scope makes my head ache."

Alex put her hand on Marta's knee. "Take your time."

Marta took a breath and let it out slowly, "I fell in and floated around. Lost my coin. But instead of losing everything, something happened. This *thing*, this *entity,* came to me." She paused. "It was a consciousness, nothing more. A mind. I think it figured out I knew you. It kept sticking its—I don't know what you'd call it, it didn't have a body, but it was like it put its fingers in my head and squeezed my brains. It pulled information out of me. Eventually, I understood the questions it was asking, and it didn't have to squeeze my brains so much to get answers."

Marta's face twisted as she struggled to find words to explain what happened.

"I gave myself over to it—to him—and he to me. I learned what he knew. He didn't have words. His thoughts were symbolic. He couldn't tell me a story, so he swamped me with emotions." She addressed Alex's perplexed expression. "When you encounter a curved oval on a stick, you know it's a spoon because you know what a spoon is and you have a word for it, even if you've never seen *that* spoon before. If you've had neither the word nor the experience, every spoon is alien. You won't see their similarities because they're outside your understanding. He gave me his thoughts and I gave them context."

Alex nodded. Not because she understood, but because she followed. It reminded her of her father nodding at Sara.

Marta continued, "Your father took your brother out of your mother's womb and blew him away."

Alex recalled the tiny black speck as it swirled in the air, disappearing. Although she saw what had happened, truly understanding what Peter had discarded made Alex sick that she hadn't felt anything about it in that moment.

"That was part of Matthew's plan. He collected the spot. Nurtured it, fed it." Marta held her arms out. "This whole dark universe; it's all him, Alex: Your brother."

Chapter One Hundred and Two

Alex felt dizzy, as though asphyxiating. "My brother?" She'd been a twin for all of a few weeks, barely even a speck and here was Marta explaining that he's the entire dark universe she'd been trapped in.

"He saved me. There was no getting out; there was nothing to get out of; I only existed in his world." Marta explained, "I tried to teach him, but he can't learn. He isn't a body. He isn't a child. So, I shared my emotions. I explained what his memories meant, and I shared mine with him. Then, one day," she craned her neck, as though trying to resolve something too distant to see, "the field appeared. Everything changed. We had things, not just thoughts."

Alex felt frozen by the realization. How one inconsequential moment can give rise to something so spectacularly important. She was there when Matthew created the field to give them a thing to stand on. She wondered how many equally significant moments go unnoticed all the time.

"Suddenly we understood there could be things and that I could teach him. We played. We colored. We created. He and I made this house. Each door holds a memory I shared with him. I did with him all the things I thought a boy would want to do."

Alex looked at all the doors. Alex thought about all the times she was jealous of Rose and Billy's relationship. *I have a twin brother.* "How can I meet him?"

"He's here," Marta tapped her head. "I'm Alex."

Abby spoke up, "What are you getting at, Marta?"

"Alex; that's the name Holly gave him." Marta's eyes twitched. "Calling him Alex will just confuse things when I talk about you."

Alex argued, "But that's his name."

"Not really." Marta tapped her head again. "He doesn't have his own body. He isn't a person, just a gob of wordless memories and experiences and feelings. We share *my* body; he's more of a repressed personality I can access. Like a hazy memory of one drunken night at college."

Abby thumbed the staircase, "What was the foil knight act about?"

Marta grinned. "I was teaching manners through chivalry. We were playing."

Alex had to ask, "Does he remember me?"

Marta considered. "He remembers another heartbeat. Each person who fell in, he hoped to rediscover who that was: the only other person he's ever known. Somehow, he pieced together that I knew you, and he kept me."

She shivered. "It isn't like he knows you, Alex. He just knows he lost something that meant something to him, and he's got it back now."

Alex couldn't help but smile. "Is it okay if I hug you, Marta? Would that be like hugging him?"

"To him it would," Marta teared up. "He's happy you're here."

Embracing Marta, Alex was besieged by a million thoughts and emotions. With everything that has happened in the past few weeks, this was a triumph. "I feel like I should say something to him, but I don't know where to start."

"He knows," Marta said. "He knows everything I know, and I know a bit about you."

Alex grinned, wiping her tears. She recalled Heather's memory from the hospital after she tried to untwin her children and failed. Marta was the first member of Heather's Book Club. She knew Billy visited Heather. Marta probably knew everything Heather knew.

After Alex let go, Marta rubbed Abby's shoulder. "You look different," she told Abby. "Sad, I mean."

Abby's eyes teared again. Alex thought, *Not again*, and hated herself for it.

"I broke my oath," Abby said as Marta gasped. "It's okay, though. Once we get out of here, Alex promised she'd ask me to take it again."

"I said I'd think about it," Alex said before she could check herself.

Abby nodded. "Same thing."

Alex wouldn't correct Abby, but felt she was forcing her into a position. *Tell a lie enough and it becomes the truth.* Alex tried to avoid glaring at Abby, but in this moment, she resented her. *Is this who she really is or is she so desperate she'd lie to get what she wants?* Either alternative was troubling.

Abby cleared her throat, "I hate to put a damper on the reunion, but I have to ask: How do we get out of here?"

Marta fingered the stair rail. "I think I can convince him to let you go."

"Convince him?" The notion worried Alex. "Why does he need convincing?"

Marta's voice saddened. "He just found you." She looked up, her eyes shiny. "It's not like he thinks these things, Alex. They're just feelings. I think about you leaving and became sad. It's lonely here and while I've been adjusting to a place where he and I can interact and play, for eighteen years, darkness is all he's ever known."

Alex thought about that seemingly trivial moment when her father removed what was barely a fistula from her mother's womb. Her muscles tensed just thinking about Matthew taking that and raising another child—

as he stole and raised George—to be a tool or a weapon. *I need to say something to her—to them—but what words will be powerful enough to make a difference?*

Abby scratched her eyebrow, "It sounds like you're not coming."

Marta shook her head. She pointed at her chest. "I don't have a coin." Her voice quivered as she fought back tears, "Besides, he needs someone to teach him about the world and how to be a boy and eventually a man. He's barely capable of interacting with your world because he doesn't understand what he sees. Matthew has been the only interaction he knows, and he's learning he doesn't like it."

"Marta," Abby pulled herself to her feet. "I never thanked you. You pushed me out of the way. You saved my life." She bit her lip, her eyes searching for the next words. "There's got to be a way; I can't lose you to the dark again."

Marta took Abby's hand, holding it a moment. "Missing me and losing me are two different things. I'll be here. I'll teach him. One day Matthew will summon him, and we'll take Matthew instead. Once he's here, I'll let Alex," she pointed at her head, "deal with him."

Abby asked, "You want to stay?"

"Whether it's fate or destiny or just, crap, I don't know, bad luck, it's where I am. People rarely get to choose their fate."

"This sucks," Abby paced between the stairs and the door. "Can we help, maybe? Stay a little while and play or try to teach him some stuff?"

Marta's mouth elongated into a thin smile. "You don't have to accept this, Abby. You and Alex have a much more important fight out there." She pointed with her chin as though just outside the door they'd find the place they came from.

"Marta," Alex pulled on the banister to stand. "Let's just say you had a coin. Like, let's say someone got thrown in and you could take theirs."

Marta's eyes widened, "I wouldn't feel comfortable stealing a life like that." She thought a moment, "Although, I guess it depends who it is."

Alex grinned with one corner of her mouth. "Let's say you were okay with it."

Abby asked, "Who are you thinking? Matthew?"

"*Who* isn't important," Alex said. "Let's get past the who and discuss the what."

"What's the what?" Marta looked at them both.

Alex gestured at Marta, "I need you to tell me what could happen if you got a coin?"

Marta pursed her lips and scratched her head. Her eyes glassed for a moment. "I mean, this is my body." She gestured at herself. "If I had a coin, I could pass from here to reality."

Alex humphed. "Just you?"

She poked her forehead. "He's in here. I'm pretty sure I'll take him with me."

Alex looked around, "What happens to all this? Will this place cease to exist or stay behind?"

Abby asked, "Does it matter?"

Alex comprehended the source of Abby's impatience. *The sooner we get out of here, the sooner she thinks I'll ask her to take her oath again.* "It does matter." Alex turned to Marta, "I think it might be important," she said. "What happens?"

"I was hoping you wouldn't ask me to explain this," Marta laughed bitterly. "It's mind bending to think about. This place—not just the house, but the whole darkness—is an entire unexplored universe. This is Alex—your brother. Right now, he doesn't want to leave this place I created, *this house*, but there's a whole world out there for him to create. Everything here, everything you see, the house, the campfire, the frogs, even you and Abby—right now—are in his head. He's in my head. You're here with me. Maybe when we leave here, all this stays in our head," she pointed between her eyes. "Really think about that, Alex. You're in him, his spirit, his mind, whatever you want to call it, his consciousness. He's getting to know you better than he ever would, had he been born. He knows the version of you right now that you barely know yourself."

Alex nodded. She had no clue what Marta was talking about, but she was willing to follow, "I think I get it, but…."

"Yeah, me neither," Abby confirmed.

Marta took a deep breath. "You think we all live in the same place. Like we're all together. We interact, we connect, we touch. You see someone walking down the street and assume you're walking down the same street. But that's not the same street. The person that's walking is not the same person that you see. We believe we all live in a shared universe. There's something that separates you from you from me," she pointed around. "Your head is so full of sensation and emotion and thought, yet you can't even get the most basic sense of what's going on in anyone else's. Everything inside is completely unavailable to everyone else. Why do you think that is?"

Alex shook her head. Abby laughed, "Are you gonna tell us?"

"Look around, guys," she gestured to the room. "Everything that's here, everything that's not but could be by just imagining it, this entire universe is *Alex*. We're in *his* universe. It's a collection of his experiences, of everything he knows and feels. It's what he is. Until recently, it was empty." Marta watched them intently, waiting for them to catch up. "He is a universe, and before you were inside him, you were alongside him. Get it?"

"No," Alex said blankly. She felt like her fingertips kept bumping her mind's ability to grasp this concept a little further away. The moment she thought she understood, she realized she didn't.

"Each one of us is inside our own universe. Our world. Our experience. Our feelings. Our reality. We touch one another, that's how we know that other people are here with us, our experiences overlap. But it's more like we're inside of soap bubbles. Sure, we touch and cling together. We connect, we touch, we love, we hate. But we're always separate. What exists inside your world, your reality, may be really similar to other people's experiences, but it will never be the same. You can never experience what someone else experiences, even if you have the same experience because you're in separate soap bubbles. Always separate, for as long as we live."

Abby asked what Alex was thinking, "And when we die?"

Marta shrugged, "I guess you have to do it to know."

Messages from the universe. Alex felt like she'd achieved an epiphany. Like Marta revealed the reality of the universe to her. She pictured people in their own soap bubbles moving about the planet, bumping into one another, the bubbles attaching, momentarily sharing a common edge, but still separate. Like that woman she saw crossing the street when they first arrived in New York City. Just looking at her, Alex could tell she had a story, from the large portfolio she carried, to her clothes, to her purposeful stride. And yet, she was unknowable. *She's out there now, going about her life, but because I can't see her anymore, she doesn't exist in my universe.*

Abby laughed. "I wonder what my universe looks like."

Marta grinned; her point made.

Alex took the silence to consider her next steps. She knew what she wanted to do, but it was too easy for Marta to decline, claiming the sacrifice too great.

Alex concentrated until she felt her coins glow, just below the glass charm Abby made for her. She opened her eyes and took her coins into her hands. While Marta and Abby watched, Alex gently pried them apart. Normally, she'd turn them around and snap them together. Instead, she held one out.

Abby and Marta asked simultaneously, "What are you doing?"

"I can't take that," Marta's hands raised as though deflecting an accusation.

"Yes, you can," Alex said. "You're not taking it from me. You're taking it *back.*"

Marta processed silently. Maybe it was her brother thinking.

"This is *his* coin," Alex told them. "I've kept it safe. It was never mine to keep."

With great hesitation, as though struggling against substantial weight or gravity or uncertainty, Marta took hold of it. For a moment they both held the coin.

"Are you sure?"

Abby asked, too, "Yeah, Alex, are you sure about this?"

"Please," Alex whispered, "it belongs to you. Always has."

"Alex, think about this," Abby hissed. "How are you ever going to *hide*?"

Marta hesitated, her fingers not releasing the coin, but Alex could tell they might. "You have to be certain, Alex. I can't—we can't—if you aren't absolutely certain."

Alex smiled. "In one act, I bring you back to life and get my twin brother back."

Chapter One Hundred and Three

arta's mouth warmed into a smile. Alex couldn't put her finger on what about her looked different. She waved a finger around Marta's face, "Is that Alex?"

Marta eyes glistened. "He's never known this feeling," she said. "It hurts, but in such a warm, wonderful way. You're bringing us back to life. How are we supposed to feel about that? It's too big to accept."

Concerned Marta would withdraw her hand from the coin, Alex stepped closer. "Take it, Marta. There are no strings attached." Alex winced at the poor choice of words, her own sparkling silver thread connecting the coin in her hand to the one glowing in her chest. "Alex might only know the way Matthew treated him, but this will let the two of you make your own destiny. Please. Take it and let's all go home."

Watching Marta's cues, Alex surrendered the coin. Her fine silver thread still strung between them. Marta held the coin close to her chest "Whatever destiny we have will be with you."

As Marta pressed the coin to her chest, her own thread connected her to it.

Like the release of pressure from a soda bottle, sensations flooded into Alex. Too much came too fast to untwine. These weren't emotions, these were raw, unprocessed sensations, feelings untranslated by experience and intellect. For one moment, half an eye-blink, she and Marta and Alex broke their soap-bubble wall. For that whole moment, they were no longer separate, but singular, sensations and thoughts freely traded between them. Then Alex's thread dissolved in the air, abruptly severing the connection. The sensations evaporated. It was all too quick, and she felt lesser for losing it. Stirring in the fading echoes, Marta and Alex's fear and joy and loneliness and hope touched her in their rawest states. Unlabeled and lacking comprehension, they existed as twists in her gut or flutters of her heart. Alex wondered if they experienced hers and if she made their stomachs twist and their hearts palpitate.

Marta pressed her hands over her heart, concealing her new coin, tears welling. Her entire face grinned. "You are amazing," she told Alex. "Thank you for this," she looked at her coin and back at Alex, "and for that. Wow." Marta stared but a moment longer, as though in awe.

Alex took her by the shoulders, their first contact since being one, and for a fading moment, she was certain she understood what her contact meant to Marta and her brother. With a stutter, Alex said, "It's time for us to go."

Marta looked around. "Say goodbye, house."

Around them, the house and everything in it brightened, every surface shining with light. Alex expected things might spin, but before anything moved, she stared out large windows overlooking the Manhattan skyline.

The juxtaposition left her dizzy. She grabbed at the white leather sofa to still herself.

Marta and Abby stood near the kitchen; the floor between them scorched: Her spell dropped when she disappeared. *What a shock it must have been to Matthew, to have me vanish and my destruction linger.* Marta and Abby were recovering from the same motion sickness settling in Alex's stomach. She waved them over. Without hesitation, they came.

Abby looked nervously about the room. "Where's Matthew?"

Marta looked around. "This is Matthew's apartment? Fancy digs."

Abby huffed at the modern sterility, "Couldn't you tell?"

Alex nodded to answer Marta's inquiry. "I don't know where he went. We've been gone, what, six, maybe eight hours?"

"That wasn't nice," Marta hissed to herself.

Alex didn't like Marta's tone. "What's not nice?"

She gave Alex an apologetic look. "He wanted to have you for as long as possible. He slowed time down."

"You can do that?"

"In your own universe, you can do anything." Marta looked sheepishly away. "It's been a week."

The idea shocked Alex. She recalled the rate at which the crayon sun rose and set and rose. *Was that really a day? It felt like an hour.* Anything could have happened in a week. *If Rose escaped the Library* was compounded by too many other *what if's* to contemplate. Alex's stomach soured. If they had escaped, after a week everyone would assume that she had died, or worse, ran away in fear.

Abby asked, "Do you think Rose and the others got out okay?"

"I really wish I knew." Color drained from Alex's face as she voiced what she'd been thinking, "If they did; it's been a week, Abby." She felt chilled.

Abby uttered what Alex was thinking, "By now they think you're dead."

Alex whined, "I have to find out. To tell them. Come on. Rose needs to know that I'm okay, that I didn't abandon her. What if Matthew's gone to them, to replace me with Rose."

"There's no need to rush," Abby soothed. She held Alex firmly by the arm. "Ask me."

Alex's head was so consumed with thoughts of Rose and the Book Club that she asked, "Ask you? What?" As soon as the words left her, Alex realized what Abby meant. As Abby replied, "To take the oath," Alex blurted, "No," and saw the power one word possessed. It struck Abby worse than any spell Alex might have mustered.

Abby moaned, "You promised—"

"I promised *to think* about it, Abby," Alex interrupted. She half-pitied, half-resented Abby, but her tone carried only the latter. "Once we got out. We're out. I promise I'll start thinking about it."

Abby's eyes welled with disdain, cutting Alex to the bone. Never had Abby asked anything of her. *This one thing is all she wants, and it's too much. But she'd be happy. It's not real joy. She'd be my slave. But it's what she wants. Don't I owe her that? Is thinking she's happy as good as being happy? Can I be morally right and still be wrong? Can I live with myself if I ask her?*

"It shouldn't be a hard decision, Alex."

"Abby, I'm sorry. I can't. I need time to think about it. I love you too much." Of everything troubling Alex's mind—what happened to Rose and the others—the more Abby pressed, the more she resented her.

Abby shook her head like she was clearing water from her ears. "If you loved me, you wouldn't have to think twice."

"Abby, please," Alex pled. "Don't do this. Not here, not now. Matthew—"

"Guys," Marta said, pointing to a doorway beyond the kitchen, "Someone's coming."

Alex heard it too. She would confront Matthew. She would resume searching for Billy. But before any of those things, she needed to know what fate befell Rose and the others. If they were alive, it was fine if they thought she was dead. Once she knew Rose was safe at home, if Carrie and June and Rachel and Nancy were alive, that would be enough for her to face Matthew. But Matthew was the barrier to that knowledge. He was moments from entering the room, perhaps startled to see them after a week, and then they would fight. "I'm fucking tired of this," she muttered under her breath.

Electric bolts flicked from Matthew's fingertips as he cleared the doorway from his bedroom, startled by the sight of intruders. His anger melted to shock, then to horror as realization set in who the intruders were. Sparks sprayed the three of them, burned the back of the couch, and shattered one of the large panels of glass overlooking the city, letting in wind and a din of urban noise.

Alex winced at the burn on her arm, the voices in her head shouting. Abby sprawled to the ground, knocked hard by the strike to her abdomen, landing on her backside, her feet splayed in the air.

"Get behind the couch," Alex cried to Marta as she turned to face Matthew. "We're not doing this," she told him. "I need to go home. I need to know the others are okay."

Matthew looked at her like she was speaking backwards. "You're not going anywhere. I have a surprise for you." He regarded his Book. Then he saw Marta and stared.

If Matthew was the door she needed to walk through, so be it. She would fight Matthew; she would pass through him to get home.

Alex raised her hands, static dancing across her skin like glowing cactus spines.

Alex primed her emotions. Everything was unknown. Did Rose survive the Library? What of the others? Did they have news about Colette and Lydia? Had Jeremiah lied to her and slaughtered everyone she loved once she was gone? She didn't know. Couldn't know. Until Matthew was out of her way.

Alex's vitriol rose like a storm surge. Instead of the flotsam and jetsam of the sea coming to inundate the land, what came on this rising wave was all her contempt. It swelled her shoulders, rounding them. It pulled her arms forward. It scowled her face. Matthew saw it and backpedaled—skidding on the polished wood floor—into the office while trying to read from his Book. The explosion of heat from Alex's fingers shattered the wall and the doorway as she screamed his name.

The dissipating waves of heat shot through the room as plaster and beam collapsed around the bedroom doorframe, the wall and parts of the ceiling shattering. Before the debris had settled, still falling in chunks and billowing clouds of dust, Alex charged into the wreckage. With a fling of her hand, a howl of wind plowed the debris against the far side of the room. Her eyes hunted Matthew.

The closet door shuddering open, revealed his hiding place, as a lightning strike threw her to the wall, her right side in blinding, searing pain.

"We don't have to do it like this, Alexandrea," Matthew shouted. "We're not enemies, you and I."

Alex regained her bearings. She ached. Her blackened shirt threatened to stick to the moisture her raw and blistered skin oozed. Her neck and back wrenched tears to her eyes as she stood, drywall and plaster dust falling from her like fine snow. Her ears rang with an electronic squeal, too loud to make out the words her brain was trying desperately to decipher.

"No one is coming to help you," Matthew warned. "The whole floor has been protected. No one has heard a sound." Then Matthew read.

With an explosion of blinding pain, like a thornbush was yanked through her arms, the room lurched and spun. She wanted to grab the wall, the floor, the ceiling, as they spun past, to stop the movement as the sudden and unexpected strike threw her, crashing like a ragdoll, into the kitchen.

"Please, Alexandrea. Hear me out. It doesn't have to be this way."

Alex lay still, certain at least some of her bones were broken. Her hands trembled from the pain that rattled through her body and shook her stomach to the point she wanted to throw it up. Pressing her hands to the ground to push herself up, she was shocked her arms didn't buckle at some new joint.

"I didn't think you were coming back," Matthew called. He looked at Marta again as he spoke to Alex. "You fell into Oblivion, and I waited all night."

"Sorry I took my time," she groaned. Gritting her teeth, Alex pushed herself up. Her trembling legs threatened to turn into jelly, but they held her. She tried to hold the countertop, but her hands hadn't the grip.

Matthew peeked from behind the wrecked office wall. Behind him, dust blew in the disrupted air, pieces of drywall, light fixtures, and wiring hung like old party decorations. "Alexandrea, do you understand what I'm saying?" Seeing her look in his direction, he ducked away. "It's been a week. I resigned myself that I'd failed. I thought my whole plan was over and I didn't have any options left."

Chills ran through Alex's body. She'd read about endorphins, but never felt her brain flooding her body with them. "I bet you can't wait to smash my hands to get your magic."

Alex sought Abby and Marta. Turning her head was excruciating. Marta's forehead peeked over the white sofa. Abby was on the far side of the sofa by the fireplace, her Book in hand. Marta whimpered, "When can we go back to the house?"

"Stay down," Alex hissed. "I'll keep you both safe."

Matthew leaned from the doorway, "How do we resolve this?"

"Once I know the others are okay."

Matthew shook his head. "I can't let you leave, Alexandrea. Not yet."

Deliberately, Alex faced him. They could keep fighting until they brought down the building. Or she could accept his truce, and nurse her wounds, and stop feeling pain, and take a moment to hear his promises. It was enough time to get Marta and Abby somewhere safe. Maybe she would never learn what happened, but they would. Every time she trusted him, it turned out worse for her. She couldn't know her Book Club was safe until Matthew was no longer in her way. She was done. There was no time to deliberate. Her anger felt like a kettle, too long on the boil.

"I'm going home!" She tried to conjure a response. Matthew screamed as the office floor heaved up like ocean waves, splitting boards and tossing furniture into the air as if they were cotton balls. The shock wave blew drywall from the back wall like breath blows dust from a book. Only metal studs and tangles of electrical wires delineated Matthew's apartment and the common hallway. Dust swirled in the air as it descended through the broken floor to the spaces below.

She could think of Rose and imagine her safe at home, in bed. She could also imagine her twisted body at the base of a bookcase in the Library. Both felt equally possible—equally real. Her chest ached, buoyed by hope, smashed by doubt.

There were no signs of movement amidst the settling collapse. "You okay, Matthew?" she asked rhetorically, hoping he wouldn't answer. Her taunt felt unnecessarily cruel, but she didn't care. Her entire body trembled. Her whispers roared like an erupting volcano.

She shouted to the rubble, "I am going home. If you don't want me to leave, then toss your Book to me."

Silence.

Marta and Abby crept from hiding. Abby muttered, "I don't think he's coming out. Ding-dong and all that."

Alex turned to caution Abby.

Matthew lurched into the open. Abby's face at once turned pale and blue. "I wouldn't," Matthew warned, his spell read. He countered Alex's sudden movement with a single, pointed, "Don't!"

Abby clawed at her mouth like she was trying to hold her throat open from the inside. Marta was at her side, trying to discover the cause of Abby's strangulation.

"I'll kill you if anything happens to her," Alex screamed as she ran to Abby. "Leave her alone."

"I can't, Alexandrea. Not until we declare a truce."

Marta's face was white with helplessness. She communicated with a single look there was nothing she could do for Abby, whose wheezing inhalations sounded like a poor attempt to whistle. "She doesn't have long," Marta urged.

Alex squared off to Matthew. She hadn't the need to marshal her emotions, already sick with worry. *Abby's going to die thinking I hate her.*

"I'll crush her throat," he warned, scowling; red rivulets ran like tears down his abraded face. "I'll be dead, but so will she. All I'm asking is for you to hear me out."

Abby's eyes bulged as Marta forced her fingers into her mouth, digging for an obstruction. Alex kept waiting for a, "She's okay," that didn't come.

Alex felt trapped. She was prepared to obliterate him, but what good would it do if she lost Abby? *As many as it takes*, Banhi had told her, but when those she loved were the expendables, she couldn't bear to lose even one.

Saying the words was like vomiting and holding the bile in her mouth. "I'll stay. Let's talk." Abby wheezed. "You have my word!"

Abby's eyes swam in her head; she was moments from unconsciousness.

"Your word isn't good enough," Matthew threatened. "How can I trust you? No one is as good as their word."

She wondered if he was as worried about her going back on her word as she was of losing Abby. "Stop, please," she said in a hushed voice. "I can't lose her. Please, I don't know how else to make you believe me."

Matthew turned his attention to Abby, who gasped a breath and collapsed. Marta rolled her onto her back and held her head to open her airway as she gulped breaths.

Alex put her hands on the countertop, fingers spread, palms down. "Is this what you want, Matthew?" She motioned to her hands, ready for the hammer.

He rubbed his face with his forearm, smearing dust and blood. "That's not what we need to discuss." His awkwardly bent neck leading the way, his strut duck-like, passing the kitchen and entering the living room, his back to the closet-lined alcove leading to the front entry.

He ushered her, "Why don't you come out from the kitchen? Here, sit," he patted the sofa, "let's talk."

Chapter One Hundred and Four

s Alex left the peninsula, she noticed people gathering in the hallway, staring through the dusty rubble that had once been an office, gasping and pointing. Someone called to her, "Is everyone okay in there?"

Matthew raised his voice, "We're all fine here. Everything's fine. It was just a gas leak or something. You should go." Concern flashed across Matthew's face. Addressing the concerned interlopers, he hissed at Alex, "Is this how you want to lose to Jeremiah? Because we cannot see eye-to-eye?"

"Okay," Alex offered, stepping into the living room, approaching the sofa. Matthew's raised hand alerted her she had come far enough. "What now?" she asked, weary he was bluffing to get her to lower her guard.

His lips twisted over his teeth as he contemplated what to say. Finally, he spoke, "A plan must be adaptable to any situation, Alexandrea. The plan was for you to take all the Books from the Library. But you didn't, did you?"

Would bluffing serve any purpose? Abby was recovering, and right now that was enough. "No," she replied.

Matthew rubbed his furrowed forehead. "It doesn't matter, then," he told her. "Without all the Books, there's no defeating him."

"The Books aren't the source of his power," Alex repeated what she'd been told.

"I'm impressed you came to that conclusion on your own." Matthew reacted by stepping back, the tension between them crackled like electricity. Each time she moved, he countered, like a dance or a chess match. "But I believe taking them all might give us a chance to defeat him."

"You believe?" Alex was aghast. "All this on *You believe* and *might* and *chance*?"

"It's stronger than belief," he said, almost as though convincing himself. "It's true belief. Blind faith. It *is* true. I *know* it is. I'm not the first man seeking to take his power away, not by a long shot. Each failure guided the next man's attempt, getting him a little closer to success."

Marta cradled Abby. They intently watched the exchange. Alex watched them and him.

Matthew started speaking again, but Alex interrupted, "What is this all about, Matthew? What are you waiting for? What's your big surprise? How are we on the same side? Just reveal your evil little plan and be done with it." Without taking her eyes off Abby and Marta, Alex retreated to the windows, where she stood, the wind blowing her hair around.

Laughing, Matthew placed his hand on his chest. "My evil plan? Alexandrea, everything I've done, even what I've done to you has been in the service of the greater good. Taking magic away from Jeremiah. Protecting it. You'll see soon." He looked at the clock on the wall beside the fireplace. "It's time."

"For what?" She panicked, but Abby's countenance hadn't altered.

"For my surprise. The big reveal. I keep my promises. I am returning William—Billy—to you."

Alex's heart leapt. For the first time she felt close. *Billy?* She wanted desperately to believe he was telling the truth, but Matthew had lied too many times. She tried to make herself disbelieve, but it was like stomping on wrapped presents rather than opening them and potentially being disappointed. She asked, "What's the catch?"

Matthew's tone sounded sad, like they'd reached the end of their conversation and he still had more to say. "I keep my promises, Alexandrea. Only through trust can we know truth. But the outcomes we seek rarely come with the results we desire."

Alex checked the clock. Nearly six. She found her patience had an expiration measured in seconds. Waiting bored even her whispers. She was strong, probably strong enough to dispatch Matthew, but could she find the right emotion to keep Abby breathing? Until now, she allowed the emotion to dictate the spell. What left her fingers wasn't always what she expected. She'd learned to associate certain spells with the emotions that conjured them. Lightning and heated anger. Wind and a mix of frustration and rage. Should Abby die, would she still be able to defeat him? How would her breaking heart alter her conjuring?

She hadn't thought of Rose, until recognizing that she hadn't. If she could have Billy back—if Matthew was being honest this one time—then it was worth the wait. She couldn't stand the tension of anticipation. Which Billy would be returning? The child she lost at Picnic Rock or the man who visited Heather at the hospital all those years ago. Which didn't matter.

All four startled when two near-simultaneous pops momentarily reversed the flow of air through the window, popping their ears. It wasn't as loud as being too close to a firecracker, but it had the same effect. Having two people appear in her vision, filling emptiness, made her brain feel like someone was squeezing it. Realization caused her heart to stomp on the floor of her chest at the shock of seeing George standing beside Matthew and beside him....

Alex recognized him. He was there, in her bedroom, ensuring she took Matthew's Book before returning to Picnic Rock. He was in Heather's memories, visiting her in the hospital. Judging by his clothes and condition, he'd just left her there. From Heather to Alex in a moment, but seventeen years apart. She couldn't take her eyes off him, seeing Billy—her cousin, now older—and Heather's son—her son. Parsing Heather's memories from her own were nearly impossible. She understood how much this moment meant to Heather, because she felt the overwhelming relief in her chest. But she also felt the overwhelming terror to be this close to him, but still in grievous danger. Anything could happen to cut their reunion short. To prevent Billy from ever coming home.

She swallowed to unclog her ears as he said, "I'm so glad to see you, Alex. I have so much to show you."

George smiled at her, "Hi Alex."

"Billy." It sounded like a question, and in some ways it probably was. It was her ultimate confirmation that Heather hadn't been duped; this man was the boy she knew.

He nodded with an impish grin she recognized right away, the child hidden in the older face. "It's a good day to see you. The right day. It's been a very long time."

Her heart swelled too big for her chest to hold it. *Billy! Billy's back!* She couldn't wait to bring him to Rose. In a flash, she imagined his reunion with Rose, with Heather, getting him home and safe and waking up tomorrow pretending none of this happened. For once, Matthew didn't matter. Jeremiah didn't matter. All that mattered was Billy finally returning home.

Then she remembered. Heather was gone. There'd be no joyous reunion.

Billy was easily ten years older than he'd been when he disappeared, a week ago. Alex could just hear her frustrated cousin complaining he'd lost ten years of his life because Alex failed him—if Rose survived the Library.

Billy and Matthew shared a glance. It possessed the familiarity of old friends. Billy, his face glowing with joy, looked at Alex.

Alex forgot all about Matthew; all about George. Her arms out, she leapt towards her cousin.

He raised his arms as though to hug her, but his hands instead grasped her by the shoulders. This was no embrace; he was keeping her at a distance, pushing her away. He tipped his head up to the ceiling. She followed his gaze, anticipating something bizarre or dangerous lurking above.

Suddenly, Matthew's arm lurched around Billy's shoulder, then flinched away. Billy looked shocked as he inhaled frantically. Then, all at once, a gaping grimace opened in his throat, spraying frothy, bright red blood as he exhaled and crumpled into her still extended arms.

Matthew disappeared out the door.

Chapter One Hundred and Five

illy collapsed into Alex, her hope, her excitement at finding him collapsing with him. He crumpled, slamming to the ground without bracing himself. Then he was still. Alex's insides twisted into her throat, her stomach rolling as she watched, waiting for the revelation, the gag, the moment the stunt was over and none of it would be real.

Abby covered her mouth in shock and disgust. Marta hid her eyes. George, eyes wide, face drained by fear, backed against the wall as though it was his only stability. Matthew hadn't looked back as he disappeared through the front door. The bloody knife sputtered on the floor where it lay, dropped.

Incoherent thoughts raced through her brain, the screaming voices in her head drowning them out. She dropped beside Billy. Her hand replaced his, pressing the gash. She wrapped her hands around his throat like she was choking him, the wound grinning like an opened mouth against her palm.

Hope abandoned her. Her insides felt like they evaporated, leaving her a hollow sack of formed skin, crumpling to the ground.

Billy, no. Please Billy. She didn't know which words she spoke aloud, and which were thoughts screaming inside her head. *Hold on, Billy. Please don't die. I just got you back. I can save you. I can heal you. Please. Please stay alive.*

She pulled him closer, to embrace him, to heal him.

His white face. His purple-blue lips. His shock-wide eyes looking at everything and nothing all at once. She pretended this older man wasn't Billy. But in his face, the little boy's fearful expression tore her heart in two.

She tried not to think about what was happening. That her hand tried to silence the bleeding mouth on his throat. That her clothes soaked in his warm, wet blood. That he was gone.

Marta and Abby spoke, but her grief made their words incomprehensible.

Closing her eyes, she struggled to replace the sensations—the soaking clothes, the body in her arms—with images of the child this man used to be. Billy. The boy. Her cousin. His limbs thin and knobby. Completely ungraceful. Walking to the park. To Picnic Rock. Almost three weeks ago. His excitement. His bright eyes. How she loved him. How she adored him. He was the sweetest boy. Sitting in his and Rose's bedroom, joking. The laughter. The joy. They were so happy. She could hear him laugh, his giggles tingling in her ears. Laughter making her heart race.

She pulled him tighter. Her eyes squinted closed. *Alex*. She pressed her face against his, her muscles tensing as she pulled him tight, making sure *Alex* there was no room between them, no *Alex* gaps, so that every *Alex* inch of her *Alex, please*, was in contact *Alex* with every inch of….

"Alex!"

Jarred back to the last place she wanted to be, she was about to ask Abby *what the fuck she wanted at this moment* when she saw.

The child, steps away, one pudgy hand resting on its slightly bent, dimpled knee, its sad expression tempered by its other reaching, covetous hand.

Alex absently licked her lips, flooding her palate with the chrome taste of blood.

"It's okay, Alex." The voice was Billy, the adult, the man who Matthew called William, half-sitting from his pale, twisted body. His coin glowed, the thread between it and his body also crisscrossing the room over a dozen different ways like a glowing spiders web.

His body slipped from her and lulled listlessly. Surrounded by her bloody handprint, a thick, gory scar replaced the once gaping wound. *I healed him and he's still dead?*

"It's okay," he repeated calmly. He touched her hand, not leaving a mark. "I knew," he soothed.

"It's not okay," her eyes welled. "I just got you back."

He touched the coin on his chest.

"You can't Billy," she whined and didn't care how it sounded, how wet her eyes were, or how her nose ran. "I can heal you. I can fix this. I can make it all better."

"I know you can," he said. "But not today." In his extended hand his glowing coin illuminated his palm.

Her eyes locked with Charon's. Her last encounter with the child nearly resulted in her death. She convinced the two men who had attacked her and Abby to retrieve their Books from the burning basement. Charon did not take her intervention well, becoming the Reaper. Had she not darkened her coin, she was loathe to consider what it would have done to her. She wondered if Charon remembered.

The child tipped its head, as though unsure who was hiding under the stain of blood. Sudden realization sneered its lip. Realization withdrew its demanding hand. Realization ripped its skin and shredded its folded rolls of fabric as it deformed into hulking terror, with razor claws and bones decorated with scraps of ancient flesh and bleached fabric.

Alex blanched: it remembered.

The Reaper reached for Billy's coin, its slashing talons whistling the air.

Alex jumped to her feet. "Get back in your body," she ordered.

"Look out, Alex," Marta and Abby and George all screamed at her.

Grinning at the Reaper, she grabbed her coin. A damp chill ran down her back and through her bowels: Her single coin. It was so easy to forget that by returning her second coin to Marta she sacrificed her ability to hide from the Reaper. Panic grabbed her like worm-laden hands. Her arms raised to protect her face from the brunt of the reaper's slashing claw.

Her guts twisted with stinging anticipation of grievous injury as the bony paw raced through her flesh. Her hands trembled. Realization established a firm conviction as the Reaper's hulking form inched forward: She no longer fought just for Billy's life.

She retreated to avoid the next slash, tripping over her cousin's body, knocking him about as though he were a rubbery doll. Back to the wall, she had nowhere left to go.

With a breath, she throttled her fear. If she were to confront the Reaper, she could not fear it. Her cousin was dead. Her aunt was a zombie. Her friends murdered or missing. Death hunted her. This creature always claimed its coin. Alex's hatred and anger boiled inside her.

She whispered to herself that she was unafraid.

Lightning struck the skeletal nightmare. It withstood her attack, unmoving. Her emotions rising, her anger balling her hands into fists, the bolts of energy were joined by more and more until her fists disappeared in the radiance of hundreds of sparking, snaking, charged bolts of lightning. The Reaper thrashed in the thrall of energy, its bones groaning, its hollow insides a nest of arcing electricity. Finally, it inched back.

A new resolve filled her. She claimed its abandoned ground.

With one hand she struck her cousin's body, holding firm. With one thought, she summoned the thud of a heartbeat.

Lightning, thunder, wind. As she unleashed each spell against the nightmare, watched it shudder, watched it wince, she felt her fire growing. She stared Death in its eyes, and it flinched.

Three sparks whizzed past her, bright illuminations that joined the growing orange glow fading from her sight. Two struck Abby, one shattered another window, sending a giant pane of sparkling glass to the street below; more wind and city noises intruded.

Furious at the interloper, a ball of plasma grew in her hand, heavy and dense. The blinding orb cast wildly dancing shadows on the walls and bright, shuddering rectangles on the buildings across the way. Abby appeared her book and muttering gutturally, threw sparks of her own.

The man lunged at Alex. Her spell was not ready, but she let the monster have it. Hot, glowing light splashed on the Reaper and dripped between bones, charring them, sizzling the remaining bits of flesh and fabric to carbon. The room quickly dimmed. The clawed Reaper scurried back a step, writhing at the heat and the dripping fire that oozed from one rib to another, glowing embers within them popping and snapping like burning firewood.

"Alex, quick, let's get out of here," George had his Book in hand and joined Abby launching a barrage of sparks at this other man.

Behind Abby, Marta was holding her head, tears rolling down her face, like a terrified child. Bolts of energy sizzled past or struck too close, and she howled in terror, hunkering behind the sofa.

With one hand, Alex conjured heartbeats. *Come on, Billy, come on.* Struggling to manipulate two spells at once was proving difficult as her attention could only manifest one spell at a time. The continuous battle stilled Billy's heart as she produced jagged bolts of lightning, sparking and snapping whips of light, that danced between her and the thrashing terror. Then again back to her cousin. The play of emotion exhausted her. Agony of loss, hatred of death. Pain. Rage. Fear of confusing them required intent, fierce concentration.

The creature inched forward when her attention reverted to Billy. Then again. And again, until she'd lost all gained ground. She skipped a few beats and with screaming resolve, her lightning and shock waves shattered bones.

Fighting was futile. With concentration, she could bring Billy back to life. Or she could repel the Reaper. But not both. The clinking death fought closer one missed spell after another. Then she'd knock it back, then a beat. The monster gained more than it gave. She was losing on both fronts. She skipped a heartbeat and unleashed her frustration and anger.

Struck by another spell, Alex saw Abby and George trading spells with the intruder, a man who looked like he'd wandered off the street but was practiced with his Book. Battling two against one, his hardened face bleak with determination, he made Abby and George suffer for their loyalty to Alex. Whenever he tried to attack Alex, however, their injuries never slowed their response, keeping his attention well placed on them.

The creature retreated, its battered form fitfully trying to escape Alex's spells.

This won her confidence. Another heartbeat; her own chest pounding. Wind whipped through the apartment as sparks streaked across the room, from Abby and George to the intruder and back. A revelation struck her like another spell: back in her bedroom, one of Matthew's men pushed Matthew's Book to her. *Matthew thought William was his man, but Billy was working against Matthew to keep me safe.*

The connection hit her with stunning force; her hands losing purpose. At her feet, her dead cousin, the boy she knew, had been there, protecting her. She heard his words from that first day at Picnic Rock, *I try to protect you*.

The Reaper charged, slashing. Inside her head, voices gurgled and drowned as though the wounds were more than to her body.

Wounded, she scurried backwards, bravery escaping her. Lightning withered at her fingers, no longer troubling the Reaper. For each inch her retreat gained, the monstrosity closed two. She'd never noticed the stink of its rotting bone, the chocking decay of the flaps of mealy flesh. The scents assaulted her likewise, as though with fantom claws the creature reached into her skull and made the nauseating stench unassailable. The creature exuded heat, likely from her spells. As it closed on her, as she could only see the apartment through the cage of its ribs, as it swallowed down her last morsel of courage, as it cornered her against the wall with no hope of escape. She wiped perspiration from her forehead with trembling hands, and as her fitful stomach calmed, fate settled upon her.

Through the prison of ribs, Abby and Marta and George stared back at her. Hope abandoned them, too. The room filled with utter dismay. They steeled themselves. Unprepared to witness the Reaper dismember her. The new intruder hadn't yielded. Her friends suffered his attack. No longer fighting back. In her last moments, she feared witnessing the intruder take her friends apart.

The wall against her back. The skeletal form before her. Alex, trapped. Billy, half out of his body, frozen, waiting for Alex to join him among the dead. Their mouths all moved. Silent cries, as though her brain couldn't waste energy on hearing, as though their terror was too great to allow them sound.

The Reaper's clawed, bony hand pierced Alex's abdomen and pushed inside her. She had never experienced pain of its kind; the intense pressure, the burning, the screaming nerves. The slightest movement an agony, like her insides were scraped out with a rusty spoon. She couldn't so much as groan. The creature hunkered down, the grinning clench of teeth studying her, forcing her to stare into its dark, vacant sockets as it forced itself deeper into her. She felt the compression on her lungs as her feet left the ground, the ceiling lurching closer. It felt like the Reaper was attempting to wear her skin while she still used it.

More sparks, flames sputtered on the couch. Marta cried, struck a third, a fourth time. Abby's face twisted with concern, washed with worry, melted to despair.

The scorched skeletal face studied her, as though it tried to understand why she disappeared before and didn't now. Its empty sockets captivated Alex, demanding her attention. Until she saw Abby.

She was so proud of the way Abby, standing amidst a melee of sparks, turned away from her. She put herself between the intruder and Marta. Abby fired sparking bolts. Alex hung, watching all her hopes and plans fall apart like a bottle of milk knocked from the counter, tumbling on its descent to the tile floor.

Alex groaned, thrashed about as the Reaper pushed itself deeper. Perhaps there was one more thing she could do. Rather than vainly try to save herself or save her already deceased cousin, she attempted one last spell. She rallied against pain to conjure one clear imagination. In her head, she pictured the safest place she knew. It wasn't hard, even with the claw swimming through her viscera. It was where she would be if she could awake from the nightmare. "Go home," she croaked to them. The skull obscured them from her sight. The smoke in the room suddenly pulling towards a common center was her only indication they vanished.

Chapter One Hundred and Six

"No one survives the Reaper, Rose. No one cheats death." Abby's words both demanded and begged Rose to stop belittling Alex's final attempt to bring Billy home.

Rose looked about the room, as though her response to Abby might be found lurking there. It wasn't hiding among the burns on the walls and furniture. Nor with the dead man who had attacked them, chasing Abby and Marta. Nor with George who fought alongside them. Nor with Heather, who had somehow returned to life during the intruder's assault.

Rose's eyes narrowed to slits. Alex was everyone's hero even when she failed, and Rose was sick of it. No one held even one of her successes with half the esteem as they held Alex's failures. At first, Abby's words stung her like another slap. Then the finality seeped in. *She's not saying Alex failed. She's saying Alex is dead.* It didn't seem fair that the one person who was supposed to bring Billy home was never going to come home herself. She pointed at Marta and Heather. "But they came back, couldn't Alex…."

"That's different, sweetheart," Heather stroked Dolly. "I read from a Book. Dolly found me in it and brought me back." She laughed bitterly. "All this time. Always sitting on my newspapers. Witches and their cats." She looked at Dolly, her tone suddenly infantile, "You save witches from Books. You saved me. Yes. You did."

Marta explained, "And I was in Oblivion. Alex gave me one of her coins. Had she kept it, maybe she'd still be alive."

"It's not your fault, Marta," Heather said softly. "She would do anything to save you and Abby."

Rose feverishly searched for proof they were wrong. She expected losing Billy to hurt more than this. She didn't feel like her twin brother was gone. If she felt anything it was contempt over how easily these women accepted it. Even if they believed it—if her mother believed it—if Abby, Alex's Familiar, saw it with her own eyes—it had to be a lie. A catastrophic misunderstanding. Rose wanted to beat her fists against someone to make them hurt worse than she did.

She wanted so desperately to shove their words back down their throats, to call them liars. As the idea came to her head it spilled from her mouth, "I'm going to destroy Matthew. I'll find Billy. You'll see. I'll even find Alex. I'll bring them both home."

"Rose, sweetheart." Abby's words were like the stomping feet of a temper tantrum, "Alex is dead." The air sucked from the room. Her words stilled everyone, burying them like an avalanche.

As though on cue, the child appeared.

Rose jumped at the sight, her heart jack-hammering her ribcage. One of the child's feet stomped the floor. The other dragged. It scanned the room. Abrasions and bruises kept one large, dark eye from opening. With its one hand, it tugged its tattered folds of fabric.

This child was disfigured. Feral in its movements, as though both terrified and ferocious. Rose swirled her hand at her side, fishing for her Book before she'd brought the mist containing it.

Heather waved her hands, *no*, as Dolly, frightened by all the chaos jumped down and ran off. Rose hesitated. Someone had beaten the child horrifically. No toddler should be so abused, and whoever had done it could be following.

Then the child saw the dead man, all its focus narrowed to the body. It took one step, dragging its other leg. Its chubby fingers opened and closed on an upturned palm, beckoning him.

Marta clasped her chest, hiding her now-glowing coin: the coin Alex gave her.

Rose covered her glowing coin as well; the missing edge and spiderweb of cracks casting dark shadows where the glow cast across the floor.

Abby shrank back, her bulk receding, frail and trembling. Eyes flicking through the room, as though judging distances for escape.

Arms trembling from the effort, Heather pushed herself off the couch, using the wall to hold herself upright. Behind her, the dead man rose from his body. He had no coin, no thread. Heather seemed unaware of his presence as she cautiously started forward, her unsteady legs made her look like she balanced on a beam.

"How dare you!" Heather rounded the couch, her fingertips crackling with static. She pointed an accusatory finger at the child.

Rose wasn't sure what was about to happen. Her mother screamed at the battered child, the undead spirit behind her holding out his coin to pay Charon.

The child didn't back away from Heather's threatening advance. Its swollen face wrinkled into what may have been a snarl.

"You took our Alexandrea. You are not welcome in this house," Heather threatened the child with static discharge snapping from her fingertips.

The child's backwards step went unnoticed until its other foot dragged back.

"What are you doing?" It was the man.

"He doesn't deserve to pass over." Heather's voice dripped with disdain. Chiding the child, she said, "Get out of my home."

"What are you doing, Mom?" *I thought the kid turns into the Reaper when it's pissed. What's she trying to do?* Rose wondered if her mother, newly returned to life, was throwing herself on Alex's funeral pyre.

"Please," the man begged. "I was only doing my job. Jeremiah sent me to—"

Heather roared, "That name is not to be spoken in my house!" She turned her disdainful glare to the man. "Just following orders is not an excuse!"

The man withdrew any hope of reply and remained frozen, his hand offering his coin lowering in disgrace or defeat.

"You killed our Alex," Heather screamed at the child, racing tears streaking her reddening face. "And you come here? For him?"

The man edged forward, abandoning his body to the floor. His glowing coin leading his way like a lantern.

The child's eyes focused on the coin with rabid hunger, snatching glimpses of Heather as it limped towards the offered coin.

Heather shrieked, "It's not fair! You can't take our Alex and reward him! He's against us!"

The child claimed their attacker's coin and turned back to Heather. It showed her the coin in its palm. It seemed to be gloating, and yet its battered expression was so matter-of-factly as though it were telling Heather this was how it always ended.

Heather ignored the child. To the dead man Heather hissed, "Get out of my house."

She turned to the child, "Now go! Shoo!"

Abby hid behind her upturned arm, averting her eyes in case the child became the Reaper.

The child half-turned from Heather.

"That's right, keep going!"

With another step, Charon disappeared into mist.

Heather turned to Rose, her chest faint with a glow.

Alex took my mother's coin—where'd that come from?

"What the fuck was that?" Carrie was demonstrating her shaking hands but raced to catch Heather as she collapsed. Carrie cushioned her head as Heather's body thudded to the ground as though dropped in pieces.

Abby and Marta aided Carrie, collecting Heather in their arms and depositing her on the couch.

George hadn't moved from his chair, his palms on his thighs.

"Mom, are you okay? What happened?" Rose wasn't sure she understood what she'd just seen.

Heather reached for her daughter, "Come here, baby."

Rose started forward but paused as though finding conflict between her mother's words and tone. Heather was dead, but now wasn't. Catching her breath, she recalled there was something she was about to do, but action startled it from her. Instead, Rose reluctantly embraced her mother.

"You're all there is," Heather whispered, panting between words. "Everything is resting on you, now."

Rose pulled back, breaking her mother's grasp. "Me?" Finally hearing the words she craved—made her question carrying that mantle. Was her mother telling her it was her responsibility?

Heather scanned the room, taking everyone in before collapsing against the back of the couch, her face pale and dripping perspiration.

Marta fanned her with her hands. "Heather?"

"Give her space," Carrie pulled Abby, stepping away herself.

Heather took a deep breath, swallowing several times. "I'm so weak," she winced. Her fingertips touched her chest. Her coin dim. "There was so little of me in that Book."

Little? Rose picked up her mother's Book and thumbed through it. The pages were all aged and stained, but evidence of ink had vanished. "How are you back?"

Heather pointed at Dolly, who cowered beside the stairs. "Witches and their cats," Heather panted. "That's why they always sit on books. They can't tell whether or not it's one of those," her trembling finger pointed at the blank Book in Rose's hands. "I always found it annoying when I was trying to read. I never realized. Dolly was protecting me."

"I don't mean to interrupt," Abby said, "but what about...," she pointed at the body and George in his chair, making a buzzing sound for each.

Why is she interrupting? My mother was about to explain what happened. Rose paused. *Is that really my mom? There was* another *woman in that Book.* "They're not going anywhere."

Abby tried to say, "But—"

Carrie spoke to Heather over Abby, silencing her, "You mean the cat brought you back?" Carrie gesturing at the cat, the Book, and Heather, "How?"

Yes, how? Rose edged closer.

Heather didn't answer. She stared at Abby as though the two hadn't met before.

Abby withdrew like the stare burned, "What?"

Heather's laugh sounded like a sigh. "There you are, Abby. I've missed you. It's been, what, twenty years? How are you?"

Abby's tears welled in her bloodshot eyes. "My heart is breaking," she sobbed.

Without getting up, Heather summoned Abby over and pulled her into a desperate embrace. "Oh sweetheart," Heather rubbed Abby's back. "I'm so sorry you're not her Familiar anymore."

"I miss her so much," Abby croaked, her face mashed into Heather's bosom. "It hurts so much."

Heather rubbed Abby's back as though soothing a gigantic red-faced crying toddler, "My poor Abby."

"Mom?"

Abby slipped away; Heather acknowledged her daughter with a grin.

Rose felt like the only one in costume at a party. "Why are you smiling at me?"

Heather reached out, "Sit with me, Rose," she guided Rose by her wrist. After rubbing Rose's back, she motioned for the others to join them.

"Are you really Heather?"

Carrie made a face, as though finding chunks in her milk. "Of course it's Heather. What are you thinking?"

Rose touched her chest. "Alex ate her coin." That should have been enough. This woman emerged from a book. "Her coin was gone. Now we're supposed to trust that it's really her?"

Carrie's defensive certainty eroded like a sandcastle facing the encroaching tide. She turned to Heather, silently echoing Rose's question.

Heather answered, "We've each read a Book." She waited until she had their attention. "You give something up to get something back." She motioned at her blank Book beside Rose. "There was a little of me still in there."

Rose's concern registered on Carrie's face, saying, "How little?"

Heather hadn't the strength to laugh. Even her gestures looked weighted with exhaustion. "Like a single symbol in that entire Book." She judged their expressions. "There is an entire Book in each symbol, and an entire Book in each of those. Remember? In each drop of ink, there's everything."

Marta leaned forward, "How did *you* come back from that?"

To Marta, Carrie's tone condescended, "How did *you*?"

Abby gave Marta a knowing glance. She told Carrie, "Alex."

The name alone seemed enough to satisfy Carrie. Her face softened. She eased back in her seat and rubbed her eye like she had an eyelash in it.

The effort to speak nearly overwhelmed Heather. She started twice but never got out a sound.

"Dolly saved you?" Rose wanted to stay on subject. If Dolly made it so Heather didn't need a Book, Rose wanted to understand how. Before she got her hopes up, she needed certainty, which had recently been in short supply.

Heather nodded.

"Wait," Carrie said three times. "That cat pulled you out of the Book and put you back in your body?" She didn't wait for confirmation, "You didn't read from a Book just before; I saw you." She gestured at the door, as though the past lingered there for them all to see, referring to when Heather, springing to life, shot sparks from her fingertips. She added, "You were casting spells. Without a Book. You do that without a Book now? Does anyone else understand what that means?"

The room fell silent. Everyone stared at Heather. Rose had seen her mother shooting sparks from both hands, no Book in sight.

"She did magic like Alex?" George, perplexed, asked meekly.

Everyone turned to George. He shrunk from their stares as though pained by them. He gestured to let them know he wouldn't interrupt again.

Abby sobbed at the sound of her name. Carrie slid closer to her and rubbed her arm to comfort her, "I know. I can't believe she's gone. I miss her, too."

When she had the strength, Heather repeated herself, "Witches and their cats."

"What happens," Carrie speculated, "if we got kitty—"

"Her name's Dolly," Rose interrupted.

"Dolly," Carrie corrected. "Let's say, theoretically, that we got *Dolly* to sit on my Book." Her voice got louder, faster, more excited. "What would happen? Would I get magic, you know, in me? Would I be like you and like… Alex?"

Heather stared, either with intense concentration or exhaustion. She drawled, "Or it would kill you. You saw what destroying the Book did to Betty."

Breaking their brief respectful silence, Marta practically cried out, "Wait, what? Betty died?"

Carrie nodded. "And Donna."

Abby added, "And Colette and Lydia are missing."

Carrie cursed. "That's optimistic of you."

"He took them to that Farm," Abby started to counter. "You think that was just another lie?" She didn't need Carrie's reply to give her confirmation. "Oh dear."

The room fell silent.

Marta's words came out as breath until she added volume to them. "What happened?"

Rose wanted to scream. *Now they're going to spend an hour telling Marta what she's missed?*

Before Rose could speak, Carrie's train of thought barreled forward. "Let's pretend that this is different than what happened to Betty. If Dolly sits on my Book," Carrie bit her lip, nodding, "maybe it'd give me magic. Like it gave Heather. Right?"

"Or it might kill you," Abby repeated.

"Or give me magic," Carrie shouted.

"Or that," Heather agreed.

George raised a hand from his sequestered seat, "Are you sure you only get *you* back and not the other woman, you know, from the Book?"

Rose glared, "No one asked you." *That's all I need, my mother to have another reason to keep me from doing this.* She was glad it was Carrie pressing the issue. Rose was sure her mother wouldn't stop the tattooed chef from taking her chances.

George moved his hands as though trying to deflect each letter of her words from battering him. "Sorry," he withdrew, curled up as though trying to hide himself.

"He makes a good point," Marta mused. To Heather she asked, "Are you sure it's only you in there?

Heather shrugged. She sat quietly as if about to nod off. "If she's here, she's awfully quiet.

Carrie slapped her thighs. "There's only one way to find out." Carrie appeared her Book and tossed it on the couch beside Heather. "Quick, get the cat." She grinned at Rose and said, "Dol-ly." She tapped the Book. "Let's see what happens."

Abby urged caution, "Don't we want to think about this? This isn't something we want to rush into." She looked down. "I don't think I can bear losing anyone else I care about."

Marta agreed, "Maybe we should have a plan."

Carrie rubbed her tattooed arms. "Do I strike you as an impulsive person?"

Abby wasn't sure how to respond.

"It's worth the risk," Carrie finished her thought. "If it works, we can all have magic without Books."

Rose watched each of their faces, waiting for one of them to object. Her Book, its binding torn and twisted, the aged pages crumpled, their creases becoming cuts, was barely held together with clear tape. *That's what happens to books. I'd* have *magic. Just like Alex.* She took a breath. The sensation it brought was like a wave, excitement at the crest, desolation at the trough. *Just like Alex* did. She felt so angry she wanted to cry. Her heart ached. If Alex was truly gone... she refused to take the thought to its logical conclusion. She refused to believe Billy was anything but missing. She hoped something would happen to give her the strength to soar over the mountain of emptiness that was growing in her chest.

Carrie waited expectantly for an objection.

Rose made kissing sounds with her lips and skulked towards Dolly.

Dolly became anxiously alert to everyone's attention.

Rose slunk past Abby. Just as the cat bolted, Rose scooped Dolly in her arms. Dolly squirmed and hissed.

"What is wrong with you, cat?"

Carrie whispered, as though she didn't want to be heard but had to say it, "I thought her name is *Dolly*."

The cat wriggled as Rose brought her closer.

Carrie patted her Book. "Put her here. Quick, please, before I lose my nerve." She shook her fists in the air and squealed gleefully.

Once in proximity of the Book, Dolly fell docile. Rose stood beside Carrie, aware of the heat radiating from the other. Carrie's forehead and neck beaded with nervous perspiration.

She held Dolly above Carrie's Book. "Ready?"

Heather pointed at Carrie, her features balled tight with a constipated mix of terror and excitement. "Yeah. Do it, do it, do it." Carrie gulped, clenching her eyes and tensing her body.

As Rose lowered the cat, Carrie burst, "Wait-wait-wait."

Rose raised Dolly higher. The cat growled.

"If I scream or burn or whatever, please-oh-please take her off."

Rose showed Dolly to Carrie. "Ready?"

Carrie froze, eyes focused on her Book. She squeaked, "Do it."

Rose lowered Dolly on to the Book.

Carrie peeked from her pose like a clenched ball. Dolly paced a tight circle on the cover and dropped into a comfortable position. She looked at the five of them staring back and groomed her front paw, admiring her claws.

Carrie complained, "Nothing's happening."

Marta leaned forward, "Maybe it's one cat per witch."

Carrie groaned, "I am not adopting a cat just to see if this works."

Rose nudged Dolly. "Come on, Dolly, do your thing."

Abby stepped closer. "Are you sure nothing's happening?"

Rose poked Dolly, who swatted her, claws extended. "Maybe she needs to recharge; like it's too soon or something."

Carrie sighed. "Fuck. We tried." She stood. "Where do you keep your liquor, Heather? This girl requires a drink."

Heather was too intent upon the cat to answer. So was everyone, save Rose, who watched the others. Disappointment swirled around Rose. She'd so hoped this would work so she could have real magic. So she wouldn't need her stupid broken Book. She tried not to get caught jealously glaring at her mother.

Heather pressed the cushion beside her. "Maybe you should sit down," she told Carrie.

Carrie lowered herself to the couch. Heather squeezed her knee.

"I know," Carrie's disappointment slowed her speech. "It would-a been so cool."

Rose couldn't understand how Carrie could be so blasé about the most amazing thing possibly not working. She poked Dolly, pushing her. Ordinarily, the attention would perturb Dolly, but the cat refused to move from the Book and hissed.

"Give it more time," Heather proposed. "She's content. Maybe she needs to feel right about it."

She's suddenly an expert on cats? Maybe there's a reason it's not working. What if she's only got one? What if she's only got two and Carrie takes the last one? What if it kills her? She inspected Dolly for signs of an eminent explosion. Dolly seemed perfectly normal.

Dolly just washed her face. Then, with a thud, Dolly hopped from the Book and rubbed against Heather's legs.

Heather slapped Rose's hand away before she could examine the Book.

"What'd you do that for?"

Heather pointed at Dolly. "Let her do her thing before you disturb it."

Dolly sniffed at Carrie's hands. She purred and stood, stretching against Carrie's knee before jumping into her lap.

Carrie asked Heather, "How will I know it's working?"

Heather offered a tired shrug. "It was probably different for me. I felt like I dug myself out of a grave and saw light for the first time."

Carrie kept her hands in the air as though touching the cat would have cataclysmic results. "I wish I knew something was about to happen," she groaned. "I feel like an idiot sitting here." Slowly she lowered her hands and stroked Dolly's soft fur.

Marta pointed, "Cat seems happy."

Carrie agreed. "How long should I wait? At what point is this just, um, Dolly making a warm spot on me?"

Rose shaded her eyes, "I think it's working." Carrie's coin was blinding.

Rose tempted another slap that didn't come. She raised the cover to examine the pages as they fanned open: Yellow, stained, but blank.

Chapter One Hundred and Seven

ime froze; everyone held their breath until Carrie's coin dimmed to a more convivial brightness. Dolly's legs twitched as she made an arched-back stretch. Then, without regard to Carrie or anyone, she hopped to the floor and padded away.

Carrie's face alighted with excitement. She asked Heather, "How do I make it work?"

"It's emotional," Heather explained. "When you read a Book, you're just reading. To cast a spell now, you have to feel the rage or the love or the desire." She took a breath. "But I think you can still only do what was in your book."

"But how? I just get mad? That sounds too easy. It was hard for Alex, wasn't it?"

Under her breath, Rose grunted, "Obviously."

Heather made a face, "I haven't had magic very long."

Rose pointed at George. "See if it works on him."

Without a word, George let everyone know the idea didn't sit well with him.

"What?" The very notion repulsed Carrie. "I'm not going to hurt someone who doesn't deserve it."

Rose put her hands on her hips. "I guess we'll wait until Matthew or Jeremiah comes calling to find out if you have magic. That'll be convenient." Rose picked up Carrie's Book and dropped it with a thud. "This is useless now. If she doesn't have magic, that was a total waste of a good Book."

In a swirl of dust sucked into the air, Carrie disappeared.

"What the fuck?"

Heather pursed her lips and gave her daughter her best disappointed face for her language.

Marta stood. "Where'd Carrie go? Did she go somewhere or did he… did he…," she couldn't finish the sentence.

"Holy crapola, that was amazing," Carrie shouted from outside. She tiptoed into the front door, stepping over the body. "I did it. I totally freaking did it. I was sitting there thinking about what I might do, and I realized I could send myself places, so I thought really hard about wanting to be outside." She threw her arms in the air, "Yes! I have magic!"

Before Rose could say it, Abby blurted, "Quick, get Dolly!" She appeared her Book. "While she's hot, let's get everyone done!"

As though sensing their intent, Dolly started up the stairs when she disappeared from the staircase. "Hey, that's my cat," Rose shouted at Carrie when Dolly popped into the air an inch above the couch.

A very confused Dolly looked around, unsure how she arrived on the couch from the stairs.

Carrie raised her hands, "Sorry," she giggled. "It's just so cool. I wanted to get the cat and… magic."

Rose put her hands on her hips. "Have some self-control for a change. That's my cat."

Heather started telling Rose to relax when Carrie interrupted her, "No, she's right. I'm sorry. Really. Truly." Lowering her voice, she asked, "It's cool, though, right?"

Abby placed Dolly on her Book. *Sure, leave me for last. It's not like they're using my cat.*

Carrie pointed at the body. "You want me to take care of that?" She rubbed her forearms as though pushing up invisible sleeves.

"You are not disappearing a body," Marta chided. "There's no telling where it would go or what could go wrong. The last thing you want is for it to appear somewhere it shouldn't."

Carrie's shoulders fell in disappointment. She thought a moment, looking at Dolly on Abby's Book. To Abby, she gushed, "To think you really couldn't use magic before and now you're going to have it. That's got to be amazing."

Abby tried to still her trembling hands. "Every time I have a quiet moment, this feeling creeps in. It's like I have all this aching emptiness to fill. It hurts so much."

"I think we're all feeling a little empty these days. Alex is gone. Just when I distract myself enough to feel normal, something reminds me of her and I'm hollowed out again." Carrie rubbed her eyes, unable to hold back her tears. "I was so thrilled about doing magic and you say her name and… I'd give it all back if she'd walk through that door."

"She's not *truly* gone," Marta whispered, touching her chest. "She brought us back." She rubbed her eyes. "She's here," Marta pointed at Abby's Book. "And in you," she pointed at Carrie. "She's the magic we all use. She gave everything to us."

"She didn't give me my magic," Rose rebuffed. "I took it from him," she gestured at George.

Dolly stirred and Abby sat, rubbing her lap to attract Dolly. "Maybe you should all stand up so as not to confuse her."

Despite all the laps, Dolly found a comfortable place on Abby's lap.

Abby grinned broadly for a moment, but her eyes welled again. "I miss her." She turned to Heather. "That feeling I got whenever she wanted something, you know what I mean?"

"The feeling that made you her servant?"

Carrie looked between the two, "What?"

"My oath." Abby's cheeks reddened. She rubbed tears from her face and snorted. "It's how being a Familiar works. Satisfying Alex's needs filled me with joy. All I ever wanted was to do things for her. It made me so happy. Or, like, if Alex liked or wanted something, part of me would do anything to get it for her, even if she didn't vocalize it. I just knew. Like these shirts," Abby pinched the shoulder of her faded muscle tee. "I must have worn one once and she made some crazy association. I can't pass one in the store without buying it. Doesn't matter if it's freezing, I wear one under my jacket."

"That's crazy," Carrie stared slack jawed. "And you never hated her for making you do all those things?"

"That's just it. I *loved* her for it." Abby's enthusiasm gushed even as tears fell. "Every time she saw me in one of these and that association clicked," she made a fist over her heart. "I felt so freaking proud: I'd made her happy."

Rose heard an echo of Jeremiah in her head, when he told Abby, *When you discover what she's done to you....*

Marta leaned forward, "And now?"

Abby stroked Dolly's back; the cat's hind legs stretched as she raised her rump. "Now, it's like the biggest, deepest, darkest, coldest hole. I feel... what's the word that means empty but really empty? Bereft? I feel like I could take the whole world and everyone in it and it wouldn't come close to filling up that hole, not even halfway."

Marta rubbed her temples. "You sound like an addict. What you're describing sounds like withdrawal."

Abby looked offended.

Dolly still hadn't moved from Abby's lap. *How long before it's my turn? Marta'll probably go next. Save the kid for last.*

Abby looked at the floor and whimpered, "I have free will for the first time in almost twenty years and I don't want it."

Carrie rubbed Abby's shoulder. "Maybe the magic will help?" Her face suggested she didn't believe in the hope she was dealing.

Abby offered Carrie a half-smile. "What?"

Everyone shielded their eyes from Abby's blinding coin.

Dolly hopped to the floor. *If no one else will check..., it's probably my job now.* She pinched Abby's Book's cover open. She yawned, "Yup, empty."

Marta looked at Rose, "Me? Or…."

Rose looked at her mother. *Once I have magic, real magic like Alex, no one can stop me from going to find Billy.* Rose was ready to elbow her way to the front of the line, but reconsidered. *No matter what I want, Mom'll let Marta go. But if I tell Marta to go before me, I can use that if she tries to stop me.* Dolly squirmed in Carrie's arms. *I hope she can take two more. My luck, she'll explode after Marta.* It felt like if she didn't go next, the shop might close and leave her forever in the cold. She could taste the magic. It was so close to being hers. She wouldn't need her busted-up Book anymore. Hoping she wasn't going to forever regret her decision, Rose said, "No, it's okay, Marta. You go."

Marta face lit up. "Thank you, Rose. I'm sure you're busting to go."

"I'm alright," Rose tried to keep the lie from painting her face. *I thought Marta got sucked into a black hole-y thing.* Rose eyed the room suspiciously. Everyone was fine with Marta being back just as they were fine with Heather.

Marta placed the Book on the floor. The cover was crooked. The pages uneven. Several stuck out, ripped from the binding. This was the Book Rose took from the dead man and tried to tear up, like her father did to hers. Only when her father tore apart her Book, it hurt every fiber of her being and fractured her coin into a spider web of cracks. *It practically killed me but didn't even tickle him. So not fair.*

Abby stopped Carrie—with Dolly—from approaching the Book with her arm. To Marta she asked, "I didn't see you read from it."

Marta pointed at the body. "I read it after Rose dispatched our ottoman over there."

Carrie snorted and giggled.

Rose watched, her heart pounding. The anticipation, watching Marta's lopsided Book on the floor, waiting for Dolly, made her sick.

At first, she couldn't wait to go next. But when she fantasized about her turn to set her Book on the floor, everyone would gasp at the Book's condition. *How did that happen? Did you do that? You should be more careful with your things.* The weight of their questions waited for her, like water behind a failing dam, moments from disintegrating the structure and drowning her.

Carrie lowered Dolly onto the damaged Book. The weight of the cat twisted the spine, further skewing the pages. Rose was nauseous.

Standing, Dolly meowed, looking at the Book and the surrounding floor. The unsteady Book tested her balance. As though her legs gave out, Dolly dropped and laid on the cover, her head proudly raised as she silently studied the women with sharp golden eyes. When she looked at Rose, she hissed.

"She's been doing that all week," Rose excused the behavior. "I don't know what's gotten into her."

"Don't take it personally, Rose," Heather said, leaning forward, straining to pet Dolly. "We're asking a lot of her today."

Don't you dare say it, Mom. Rose was ready to hear Heather tell her, *That's enough for one day. Dolly needs a break.* Each second that Heather didn't say it, Rose became more certain it was coming.

Marta sat on the floor, crossing her legs with her feet atop her knees like she was meditating. "I can't believe it's about to happen. Magic." She turned to Abby, grinning expectantly.

Carrie placed her arm over Rose's shoulder. Carrie was a little taller. She whispered in Rose's ear, "I don't know how you're doin' it, Rose. You and Alex were like sisters. I'm so sorry. It's got to be tearing you apart and we're getting silly over these Books."

Rose groaned. She missed whatever Marta and Abby were saying.

"I know," Carrie rubbed her back. "I miss her, too. Alex was somethin'."

Rose didn't know how to shrug Carrie's arm from her shoulders without it seeming ungrateful. She endured.

Carrie rubbed her forehead. "Shoot, I'm late for work." She looked around the room, shaking her hand nervously. She asked Heather, "What do I do? What should I do?"

"You've got to go to work, Carrie." Heather nodded towards the door, and the body in front of it. "Everything's under control. We'll take care of things."

Carrie released Rose. "Okay. Yeah? You're sure? You're not just saying that?"

"Go," Abby urged. "We got this."

Carrie turned to Rose. "You'll be okay if I go?"

Rose nodded.

"Cause," Carrie hissed, so the others wouldn't hear. "The other day," she circled her finger in the air around Rose's eyes.

Rose tried to swallow her anger and hide her glare. That was the night she tried to smother her mother and her father almost killed her, tearing apart her Book. It left her eyes bloodshot, filled with burst vessels. Carrie said nothing about it, but Rose anticipated an interrogation with every encounter. She stared at Carrie, trying not to think the angry thoughts invading her brain.

"Go to work, Carrie," Abby shouted.

Their staring contest broken, Carrie's face erupted in excitement. Just as Heather was saying, "Take your motorcycle…," Carrie disappeared.

Chapter One Hundred and Eight

Rose stood beside Marta, facing her mother. Dolly's back feet held their place as she stretched as long as she could, and only then did she fully step off the Book.

Marta waved her hands in the air like she was a nesting bird taking flight from an approaching cat. Dolly meowed politely and circled Marta, rubbing her entire body against Marta's back and finally coming to rest in the bowl of Marta's crossed legs. Dolly tossed her body around until she nestled on her back, purring as Marta pet her white stomach.

Rose took an impatient breath. *How long do I have to wait?* She briefly thought about putting her Book down and rushing the process.

Out of nowhere, Marta gagged. An eruption of perspiration stained her shirt. She dry-heaved and shivered. Her hair wilted as her scalp dampened. Her back curved, her spine showing through the knit of her shirt as her body clenched. She grimaced, showing all of her teeth, making her look joyfully insane.

Abby grabbed Marta's shoulder. "Are you okay? Marta?"

Rose crept backwards a step. *Is this because the Book was damaged?* She pressed her hands against her stomach, trying to hold back the sick.

Heather hushed, "Marta, dear, what's happening? Tell me what I should do. Is it Dolly? Should I move her off you?"

Marta's eyes bulged. Her hands clenched and shook in the air like disfigured claws. Her lips turned blue. She looked to each of them, Heather to Abby to Rose, all the while gagging, her arms flapping, veins strained against the skin in her neck, twisting and flopping her head from side to side and front to back. Her eyes flashed desperately, pleading for them to do something but not indicating what that something might be.

Am I watching her die? Am I going to stand here and watch her choke until the life literally spills out of her? What am I going to tell them when it's my turn? Rose wanted to—but didn't know if she could—pretend this was a Marta thing and had nothing to do with the condition of the Book.

Heather yanked Dolly from Marta's lap. The cat seemed suddenly shocked at being tossed across the room and—once catching her footing—sneered at the ungrateful witches who could so casually discard her. She walked back to Marta, as if determined to complete the job, and when Heather held her arm in the way, Dolly slapped at her with two lightning-quick strikes. Heather withdrew with a wince, the tracks reddening as blood swelled to the surface of four parallel sets of scratches on her forearm.

"Mother-fudger," Heather winced, smearing the blood as she rubbed the stinging wounds.

Dolly approached Marta, who had collapsed as though all her taught muscles had turned to pudding. She pressed a paw on Marta's leg, as though testing her solidity.

Dolly hissed at Abby's attempt to remove her, contented to stay exactly where she was.

Abby looked at Heather, her eyes wide with concern. Her arms remained extended, at a standoff with Dolly's claws.

Rose grabbed Dolly, despite being menaced by Dolly's claws, and pushed the cat from Marta's lap. Dolly sneered, hissing, and then in a fit of pinwheeling limbs and tufts of hair, tore out of the room and up the stairs.

Rose watched as her one opportunity to become a real witch disappeared down the hall. She wasn't sure whether she felt relief or disappointment. She wondered when her mother would announce that they were done for the day. Whatever she was feeling would crystallize at that moment.

Heather, however, didn't speak, only helped to ease Marta as she collapsed against the couch, the seizure wearing off in cycles, like someone kept touching two wires together to pulse current through her.

She panted and wheezed. She pulled herself to her knees and took deep, trembling breaths.

Rose watched. Heather lowered herself and allowed Marta to lean against her while Abby kept her steady.

Rose side-stepped around the others and opened Marta's Book. The pages were blank. She studied Marta with eager anticipation.

"I'm okay," Marta panted. She nodded her head and pushed a subtle distance between herself and Heather. "We're okay."

Abby inquired, "What happened?"

Marta nodded.

Those two know something. Rose stepped forward. She was bursting. Wanting to know if she could finally go next or if she'd waited too long. Was Dolly spent or was it the Book? She demanded to know, "Was it your Book? Is it because the Book is broken?"

"No, I, um," Marta stammered. She glanced at Abby out of the corner of her eye.

Rose checked Abby. *That's not it. They're hiding something.* "Out with it, Marta."

Heather erupted, "Rosemary!"

Rose glared at her mother. Heather lost the strength to respond.

Rose stormed from the room.

Climbing the stairs, sweat dripping down her back, Rose could hear Heather apologizing to them, "She's not handling Alex's death well."

Rose clenched her fists. She wanted something to pound. *Not handling Alex's death well? What about Billy, you bitch?* Her eyes teared up. She turned to her room, not sure if she wanted to upturn the furniture or scream into her pillow until her throat bled.

Dolly stared at her from Billy's bed. She blinked politely, as though happy to see Rose. Rose mocked Marta, exaggerating the hint of an accent, softening her consonants, "It's my Bo-oo-ok. It's the Bo-oo-ok that did that."

Dolly was indifferent when Rose swept her into her arms and pounded the treads down the stairs.

"One last time, Marta," Rose screamed, Dolly squirming at her volume, "what did that? Was it your Book?"

Before Marta could find her composure to reply, Rose appeared her Book. The three of them gasped as Rose threw her Book at their feet.

Rose glared, daring any of them to say something.

The spine of the Book was torn open and revealed the binding like guts of thread spilling from a wound. The cover was skewed and creased; the pages stacked unevenly. Her heart was pounding like the echo of her feet stomping down steps. She felt like her pulse expanded her temples and was sure her pulsating veins distended her forehead.

The Book sat on the floor, moving, as though slowly deflating from a leak, its own weight bending the remains of its broken spine. The Book was in desperate, piteous condition; a broken, wounded thing, slowly falling still as life left it.

Rose stood there, the cat in her arms, sick with conflicting emotions. She wanted magic, like they had—like Alex—but if the Book's condition would harm her, she needed to know if the risk was worth it. *Does Marta have magic or not?*

"Rosemary," Heather's concern shot her words out rapidly, "what happened to your Book? Sweetheart, dear, who did that? What happened to you?"

Shut up, Mom. "Tell me," Rose threatened Marta, holding Dolly in the air, "was it was your Book?"

"Rose, what did *that* to *you*?" Abby cupped her mouth at the sight of Rose's glowing coin, at its spider-web of crack and rough edges.

Heather pushed Abby's meaty shoulder. "Please, stop her."

Rose released the cat. Dolly unsheathed her claws as she extended her limbs and landed on the Book with four simultaneous thuds.

"Last chance," Rose warned. "Was it the Book?"

Marta shook her head like she didn't want to answer. *What's she hiding?*

Even Heather seemed to notice the way Abby and Marta kept looking at one another.

Before Dolly could be shooed from the cover by Abby, Rose held Dolly firm. The added weight splaying the book like a deck of cards spread across felt.

She glared, willing her eyes to rip holes in them. *When I have real magic, you won't dare hide the truth from me. You'd never lie to Alex.*

"Abby, Marta, what's going on?" Heather's tone verged on the phony calm before the screaming storm at misbehaving children.

Time seemed to slow down.

Abby turned to Heather.

Marta turned to Heather, her hand gesturing at her Book.

Rose picked Dolly up and dropping to her butt, tucked Dolly on her lap.

"I can't," Marta whimpered like a child, fearful of a lashing.

"She can't," Abby confirmed.

"Explain," Heather demanded of Marta.

"Men can't have magic."

Rose's head turned so sharply she heard her neck crack.

"You're trans? You're not trans." Heather was trying to find logic in Marta's confession.

"She's not trans," Abby said.

"I'm Marta," Marta confessed, "and I'm Peter's son, Alexandria's twin brother; Alex."

Rose screamed.

Rose felt the air rapidly leaving her throat, but the sound it made was distant, like a train whistle, ten winter-miles away. Darkness had crept in from her peripheral vision, covering everything in a cobweb of light and darkness, blinding her to everything but their eyes. They looked like deer on a moonless road, their glowing pupils the only telltale sign of their existence. They might have been across the room or light-years away.

Chapter One Hundred and Nine

"What happened to her coin?"

The words were distant, deep, and earthy, like wet loam.

"Her coin?"

"Look at it."

"Oh my Rosemary, what have you done?" the voice continued to beg and plead.

"Did the Book do that?"

"No. I saw it as soon as it glowed." That deep voice took pity on her, "Someone did that to her. Maybe whoever did that to the Book."

Rose's skin tingled with vengeful vibrations to remind her of the excruciating torture that had finally passed. Worse than the burning pain caused by her father attempting to destroy her Book, this was an agony as though the fissures in her coin were being slowly, tediously carved through flesh and bone. She lay still as though accounting for the pieces she'd been hacked into, still uncertain as to the whereabouts of at least a few.

"Don't move, Rose, sweety, stay still."

Slowly her eyes opened. "What is he doing here?"

Heather grabbed George's arm, preventing him from leaving Rose's side.

"He saved you," Heather claimed. "He took Dolly off of you."

It came back to Rose: The Book. Dolly. She put Dolly on her lap and her coin felt like it exploded. Her whole body felt like a porcelain doll dropped onto concrete. The sensation of shattering—of being torn apart ended only once unconsciousness spirited her away. "My Book," she strained to sit up. Abby and Marta held her down. "My Book," Rose reached, but it was too far away.

"That Book," Heather muttered. "He said it'd be trouble."

"Mo-om," Rose protested.

"Sweetheart," Heather stroked Rose's forehead. "We thought we were going to lose you, baby." She pressed Rose's clenched fist to her lips. "You were screaming. Your coin was bright and damaged; it kept breaking. The cracking sound was so loud. I thought you…" She couldn't finish, but Rose feared she understood.

George touched her chest with two fingers, as though afraid her breasts would bite if he used three. "Your coin," his voice trembled with uncertainty, fearful of her rebuke. "It's shattered, Rose."

"My Book," she demanded as forcefully as she could muster.

George slipped from her side. She could hear the dry, textured sounds of his hands skimming the pages. He took an audible breath, his mouth opening and closing as he lubricated it.

Rose was certain he was taking this opportunity to steal back her Book.

Abby turned from her. "Speak, George!"

He carefully held the Book up for them to see, practically juggling the dismembered pages to keep it together. "It's not blank," he worried. "She can't have the magic."

Rose cursed and thrashed, fighting their hands. Residual pain clung to her limbs with every movement like her joints were rusty. "Get off me," she forced herself upright. "I'm fine," Rose protested, pushing their attentive hands away. "Stop it, I'm fine."

"You don't look fine," Abby whimpered, "you look like bloody hell."

"Give me my Book," she stretched.

Reluctantly, George handed it to her. The Book was even worse for wear, but not a missing mark or an altered symbol. "Fuck," she cursed the Book, tossing it abruptly away and immediately regretted doing further damage.

"I guess I'm like you," she told Marta. "Too pitiful to have magic."

"Um," was all Marta offered.

She took to the stairs when she heard Heather take a breath. *She can't wait. She's got to ask.* Rose anticipated the question like a child trying to pretend the broken lamp had always looked like that.

"Sweetheart, can you tell me what happened to your coin?"

Rose climbed the stairs, letting her stamping feet answer for her. She could hear Heather's anticipation in her mother's breathing: Heather waited either for Rose to answer or enough time to pass to pretend her daughter hadn't heard the question.

Rose stopped at the top of the stairs and waited for the moment Heather took her preparatory breath, then interrupted her from repeating the question. "You know the day, Mom," Rose's tone caused the others to take a step down, lest they be too close and grant her the high ground. "Remember, when I tried to smother you?"

Abby and Marta gasped. "What? When?" they asked. George disappeared into the other room.

Heather's expression hadn't changed. *She remembers.*

She answered Abby and Marta, "I couldn't do it. She didn't deserve to live like that. It was… degrading. Killing her was the most humane thing I could imagine doing for her. But I couldn't. I was too *weak*." Tears almost welled in her eyes. "I didn't know," she gestured at Heather. "I mean if I knew all she needed was the cat to sit on her Book I'd've done it weeks ago."

Heather's tone was frosty. "That's not what shattered your coin." Although looking awkwardly up at her daughter from a lower step, Heather never turned away.

"I visited my father. When he saw I had a Book, he took it and ripped it apart. It was like with Betty."

Heather touched her lips. "That son-of-a-bitch."

"My father tried to kill me." Rose turned and disappeared into her bedroom, slamming the door.

So, I can't have magic. Neither can Marta, right? It's not only me. It's because my father damaged my Book. He hates magic so much, more than he cares for me. He didn't even see me. All he saw was my Book. Rose felt longing for the splayed pages downstairs. She had left it alone, with them. She hadn't been this far from her Book since the day she ripped it from George's hands. *He's probably looking at it right now. He'll probably try to tell me it was never mine and find a reason why I can't have it back. Mom'll be fine with that, too.*

In her head, she impersonated her mother, *You know, sweetheart, I never liked that you used that Book. You should return it to the nice man.*

After several minutes, Rose decided that it was better to face them than leave her Book abandoned a moment longer. She opened her door and escorted her mother downstairs.

George stood beside the couch, gently cradling her Book. He held it like he'd finally been reunited with his missing infant.

Rose took a breath, ready for the fight she was sure was coming.

George held out the lopsided tome, his wide-set eyes locking with hers before darting off. "Here, Rose. You probably want to keep this someplace safe."

Rose half expected him to tease her and pull it from her reach. She snatched it and he backed away. Once in her hands, the uneasiness settled. It was as though the cradled Book comforted her.

George seemed to sense her expectation of him. His nerves chopped his words into stutters, "I, I know it was mine once. But it's better you have it now."

"Thanks," Rose said, sounding like a question.

She barely looked at it, tucking it carefully into a pocket of mist for safekeeping.

"What's the deal?" Rose asked Heather. "Does Marta have magic or not?"

"Rose, please," Heather groaned. She collapsed onto the couch. "I'm so tired. I can't waste my energy on this constant bickering."

"I'm not bickering," Rose blurted. "I want to know what happened. We both had broken Books, but hers is blank. Where'd it go?" Rose looked around. They were alone. "Where'd they go?"

Heather waved at the door. "Taking care of our guest."

Rose hadn't noticed the missing body until her mother pointed it out.

"You have to understand what's happening," Heather rubbed the seat beside her.

Suddenly she sensed that she was late—delayed from her journey to save her brother. Why didn't she leave when she had the chance? Why did she let them distract her? She'd stayed because she wanted to get magic, and look where that got her. Now she was going to have to listen to her mother explain why something she did was wrong. Rose chose not to see eye-to-eye with her mother. "I'll stand."

Heather's face flashed indifference. "Rose, dear, try to understand, things are messed up right now."

Rose crossed her arms. She wanted to tap her foot, but that felt too obvious.

"Alex is gone. Your brother is gone. You saw what Jeremiah did to us. To me. We thought we'd lost, that the fight was over."

"I thought so too." Rose's softening tone came as a surprise. Considering the events of prior days—the last week—diluted her anger and her bravery. Just recalling Jeremiah made her insides quiver, bringing tears to her eyes. While Heather was a zombie, while she had Carrie and Rachel looking out for her, Nancy helping her clean her mother, it was easy to forget the horrors of the Library. Watching Donna die, Betty and her Book burning up, Caleb, Colette and Lydia taken to whatever dreadfulness awaited them at the Farm; these memories stubbornly refused to be forgotten. "What changed?"

Heather crossed her arms, then uncrossed them. She dragged her fingers through her short brown hair. She appeared to be watching a chaotic swirling of words, waiting until the right one came close enough for her to snatch it and start her talking. "Marta. You. Me. The Books. It's all changed. Your brother was right."

"Billy? Right about *what*?"

Heather nodded, as though defending her words before Rose could call them a lie, "He visited me in the hospital. A long time ago."

"Visited you? When?"

Rose sorted her confusion into coherent questions when Heather continued, "When I was pregnant with you both. He visited me." Heather told the story, how Marta was her nurse and Billy came, only he was older, and how he said they would both die. Then she said, "He said to me, *You'll think Alex is amazing, but wait until you see Rose.* He warned me about your Book. He said it would be trouble, but not what that kind of trouble that was. Then he told me: *Rose is the key. Rose is the key,* he said to me. Rose, sweety, you think you're the only one here without magic, but that's not the point. Of us, you're the most important one. You were brave and took that Book from George and saved us all. It was never about Alex. It was all about you."

This was not the speech Rose expected. "How am I the key?"

"You taking that Book gave Alex the idea to give each of us ours." She motioned to George. "Tell her what you told me."

George entered the conversational space around the couch. "When men read from Books, that's what we do. It's different for women. You get pulled into them. It seems you're paired with them." He motioned to Heather. "The cat brought Heather back. But your mom didn't just return alone. She has magic, too."

Mom has magic, the way Alex had magic, maybe even better, because she doesn't have those voices in her head. "I'm the key because I started this?" *I guess I'm done then. I can get on with my life.* She almost spoke. *Is that why I couldn't read another Book?* She had tried, at the Library, but it was like that Book was dead. *I can only ever have one?* She thought of the condition her Book was in and wondered how much more damage the Book could take before it stopped working. If there was some point when that stupid rule would no longer apply.

George deferred to Heather. "That's all we know, Rose. You saw Carrie and Abby. Marta, well, she's...," she looked at George, who shrugged. "And you made that happen."

Rose felt left out of the club she created. "Are you saying I did my part and don't matter anymore? You all get to be special. All I get is a broken Book. What, Mom, are you going to leave me home again because I don't have real magic? Because I have some second-class Book magic?"

"Book magic isn't bad." George regretted his utterance at their glare.

"What are you talking about, Rose? Leave you home? Don't matter? Of course, you matter."

Rose crossed her arms and widened her stance, glaring down at her mother. "Like before. With Alex. You, keeping me *safe*."

Heather sighed, "Watch your tone with me."

"Or what, you'll cast a—"

"I'm not going down this path with you," Heather spoke over Rose's protest. She took an exhausted breath and evened herself. "No one is leaving you anywhere, Rose."

Rose let the silence fester. "He told you I was the key, yet you took every opportunity from me."

"What did I take from you, Rose? He said your Book would be trouble. I didn't know what that meant. When you got it, I worried about what it would do to you. Didn't you see what magic did to Alex? Did you? It tortured that girl. Every minute of her life was excruciating. She was either cursed without magic or cursed with it. I was terrified the same would happen to you."

"It's always about Alex."

"She suffered because of what we expected from her. It killed her, Rose."

"She sucked at magic and all you ever did was make excuses. I save everyone and you yell at me. What did you see in Alex that you don't think I have?"

"I know what you're thinking, Rose, and I don't."

"What?"

"I don't wish she were my daughter."

Rose looked away. She couldn't hear her mother lie. She glared at George until he returned to his chair. She didn't know if she wanted to utter the words she was thinking. "It was supposed to be me, you know."

"What was supposed to be you?"

"You took it away from me," she accused Heather. "You. Because you're always jealous. Your brother had the special daughter. Your daughter had the special Book. What did you have?"

Heather looked slapped by the accusation. *She knows I'm right.*

"And when Jeremiah called on me, you took my place."

In spite of her exhaustion, Heather sat upright in her seat. "Of course, I did. I thought he was going to murder you. I would do anything to save your life."

Rose's volume increased through her accusation, ending in a scream, "You couldn't bear for me to have it. You took my place and now look at you. You have magic. It was supposed to be me. I was the key, and you stood in my way. You took it from me because you're a jealous, petty bitch! It was supposed to be me! Me, Mom, me with the magic!"

Heather's mouth hung open. She looked furious and hurt, slapped and fuming. Through clenched teeth, she seethed, "Do you know what seeing that happen to you would have done to me? I would rather die a thousand deaths than watch you die once. How dare you!"

"It's always about you," Rose spat back. "Oh, poor Heather. She can't bear watching her daughter die, so she has to make her daughter watch her die."

"It's natural for parents to die before their children."

Rose gestured frenetically, "You're not dead! You didn't die! I've spent the past two weeks washing shit from your backside."

"No one could have known that at the moment, Rose." Heather's whole body trembled—whether from anger or exhaustion, Rose couldn't tell. She was searching for an excuse, something to say after the fact to justify what happened, and she wasn't disappointed. "Your Book is damaged, Rosemary, sweetheart. If it had been you, Dolly would never have been able to bring you back."

"And who did that?" Rose screamed. "Who damaged my Book?" How close had she come to being trapped in her own body? A zombie forever. Heather didn't save her by volunteering herself. Her father ruined everything. *He's the reason I don't have magic. He's the reason I'd still be a zombie and not back like her. He's the reason my coin is broken.* She suddenly didn't feel ready to save Billy; there were loose ends that needed to be snipped away, needed to be cauterized so there'd be no more unravelling, no further opportunity for other people to take away her destiny.

Rose huffed, disregarding her mother's argument, her chest heaving as she tried to catch her breath. She thought on her Book. It practically called to her.

"It should have been me, Mom." Rose heard her voice whine and tried to repeat what she meant. "Billy told you what would happen, and you took it just when it was supposed to be my moment."

Heather tried to assuage her daughter, but Rose vanished in a cloud of mist.

Chapter One Hundred and Ten

arkness concealed Rose. She stood at the foot of a plain wooding landing leading to the door of a white mobile home. She was here three nights ago. She came, her heart breaking, hoping her father might—she didn't know what she wanted—take her in or say anything to make her feel less alone. Instead, he took magic away from her.

In her mind she could still see it, hear it, feel it tingling like a parasite chewing through her skin. The explosion of motes as the Book broke, the spine snapping, the pages tearing. It was the Book—it was her body, her coin shattering—as her father attempted to break her in two.

Rose waited, taking deep breaths. The odor of the burned-down house behind the trailer was fading. The stairs. The door. These were not barriers. They were lines to be crossed, lines that once crossed could never be rolled back. Once she chose to step forward, the consequences of her actions could only multiply. She could turn away and no one need ever know she was here. Or she could open the door that could never be closed again.

He deserved whatever happened. He took magic from her. He tried to kill her.

She swirled her hand into the mist and extracted her Book. She allowed it to fall open, cradled in her arm. It was like a fidgety babe. As she marched up the stairs, intent on bashing her fist into the door, she took notice of the page the Book had fallen open to. Perhaps she needn't open the door herself. Grinning, Rose read.

The main door, the screen door, and most of the surrounding frame wrenched from the wall, decomposing to splinters in a roaring cacophony of wood and metal and plastic crying at being torn to shreds. Rose walked through the gaping hole, entering the vestibule, the kitchen just beyond. Eric and Jennifer sat at the table; their faces startled white. In the living room, to her left, Hunter and Caitlyn, who were watching a teal inchworm preparing tea in her living room on television, were now screaming in terror at the sight of her.

Eric's chair screeched as he leapt to his feet. Rose could almost hear his heart pounding; he was out of breath before he was standing.

Her shattered coin aglow, guttural words spat from her lips; red electricity flew from her extended fingers, striking her father in the chest, burning his gray and red college sweatshirt, knocking him hard against the wall, grunting and pissing his jeans.

Jennifer screamed and threw herself into Rose's line of fire to protect her husband. The strike spun her around and dropped her; her face striking the tabletop, mid-fall.

Rose pulled her hand back like her fingertips touched a hot stove. Jennifer grabbed her face, blood pouring from between her lips. She whimpered pathetically. *What did I do?*

Eric dropped to his knees and cradled Jennifer, her face smeared with blood from her nose and mouth as she coughed and choked on it. Hunter and Caitlyn, ignoring the danger, ran to their parents, trying to wrap their bodies around them, as though hiding amidst their parent's arms and legs could protect them. They cried and sniveled and begged their parents to be okay.

"Is she okay?" Rose's words were too small to be heard. She took a cautious step forward. "Is she okay?"

"What do you want?" Eric stared at her. His disdain for his daughter made Rose retreat a step. He cradled Jennifer's head. Blood was everywhere, soaking into his sleeve, her hair, smeared on the kids, the floor.

"I didn't mean to hurt her," Rose offered. It seemed too little, too late. She took another step towards the table. The children wailed at her approach. "I can fix her," she told them.

"Get out!" Eric screamed. "You've done enough. Get out of my house. Don't ever come back. I never want to see you again, Rose."

"I can fix her," Rose wasn't offering anymore. She took another step.

Rose rounded the table, intent on undoing the pain she'd caused. She'd heal Jennifer and make everything better. The children went rigid in panic at her approach, until she was close enough to force out their screams. The children's wailing made them shake in fear, screaming at Rose with squinting eyes and grimacing mouths that sneered with fear and hatred that felt so pure, Rose felt it cut.

Rose reached to embrace Jennifer even as Eric tried to pull her away. Rose touched Jennifer's arm, when her father slapped her across the face.

Rose looked up in shock. Before she could speak, Eric grabbed a ball of her shirt and flesh, pinching a fistful of skin and bra-strap. He shook her, his teeth gnashing and his eyes afire. He held Jennifer's head with his other hand as he shook Rose, the children crying and trying to hold them both as they all shook with his rage.

Rose winced at the pinch of her flesh in his hand. She pulled away from him to retreat a solitary step from his reach.

"Get out of my house!"

Rose grabbed Jennifer, pushing Hunter away so she could fully embrace her.

Rose held her, concentrating, trying to block out any emotion besides how she felt for Jennifer. *Why'd you step in the way? I didn't mean to hurt you. I was just... I was angry at him.*

Eric grabbed her like she was a sack of rice, and heaved her into the table and chairs, skittering the furniture across the room.

Rose grunted; it was like being hit with bats. Eric took her Book from the floor.

"Give that…," she started to get up, but he pushed the table into her, knocking her into the wall. Caught in the midsection, she couldn't inhale, like the table cut her in half.

Eric retreated to the gaping hole where the door used to be. He carried her Book like he knew she'd doggedly follow it like it was some rare beef and she was a hungry lion.

Rose pushed the table away and caught her breath. "Give that back," she panted.

Eric tossed it, fluttering, disappearing into darkness outside.

Rose still could barely breathe; she raced towards the door. Eric skirted the room as though they hunted one another around an invisible tree.

She paused in the gutted doorway. She watched Eric collect Jennifer and the kids. "Mommy's going to be okay. We're all going to be okay," he assured them. He looked at Rose, his eyes unmoving.

"I—"

"I don't care," he spoke flatly.

"You don't know what you've done," she told him.

"You know *exactly* what you've done," he replied.

Rose had a thousand retorts. None of them fit what she saw, what she'd done. He'd taken magic from her; what did she almost take from him? This was supposed to be her way of reining consequences down on him. It was unfair that she had to suffer them because of what others did, because they were incapable of recognizing the errors of their belief.

"What are you waiting for?"

Rose stared down at her Book. It lay broken amidst the parts of door and wall, skewered on a splinter of lumber.

"I didn't mean for this," she couldn't bring herself to finish.

"It's magic, Rose," Eric coddled his family. Jennifer kissed her children. "When you have that kind of power, it lets you think you have the right to use it."

She couldn't take her eyes off them. If this was all Eric's fault, why was she the only one feeling guilt? *What have I done?* She saw the gaping wounds she left in the trailer, saw the scorch marks on the wall. Even after she left, this memory of her would remain far longer.

"I'm sorry, Daddy. I didn't…."

"Rose, what can I say that'll make you leave?"

"I was angry. You took magic from me and—"

"I took your magic?" He laughed. "This is you *without* magic? Maybe that's not a bad thing. I'd hate to see what you do *with* magic."

She couldn't understand when his fault became hers. "The others have it," she whimpered. "But not me. I can't. Because you ruined my Book."

"Others? You mean besides Alexandrea?" he asked slowly, his words precise.

The question left her irritated. Everything was compared to Alex. "No, not Alex," she said, trying to hurtle the words at him. "Mom has magic. She's back and has magic. She's an actual witch now. Abby, too."

Eric shuddered. "Abby? Abby has magic? Is that possible?" He whispered to Jennifer, and she took the kids as he stood. "You're certain, Abby has magic?"

Rose nodded.

Eric wrapped his fist against the table and cursed. He stared at Rose. "What happened to Alexandrea?"

The crushing wave washed over Rose like an ice-cold tsunami. She felt spun around and dragged by the undertow, spinning in currents she couldn't control, dragged further and further out to the dark, cold, unfathomably deep sea where she'd be forever lost in the truth that finally came to her lips with all the meaning she'd denied until this moment, "Alex is dead. She was murdered."

Chapter One Hundred and Eleven

he echo of Rose's words, *Alex is dead*, crept back to her from every corner of the little, destroyed trailer. The words haunted her, like a green-faced ghoul. The power contained in the trinity of words drained the blood from her father's face. His frame decreased, as though the words deflated his stature. His shoulders slumped, rolling forward like he might collapse into a ball. He leaned against the table. His head fell. He half-sighed, half sobbed. She hadn't the heart to tell him about Billy. Hadn't the strength to be the one to say it: *Billy's dead, too.*

Rose didn't move, her own words working against her like a pickaxe, chiseling away her hardened edges. Saying the words—seeing the devastation they wrought—made them true. Making them true was almost like committing the act herself. For the first time since Abby told her Alex was gone, Rose felt the empty loss consuming her chest from the inside, like an apple being devoured by a worm. Her eyes welled and she cursed herself for feeling weak.

Jennifer and the kids made their way to the sink, all the while her eyes suspect of Rose. She wet the end of a dish towel and began mopping blood from her face.

Rose's Book, the torn pages flapping in the breeze outside, called to her; a jagged splinter of framing like a stake through its paper heart. The rough flapping of the pages, as though the wind perused her Book, laced her with a jealous anxiety as though she feared it disappearing. She so wanted to reclaim it, yet departing without her father's attention felt like fleeing. If he were glaring at her, seething in anger and resentment, that was one thing. But it was Alex consuming his attention, detaching him from all else, and Rose didn't know how to draw him to her except to leave. At least she'd have her Book.

She grabbed the rail and began down the stairs. She felt no eyes on her back. It was like his anger turned her invisible. She'd never felt so unwanted. Her aching bruises punctuated how alone she felt. How long before they knew she was gone? Then her father called, "Rose, wait."

Freezing, she didn't want to turn around until she heard whatever cruelty her father might cast at her. She stifled her inclination to blame someone else: *Jennifer got hurt because she stepped in the way.*

"Where are you going?"

Rose turned slowly. "I, I," she stuttered. An interrogation likely waited for her at home. "I don't know." A thousand answers danced through her head. A thousand places to go and hide and kick the walls and break things. She wondered why her father cared. Perhaps he wanted to know she was going far from them. "Why?"

"Billy, too?"

She froze, uncertain he was asking or telling. The reply caught in her throat. The sudden swarm of tears running down her face drove her to nod furiously.

Eric closed his eyes and sobbed into his hands. "I never believed her. I figured she was stoned on painkillers and imagined some orderly was her son." He beat his fist against the wall.

Jennifer froze, her face laced with horror and sadness, her expression changing as rapidly as her gaze shifted between Rose and her father.

Rose's reply came out tiny as if spoken by a mouse, "Abby saw it."

Gaining his composure, Eric stood. "This changes everything." He did his best to shake off Rose's attack. "I need to make sure you're safe before I go," he motioned to Jennifer and the children, clinging to her, having cried themselves to trembling statues.

Jennifer's bloody jaw dropped open. Aghast, she hissed, "What? Where are you going? Now?"

Eric's face registered a round-robin of emotion. "I made a promise," he told Jennifer. He ran his fingers in his shaggy hair, snagging fistfuls. "It's happening. In a hundred years, I never imagined it would." Turning to Rose, he said, "It's time for me to do what I promised your mom."

Rose looked at him. "I think it's a little fucking late for that."

Jennifer hissed at her language in front of the kids.

"I don't mean the *thing*." He took his kids' hands and brought them around the table to sit. "It's easy to make a promise when you think it's impossible that it'll happen. I guess only improbable. I swore to them, to Heather and Peter." He was looking into a middle distance, as though he saw something far away. He took a deep, deliberate breath. "That I'd be there when Alex needs me."

Jennifer threw the bloody dishrag into the sink with a thunk. "Alex is dead. Didn't you hear?" She pointed apoplectically at Rose, trying to get the words out, "She tried to murder us."

Rose pointed at her father, "Only him."

Eric took his wife gently in his arms. "I don't expect you to understand. It was Heather's deranged fantasy. Then Alex went and kicked the hornets' nest and got killed for it," his words drifted to thought. He asked Rose, "She's killed us all, hasn't she?" Returning to Jennifer, he continued, "I can't protect you. Not by staying. Peter warned me all those years ago, but I never believed it would come to this."

"What are you talking about? Come to what?"

"The people who killed Alex, they're going to come for Rose next."

Jennifer laughed; Rose was certain it was forced. "Am I supposed to care? Should I be heartbroken? Tell me why someone going after your psychopath daughter should upset me. Serves her right." She looked at Rose, perhaps ashamed for speaking ill of her in her presence. "No offence," she offered reflexively.

"They're going to come for Heather after that," Eric added.

"What about us? What about your family, Eric?" She rubbed the children's heads as she surveyed the derelict trailer. "You're not married to Heather anymore. You don't owe her anything. What are you doing to protect us?" She shook with rage at his silence before muttering, "Selfish asshole." She took her children's hands and led them through the living room, disappearing into the bedroom.

In her absence, Eric wouldn't look at Rose. His gaze remained on the walls, the floor, the ceiling; everywhere but his daughter.

"You can run if you want to," she said, uncertain he was even listening.

Eric shook his head. "I was there when this all started. I planned with Heather, but I didn't believe." He looked at his hands. "I lost my boy," he whimpered.

Rose felt excluded, as though he'd just told her he disowned her.

Jennifer returned. "You made me lie to my kids," she said to either Rose or Eric. "I told them this was scary but all fake like a movie and they shouldn't be afraid. Fuck you both for making me lie."

Eric tried to speak but Jennifer continued, "There's no way they're sleeping tonight. First the fire, then this? They're devastated and I haven't even told them their father wants to leave."

Eric rubbed his forehead. "I don't want to leave," he petitioned. "But after they're done with Heather, they'll come for me. That means they're coming for us."

"What are you talking about, Eric?"

Rose rubbed her eyes. "Jeremiah warned us: *Everyone who knows her. Everyone she's ever met.*"

Eric gestured to Rose as proof. "That's his way. That's how you extinguish an idea. Take out everyone who it might have infected." He looked at Rose, "You understand what that means, Rose? She got to them. For them to risk the blowback and kill her, she got to them."

Blowback? Rose wanted to tell her father that he'd gotten it all wrong. *Alex died because she was incompetent. I'm the only one who can finish this.*

Jennifer collected her bloodstained dishrag and held it to her jaw again, "Wouldn't someone notice all the killing? I mean, how realistic is this fantasy of yours?" She positioned her hands near her mouth as though keeping her words from waking the children through the paper-thin walls, "Won't the authorities notice when people start being murdered?"

Eric glanced at Rose before taking a step towards Jennifer. "Who has noticed this far? You have no idea who these people are. They're some of the very people you'd call for help. They're everywhere and nowhere. Peter was one of them, before. That's how close we are to them, separated by one degree." He saw Jennifer's doubt. "I said Heather was crazy. That doesn't mean she wasn't right."

"But you stayed out of it, Eric. That's got to count for something. Couldn't you explain—"

"There's no explaining, Jenn. Guilt by association. Alex got to them. She crossed a line and hurt them, so they killed her. That's the only explanation. We know the truth, that Alex was real, that magic is real, and that makes us dangerous. We can run, but they'll find us. It'll be a cop on the interstate pulling us over for a taillight that's not really busted or a trucker who sees us at a rest stop or a clerk when we check into a motel. There's no knowing until they open their Book. The only way to keep you safe now is to help them."

"Couldn't you give them something they want? Proof you aren't a part of this?"

Rose gasped.

"Hun," Eric petitioned his wife, "even if I murdered Heather and gave her body to them, there's no saying they would leave us alone. They'd, I don't know, demand I brought them Rose." Jennifer still wasn't convinced. "Or you, or you and the kids. They'd make it so uncomfortable there'd be no way out."

"You're just making things up now," Jennifer accused.

"He's not." Rose was hushed by Jennifer's glare.

Eric lowered his head. "I was a part of this until it got uncomfortable. I know more than I ever let on. It's only a matter of time before," he gestured to the gaping hole where the door used to be, "they come through our front door and take care of all the loose ends. Alex was here, remember?"

Rose couldn't tell if Jennifer was beginning to believe or was humoring her husband. "Why don't we run? We don't have any belongings. We have no house tying us down. Why don't we put all our crap in the minivan and vanish?"

"And go where? I know you don't believe how serious this is, but you have to trust me. There is no place safe from them. But maybe I can work something out. Maybe I can negotiate a truce." He looked at Rose, who nodded when he said, "Heather and Abby have real magic now. A bunch of them do. If she's anything like Alex, that might be enough to tip the scales. There needs to be a level head, someone to mediate both sides." He was speaking aloud, but he didn't seem to be speaking to either Jennifer or Rose. "We need to show them that we're dangerous. That we'll bite when they come for us. Negotiations only come from stalemates." He said to his wife, "I need you to grab the kids and go to your mom's. That's the only way I'll know you're safe."

Jennifer's mouth opened wide. "That's why you were such a dick when Alex was here? You weren't mocking her; you were afraid she'd start this. You knew this would happen, didn't you?"

"It was a long shot, but it was a possibility. They gave her magic. They started this that night, in our home."

Jennifer left the counter, approached him, slapped him. She stared at his face for a reaction and, finding nothing satisfactory, slapped him again. Nursing her palm, she slapped him a third time with her other hand. "Fuck you, Eric." Turning away, she started toward the bedrooms. "You fucking knew and never warned me?"

Nursing his reddening cheeks, Eric offered five starts before he settled on, "What could I have said?"

Jennifer stopped. "Anything. Any truth. You told me your ex-wife was crazy. I figured it was the speech every second wife hears. I assumed she was a little batty, that you exaggerated things to prove there was no love left between you, so I wouldn't feel insecure. All the magic and stuff, I thought that was all fantasy. So what, she thinks she's a witch? My first husband thought he was a genius. You never bothered to say it was *real*."

Eric kept trying to interject, but Jennifer wouldn't stop. Rose let her amusement show on her face.

"Now you tell me Heather wasn't crazy? She was freaked out because there was real danger that could kill us all. And what, you thought by burying your head it would go away? Worse, you called her crazy so no one would heed her warnings!" Eric tried to interject, but Jennifer shouted over him, "I'm not done yet. You lied to me. About everything. She really is a witch?" she gestured at Rose. "You thought making me believe the lie would somehow protect us? Magic is real and you knew all this time and never told me the single biggest fucking secret to the universe? So, tell me, Eric, which one of you was nuts? The one who spent her whole life prepping, or the one who denied it existed until it burst through his front door?"

For Jennifer's entire speech, all that came out of Eric's mouth was a series of vowels. He offered two more before turning to Rose and saying, "You said you can fix her."

Rose shrank in the spotlight. Outside, she could hear the flapping of her Book, the wind molesting the pages. She hoped it hadn't blown any torn pages away, imagining them tumbling across the lawn. The Book wasn't pretty, but at least it worked. If she lost even one page, she dreaded what that could mean. "I need my Book to do it right," she offered.

"She's not touching me," Jennifer said simultaneously to Eric's, "Get it."

Chapter One Hundred and Twelve

nside, Eric and Jennifer shouted over one another. Outside, freeing her Book, Rose wondered if the point was just to shout their grievances past one another. When Rose heard that in no uncertain terms, Jennifer would rather die than have Eric's filthy bitch daughter touch her, Rose winced. It felt unnecessarily cruel, yet she couldn't clear her head of Jennifer's face slamming into the table. *I didn't mean it. If she'd minded her own business….*

Rose returned, her Book tucked under her arm, pages sloppily dangling out in every direction. It was a wonder it stayed together. She stood far enough from the argument so as not to be drawn in. Eric was now wearing only boxers, his pee-soaked sweatpants in the sink.

Eric raised his hand; for a moment it looked like he might slap Jennifer. Rose opened her Book, ready to put an end to him. As much as she loathed Jennifer for her accusations, she would not tolerate her father laying a hand on her. She watched Jennifer's face. Jennifer dared her husband to do it, lowering the washcloth to offer a bruised cheek. The upraised hand, however, was his signal for them both to stop. "Please," he begged, "both of you. Shut up and listen to me for one damn minute."

Before she could check herself, Rose said, "I wasn't talking."

Jennifer looked uncertain which of them deserved her glare.

"You," he pointed at Rose, "show her." He pointed at Jennifer, "You, let her." He reached into a drawer and said to Rose, "You hurt her even a little and I will stick this knife into you so many times…."

Jennifer glared at him.

He answered her glare with one of his own.

Rose shook off his threat and approached Jennifer, who held her arms out and turned her head away, her eyes shut tight. "Go ahead," sounded like a dare.

"Um, it doesn't work like that," Rose said as Jennifer edged away. "I need to hug you."

Jennifer was repulsed. "What?"

Rose repeated herself. "For it to work, I need to hug you. You know," she pantomimed an embrace.

Jennifer turned to Eric, but he wasn't sympathetic. She closed her eyes. "Fine."

Rose wrapped her arms around Jennifer. Pulled her close. She could feel Jennifer straining to lean away. It felt strange to hug someone and not be hugged back. She tried to ignore it, but it bothered her to feel not just unloved by someone she cared about, but loathed by them.

Closing her eyes, Rose reminisced on her memories of spending weekends in the summer with Jennifer and Eric and Billy, before Caitlyn and Hunter. When Jennifer at least pretended to care for Eric's children like they were hers. These were days free from Heather, free from daily rituals and expectations. It didn't matter that it wasn't Jennifer she loved, but the time away from Heather. Freedom with Billy. A family with a father who behaved like a different man, never arguing with his wife about magic. A new family with this new mother who showered them with generosity as if to buy their love. She felt so important; they did everything to prove their love for her. Her and Billy. She felt her heart swell. She longed to touch her brother again. To hear his stupid laugh. To be disgusted at his teenage body odor. To be annoyed at his stupid boob jokes or how he was the first to laugh at them. She sobbed. She missed them so much—Billy, and those days. She was carefree. She'd lost so much in so short a time and just wanted to linger in this sensation a little longer. It caused her to ache, but she'd rather ache than feel nothing. She'd rather miss Billy than forget him, no matter how much his absence tore into her like a rusty axe.

Rose thought of Alex. *Her magic tore everyone apart. As soon as she's gone, everyone comes back together.* It was the first time in a while that thinking of Alex brought a smile to her face.

Jennifer gasped, and Rose pulled her tighter. *Billy always smiled and laughed more when we were here.* She remembered how her strict father, once he left Heather, let them do whatever they wanted to show his new wife how much his children loved him. Here they could stay up late, go out and play after dark, ask him to drive an hour for ice cream at their favorite stand. She could almost hear Billy laughing off his sugar high, his hands sticky with ice cream, trying to stick sprinkles to her hair. She'd do anything to see her brother. She ached to know he was asleep in the bed across the room. Except Abby saw him die. She clutched Jennifer, willing to give up anything to know her stupid brother was safe at home. The longing became too great and Rose couldn't hold it in. She sobbed aloud, her hands nearly clawing at Jennifer's shirt, desperate to feel anyone hugging her back. Billy was gone. She pictured him jumping off that rock, that day weeks ago, leaping to the stones below. Only he never landed. He just disappeared forever. He was gone and how it happened didn't matter nearly as much as knowing she'd never hold him, ever again.

Slowly, she slipped away from Jennifer. "Sorry," she whispered, apologizing for leaving wet tears and snot on Jennifer's neck.

Jennifer touched her face. Her lips were barely bruised, and pinching her nose no longer elicited a wince. She attempted to wiggle her teeth and looked from Eric to Rose, her eyes wide with surprise. "That's amazing," she hissed. "Can she teach me to do that?"

Rose had barely made a sound when Eric replied, "Not a chance."

Rose slunk away. She disappeared her Book; with all the pages precariously dangling, it felt vulnerable and fragile, in covetous need of protection, especially considering her father's history with it.

Eric said to her, "I need to help them pack and get them on their way. I can drive you to Heather's in the morning."

Rose thought a moment. Healing Jennifer left her craving actual human connection. "That's okay," she whimpered.

Jennifer's voice softened, "It's okay for you to wait."

Rose looked at her. *Why is she always nice to me?*

"I think you and your father should talk," Jennifer said, "without me around."

Rose looked at Eric. He was no replacement for Billy, and that's all she wanted right now. "It's okay," she told them both. "I'll get back myself." She faced her father. "You'll be over tomorrow?"

He looked at Jennifer for approval. "Once they're on the road. I'll be at Heather's after breakfast."

Jennifer finished wiping the blood from her face. She looked better than could be expected. "You sure you don't want a ride? It's a long walk."

Rose appeared her Book. "It's longer by car." Grinning, she opened to a page and with some guttural words, disappeared.

Chapter One Hundred and Thirteen

"Where the hell have you been?" Heather sat on the couch, nestled against the arm. She sounded like she'd just woken up.

Rose froze in place. Although she'd left her father's trailer an instant ago, her first fear was that his snitch phone call beat her home. Realizing that couldn't be the case, Rose huffed. Heather was giving her grief; waiting for her response. Rose's natural inclination was to make something up. *I needed to clear my head. I went looking for Billy. I did something to accomplish some other thing.* Anything but the truth. Unfortunately, her father was coming tomorrow. Was she going to bet that the truth would come out? In the past, he wouldn't burden Heather with tales of Rose's occasional misbehavior, even when he threatened Rose with it. This was different. What trouble could she have ever gotten in from staying up too late or talking back to her father? She intended to kill him. *To kill.* The word seemed so strong given the fact they'd have a family reunion and finally, after all these years, Mommy and Daddy would be on the same side.

"I was angry," she began. "I went to see Dad." So far, no lies.

"Oh?"

"He should be here in the morning."

Heather's voice became stern, "What?"

Rose didn't know what to say. *What do I tell her? Everything or just the parts she needs to hear?* "Some things happened. When I told him about Abby...," she paused and looked around. "Where is Abby?"

Heather spoke like she was making an accusation, "She went home to sleep. Marta is in your brother's bed. No one knew where you went."

You let Marta sleep in Billy's bed? You found out he was dead hours ago. "When I told him about Alex," she stumbled. "I mentioned Abby had magic, and he knew that only meant one thing."

Heather grinned, her eyes sparkling devilishly in spite of the exhaustion plaguing her voice. "And what did he have to say about that?"

"He's packing Jennifer and the kids up and getting them somewhere safe. He says he knows what's coming."

Heather nodded in the patronizing way she did to show Rose she was wrong about everything. Rose hated it. *Why doesn't she just say something? Why does everything have to be an act with her? If Alex were here, they'd go off into the other room to complain about me.* Rose's thought drifted off. Heather always complained to Alex about their latest tiff. And Alex would listen. And Alex would unravel Heather's anger and explain away Rose's fault. Not all her attempts were successful, but whenever

Heather disappeared with Alex, she knew she had a champion on her side. Alex's absence suddenly had substance; watching Heather react, Rose knew there wouldn't be a counterbalance.

"We're going to sleep," Heather said matter-of-factly. "And tomorrow we are going to make proper witches out of Nancy, June, and Rachel."

"And then we're going to—"

"And then we're going to figure out how to get to the Farm and bring Colette and Lydia home."

"What about Matthew? Daddy's going to want to kill Matthew."

"Who cares what he wants?" Heather leaned forward slowly to take Rose's hand; Rose reflexively pulled away. "My heart is broken, Rosemary. I've dreaded this day since before you were born. There's time enough to hunt him down. But first, we have to save the people who are still alive. It's the right thing to do; it's what Alex would want." She pushed herself to her feet, taking a full minute to straighten her body. "You should get some sleep."

Rose stood, frozen. Heather didn't budge, just swayed slightly as though straining to stand. Her expression told Rose she had been dismissed.

Rose retreated to the stairs. "It's what Alex would want," she mocked under her breath. She paused. She wanted to look back and see if her mother was still standing with the disappointed expression on her face. But something about Heather bothered her. Although Heather was solid and real, there was something transparent about her, as though she was evaporating. Rose didn't turn around because she feared when she did, her mother would no longer be there. If her mother was still here in the morning—if her father held true to his word—Eric would tell Heather what Rose had done. Rose's stomach twisted with anticipation. *She'll be furious.* Rose turned back to see Heather collapse into the couch, looking only at her hands, which made and released fists as though lubricating her joints. Rose climbed the stairs. *That decrepit woman's not my mother.* Rose appeared her Book. *But she's got magic. When she comes to punish me, I'll be ready.*

Chapter One Hundred and Fourteen

he Reaper pulled Alex closer. She could nearly taste the ancient, burned dust of its bones, the death it traded in.

Clasping its mandible, she tried one last lightning strike. Too weak for anger. Its eyes glowed; opening its filthy maw, it threatened her with devouration.

Billy pleaded she stop fighting, "Alex, there's no defeating death. Not with fear. Not with hate."

The room was empty. Too weak to control her spell, she had sent them all away. Hopefully home. The three of them—Abby, Marta, and George—could dispatch the intruder.

They were safe. She was alone. With Billy. No one left to protect. No one to worry about.

Alex fell limp. She hung on the hook of the Reaper's claw like a slab of meat at the abattoir. It wouldn't be long. Life drained out of her, dripping along the tibia and ulna protruding from her viscera. Her head lulled and she found herself gazing down at Billy as the Reaper forced its claw nearly to its elbow. She knew it hurt; it was a constant excruciation, but it was like one person's scream during a riot, too singular to be heard above the din. She kept her eyes on her cousin. She'd failed. Failed him. She would keep looking at him until she was no more.

Alex felt projected through the strands of Billy's glowing thread crisscrossing the room like an infinitely complicated cat's cradle, a gordian knot of light. As her vision dimmed, the bright lines held their glow in the darkness, always coming back to Billy. There, in the center of the complex designs created by the repeating, overlaying thread, Alex stared into the paths of time, and it seemed like time stopped. The creature was still. Billy froze in his body like he was emerging from a chrysalis of his shedding skin, a glowing coin forgotten in his open palm. Half-hidden in his terrified face, a fearful boy peeked out.

Alex's heart broke, shattering spectacularly as though its fine glass form was dropped to a hardened floor, pulverizing immediately to a spreading cloud of dust. Not only did Billy have to die, but he did so witness to her unravelling fate. She wanted to tell him it was okay. To tell him to hand Charon his coin and move on to peace. Only Charon was the Reaper, and how could Billy find peace after watching it shred his cousin to ribbons. She wanted to comfort him. To protect him.

Anger and fear and hate could not overcome the creature. These were the emotions of magic, the spells of battle. What was left for her to do?

Beyond her dangling feet, through her unfocused vision, she resolved the boy within the man. Despite her own predicament, her only regret was losing him. If she somehow survived this day, she would gladly return here to sacrifice herself, if only to spare his life; she loved him so.

Love? How could she think about anything with the burn of her nerve endings screaming their pain throughout her body, like pins in her fingertips and fire at her earlobes. Looking into the eyeless face of death itself, Alex understood: This creature was her only destiny. There was a moment when fear broke like sweat ending a fever. She was dying.

Love? This monster and the child were not human. In moments, the Reaper would resume its slaughter. Rip her coin from her chest and—if she were lucky—allow her to leave her mutilated corpse to pass to the afterlife. What more could she do? Billy was right. She could not fight death with fear or hatred.

Love? The exquisite pain took her thoughts, transporting them. It reminded her of how she felt within Sara, Matthew's hammer smashing bone, regurgitating magic. With death such an inevitability, did it matter that she ever lived? What had she accomplished? What had she left behind? Life seemed meaningless. She was like a thread pulled from a sweater that refused to unravel. It was so much bigger than her. She was dying for a life she couldn't save. She prevented the child—Charon from claiming Billy's coin. Her selfishness to save Billy stole from him the death he deserved and instead forced him to be a witness to hers.

Her vision went dark. No longer seeing the room, her thoughts projected Billy onto her blackness. His smile. His laughter. His goofy humor. His silliness. She loved her cousin so. She'd do anything to protect him.

Love. Emerging from a point in her darkness came a light so pure and intensely white she winced at its brightness. She assumed she was passing over, going into the growing spot, but as it spread, it illuminated the room, the Reaper, Billy. It filled the apartment and cast stark shadows on the buildings across the street, humiliating the sunlight. The Reaper winced from it; rage drained from bony features. The light exploded from her hand, swelling and opening like a petaled flower. Light threw the nightmare away from her, its clinking and shattering bones fracturing in sprays of ancient dust, colliding with the far wall like a shattering plate. Two clean-severed bones protruded from Alex's abdomen: a severed hand still within her.

The creature clinked and writhed, protruding from the broken wall, its ruined limbs twirling insect-like around its torso, trying to right itself, shattered and broken bones doing little more than carving panicked grooves in the floor.

Alex collapsed, grasping her stomach. Her hands pinched the edge of bone and with tormented disgust, pulled, yelping as though removing her own insides. The wet, bloody claw slipped from her, clattering in her hand like a party noisemaker, its extrication her only relief. She anticipated no pause, expecting the Reaper would—in her next breath, perhaps—slice her remains apart, finishing her. She had no strength left to resist it.

Bundled in the corner, lacerated and bloody, shaking a bloody stump of arm, the bruised child Charon gaped at her, its dark eyes wide in fear. Seeing her gazing back, its feet kicked, pushing it hard against the fractured wall. Its face twisted in pain and fear and terror of the girl who looked upon it and pitied what she had done.

Chapter One Hundred and Fifteen

haron's visage was of a toddler, no more than three or four years of age, bloodied and broken, writhing in terror of Alex. It shrieked at her glance, howling inhumanly, fearfully, the only sound she'd ever heard it make. It cried because of her. She'd hurt it, perhaps worse than the child had ever been hurt before. Understanding the pain she'd inflicted, spelled out in explicit cries and thrashes, made her wish for some way to take it back. Charon cowered as though her eyes seared its skin as they lingered too long.

She still possessed the bloody claw, wet with her blood and clogged with her meat. She found it impossible to release, unable to let go out of fear this severed hand might yet cause her harm if she no longer controlled it. She feared what might happen if she returned it to the child, and she feared what might happen if she didn't.

Billy gaped, standing in his body, his face painted in fainting horror, his eyes locked on the severed claw in her grasp. He stared as if both horrified at what had happened to her and at what she'd done.

She reached for his body, her eyes demanding he lay back down. "Please," she choked, her mouth sticky and coppery. She was so parched, so thirsty and cold, she couldn't swallow the dryness.

Billy moved further from his corpse, separating himself from his body, his coin no longer tethered to flesh.

Seeing his desire not to be saved pulled from her the last of her will. Her focus—once to save Billy—was listless and lost. She slipped from him to the ground. Her body shivered. The bony appendage rattled at her tremors. She twisted her neck and spied Charon had vanished. She stared at the empty, damaged wall. It was over.

But it didn't feel over. The sudden relief, the great rest steadily creeping up on her offered no solace. Hurt as she was, beaten, battered, she wasn't ready to die, but not even the whispers inside her head offered any alternatives.

If she had it in her, she would cry. Charon was no longer here to claim Billy. Or her. Could they cross over on their own? Her coin could no longer be flipped. She wanted to close her eyes and pretend she might awaken from this nightmare. But the nightmare was her own making, and before she could rest, she needed to find the determination to unmake it.

"Help," her mouth pantomiming speech. "I need help."

Raising her head from the blood-sticky floor took more strength than she had.

"Help me," she begged. Delirious and too weak to move, shivers kept her perpetually in motion. *Who can I call? Who could come? Who knows where I am?* She felt so alone.

The voices in her head were but moaning whimpers. She was not one dying woman, but the remnants of thousands, perhaps millions of women; the only proof any of them ever existed. *Lesedi was right. Books would be better.*

She told Billy, "I failed."

Billy knelt beside her. "Alex, you haven't failed. Not yet."

This elicited a laugh which gave her strength to say, "This doesn't look like failure?"

"It looks like a lot of things," he told her, "but not failure." His voice softened. "You have a choice, Alex. I've seen my death a thousand times. Its certainty has haunted me for nearly twenty years."

"I have no choice but to let you die?"

"You cannot save me." Billy held out his coin. It didn't dangle from a thread, but floated, suspended by dozens. "This is your choice," he told her. "You have Charon's hand. You can use it. Use it to take my coin and lead us to the afterlife."

"Lead *us*?"

He nodded. "That's one choice. You don't lose me because we *both* die." With a sigh, he knelt as if to comfort her, but didn't. "It probably feels like the right thing. You fought so hard. No one can say you didn't try. You beat death, and that's never happened before. But you think it beat you. You don't see that you succeeded, only how you failed."

In spite of his comforting tone, his message felt condescending. Like he was saying here was the choice only a quitter will take. "What's the other?"

"You know what it is."

Alex took a few slow, deep breaths. She hoped to have the strength to push away his hand and the coin it held. "No," she said as firmly as she could muster. Lacking the strength to turn away, she closed her eyes.

"This isn't a choice between something you want and something you don't. This is a choice between dying and surviving. I came to you today to die. If I lived, you would fail." He sighed in frustration. He looked to the ceiling, as though searching for another way to convey his truth. His eyes lingered on the ceiling as he said, "When people die—when their bodies die—and they hide from Charon—or Charon deems them unworthy—they become horrible, terrible things. You believe you can escape this choice by not choosing, but that means the universe decides for you. The universe will choose an eternity of pain for us both. We'll be unable to remember our humanity except for our pain." He looked at her, his eyes showered her with pity. "This should not be easy, Alex." He regarded his coin. "Please. Take it."

His pleading took the air from her lungs and trampled it all out. She felt faint and sick and violated for just knowing. *How many indeed?* She thought of Jeremiah feeding her Heather's coin, telling her it was but her first. Taking Billy's coin felt like handing another victory to Jeremiah.

"I can heal you."

"No." He took a preparatory breath but was silent for a moment. "Alex, I am dead. Why won't you save yourself?"

Because saving him was all that mattered. Before Alex could vocalize her argument, he interrupted her, "Leaving me here, dead, tied to my corpse is cruel, Alex. Once you die, you won't be able to use Charon's hand. You won't be able to lift it."

Alex stared at him a moment. *When did I stand up?* She wobbled, barely able to maintain herself upright. Deep inside, she knew he was right. Her hands fell to her sides. "Oh, Billy," she sobbed.

He touched her shoulder. "I can't do it for you, Alex."

"No," Alex whined. "No." She closed her eyes. She wanted to rub her face but still held the claw. She threw it. "No," she screamed, as it clanked against the wall, falling to the floor like a creepy doll. "What kind of choice is this? Consume your coin?" Her hands balled into fists. "Everything I've done has been to bring you home, and now you're telling me I have to be the one to end you?" Her mouth made shapes of words she never uttered, her heart aching, her emotions such a whirlwind she couldn't focus on a single thought.

Billy took her hand and turned it, palm up. Gently, he opened her fingers. Then he placed his fist on her palm. "It's not ending me." He managed a smile, the boy peeking out of the man's face. "It's making me a part of you. Please, Alex. Bring me back to my mother."

She turned away, unable to look at him, knowing what she had to do. "I don't think I can."

"If anyone is strong enough, it's you, Alex." Billy waited for her acknowledgement. When he resumed, she interrupted him, "You're sure you want this?"

"Why wouldn't I?" He gazed at her with wonder. "To become a part of you? To know in my final moments that I gave everything to help you succeed. Who wouldn't want that?"

She couldn't help but smile. That dopey kid became a wise, kind man. She poked his head, "Is there anything in there you don't want me seeing?"

Billy laughed. "It's a little late to worry about that." He opened his fist, releasing his coin into her palm. "Have it, then. I give it to you. Willingly."

Alex felt the struggle leave her. "I feel like this is a—"

"It's not a test, Alex. This isn't about if you can be a better person than Jeremiah. It's about doing what it takes to defeat him."

"How do I beat him?" Her voice sounded so small.

"I don't know." Billy tapped on his coin. "The answer isn't here."

She gazed at the coin in her hand. "To think all I have to do is swallow it. I wish it wasn't this easy."

Billy grinned. "This was easy?"

Alex shook her head, tears running down her cheeks. "This is the hardest thing I've ever had to do."

His mouth formed words as though testing each to see if it could lead out his thought, "You're not killing me, Alex."

"No?" She couldn't stop her tears. "Then why does it feel like I am?"

He addressed the body on the ground. "Matthew did that."

Alex squinted at him. "But you knew? You raised your head. You let him—"

"Take my coin. The answers are there. All my life, I've done my best to protect you. I can't always do what they want, but I do my best. This is the last thing I can offer you. The last thing I can do for you." He looked at her, the faintest grin on his face. "Save you."

Alex raised the coin. She practically gagged, dry heaving at the thought of putting it in her mouth. She looked to Billy, and he nodded. She recalled how it felt being forced to eat Heather's coin; the violation at having it shoved down her throat. That was easier. That was forced on her and she could tell herself she didn't do that. There would be no plausible deniability here.

Alex almost couldn't find the words to speak. "I love you, Billy." She placed his coin on her tongue. She sobbed and swallowed.

The coin descended through her throat like something she hadn't chewed thoroughly, distending her esophagus. She felt it grow; she felt it expand into her, warming her. She recalled the sensation of consuming Heather, the warmth, the comfort, the love she felt. Some part of her craved that, expected it now, suddenly eager to be consumed by the life she took.

Memories flooded into her head. A cacophony of recollection, of experience, of knowledge. They came as a deluge of images and emotions, thoughts and recollections, like someone disordered an entire library and dumped it straight into her brain. She felt like her head was exploding. She expected the settling, when—as Heather's memories had—they organized into a life, came together and made sense; like someone filmed all the pages being torn from a book and threw them into the wind and watched them whip all around and then played that movie backwards, creating order from chaos. Instead, this maelstrom of moments swirled in her head like shards of glass in a tornado.

Alex might have dropped to her knees. She might have clutched her head in agony. She might have screamed. All she knew were the memories. They overlaid and intertwined. Like a knotted ball of string, the path through life was never clear. They played over and through one another as though each moment in Billy's life happened simultaneously to every other without order or cause and effect.

She saw moments, Billy as a child, walking to his room, but he was also a teen and a man, standing with Peter, negotiating with Matthew. He was in the Library, he was in his bedroom, he was in the air, mid-leap from Picnic Rock. Alex struggled to tease one moment out of the mess, like finding a corner of a jigsaw puzzle. Then, she grasped a memory of her own and matched it to one from the storm and drew him back.

Chapter One Hundred and Sixteen

arkness.

Billy is aware of his body. Warm. Racing heart. Arms not moving.

A moment ago, he was in the air. Anticipating crashing on the rocks below. Fearful of gravity returning: His body will be broken. Until then, he sits. He waits.

Billy is with Alex and Rose. Alex pulls out a bottle of sunscreen. *Your cheeks are getting red*, she proffers the bottle. Rose smears some on her face, before turning to him. *Give me your face,* she smears it on him. *Rub it in yourself.*

The goop feels cool on his face as he rubs ferociously. Something about this place feels off today. Making him anxious.

Alex sighs. *It's so beautiful here. It's like you can see forever.*

Lately, Billy sometimes sees further than normal. Not further as distance; further as time. This morning, when Alex said they would go on a hike, Billy saw Picnic Rock. Everywhere he looks, his eyes show him a flash of Picnic Rock. It calls to him, telling him to come. It happened before, these visions that flash before his eyes, suggesting what he must do. Today it is Picnic Rock. This really is the right day for a hike.

Unfortunately, sitting on Picnic Rock, looking over the expense of the verdant valley, it is the furthest he can see. It is as though later is no longer.

Almost, Billy remarks. *Some things I can't see from here, no matter how hard I try.*

Rose muses, *I sometimes dream about this place. I'm in the dream, and there's a trail right over there*; there is no path where she points.

As Rose describes it, Billy remembers it. He's never been there. He sees it clearly; a house: smallish on the outside, a warren of rooms inside. He's never had so many visions in one day. He wonders if he has a brain tumor. What other explanation can there be?

Rose continues, *Sometimes I expect to see you, Alex, but you're never there. Billy usually is. He never says anything to me. He just sort of stands watch. He's so serious. I think he's protecting me.* She pats his shoulder. *You're a good dream-brother that way.*

That makes him smile.

Billy is standing in the kitchen. There's a stone fireplace to his left; the fire is roaring, crackling, and radiating waves of dry heat. Visible through the large opening is the living room, and in there, he spies Rose. She looks about, touches the chair, and examines the large doily covering the headrest.

This is so weird, she says to herself. *This wasn't here last time*. Then she notices him. *What're you doing here?*

She enters the kitchen, staring at him as though he's a sculpture she doesn't comprehend. He wants to embrace his sister. The crushing loss in his chest feels like cold milk that's curdled. He doesn't understand the ache. He doesn't understand why he misses her, as though he hasn't seen her in weeks or months, as though he knows he won't see her again. She leaves through one door and comes in another, as though the disparate doorways are mystically connected. The fifth or sixth time he realizes her clothes are changing. The furniture rearranges itself and evolves. Rose is randomly older and younger. He thinks he understands: He misses her, so he visits her. All different times are the same for him. Because one day he will stop seeing her. Until then coming here is the only way to stop his heart from breaking.

Did he leave Picnic Rock? He was in her dream house for hours or days, yet he doesn't seem to have missed a syllable. No one seems aware he left. No time has passed. He can barely catch his breath.

He tells his sister, *I like the fireplace. The one in the kitchen. You can see through to the living room.*

Rose looks back at him. *You dream about it too?*

Does he dream about it? He hasn't yet. He remembers he *would*. He will have done it by now. For Rose, he'd been there even though he hadn't yet gone. How else will he make her memory happen? It hurts his head to reconcile his *when's*.

Only when you do.

Rose looks at Alex like she sometimes does when he's being dumb or creepy. He knows she doesn't mean to hurt his feelings, but she is making fun of him.

Alex, Rose's tone sounds deliberate and mocking, *why don't you visit my house in your dreams?*

I guess I've never been properly invited. She replies, *Honestly, I feel a little left out*.

Do you ever have a dream like that? You know, where you're somewhere you've been, but it's different?

Billy's hands have started trembling. Billy's heart pounds. He's sweating. He's at the foot of a staircase. Alex is up those stairs. She's in grave danger. Matthew climbs ahead of him, ahead of them. Only Matthew is on Picnic Rock, listening to Alex reveal her secret, explain an event that happened to her years earlier. He feels sick that, as she retells the story, she'll recognize him. She'll make him explain something for which he has no explanation. He holds his breath, knowing exactly what Alex is about to describe, even before she says the words.

At last Alex answers Rose, *I have a dream where I go somewhere, but it's not pleasant.*

Where do you go?

Billy is watching Alex, her mother a bloody mess, a small child demanding her coin. Charon. That child's skeletal hand was in Alex's hand. He is dying. *Choose,* he tells her.

Billy can almost recall each moment before Alex says it. *I'm in my bedroom. I mean where I used to live with my mom and dad–when these men come.*

Alex shushes Rose when she interrupts and continues. *My parents are just like I remember. Probably the same age they were when the accident.... Dad was, I don't know, strange. In the dream, I mean. He was always like a zombie; you remember?*

Billy remembers Peter. *I want you to meet my sister*, Peter tells him, when they were friends.

Billy shrugs. *Sure.*

Peter smiles. He's no zombie. Peter is young, gregarious, excited. Then Peter is older, just a few years, a gaunt, shuffling creature.

Billy whimpers, *He made me sad.*

Alex continues, *In the dream, it was like he knew something was happening. Then these men come, and a bunch of stuff happens. Then my dad has a gun and is screaming at me.*

He wasn't a zombie? Rose dares Alex to admit her contradiction. Billy wants to shout at them, *That was Matthew, inside of Peter.*

He was, but he wasn't. I think my mom exploded him to dust.

Billy starts up the stairs. He witnesses Matthew blast across the hallway, the wall shattering as his body slammed into it. It is brutal to witness, heartbreaking, because he knows in that moment, Peter is gone. And Matthew is so gravely injured he will always hold it against the girl who was supposed to be his to control.

How did he know? It's like a memory, like her words helped him remember something he'd forgotten for a long time. Only, he is remembering something that won't happen for years and also happened years ago. Had. Will. Two expressions of the certainty Billy feels in these moments. Past. Future. They are the same.

Then the wall turns to mist, and all this other crazy stuff happens.

Rose hisses, *Crazier than your mom exploding your dad?*

Billy wants to scream, *She didn't explode him. Matthew did. Matthew didn't understand that Alex was there, only she hadn't been there again, yet.*

Alex motions with her hands by her chest, *These silver things start appearing on everyone. They look like glowing disks. There's this little cute kid, but then it's this horrible monster. It's like this giant skeleton.*

Alex is battling the Reaper. She's so powerful; stronger than even she realizes. *You can't defeat death, Alex. Not with hate, not with fear.* Then something happens. She stops allowing her rage to cast her spells. What comes out of her, a blinding flash that tosses the monster across the room like a broken pile of twigs, is love. *Her love for me. She cares for me so much.*

Gary tries to take Holly's coin. The Reapers slays Gary without hesitation. Why is it so covetous of the coins?

Rose's voice cracks, *Go on.*

The little kid goes like this to mom. Alex holds her hand out. *It sounds so ridiculous when I say it out loud, but it's the same, night after night. It seems so real. Anyway, my mom gives the monster her disk. It turns back into the kid. I'm scared, but she tells me to go, so I walk into the mist. Then I wake up.*

Billy is looking at Charon. The child looks piteously at him, hand extended for his coin. It makes him want to give Charon his coin, but he cannot. Is Alex hurt? She's covered in blood. Wait, he thinks, is the blood mine?

You don't give your silver coin to Charon, Billy looks at his hands, cupped in front of his chest.

Is he asking about her coin or his? He so wants to give Charon his coin.

Rose looks up. *Billy, what did you just say?*

Charon recognizes Alex. A spark of recognition crosses the child's face, and almost as suddenly, the child is torn apart becoming the Reaper.

Charon. The child—the monster. It looks scary, but it's not, unless you try to trick it. You can't cross over unless you pay with your coin.

Coin? I don't have a coin, Alex answers.

You don't? Billy remembers she doesn't now and does, later.

Look at this, Peter says to him, holding up a Book. Billy won't look at the open pages; he cannot; he must not. *I can give her a second coin.* He slaps the cover closed; his excitement palpable. He knows a secret he believes Billy doesn't, but doesn't understand he already told Billy, even as he says the words for the first time, *It'll be like they cancel one another out. Instead of glowing, they'll appear dark. My daughter won't be able to do magic, but Matthew won't be able to find her. Do you know what this means, William? We don't have to give her to Matthew. We can hide her away. We can protect her.*

Coin? I don't have a coin, Alex confirms.

You don't, Billy tells her, *because you're dreaming.*

The sky is dark. Across Picnic Rock, Matthew walks towards them. Billy can feel Matthew's magic making lies in his head. He sees untrue things. It forces him to do what Matthew wants or he sees his mother die or Alex die or Rose die. The hallucinations are so real, his guts twist and his balls twist and it squeezes all the hope out of him. He knows it's not real because he sees it only now. He hasn't seen it before or later, and right now memories are lies. Rose doesn't know the memories aren't real. He can see the pain and despair cross her face each time she sees Alex. He sees Alex and the flames, burning her alive.

Alex breaks his concentration with her stare.

Alex is in the flames. In the blink of an eye, a Book falls from her hand. The flames die out.

Matthew whoops in celebration. *You did it*, his eyes brim with tears. *It worked. I knew it! I had to coax it out of you!*

Burn her, he told Matthew.

Burn her? Seriously? Matthew looks like he's waiting for the punchline. *What about Oblivion?*

Billy shakes his head. *Keep that thing away from her.*

Matthew studies him. Billy fears Matthew senses his uncertainty.

He's untwining her tonight? Why are you telling me? Matthew sits forward on his sofa. He has youthful confidence—his neck hasn't yet been broken. Matthew glares, and Billy thinks he's slipped up until Matthew says, *Out with it. Why are you betraying him to me?*

Because there'll be something left behind. Something you need. Billy holds back some of the truth. *There'll be a miniscule darkness left. It'll dissipate without your intercession. Take it. Nurture it. It'll harvest coins for you.*

I said burn her. On that big rock near the witch's house. As Matthew nods, convincing himself this is a good idea, Billy is sick. He's seen Alex, her blackened fingers fruiting blisters the size of cherries. All the pain she suffers is because of him.

The ropes collapse from around Alex, and lacking their support, she drops to her knees. Her clothes are burned to her skin, her body red and black and oozing moisture. She shivers uncontrollably. Rose creeps to her, kneels beside her, and with all tenderness, holds her.

Matthew sees the Book. The expression on his face makes Billy watch him closely. At this moment, Matthew understands the depths of his betrayal. He thought the Book was lost or left and now she has it. He eyes Billy with uncertainty. With fear.

When did you get that?

Alex pulls the Book closer, scraping it through the ash.

The day I broke my neck. His voice drops to a whisper, *That was... you.* He smiles. Matthew understands now. *That's why I can feel you.* He nods his crooked head. *Clever Holly. I thought I saw you, but it wasn't you then. It was you,* now. He laughs. *That's why you couldn't do magic.* He can't stop smiling. He understands. *You have it,* he beams. He finally has the woman who can empty the Library and give him his Book. She is weak and hurt. But finally ready. He laughs, jumping a little. *You have it. You finally have a soul.*

It's not a soul, Alex screams, *it's a coin, for paying passage.*

Billy continues for her, *You give Charon your coin, just like the stories say, to pass when you die.* Billy is sitting with Alex and Rose on Picnic Rock, the sun shining and warm. Matthew staring at him in confused wonder, the sky black, the coals of the fire still radiating heat. *You throw a coin in the fountain for luck. Silver dollars are the luckiest, but most people throw pennies. They never get any luck, though. But you're not buying luck; you're tossing coins to confuse Charon. I think that's where the tradition really comes from. Toss a fake coin so Charon goes looking for it and won't come for the real one. They're not the same kind of coin.* He looks at Alex, still in Rose's arms. *I keep you safe.* He lied to Matthew about her. *No. My sister isn't special. My sister plays no part in this.* His heart is pounding. He is terrified. He knows what comes next, the start of his journey and the end of it. His birth, his death, in one solitary leap. The circle feels infinite. *My coin is tarnished because Mom didn't keep it safe for me. She ruined it. She meant to but didn't mean to.* He faces Rose and Alex, his focus shifting slightly, *I protect you, but I can't do everything that I should do to keep you safe, but I will when I have to.*

Rose stares at him. He knows how much he will be missing her. *Billy, what are you talking about?*

My job. I keep you both safe.

Heather is in the hospital, pregnant with twins. Rose and him. His coin dangles from a spider-web of threads, his dead body on the ground. His birth, his death. Simultaneous. He feels the end rushing inevitably towards him, a memory he knows he hasn't yet experienced. He starts to cry. *Don't tell Mom. I have to keep you safe.*

Billy misses his mother. He misses his sister. He misses his cousin. They are right beside him, yet he is always running, always preparing. He knows in a moment he won't see them again until he dies. He feels his heart withering. He wonders what he might sacrifice—if the opportunity presents itself, which he knows it won't—to step out of his loop and live his life like a normal man. Would he? Could he? The thought feels selfish; Alex won't. Every time she is presented with the chance to concede, she continues. He would stop if she stopped. The future is his blind spot; he has no concept beyond his own existence. Once he jumps off Picnic Rock, it all ends. This was all for her. He misses her desperately. He cannot help but break down.

Alex crawls around Rose to soothe Billy.

Rose wraps an arm around them both. *I think we should start walking back.*

Alex agrees. *As soon as Billy's able.*

After a minute, Rose asks, *Are you ready to start back yet?*

Another minute, he answers. *Please don't tell Mom.*

Okay, Rose tells him. *This is our secret.*

Rose is lying. He overhears her admitting it to Alex. He is grateful her concern for him is greater than a promise. Had she kept her promise, would Alex tell Heather about her dream? What would happen if Heather remained oblivious to the impending danger.

Alex left the flames without her coin and now she has returned. She cries out in pain. Matthew did it, he pushed her just far enough. Matthew is ready to claim his prize, but Alex is no one's prize. Anything more, in Alex's weakened state, might kill her. Billy knows he must stop Matthew.

Billy is holding Matthew's Book. Daylight. Nighttime. Matthew is furious. Billy never told him this would happen. A small part of Matthew is joyous for her pain, revenge for his unrepairable broken neck. He still doesn't know the spell that obliterated Peter, that nearly killed him, was his own. He doesn't trust her. To him, she's like a dog that already bit him once. He's jealous of her power and wants it for himself. He's hurt by Peter's betrayal, and now he realizes everything was orchestrated by the one person he trusted. He questions that trust. He thinks this moment is when his luck changes and his plan lands on its rails, full steam ahead.

Billy, the Book in his hands, lit only by torchlight.

What's he doing? Alex squints into the sun.

Alex reaches for him, her fingertips brushing his shirt as Billy leaps out of reach. His arms ensnare Matthew and together, they tumble into darkness.

Only Matthew isn't here now. Matthew is there, later. Without Matthew, without understanding why he can see or where those threads lead to, his body smashes into the rocks below, coming to rest on the steep cliffside dropping into the valley.

Picnic Rock disappears beneath his feet, replaced by darkness. Matthew twists in his arms as they fall. His head swims as they crash in the pitch, Matthew tumbling away. Billy anticipates the agony of torn skin and broken bones.

Picnic Rock—a shadow of it—rolls over him, tearing up the soil and disappearing into the darkness of a night that has yet to come.

✻✻✻

Billy is in blackness. He hears his own panting breath. He hears the breath of another. A door opens. He can barely catch his breath. Why is it always dark?

The darkness brightens as his eyes open. It was dawn, and he is damp with dew, his clothing crusted with dirt. Looming above his head, silhouetted by the blue sky, is Picnic Rock. The stone face overlooking the valley is mottled with lichen except for one perfectly cleared rectangle. In this space, where the lichen had been fastidiously scraped away, are carved the letters, *Johnathan William Frost, 1*. Chalk marks what has yet to be carved. It will be completed later today.

He climbs the steep hillside. It's treacherous but not yet as eroded and steep as it will be when he is younger. Beyond it he spies a path; unlike the blazed trail he and Rose and Alex will one day walk, this is barely an animal path worn in the undergrowth. He follows the path. It seems different from how he remembers it two hundred years from now.

Not far ahead, there is a clearing. The trees and the undergrowth have been tamed back. Situated nearly in the center is a new house. A very pretty woman works outside, in the garden. *Sara*, he whispers to himself. She collects weeds in a pile to her left and places herbs in a pouch strung across her dark dress.

You don't understand, Peter, he is trying to raise his voice and not raise it at the same time. Their privacy is an illusion, secluded amidst towering bookcases. Solitude can never be an expectation, and their words risk excommunication—to the Farms, or worse—should anyone hear the heresy Billy is about to voice.

Okay, Peter says, *tell me again.*

What I'm talking about isn't magic. It's time. Time is infinite, but if you take a moment and remove it from time, he has an idea and slides a single Book so it overhangs the otherwise compulsively ordered shelf, *it has a beginning and an end you can send someone to.*

And why do I need this again?

Your Book, Peter. You told me that Sara Frost has a spell that could be used to untwin.

I think that's how it could work. Lot of good it does me, Peter complains, then lowers his voice again. *As it's writ, maybe it'll cause a miscarriage. Only Sara, with emotion, could use it to untwin.*

And how do we give this theoretic untwinned daughter of yours magic?

I've told you a thousand times, William. She needs to be in a witch the moment she has her magic removed and made into a Book. Then we give her that Book and—or so the theory goes—she'll absorb the magic because some of it was hers. She'll absorb any Book she touches after that.

Well, what if the witch who has her magic removed is also the one who has the untwining spell?

Peter is confused. *Sara died a hundred and fifty years ago. How would we—*

You have her Book, Peter. You've read Matthew's notes on the incident. We know it worked. Besides, if we use her, we already know how and when Matthew kills her. It's a win all around, Billy presses forward. *You get Sara to untwin Holly, and you put your daughter in her, too.*

Who's there? The woman looks up from her gardening. Billy freezes. She looks directly at him. Billy does not want to meet Sara. He does not want her to be kind to him. He knows what this day brings her.

A man exits the house, distracting Sara from her search. Over his shoulder he's looped a length of rope and a belt with a pouch of stone carving tools. *I am off to finish my claim on the rock,* he tells her. *Last day, I promise. Then no one can take this land from us.*

She looks off into the woods again, then shakes it off. She kisses her husband, and he begins on his way. Pausing, he tells her, *I will return for midday. I promise not to forget this time. I will not be late.*

Sara waves him off with a grin.

Disguising his own footsteps with Jonathan's, Billy continues on his way.

Eventually he comes to the edge of the woods and steps into a meadow of tall grasses and wildflowers. *Fallow farm field,* he says to himself. Maybe one day it will be a farm, complete with neat rows of vegetation, and then it will be left untended for years.

Only now, the meadow continues through scrub brush. For the better part of the morning, he walks. Without roads, without houses and cars and people, this area at once seems vast and tiny. Places seem so much closer together without roads separating them. This place is where his family will one day live. He misses his family. Even though it'll be dozens and dozens of years before they are born.

Ahead, not far from a narrow dirt path that constitutes the only nearby road, Billy spies a small shack. Unlike Sara's house, the hewn boards are tacked carelessly together to create four walls and a slant roof. There is a door but not a single window.

I remember the day we met like it was yesterday, Matthew tells him.

Billy recalls the shack before Matthew mentions it.

I was holed up in some half-way shack. I think it was a waypoint for people to overnight on their way further... anywhere. You were just some kid. Dressed so strangely. Matthew looks like he's daydreaming. *I worried I'd have to kill you.*

Walking to the shack, the door shudders against the doorframe each time Billy knocks. Nothing about this place feels sturdy.

The door groans open. A slash of light cuts brightly across a peering eye. *Move along,* the man grunts.

The nervous eye verifies Billy is alone.

And just as I'm trying to decide, Do I kill the kid if I can't chase him away, *you say to me….*

Matthew, Billy tells the man, *I've come to help.*

The door creaks wider.

I mean, the balls on you, William. I'm here to help? And just as I'm ready to crack your skull with my hammer, you tell me everything I know about Sara.

Matthew's face is a mix of fear and wonder. He releases the door. It wobbles on its hinge, opening wider until it settles and stills. *What did you say?*

I know you're going to see that witch today, Billy tells him. *Sara Frost. She's still got magic. She's the last one with enough magic left.*

Matthew looks over his head, scanning the road and the brush along the sides. *Jeremiah send you?*

Billy knows Jeremiah only through Matthew's description. Matthew has been true to his word and keeps Billy safe from the ancient one. *No,* he tells Matthew. *Jeremiah didn't send me. You're not going to want to believe me, but you did.*

Matthew is laughing now, recapitulating his story. He wipes his eye. *You did,* he repeats as though it is the funniest punch line of the ages. *I had that hammer behind my back. I was ready to cave in your skull and call it a day. Then you tell me about how I grew up in a rowhouse in Brooklyn. How Jeremiah found me when I was fifteen. You told me about the door that led to the Library. You described my every memory, from the tri-foil hats to the maze.* He quiets. *Then you told me about the day I met Laurent Robaleaux…*

How do you know Laurent? Matthew accuses, his voice jittery. *He has been dead thirty years.*

…You will tell me about him, one day. He told you about all the others who tried before. He took you under his wing. You weren't convinced at first, but you came around. There were so many who tried and failed, most lost to history. Even those remembered aren't known for what they really sought to accomplish.

Matthew gulps. *Tell me, mister future boy, what happens today?*

You go to Sara's house. You cast a spell to mute her magic. Her husband comes home. While you're taking the magic out, you'll see someone, in Sara's eyes.

Someone? Who?

Someone who won't be born for over a century. Someone I will lead you to.

Matthew grins. *Oh, William. I am so sorry I threatened you. You told me about George and Abigail. You told me that when one of my boys murders her husband, I had to kill him. I thought I was so smart.* No killing, I told them. *I figured that would prevent your prophecy from coming true.* He nods his head. His neck's been crooked for so long, it looks wrong straight. *I guess I should invite you in, William. Welcome you to our family.*

Matthew steps aside to allow Billy entry. Billy lets them think they've surprised him when Matthew's henchmen leap from behind the doorframe and tackle him and tie him down to a solitary stool in the center of the floor.

****

He knows Matthew is serious when he shouts, *I will slit your throat when we return, unless everything you promise is exactly as you say.* He knows Matthew won't, because even as he sits there, his hands tied, he knows it is a threat that takes centuries to be completed.

Billy is alone. The door is closed and a thick branch leaned against it. Why isn't he terrified? Because he knows this day turns out just fine. He can't quite figure out how he knows, but doesn't question his lack of fear. With nothing to look at, Billy sleeps, slipping in and out of dreams. In one, he is also tied in his chair, his eyes covered. A door opens. Someone beside him moves.

Billy opens his eyes. Thin scars of light slash the darkness around him, dust motes glow in the still air that smells heavily of dirt. His arms bound behind his back with coarse rope, each piece laced with sharp, frayed threads that scratch; he waits for Matthew's return.

Matthew will leave momentarily. George is beside him, Abby and Marta across the living room. Beyond them a panorama of New York City. Facing him, it takes Alex a moment to see through the years on his face, and as soon as she does, her smile alights. Her smile carries so much weight, it rises slowly. She is happy, but also, life has left her haggard and exhausted. He holds his arms forward to stop her from getting closer; she mistakes this for the offer of an embrace. He raises his head, offering his throat. He makes certain Matthew's slender blade will cut deep. There is no second chance to get this right.

Matthew slit his throat so many times it lost its shock. The knife parting his skin comes as expectation; his nightmare will be over soon. So much so, he now welcomes it.

Why did he experience moments in time when people speak of them, but when it comes to himself, he can only see his death? It is a cruel trick of time that he can be blessed with the ability to see the future, but know only how his life will conclude.

And yet, while he has lain in his blood so many times, knowing this is finally the end of his journey, it is the darkness that troubles him. It is absolute and eternal.

The door creaks open. Matthew tells the other men to wait outside. Babies are wailing. Matthew's clothes are soaked through with sweat and splattered with maroon bloodstains.

You saw her. Billy isn't asking. Matthew often recounts their exchanges when chatting with others. He's told Peter about near every conversation they shared, but this.

Matthew walks right up to Billy. His pace suggests violence, coming to an abrupt pause at Billy's feet. He huffs dramatically. He paces, his leather-soled shoes scrape the dust into the unfinished wood flooring. He rubs his forehead. *We took every drop of magic from her.*

Billy repeats himself, allowing his inflection to rise, *You saw her?*

Matthew holds his hands out, demonstrating how they tremble. Without looking at Billy he states, *You knew I would spy her in there.* He lowers his hands. He still isn't looking at Billy. *How did you know?*

Billy leans forward only a little. It's been a long time in this shack. Hours for them, but years for him. Years doing other things. Meeting Peter. Plotting with Matthew. All the while, he was always here. *Untie me.*

Matthew hesitates. *I was doing those unspeakable things to get the magic out, looking right into her eyes. I saw her in there. Just like you promised. How did you know?*

Billy feels sick. Matthew needs to know. Alex told Rose, who told him. She was in Sara when Matthew murdered her. Did that happen because of him? Had he not told Matthew, had he kept quiet, would that have happened—did he make that happen the moment he told Matthew she would be? Instead of expressing doubt, Billy says, *That's not the way this works. If you want your plan to work, Matthew, there can be no questions. I tell you what you need to know. Not how I know it.*

Matthew rubs Billy's back, still laughing at the absurdity of his story. *I was still considering my options. Do I kill the kid or do I trust him? I was so unsure. The things you said, the knowledge you had, were things so personal to me that they could only mean that Jeremiah knew every facet of my agenda and sent you to humiliate me. You told me that's what I was thinking. That the reason everyone before me failed was because they didn't know the future, they didn't know the people they needed to complete their plan.* Matthew slapped Billy's back. *Then you asked me what happened when Sara's husband showed up.*

Matthew blanches at the question. Matthew sneers but doesn't respond. He covers his eyes and rubs his forehead. *There has not been a real witch seen in almost thirty years. The Books we make are thin and weak. This one,* he laughs unemotionally, *she was filled with magic.* He turns away from Billy. *And those eyes. I could see them, staring at me. Hating me. Not her eyes, but those other ones.* He turns back, *Who is she, the one inside?*

The Book you made today contains the magic of two witches, Sara Frost and the one I will help you put inside her.

This stops Matthew's pacing. *Help me put...? When did we do that?*

She hasn't been born yet. Neither has her father or his father or his. When the time comes, you will find her father. He'll do it for you. He'll make today possible.

Who sent you to help me?

Billy laughs. He can smell Matthew, his face pressed against his sweat-soaked shirt as they tumble from Picnic Rock into darkness. *You did. The day you put all that magic back into that girl, you sent me here, so I could be your guide, returning you to that moment.*

Matthew is silent, deep in thought. Several times, he mutters to himself, *I sent you?* Each time the inflection changes as he ventures from rhetorical question to defining statement.

Once Matthew has finished convincing himself, Billy speaks. His words come slow and certain. *Jeremiah is all powerful. You've seen his golem army. He doesn't need a Book to cast a spell. You've heard rumors that he's as old as time itself. I know what you're thinking, Matthew, when you think about Jeremiah. That's too much power for one man to wield. He must be stopped. But you're only a man. Laurent gave you the knowledge of those who came before. Hundreds of them throughout history, perhaps since the beginning, sharing their experience with each successor. But you know that's not enough. How could it be if they all failed? You're afraid and have no one to help you because these are the sorts of thoughts that get a man killed. Today, you're not alone. Today you have knowledge that wasn't passed to you from any of those who came before you. Today you know the path you're on leads you to a place none of them ever reached. How do you know? Because you sent me here to tell you. Because together, we found the way.*

Matthew never sent him, but Matthew telling him he did made it no longer a lie. *I sent you back to guide me on this path. It's the most brilliant thing I've ever done. When does it happen?*

Not yet, is always Billy's reply.

✳✳✳

Billy sees the way the hellish flames alter the shadows across Matthew's face, transforming his scowl to a mad grin, shifting it back and forth as he watches Alex burn on Picnic Rock.

Matthew reaches into his pocket and withdraws and opens a pocketknife with a burl wood handle. *I guess I won't slit your throat.*

As Matthew cuts the ropes binding Billy's hands, Billy says, *Not today.*

He can feel the knife, kept razor sharp for over a century and a half, slicing through his skin, a sting like electrical fire burning his throat. It's like he's swallowing salty warm water and it all goes down wrong.

As though that wasn't all enough, Matthew says like he's about to reach the punchline of a lengthy joke, *you tell me about the two other men who helped me. One of them'll betray me but you don't know which, so I have to kill them both.* Matthew shakes his head. *I guess what I did to that woman made that easier.*

Billy doesn't know how they'll betray Matthew. But Matthew said they would. Because Billy said they would. Because Matthew said they would. They each confirmed one another so many times Billy could never be certain who said it first. Could they have both said it because the other one told them; an infinite loop, a snake of lies or truths eating itself.

Matthew nods and leaves Billy in the shack. Matthew utters the guttural chant to cast his spells. The pleading men drop. The babies howl.

Matthew returns and hands Billy one of the swaddled infants. *This is George,* Billy tells him. *He's important to our story.*

What else will you have me do? He holds up the girl. *Slaughter an innocent babe?*

Billy shakes his head. *No.* He touches George's nose. *When this boy is ready, he'll make a Book from her.* Billy's nose wrinkles as though George is soiled. He wishes George could have been kind to Abigail. George believes cruelty makes the Books.

Matthew hides his shock well. *Anything else you have to tell me?*

For now, all you need is time. Lots of time.

I left her coin, Matthew gestures over his shoulder as though pointing to Sara's house. *If I need to live that long.... You should have told me before I left her for dead.*

Billy looks down shamefully. *Don't you worry, Matthew. You'll have plenty of coins.*

****

Billy stands beside a desk in the Library. A stack of closed Books leans precariously against the bookcase beside him. He doesn't touch the covers or attempt to read them. He wants nothing to do with them. He remembers his mother taking him and Rose to visit his cousin, Alexandrea, and seeing her father, Peter, wander around the house like a zombie. That was years ago; Billy was a child.

He helps Matthew raise Sara's child, George. He's an easy baby, happy much of the time. He called Matthew *Daddy*, and Billy *Willy*. He's a precocious child and an adventurous teenager without a rebellious streak. He was told from early on he was born for trying times. Billy tells him a little about Sara once he's old enough. Matthew fills in the rest, peppering his story to hide the bad taste George will eventually have to swallow when he meets Alex and learns the truth. George never connects Billy to William. He never sees the similarities. In spite of the years he's lived it's perhaps never important enough for him to care.

Billy had been to the Library before. But this might be the first time. Baby George is two. Matthew wants to gift Billy a Book all his own. The three of them stand in one massive aisle. Baby George grasps the spines of the Books within reach on the bottom row and pulls them, disrupting their neurotic order.

It doesn't matter which, Matthew tells him. *Take one. You can't tell what spells it has, until after you've opened it. It's a crapshoot.* He watches Billy a moment, misinterpreting his reluctance for hesitation. *If you pick a dud, you can try again, but I'm told that reading too many Books drives men mad. It's a final witch's trick. Whether it's true or not, it's left dozens of men carrying around Books that can't do much more than loosen knots or divine crochet patterns. Hope you get one that is good enough on first pick.*

Billy looks about the aisle at the amazing disparity of Books. Some are no bigger than pamphlets, others are too immense to do anything but sit pretentiously on a display table.

At the far end of the row, he spies several desks, places where one might sit to study, just like at a library whose books contain literature. He stares, trying to uncover the fondness he suddenly feels, as though those desks possess meaning he's forgotten. Or has yet to recall.

You remember the boy I've told you about?

Matthew laughs without humor. *Peter.* Matthew doesn't believe him. It's too perfect a prophecy: *One day this young man will come along, and he'll become your prize student. Through him you'll make the special girl who will empty this Library. She is your key to defeating Jeremiah: Your one Book.* It is through sheer repetition that Matthew begins to either believe or at least humor Billy his endless descriptions of this Peter who has yet to be born. The Peter whose parents aren't yet born. *What about him?*

Billy points at the desk. *I met him right there.*

Met? When?

Billy stares blankly, trying to remember. *Soon.*

Matthew grabs baby George by the collar and drags the toddler from the bookcase. He was putting scraps of dry leather in his mouth, torn from Books. *You said he wasn't born yet. You said he won't be born for a very long time. Which do you mean? A long time or soon?*

Billy exchanges his gaze from Matthew to the desk. He passes Matthew, walking towards it. He turns around. The aisle is empty. Further down the aisle, beyond where he expected Matthew, another man examines a Book and replaces it on the shelf, taking the very next one. He looks up and regards Billy, his eyes judging the style of Billy's dress. Billy has seen clothes like this man wears in his mother's mother's old photographs. He turns away and continues towards the desks.

Waiting there, his leg twitches. The stack of Books dares gravity to topple them over. Loitering is discouraged in the Library. An unwritten tradition. A belief that people without purpose loiter, and purposeless people shouldn't have access. He isn't about to examine these Books, even for appearances. He has purpose, and it is to loiter. To hell with tradition. In a few minutes, a boy a few years younger will show up, having entered the Library for the first time. Or so he remembers.

Billy ignores the stares burning into the back of his head. He can almost hear their disdain at his idleness. He is not reading or studying or looking for spells or doing scholarly work or making repairs to save the older, decaying Books before their pages are beyond repair. He wants nothing to do with them. He knows Alex will eventually take care of them. He'll never be here when she is.

Excuse me, the voice is one used to confidence, but heavy with uncertainty.

Hi Peter, Billy greets the newcomer with an extended hand. *Nice to meet you. I'm William. Matthew sent me to get you started.*

Disappointment weighs Peter's voice, *Okay.* Billy guesses he was expecting Matthew.

Billy puts his arm over Peter's shoulders. *I'm glad you found your way. I'm told that maze can be, well, intimidating.*

Peter guffaws. *I practically shit myself when I saw it. Matthew said I should just charge in and walk. It's confidence that gets you through, he said, but after a while I started to think I was going to die there.*

Billy nods as Peter speaks.

But I'd walked too far to ever find my way back. I wasn't going to give up. Part of me was panicking that I was lost and the other part figured if I walked long enough I'd find my way through. And then there was the door... the three doors.

Everyone has a theory. Matthew told me that when this place was made, someone must've calculated how long a man's will can hold and made it take exactly that long. How did he know? Did Matthew tell him that? He would, one day. *That labyrinth,* Billy continues, *can make even the most confident of men rethink their life choices. That you made it through says all I need to know about the person you are.*

Peter takes Billy's words in. *William, is it?* Billy nods. *Matthew wants me to be his pupil.* Billy nods. *It seems so, I don't know, coincidental.*

Billy laughs. *I'm sure it does.* He looks at Peter's face, his suspicious light brown eyes, the life and joy and energy in his lanky frame. Billy's smile fades. Peter has so few years left before he will become broken and gaunt and empty. This boy exudes life. He is charged with it, like electrical charisma. He knows nothing of that journey, of the decisions before him. Of the multitudinous paths he could choose. Because Billy will light but one. The notion is crushing. He feels buried by the weight of his guilt. Although he knows they are the same, when he looks at this Peter, he cannot see the shuffling zombie, his face slack and drool-shiny. Yet, when he is near zombie Peter, all he can see is this one. His youth bled dry. His life wasted for the benefit of others. This young man, this boy, is his uncle. His mother's twin brother. He is eighteen. Billy almost can't breathe, overcome with the knowledge that on this day, the day Peter and Billy meet, Peter's fate is sealed.

Peter, perhaps sensing doubt in William's thoughts, says, *There's something so familiar about you. Did we meet before? Did we go to the same school or something?*

Billy shakes his head. *I was homeschooled by my mom. Me and my sister.*

Twins?

Billy nods, thinking of Rose. He sees her. In the field George led him to. The field with flames soaring into the air, other men screaming and running. She is amazing. She is powerful, too. Crazy powerful. Scary powerful. Something about her magical ability seems too natural to come only from her Book. He sometimes tells George about his sister. He feels like he's bragging, considering Abigail is being raised at the Farm and will one day be made into a Book. Billy pauses. He wonders if this is why George lets Rose have his Book there, in the field.

You don't understand, George tells Billy earlier that day. Billy's heart aches for the constant pain George must be in. He brought Alex to the Library and showed her Abigail's Book. Then she burned him. Why was he bragging to her? Trying to prove how capable he was? George continues, *Jeremiah is bringing an army. Matthew says the Library has never been organized like that. You see how it is. Most patrons don't even know Jeremiah exists. Someone invites them, like Matthew and you invited Peter. They show up and study or do magic. Most of them don't even know how the Books they study are made. Jeremiah is a shadow. He controls and manipulates from afar. It gives him far more power than if he were some obvious leader. I expected Jeremiah to have his golems. He's suspicious of me. He's suspicious of Matthew. Matthew wants me there, so he knows right away what happens, but Jeremiah's going to figure it all out and kill me.*

Relax, Billy tells him. *Like you said, Jeremiah likes being a puppeteer. He's going to underestimate Alex today. It's only a matter of time before she has the entire Library.* Billy has no idea that this will happen. Alex's future is part of the darkness ahead.

George shakes his head. *Didn't you listen to Matthew? It's not that simple. Jeremiah is the Library. He says no one understands how deeply everything is entwined.*

Billy's never heard this before. *What do you mean, entwined?*

George explains, *I don't think he cares about the Books. It's like they aren't the real magic. They're just books and the magic is something else.*

What do you mean?

Like if Matthew succeeds and Alex burns them all he doesn't care.

How do you suppose that changes things? Billy isn't sure he believes. Everyone knows a spellbooks magic is writ on their pages.

What if the Books are just women, and when we read, we're not reading magic, but waking her to make the spell. What if the Library is the magic? What if Jeremiah is the magic? What if something we've never seen before is the magic?

I'm a twin, too, Peter replies, jarring Billy from the field. *You kinda remind me of Heather. She's my sister, although she'd kill me if she heard me say a guy reminds me of her.*

Heather Hawthorne? The name spills from his mouth before Billy realizes. Of course, Heather is Peter's sister. But meeting Peter makes Billy wonder how the years will change his mother.

Peter's eyes widen, *You know Heather? She's here—I mean in the city—she and our friend, Abby. We all came together. You should hang out with us later. Maybe we can sneak into a bar or a club or something cool like that.* He makes certain no one is close enough to overhear. *If you have ID, maybe, you know, we can all get in. That would be so cool.*

Billy grins. What would hanging out with his mother be like? He'd be older than her in this moment.

We're almost too behind schedule for that, he tells Peter, turning away. He hopes Peter perceives his disappointment. He wants Peter to want to please him. He is just enough older for the other to look up to him. Not older like Matthew. Peter thinks Matthew is old. He has no idea *how old*.

This makes his trusting Billy a simpler matter. Billy can push him in the right direction. But before he will take a single step, he needs Peter to believe he can walk. He needs to believe the choices he makes are his own. *You know how many Books the Library contains?*

Peter looks around. *Millions.* There is a nonchalance to the word.

You know how they're made?

My mother said…, Peter hesitates. *I've heard*, he pauses, unable to finish, panic creeping across his face. The stains in his armpits are dark and fresh.

Billy nods confidently. *Your mother was right.*

He selects a Book from the pile, sliding it out from between others. He hands it to Peter. *Open it.*

Peter's hands hang in the space between them. *I don't think I should*, he says at last.

Billy urges the Book forward. *You should. Open it. Read.*

Peter's face blanches. Sweat beads across his forehead.

Billy forces a grin. *You're not afraid, are you?*

No, Peter defends. He still hasn't taken the Book.

Billy holds it awkwardly cantilevered between them. He whispers, *They beat the magic out. Break their bones and pluck out their eyes until they regurgitate it.* Should anyone hear him, he would find himself a guest at the Farm, but it needs to be said. Peter needs to know his old mother's tales were true.

Peter is captivated by Billy's whispers. His mouth hangs slightly open, closing only to swallow.

I know you understand, Billy hisses, *how cruel it is. You know it has to stop. It could be your sister… Heather could be next.*

Peter pushes away the Book, *Don't threaten my sister.*

Take the Book, Billy forces it at Peter. *Only you can make sure it never comes to that.*

Peter hesitates. The established trust between them is too easily bruised. What Billy is proposing is heresy. Peter will someday tell him he was worried this was a test.

I'm not testing you, Peter. And I'm not threating Heather. I'm protecting her. Take the Book. I can't make you trust me, but you will. I want to show you this, and you won't understand until you do.

Peter reluctantly slides the Book from Billy's hands.

He opens it.

Billy hides the page with his open palm. The dry paper against his skin is as close as he ever cares to come to a Book. *Pay attention to the feeling you get as you read it. She'll tell you what happened.* Billy withdraws his hand and steps back, crossing his arms.

Peter casts his eyes to the page. Billy can't help but grin at Peter's expression when he sees the nonsense written there. He thinks this is a joke, that Billy is hazing him. Peter nearly looks up to ask—to accuse—when he sees something. This is the first Book he'll read. It won't be the last. Matthew's fear of madness is unfounded. Peter will read from countless others after this.

You'll feel her, like the flutter of eyelashes. Listen carefully. She'll tell you.

The writing is gibberish. It's not even letters. It makes no sense.

It never will. You don't read it. You control her. You make her do it for you.

Peter breaks eye contact with the Book. *I make her do it?*

The truth is brutal. Unless you've wielded the hammer, you cannot accept what happened. None of them can. They pretend the Books give them the magic. They pretend they are studying Books. Pretending to be scholars of magic rather than complicit in the bondage on the page. Billy points his chin generally to the Library. His voice is deep and low. *They'll never tell you these things. They will never willingly believe it's not them making magic. That magic is what remains of her, scribbled upon the page.*

Billy's words work across Peter's face. Billy never appreciated Heather's rants about men and magic, but is grateful he listened, otherwise how would he know what to say to his uncle?

Billy's stomach twists with a pinch of anxiety. He wonders if when he leaves the Library, Peter will share this experience with Heather. Will that drive her furor? Could he once again be creating the feedback loop that informs his decisions? How much of the information upon which he relies has he authored?

Peter looks up from the Book after several minutes, his eyes wet, his face ghost-like. *I never want to read another Book as long as I live.*

Billy puts his arm around Peter. *You understand why we need to end this?*

Peter nods.

Then you'll have to read more Books. Many more.

Peter's eyes beg for explanation.

Matthew sent you here to meet me. He needs your help.

What does he want me to do?

It's not you, Billy confides. *It's your daughter he needs.*

Peter's face darkens. *I don't have a daughter. I've always worn a condom.*

Billy giggles. *You don't, not yet. But you will, and if she's going to be capable of ending all this, we've got a lot of difficult work ahead of us.* Billy leans so close to Peter he is sure his breath tickles the hairs in Peter's ear, *Matthew must always think we're working with him, even when we're not. That's the only way we keep Heather safe. You and me, Peter. This circle of trust includes no one else. Understand?*

Okay.

Billy can hear the reluctance in Peter's voice. Peter is worried his loyalty is being tested.

I've really put myself out there for you, Peter. I know you think you're the one being compromised, but you'll soon learn you're the one with all the power.

✳✳✳

You meet with Matthew tonight?

Peter leans against the desk, the one at the Library where they first met, years ago. *Yeah,* his lips tense as he fails to hide his growing grin. *There was a particular book out on his desk.*

Billy stared at the city through the large window in Matthew's apartment. Matthew paced. *Shouldn't Peter be here by now?* Sometimes it is so hard for him to tell the order of events.

Matthew stared at Billy. *You slip?*

Come again?

Matthew walks his fingers across the desk, *That thing you do. One minute you've gone somewhere. Then you're back. Done something you don't remember. You don't even realize, but everything's different. Sometimes you're older, sometimes your clothes have changed.*

Billy stares at Matthew as though the old man is insane. *I didn't slip.* He doesn't remember the clothes he put on this morning and is concerned he's wearing something different. If he wore the same sorts of things everyday, this wouldn't be an issue. He looks himself over, becoming more and more uncertain. *I didn't slip,* he repeats, as much for his benefit as Matthew's.

Lately there is tension between them. Billy fears that Matthew senses Billy isn't being forthright, senses duplicity among his loyal team, senses Peter is hiding things. He has no evidence to any of this. He's learned not to act on his gut and risk alienating the only men who he believes are capable of steering him to success. Instead, he stews. He lashes out. He is curt and abrupt and abusive. It passes when what Billy said would happen comes to be. Which it always does. Some roads make the journey feel so much longer.

Matthew regards his clock again. He leaves Billy in the study. *You thirsty? I need a drink. What do you want? You told me this kid's the one, but it's like he takes nothing seriously. Typical of his generation. Slackers, every last one of them.*

I'll have whatever you're having, Billy calls after him, his shorthand for a glass of water with ice. He turns to follow, but not before hiding a thin book between two others on Matthew's desk.

Matter-of-factly, Matthew adds, *Dany's doing great work in Paris.*

Billy nods. Dany is Matthew's answer to Peter. A backup plan. A kid from some nowhere called Angers. *Awnjay,* Matthew pronounces it. Billy always laughs when he sees it written; a place spelled like anger is too ironic not to find humor in it. Matthew secreted him away to a safehouse somewhere in Paris, where Matthew has forbidden Billy from going. If Peter fails, Matthew will have his loyal follower to pass his knowledge to when the time comes. Billy is somehow sure they've met. Maybe at the Library. Maybe another time. *Dany, you'll know what to do.* Billy doesn't take it to heart that Matthew has a plan B. That after all these years, Matthew still harbors a modicum of distrust. The proof Matthew requires to trust one person is one notch above absolute certainty. Even knowing the future isn't enough to satisfy him.

Peter leans on the Library desk. *Yeah, not just any Book.* He holds up the thin text, a grin plastered across his face so large he looks in danger of popping out his eyes. *I got to his apartment late, like you told me. He was filthy drunk. He was all,* You're late. I need to lie down. Go see what I dug up for you in my office. *I went in and the first book was his. You know, the book he wrote detailing Sara Frost, how he took her magic, what he thinks it does, yada-yada. There were others, analyzing specific types of spells and whatnots. One on the theory of looping time onto itself.*

The time loop, Billy complains, *it's all just theory. Just a lot of big words separated by a lot of maybe's and perhaps's. There's not even a clue how to make it work.*

Billy puts his arm over Peter's shoulder. *You worry about the spells. Leave time to me.*

There was one on untwining. Studies on Charon. Some ridiculous treatise on how the afterlife wasn't always the after. He laughs. *One big pile of mostly bullshit, but tucked right there was this baby,* he pulls a book from behind his back. *It theorizes doubling a coin and all the things that could, theoretically, achieve.* He waves the book in the air, his voice a shouting whisper. *It's exactly what we need!*

✳✳✳

The drive from Matthew's apartment to the country feels endless. George drives their Toyota sedan. There is still novelty in motor vehicles for him. Pausing at a rest-stop on the turnpike, Billy behaves like a seven-year-old, pinching his crotch and complaining how badly he needs to piss.

He enters the stall and pulls a flip-phone from his pocket. He bought it weeks ago. He'd set it up but not yet used it. He hopes it works. There is one contact. No name, just a number. He dials and waits.

There's irritation in the answering voice, *Nurses station. How can I help you?*

He recognizes the voice immediately. *Please listen to me, Holly,* Billy pleads. *I'm an old friend of Peter's. I'm calling to tell you... it's happening today.*

The phone holds, silent. Eventually, Holly says, *What do I do?*

Nothing you weren't already doing. One change in your pattern fucks everything up.

Why are you helping me?

I'm helping her.

Holly is silent.

We still have hours to go. You must be there. He hesitates to hang up, waiting for Holly to say anything else.

You'll make sure she's safe?

That's my whole purpose.

It sounds like Holly is crying. *I've always known he'd come. But finding out today is the day I'm going to die... It's like the day I waited for Peter to come home. I'm so tired of waiting.* It sounds like she wiped her face. *I don't know if I'm ready.*

Billy fears she's going to back out. In his panic, he tells her something he hadn't planned to. *There's something else. You're going to have help. Just before we get there. The girl who escapes tonight and grows up is coming back to help you save her. You can see how she turns out. Peter explained to you how to fix her?*

My daughter's coming back tonight?

Billy repeated his question, *Peter explained how to fix her?*

Flip the coins. Yeah. I get to see my baby grown up? It's really her?

His heart aches. He knew Holly when he was a child, saw her when they visited Aunt Holly and Alex. Despite her façade, he always thought she seemed sad, burdened by grief. She'd reminisce about her husband as he wandered room to room. Always the same, like it was a rehearsed speech. Now here she was, learning that the moment she'd anticipated and dreaded is here. He sympathized with what he imagined she was feeling.

Forestalling his ending the call, Holly asks, *William; it's William, isn't it?* Billy doesn't answer, which is an answer in itself. *Like Heather's son. I bet she named him after you. Peter loved you like a brother. Anyway, thank you. For letting me know. For protecting my baby.*

Billy closes the phone. He stands and as the automatic sensor flushes the toilet, he drops the phone into the whirlpool and watches until it disappears. It takes with it all his angst for being one of the men who, having warned her, would try to take her daughter and her life.

***

George turns into the driveway and pulls to the end of the gravel. There's a car parked right up against the house, and Billy holds back telling him to pull up onto the grass.

George shuts the car and unlocks the doors. He turns to Matthew, in the passenger seat.

No one says anything.

Matthew turns to Billy, unbuckling his seatbelt to do so. *She's definitely here?*

Billy nods. He wasn't sure Matthew asked or stated, but he confirmed. Matthew won't realize for some time that they're both here. Alex and Alexandrea. Matthew doesn't realize he's about to have his neck broken. He doesn't realize how close this house is to the shack where they first met or to the house where he murdered Sara. If he did, he wouldn't need to ask. He'd know his journey is nearly complete.

How did you know? I think I sensed her a few minutes ago. Like a lighthouse at night. She suddenly appeared like a flash. How can feel I her now? Why today and not fifteen years ago?

Billy has made his career on Matthew's disbelief. He's survived on it. Always having an answer that leads them to the right moment. *I haven't let you down yet, have I?*

Matthew grins. *Not even once, William.* He looks at George and then at Gary. *What are you two numb-nuts waiting for?*

Gary is the relative newcomer; taking Peter's place when he disappeared. As to where Peter went, Matthew has only unconfirmed suspicions.

They all open their doors and step onto the gravel.

****

Reaching the front door, the three men step wide while Matthew wraps the storm door with his knuckles.

As the vibration of the aluminum door settles, Billy finds himself buzzing with anticipation. The moments that follow are everything. The culmination of—at least in Matthew's case—centuries of planning. The culmination of sacrifice. The culmination of magic. Everything could go wrong. There are so many moving parts in so many different timelines that Billy can't keep them straight. He is on Picnic Rock with Rose and Alex. He is at the door to Alex's house. He is on Picnic Rock with Rose and Alex and Matthew. Alex is inside, her coin flipped, finally about to discover magic. Alexandrea is inside, her coin dark, about to flee for her life after watching her mother and father die.

Just because he remembers all these things, just because he is doing all these things, offer no guarantees that each person will behave exactly as he remembers. It is time that is fluid, not him. He feels stretched so thin when recollecting the different moments, as though bits of him need to exist in each of them, so that all of him exists nowhere together. He holds his breath for fear if he tried to breathe, he'd be unable to. Seconds tick by, the four of them waiting at the door, not speaking.

Billy eyes Matthew. His nervous hunger is palpable. He feels Alex—senses her—for the first time. For millennia, his forbearers strove to find a way to depose Jeremiah, and here he is, a door separating him from his prize… or so he thinks. He does not envy Matthew the disappointment he will experience when he awakens to discover that not only did they fail, but the effort killed Gary and nearly killed him.

Matthew's hand abruptly raises to knock a second time, but hesitates, before striking the door several times, more forcefully than before.

A face appears in the window beside the door: Peter shuffling past. Matthew sees him. He makes as if to speak before shaking his head, clearly upset by the sight of Peter. *Stupid fool*, he whispers under his breath.

The door muffles the brief conversation occurring inside. The wooden door opens. Holly is framed on the other side of the storm door. Matthew's mouth twitches as his lips snatch the breath away from whatever words he nearly uttered. Matthew doesn't wait for an invitation and pulls open the storm door; the yowling, screeching metal startles them all.

Hello, Holly, it's been some time, Matthew says as though uncertain what else to say.

✳✳✳

Conflict twists Matthew's features as their exchange continues. This is Holly, Peter's wife. He's known her for years. Watched them date and marry and watched her throughout her pregnancy. Then they went into hiding. Perhaps he understands their motives. Perhaps he is processing the betrayal now that she's standing before him. Perhaps he's feeling things he hadn't expected to feel after so many years. *You stole her from* me. *You went with the plan until it stopped suiting you.*

He barely finished speaking when Holly snaps, *She was never going to be yours.*

Matthew is angered by her verbalizing the betrayal. He hisses, *That wasn't your choice. Peter was willing to die for our cause.*

Peter knew what he was sacrificing. He did that willingly, not for you.

And where did that get you? Look at him. Matthew's hand gestures at Peter, who is barely a shadow of the man Matthew and Billy remember. *The plan—my plan—never involved the sacrifices the two of you have endured. My plan would have—*

Don't you dare, Holly interrupted.

Matthew's surprise melts to resentment. His questions come barbed, intended to inflict nothing but pain. *Was it worth it?* He pauses, but not long enough to allow Holly time to respond. *Fifteen years, wiping his ass?* He looks at Peter, who was staring blankly at a wall. *Maybe Peter knew what he was sacrificing, but did you?* Holly's face reddens with anger. He'd struck a nerve and now he'll season the wound, *Tell me, Holly, is your life everything you expected?*

Holly's response echoed of how harsh she'd found his questions. Although her tone tried to remain forceful, the emotion in it shook her vowels. *You'll never understand. It was always me and him; there was never room for you.*

While George's face is cast in self-satisfied amusement, Billy can't hide the disgust from his. Holly doesn't deserve to be treated like this. Matthew will never understand that this was the only way it could work. Had they handed Alexandrea over to him at birth, he'd never succeed in getting her into Sara. She'd never be anything more than a girl he eventually makes into another Book. It's easier for him to blame his current lack of success on Holly rather than acknowledge—as Billy has tried fitfully to explain—that Holly did exactly what she needed to do.

Gary backhands Matthew's arm. *Why are we talking to her?* He snarls, speaking as much to Holly as he is to Matthew. *What are you waiting for?*

Billy groans. Gary only knows Holly through Matthew's vitriol and disappointment. Matthew asked Billy to procure a man who would do whatever Matthew needed, without regard to morality. Everything about Gary disgusted Billy, but when the two met on a frigid January afternoon on Staten Island, Billy knew he was the man for the job.

Something wrong with you? Gary hasn't released Billy's hand after shaking hands, following introductions.

It's just the wind, Billy lies about the expression Gary saw him make, *freezing my eyeballs.* He enunciates like a New Yorker, all his emphasis on *balls.* As he shakes Gary's hand, the Reaper rips out his coin. The sudden violence, the screams, the stench of putrid dust in the air, the chaos, and the screaming practically overwhelm Billy. He is looking into the face of a man as he witnesses his brutal death. Bringing Gary into their fold will be temporary. Knowing he is cementing Gary's destiny gives him some reservations, but none so significant as to change his mind.

I'm not waiting, Matthew tells Gary. *She's upstairs. I can feel her. I've never been so close, and I'd rather have Holly's cooperation.* He looks directly at Holly. *Deep down you know this is happening no matter what. I'm letting you choose to be on the right side of history. Why else were you willing to make any sacrifices if not to prepare her for Jeremiah? You had to know giving her magic would attract his attention eventually.*

Your sick plan is to kill my daughter. At what point did you ever think I'd go along with that?

Matthew glances sideways at Gary and then turns back to Holly. Gary misreads the intent and pushes Holly as he says, *Come on, Matthew, what are we waiting for?*

Holly retaliates to Gary's aggression by pushing him.

Gary appears his Book. In a fluid motion, he opens and reads.

Both Matthew and Holly recognize escalations beyond their control. They've always had an adversarial relationship. This dance is not new. As Peter's girlfriend, then fiancé, then wife, Holly had been the distraction that took Matthew's most prized student from him.

Matthew makes himself a drink, looking not at what he is doing but at the view from his apartment, overlooking the dusky city. He slams his glass on the counter. Billy cringes, anticipating the shattering of glass and fallout of Matthew's charged temper. *Look, William, I get it. Peter needs to have a wife. He's not going to give birth to the girl alone. I just wish it was someone... pliant. Holly Tylerson is a pain in my ass.*

Billy approaches the counter. Rather than risk Matthew finally breaking something, he pours the gin and adds a splash of tonic to Matthew's glass. *You always obsess over the now. Never how it will play out. For someone who's lived as long as you have, you're impatient.* Matthew grins as he always does when Billy speaks a truth with which Matthew wants to— but cannot—disagree. *If Peter found someone who didn't captivate him, might he be more devoted to his study than his family? That means no children. Holly will demand Peter's devotion, which makes him more devoted to the cause. You can see that, can't you?*

Matthew laughs, shaking his head. *I can only judge the future by how I perceive the present.* He takes a sip of his drink and replaces it precisely in the ring of moisture it left on the counter. *How are you always confident it'll all work out?*

Peter, I'd like you to meet Steven. He's a friend of mine. Billy introduces the two. He'd met Steven a few weeks earlier, a purposeful encounter. He'd recognized Holly's brother in an instant. In a few weeks, Peter will take an exam and Holly will think he's cribbing off her. When he asks for her number, Peter puts together that he knows her brother. And she will put together that this is the Peter her brother has talked about. Then she'll give him her phone number; knowing he already has it.

Billy tells Matthew, *I'm just lucky, I guess.*

Matthew squints, *You just did that thing again, didn't you? Where'd you go this time?*

Don't worry about it, Billy dismisses. *If I told you every time, we'd never get anywhere. Sometimes it's harder to keep track of where I am than where I go.*

Sparks fly from Gary's fingertips; a sharp crack of electricity strikes Holly's hip.

Billy doesn't need to see Matthew's face to know he's furious. Billy tackles Gary.

Matthew turns to Holly. However he wanted today to go, that ship had sailed. Billy warned against Gary. *I get that you want him loyal, but remember, all dogs bite.*

Matthew shrugs. *You see something that turns out wrong?*

Turns out wrong? Billy plumped his bottom lip. *No.* Billy sighs. *If you get lost but still arrive on time, did things go wrong?* He doesn't wait for Matthew to reply. *He's an asshole.*

Matthew rubs Billy's shoulders. *I don't care if you like him. I need a third set of hands to replace Peter.* Matthew stares at Billy. *I know what you said. It still feels like betrayal to me.* Matthew shrugs. *At least I have Dany.* Dany from France, Matthew's Plan B. Proof that as much faith as Matthew puts into Billy, there's always room for doubt. *If we have to dump this guy afterwards, that's fine. I just want someone who can get the job done.*

Billy stares into middle-distance. *He'll never sell you out. He hates Jeremiah, almost as much as you. He's got an odd morality. He has no qualms about kidnapping a child if she's a witch, but he won't do dirty work for Jeremiah.*

I'm cool, get the fuck off me, Gary curses, his open palms demonstrate he is done fighting. Billy disengages and stands, disregarding Gary's extended hand. He turns to Matthew, *I told you so* written across his face. Gary mutters a stream of obscenities as he climbs to his feet.

Enough games, Holly. She's right up those stairs. I'm claiming what was never yours to keep.

Billy's gaze follows the instruction in Matthew's words: She's right up those stairs. That's Alex, his cousin. Alexandrea, his cousin. She's about to watch her parents die and he's complicit. He's going to tell her he adores her and tries to protect her, yet he's about to be the cause of her greatest heartbreak. Standing in the very crowded vestibule, Billy is alone.

She has a name. Holly's voice is laced with acid. *She's a child, my child.* As Matthew walks past, she backpedals and steps in his way. *Why her? Why now? There's got to be some other way. Some other child. Just leave her alone!*

You knew, he retorts. *Or why hide her? Jeremiah doesn't know, but he's no fool. He'll figure us out, and when he does, he'll destroy us all.*

Holly seethes. She isn't buying the excuse. *Everyone knows his name, but no one's seen your bogeyman. Maybe you made Jeremiah up to scare children. As though you'd need help.*

Billy isn't sure if she is accusing Matthew of fabricating the whole thing or downplaying the urgency and danger for herself.

Matthew tries placating her. *Holly, Jeremiah is very real. He won't talk. He won't negotiate. Not when he figures out we've betrayed him.* He leans closer, his tone dancing with condescension but never crossing the line. *You understand that, don't you? If we don't go through with this, we're all dead. She's the key, the only chance we have. There's no other way.*

Why her? Shouldn't she have a say? Shouldn't she hear what you plan for her?

He chuckles. *Holly, we all agreed to this,* he explains. *You lied; you stole her; you hid her. You had to know I'd come looking. You had to know I'd find her.*

I knew you'd try.

As though he's had a revelation, Matthew's question doesn't quite sound rhetorical. *All those years, you've lived dreading today would come, didn't you?* He shakes his head as though pitying Holly's reality. *How sad, always looking over your shoulder, waiting, knowing I was behind you.* He takes a breath and looks at Billy and George and Gary, his eyes urging them to hold. He returns to Holly, referencing Peter, *You're both such idealistic fools. Did you really think you could betray me? You made promises, swore oaths and broke them. Where did it get you?*

Stop it, Matthew! Holly's eyes betray the seething anger in her voice.

As though on cue, Peter shuffles towards them. Each time he sees his former student, Matthew's expression softens, if only for a moment. *Look at Peter. There's nothing left. He gave up everything! He made that sacrifice for the greater good. Not for you or even for her.*

Holly referenced Peter. *You can't know him and say that. Peter protected her.* Holly seemed at a loss for words and sobbed, *Don't do this to my little girl.*

Enough stalling, Gary complains. *Why are we talking to her if the girl is here?*

As he speaks, Matthew approaches Peter as though greeting an old friend. He places his arm over Peter's shoulders and appears his Book, showing Peter the open page with the same glee of a twelve-year-old boy sharing his first nude centerfold.

If you think I'll just hand her over, you're crazy.

Then Matthew is gone. With a single step sideways, he disappears into Peter. Every one of them—Billy, Gary, George, even Holly—shake their heads to clear the mental confusion. It is as though their eyes uncrossed and double vision disappeared; Peter and Matthew becoming one, except now Peter held the Book, grinning.

Peter looks at the other men. *Now she'll come right to me.*

Peter? How? Matthew, stop it! You're hurting him. What are you doing to him? What have you done?

As Peter takes to the stairs, Billy grabs Holly by the shoulders and draws her into a bear-hold, keeping her from attacking Peter. Although meaning it, Billy shouts for dramatic effect, *We don't want to hurt you or Alex. Don't make this more difficult. Don't cause someone to get hurt.* Her struggle falters. He releases her. She turns and stares at Billy, her face alight with recognition, and sobs.

She takes a step after Matthew, quick enough to be threatening, *You are not taking my daughter. Not today. Not ever. I will not let you have her.*

Holly, please. You're giving him no choice, Billy begs.

Really, Willie? Just put the bitch down. Gary storms past, clipping Billy's shoulder.

Billy is so disgusted by Gary he can barely tell what he's doing, tackling Gary from the stairs, slamming into the side chair and sofa. The two men wrestling on the floor. Gary pushes himself free and re-appears his Book.

Holly cries out, *Alex, don't let them take you!*

Gary fires a warning spark at Billy. *What's wrong with you? Quit fucking with me.* He fires at Billy again as Billy crab-crawls backwards, knocking over the coffee table, then at Holly, who used the distraction to make for the stairs.

Enough, George shouts, stepping between them, his hand falling on the flat page of Gary's Book. His gaze falls to Matthew—Peter—at the top of the stairs. *Are we here so he can do this alone?*

Gary gestures at Billy, *He—*

I didn't ask who started it. George helps Billy to his feet. *He's up there alone,* he warns, as Holly races up the stairs behind Peter.

The three men start up the stairs. They hear the muffled dialogue upstairs. Matthew says something.

Holly screams, *Get out Alex!*

What happened next… Billy can never be sure of the exact order of events. Each is such an individual experience that memory stacks them in different orders with each recollection.

A crack; the usual discharge of static electricity from a spell, but louder, more powerful.

Someone screams; a cry so emotional, so heart-wrenching, it slaps each of them to attention.

A wave of hot air rushes past them.

A whip-snap of a sharp explosion; like a hot glass cracked with ice water, but so loud the glass would be the size of the house.

A shock wave twists Billy's guts, passing through his body.

Matthew flings across the hallway, his body shattering the wall head-first. He looks caught in the shockwave of a nuclear explosion or whipped up by a tornado and tossed at incredible velocity, his accordioning body stopping only once he crunches through the wall.

George races up the stairs, nearly tripping over Matthew, and disappears into the bedroom.

Gary attends Matthew.

Holly is crying something to someone. Telling them they have to go.

Matthew's neck is broken. Gary shouts, *George, did you hear me?*

From the bedroom, George replies matter-of-factly, *Yeah, Gary, I heard you. Is he dead?*

Billy makes his way to the room, watching Holly speak to two versions of her daughter.

George, like he's giving an order, shouts, *Gary, I asked you a question!*

Gary was rising but kneels and touches Matthew's neck, *He's alive, for now.* He sees the empty shoes. *Peter's obliterated. George, it wasn't supposed to happen like this. No one gets hurt, remember?* He rises and turns into the room, spying the young, terrified girl. *She wasn't supposed to be that strong yet.*

Billy grins. She wasn't. Not the little girl they see.

George shakes his head. *She did this?*

Billy pushes past them. He grins at Alex. She is like the blur of a wave of heat. She is here but not; she is here but somewhere else. Sometime else. He answers them, *It was her.*

George urges, *Be careful, William.*

William nods. *I am.*

Billy watches Alex, watches Alexandrea. How different they look, the sixteen-year-old girl and the young woman, who lived through Sara's life and is now on Picnic Rock with him and Rose and Matthew, burning alive.

Whereas Alexandrea is panic-stricken, her eyes unable to stop scanning the room. Alex is staring right at him, her eyes narrowing as she tries to make sense of the familiarity. Billy so wants to tell her, but there isn't time.

Holly urges her daughter, *Alex, please focus. Go back through the mist. Take Matthew's Book. I love you.*

Billy sees her, sees the flames, Matthew's Book in his hands. Matthew gazes nervously into the flames consuming Alex, who screams and begs and cries. Matthew, whose neck is distended forward from his shoulders. Even Marta's coin couldn't heal his neck. Nothing could. He blames Alexandrea for disfiguring him. They bring Matthew back to his apartment. They leave the car in the driveway, using their Books to return there. They are men and can't heal him. They debate bringing him to the Library, to the Farm where Jeremiah stores his women, where they wait to become Books. They could force those women to heal Matthew. George insists they try.

Do you even know how to find it? Even if you knew, men are forbidden from entering the Farm, Billy argues. Matthew told him so.

George ponders Matthew's mangled neck. *We owe it to him to try.*

Billy doesn't have a retort. Then Matthew speaks, his voice choking on his crooked windpipe. *William said it turns out the right way. Listen to him. Find me a coin and I'll heal my own damn neck.*

Without so much as a breath, George says, *I'll be back. I'll find someone no one'll miss.* He makes for the door.

Wait, is all Billy can say. Wiping gritty perspiration from his forehead, he sees the mud of dust and sweat on his palm and realizes this is all that remains of Peter.

His stomach feels like a sack of toys a child shakes to dump them out. He races to the bathroom and heaves into the toilet.

Holly is ordering, but Alexandrea stares at her like she is mad. Billy wants to tell her it'll be okay, but the back of Holly's shirt is burned away, the skin seared, exposing charred meat. He cringes at the sight. Her motherly drive masking the excruciating pain so she can protect her daughter.

Gary gives up on Matthew: Matthew is alive. So long as Matthew lives, Gary still has a job to complete. *Alexandrea,* Billy hears Gary's anger, but also the tremble of fear in his words, *That's not your mother. Don't listen to her.* He snatches at Holly's glowing coin, as though reaching into her chest. His fist glows red. *Not anymore.*

Alexandrea watches in terror and cries out, *Mommy!*

Billy wants to intervene. Enough, he wants to scream, this has gone too far. There is his cousin, his dear Alexandrea, her whole short life ahead of her, and here she is, more terrified than any creature should be. He isn't half as afraid of the knife that is coming for him as Alexandrea appears, trembling before her mother as Gary extracts Holly's coin: Taking it for Matthew.

Gary tugs on the coin to sever the thread, but Holly's will is greater than his. It yanks from his hand, momentum knocking him to the floor.

Billy tries to be sooth Alexandrea, but he can't catch his breath. Charon would come soon, and Alex is standing beside him, watching her mother die again. He tries to sound calm and caring, his words come out too harsh. *I know you're scared, but things will be okay.*

Alexandrea stares right through him. Maybe she sees her young cousin somewhere in his face. Maybe she is distracted by something else.

George shouts, *William, what are you doing? Grab her!*

William hisses, *I won't touch her.* He doesn't want to touch them and disappear to another place. It was time for Alex to go.

Alex, please focus, Holly shouts, tethered to her supine body. She pulls Alexandrea towards Alex. *Go back through the mist. Take Matthew's Book. I love you. Now GO!*

As Alex says to her mother, *Don't make me leave you again. How many times do I have to watch you die?* Alexandrea is asking, *Mom? What?* Alexandrea hears that her mother is speaking to her but cannot discern when Holly is speaking to Alex and not to Alexandrea.

Don't touch that wall, Gary orders. Then to Holly he says, *Tell your daughter, or I'll do unspeakable things.*

Mom?

Go, Holly orders. *Now.*

With his foot, Billy pushes Matthew's discarded Book closer to Alex. He hisses, *The loop is closed. Get out of here.* She stares at him with determined but fearful eyes. He can hear the flames as she reaches, her eyes daring him to try something, collecting the Book.

She doesn't thank him but turns and disappears.

****

Alexandrea drops beside her mother; tears stream down her face. *Mom! Mommy?* and then, *Holly? Say something, Holly.* Then something catches her attention. Her tone changes and she asks, *Where'd you come from?*

Charon reaches to take his coin after Matthew's knife opened his throat, and Alex tries to fight it off. He sees every act, every spell, feels his revulsion and horror when the Reaper impales Alex on its claw. She writhes in pain as it lifts her off the floor.

Billy shouts, *We need to get out of here.*

Calm down. Charon's come for the mother, George reassures, his tone belying his words.

Gary shoots back, *I'm not leaving without the girl. Matthew needs her*, he motions to the crumpled form in the hallway, *more now than ever.*

Charon kneels at Holly's side, its palm demands payment.

What's happening Mom? Billy can't help but wonder if Alex and Charon are always destined for one another. The child knows her family more than most. Looking at the toddler, seeing it across Matthew's apartment, he is overcome with an overwhelming sense of peace. The extended hand, the large, impossibly dark eyes, the creature so empathetic as to relieve him of his pain, as if to say, *I am here so you can rest. Hand me your burden. Let me carry it a while.*

Holly is unrelenting, *Not yet. I've got to see my daughter safe.* Holly begs her daughter, *I can't stay, but I won't leave until you're safe. Go. Please, Alexandrea,* she motions with her head towards the wall of mist, *walk into it.*

Billy and George retreat to the door. It makes them uneasy the way Charon's presence makes everyone's coin glow, as though it might decide to take any of them instead.

Both William and George shout as Gary again reaches for Holly's coin, *Don't do that.*

Charon's face contorts with rage. In an instant, it becomes a slender mass of bone, sinew, and tattered fabric. Before Gary can lurch away, raise his hands defensively in the air, the gigantic nightmare slices his chest with a bone-clawed hand, extracting his coin as though his flesh and bone separates at its touch. With a crisp snap, the glowing tether between Gary and his coin breaks and disappears as falling sparks.

Gary crumples to the floor like a discarded suit at the foot his standing form.

Billy's seen it so many times, but each time, the violence is so abrupt his heart leaps from his chest.

George races into the hallway. Billy hesitates. As much as he tries not to, he can't help but hear the horrible clinking of bone as Charon claims Gary and sends him to the beyond. Like when it comes for Alex. Alex fighting, failing, he despairs. She is incensed. She is enraged, repulsed. The Reaper attacks her with the ferocity of an animal lost in the frenzied moment.

Struggling on the meat-hook like claw, Alex is lost but doesn't yet know it.

Billy wishes her death in peace, *Alex, there's no defeating death. Not with fear. Not with hate.*

Alex stares at him. As though too stubborn to die, she looks away, as if his words of comfort were a slight. Bleeding from Alex's whole being, blinding light unfolds and unfolds and unfolds like a blazing flower or a supernova of pure energy. Everything turns black.

He hears his breath. The breath of another. A door opens, glass panes rattle, the hinges barely squeak. Someone enters, others follow. Many uncertain footsteps. Hands touch his head. He anticipates the blackness peeling away to finally reveal who has come to render his final death.

As brightness comes into his eyes, he sees George attend Matthew in the hallway. He says to Alexandrea, *It's okay now. No one will hurt you.* He starts to leave and pauses. *He won't stop, you know. Matthew needs you too much. He thinks he's the only one who can stop Jeremiah. He doesn't understand.* He retreats and kneels beside George and Matthew.

He won't survive the drive, Billy says.

Fuck the car, George appears his Book.

****

I'm fairly sure it was her, Matthew collapses into his white leather sofa.

George comes out from behind the kitchen peninsula. *You think? You don't know?* He is still drying his hands with a small white towel which he nonchalantly tosses onto the counter. Matthew bristles at the misplaced towel. *Didn't William tell you she'd be there?*

Matthew rubs his crooked neck. It still hurts him terrifically years later. The fact he is even alive is a testament to his and their magic. *I expected something.* He twists in his seat to look at Billy. *You're really sure she can't?*

Like I said, Billy replaces George behind the peninsula and pours himself a glass of water, folding the damp towel and tucking it away. He hasn't eaten in days; the constant vision of the knife lingers behind closed eyelids. *She can't. Peter protected her. Cursed, maybe. Made it so you can't find her. Made it so she's incapable of magic.* As true as his words are, to tell Matthew that the Alex who broke his neck four years ago still hasn't discovered her magic would be like admitting his disloyalty.

Matthew slaps the back of the couch. *That's bullshit. How is that possible? Peter wasn't that talented. How'd he manage that?*

George replies, *Isn't it clear? He had help.*

Matthew turns to his reflection in the window, framed against the city outside. The sky is its usual golden-gray; not even the stars can compete with the innumerable lit windows and streetlights that make the city before him twinkle like a celestial miracle. *Who? Who could have helped him?*

George stands with his back to the windows. *The better question is when do we scoop her up? If she doesn't have magic, she's prey.*

If she doesn't have magic, Matthew growls, *I've wasted my whole fucking life. She's useless.* Repeatedly, he slams a fist into the cushion beside him.

George eyeballs Billy, silently transmitting his concern that Matthew is in danger of becoming irrational. *Maybe we should scoop her up anyway*, George proposes. *William said she needs to be provoked. If we had her, you wouldn't need to resort to stupid tricks in the forest. Maybe all she needs is a good prodding.*

Billy squints at him, *What's that supposed to mean?*

George shrinks from the accusation in Billy's tone. Billy hasn't forgiven him for Abigail. After a century George can't understand Billy's grudge. He was told to make a Book. That's what he'd done. Billy feels George didn't need to be so eager, so cruel about it. George replies, *Maybe she'll respond if her life is in real danger.*

I chased her through the woods, Matthew replies. *I used all the stupid horror movie tropes. Let them see me one moment and not the next. I got close enough that I could smell their body odor. It was dark. They were terrified. What more should I have done to provoke her?*

Billy's limbs are threaded through the rough branches lashed together, every movement jarring him. He thinks he's hallucinating a bent-necked man traipsing through the woods.

George gives Billy his look. It is a throwback to childhood, when Billy was teaching him there is more than one way to satisfy Matthew's requests. If he can understand what Matthew is trying to accomplish, what Matthew asked for is irrelevant. Billy understands; George has concocted an alternative plan. Without knowing what, Billy nods his encouragement.

George says, *We scoop her up. Maybe you weren't the threat you thought you were. If we have her, we can see if it's fear or terror or pain she'll respond to. A controlled experiment.*

That's not without danger, Billy warns. *Remember what happened to Peter, her own father.*

Matthew glares at him. *That wasn't her*, he spits the words at Billy. *I don't disagree with your idea*, he tells George. *We need to have a plan. What's the execution?*

George shrugs. *Figure out when she's vulnerable and swoop in. What do we have to worry about, her Familiar? What's that fat broad going to do that we can't handle?*

Matthew shakes his head in disappointment. *Beware the Familiar, boy*. William knows George hates being called boy. Matthew made sure he kept his youth, remaining twenty forever, even at well over one hundred. Always the child even though he was seventy-odd years older than Billy. *They're fiercely loyal and resistant to magic. They'll withstand ten times what'll drop an ordinary man. You don't want to go toe-to-toe with one of them, even with the right Book in your hands. You don't fight a Familiar with magic.*

How do you beat a Familiar, then?

Matthew punches his palm. *Old fashioned pugilism.*

Watching this broken old man make a physical threat causes George to grin. He says, *Okay, but there's three of us. I can take Alexandrea. If she doesn't have magic, she'll be easy to grab. You think you two old men can manage the Familiar?*

Matthew's mouth downturns. He is considering it. *What do you say, William?*

Billy finishes his water and pours another glass. *There'll be two of you. I've got someplace to be tonight.*

Matthew takes two tries to twist around in his seat. He stares at Billy for a long, uncomfortable, two minutes. Billy had never not been a willing partner and Matthew was digesting what this meant. Finally, he says, *Is this the day you warned me about? You're leaving?*

Billy stands silently a moment more. *I've done everything I need to help you, Matthew.*

We don't have her yet, Matthew counters. *One more week. Give me that, until we know for sure she's got it.*

Billy empties his glass a second time and deposits it in the sink. *You'll go after her tonight. They'll be at the hospital first. Heather's kids both need care. She'll send Alex and the Familiar out alone. Grab them at Heather's house.*

Matthew looks at the clock, *Tonight? That's hardly enough time. You mean to tell me you can't even join us for that?*

Billy shakes his head.

Why won't you give me this one last thing?

George agrees, *Come on, William. Give us one more night. We're so close. You've got to be there when we win. Whatever you've got to do can wait one more night.* His whine sounds genuine and needy.

I can't, Billy steps out from behind the peninsula. He heads for the door.

Wait, when do I send you, you know, back to the day we met?

It's a great question, and Billy hopes Matthew doesn't work out that if he'd never sent Billy back, then everything about their relationship was built on a lie. Billy takes a breath, feeling like he's off balance on a high-wire, without a net, over a pit of spikes. *The time's not yet*, Billy tells his lie.

That's it? You're just leaving? After all these years?

I'll be back, Matthew. The next time we meet you'll have her with you. You'll succeed without my help. That damn dark cloud of yours will be gone. You'll promise to return her cousin: me. Billy pauses, watching Matthew process what his words really mean: his next effort to get Alex will fail, but eventually he'll succeed. *When you see me, I need you to do something. You're not going to like it, but it's got to be done.*

Tell me. I'll do whatever you ask.

Tell us, George begs. *Tell us what we need to do.*

You need to understand the whole picture. She'll have magic, eventually. Keep trying until you provoke her. Show her The Library. Tell her about your plan. You'll figure it all out in time.

What if I can't figure it out without you?

He sees Alex on Picnic Rock. *Burn her*, Billy says, regretting the words. *Like a witch.*

That's it? Matthew is nonplussed by the suggestion.

It'll make sense eventually. Don't give up. You're so close. Just two or three weeks.

You haven't told me what you need from me.

Billy slightly raises his head and drags his fingers across his throat, *I need you to cut me right here. No magic, just your pocketknife.*

William, Billy, Bill, Matthew tries sounding gregarious. *Why would I ever do that?* He looks at George and laughs, trying to look like they share the joke, only George returns his laugh with a look of shock.

Billy likes that Matthew finally knows what the uncertainty of thinking he is being tested feels like. *Give me one good reason why.*

Billy opens the door. *Because I'm the reason Peter betrayed you. I helped him hide Alexandrea from you. Because there was only one way to make your plan work, and if you knew, you'd fuck it all up trying to do it your way.*

Matthew usually strained to climb off the couch, but he is on his feet in a heartbeat, coming around it, appearing his Book. Billy slams the apartment door as he exits to the hallway. He hurries down the dimly lit hall, and hears the door open behind him. He knows Matthew is coming for him, furious at his admission, eager to make good on his request right away. Billy turns back. The woman approaching him is tall and impossibly thin. She doesn't look happy that he is still waiting.

❋❋❋

She said she'll see you, Marta says once she is close enough to use hushed tones. She pokes his arm. *I'll be right outside the room. Try anything and getting ass-raped in jail will be the best thing happening to you tonight. Get it?*

Billy nods solemnly. The knife hangs in the air before him, a vision no longer linked to its own time but waiting for him in his.

Marta shows him her room. *Heather H* is written in block letter magic marker on a piece of surgical tape covering a metal slide beside the door. Marta gestures to the door. He hesitates; his stomach is gurgling, like an upturned bottle, its contents glug-glugging out.

How long has it been? How old is he now? He was sixteen when Matthew kidnapped him and Rose, and Heather hasn't seen him since.

He left the Library with Peter, who was eager to introduce his new friend to his sister and their friend, Abby. He showed Peter how to work the magic in the Book to find them, and it was in the crowded subway when Peter called to them, *Heather, Abby, hold up!*

They eagerly approached Peter, who says, *Hey, I want you to meet my friend.*

Hey, Billy says, looking at this child who would one day give birth to him and his sister. Seeing his mother takes his breath away. She is completely unaware of what her life had in store for her. He did. He is so proud of her. So sad for her. For all her youth, her strength, the years will not be kind. He could tell how cruel they will be in how old she'd be before he'd know her again. As though time were a vampire, sucking the life from her.

Standing there, his chest aches and head throbs. The temptation to tell Heather and Peter and Abby what was coming is so great, but he wonders for whose benefit it would be.

Hey, Heather shouts, a smile widening on her face. She holds out her hand.

I'm William, he takes her hand and holds it. She grins, likely at the way he sandwiched her hand in his. He is comforted by her smile, by the warmth of her hand. *I love you, Mommy*, he might have said.

What? I can't hear a thing, she screams back, barely audible over the grunt of people pushing around them in both directions. He feels like a rock in a stream. The world moving around this singular moment.

She keeps smiling at him; Billy wonders if she is subconsciously aware of their relationship. He can't take much more of this. Seeing her this long is killing him. He feels like his heart is being pulled back to a time in his youth before Picnic Rock, before he started slipping through time, to when he was just some kid who made bad decisions.

Dude, he leaned to Peter, using his thumb and pinky to mimic a cell phone. *I've got to take a call.*

Peter looks at him like he has rats for hair. *Take a what?*

Billy shakes his hand as though dropping his imaginary phone. Cells aren't even a thing yet. Sometimes he gets confused. *Sorry, I have an appointment. I gotta go.*

Peter starts saying something. See you soon or catch you tomorrow.

Billy waves to Heather. *Nice to meetcha.* He smiles at Abby who has been shyly lurking beside Heather. He departs, feeling Peter's confused glare burning into his neck. Seeing Heather felt too real. Seeing her so young made him realize what he's missed. What he's done. How he's hurt everyone he loved. When he next sees his mother, a few years later for her, five minutes shared in a city subway won't be remembered.

He turns into a doorway to catch his breath and enters Heather's hospital room. Did he just visit with her and Peter and Abby in the city, or was that years ago? The memory is too fresh to be old, yet he can't be certain any longer, as the odor of the subway dissolves in the anesthetic around him. He can't be certain of anything any longer. One moment he's talking Matthew down from his rage at Alexandrea's disappearance and the next moment he's showing Peter how to hide her.

He hasn't eaten more than a few bites for the past two weeks, completely unable to shake the feeling of the knife entering him. It is always there, always slicing through him. Seeing Heather makes him forget the blade. He feels dizzy at the sight of her. He grasps the doorframe. He stabilizes himself, hoping she doesn't see how gaunt and lightheaded he really is.

All children think their mothers are pretty. But seeing Heather, impossibly pregnant with twins—with him—she seems to glow. Her skin is plump and radiant. Seeing her makes him realize how much he misses his mommy.

Hey, he nearly whispers, unable to find his voice, *it's so good to see you again. It's been,* he struggles to catch his breath, *a really long time.*

Heather's face softens. *Marta said your name is William.*

He nods. *Yeah. You let Eric name me. You once said he hated his name because he could only ever have one. He wanted me to have as many names as I wanted. You called me Billy when I was a kid.* He sighs. *I think I would have been okay with Chris, though. I was always jealous of Rose's name.*

Rose?

Billy nods. *Rosemary. It's what you're naming my sister.*

Heather hisses, *How the fuck do you know that?*

William is afraid he'll leave this moment if he focuses too much on other times. There is no place he wants to be more than with his mommy. Just to feel her comfort one last time. He can feel Marta's lingering presence right behind him. *Is it okay if I come in? Just out of the doorway?*

Heather nods.

Billy enters cautiously, pausing at the foot of the bed. *You did it, Mom.*

Did what?

He touches his own belly, *When you, you know, the thing.*

Heather's disdain at the accusation washes across her face, *What thing?*

When you reached into your womb and grabbed my coin. Two days before Christmas. You thought you failed. You pulled and pulled, and it hurt, and you couldn't do it. Her face shows the pain his words are causing her.

He has more to say but can't because he can't bear to cause her more. Finally, he tells her, *But it worked.*

Her curiosity struck, he continues, *You damaged my coin, Mom. Bruised it. Tarnished it. Ever so slightly. I'll seem normal, but never quite right. I'll make stupid decisions. I'll do things you hate. Everything, whether you know it, whether I know it, leads to what happens tonight.*

Tonight? What are you talking about?

He's about to tell her the truth, tell her what happens to the little boy in her belly, and his head swims. He braces himself with his knee on the end of the bed. *My coin is broken in time, Mom. I'm twenty-eight years old and I haven't been born yet and I haven't seen you since I was….*

Since you were what?

He doesn't remember. Sixteen? Twenty-one? Twenty-eight? Is this even happening now or is it a memory? His life flashing before his eyes as the knife opens his throat. *I can't tell you, Mom. Shouldn't. If I tell you when, you'll make it so it can't. It has to, Mom. Just like Peter had to.*

Don't you dare talk about Peter. You don't know him.

I do, Mom. Maybe even better than you. I helped him. I helped him hide Alexandrea. I helped him figure out how to let you cast the spell to end her curse. You haven't done that yet. Her face knots with concern and confusion. *It works, you know. You do it.*

She pushes herself upright, struggling around her swollen stomach.

And Rose, he gushes, *she's amazing. You think Alexandrea is special. Wait until you see Rose. She will do amazing things, Mom. She's the key. Only...* He sees Rose again in the field, lightning shooting from her fingertips. There is Alex, covered in her own vomit, seizing in the tall grass. He sees Rose's eyes, the excitement, the passion at her newfound power, and that disturbs him a little. She's enjoying this. She's trying to slay their attackers and she's reveling in the power she has found.

What? Tell me, William.

The promise of power has brought out her cruelty. He saw that in George, bashing magic out of his own sister. The men in the field believe she's the enemy. They suffer her mercilessness. He hopes Rose will learn— that George will learn—to wield their power with compassion. *It's that Book. It's going to be trouble for her. And you.*

Heather whispers, *Book?*

He's lying on a gurney, being transferred to a bed, hoisted in the bedsheet like it was a sling. His leg, his arm, his head. Everything feels broken. The nurses ask how he fell. He tells them he jumped. Then he's back at Heather's bed.

It's funny, that happens right here, in this hospital. Just not yet.

What are you talking about? Nothing you're saying makes sense.

Billy wonders, Am I here? *It will. In time. For you, tomorrow is the future. But my past. I'm not born yet, but I lived most of my life before today. It's still linear for me, confusing to describe things that haven't happened yet. Hard to tell you enough but not so much that you do anything different. Because you can't. Everything you have yet to do has already been done for me, but it can't happen until you do it.*

Billy is unsure whether Heather is staring at him because she believes him or thinks he's insane. Until she asks, *What happens next?*

William shrugs. He doesn't have the strength to tell her about the knife.

When will I see you again?

The question saddens him. The knife is his only future. *When I'm born.*

Heather reaches to him, *I mean you, see you again.*

George is nearly frantic and out of breath when he rests his hand on Billy's shoulder. *Here you are. I've been looking for you.*

Billy nods calmly. *I've been here, waiting for you.*

We could have used your help, George says, failing to make him feel guilty. *Where the hell have you been the past few weeks? Where'd you go when you left us?*

I think I visited my mom.

George looks sad and confused, his puppy-dog eyes telling Billy that was impossible. *You didn't hear.* It's more a statement than a question.

Billy doesn't have to ask; George understands it's cruel to make him ask. His words carry with them the weight of the many wounds he'd suffered since Billy abandoned them. *Jeremiah killed your mother. Sending Alex to the Library backfired. I've been looking for you everywhere.*

Killed Heather?

Matthew will kill Alex if we don't get you there. Or she'll kill him. We have to get you there.

The knife.

His instinct is to go. He's got to protect her. *He won't kill her.* Billy takes a deep breath. Hearing Heather is dead give the words sudden weight. It feels like every memory of his mother is sinking in his body, leaving his head and filling his heart, swelling it, making it ache because it should not have to hold so much. *We should go. He's expecting me.* Him and his knife.

Billy answers his mother's question, *You won't, Mom. We both die before we see one another again.*

She gasps.

The expression on Heather's face is more than he can bear right now. Here she is, alive, glowing, at the peak of her life and there she is, dead, in the same moment. The expression of shock on her face is echoed by his heart, the weight of those descending memories pulling on the connective tissue, threatening to dislodge the beating muscle and have it just fall out of him.

He sighs. *You'll know, but when it's time, follow Rose. She'll want to look for me. You'll know she won't find me. Don't stop until she stops. You'll be looking for me then and I'll be here, talking to you right now. And after right now*, the knife drifts closer, *I don't know. Everything else is in my future, and while I've been able to see all the places I've been before I went back to them, I can't see past tonight.* Except for that other place he's been, the dark place. When is that?

Tonight?

William nods. The knife. *Tonight. Alex will try to save me. I'll die. Death comes for her, too.*

Who's Alex? She looks confused, the name meaningless.

William can't help but smile at the memories that spill into his head as he says, *Alexandrea. You'll see. She'll come to live with us. You think everything started with Peter, but that's the real beginning.*

Why does she live with us? She's just a baby. Where's Holly?

He is with Holly at the bottom of the stairs, moments before she will die protecting her daughter. *Mom*, William warns, *if I tell you everything, you'll try to fix it all.*

Shouldn't I?

Everything seems so carefully connected that pulling on one errant thread would unravel everything. *It's all in motion, Mom. You did it. I'm telling you so you know you don't fail. You can face anything and know you'll succeed. You must be so strong, Mom.*

Heather's face is washed with concern. *But, why do you have to die?*

Billy snorts. *You know, Mom, you always told me I make really stupid decisions. It's like a shorthand between us because sometimes they're not really my decisions. I just see where I need to be and I go. I can't help myself. Alex is coming to save me. I've got to be there. It's the only way, and I've got to die for it to finish. If I don't go, everything falls apart.*

Heather nods somberly. *I think I understand. You're really my son?*

Billy puts his hand on his chest. *I swear.*

Billy comes around the bed. Heather reaches out. They touch, embrace. Billy struggles to hold everything in, a flood of emotion easily overwhelming the flimsy damn. His face buried in her shoulder, there's familiarity in her scent, but it's not exactly the same as he remembers. It's just enough for him to hold it all back as they separate. *I can't believe I'm in there, too*, he says, touching her stomach. *Watch.*

What are you doing?

He doesn't answer. His coin glows. A web of strings fills the room, each leading a different direction. Only one goes to her belly. Heather gasps.

Pretty cool, huh? Everywhere I've been. He wonders which one leads to the knife? He points at her stomach. *Waddya say, I'll see you in a few months?* William stands, somberly. *Time to go. Destiny, and all that.*

Heather sobs. *Can't you stay a little longer, maybe tell me a little about yourself?*

How he would love to stay. He knows which thread is the last. It pulls on him. *Those things are best learned for yourself. I love you. I'll see you, Mom.*

Heather smears her tears across her face. *I'll see you, Billy.*

✱✱✱

Sitting in his and Rose's bedroom at Eric's house. Alex says, *I can tell you a little.* Alex has a look on her face. She'll be leaving soon. She won't stay in Eric's house. Billy wants to tell her that it's okay.

Alex begins, *It was so weird. You met the Book Club, all those women. They seemed normal, right?*

Yeah, Rose answers. *Mostly.*

Billy rubs his arms, *Except the one with the tattoos. She's a badass.*

Alex continued, *I thought they were all out of their minds. They took me to the stone foundation, you know, the Old Witch's Shack. They put on these black graduation gowns, I guess like witches' robes.*

Witches' robes? Rose says like she's concerned Alex is pulling her leg.

They made circles of salt. Then they cast a spell. All at once, there was a house there. I was there—as in a long time ago. Then she came out. Alex adds drama by deepening her voice, *The witch.*

Billy can almost picture the scene in his head—as though he'd been there. The house in the woods, the garden clearing, and the stunning woman, kneeling in the dappled sunlight, tending her herbs.

Rose's wide eyes narrow as she grins. *You're lying.*

Alex shakes her head.

What did she look like? Rose insisted.

Billy is confused. Was she beautiful? He's thinking maybe he heard this story somewhere and she wasn't. The words just slip out, *Was she old and all ugly?*

When I first saw her, I thought she was horrible. Alex's eyes well. *Then, I saw her when she was younger, and she was the most beautiful woman I've ever seen. And these men came to punish her.*

Rose is silent for a change. Billy can't quite place the feeling in his gut as though it was his fault this woman from long ago was hurt by these men from long ago. It feels like a dream he just forgot upon waking. Recollections of recollections. But he's heard this story. His stomach sours with certainty that whatever Alex is about to say will implicate him. As though she's about to accuse him of murder and with the utterance, make it true, conjuring his memories out of thin air and jamming them in his unwilling brain. His hands start to shake, the emotion rising inside him like a volcano, and when it reaches his neck, he can feel his jaw clench and his eyes begin to weep. *I don't want to hear about what the men do.*

Billy doesn't know how, but he knows two children were orphaned. The woman was murdered. He can feel in his guilty heart how much Alex hurts.

Rose reaches over to rub his arm. *It happened a long time ago, Billy. Right Alex?*

Billy wishes he was anywhere else but here. He wants to cover his ears and scream to keep the knowledge out, but whether from Alex's words or the thoughts seeping into his mind, they won't stop.

Alex might not understand what he's feeling, but she seems to sense his pain. She tells them, *If he doesn't want to hear it, I'll just tell you another part.*

No, Billy pleads. He doesn't want to hear any part. It all feels too real, as though beaten and bloody Sara is right there, in the doorway.

Rose chides, *What's the matter with you?*

Billy doesn't know. He feels assaulted. Ever since Picnic Rock. He was there with Rose and Alex. But then the man with the crooked neck was there. It was day. It was night. Billy's chest feels tight, as though everything inverted and the whole world now rests upon him. Thoughts and memories pummel his head, and all he wants to do is hide inside a drawer inside a closet, inside a very deep hole. Anything to make it stop.

In one flash, he sees his mother, young and pregnant. In another, a web of sparkling threads. In another, a young man who looks like his zombified Uncle Peter is telling him something about untwining. Sara the old hag. Sara the beautiful woman. Sara, Alex. Alex, Sara. A hammer. Destinies all tied together like the tangle of threads coming from his coin. The knife. Slicing across his throat. Opening him up to the world. Releasing the pressure. Sudden relief. It terrifies him and yet, seeing the flash of steel, choking on his own blood, he feels peace. He knows.

Oh, he turns back to Heather, *I almost forgot. You don't have to remember, but I have a message for Alex.*

If I won't remember, Heather trails off.

Billy nods tearfully. *Alex*, he says, *I know I contributed to everything you've been through. I'm so sorry. You never asked for this, and it's far from over. I know you want to rest. You're so tired. There's so much I want to tell you. I hope one day you can forgive me. You don't deserve the sacrifice you must make.*

What does that mean? How am I supposed to remember? When do I tell her?

Billy knows she won't have to. He knows he's telling Alex. His mother is gone and his and Alex's destinies are about to collide. *It's nothing. Something I needed to get off my chest.* Turning to leave and Alex is in front of him. He holds out his arms to keep her at a distance. She misconstrues it as a hug and attempts to embrace him. For the first time he is certain what comes next and tips back his head. With little more sensation than a sting, the knife opens his throat.

Everything is black.

Billy is still. He is warm. His heart racing. A moment ago, his throat was slit. A moment ago, he was in the air. A moment ago, he leapt from Picnic Rock. Now he's in darkness. Still catching his breath, his body still anticipating being dashed on the rocks. He sits. He waits.

He can hear his own breathing and little else. He hears someone beside him. Every so often, they shuffle their limbs.

A door opens. Glass panes rattle when the sticking door gives. Familiar voices. Not all speak English. Warm hands touch his face and roll back the dark blindfold.

Billy takes a breath. Everything is done. His journey is complete. The time to rest has arrived. There is only death now to face.

As his eyes adjust to the light. He is face to face with Alex.

Chapter One Hundred and Seventeen

waking from the whirlwind of memories, into the epic confusion and utter turmoil as they assimilated into her own, Alex collapsed. They'd been delivered all at once, jammed into her brain like the crush of a crowd fleeing a fire through a doggie door.

Ticking dust and groaning debris settled around her. A few drips. Wind moaning through the shattered windows, carrying on the warm muggy breeze, the cries of traffic and sirens.

To her side, there was no mistaking Billy's condition, his throat a joyless grin. She understood what brought him to ruin, knowing the boy and the man intimately. She now thought of Billy or Heather much the way she thought of herself. Their memories were her possessions. These cherished tatters were all that remained of them. They didn't cross to the Between, ceasing to exist except in her mind. She choked down her tears, knowing if they came, she'd ultimately succumb to them.

Her own body was in revolt. Her limbs leaden. Her abdomen on fire. Uncertain if it still bled, the perception of heat radiating from the wound menaced her with immolation. For the first time, she understood the notion of a spark of life. Hers lacked the luminance to power the engine of her body. She lay in her and Billy's mess, the last of her spark stammering like the final flickers of a candle wick when, the fuel spent, the flame withers to a red glow visible only in darkness.

Her body was done. She'd harmed Charon; she'd never felt such pity as when the child cowered and kicked in fear of her. Dread haunted her, that the child who claimed the dead had abandoned her among rotting corpses.

She clasped Abby's cold glass charm like a religious token. *It's not that kind of charm,* Abby had once said. But it made her think of the woman who gifted her the beautiful glass. She hadn't yet known Abby was her Familiar, so she hadn't thought to question the gift. Now she second-guessed everything Abby ever did for her. But inside the charm were the remnants of her father's coin. In spite of everything he put her through, she now possessed the context of his decisions—told through Billy—and finally understanding him, missed him desperately. Missing someone she never really met—someone she only knew through other people—did not diminish her need.

She ached to collapse into a caring embrace and be held and told everything would be all right. But there was no one left for that. Heather was gone. Abby was no longer her Familiar. But there was one other, despite the fact that she'd been dead for years: Charon had taken her mother, brought her to the Between, where the living go to dream and the dead dream endlessly.

She summoned all her strength to pull herself from her body. Her thread weighed on her as though her body was an anchor tethered with thin, sparkling monofilament. Accomplished in her task, Alex stumbled backwards at the horror of her body's condition. She looked mauled. Abraded and broken. Where her tattered clothes didn't cover her skin was a kaleidoscopic mess of congealing blood and bruises.

Each inch she put between herself and her near-corpse strained that thread. Each inch felt like she dragged that anchor through the bottom sand, the thread so tenuous it threatened to snap.

She surveyed the scene mournfully, not just for her cousin, but herself. The destruction utter. The apartment, the bodies; all ruined. Yet her corpse continued to pump blood and breathe as though stubborn even at the bitter end. Perhaps Charon's infliction possessed some magical quality denying her death. Perhaps Billy's coin gave her just enough strength to continue on. It certainly didn't give her what Heather's coin had. *Perhaps that's why men eat women's coins? Because men's coins don't have any life to give?* Billy had one memory—seeing Alex again—that she didn't remember. Perhaps she'd forgotten? Perhaps it was the key to his survival that she'd been to distracted to fulfill. Bereft of choices, survival did not exist for her here.

She conjured the mist and passed through, entering The Between.

For so long Billy's safe return had been her motivation. There was no hope for that any longer. No quest to distract her. She'd lost so many she loved. Rose was the only one left; her only family. She imagined Rose discovering the scene and blaming her. Even though it was her imagination, she resented Rose for her rush to judgement. The only justice she might have in her cousin's eyes would be if she made things right, but what was right? Matthew's duality left her feeling like she'd been abandoned at the top of a seesaw. He'd murdered Billy. But Billy motivated him to it. She now saw Matthew as more manipulative than evil. He had said they were on the same side. Perhaps a monochromatic worldview had no place in reality.

Billy's jigsaw of memories felt complete save for some errant piece that alone revealed the whole image. The frustration enraged her. Not knowing, not understanding after so much suffering infuriated her. The only way to find the correct piece and solve Billy's puzzle was to live.

"Help me," she cried out, her heart begging for her mother to hear.

Unwilling to wait for her mother to sense her need, Alex wandered. She walked, she flew, she searched a barren Between, always fearful that pushing herself too hard might fatally harm the withering body at the terminus of her thread.

Eventually, she spied her mother's house below.

As she landed, a gentler crash than usual, she was relieved to be here. Although this version of her wasn't battered and broken, although she was free of the pain and the wounds, they were a thread away. She couldn't feel them, but was very much aware of them. She knew Holly wasn't capable, but the child part of her wanted her mother to kiss everything better.

Billy's memories had pushed her here. Understanding that she came home from work that day knowing she would die to protect her daughter reframed the entire moment. Alex never understood the true cost of the sacrifices her parents made until now. It had always seemed like a guilt-trip or a burden to carry rather than a statement of love. Unfortunately, her mother's death kept getting in the last word. She wanted to see her mother and leave her peacefully again. The sight of her mother's corpse—much like her own—kept haunting her.

Approaching the porch, Alex remembered the actual structure this house was based on no longer existed. She had burned it to the ground. She couldn't help but consider the two men Jeremiah had sent who died within it. As much as she tried to blame them, she was beginning to believe it was time she took responsibility for the deaths that occurred in her wake. Whether or not she caused it, they died because of her. Rat eyes and his cohort. Billy. Her mother. Heather. Betty. Donna. Lesedi. The countless others—women she didn't know. Blaming others could only push the guilt and blame away by arm's length. It was an exhausting acrobatic trick to keep believing in her own innocence. That innocence ended when Heather cast that spell. When Matthew beat the magic out of Sara. When she took it back. When she understood what she was up against and still strove forward. Each time she made the decision to continue, she lost the ability to claim innocence. Each time she did the right thing, the higher the guilt was piled. She hoped she could continue to bear it.

Before she rattled the storm door with her knuckle, it crept open, creaking wide. Alex wasn't without trepidation as she entered.

There was nothing unusual to suggest why the house was vacated. Everything appeared just as it was. Alex wandered room to room, calling her mother's name. She even ventured into her parent's bedroom. She anticipated seeing Holly's imagined version of Peter, all gregarious smiles and endless I love you's, but even he was absent.

Alex wandered into her old bedroom. The once-discarded toys loved to ruin, which her mother was fond of, were replaced on their shelf. A yellow bunny with pink velveteen ears, a brown puppy so well loved its head was permanently tipped, its felt ears teethed to tatters. This wasn't her room; it was her mother's frozen reconstruction of an era she herself could barely recall.

Alex rested on the bed, taking a moment to recharge.

"I wasn't expecting you," Holly said, stepping into the doorway. "What's happened?"

Holly's heartfelt concern nearly brought Alex to tears. She looked at her mother, trying to explain while holding the tide of emotions at bay. She was dying, alone, and wanted her mommy.

"Sweetheart," Heather swaddled Alex in her arms and gently rocked her daughter while making soothing shushes in her ear.

Suddenly safe, the armor of her mother's love gave her strength to finally let go of the flood she was holding back. She sobbed into her mother's shoulder.

"I thought I was protecting you," Holly finally said once Alex's sobs had stopped. "We got swept up. We believed we had the hardest part. We couldn't have imagined the pain we were creating for you." Holly didn't move to loosen her embrace.

Alex found her words caught in her mouth. No matter how many times she rearranged them, she had too much to say, and none came out.

"You came to me for help, and I thought I could spare you more pain. Tell you the *scary* truth and make you run for your life."

Alex stopped trying to speak.

"You are your father's daughter," she said after a breath. "You took what I said and used it as fuel."

"What was I supposed to do?" Alex's words were spoken as if by a mouse.

Holly looked away.

"My father gave his life for me to have these... abilities. You gave your life and saved me, twice. What was I supposed to do? Let your sacrifices be in vain?"

"Yes. Yes, a million times, Alexandrea. We didn't know what we were asking you."

"You really believed I'd be born, and everything would change?"

Holly was silent, as though the question struck her and peeled back the cover on a truth she'd kept hidden for too long. With a sigh, she answered, "I don't know what we were thinking. We were kids, caught in a moment. We believed our sacrifices were just and noble. We had no idea. Children never understand how dire consequences can be until after it is too late."

Alex tried to think on her mother's answer. Was this why her father disregarded Sara's warning? Did he believe his sacrifice was all that was needed? She shuffled through Billy's and Heather's memories, and however faint the recollections were, they included the group of them: Heather, Peter, Holly, Billy, Abby. They fed off one another's ideas and enthusiasm and expectations. A massive, misinformed feedback loop. Pulling free from her mother's hug, Alex said, "They're all gone, you know?"

Holly stood, *Who?*

"Heather and William." She hesitated, "And kinda Abby."

The news struck Holly like a sledgehammer. Her knees wobbled. Had it not been for the wall, Alex wasn't sure Holly would have continued standing on her own. "What happened?"

Alex looked away. She explained Matthew's duplicity, sending her to the Library thinking Billy was being imprisoned there. "For a long minute, I thought I was winning. Then everything turned upside down and Jeremiah forced Heather's coin down my throat." She could tell from Holly's horrified expression that her mother understood Heather trod the same road Peter took. She finished explaining what happened next with "… and then I made Abby break her oath."

Holly collapsed ungracefully into the wall. "Why?"

Alex didn't have an answer anymore. "To top it all off, I ate William's coin."

Holly looked at her with an expression that might have turned her to stone. When she finally whimpered, it was to ask, "You killed him?"

"Matthew did." As Holly screamed her anger, Alex shouted over her, "William wanted it that way."

Holly abbreviated her lament. "What?"

"William knew it was the only way to save me."

"Save you from what? Matthew? Please tell me you killed him."

Again, Alex shook her head. "He fled after. I tried to protect William. I wouldn't let death have my cousin."

"What? Who?"

"William. My cousin Billy."

Holly's laugh was a demonstration of her confusion. "Again, what?"

"Billy, Heather's son, remember him?"

"Yes," Holly answered, stretching out the vowel.

Alex explained how Billy was untethered in time. Holly was shocked to learn William's identity. She reacted as though discovering the Holy Grail had been her morning coffee mug.

Alex continued, "I tried to protect him from death." Alex explained her prior encounter with Charon and the Reaper at their actual house. "I burned it down." Then, how Charon recognized her this time. How they fought. How badly she felt knowing she denied William his afterlife.

"You beat Charon? Is that what you're saying?"

Alex recalled the grievously injured, fearful child as she held her abdomen. "I'd call it more of a draw."

Holly let go of the wall and stood on her own. With trepidation, she approached her daughter, took her hands and drew her from the bed. "The universe," Holly said, "it knows things. It speaks, but only if you know how to listen. It's like the creak of an over-tightened screw or the burbling of water through a pipe. The right person knows what these things mean."

Alex wasn't sure she understood.

"You don't defeat death, Alexandrea. It's the single eternal truth. The greatest force. *Everything ends.* Yet here you are, still living."

In her mother she could see her godmothers, Lesedi, Banhi, and Khowla: *How are you yet living?* It made her miss Lesedi even more. She was the first person as a direct result of helping Alex.

Holly continued, "I don't know what Jeremiah did to be as powerful as he is. I don't think anyone knows. He's rewritten his own history so many times every myth tells a piece of his story. But the universe bemoans its dark heart. It's not supposed to be, it's like that over-tightened screw, the wood crying to be undone, if only a little."

"How do I fix it?"

Holly led her daughter down the stairs. As she descended, Alex looked at the storied steps. The part of her that was Billy remembered each tread, the way his heart pounded climbing each one in pursuit of Gary, the knowledge of what was about to happen echoing in his head.

"I think some part of your father believed that once you could do magic that would be it. Matthew warned him, but Matthew's lineage is cursed with failure. We snickered behind his back. We thought we'd discovered a new way. We were so sure we were smarter."

Alex didn't know what to say. She'd always projected some sort of omnipotence onto her parent's decisions. Hearing her mother confess to not knowing made her realize they were as lost as she was.

Vocalizing her doubt, Alex said, "I don't know what to think of anyone anymore. This whole thing started with this one good and that one evil. The more I learn, the less I'm sure about anything."

Holly brought Alex to the kitchen and poured her a glass of water in an orange-colored cut-glass she'd used her last visit. Alex didn't realize how thirsty she was and gulped it down, unsure how she was feeling thirst or if this water actually sated it.

"Everyone does what they believe is best. Intentions are evil, not people."

Alex shook her head. "No, people can be evil."

Holly stroked Alex's hair. "You know, I always had hope that with each sacrifice, we'd somehow turn a key that solved the puzzle. Hindsight has shown me how foolish we were to believe such childish things."

Alex rubbed the rim of the glass with her finger. "I don't think it's foolish. Wishful, maybe."

"You came to me because you were hurt. When I saw you, I assumed we'd lost."

Alex put her glass down solidly. "That sounds like a *but* statement."

"*But*: You defeated Charon."

"I didn't defeat death, Mom. We both crawled our separate ways."

Holly rubbed her daughter's shoulders. "Whatever you want to call it. It isn't supposed to happen. Charon always gets the coin."

Alex used Billy's words, "It's kind of covetous of them."

"I once told you to run away and hide, and now I look on my daughter and I can't help but wonder."

"Wonder what?"

Holly took a moment to answer as though what she was about to say was heretical. "If you defeated Charon, why not Jeremiah?"

Alex's mouth felt suddenly parched. "They're not the same, mom. Charon is...," she couldn't find the words, so she made do with what came to her. "There's part of the child that cares. It's nothing like Jeremiah." She shivered. "He's horrible. He doesn't need a Book to cast. He *is* magic."

"He doesn't need a Book? I thought all men need their Book."

"I thought I burned him to death. He just transformed himself. He looks like a man, but I wonder if he's only pretending to be human."

"I only knew of Jeremiah through Matthew." She looked away from her daughter. "Part of me wants to tell you to run away. To live your life. Find someone to love and do whatever makes you happy." Holly continued, "But they'll never let you. As long as you have the will to fight, you should. You must."

Alex touched her stomach. It was perfectly fine; here. "Charon killed me, Mom."

Without touching it, Holly ran her fingers along Alex's thread.

"I know I'm alive," Alex protested. "The Reaper tore me apart. I'm lying in Matthew's apartment." She took a deep breath, trying to stand tall. "I'm torn open and bleeding, but because of what I did, Charon doesn't want me. I think that's why my body won't die. I'm just lying there, wasting away." She looked at her mother. "It's horrible, and I don't know what to do. All I could think about was seeing you."

Holly stepped back, tears flooding her eyes.

"I need you, Mommy."

For a moment, Holly hardened. "You cannot stay here, Alexandrea. I'm already dead. I can't offer you anything but faulty advice." Holly swallowed back her motherly instinct. "You're the most powerful witch, maybe ever, and you came to me for help? You need to go back. You must keep going."

Alex reached out to her mother, "What if I don't want to? What if I want to stay here? With you?"

Holly shook her head. "Dreams are short for good reason, Alexandrea. They leave us wanting things we should never, ever have. Visits here mustn't be long." Holly pointed at Alex's coin and warned, "There are other covetous things."

"I can't, Mom. I can't go back. To that body? I'd dead, but I won't die."

Holly pointed to the door. "Please, Alex. There's still hope."

"Why are you throwing me out? Don't you love me?"

"It's because I love you." Holly looked at the ceiling as tears poured from her eyes. "I know it feels like I'm sending you back, but that's not it. If anyone can kill Jeremiah, it's the girl who beat death."

"I don't have the strength. I'm so tired of fighting. I just want to stay here, with my mommy."

"I am not the person you want me to be, Alex. I am your mother and as much as I want to protect you, I see the mistake you're making. I can't protect you and let you make it."

"How do I fix this alone?" Alex referenced her body as though Holly could see the damage.

"Since our last reunion," Holly said, "I've been thinking about all of this," she gestured at the house. "I'm holding on to something that is gone. A memory of another time. I told you that one day I'd move on from the comfort of these memories. They gave me a place to hide from what happened to us. They won't become a place to let you hide."

As though sublimating from solid to gas, one after another, parts of the house vanished around Alex. Cabinets left piles of plates and glassware floating in the air. One by one, in near immediate succession, objects evaporated, even the house. A few remaining objects: a pile of forks, a photo album, a wool throw, all floating as though balanced by invisible forces, until they, too, disappeared.

"What did you do?"

Holly was stoically silent for a long moment, surveying the empty space that was once her home. She nodded as if answering an unasked question. Turning to Alex, her voice was soft and compassionate. "What you have to do is too important to allow you another moment's refuge in the fantasy I created." She pointed along Alex's thread. "Your father and I made a choice to sacrifice everything to put an end to Jeremiah." She spoke with extra determination. "End the Library. Stop them from making any more Books. Return the magic. I love you, Alexandrea. I will keep sacrificing to see this to the end, no matter what it costs me."

"What about what it costs me?"

Holly didn't seem to have an answer, her face registered painful understanding. "I'm sorry, Alex. People don't always get to live the life they want. Wars, disasters, bad luck can change everything." Holly embraced her daughter briefly. "You came to me because you're hurt and I'm sending you back. I'm sure it feels like I'm being cruel. I wish I could take the burden of your suffering. But you're the only person capable of doing this. If you give up now, all our sacrifices—mine, your father, Heather, William—will have been in vain." Holly touched her cheek. "I love you Alex. I wish you could understand how much I love you and how proud you've made me."

Alex's head drooped. As huge a responsibility she believed her parents had placed on her, her mother had just increased it exponentially. She wanted to be angry. She wanted to feel abandoned. But what she felt was foolish. Childish. Her parents had sacrificed their life for a cause she, too, believed in. Here she was, begging to be done, but still alive. Her parents were dead, and her mother was still willing to make sacrifices. And here she was, still alive: she still had more to give. Jeremiah had taken from her everything she believed was worth living for, her family, her friends, her life. But that life he'd taken was college and boys and the things normal people were expected to do. But she was still alive. He hadn't taken that. And until he did, Alex understood there were still sacrifices for her to make.

"Where will you go now?" Alex asked of Holly and her disappeared home.

Holly shrugged. "Who knows. I never thought in death I'd have something to look forward to."

She wanted to tell her mother that she understood. That she was sorry it took her mother losing everything before she learned the lesson. The anchor at the end of her string did not hurt with the intensity her heart now ached. Her parents sacrificed everything for her to accomplish great things. And great things required even greater sacrifice. Her thread still attached to her living body was testament to her not yet failing. Before she could resume her fight, she needed to heal it.

Alex embraced her mother. She held there as long as she could. Until her mother tearfully told her it was time to go. To continue forward.

Alex understood what she needed to do. But first, there was someplace she needed to go. She'd witnessed such destruction on the Between, witnessed such pain all because of her. She felt drawn to return there, as though in the destruction, she'd left something unfinished. Something that needed correction before she could continue forward.

Chapter One Hundred and Eighteen

lex wasn't ready to return to the real world. There was someone she needed to speak to.

Time was essential, so she took to the air. Not far ahead, she spotted the ruins she sought, the market, looking like a massive, half-buried pile of broken holiday decorations.

She swooped lower and rolled to a stop with only a bruise. She dusted sand from her hair and shook it from her clothes. Ahead of her, a path through the ruined market led straight to the square.

In the skewed angles of the collapse around her, she saw jigsaw pieces of beauty that once lined this aisle. She mourned her awe from when she first witnessed what a wonder this place had been. Now it was a pile of rubble, a catastrophe of jumbled thoughts.

The ruins were a visual assault, a cacophony of sharp colors and jarring angles. She alone was responsible for the mounds of debris lording over her. Their sheer scale was overwhelming, casting her into jagged shadows. Debris hung in menacing heaps. Now and again, a distant groan or creak preceded a distant thundering rumble setting off a chain of further disintegration.

She wondered if this was to be her legacy. Would this fight result in the whole world ending up like this? If so, what exactly was she fighting for? She tried to remember the market that was. Her memory failed to recall the grandeur she thought she remembered. What she could recall, and with greater clarity, was the shades destroying it.

This is what I've done to the world. Everything I touch turns to this. She thought of hers and Billy's splayed and bloody bodies. The transformation of Heather as she lost sentience. Of Donna burning away. Of Betty. All gone. She could hear Abby begging her, *Please ask me to take the oath*. She ruined everything.

Ahead, was the neatly stacked pile of stones under which she buried Lesedi.

Alex wondered if she might have saved Lesedi. Sent her away sooner. Waited until they were safely home before leaving them. Her fairy godmother's death was a cruel foreshadowing of what happens to everyone Alex loved.

Approaching the pile, she thought, *This is not Lesedi. Lesedi is gone. This is what I believed.* Approaching the grave, the desire to unburden herself to Lesedi—which moments ago felt so important—now seemed foolish. Why had she come to this abandoned place? This was no longer a place for the living, but a graveyard of hopes and dreams.

She sat beside Lesedi's grave. "It seems such a waste, doesn't it? You wished me joy. You said you'd rather be made into a Book than die. You lost your life because of me. And I'm miserable." Alex couldn't take her eyes off the pile of stones. *I'm such a hypocrite, complaining to the dead.* "What should I do, Lesedi? It's so unfair you're not here to tell me. To say something that makes me laugh."

Her thoughts stilled, giving her a moment of peace from the haunting destruction. "Child, I wished you joy. That does not mean you will have it. It means if you search for it, you will find it." It wasn't Lesedi, but Alex's imagination conjured enough of a likeness that she couldn't help but smile through her tears, listening to her friend. "But you cannot find it while you search for other things." Imaginary Lesedi looked around the ruined market. "Look here, child. That man comes and takes everything from us. His harm to you is worse when he harms those close to you. The destruction he leaves reminds us all that he is here. What do you leave behind to remind us that you are here?"

Alex moved a stone on Lesedi's grave to demonstrate her answer.

"What is that? A grave? For whom? Not for me. I am alive in your imagination. My body was found in my bed. No part of me is here except what you believe." Lesedi knelt and placed her hands on Alex's shoulders. "You never knew real pain before becoming a witch. But you are only as strong as you believe. It is time for you to stop this self-pity and search for your joy."

"I can't, Lesedi. Not as long as Jeremiah is alive."

Lesedi smiled. "See there, child. Now you know the truth about where your joy will be found. I wished you joy. If you look for it, you will find it."

Alex couldn't help but smile, even once her imagined Lesedi was gone.

"What do I leave behind to remind them that I'm here?" Alex spoke to no one. Matthew created a field of grass by thinking of it. If he could think things into being, if Marta could make an entire world within her brother's universe, then she could do the same. But first, she had to excoriate the market of Jeremiah's existence. All around her, the mounds of angled and fragmented dream collapsed to the ground in a torrent of liquified sand.

What should I leave behind?

Alex closed her eyes. She recalled the fountain that used to be here. The round pool, its surreal size…. *I can't remake it. It has to be mine.*

She pictured a mosaic of tiles, small triangles of hundreds of shades of azure ceramic and cobalt glass. Up close it seemed a riot of shapes and colors, but from a small distance it became the deepest blue of the ocean and the brightest blue of the sky, the sparkling tiles tricking the eyes into seeing undulating waves below wispy, windswept clouds. It appeared always in motion in her mind's eye. It wasn't round. No, the main part of the pool would be star-shaped, with five long arms radiating out to sleek, slender, elegant points.

The base of the fountain would be—she struggled for a moment, trying to picture it—made of highly polished black stone. One giant, perfect sphere. Variations in the stone refracted the light, so as she walked around it—in her mind—it sparkled, as though trapped glimmers of a rainbow exploded out of it.

This is hard. It was easy to appreciate creativity, to recognize someone's original take on something, but so much more difficult to be original herself. She considered the creatures that graced the original fountain. The menagerie, how the rippling water over their flexed limbs gave them motion. There were more types of phantasmagoric life on that one spire than she'd ever encountered in every fantasy book and movie and dream. How could she top that?

Alex, her eyes still closed tight, thought of those creatures. They scurried up the length of a tower, like an immense cathedral spire. She could recreate what had been, just taller or bigger, but that felt like cheating. Instead, she took away the tower. The creatures themselves became the tower, one reaching to another, to another. There would be unicorns and flying horses, dragons and centaurs, griffins, and all manner of mythologic creature she could recall, and chimeric creations of every variation she could imagine—sharks and bison, fish and tigers and salamanders, dogs and dinosaurs and eagles and crabs, snakes and rams, antelope and elephants, and sheep and reindeer and lizards, and…. She envisioned sculptural representations of plants and flowers and vines, of the wind, the soil, the rain, the sun…. On the globe, it seemed only fitting that there should be a reminder of who made this sculpture. A stack of Books knocked askew by their opening covers, with flames racing to the clouds. Like that old Book Caleb gave her, all these creatures sprang from the burning pages, birthed from the flames like a phoenix (which also sprang from them). As water began racing down the fountain, it splashed and swirled, capturing and refracting the light so it appeared as flame. Splashes of water become sparks and embers and quick bursts of fire with these animals and chimera all in a frenzy about it.

She nearly had it fixed in her mind—the fire, the pool, the animals— but it felt unfinished. This was her message for them. It had to recognize their loss, and so in her mind, way at the top, she pictured a solitary woman, her hands out at her sides, overlooking the fountain and the square, as a protector and friend. For a moment, Alex considered Heather, but this was not her memorial, this was theirs. She recalled Lesedi's features, her hair, her ever-smiling face, her sparkling eyes that always seemed to shout, *Hello friend*, whenever they looked upon Alex.

She'd imagined every detail, but it only existed in her mind. *What do I do to make it real?* She imagined the sand and the dust and the water pulled into the air. She imagined the blood spilled here. All of it forming and transforming, making just as she unmade. But this was just fantasy; wasn't it? *No. It's imagination.*

Alex opened her eyes.

The market and all signs of destruction were gone. What stood before her, immense, towering, took her breath away.

"This is so much better than a grave of stones," imagined Lesedi said to her.

"Thank you, Lesedi," Alex said to the fountain. "For showing me what I must do to find my joy."

Chapter One Hundred and Nineteen

eturning to Matthew's apartment was a shock. Seeing the destruction, not just to the apartment but to their bodies, made Alex cry. It was so easy to decide what to do when this view was hidden from sight. But standing before it, recollections of twisting agonies slowed her approach. Her body was still warm. It breathed. She had seen herself from outside her body before, but never like this. She pitied that girl.

She'd healed herself before. The burns Matthew gave her, wounds and scratches. *Healing isn't about wounds, it's about love. I wasted so much time. Why didn't I realize I could do this?* Alex knew why: She doubted herself.

Alex took a breath. She closed her eyes. She needed not just to believe she could but to know it. Although she stood beside her body like it was a sloughed-off costume, she felt her wounds knitting. The dull, itching ache, swelled in her gut as her skin tightened, as tissue mended to tissue.

Staring down at her own body wasn't like looking in a mirror. It was like seeing someone who was very familiar. The misplaced features opposed what the mirror showed her. She knelt; sliding into her body was like slipping naked into bed on a chilly night, hardly disturbing the covers to avoid letting in the cold. She'd slipped into herself before, but this time the ephemeral comfort was replaced by the onslaught of all the pain she'd avoided.

She lay still for several minutes, breathing through waves of anguish. They eased, leaving the itching burn of mending flesh and tissue. Reconvening with her body was a shock. Her strength dissipated instantly, evaporating as if into a vacuum. Every breath took shocking effort. The ground pressed hard into her back. Her shirt, wrinkled and folded beneath her, pressed against her like sharp, uneven stones. Ignoring the pain and discomfort and focusing on making it go away was not without difficulty. Her concentration was so great, however, that it took a minute after the hurting subsided for her to realize it had gone.

With a gasp, Alex moved. Her abdomen ached, the flesh tender, the muscles protested the effort; her wound angry, enraged, but closed.

Alex lay, trembling and weak. She tried to push from the floor, and while she could move her limbs, they were incapable of bearing weight. Billy's corpse lay feet away. Realizing his memory lived within her wasn't enough to prevent the despairing chasm within her from widening. Had she the strength, she would have sobbed, but her exhaustion was overwhelming.

Like a ringing in her ear, she became aware of droning sirens. They grew louder, more desperate, and anxious.

What happened? When she had Heather's coin, power surged through her: She had never felt more amazing. It was terrifying and wonderful and addictive. So much so that when Billy suggested she take his, a part of her didn't want to hesitate, to accept his offer without consideration, if only to feel that way again. But this was different. Billy's memories were how he experienced his life, a confused, unsolvable knot of recollection and time. It was no wonder life wore him down; it had been a spiral of confusion, the past the present the future, all the same. He experienced his life as though secreted within each moment was every other, until finally, inevitably, he returned to Matthew's apartment to sacrifice himself. Even his death, occurring so many times during his life, was a confounding, endlessly repeating snarl with no perceivable terminus. Except for the haunting memory of Alex looking at him.

Outside, the sky was clear and blue, a thousand glaring suns reflected in a thousand windows. A perfect day viewed through shattered windows. A few feet away, still stained by her blood, Charon's claw sat, curled, like a macabre, discarded doll. Seeing the bony hand caused Alex's head to spin slightly. Admitting Billy's memories to her own made her more recent experiences recede to a lifetime ago.

The sirens were so loud now that Alex half expected to see the trucks pulling right outside the window. She tried to stand. It took more energy than she had. She pulled her way to the couch and pulled herself into it, throwing herself against the white cushions, smearing them with her dark blood.

It was like her veins pumped concrete. She stretched wearily. Each time she considered one of his memories, her head ached at the recollection, as though retrieving it was a Herculean task beyond its willing capacity. She looked at her cousin's body. It was still shocking to see Billy dead and jolted her each time as though while she knew to expect it, she was stumbling upon it anew. *No wonder he was willing to die.*

In the distance, men were calling out.

Alex strained but failed to push herself upright. *I'll be fine. Maybe they'll arrest me. I'm covered in blood, so maybe they'll take me to the hospital. As soon as I'm strong enough, I'll escape.* Even if that was not how it turned out, she couldn't imagine a jail cell that could hold her, so long as she had time to regain her strength.

Sounds of movement echoed up the stairwell leading to the hallway. Alex's heart startled and raced. She hadn't been concerned about being found with Billy's corpse until it was clearly about to happen.

Echoing footfalls pulsed into the hallway, accompanied by the electronic chatter of two-way radios. Voices spoke of reaching the source of the explosion and beginning their search.

Alex's eyes went wild with emotion. Her heart thundered inside her chest. Someone began pushing rubble aside, testing their footing. "Watch that, watch that!" someone urged. Alex didn't care. Someone called out, "Police. Shout to me if you're here!" And then, "Anyone in here? Is everyone okay?" The speaker grunted as he waded through creaking wreckage that was once a bedroom.

A police officer stumbled into the living room. Seeing the body and the blood, his hand snapped to his waist. "I'm officer Gonzalez. Are you alone?"

"Yes," Alex spoke as confidently as she was capable.

"Where are you hurt?"

Alex shook her head. The answer was too complicated.

He keyed the radio mic on his shoulder to report the situation.

Following the police officer, a chubby, middle-aged man, his full head of dyed black hair, wearing a dark grey bowling shirt with black slacks, black socks with sandals, climbed from the sea of debris. "Everything's fine here, officer."

Alex knew that voice. It sent chills through her, like a fly caught in the web of Billy's memories. Those four words turned her skin sweaty and cold. She wanted to warn Officer Gonzalez, but was unable to explain why.

Officer Gonzales mistook her intent and grabbed her, easing her against the couch.

Alex's warning—the only thing she could think to say—only confused the officer, "Abby's barn."

As the man introduced himself, "Hi. My name is…," Alex said with him, "Johnny Corteze." He continued, "I live three floors down. This is my friend's apartment. He's remodeling. As I'm sure you can see. You can go."

The man in Abby's barn. Jeremiah's. The one sent to *see* if she had magic.

"You need to leave, sir," Officer Gonzalez warned, his hand popping the flap holding his bright yellow taser. "This is a crime scene."

"That's just the thing, officer," Johnny began, appearing his Book and continuing to speak as though anything he said might make sense. Confused by the guttural words, Officer Gonzalez stood no chance. In an instant, he was sprawled on the floor, his charred chest smoking. Johnny lowered his Book to investigate.

"Fucking vest," he muttered as the cop struggled to pull his gun. Dispassionately muttering again, he fired a barrage of bolts at the officer.

"Stop," Alex screamed. She pushed herself from the couch, her hands generating a single spark that spun the Book from his grasp.

Alex dropped to her knees, panting.

He froze. Cautiously, he knelt to collect his Book, his eyes never leaving her. When he stood, repositioning his Book in his hands, he studied her, as though waiting for what would happen next. A grin formed in the crease of his mouth. "That's all you got." His question came dressed as a statement of confidence. Still, his eyes never wavered as he blindly flipped the pages to find his place.

Alex couldn't catch her breath. Her limbs trembled from exhaustion. The officer groaned as he flirted with consciousness. She couldn't tell who Johnny would attack next. Or how much she could take, as he found his page and began reading.

Swallowing her panic, taking gulping breaths, she primed her emotion. She stared at Billy's corpse.

These men came wielding magic as though it gave them the right to inflict harm. As though the Books were their possession. As though the magic writ within them was theirs. They didn't see the destruction they wrought. They blamed her. Or they just didn't care. In an instant, she considered all the things that could happen next if she didn't, if she couldn't act.

Electrical sparks shot from Johnny's outstretched fingertips.

Like an engine with all its wires disconnected, it didn't matter how much fuel she could force into the motor; the energy fizzled within her, unconverted emotion twisting her insides as her body was battered and burned.

Summoning all her remaining strength, she threw herself. The collision sent them both sprawling. Johnny was quick to toss her aside like a bale of hay into the wall. She wanted to right herself and prepare her defense, but her limbs were exhausted. All he had to do was claim his Book and cast a spell to end her.

She recalled the panicked child, Charon, in this very spot, trying to flee from her and realized she was now the one afraid for her life. Was she as pathetic to Johnny as Charon appeared to her? She would not find the same compassion, no matter how pathetic. The child was not the only thing that came to rest here. She reached blindly to where she had last seen it and discovered the discarded claw.

He claimed his Book. Gritting his teeth, he turned to Alex. His eyes were slits, his sweaty skin collecting dust in his wrinkles and creases, exaggerating his age and his anger. His eyes lowered to read but instead were drawn to his glowing coin as it began tipping from his chest.

Alex crawled forward; Charon's claw clutched in her left hand. She held it out, the bony palm clinking open, sounding like a fall of dominoes. "Give it to me," she demanded.

He laughed, nervous and uncomfortable. He couldn't know it was the Reaper's claw. As she struggled to her feet, he returned to his Book.

She stepped forward, step for guttural syllable. His voice rose in volume as the coin spun, pulled on its string from his chest. His eyes racing from her to the claw to his coin.

She thrust the claw at him and, as though alive, the bony fingers ensnared his coin. Drawing it back to herself, his thread sputtered sparks. *I hope this doesn't kill me.*

"What are you doing?"

Alex didn't answer. Even when he asked again. Even when he screamed his question at her. Even as she claimed his coin from the claw. Even as she swallowed it.

Chapter One Hundred and Twenty

his is bullshit. Come on Marco, you're setting me up for a B-n-E.

Marco, just out of his teens, his dark brown hair buzzed in a high-and-tight, laughs. He smooths out the facial smudge he has the nerve to call a moustache. *Johnny, buddy, I'm tellin' ya. You gotta meet him.* The two have been best friends since Marco got left back in sixth grade. He shifts his weight from foot to foot, a move that looks almost like he is dancing.

Johnny puts his hands on the large knob. He attempts to turn it before turning back to Marco, *It's locked. You're such a dick.* He smooths out his hair. Unlike Marco's, it is long, all in the back. Dark brown and glossed stiff with product.

You're the dick. I told you. Hold it. Like Theresa is naked and waiting right inside that room an' you ain't got no key. Turn it and hold it like you're gonna break it.

Johnny offers Marco the door. *You do it. Show me since you're so smart.*

Marco holds his hands up. *I told you, dude. He wants you and he wants it this way. Told me hisself.* Johnny isn't convinced. *Dude, come on. Just try the fuckin' door like I said. Grab the knob and turn and hold it. Do it for like a two fucking minutes. I swear I'm not fuckin' around.*

Who's this guy, again?

He's the guy, Johnny. I told you. The guy who owns this place.

Johnny looks at the battered green door with the nails and the large brass knob and steps back to look at the building. *He owns* this *dump?*

Marco shakes his head. *This place,* he says with his arms out wide. He lowers his voice, *Everything.*

Is he gonna sell me a bridge, too? Am I supposed to be impressed?

Tell me if you're impressed when you get inside.

Johnny is sure Marco's prank requires his hands occupied on the nob. For insurance, Johnny tightens his belt a notch before grabbing the knob. *Like this?*

Are you tryin' to turn it?

It don't turn.

Yeah, but are you tryin'?

How the hell do I turn somethin' that don't turn?

Just hold it. Hold it like you're gonna turn it if it turned.

That's what I said I'm doin'.

Marco realizes Johnny is making fun of him. He crosses his arms in a huff.

Why am I holding this fucking knob for no goddam reason like it's my johnson?

You hold your johnson for no reason?

Johnny laughs, *Nah, that's your mother's job.*

Marco winds-up a cartoonish punch. They're both laughing. Johnny offers his arm. Marco fakes, but Johnny flinches. Marco grins. Now Marco gets a freebee. No blocking or retaliation allowed. As Marco strikes, the door opens. Johnny leaps over the threshold and slams the door, unstruck.

Johnny is still laughing, still trying to catch his breath, when he realizes he's on the other side of the door. His laughter dies when, turning around, he sees this room can't possibly fit under the stairs. He sees the rows of free-standing coat racks covered with jackets and cloaks and the strangest outfits he's ever seen. It looks like an abandoned Halloween store for men.

Johnny opens the door, expecting to see Marco, expecting Marco to laugh at him and probably connect that punch. He's looking over a dark and stinky alley. It is raining gently, awakening the scent of wet trash and rotting food. The largest rat he's ever seen scurries past. It regards him like it's disgusted. He slams the door.

To no one, he mutters, *Where the fuck was that?*

He creaks the door ajar. A two-foot-high wall of snow collapses against his shins. The wind howls in, the coats wave about and a large cap lifts from the rack. It tumbles to the floor, disintegrating on impact.

He pushes the door closed against the snow. He wipes the ice from his jeans. *What the fuck?* Maybe this isn't a joke. Maybe Marco really has sent him to meet with the man. *The man.*

His stomach feels sour. Behind him is an archway that exits this room. He remembers what Marco told him. *One big fucking maze. The sort you think you'll die in.*

The door opens. Marco falls to his knees in cackling laughter. *Dude, you gotta see your face!*

Fuck you, Johnny curses. *This is real? You were serious?*

Marco reverentially closes the door behind him. *Come on*, he says, walking past, heading for the archway. *He wants to meet you. He's looking for the right guy. I told him you was it.*

Johnny stiffens and shakes off his nerves. *What're we waitin' for?*

Marco grins. *I can't wait to see how you do. You know how you talk about wishin' you could be paid to crack skulls?*

Johnny lies, *I don't know what you're talkin' about.*

He's got plenty of skulls in need of crackin'.

Johnny rubs his forearms. *He pays well?*

Marco put a hand on Johnny's shoulder. *You know what want is? Like bein' hungry?*

No, like wanting somethin'. Anything.

What about it?

You'll never know what it is again.

Johnny watches Marco's face, waiting for the tell that he's joking, but it doesn't come.

Come on, Marco disappears into the archway.

❋❋❋

He has on a suit. Not something off the rack; he hadn't worn crap like that since his communion. A woman with no English and a mouth-full of pearly-pins had made this for him. One of ten. Navy that was almost black. Fine blue pinstripes. Robins-egg, the pin-woman's assistant had said.

He is waiting by the door. Crummy New York City street, Hell's Kitchen. Rows of crumbling brownstones probably owned by foreign investors, every floor rented out to some stupid tech bro. Most men who go through the door leave the Library magically, but Jeremiah told him to be here. Even he knows this guy's a douche.

Johnny picked him up and brought him to the door this morning. They didn't speak. The guy never made eye contact, like his shit didn't stink and all he could smell was Johnny's. But Johnny knew him. Douche was on television every fifteen minutes, jerking off about how immigrants were killing the city or how taxes were sucking him dry and people should just get to work. Douche claimed to be worth billions and minimum-wage pin-chewing immigrants were the cause of his problems? Not that Johnny cares, but this is easier because he's such a douche.

Johnny's cell rang. He answers, *Yeah?*

The voice on the line says, *Take our friend home. He's uninterested.* It isn't Jeremiah. It was someone else, someone Johnny probably never met. A bookkeeper or lawyer or sum-such who saw that ink was properly dried on contracts and agreements.

Johnny tucks his phone in his breast pocket. *It doesn't bulge,* the pin-lady's assistant said. She was right.

The door opens and Douche steps out. Johnny opens the back door of the colossal black SUV he rented for the day and stands there like he's got a stick up his ass.

That is something, Douche says with a grin as he steps out of the door. He notices Johnny and his face melts to seriousness, like the help can't see him happy.

They get in the SUV and Johnny starts to drive him home. Only he doesn't take the West Side Highway, they sit in traffic. He wants Douche to stew.

When they're two blocks from Douche's glass apartment building, Johnny clears his throat. *You know,* Johnny says in his tourist-trivia voice, *I drop a lot of guys like you at that door. Most don't come back out that way.*

The Douche doesn't so much as look at him.

Normally I'm the one who takes them in, you know, shows them through the maze. Johnny pauses a moment. *Jeremiah must think you're special for the show you got this morning.*

He doesn't look up. *You know who I am.*

Johnny grins. *I sure do. You came out the door because you didn't take Jeremiah's deal.* Johnny looks into the rearview, silent until they make eye contact. *Most people see the wisdom in aligning with….* He trails off and waits.

Who do you think you are, talking to me?

Johnny grins away the condescension. *There's a cellphone in the cupholder. It's got one number. I'm the guy who is going to get you to call it.*

Douche doesn't take the bait. That's fine. Johnny starts to ask, *There's one the thing I don't understand—*

Black SUV up the block, yeah, Douche interrupts into his phone. *Send Branden and Manny.*

Johnny's eyes go wide purely for effect. He pulls over, jams the SUV into park. He turns in his seat. *Who are Brenda and Fanny? Security detail?*

How do I get out of here? Douche is pulling on the handles and banging his shoulder against the door.

Outside, two gigantic men approach. Dark suits, dark glasses: the standard uniform. No one makes a bespoke suit look blue collar like muscle-lunk security. Johnny hops out of the car. *Girls,* he calls to the giants, *you're dismissed.*

One giant orders Johnny to let Douche out while the other begins pulling on the door handle like he's trying to clean-and-jerk the SUV.

Johnny likes to rile the muscle, but there's a fine line. He wants them ripping pissed, at the stage where they threaten bodily harm, but before they consider laying a hand on him. *You girls need to get away from the car. Whatever he's paying you, it's not worth it.*

While the door-guy bangs on the window, the other lunkhead circles the car towards Johnny. *Sir, let him out of the car this second or I will be forced to compel you to unlock the doors.*

Compel me? You? Don't get your panties wet. I'm going to count to three. I'll stop if you walk away. Either way, you won't hear me say three.

At *One*, the lug-nut hustles towards Johnny. Johnny appears his Book, says *Two*, and reads. He never gets to *Three*. He's already alone again with Douche. He opens the car door. *Don't forget the phone*, he sneers, his Book still in hand.

Douche stares at the one mountain crawling to the sidewalk, his suit a smoldering mess of molten polyester. The other mountain turned the corner and isn't coming back.

That was something, Douche tells Johnny. *Can I see that Book?*

We're going up to your place, Johnny tells him.

Douche looks surprised. *I'm uncomfortable with that. This is business. That's my home.*

Johnny reads the Book and fires one electrical bolt at Douche's leg. He cries and hops out. Johnny tells him, *This is all business. Your home is business. Your life is business.* He points up at the glass apartment building. *From this moment forward, that phone is the only friend who will help you.*

He grabs Douche at the elbow and leads him to the door. Douche doesn't even try pulling away. The doorman opens the large glass doors with some hesitation. *Everything all right, sir?*

Johnny knows what Douche is about to say and reads. Just as Douche says, *Does everything look all right to you?* The doorman is crawling behind his desk.

Please call the police, Johnny politely tells the doorman. *One of your residents is about to die in a murder-suicide.* He pulls Douche through the lobby and into the waiting elevator.

Murder suicide? Douche asks once the doors close. Johnny presses the PH button. *No exit strategy?*

Johnny lowers his Book. *I have a dinner reservation in twenty-five minutes*, he tells Douche. *You're the suicide. Your family and staff are the murder.* He gestures at Douche, *Unless you make the call.*

Jeremiah thinks he can intimidate me? Douche laughs. *He knows who I am. He can't send some thug to rough me up and expect me to cooperate.*

Sir, Johnny says calmly, *I've done this a few times before. Before I begin, you should know two things. First, everyone breaks. It's hard to watch me roughing up your family. Harder when I start killing them. Eventually, everyone breaks.*

And the second? Douche asks as the elevator doors open.

The second thing. Once I start, I don't stop. Not until you make the call. Or when you're dead.

Douche laughs as they step out. *Doesn't killing me defeat the purpose of coming here and trying to get me to make that deal?*

Johnny shrugs. *I don't like killing, sir. It's my job. I'm good at it. The thing to remember is that if you don't agree to work with Jeremiah—*

What he's asking is hardly working with him. It's doing his bidding.

Johnny continues as though he hadn't been interrupted. *If you don't agree, then I make you a lesson for the next guy. It's important for people to understand their decisions carry consequences. Certainly you've heard the rumors.*

Across the foyer, from the kitchen, Douche's wife and three teenage children look up from the table.

Johnny raises his Book. He begins reading.

Douche dials the phone.

Johnny lowers his Book as Douche grovels apologetically. When Douche finishes the call, Johnny turns to leave.

Don't you want to stay for dinner? Douche's wife calls from the kitchen.

Thank you, ma'am, Johnny says. *But I have a dinner reservation.* He grins at Douche. *Maybe next time.*

✷✷✷

See if she has magic. Johnny feels insulted. He's got to accompany this ugly freak to visit some girl. Why Freak is still alive, he doesn't understand, but he doesn't ask Jeremiah, either. Johnny has worked for Jeremiah long enough to understand he's not quick to kill his enemies. He studies them. Watches their methods and charts their connections. He lets them think they're operating in secret, all the while learning everything there is about their entire operation.

Freak is a bundle of nervous warnings about the girl. He rattles on endlessly about her magic and her importance. The only thing Johnny gets out of it is heartburn, no matter how he tries not to look at Freak's badly burned face.

They're watching the girl and her fat friend chatting, a car drives off, and the fat friend goes into some dilapidated barn with a trailer next to it. Johnny grins at the scene. *Real American shit right there*, he tells Freak. They enter the barn and Johnny sees the tanks of gas and equipment that's completely foreign to his eye. *Are you baking meth?* he quips.

Fat friend startles. He threatened her with his Book like it's a gun. *Not a word*, he tells her. *Cooperate and no one gets hurt. We're here to talk to her.* He tells Freak, *Explain to her.*

While Freak chats with Fatty, Johnny waits impatiently. The girl takes her time. When she comes in, all nerves and jitters, he watches. He's learned this from Jeremiah. You can learn a lot about a person by how they react.

They stand in silence. This girl is a child. Not even that pretty. From all Freak had to say, Johnny expected something more. Maybe there's been a mistake. This tall, gangly girl can't possibly be important enough that Jeremiah would waste his time. He verifies, asking Freak, *This her?*

The girl startles at his words. That alone tells him all he needs to know about her.

Freak sounds like he's introducing his ninth-grade girlfriend to his father, *Johnny, meet Alex.*

Might as well get this show on the road, he thinks. He introduces himself, *I'm Johnny Cortese. I'm here to see what you can do.* He pictures some cartoon he once saw, a bunny made to dance as a gunslinger shoots at his feet. He finds the thought so amusing he adds, *Go on, show me your stuff.*

For a moment, she looks ready to answer. Then the girl makes her first mistake. She asks Freak, *Where's Billy?*

He's heard that name. Freak must have said it twenty times. Johnny has no recollection of who Billy is or how he plays into this. He asks, *Is that the kid you mentioned?*

Freak answers yes.

The girl asks, *Where is he, George?* Johnny puts two and two together. Freak's name is George. Figures.

Freaky George responds, *Alex, Jeremiah sent us to—*

You're talking to me, Johnny snaps, interrupting. He's already bored and needs absolute confirmation the girl is or isn't as Freaky George says.

The girl turns to him like she's about to offer a lesson on manners. He waits for—and is disappointed he doesn't get—fists on her hips or even a wagging finger. Then she makes her second mistake and tells Fatty, *Come on, Abby. Let's go.*

Johnny can't believe his eyes as the fat one starts to leave. He grabs her wrist and growls, *Neither of you are goin' anywhere. Show me what you can do.* The girl doesn't look old enough to be a mother, but why else would she be so concerned about some kid? He offers, *Then Jeremiah delivers your kid.*

Fatty is practically shaking. Johnny expects her to pee herself. Then the girl makes her third mistake. Glaring down at Johnny, she tells him, *I don't do party tricks.*

Johnny glares at Freaky George. Jeremiah doesn't care what happens to Fatty or the girl—unless she has magic. Any reasonable witch would have cast a spell by now. Clearly Freaky George is mistaken. Time to wrap up this mess. He summons his Book. Fatty pulls away, nearly knocking it from his hand as he reads, disgusted that he's been sent on this bullshit job.

Bolts leap from his fingertips. Johnny wants to laugh at the cartoonish way the lightning strike knocked Fatty down, feet flying up in the air as her convulsing muscles made her dance and jump. But Fatty turns on him like a feral animal. He's shocked she has the balls to punch and claw at him, trying to pull the Book from his hands.

As he's struggling with Fatty, Freaky George talks to the girl. He tries to throw Fatty off, feeling her weight in the side of his gut. He thinks he's given himself a hernia. She uses the distraction. His eyes see only white for a moment, the full-fisted punch to his nose echoing in his skull. He felt it in his ears and teeth. He can feel the hot gush of blood on his face and tries to pull back. All he wants to do is reclaim his Book and put these two—hell, these three—out of their misery.

He uses the space he'd created and punches Fatty repeatedly. Just when he thinks he can read again, the girl jumps into the fray. She's frantic like a rock climber losing her footing, reaching for his Book like if she can't grab it, she'll fall to her death.

Johnny grunts, *Gimme a hand, you piece of shit!*

Freaky George doesn't hesitate and pulls the girl away. Fatty turns for just a second, but it's enough for Johnny. In his two hands, the Book strikes her skull, again and again, until—her eyes rolling figure-eights—she drops like a sack of shit.

Johnny opens his Book and reads, firing a few bolts into Fatty's back for good measure. Turning his attention to the girl, Freaky George is still making his moves. Freaky George dances when a bolt hits him right in the ass. *Get away from the girl, George!*

Freaky George whines, *We're supposed to* check *if she has magic.*

Johnny lowers his Book. Did Freaky George just talk back? Clearly no one here has magic. He sneers at Freaky George, *What do you think we're doing, you ugly freak?*

He smooths back his hair. It gets unruly when he perspires and if it stands up, it gives the appearance he is thinning at the crown. He stares at the girl to watch what she does as he snaps open his Book. He reads. She is like some puppy, giving eyeballs because she clearly has no clue what is going on. A girl with magic? Such bullshit. More like a freak with a crush. His electrical bolts strike Freaky George, who howls, dancing like that bunny he'd thought about earlier, making him laugh.

This is a waste of time. There's no magic here, just a freak with an unrequited boner. He screams at the girl to mock Freaky George, *Show me what you can do!* He reads and watches her convulse as the bolts hit her. It would be funnier if it weren't so annoying. This is a waste of everyone's time.

The old man must be confused, Johnny tells Freaky George, his tone marinated in sarcasm and disdain: Because Jeremiah is never wrong. Freaky George looks like a slug wishing it were a snail. *The girl wouldn't even fill a single page, much less a Book.* He hopes Freaky George understands that he doesn't work for free and one way or another, he'll extract his fee. *This is a waste of my time.*

Johnny looks around the barn. No one has magic. If he leaves now, Jeremiah will ask him how he is sure if everyone was left alive. It didn't seem fair that this girl should die because Freaky George has some delusion, but that is why fate is a cold bitch. He thought about the kindest way to end her. It's just a job. Like putting down a lame puppy. It sucks, but it's the humane thing to do. He decides that if Freaky George says even one word, he'll be put down, too. He'll give her one more chance. He pulls his punch, startling the girl. She is trying so hard to be brave.

With an exasperated sigh, Johnny reads his Book. The girl looks like she considers running—he still hadn't decided whether he'd let her go or not—but she doesn't move. Her body is twisted towards the door, but her eyes are locked on Fatty. The electrical bolt brightens the barn and casts terrifyingly large shadows up the walls, striking the girl and throwing her in the air. Johnny can't decide which is funnier, the girl's ungainly sprawl or the shadow-puppets she made on the walls.

Fatty leaps like she was overwound and her spring snapped. In an instant, she is protecting the girl. He fires at her. The bolts hit her with static snaps. Burning cloth and flesh smoke and stink as he keeps reading and firing. Fatty should be screaming for her life, instead, she holds her own as Johnny reads and re-reads.

This couldn't be anything but magic.

He wonders, *Why is the girl letting Fatty suffer?* His eyes narrow as he studies her, firing relentlessly into Fatty's back, wondering when the girl will act.

Then Freaky George opens his stupid mouth, *Do something, Alex! You have to—* He screams when Johnny sends a strike his way.

Fatty is saying something to the girl. Even as he turns her backside into well done chop-meat, she is protecting and coaching her. Now he can't stop. Magic is in play, even though not a spell had been cast—how else is Fatty enduring this? Johnny dealt with some of the most powerful men. Even the most resolute among them broke after four or five. He lost count after ten, but he keeps reading.

The girls face changes from fear and concern to disgust. A commotion erupts behind him. He doesn't mean to glance, but the deep rumble of boiling water makes him turn to see it gushing out of the barrels. Tools danced across the tables. The entire barn trembles. Dust cascades from beams and seams as explosive tanks wobble. Shelves collapse and the large piece of equipment that looks like a stone safe cracks in two, glass objects obliterating as they crash to the floor.

Johnny watches in dumb silence until Fatty asks the girl, *What are you doing?* And it became clear he has witnessed her magic. It didn't feel like a show, like she was rattling some tools to frighten him. The whole room trembles the way an obstinate three-year-old with a red-face shakes as it holds back its rage. This isn't power she flaunts; this is her control: slipping.

The beams above them groan and snap. Dust swirls in the air, pouring down like the barn was the lower half of a gigantic sand-timer. Freaky George begs, *Please Alex, don't burn me again!* Fatty tells the girl to focus. The roof begins caving in.

Johnny has never felt so much energy in one place. It is bewildering and terrifying. He's never seen emotional magic at play and this emotion is rage. It is like standing in the middle of an empty eight-lane highway, a single truck barreling towards him so rapidly the pavement is breaking apart around it. He's frozen in the glare of the headlights as the engine's rumble courses through his gut, making him feel like he might crap himself.

Then the girl looks at him.

Johnny feels her focus.

It is like the heat of the engine of that semi moments before it liquifies him.

He feels the pressure of her energy. The agitation as the air presses against him, vibrating him apart. This is no emotional outburst; this is controlled and precise. The immensity of her magic is bewildering, but she is holding it back, even as his joints begin separating, as she slowly pulls him apart.

He's already reading as his skin reaches its limit, like he's stepped, naked, into the very vacuum of space. He can't read fast enough, his nerves crying out as each ending is pricked. For a man who hasn't had the need to be afraid in so long, he's terrified. Even once he pops into the Library, panting and whimpering, his shaking hands won't let him still.

He knows the first thing he should do is report to Jeremiah. But there's no way he's going to Jeremiah like this. Slick with sweat, covered in dust, and—he's pretty sure—stinking of shit.

✳✳✳

Is Marco coming? Johnny says to no one.

Johnny waits in a large, sparsely decorated room. There's a couch, a chair, and a few end tables. Standing in front of the couch, as though saving it for a friend, is a young strapping man with tousled blond hair. Johnny eyes the newcomer in his jeans and T-shirt that shows his physique.

You new?

You could say that, the younger man says flippantly.

Jeremiah send for you? Johnny's impatience grows exponentially in the time it takes the blond man to answer. He'd never met this guy before. Never worked with him. It seemed strange they'd be called together unless…. Johnny doesn't want to think about it. He's always been good to Jeremiah. One of his best, or so he thought.

Johnny's armpits are suddenly soaked. He hasn't sweat like this since he was a teenager. It's about the girl, he thinks. Yes, he found out she has magic, but he also lost Freaky George. And then the girl comes to the meeting with Jeremiah and wreaks havoc on everything. Johnny wasn't there, but he's heard the survivor stories. You'd think they were in Normandy or 'Nam or Afghanistan. Jeremiah is questioning if he's lost his touch. Is the blond his executioner?

Johnny squirms. He looks around the room, nervously. Screw this, he thinks. After everything, he's not going to kill me for that. I warned him the girl had power but no control.

Blondie orders, *Look at me*.

Johnny rolls his eyes. *You're not my type*, he replies flippantly. He's got two choices: follow instructions or put the punk in his place. *Look, you and I are here, probably because the big man wants me show you the ropes.*

I'm young, so you assume I'm new? The blond laughs. *I imagine, considering what you do for Jeremiah means you cannot underestimate anyone.*

That's right.

But you underestimated me.

Johnny's back is suddenly soaked. Is blondie screwing with him? His confident body language feels too familiar, but Johnny can't place from where.

Blondie calmly asks, *What would you say if I told you I'm Jeremiah's replacement?*

I'd have to tell you I work for Jeremiah and only *Jeremiah.*

And if I promised you riches beyond your wildest dreams?

I already want for nothing. Johnny hopes he's neutralized the snare. He hesitates, uncertainty troubling his normal confident demeanor. *I'll admit, you've got balls.*

I believe in consistency. I've kept my appearance for nearly three hundred years. Give or take. But I decided it was time. I did it for the girl.

The girl? Who else knows about her? Could the blond be telling the truth?

The blond nods. *She didn't relate to the old man. I thought this would appeal to her, reinvigorate the brand, as they say these days.*

Johnny senses something serious is happening, but his concern at being played clouds his objectivity. This either is or isn't Jeremiah. Blondie's in the right place, saying the right things. His heart beats fast—faster than when he's walking someone to their home knowing he's about to beat the living shit out of them. He dreads what is coming. The girl was like standing inside a nuclear reactor. He tries to sound cool, but his nerves are shaking his vocal cords. *Talk about giving it up for a girl, Jeremiah.* He adds weight to his boss' name.

Jeremiah smiles. *She's powerful. I wanted to understand what she was willing to do with that. The old man was immediately adversarial. I decided to see what she'd do with someone her own age.*

Johnny feels a cold chill wash over him. His balls retreat into his abdomen. He doesn't like this. The youthful appearance was throwing him off. Jeremiah isn't chatting. He's setting up his next job.

I already sent Marco.

Johnny's wounded pride wants to ask, *Why'd you send Marco first?* His concern for his friend wants to ask, *Why'd you send Marco first?* But it is his cold pragmatism that takes the floor and asks, *Did Marco know what you were sending him into?*

Jeremiah responds by saying, "You were close, weren't you?"

A chill settles in Johnny's gut. He can't let Jeremiah know how hard Marco's death has just hit him. He steels his face the way he does when he doesn't want to but has to finish a job.

Jeremiah grins. Johnny wants to slap the smug look off the kids face. When the old man made that same expression, it suggested confidence and experience. Now it just looked cocksure. Finally, Jeremiah starts explaining. *It's the end of an era. What started four-hundred years ago with Laurent Robaleaux ends tonight with Matthew and the girl. It's sadly predictable how charismatic revolutionaries are at the start of a movement and how like inbred deficients riding the coattails of their predecessors they are by its conclusion.*

I've heard things, but when the stories are about people who cross you and almost succeed, I'm disinclined to believe them.

Jeremiah looks contemplative. *Where do I begin? You're a native-born American, so I assume you don't know a lick of European eighteenth century history.*

Johnny nearly argues the point, but the only eighteenth-century history he's heard of is Napoleon. But he's not sure if the little general was

European or French. Before the silence demands he say something, Jeremiah begins to explain.

There's a cult of neophytes who believe I'm like the devil or something. It's nothing new: One comes along every few generations, usually once enough history has buried the prior organization. This time around, it was Laurent Robaleaux. It's nothing I hadn't anticipated. You show a man magic and power and suddenly they doubt the hand that managed it secretly for millennia. It's selfish jealousy disguised as a noble quest. All they really want is to control it themselves.

As usual, I let the revolution play out. Usually power-seeking men find other like-minded souls and in time the growing organization cannibalizes itself. Men seeking power won't be subservient for long. But Laurent was different. He found ways of subverting the narrative to keep his people fearful of being discovered. Working in the shadows, he raised the largest insurrection that I'd ever seen in the modern era. His actions destabilized most of the Continent. He started wars with ideas. The notion of powerful governments working together was unheard of before then. His ideas were infectious. I had heard them before, in Athens, in Rome, so I let them fester to see where they'd go. He consolidated his power and massed his following. It eventually led to the war in the America's. He clarified, *with England. This spread back to Europe. Overturning one government after another. Nearly joined all of Europe under a unified flag, but allies in war are only temporary.*

Given enough time, the ideas that birth nations seem quaint and old-fashioned. Laurent's followers were gradually undone by their own mortality. Time wore his revolution down, grinding the stone into dust, until eventually only one man remained to carry on the cause.

Matthew was Laurent's student. He lacked his mentor's charisma, but what he had was fortitude. He has carried on the cause for two centuries now. I sent the girl to kill him.

Johnny has been nodding all along. He hasn't yet heard how he will be put into play. *And what do you want me to do?*

Make certain this is finished.

This is the point where Johnny usually asks for specifics and details and leaves. The specter of uncertainty prevents him from moving. *Why not send me and Marco together?*

Jeremiah regards him with a dispassion Johnny hasn't experienced. It's chilling. He understands that to someone as long-lives as Jeremiah, a human lifespan, be that ninety years or fifteen minutes isn't temporally different.

Jeremiah explains, *It is a test.*

Of me?

Of the girl, Jeremiah corrects.

Johnny remembers all too well the girl's wild power. If she's learned even a modicum of control… he doesn't want to consider it. *So, if she defeats Marco and me—*

When, Jeremiah interrupts as though the outcome is written in stone.

When, Johnny says as though the word is wrapped in thorns. *What has your test proven and what comes next?*

Jeremiah's eyes twinkle a little. *You're afraid but you're still willing to go.* He smiles. *This is why I have rewarded you all these years. You believe in the cause and will sacrifice for it. Like Matthew.* He sighs. *I will have learned that my two most adept soldiers are no match for the girl. I will understand her abilities. As for what comes next, I will scorch the earth of her.*

What all *do you mean?*

Jeremiah shrugs. *Wipe her from existence.*

Johnny has never seen Jeremiah outside of the Library. *You're going after her?*

Jeremiah's expression told him everything he needed to know.

Oh. You're sending your men *after her.* Jeremiah didn't like when he called them Hipster Clones, even though that's what Johnny thought they looked like. They weren't men. They creeped him out.

Jeremiah grabs Johnny's shoulder with a slap and squeezed. *That's all assuming you fail. You've met the girl before. She won't be expecting you. Take advantage of any opportunity to destroy her.*

Johnny understands. Like overpacking a suitcase, he pushes his fears and concerns down hard and zips them away. He retools his posture and tightens his expression. *Is there a Book I should take?*

Jeremiah points to a corner table and the Book resting on it.

After a quick perusal, Johnny appears his current Book, exchanges them on the table and disappears it. *Where am I goin'?*

Matthew's apartment in New York City. Jeremiah nods as though he's reviewing a list. *You'll have ten minutes before the others arrive. Take comfort in that.*

Chills run up Johnny's spine, the fine hairs on his neck stand and shiver on their own. His survival might be in the hands of the Hipster Clones. He never imagined he'd hope to see those creepy motherfuckers.

****

Jeremiah's words disappear into the distance as Johnny finds himself in a ruined apartment building hallway. It reminds him of the barn where he met the girl: in a state of catastrophic destruction.

The air he inhales differs from the air he exhales. It's heavy with dust, it's warm. Ahead, studs and wires and slabs of wallboard are splayed about like giant playing cards. He rolls his shoulders. The girl still doesn't have control, he thinks: This is his advantage.

A door creaks open down the hall, a tide of debris collapses into the stairwell. A moment later, a police officer awkwardly steps over it, entering the hallway. Johnny flattens himself against the wall, hoping he's concealed by the dust and darkness.

The officer calls out, *Anyone in here? Is everyone okay?* He pushes through the hallway, disappearing through the enormous, wrecked hole that once was a wall.

Johnny creeps forward, listening to the exchange, trying to understand what it means.

I'm officer Gonzalez. Are you alone?

Johnny strains to hear the answer.

Yes.

This is the voice he remembers, but not the quality of it. She sounds tired. That could mean the magic wore her out or she's hurt.

Where are you hurt?

Where—not are. He follows the officer.

The officer is reporting the situation into his radio mic on his shoulder. One patient, needing medical attention. Johnny doesn't need more people making this more difficult. He looks at his watch, wondering how many minutes have passed since he arrived. He estimates two. Eight to go, he thinks. Only eight. He enters the apartment confidently. The officer startles as Johnny tells him, *Everything's fine here, officer.*

Chapter One Hundred and Twenty-One

ohnny Corteze faded. Memories dissipated and dissolved into Alex's own. It wasn't unlike awakening from a vivid dream, or like holding a picture made of colorful sand, only to watch it sift through her fingers, going from a cohesive memory to dust in moments.

Alex shook off her disgust. A lifetime of memories filled with violence and excesses from service under Jeremiah were sickening and repetitive. Not all his life was horrors. He had tender moments. Friends and lovers, some of whom he actually cared for. She now understood more about male anatomy than she ever cared to. It was an entire life she would happily forget—if she could.

Alex's heart pounded like an orchestral bass drum; a moment ago, she could barely stand. Now she felt adrenalized, ready to do cartwheels. Everything Billy's coin took from her, Johnny's replenished, and then some. It electrified her.

Johnny now explored the remains of the apartment like a robotic vacuum, striking debris and turning about, his lobotomized expression never changing to express frustration or anger or concern.

A quick survey: The doorway to the damaged bedroom. The bloody mess of Billy's body. It made her heart ache. *He's gone. I took him*. A groaning, half-conscious police officer. One zombified hitman. His Book. And to top it off, one skeletal hand.

Staring at the hand, *What do I do with you*?

A spark in her brain nagged at her. Like a pull on a sweater, the more she thought about it, the worse it became. *What do I need to remember?*

The thought became whole—*ten minutes*—just as sparks struck her.

The first few impacted Alex like bricks, tossing her over the couch. One after another, men appeared and kept appearing. *Two, three, five, seven... are there ten? He sent* ten *men after me?*

She peeked over the couch. Jeremiah hadn't sent ten men: He'd sent ten Books. Johnny's thoughts still fresh in her head, she giggled: hipster clones.

There seemed no sense as to why he'd send one man and then ten, even if they were golems. Alex almost felt honored. The odds weren't fair. Jeremiah wanted a problem solved. Or a bigger problem started. Her racing heart, flooded with adrenalin, beat like a hummingbirds'. Her hands trembled, but not with fear—with excitement. She felt so juiced from Johnny's coin she couldn't help but grin when she heard them speaking in their guttural tongue, projecting their sparks at her, scorching the couch, and blasting the windows.

They moved, attempting to flank her. Her fingers tingled. She looked at Billy's body and refused to take her eyes off the bloody mess to replenish her anger. How many had they taken from her? This was enough. Her grin faded. Taking a deep breath, Alex leapt to her feet, and from her fingertips her anger produced a shockwave that threw half their number—the right flank—through the air like feathers in a hurricane. The wall behind them vanished in a glittering explosion of wallboard dust, the rolling destruction warped the floor and ceiling like an ocean swell.

Dust choked the room; the air pressure flowing from the shattered wall that now opened on the stairwell pushed it out the broken window, swirling and furious.

Sparks stung her back like wasps. Turning to the left flank, screaming, this lesser wave of energy brought the ceiling down atop them.

All along, Johnny Corteze shuffled around the apartment like a shooting gallery target.

Officer Gonzalez asked, "What the fuck's happening?"

Alex knelt at his side. "Can you stand? You need to get out of here."

He looked at Johnny with suspicion, "What's with him?"

"He won't bother you."

He poked at his chest. "He shot me?" He looked at Alex, reached for her shoulder, "Are you okay?"

Sparks showered them as several Books dug themselves from the rubble. Thrown into the wall beside Officer Gonzalez, Alex left a semi-circle indentation. She hadn't yet regained her bearings when sparks barraged her again. Extricating herself from the broken wall, her body pummeled as if stabbed with knives. Officer Gonzalez cried out; drew his gun and fired until empty. The sparks never stopped; the bloodied, wounded Books turning their attack entirely to him.

Alex screamed as she stepped into the line of fire, protecting Officer Gonzalez with her body. Her hands raised as though to protect her face, her concentration drawing the electrical bolts to her palms as though they'd been magnetized. Her palms burned and the growing agitation of the electrical magic gave it weight and mass, as though she tamed molten metal in her bare hands.

Behind the attacking Books, others began pulling themselves from their rubble graves, emerging broken and bloodied and missing pieces, looking like reanimated corpses. Officer Gonzalez muttered a stream of expletives as he reloaded his gun. Once that was empty, fired his taser to all the effect of a party popper. The golems collected together, taking hold of one another like schoolchildren on a field trip, one hand to the next shoulder.

Alex threw their collected lightning at them just as one of the connected golems became an explosion of dust. The blinding shot hit her squarely in the torso, like a speeding truck, knocking the air from her chest and her feet from the ground. The room was a kaleidoscope of spinning walls, floor, and ceiling. Her ears popped and everything groaned in a deep rumble punctuated by the sharp snapping tinkle of glass.

Emerging from the apartment in a whirl of chaos, the cool air left her like a bubble popped in humidity. Her stomach rose into her chest as the golems and the apartment shrank from view. It didn't make sense to her brain, which still commanded her arms to reach for purchase that was too far away.

Windows blurred by; the ground rapidly approaching.

Oh fuck.

She whizzed towards the ground. Her brain flabbergasted by her predicament. Debris exploded below on the pavement. There was nothing left for her to do but crash.

Horns and screams and crashing rubble roared.

Her eyes locked on the ground. On people looking back at her. Distance measured in seconds. No time left. Preparing for impact. Twisting to not land face-first. Familiarity in the motion. Thoughtlessly, she twisted and stretched.

The ground roared past and then away even as the last of the falling flotsam battered the street and the people on it.

It took a moment to register that the ground was receding. *Flying isn't possible in the waking world.* Even as the evidence proved her wrong, she couldn't help but doubt her own experience.

She slowed, just a few stories from the ground. A crowd of gaping people watched her through their phones from behind a window. She feared looking down would break this spell of levitation.

Cries of the wounded became shouts as people on the ground discovered her, floating in the air. They cried at and to her. Glancing down, panicking at seeing the ground so far beyond her feet, the sea of people looked like an army using cell phones for shields.

Gulping a much-needed breath, Alex wasn't sure when she'd last taken one. She gave over to instinct, her body more adept at controlling flight than her mind. With a slight stretch—her mind terrified of the bold flight moves she made on the Between—she rose gently on her return to Matthew's penthouse.

Her body coasted upwards as if pulled along a fine thread. Any time her mind attempted to control her, she tipped and wobbled. Giving flight over to her body, she gained speed, gained altitude, closing in on the window.

Shouts and screams called to her from the street. Wonderous, hopeful, rude, disgusting commentary from below. She gave them no regard; as soon as she reached the penthouse, sparks sprayed from the windows. Most missed her, shattering the windows across the street.

Her initial reaction was to duck, but the result was to fall. Her drop accompanied by cries from the crowd. She steadied and their concern diminished. She rose slowly to cheers. She hesitated, pausing safely below the window to their collective sigh and reminding shouts of *Watch out!*

There, she hovered, one stabilizing hand pressing the wall as she caught her breath. Her trembling hands stilled; her heart slowed until she could tell one beat from another. She looked at her hands. *If I cast a spell, will I fall?* There seemed only one way to find out. Before kicking off again, she made the mistake of looking down. Her feet dangling so far from the ground was nauseating. It felt like reaching blindly for a ladder rung but never striking it. She could descend to the street and never have to test her theory. But Officer Gonzalez was trapped. Would the Books let him leave? Also in the apartment was Johnny Corteze's Book. Jeremiah sent her a message. Perhaps it was the energy of Johnny's coin pulsing through her veins that made her want to ensure he received her reply.

She jetted up into range of the window. It was like being thrown into a hailstorm, except instead of rocks of ice, her skin sizzled and bruised, struck by hot electricity. She propelled herself at sudden, terrific speed, launching herself through the shattered windows. She still sucked at landing, crashing beside Johnny Corteze's Book. Bolts struck her as she opened the cover and glared at the pages.

Continued strikes battered her like they cast bricks, but as the Book incinerated, they left smoking craters in the wall, shooting through her fiery form.

Her flames expanded throughout the room, embracing the Books whether they fired at her or languished, pinned beneath rubble. She walled off a bubble of air around Officer Gonzalez, who watched her flames in expectation of an incineration that never came. She kept her heat from Billy, too. She'd already taken so much from him that using her flames as his cremation pyre seemed a step too far. Not to mention, after how his coin had damaged her, she wasn't willing to risk it.

She turned all the Books—the Hipster Clones—to ash. She blackened the walls and darkened the windows.

The power in these animated golems was different. As though by giving them life, the magic within them was amplified. The energizing sensation was nearly orgasmic. She believed she was momentarily capable of seeing unseeable patterns and congruences. For a moment, Alex thought she understood the entirety of the cosmos.

The charred and smoldering hull of the apartment creaked around her. Her body trembled convulsively. She thought she felt every hair, every breathing pore, every cell in her body, as she resonated with the recollection of multitudes.

She fought to catch her breath. It was almost too much. Yet, even as she felt she might be sick, as though the power she consumed was so great it would explode from her, pulling her insides out with them, she craved more.

The whispers screamed, but not of fear or of pain; they celebrated. It felt not unlike a rave in her skull as they hungrily devoured the excess energies and felt that much closer to being alive. Her breathing stilled as she surveyed the apartment. Even Johnny was incinerated. Only Officer Gonzalez remained.

Her eyes met his, and he flinched, as though expecting her to strike. When he was mostly certain she wasn't killing him, he asked, "Who the *fuck* are you?"

Alex realized he wasn't asking for her name. There was only one answer. She repeated his question back to him, "Who am I?" She took a breath to answer, "I'm a witch."

She held out her hand—the universal sign for *let me help you up*—and waited. *There will be more, won't there?* Johnny thought Jeremiah had a hipster clone army. How many did Jeremiah have? The Library was immense; he could spare thousands of Books. Could Jeremiah make more? How many could she handle? The hipster clones were one thing. The true believers, the Johnny Corteze's, were another. This was how Jeremiah meant to harm her. There was no winning this fight without suffering, and she had to be on the receiving and the giving end of it. How many coins? How many lives? At what point would she be just as bad as Jeremiah? The hundreds of thousands of voices in her head reminded her she had a long way to go before that happened.

Officer Gonzalez took her hand and climbed to his feet. "You need to leave," she ordered him. It felt awkward to embrace him, cementing a lie by telling him he was her hero, and force him—make him—want to leave. It didn't feel right to pander to him after what he'd witnessed.

He stared at her, his chest puffing his shredded vest and his tattered uniform. His eyes wouldn't settle on anything, flashing back and forth across the destruction—like he didn't quite comprehend what he'd experienced. She anticipated he might invoke some chivalric statement, like an action movie hero, and he didn't disappoint. "I can't leave you here."

"I'm not staying," she warned, "but more of those tattooed men are coming."

It was obvious that Officer Gonzalez wanted more than anything to leave, but he had his duty. If she—a girl—could stay, a tough cop couldn't turn tail.

If he wouldn't leave, she wouldn't let him hold her back, either. Alex dug along one wall through the soot and ash until, blackened and half buried, Alex reclaimed the skeletal hand. The skeletal claw clacked opened, and the cop's coin glowed.

"What the fuck is that?"

Uncertain he was asking about Charon's hand or his glowing coin, Alex answered the simpler question by pointing at his chest, "It's your heart-star. Your soul. You'll leave if you want to keep it."

Officer Gonzalez stepped backwards, tripping over debris. Catching himself against the wall, the ceiling above them groaned, lamenting its compromised state.

How many people are still in the building? How many in the street below? Hundreds could die, the next wave of Jeremiah's sycophants was inevitable.

He assessed the ceiling like engineering was his career. "It's not going to hold much longer. I've got to get you out of here."

"Be someone else's hero," she told him. "There are more people in the building."

She saw it in his eyes: she was just a girl, reciting action catchphrases.

He forcibly grabbed her arm, insisting, "I'm not leaving without you."

Alex appreciated his protective temperament, his bravery in spite of danger, but in the coming moments he would be her weakest link. "Thank you," she crooned like a distressed damsel, and sprang to embrace him. Her mind conjured images for him, racing floor to floor, a heroic Moses leading residents to safety.

She slid away; his dumbfounded expression accepting her visions. Without another word, he cautiously navigated the remaining debris, disappearing into the hall. His shoulder radio-mic chirped and he asked his dispatcher to notify the responding fire departments that the building needed to be evacuated. "The top floor is rubble," he reported. "The whole thing is gonna collapse."

Alone, she looked at Billy's body, clearing a few pieces of debris from him. Wiping the soot from his face. The dirt made him look more like the boy she knew. Leaving him felt wrong, but there was no other choice. This was no longer Billy, just like it was no longer Lesedi. She ached with loss, she felt empty. She pulled her hair from her face, examined her shirt to see how burned it—and she—was. Bruises polka-dotted her body purple.

She felt like she was in the eye of a storm: A moment of mourning peace before Jeremiah's reinforcements arrived. For the first time, her path forward was no longer clear. Matthew deserved to suffer, but Billy had showed her he knew more, and his knowledge was too important for revenge to destroy.

Alex's insides spun like an emotional whirlpool, enough to make her dizzy and reel. Confronting Jeremiah had been terrifying: He was unstoppable. No matter what she did, he shrugged it off. Or so it seemed. He said he was the magic. If the magic was inside her now, how didn't he control it—or her? *He lies about everything. Nothing he says is ever really the truth.* She was tired—no, exhausted. She was carrying a burden of grief that she hadn't had a moment to unpack to determine its true dimensions. It felt immense. Billy was just the latest casualty, and yet had been such a driving force. His life had been a masterful chess game, sliding pieces to keep the game going, check always two moves away. There were so many people who believed in her. Stopping now felt like a disregard of their suffering.

Lesedi once told her that no one ever takes a stand when winning seemed inevitable: Stands are taken against defeat. That was always the point. One by one, her options exhausted until all that remained was her stand.

The idea terrorized her. Not because she would die, but because anyone foolhardy enough to stay at her side would die, too. *Wouldn't that be their decision?* She imagined Carrie at the Library, reading her Book; fearlessly. Her tattooed warrior-chef. She wondered why, given all of them, Carrie came first to mind. *Would Carrie die at my side? Abby? Marta? Rose?* Knowing that these women might willingly sacrifice themselves complicated her stand. It was one thing to face her fear. It was another thing, when, because she did, so would they.

For now, she couldn't worry about Jeremiah. He was sending his reserves. She recalled hovering over the street and looking down at a sea of phones. Once she was outside in the street, would he be so quick to send more? If his secret—that magic was real—was out to the world, what would he do to compel that genie back into its bottle?

It was Matthew she needed to track down. Part of her wanted him to suffer. To use his hammer and break his fingers and ankles and arms and skull. To turn him to ash and turn his ash to atoms. She wanted him obliterated.

Billy showed her she needed his knowledge. The thought disgusted her. He had to answer for Sara and Billy, and yet, hadn't that all been Billy's doing? Hadn't there already been a reckoning? She felt conflicted and confused, uncertain where to place her blame. Not that she wanted his two-hundred years of memories, but taking Matthew's coin offered the only compromise.

She approached where the wall of windows once existed and peered over. For a moment, vertigo forced her back. Did she imagine slipping over the edge? She questioned her recollection of reality. *Did I really fly?* Perhaps she imagined it. The fight had been brutal. Although her body turning to flames had healed her flesh, she couldn't put away recollections of searing pain as she was struck again and again. Had falling been a fever-dream? It wasn't like magic; she hadn't cast a spell. It was like what happened in a dream or on The Between: it wasn't will, but the absence of doubt that she would fly.

She stood somberly in the smoky wreckage accompanied only by her thoughts and Billy's body. Her eyes closed, thinking only of Matthew. Picturing him. Trying to recall how she felt when he was near, recalling all the details she knew about him.

She understood now how Matthew felt her presence all those years ago. It required intimate knowledge and all-consuming thought, but she sensed him. It would be stronger if he read from his Book; he'd light up like a flare. But now, he was like a glowing cigarette at night, twenty miles away.

She carefully reconvened with the edge, peering down.

In the street below, amidst wrecked cars and shattered glass and broken furniture and the police cars and the fire trucks and the crowds of spectators, Matthew waited. Watching. He could not run; without her, he was nothing but a man with a Book.

Could she muster the courage to leap from the edge and soar to the ground? For millennia, Jeremiah worked diligently to hide magic. What would it do to her—to him—to the whole world—if, witnessed by everyone on the Internet, she flew to the ground and ate Matthew's coin? The act would replay a thousand times on every screen on the planet before the hour was up. What would that do to Jeremiah, if suddenly his secret was no more? Might he disappear into the shadows to outlive the excitement? She wouldn't know until she made it happen.

She took a preparatory breath, listening to the city below. The wailing sirens, the police on loudspeakers, the traffic. Beyond this block, beyond this crowd, did anyone know this day was going to end very differently than any day which preceded it? She looked out into the city, at the buildings and the canyons they made. To experience this wasn't her destiny. Like passing those carts of delectable-smelling foods on the way into the city, to the Library, there were so many experiences of life she would have to pass. Was her life a list of things she'd never do—or was her life a list of things no one had yet done? She had magic. She'd traveled to the Between. She'd flown. Did these experiences make up for the others? She didn't know. She stared at the city. She could allow herself one minute to see this one thing. The sun made the buildings sparkle. It was beautiful.

It was time for her stand.

She stepped forward into the void.

Chapter One Hundred and Twenty-Two

Rose covered her eyes. The morning light was unbearable, burning through her eyes to the back of her skull. She felt twisted inside out, her whole being sore and in need of a wash.

Billy's bed was neatly made; the sheets taut and crisply folded and tucked in their entire length. Her father used to say he could bounce a quarter off the sheets after Heather made the bed, but until now, Rose never understood what that was supposed to mean. Billy's idea of a made bed—when he remembered he was supposed to—was to pull the sheets up to the pillow, even if they were untucked at the feet.

The commotion of Dolly, being whored out for the sake of making witches of the others, tip-toed stealthily up the stairs. Rose tensed at the laughter, the fearful excitement. These emotions excluded her. She would never be an actual witch. She got dressed. Downstairs, at seven-thirty, her mother and her friends were having a good-ole time: festive chit-chat punctuated with drunken laughter, except magic was the only thing imbibed.

Rose took a deep breath and tried to blow out her resentment. *They better not hurt Dolly.* She pictured Dolly hitting some limit, like a counter returning to zero, and disappearing in an explosion of fur. She charged down the stairs, ignoring everyone and turning into the kitchen.

She had just started eating breakfast when Carrie came in. She saluted Rose, then grabbed her playfully by the wrist. "Leave everything and come here."

Carrie dragged Rose into the living room. Nancy's staccato laughter was so contagious the others giggled more with her rather than at what she found hysterical. Nancy draped her arm over Carrie's shoulder and raised her eyebrows in an exaggerated expression of surprise at Rose. She wore all her piercings, eyebrow, nose, and lip. She gently played with her lip-ring, wagging it back and forth. By now, Carrie was joining in the hysterics. Carrie directed Rose to Dolly, who was going from Book to Book, sitting, eyeballing the women with deep suspicion before moving to another Book.

There was a new woman seated on the couch beside June and Rachael. Rose wondered who this newcomer was. She wore a bright, three-quarter sleeved banana-yellow polo shirt. It wasn't until she looked up at Rose with bloodshot eyes, her face ruddy and blotchy from crying, that Rose realized it was Abby.

A round of laughter circled the room like a breeze. It picked up each time Dolly moved to another Book.

"What's so funny?" Rose felt like the only person who didn't get the joke, the only one not acting drunk, the only one who found nothing here amusing.

"Watch her," Carrie pointed at Dolly. "These Books are empty. It's pissing her off."

Dolly moved to another Book, pawing at the cover as though attempting to verify it wasn't empty before she sat upon it.

With an accusatory tone Rose asked Carrie, "Is this what you wanted me to see?" She scooped up Dolly and turned back to the kitchen.

"Sweetheart," Heather took her by the arm, pulling her aside, "put Dolly down and come here." Rose placed Dolly on the floor and even with the commotion in the room and all the attention on her, the cat ran right back to investigating the Books. Heather took a sharp breath. "Please don't go. Between all of us, you've been doing magic the longest."

The laughter died and everyone turned to Rose. She looked from face to face, suddenly the center of everyone's attention. Not one of them found Dolly amusing any longer. In her mind, she put emotions to the expressions she saw. Who was disappointed in her (Carrie), who pitied her (Abby), who despised her (June).

Heather rubbed Rose's arm like she sensed something was off. "Rosemary, sweetheart, we're all new to magic and we thought maybe you could share something Alex told you that you think we should know about." Heather turned to her Coven and they each nodded to Rose.

Rose felt smothered by the expectant silence. She scanned from face to hopeful face. *Is this what Alex went through? Everyone wanting her to explain everything?*

Carrie turned away. "We don't mean to put you on the spot, Rose. But Heather told us what Billy told her all those years ago. *You're the key.* Now that Alex is gone, we're looking to you."

None of you treated me like I was the key before Alex was gone. Was I not the key two weeks ago?

Carrie retreated across the room from Rose's scowl.

Rachael said, "It's okay, Rose." She turned to June, and the two exchanged hushed words, as though they didn't want Rose to hear.

At first, Rose thought Heather held her to prevent her from leaving. Now she realized her mother leaned on her to keep from toppling over.

"Your magic," Rose said at last, her voice louder than intended, "came from your Book. Can you do things that weren't already in your Book? Can you combine spells? Alex said emotions change magic, so can you start doing one thing and then do another?"

The women exchanged curious glances. At first, they appeared to be critiquing the ideas. *What did they expect? I don't know how their magic works.* Their chatter rose as they discussed the topic.

Nancy took Heather by the shoulders. "You're looking pale," she fretted. To Rose, she said, "Your mom hasn't been the same." Rose felt Heather's grip shift from her to Nancy, as she used the other for support. Nancy led Heather to the couch; Abby and Rachael and June cleared the space for her to sit. Rose couldn't recall Heather ever looking so feeble. For a moment, she forgot her disdain and found herself awash with genuine concern and jumped to help.

Heather looked at her daughter leaning over her with a world-weary sigh. "Don't worry about me. I'll be fine. I can find the energy when I need to."

Rose started to reply when Nancy drew her back. "Don't argue with her, Rose. She needs to conserve her strength."

"I wasn't arguing with her."

Carrie came beside them and drew her aside. "Rose, we're all on edge. Whether it's because we're grieving Alex or excited because your mom came back, we're still upset because it's like only half of her did. It seems like yesterday I was flirting with Alex right here," she grinned, "making her think I was talking about Colette."

Rose looked at Carrie. She had so many questions running through her head. What came out was, "Why? Alex likes boys."

"If you say so," Carrie replied.

"Besides," Rose disapproved, "you're a lot older."

"Six whole years. Doesn't matter now. What I'm saying so poorly is we spent years planning for this and it only took a few days to fall apart. Alex, Donna, Betty. Maybe Colette and Lydia, too. I'm just saying that for most of us, we're realizing we haven't lived enough life to be ready to face death."

"You're scared?"

Carrie nodded with the full mobility of her neck. "Hells, yeah, I'm scared. You remember that boy who helped us in the Library?"

"Caleb?"

Carrie smiled. "Dreamy Caleb."

"Shut up," Rose didn't like being mocked.

"I'm not making fun. His eyes were all over you to the moment Jeremiah took him away. You're a young woman, Rosemary. It's not fair that you have to lead us, just like it wasn't fair that Alex had to. You should be going on dates with Caleb, not watching him marched to his death."

"What makes you think he's dead?" Rose couldn't bear the thought he was dead, too. It was hard enough to lose the older women. *That's what happens when you're old, you die.*

"What makes you think he's not?"

Rose wanted to say, *Because that wouldn't be fair.* Even as the thought lined up behind her lips, she recognized its juvenile aspect. *Billy wasn't fair.* Her eyelids blinked rapidly.

"It's okay to cry, Rose," Carrie squeezed Rose's shoulder. "You found out you lost your twin brother and cousin on the same day. You should cry."

Rose pushed Carrie's hand from her shoulder. "That's what's wrong with all of you," she growled at Carrie. "You all get sad. I'm not crying," she wiped her eye, "because I'm sad. I'm fucking furious, Carrie. Why are we standing around having feelings when we should be hunting Matthew down?"

"Your mother has her reasons," Carrie urged.

"That's not my mother," Rose responded. "Alex ate my mother's coin. I don't know who this woman is."

Rose waited eagerly for Carrie to respond when a knock at the door made Rose want to skulk back to her room.

Heather's voice didn't sound weary at all when she chimed, "Rose, honey, mind grabbing that? It's probably your father."

Rose froze as though staring into the single light of an oncoming locomotive. She could half imagine him taking one step into the room and announcing, *It's nice to have my daughter not try to kill me today.* Her throat burned from the acid boiling in her stomach. He was going to announce her attempted murder and all the real witches would take her Book and use it to execute her, one torn page at a time.

She slow-walked to the door and, on a repeat knock, opened it.

Eric waited outside. Raw bruises marked his arms: brown and purple bullseyes. "Hello, Rosemary," he said. There was no kindness in his voice or his body language. "Are you going to have me in?"

She stepped aside. Eric stepped far enough in for her to close the door but no further. He looked around the house as though taking stock of the changes. It had been years since he set foot inside. Not since this was his house, too.

Heather rose from the couch without assistance, and they hugged. Rose wondered whether the encounter qualified as theater. Although they were often civil to one another, it was always *for the kids.* What kids were there to qualify for their civility? Billy was gone. And Rose realized she had attempted to kill both of them. Their greeting lasted—for Rose—an uncomfortably long time. Eric embraced Heather, holding her as though he was afraid of slipping away. She did the same to him. Heads bowed onto one another's shoulders. It was like on television when two lovers overcome an elongated separation. Before they separated, Eric whispered to Heather's ear.

Rose's heart pounded as she crossed the living room to the kitchen. From here she could make a hasty retreat if need be. If she had to defend herself, she reasoned, she'd first strike the snitch.

"There just aren't words," he said to Heather. "It's against the natural order of things. It's not supposed to be this way." Rose bristled at his accusations.

"Please stop," Heather begged, her words wet with emotion. "I've lived with that knowledge my whole life, alone. I'm just glad you're here. Finally."

They weren't talking about me at all.

He told Heather as they stepped apart, "I appreciate you not rubbing it in my face. Much."

Heather crossed her arms. "You have a lot of crow to eat, so I reserve the right. Jennifer and the kids understand?"

He made a face. "Let's just say that she holds a lot more sympathy towards you today than she did this time yesterday. She isn't happy with me. Says I betrayed her. That I've been lying since the day we met."

She nodded. "It's nothing you don't deserve."

"Ouch," he laughed, breaking his lamenting tone. He was being far too convivial and even-tempered for Rose's comfort.

Heather touched his arm, wincing at his bruises. "What happened here?" She briefly cast her glance to Rose.

Shit. Here it goes.

"You know how it is, Heather," he explained. "I can be a dick when the women in my life talk about magic. I banged up Rose's Book the last time I saw her without realizing what that'd do to her. I don't know if she told you she came by last night."

"She didn't say what happened."

Rose grit her teeth. She wondered when appearing her Book would be regarded as a defensive act rather than an aggressive one.

"Let's just say our daughter knocked some sense into me."

Rose waited for his next sentence….

Heather mocked a smile and spoke through her clenched teeth, "We are perfectly fine without your help."

"And it probably wouldn't have come to this, like I said, if I hadn't tried to wreck her Book."

He's not accusing me?

"You're the one who did that to our daughter's Book?" Now Heather was accusatory. Like she'd put together how the damaged Book made Rose suffer and sought to confirm he was to be blamed. Now Rose wasn't seeking to escape but ensuring this route was blocked to her father.

Eric sighed. "Look, you know where I stood on magic. It took your daughter slapping reality down my throat to bring me around."

Heather repeated, "Slapping reality?" She looked over his arms. "It looks like she held back." She looked to Rose, "Why didn't you tell me *my daughter* had a fight with *her father* last night?"

Rose shrugged. She watched her father for some sign, a wink or a nod that everything was okay, but he regarded her with cold indifference. "It was late and we," she hesitated, looking for any assistance from her father, but getting none, "resolved things."

Still no lies. She watched her father a moment more, waiting for his words to break the whole game apart, but they never came.

"So," Eric said cheerfully, "I'm here now. What's the plan?"

Heather dragged him to the center of the room. "Everyone, this is my ex-husband, Eric. Most of you met him and drank his wine. Please disregard all the shit I've said about him in the past," she grinned mischievously at him as she spoke. "He deserved that, but what matters is he's here now."

The women offered reserved *Hello*'s and *Nice to really meetcha*'s. Rose noted that no one appeared particularly enthused about his presence.

Carrie walked past Rose. "Kicked his ass, I see."

"What do you know?"

Carrie shook her head. "I know nothing." She pointed to her eye to signify she understood why Rose's eye had been bloody that day.

Eric approached Abby, holding at arms-reach. "Abby, I am so sorry. Rose told me. I can't imagine…," he stopped talking as Abby folded her hands over her face, sobbing. He looked like he'd broken a faucet and couldn't get the water to stop. He sought Heather for support.

Heather whispered, "It's been really rough for her."

Carrie and Nancy took their place at Abby's side, soothing her, helping her into the kitchen to wash her face and have a glass of water. June and Rachael were like satellites around Heather, keeping their distance but near enough should her show of strength falter. Although the strain was evident to those who knew, she wasn't showing her ex-husband that she was at all diminished.

"Hi," June held her hand out, "I drank all your wine."

Eric shook her hand. His expression suggested June's grip surprised him. "It was my wife's wine, but she's over it."

"Rose kicked your ass, huh?"

"I wouldn't say…"

"But I did," June replied, pulling her straight, long hair behind her ear. "She's shouldering a lot. I know you're her father, but she's a very capable young woman. Do not for a moment pretend that because she's young that you somehow know more. What you think passes for wisdom will come across only as condescension."

Eric's demeanor changed. His cheeks, twitching from the exertion of holding his smile, released. "You're right," he hissed, "she is my daughter. By what right do you have telling me…."

When the wind left Eric's sails, June grinned. "Let me remind you who you're dealing with. You see these women here? Every one of us has a bigger dick than you. Don't make me pull mine out to prove it."

Eric swallowed. He didn't budge, just stared at June like she'd slapped the sense off his face.

"That's what I thought," June purred. "It was nice meeting you, Eric." She returned to Rachael, who failed to stifle her laugh.

Eric remained in the center of the room, like a buoy left out at sea.

Rose approached June. "That was something."

June shrugged. "I've worked with men like your father my whole career. Sometimes they need to be *told*."

"Hey, Heather," Carrie called. Rose wasn't far from her mother and heard Carrie ask if and when they were summoning George from the basement.

"It's probably time," Heather said. "Bring him up, please."

While Heather was engaged with Carrie, Eric, apparently in the mood for contrition, addressed the room, "Rose filled me in on a few things. I'm sorry. I heard about Alexandrea. I… I can't imagine. I'm so sorry. I know. My son is gone, too. I know you heard lots of unflattering stories about me. What should matter is I'm here. I get how real it is now."

Heather pulled him by the elbow from the room's center. She walked him to the kitchen and pulled out a chair and urged him to sit. "You don't *get* how real it is, Eric. Just sit and pay attention. We've lost close friends and children. We're all grieving. Hearing your apologies just sounds patronizing at this point."

"But I mean everything I'm—"

"I'm not saying you don't," she interrupted him. "It's falling on deaf ears. We're glad you're here, but frankly, no one gives a shit what you think because you weren't there."

He nodded. "I just wanted to—"

This time her interruption wasn't polite, "No one is asking what you think, Eric. If you're going to continue to try explaining, the door is there." She pointed to the women in the room. "These women may look like that rag-tag Book Club that started meeting at our house all those years ago, but they're not. They've seen magic. They have magic. They've fought for their lives; every one of them. They've watched their friends be murdered. Until you've experienced that, no one here gives a flying fuck what you think." She seemed out of breath but was otherwise unwavering. "Just because you don't see another man here, don't assume we need you as a leader."

Eric looked like a castigated child. His frame slouched; his hands clasped in his lap. "Sorry," he muttered.

Heather huffed. "Always the last fucking word with you." When he tried explaining that wasn't what he was doing, Heather walked back and threw herself into the couch.

Chapter One Hundred and Twenty-Three

Heather addressed the room, "We have one mission right now: Bring Colette and Lydia home safe." She paused, leaning heavily on the couch, "George offered to guide us to the Library. The alternative is to go back to the door and go through the maze. I don't think anyone wants to try that ourselves. This whole thing is a disaster and we're going in blind. There's a good chance as we're feeling our way that Jeremiah will attack us, and we'd be foolish to expect mercy this time."

Rose's skin felt hot. Her whole body tensed. *Bring Colette and Lydia home? Not get revenge on the man who murdered your son?*

Carrie returned to the room with George in tow. Rose half-expected him to come up in bondage, but he entered the room with the ease of one who belonged there. Carrie pointed Eric out; George didn't budge to meet Eric's introduction.

Eric muttered, "Maze? Door? What have you gotten yourselves into?"

Heather ignored him. "There's no time to practice, and I fear that when we do magic Jeremiah will know. Let's agree on our plan and execute it. At noon, we go the Library, together. That means we have to trust George and he's given us reason to believe we can. When we get there, we look for Colette and Lydia. Nothing can distract us from rescuing them. I don't care what we have to do to find them; nothing is off limits. Grab as many spare Books as we can carry. Then we get out. Bring them home, give them magic. Then, once everyone is safe, we'll figure out step two."

"What about that boy," Carrie asked, "Caleb?"

Rose saw Carrie looking at her, as though expecting her support. *I don't care what happens to him, even if Carrie's right and he likes me. There's only one thing that matters today.*

Heather seemed to recall Caleb with some surprise. "What about him?"

"He helped Alex," Carrie reminded them. "He helped us."

Heather eyed the room, taking a mental survey of the reactions. "We're already trusting George and that one," she gestured to Eric. "If we find him, we'll do what we can. But remember, we're doing this for our friends. Is everyone in agreement?"

Everyone murmured and nodded as they looked from one to the other, getting visual cues and feedback. This show amused Rose; aside from Carrie, none of them answered without first looking to someone else. *Can't they decide for themselves?* Watching this helped cement her determination.

"What about him," June nodded at Eric. "How does he fit in?"

Heather's face lined with worry when she turned to Eric.

Eric pointed at George. "What about him, who you're trusting? Who's he?"

Carrie laughed. "He's a long story."

June interjected, "George has agreed to do whatever we tell him."

"I'll do whatever you tell me." Eric addressed Heather's continued gaze, "What?"

"I don't know," she rubbed her temples. "How does he come without a Book?"

Abby raised her hand. "I can do it," her voice wobbling, "the same spell I… cast on Alex. It should work for him, until he can get a Book."

The prospect of having a spell cast on him didn't sit well with Eric. So far, he'd only experienced Rose's spells cast on him. "What spell? What'll it do?"

While Abby sobbed, Heather summarized how Jeremiah forced Abby to take Alex to Matthew's.

Rose looked at the clock. She couldn't wait any longer. "There's someone you're forgetting."

All eyes turned to her.

"Matthew? Remember him? He murdered my brother. He's the reason all this happened. He killed Alex's parents and is why she's dead, too. And what, he gets off because we have other things to do?"

Heather chided her daughter, "Not today."

As Heather turned back to the group, Rose pressed her, "Not today? We know where he was yesterday. If he runs, how are we going to find him again?"

Heather started her contradictory reply, but Rose spoke over her mother, "That's fine. You all go to the Library. It's probably the right thing for you to do. But not me. I'm going to put Matthew down." She chortled; entirely fake, but she didn't care. "How many more of us does he need to murder before you take him seriously?"

"Rose, sweetheart," Heather started to say, "you will not go off on your own and—"

"I'll go with her," Marta offered. "I promised Alex I'd watch over her. Avenging her is the right thing for us to do."

Heather stared, slack jawed. She looked betrayed. She composed herself. "Anyone else think *revenge* is more important than saving two of *our friends*? What if you were the ones missing? Which would you have us do?"

The room was silent. Women stared from one to the other, looking for support, looking for someone to make a call.

Carrie stepped forward. "I'd prefer we all stayed together, but I don't think Rose is wrong," she offered Heather. "But finding Colette and Lydia comes first for me. Rose is your daughter, though. You need to make that call."

Before Heather could speak, Rose said, "Why shouldn't we do both?" She looked at the others, then at Heather. "You'll worry about me either way. If I come with you, you'll probably make some stupid mistake to keep me safe, like stepping in for me when Jeremiah wants to feed my coin to Alex."

Heather glared at her for the remark. Eric muttered from his chair.

"You save Colette and Lydia. Marta and I will take care of Matthew. We'll meet back here when we're done." She grinned, "Kill two birds, you know?"

"Excuse me," Heather told the room. Pushing to her feet, she led Rose by the elbow into the kitchen.

Before Heather could speak, Rose announced, "I'm going after Matthew."

"I'm never going to change your mind?"

In the other room, one after another, everyone's cellphones beeped and vibrated. Like a chorus of notification sounds, they repeated and circled the room.

Distracted by the sudden electronic deluge, Rose said, "He murdered Billy, Mom. Maybe you knew it was coming, but I didn't. I need, what would you call it, closure. Besides, Marta said she'd help." She heard the television come on. She rolled her eyes; with Heather gone, were they so bored they needed to watch television?

Heather sighed. "Her magic didn't stick, Rose."

"Her Book was *blank*."

The other room was filled with gasps and utterances like "She needs to know. What is going on. This is amazing." It was riling Rose. She wanted to run into the other room and shout, *Shut up and turn off the television!* Just the thought reminded her of her mother. "Even if her magic didn't stick," Rose said, "I can take care of both of us. By now you've got to know that."

Heather's voice fell. "Listen to me Rosemary. If she doesn't have magic, this was her choice. I don't want you wasting any energy trying to protect her. Worry about yourself."

Rose heard what her mother was and wasn't saying. "Even if that means Marta dies?"

As though called, Marta slipped into the room. Rose and Heather both waited to see if Marta had overheard. She smiled awkwardly at them as apologized for interrupting.

"That's not what I said," Heather replied to Rose. She looked at their feet. "Yes." There was a stir from the other room. A murmurous rise and then silence, with only the television providing muddled narration.

Matter-of-factly, Rose replied, "Got it."

Heather pulled Rose into an embrace. "My baby," she whispered in Rose's ear, "I'm going to be worried sick until we're together again. Please, please, please, do whatever you have to do to come home."

Rose waited for her mother to release her. "I think you know me well enough by now. I will."

Heather rubbed her nose, her eyes wet. "We should get back before they get too comfortable." She pantomimed turning on the television and shrugged.

Rose grinned. "Between you and me, Mom, I'm more worried about you. Your *Coven* doesn't seem capable of anything without you telling them first."

"They're scared, Rosemary." Heather said. "I feel like that's all I ever said to Alex: *Give them some credit, Alex, they're scared.*"

"That's what I mean," Rose replied. "Look how well that turned out."

Heather seemed to freeze, perhaps chilled by Rose's cold dose of reality. "I love you, Rosemary."

Rose appeared her Book. Rose asked, "You know where we're going?"

Marta nodded. Rose began reading.

Carrie came running in and grabbed them both at the elbow. "You've got to see this. On the television."

Heather asked Carrie, "What's on the television?"

Carrie took a breath like she had been holding it for some time. "It's Alex. Alex is on the television."

Heather tried to share her excitement with Rose, but her daughter was already gone.

Chapter One Hundred and Twenty-Four

"What the hell happened here?"

Alex recognized the voice and mid-step, spun around, nearly falling. "Who's this?"

The momentary joy of reconnection played out in a smile on Alex's face. The body, however, caught Rose's regard.

Rose's eyes flitted between Alex and Billy, a flicker of uncertainty departing her expression as though each time she looked at Alex there was some verification that confirmed her greatest fear.

Alex watched as realization dawned on Rose, hitting her with all the subtlety of a sledgehammer. Except for Billy's adult body, the smudges of dirt, the tortured way Alex's heart kept her arms in motion as though she could reach across the distance and embrace Rose—Rose might not have ever realized this was Billy's corpse, but she read that truth from Alex.

Rose screamed. Her eyes accused Alex, as though furious Alex had hidden the truth from her. She collapsed over her brother's body, wiping away the dirt and soot staining his face, as though with each rub she might push away a year or two. She saw what Alex already knew: His features, worn thin by time were but a disguise worn by her twin.

Rose cried out like an animal in anguish, giving voice to what Alex felt inside. She felt all the rage, all the pain: as though they shared that same wound. Rose howled, tears streaming down her face as she cradled Billy's corpse.

Alex wanted to comfort Rose. To tell Rose how much he loved her. Remind her of their favorite moments together. As close as Alex felt to these sensations of time past, the more alienated she felt from Rose. She possessed things that shouldn't belong to her. No matter how sincere the sentiment was, Alex realized, Rose would only receive them through an inadequate translator.

This was Rose's twin; no matter how close Alex felt to Billy—even being a part of her—her loss couldn't compare to Rose's. Any intervention would come across as attempting to minimize Rose's grief. But anything was preferable to witnessing her cousin's desolation.

Marta lingered behind Rose, watching with grave concern. Shading her eyes, she noticed Alex in the glare of the shattered window. The expressions crossing Marta's face matched an unseen replay of their last moments together, ending with surprised confusion: Marta couldn't comprehend how Alex survived Death.

Once Rose's cries exhausted to whimpers, Marta touched Rose's shoulder as she stepped first beside her and then past her, all the while staring at Alex.

"You're alive?" Marta's question sounded like a declarative.

Alex's response was barely a nod. Marta had unasked questions, but Alex wanted an intimate moment to share in her cousin's grief. It felt impossibly cruel to stand this near to the one person she loved more than any other and not make contact. Her feet crunched through the ruins as she approached Rose.

Rose looked up. Seeing Alex, Rose didn't react with surprise. Her reaction was half an *of course* and half a *you again*. There was no affection in her eyes. Alex's approach froze, her heart hardening as though frozen by the glare. The sight was so great a hurt, Alex had to look away from her. It was worse than knowing that Billy was dead. It was knowing she was dead to Rose.

Without changing her aspect, Rose dryly asked, "What happened?"

The question took the air from Alex's lungs. She refused to cry, and yet her eyes threatened to run over. "Matthew," she squeaked. Alex felt the weight of Rose's accusation and responded to it, "There was nothing—"

"Nothing you could do," Rose mocked. "You survived all this," she gestured to the ruins around them as they stood in the open, thirty stories up. "Don't lie and tell me you couldn't save him."

"I," Alex silenced herself. What else could she say?

Tears streaked Rose's face. At once she looked like a child and a woman. So young and so old. "You ruin everything!"

Alex didn't know she was speaking until she heard her words, "I'm sorry."

Rose glared as though trying to burn the words from the air. "What did you do to him? He's old."

Alex tried to find an explanation where blame couldn't be placed on her. "Since he disappeared, he's been travelling through time…." Her voice lost its will to continue.

"He's so old," Rose repeated. She whispered, "What happened to you?" Rose collapsed in a heap atop him.

Marta placed her hands on Rose's back. "I'm here," she reassured. "I'm here."

Rose rolled her shoulder to throw off Marta's hand. Her tear-red eyes went wide with rage; her teeth bared. Her chest heaved as she fought to hold in cries but screamed anyway. Her heaving sobs choked her and made her dry-heave. She pulled on her own hair as she screamed and beat her chest as though in a fit.

Alex knew there would be no fixing, no embrace to take away the pain.

Alex approached; no matter how quietly she tried, her footsteps crunched the charred wreckage, like someone repeatedly cracking their knuckles.

She knelt across from Rose and reached out but did not dare touch her cousin's shoulder. Rose's eyes wouldn't leave Billy. She wiped away her tears and snot and used her wet fingers to clean more blood and soot from his face, pushing his hair from his eyes. "How'd you get so old?" She cried to him, "Why'd you go away from me?"

Billy's memories swirled in the reaches of Alex's mind. They mingled with Heathers. She could practically answer any question Rose had for either of them but would never be believed. "He did it for us." Alex couldn't muster the conviction to say anything to Rose about her twin.

"For us?" Rose's face soured when she looked at Alex.

"He did things," Alex found that necessary words were beyond her oratory skills. "He helped my father, he guided—or misguided—Matthew. Everything he did was to help."

Rose glowered. Her eyes seething. "Everyone dies because of you!"

Alex heard herself contradict, "That's not true," realizing it was.

Rose demanded, "What happened to my brother?"

"Matthew killed him."

"You couldn't save him." Rose huffed like a bull considering a charge. "You didn't even try." It wasn't an accusation, but a statement.

Alex wearied of the defensive. She considered the claw and showed it to them. "I fought death to save him, Rose. It didn't matter; he wanted… he needed to die."

Rose mocked, "You fought death? Why are you alive?"

Alex wanted to tell Rose she was being a bitch. She unsuccessfully tried to keep her tone measured and even, "Rose, I can't imagine how finding him like this must hurt you, but why do you take everything out on me?"

Rose appeared her Book. Rose read.

Chapter One Hundred and Twenty-Five

lex was too stunned to respond; Rose's reddish lightning struck her, somersaulting her backwards. The red-glowing, staticky bolts were stronger than any others. Perhaps an indication of her vitriol.

Marta pulled Rose's shoulders. Rose strained against Marta's grasp, spitting out word after word as though it were poison in her mouth, throwing lighting, determined to force Alex through the window.

Marta screamed, "Stop it, Rose!"

"Rose, please," Alex begged, yelping and crying out as each strike burned into her flesh. "I don't want to hurt you!"

Alex bore the brunt of it, gritting her teeth and glaring though tearing eyes. Like hot knives cauterizing the wounds they stabbed, the lightning struck deep, radiating through her like touching a fork jabbed in a socket. This was Rose's retribution for failing to protect her brother, and although wanting them to stop, Alex accepted the punishment for her failure.

Rose screamed, shaking her Book, turning away only to push Marta down. She faced Alex again.

Alex collapsed amidst smoldering char, inches from the ledge. Her already stained and tattered shirt smoldered. She whimpered at the intensity of the pain, concentrating it away as best she could in preparation for whatever came next. Some spells contained in Rose's Book were worse than this.

"You don't want to hurt me?" Rose sounded bewildered. "My brother," she cried, gesturing back to him. "You ate my mother's coin!" She gasped for breath, disappearing her Book. "Tell me again how you don't want to hurt me!"

"I didn't mean—"

"That's just it, Alex," Rose interrupted, "you never mean. You never intend. You try so hard. But you fail, every time."

Alex clutched handfuls of debris, crushing them in her fists, and tried to look at Rose without hating her. "Matthew killed your brother. Not me."

"He killed Billy *because* of you. Try telling me how that's different."

Alex lowered her head into the wreckage. Hot coals smearing her face, the polluted scent of burned char stinging her nostrils. *How can I argue? She only believes what she wants to believe.*

Rose turned as Marta was standing. "Stay away from me," she spat. She returned Billy's corpse. "Take me to him," she ordered Alex. "Billy is on the Between now. You have to take me. I need to see him." Her voice was buoyed with hope and held aloft with expectation.

Words abandoned Alex as she tried explaining why she couldn't.

Rose seemed confused for but a moment. Then the truth behind Alex's stammer hit her hard enough to shudder her entire body. "Tell me you didn't." Rose didn't wait for Alex to answer, reading the truth from her cousin's face. "Did you even try to save him? My mother's coin wasn't enough? His, too?"

There was nothing Alex could say to diminish the truth.

"You stupid, horrible, evil, disgusting," Rose's stammering accusation sounded not unlike a brief spell, read from her Book as her anger temporarily robbed her of coherence.

Tears spilled from Alex's eyes. "I tried, Rose. He told me I had to—"

"You ate his *coin*? You *ate* his coin?" She screamed. Hands trembling, Rose stepped over the body. She made her coin glow and pushed it into Alex's face. "Here! Eat it, you selfish bitch!"

Pushing Rose's hand away, Alex couldn't take her eyes off Rose's coin. A spider-web of cracks covered its face, diminishing its brilliance. One edge was fractured, its edge rough like a bite taken from it. The forgotten claw in Alex's hand clinked to life. It clacked away, straining and reaching.

"Please, Rose," Alex begged, the claw squirming in her grasp. "Put it away."

Rose stared at the writhing appendage with equal amounts of disgust and curiosity. She returned her coin to her chest. She was clearly uncertain what she was witnessing. "You took his coin with that?"

"No," Alex replied before Rose's words were silent. "This is—"

"I don't care," Rose interrupted.

Alex had suffered so much pain and was so tired of always being on the defensive with Rose. Rose refused to understand how desperately she'd tried to save Billy. Alex allowed honesty to guide her. "That's right. He's dead. Because of me. Same with everybody else. Because of me." Alex choked on her sob. "I didn't ask for this. I don't want any of this." She wiped her nose and tried to catch her breath, unable to look at Rose's scowling face. "Everyone I love is either dead or hates me."

Rose's stare was more venomous and painful than any accusation. It screamed of betrayal and hatred and pain. There was nothing Rose could have said that would hurt as much.

As though taking her cue from the silence, Marta spoke gently, "Heather's alive."

Rose turned to Marta with the speed of a striking viper. "Oh, Heather's alive. That makes everything better," she mocked.

Alex thought she misunderstood. She tried not to take her eyes off Rose for more than a moment. "How?" Her voice sounded so small, lost amidst the city sounds.

"The cat," Marta's hands pantomimed, "her Book. Put her back in her body."

"Fucking Dolly," Rose cursed, her tone transitioning to a quiver the longer she spoke. "She sat on Mom's Book and-and-and, sat on her and she came back."

Alex's pain prevented her smile. "Back?" What she wouldn't give to fall into her aunt's arms.

Rose glared at Alex, "She has magic, just like you. She doesn't need a Book anymore."

The information was foreign to Alex. There were all these "What's?" craving answers. As though Rose knew each one, her barbed tone replied, "None of them needs a Book. Dolly put the magic into all of them."

Alex didn't understand. "What?"

Rose's voice softened slightly as she said, "They're like you. The magic's in them."

"It's in all of them," Marta said over Rose's shoulder. "The cat did it to everyone."

Rose explained how Carrie and Abby also got magic, frustration coloring her words. She finished by saying, "That's why cats sit on whatever you're reading. They're protecting you."

Alex asked, "You still have a Book?" Each word raised Rose's cackles.

Rose appeared and opened her Book. Alex backed a step. Rose presented it for Alex to see the broken spine skewing the pages, tape holding torn pages together. Pages turned pathetically in the draft, one, two, ten, eleven, twenty, turning in clumps, revealing breaks in the spine.

"My dad broke it," Rose whimpered. She showed her shattered coin. "It was like Betty." Rose put it away before the claw reanimated again. "Only it doesn't work on them, on men," Rose clarified. "I tore up a Book, but it didn't hurt him, even a little."

Alex didn't want to interrupt but had to. "They sent men after you?"

Marta pointed to the approximate place, "That guy who attacked us, yesterday," she said. "You sent me and Abby away. And George. And him. Rose put him down."

Marco.

"George is on our side," Marta offered.

"I don't trust him," Rose growled. She lowered her Book like its weight exhausted her.

"Heather's back? George is on our side? They're all witches?" For the first time in days, perhaps weeks, Alex had hope. "Real witches?" She turned to Marta, "You, too?"

Rose accused, "Her Book was blank."

"*I* do. *He* doesn't. We cancel each other out, like twins. Like he would have done to you, had he been born." Before Alex could ask, Marta volunteered, "I did the Book thing with Dolly. It emptied the Book into me. Only men can't get magic because it didn't *come from* them."

Alex wondered if having magic helped Abby. She realized that if they all had magic, they also weren't likely to sit around.

As though reading her mind, Marta said, "Everyone thought you were dead, Alex. They're going to the Library."

Anger returned to Rose's tone, "Heather wants to free Colette and Lydia. It's like she doesn't care Matthew murdered her son."

"Wait, what?" Moments ago, Alex believed her aunt was basically dead. Now Alex feared she was marching to certain doom. "Heather needs all the help she can get. Why did you come here?"

Rose said, "To kill Matthew."

Marta clarified, "To avenge you."

Alex groaned. "Why can't she stay put? I was about to take care of Matthew."

Rose perked up. "You know where he is? I'll finish him. You can rescue Heather."

If everyone Alex had left was going to the Library, she had to go there too. If something happened to them because she wasn't there, she wouldn't forgive herself. But Rose's desire to hunt Matthew couldn't be discouraged. And Matthew had answers she needed. If she left him to Rose, she would never learn how to defeat Jeremiah.

Alex needed to justify her conscience into submission. "We're not separating. If Heather has magic, they know what they're getting into. We'll all go after them once we get Matthew."

"Once *I* get Matthew," Rose spat.

"Whatever, Rose," Alex exasperated. She wasn't about to argue details now. Alex understood how important a small piece of information could be. She addressed Rose, "I need to get information from Matthew, just like he takes magic from witches. You can have him after."

Rose's face lit up. "Torture?"

Alex was disgusted. *Was she always so wretched?* "Rose, I need to know you understand that you can't do anything until I say it's okay."

"You're gonna let him get away!" Rose screamed like a feral animal. "He murdered my brother." She pointed her finger at Alex, "Look what he's done! He has to suffer! If we let him go, he'll get away forever. I have to show him how he hurt me, or I'll never get rid of it."

Rose appeared her Book. It flopped open to a page, and Rose started reading, her scowling face dripping with tears.

This time Alex was ready. Rose's red bolts of energy deflected into the walls, disappearing in explosions of wallboard. "I don't want to hurt you, Rose. Please don't make me," she shouted as Rose kept reading, walking forward, charged sparks leaping from her fingertips like bullets.

"Matthew must die!"

Sparks flew into the late morning air, striking the building across the street, shattering windows and dropping debris to the street below.

Alex yelled to Rose, "I'm warning you, Rose. I will not be responsible for what I do. You're pissing me off!"

Debris littering the floor began swirling like eddies in a tidal pool. Rose kept reading. The remaining windows exploded. Rose read; red, fiery bolts exploded walls. The building groaned.

Alex was doing everything to manage her anger. Rose hadn't landed a single bolt but wasn't deterred. Alex didn't know how much more she could take before she inflicted on Rose real harm. Marta raised an unhinged door and ducked beneath it. Alex's concern for the integrity of the building grew as it swayed and groaned. Even more than Rose, Alex worried about the people still in the building and out in street, the people she'd kill if the building collapsed.

"Enough, Rose," Alex cried out. Her fingertips crackled. A single, powerful shock struck Rose in the chest, throwing her down. Rose didn't move.

Alex nursed her wounds. Her shirt in tatters. Everything hurt. Her wounds healed quickly, closing and scabbing over. She was ready to leave Rose behind without checking to see if she was okay. She was furious. When she screamed to vent out her rage, the building groaned. Alex reined in her emotions, bottling her feelings.

From the ground, Rose sobbed, "Why won't you help me? He murdered Billy. He tricked you."

"I never said I wouldn't, Rose. If you hadn't shown up when you did—"

"Then let's go after him." Rose, collected her Book, absently pushing on tape and fixing pages that creased and tore when she was struck. She touched her scorched shirt, and the burned skin beneath. "That hurt," she announced. Her face twisted with anger and sorrow and madness. "Where is he?"

"I'm not totally sure, Rose."

"I don't know. I can't do it," Rose mocked. "What is wrong with you?"

Alex rolled her eyes and turned away. She understood what Rose was complaining about, but it felt like she was lying to say she knew how to do that. She barely knew how her magic worked. She knew where Matthew was. She'd felt him just as Rose showed up. She concentrated, thinking deeply of him. He was easier to find the second time. Alex pointed out the shattered windows. "He's in the street. He's been watching."

"Watching?" Rose and Marta asked simultaneously.

"He says we're on the same side. He still needs me." She glanced at the claw in her hand. *What the heck do I do with this?*

Rose fearlessly peered over the edge. There were hundreds of feet between her and the ground, anyone she spied would have been little more than a speck, but still, she craned her neck around, the breeze blowing her hair. She disappeared her Book. Leaving the window, Rose looked around the apartment, or what was left of it. "You do this?"

"Me and Jeremiah's *men*."

Rose walked through the apartment, peering towards the hallway. "Did they get away, too?"

Rose's sarcasm was exhausting. "No. I burned them up."

Rose cackled. "Nice! Bet they weren't expecting that. How many you get?"

"It doesn't matter," Alex replied flatly.

"That many?" Rose grinned.

How can she be excited by killing? Even Books—Hipster Clones— were once women. When I kill them, where does the woman go? Alex thought she knew the answer. She'd burned enough living Books to know they contained no voices. The women were sacrificed to give the golems life. Still, if there was some way to avoid the slaughter, Alex would gladly take it. "We need to go. I don't know how long he'll wait and the police and whoever else are busy evacuating the building. They'll be here soon."

Rose wiggled her fingers. "Let them try!"

"Enough, Rose. What the hell is wrong with you? It's Matthew who's the problem, not everyone. He knows what he's doing. Even Jeremiah's followers only believe what they're told. They don't know they're wrong."

"You don't know that," Rose retorted.

"Actually, I do," Alex pointed out the shattered windows. That said, Johnny was generally an asshole. He chose to believe because it suited him, not because he didn't think to question it. "Matthew will be leaving soon. I need what he knows. Are you coming with me or not?"

Rose nodded her head, her eyes begging and frenzied and ferocious.

"Come here," she told Rose, her arms extended. She waved Marta over as well. To Marta, she said, "I can send you back to Heather's."

Marta shook her head. "Your brother refuses to leave your side. So do I."

"I can't keep you safe," Alex warned. She couldn't have any distractions, not against Matthew, not when she couldn't trust Rose not to murder him before she had what she needed.

Marta nodded. "I understand. He says we can help."

"Enough," Rose growled. "Let's get Matthew, already!"

Marta asked, "What's the plan?"

Alex stuffed the claw into her back pocket. Was that her plan? Use Charon's hand to take Matthew's coin. It seemed a cathartic ending: Slipping Matthew's coin into her mouth while he watched. She'd have her answers but wasn't sure she cared to recall his thoughts. Over two hundred years of memories from someone like Matthew would be a lot to swallow.

"We're going down to the street," Alex answered. "When we find him, I'll take his coin and you can end him."

"Just like that," Rose asked, "in public? Are you sure—"

"Suddenly you're concerned?" Alex checked Marta to make sure she read Rose's hesitation correctly. "Jeremiah's kept the truth a secret for, well, forever. A little magic in the street and that's done with and over." She looked out the window, she considered her flight. *It's time for my close-up.*

"Okay," Rose sang. "Elevator?"

Alex chortled. "What kind of an entrance is an elevator?" She extended her arms. "Take my hands." Marta and Rose each took one. Alex closed her eyes briefly. Their coins glowed, the claw squirming unpleasantly in her back pocket. "Through there," she nodded at the roiling patch of fog that was the result of the Between opening to the waking world, or in this case, the Between connecting two places. "Get out your Book," she told Rose as they released hands, and stepped into the street.

Chapter One Hundred and Twenty-Six

People stared. Most held up their phones and videoed, others fumbled to do so, disappointed they missed the three women who, having appeared through a patch of crazy-strange hovering mist-fog, stood in the middle of the cordoned-off street, wondering if they'd stumbled onto a movie set.

Rose spun around, overwhelmed by the crowds, hunting the sidewalks for her prey.

Yellow "Police Line" tape and metal barricades cordoned off the street in front of the building. Rows of fire and emergency trucks and police vehicles of all sizes congested either side of the road. People clogged the sidewalks. Traffic snarled, with nowhere to get through. The road was a jumble of honking cars and taxis and box trucks with cyclists somehow finding enough space to weave through. Wreckage of debris and broken furniture and appliances cluttered the cordoned section of street, the morning sun streaming down the narrow canyon glinted off the snowy layer of shattered glass.

Where is he? Alex rotated, the sea of faces perfect camouflage to hide one person. He could be anywhere.

Rose walked a perimeter of the cordoned-off area. A police officer approached to escort her out.

Just as the officer told her they couldn't be here, Alex shouted, "Don't do it, Rose!"

Rose closed her Book in a disappointed huff and wrenched from the officer's grasp. She glared at Alex when he began forcing her past the barricades and into the crowd.

Alex closed her eyes. She could feel other officers approaching, perhaps even Officer Gonzalez, who was probably still trying to convince himself he didn't see what he saw. She concentrated, thinking about Matthew's face; the way he moved, his broken neck wagging his head; the rattle his kinked throat made when he breathed. He was nearby, but that was as accurate a read as she was getting.

A hand clasped her elbow. "I have to move you past the barricade. Is that okay? You won't, you know, do anything?"

Officer Gonzalez's uniform was shredded and his expression was pure anxiety. He looked like he was disarming a bear trap with his head between the jaws: One wrong move and he knew what came next.

"Marta," Alex called, "go with him." To him she said, "I'm looking for the man who killed my cousin. He's here." She pointed her finger in an arc, "in the crowd."

"You're sure?"

Alex nodded.

He explained, "You need to be outside the barr—" Alex's expression froze his voice.

"Ignore Alex and escort me," Marta interjected. Before he could contradict her, Marta pointed at all the phones, "I'll even struggle if that helps with the show."

He looked at Marta with bewilderment. Tall but also so skinny; Alex could tell he considered tucking her under his arm.

"I'm sorry," he whined, other officers coming to see what was taking so long. "I gotta move both of you."

Alex had an idea. "Do you trust me?"

Officer Gonzalez looked at her. "To do what?"

"To not hurt you."

"Um—"

Lately, anger was always nearby. Alex barely needed to prime her emotions. The smug faces of the cops approaching her was enough. She didn't even need to think of Matthew, or of what she would do when they next met. There was already so much bottled up—Billy, Rose, Jeremiah—that when she raised her arms, lightning crackled, nearly striking officer Gonzalez, and providing enough power to illuminate the lights and signs up and down the street. When the blinding flash dissipated, he practically leapt into the air, grabbing Marta and hauling her—practically under his arm—to safety, waving the other officers away as he ran.

The crowd howled at her demonstration. Some people backed from the barricades. Others Were fearless behind their phones. People shouted the most bizarre things at her, calling on her to do it again, to get out of their city, cursing at her for snarling traffic, and for destroying the building. More than once, a creative derivative caught her attention.

Alex caught sight of Matthew. He slipped around the barricade and approached.

"This is quite a show," he called to her. "The media will be talking about the hoax in New York City for days. Scientists will debunk eyewitnesses, saying the explosion," he motioned up to his penthouse, "released toxic gasses or some such that made people on the ground hallucinate. In a week, everyone will forget this happened."

Alex approached, watching his fingers wiggle in preparation of claiming his Book. "Why should I keep his secret?"

"Alexandrea, think. You're doing what he expects. You're not the first person to try overthrowing him, much less the first women. Look throughout history. You can tell each time there was an attempt. It's like finding evidence of fire in tree rings. They're always followed by a purge. Witch trials, pogroms, revolutions…." They each took a moment, perhaps sizing one another up. "There are still Books in the Library. You're not ready. I'm not ready. He's too powerful. I need you to trust me."

"Trust you?" Alex lowered her head, "You should have thought about that when you killed Billy."

"That wasn't my idea," Matthew blurted.

"I know. It was William's." She watched him fight his surprise. He'd consumed enough coins to understand how she knew.

He glanced nervously, "Please, Alexandrea. The prudent thing to do is keep hidden. Until we're better prepared."

Alex looked at the crowd, the people staring at her, waiting to see what she did next. Several officers marched towards her. "He wants me to hide," she referenced the crowd. "And you, you want to take what I have, rather than show me how to use it. If we're on the same side—"

"A woman?" Matthew looked visibly amused. "Stop pretending. You'll get nowhere with emotional magic."

"Nowhere?" She withdrew the claw from her pocket. She held it towards Matthew. The bony fingers opened; Alex could feel their desire to draw closer to Matthew's now glowing coin.

"What in hell is that?" Matthew asked, though it was clear he knew, his coin spinning lazily atop his chest, drawn to the bony fingers. Matthew edged backwards but the crowd pushing the barricade cut off his exit. Many of them startled, aware that they, too, had disks glowing on their chest. It was as though Charon's claw drew them just as it drew their coins.

"I took it," Alex edged closer, the coin pulling from his chest, drawn to the clinking skeletal palm, "from Charon."

Matthew blanched. He clutched the barricade for support, his hands trembling. "Charon? You took the Reaper's hand?"

Teasing him with it, Alex thrust it towards him. The crowd pushed him and the barricade forward, everyone feeling the attraction of their glowing disk to the skeletal hand. Matthew's coin danced on its edge, spinning wildly on its sparking string as the claw drew it closer.

"Don't do it," Matthew begged. He stared, perhaps with awe or reverence.

Alex's heart pounded in her ears. Her hands trembled. She wanted to grab Matthew and rip him apart. Every time she looked at him, Billy's memory bubbled to the surface and Matthew dragged the knife across his throat. She wanted to hurt him in the most unimaginable ways, but he was surrounded by the crowd. Phones pointed at her. She would not risk hurting anyone else. Besides, she needed answers. She reached for his coin.

"I underestimated you," he told her, staring at the sun-bleached claw in her one hand, the covetous grasp of her other. "I have answers. People you must meet. People who will follow you. I had no idea you could—"

Alex was on the ground. The rumble of a shockwave still echoing in her head and as it departed down, between the valley of buildings. Her head was still trying to make sense of what had happened when she was suddenly flung through the air.

Around her, people screamed. Glass was everywhere. Barricades were twisted and strewn about, battered emergency vehicles lay on their sides or crushed people. Everywhere she looked, people were brutally harmed. Body parts lay hither and thither like forgotten gloves or discarded shoes. She looked at her empty hands. Through the chalky air, she spied the claw, but Matthew reached it first. She held her breath, the maelstrom about her seeming to pause.

He held it out. She anticipated its covetously bony fingers.

"Take it, Alexandrea," he urged. "We're on the same side, you've got to know that by now. William's coin showed you."

Three reddish sparks hit Matthew, spinning him about, the claw flung, disappearing in the fleeing crowd. Rose kept firing as she raced towards them, sometimes missing Matthew and wounding others in the crowd, too dense for them to flee. People cried out in the crush or disappeared as the mass surged forward, pushing through a barrier or climbing over a crumbled building façade.

"Rose, no!" Alex screamed.

Behind Rose, a trio of officers gave chase. One unlatched his yellow taser.

Alex noticed strange patterns in the crowd, people, here and there, who did not run: men with Books.

Matthew rushed to his feet, his back turned to Rose as she fired again, dropping him to his knees. Alex spun to see what Matthew deemed so important he'd turn his back on Rose. Violently erupting through the crowd, two dozen Books pushed their way, shooting electric bolts to clear their path.

Sparks zapped from everywhere, from Rose, from the dozen or so men with Books, from Jeremiah's golems.

Matthew returned fire to the nearing Books. Two of the pursuing cops tackled Rose hard to the ground, her knees and hands scraping, her face falling practically in her Book which splayed across the pavement like a deck of cards. She shrieked and thrashed like they flayed her alive. All of it caught on hundreds of phones. Parts of the crowd hesitated and cheered on the police.

"Leave her alone," Alex cried to the police as they wrenched Rose's arms behind her back. Alex rushed them, dodging fire, collecting Rose's scattered pages. With Rose as a stationary target, some of the Books' sparks burned the pavement around her, blackened her Book, hit the cops, hit her, eliciting screaming cries of pain from each of them. Alex turned to the golems to return fire.

"Alexandrea!"

Matthew called to her. Although he was firing a barrage of sparks at the army of Books, they were targeting the crowd. They reached out to touch one another; Alex fired her bolts of lightning, but it was too late. The end Book exploded in a veil of dust, his spell blowing the crowd apart, hurtling people into the air, and skidding a car across the sidewalk, through the fleeing crowd, and into an Italian restaurant window in a shower of plate glass.

The scene so disturbed Alex, the shocks of glistening red, the cries of pain—she felt like she was back at the market, besieged by shades—and reached out towards the Books as they reconnected. Her spell struck them as they unleashed theirs. The caster vaporized to dust just as the mass of them tumbled like stuck bowling pins.

Limestone façades collapsed from the buildings like calving icebergs, splashing in the sea of the street as they pulverized to dust on the concrete below.

Sparks whizzed past, some striking her. She returned fire, separating a man from his Book. She saw another man, not engaging. He wasn't ignorant to the carnage, his expression conflicted. He offered Alex his Book as if surrendering his weapon, "What can I do?"

She pointed at him and cried, "It's them," her hand directed his eyes toward the army of golems as they massed together, intent on another spell. He looked from them to her and back before disappearing his Book and disappearing into the fleeing crowd.

Why kill innocent people? Alex was sick with dismay, the crowd dispersing so chaotically they went nowhere, the excitement of witnessing magic gone.

Alex's rising vitriol filled her body, the disgust and contempt boiling. They came to attack her, but also to maim and kill, perhaps collapse a building; all to create a plausible scenario where this wasn't magic but a faulty gas main or a terrorist bombing, just as Matthew warned. Her body vibrated with disgust, and as she raised her hands towards a separated half-dozen of these living Books, they made their connection again. What swirled from her fingertips twisted the asphalt, buckled the road in a direct line between her and them. Like a giant lizard, suddenly awakening in the street, panels of blacktop reared up like irritated scales, the ground swallowing them like a smoking maw.

Another man, in a natty suit, approached her, Book offered. "This is wrong," he said. "How can I help?"

A swirl of words jammed behind her lips and she understood he wasn't asking if, but announcing that he would. "Stop them," she shouted, pointing at the golems.

The natty-suited man was immediately joined by a bike messenger, both reading their Books, firing at the golems as they attempted to re-connect. The bike messenger told Alex, "No one does this to my city."

Matthew exchanged sparks with a duo. Strikes hit him; he cried out. His returned strikes did much the same to them.

Alex left the men to retreat to Rose. The police kneeled beside her, frozen in witness of the carnage these newcomers created. One drew his bright yellow taser, the other his handgun. The third was the target of multiple electrical bolts as he used his body to protect Rose.

Alex collected the scattered pages and shoved them in Rose's hands. Rose stuffed them unceremoniously into her Book. Alex drew her attention to a cluster of living Books and one man, who were showering a ground-floor restaurant with sparks, white tablecloths smoldering and igniting to flame as glass and wallboard shattered.

Rose complained, "Matthew—"

Alex grabbed her face and twisted her towards the Books. "Them first."

The cops were backing away, pulling Rose to safety. When she escaped them, they didn't stop to reclaim her, sparks showering them.

Rose's eyes were fiery with anger. She seemed suddenly aware of people fleeing and dragging wounded. Blood ran down the gutter. Pained cries echoed between the buildings. She sprung to action.

Rose organized her Book, which had nearly fallen in two. Each time she tried to read she needed to save more falling pages and stuff them under the cover. She read aloud at last, the sparks blackening her fingertips, but shooting a stream of fiery red lightning at the golems, drawing their attention from the building. They turned to her and fired while she sucked her burned fingertips. Rose screamed the words from her failing Book.

Alex's wrath boiled over. Her heart ached for the wounded she saw everywhere. She turned and reached out to a man she saw holding a Book. Threw him to the ground with a lightning strike. Then to the next. Then to a collection of golem. Like she drew her emotion from a bottomless well. More screams. A rattle of gunshots as the police organized and opened fire on the tattooed twins swarming through the streets. Even as new men kept appearing and joining in the fight, more of them disappeared. Others took up arms against the golems for attacking their city. Alex fired strike after strike, her lightning cauterizing the air, like a conductor trying to control a rioting orchestra.

Matthew limped beside her. Taking a breath from reading his spells, he said to her, "We need to get you out of here."

Chapter One Hundred and Twenty-Seven

All around Alex, the din, the chaos, the confusion was a raucous roar punctuated by the tinkling of shattered glass, the tang of coppery blood, the sharp reports of gunfire, the bitter taste of rock dust and gunpowder, the rumble of collapsing building façades. Dust swirled through the street, carried on the breeze as it eddied and twisted in tortured knots. Alex felt pain in the begging cries of the victims around her. Her whispers roared as they demanded her action to dampen the rubble as a doorway caved in or push someone out of harm's way or beg her to heal a teenager who lay among the wounded, clearly not long for this world.

For the first time she understood Matthew. He had told her, "We're on the same side." Here they were, standing amidst the wreckage in a city street, fighting side-by-side.

She looked at the men who appeared their Books, until that moment, they were no different any other men on the street. They were ordinary, in suits and baggy jeans and paint-splattered clothes with construction vests. They were cops and firefighters. They were everyone and no one. There was no telling which man in the crowd might suddenly turn on them, and yet, she saw some of them affected enough by the horror to turn on their own. They shot at the living Books, they shot at Alex and Matthew and Rose, the confusion was so great—the running crowds, the collapsing walls, the wailing sirens—disguised further by the pall of dust that it was impossible to determine who was taking which side. Some of these men were sent by Jeremiah, like Marco and Johnny. Some fought of their own volition. There seemed no difference between the two camps except the carnage swayed some and nourished others. *Did he think they would kill me or is he sacrificing them? Forcing me to kill?* That seemed the crueler likelihood.

The golems she understood. They were like wooden soldiers, sacrificial warriors who marched in groups through the street, linking together to amplify their magic, and unleashing devastating attacks that vaporized the castor.

In the chaotic din, a moment of clarity pricked Alex's thoughts: Back in her home, she had grabbed Matthew—when he was inside her father's body—when he cast the spell at her mother. It turned her father to dust and threw Matthew across the hall, breaking his neck. She realized she had this power of amplification, too. The sacrifice it required was too high to ever consider it.

Her stomach heaved like a wave preceding vomit; Alex didn't try to hold it back. In her head, the voices screamed their battle-cry; Alex unleashed them, willed them all to join her. She hunted for the largest group of golems she could see.

The street around her heaved in huge panels of concrete and steel, uprooting sparking underground cables. Steam and water surged upwards as the few people still recording her with their phones finally accepted it was time to flee.

Giant slabs of building collapsed to the sidewalk, disappearing people in a crush of stone and dust, the rumble of collapse and the roiling sound of spinning, airborne grit silencing the screams. Pyroclastic explosions of dull, gritty, roiling clouds consumed the street, blinding everyone in a stone fog.

Her eyes burned with grit. A strong breeze pushed the debris as it rained out of the sky like stony hail. A militant line of living Books appeared through the stony fog. Lightning erupted from her fingers, huge strikes that branched hundreds of times in the instant between her and one Book and then another. Some fell when the roadway opened beneath them. Others trembled from her electricity. None fled.

She did her best to break their connections, to turn the single group into two by incapacitating a central member, but the eight remaining were relentless. Unless killed, they would rise, wobbling on broken limbs, grimacing in clear agony, but continue, undiscouraged.

A rapid series of gunshots; several cops targeted these Books, firing until their pistols were empty. Bullets tore the Books apart, dismembering them but detaining only the most grievously wounded. Alex prepared to draw their attack to her, to protect those around her. But, before she could, the casting Book exploded to dust just as Matthew pushed her away. The line of officers exploded in a violent rush of tissue and uniforms.

"You'd never survive that," Matthew warned as debris rained down.

There appeared to be two coordinated attacks. Some living Books focused on her and Matthew and Rose and the police. The others continued their destructive impulse on the surrounding area, perhaps intent to demolish any memory of what had been seen here, to bury the recollection of magic under the rubble of half a dozen buildings. Alex realized if it ended here, if she were to die here, they would erase every memory of her.

As the façade of one building collapsed, sheared off like the building front stepped away and knelt, Alex bombarded it with a shockwave. It exploded in a fury of rubble that rained down on the fleeing crowd, stoning them. She saved them from being crushed, but couldn't disappear falling stone.

Strewn on the ground a few feet from her, the pages of a discarded Book lazily turned, the burned edges glowing red each time the breeze stoked them.

She collected the Book. Holding it brought back recollections of pain, but in her head the voices screamed about freedom. A dozen singeing sparks knocked her, trembling, to one knee.

Looking up from the Book, the approaching golems joined together. Alex closed her eyes and they screamed as the heaving road swallowed them.

She spun the Book around in her hands. There was no longer anything beautiful about the illuminated pages. There was no art or finesse in the designs. These were juvenile depictions of torture. Infantilized versions of women, their full bodies, their glories and their foibles and wonderful flaws scribed onto the page, mocked by a hand that couldn't comprehend the language it wrote. How did she ever think the pages were beautiful? Their *art* reduced women to a few shapes, a few scratches on a page. They didn't understand the truth.

Behind her, Rose was losing her fight, fumbling as her Book came apart, becoming less and less reliable. Her fingers were a scorched gnarl of burned flesh as her lightning shot fiery and red or sputtered or came not at all. Most of the police and emergency responders were either in retreat or taking cover behind debris or in some state between wounded and dead. A group of Books fired at Rose; there seemed too few remaining to sacrifice one for the sake of amplified power, so they fired lightning bolt after lightning bolt at her, knocking her first to her knees and then to the ground where she convulsed on her ruined Book.

With the road still overturning around her, pieces twisting and shattering as water gushed into the air, Alex began to burn.

Her flames leapt into the air, but she held back. She wouldn't freely turn to fire. She wouldn't allow herself to be lost to the flames.

"Don't do that," Matthew warned her. "Just the right spell can—" he spun through the air, his Book fluttering above him as he crashed and rolled amidst the shattered road and wounded and debris.

Matthew fought his way to the edge of the crowd. Between guttural utterances, he called to her, "You remember the door? The Library? I'll wait for you in the cloakroom."

Alex walked through the street, an immolating woman. She burned, or appeared to, the Book in her hands turning to ash. After what Jeremiah had done to her, returning fire to flesh, she would not allow herself to be so exposed, so changed. She walked through the street, lightning strikes sizzling through her: finding no flesh, they passed through the embodiment of her rage.

She walked right up to the Books, seeing the details in their tattoos before she blackened them. She charred their bodies black until they came apart in flakes of charcoal. She hunted through the scene, looking for rogue golems, for men who hadn't abandoned their Books. Some fled at the sight of her. Some saw what she was and revealed where more living Books hid. Some stood their ground and fired their puny sparks at the woman on fire. Likely still on camera, burning men alive was not something she relished doing. One tried to quench her with spells of water, unwilling to release his Books as the pages blistered and blackened his hands. Another found horrible spells that would have flayed her to her bone had she skin. She could not believe these men would stand, would wait, would allow her to walk right up to them, taking their bodies into her own. Were they sacrificing themselves? Did they so believe in their cause they could justify the death around them, witness her trying to prevent it, and still want her dead? She felt each man writhing within her, felt him breathe her in as she scorched his lungs. She reduced them all to ash, claiming their coins in her fire and let those become a part of her, too. Books, coins, flesh.

And then, the din disappeared. Sirens still screamed, people still cried, but the crackle of lightning, the tremulous roar of collapsing structures quieted. Alex's flames dissipated and as she spun, looking at what remained of the crowd around her, the only Books were now held closed, their handlers acknowledging her with awe or reverence.

"Alex! Alex!"

The last of Alex's flames still snapped in her hair as she faced a panicked, limping Rose.

Rose's scalp bled from a deep gash over her bloodshot left eye. "He's getting away, Matthew's getting away," she pointed at the last twists of mist dissipating in the air. Alex grabbed her and held her back.

Marta crawled from behind a smoldering firetruck, its tires flat and burning, "I'm okay!"

Looking beyond Rose, Alex saw a bigger picture. She may as well have been standing in the market. She saw the people; innocent, wounded. Jeremiah did this, too. She wondered how many catastrophes throughout history were perpetrated by the same man.

Alex closed her eyes. It seemed silly to think what worked on the Between would have success here, and yet, she attempted it. She thought of the rubble, the broken glass, the twisted steel.

Rose grabbed her shoulder. "Alex, what are you doing? We can still find him." Then she gasped.

Rubble flowed as it turned to sand. Large, shattered frames and piles of bricks simply raced away to dust. Alex placed her hands on her heart, feeling her charm, slightly cold to the touch. Her coin glowed. Reaching out with her mind, she did her best to heal the wounded.

Rose tugged on her shoulder; her raw fingertips still black but mending. "They'll be fine," she hurried. "Matthew!"

Alex turned to Rose. "What is wrong with you? Look around. These people—"

"Don't matter," Rose interrupted. She urged, "You need to find Matthew again."

"I know where he is," she snapped at Rose. "He's waiting for us."

"So, what the hell are we waiting for?"

Alex looked past Rose. "We can't leave these people like this."

Marta firmly grasped Rose by her shoulders. "Rose. Please reconsider. If Alex can help these people, if the world sees what she can do and understands she will defend them, then maybe…."

Rose pushed Marta away. "Fine, Alex. Heal them all. Heal everyone. Let Billy die but heal all the strangers you want."

Alex closed her eyes, "That's not fair." As Rose's tirade continued, Alex refused to listen. She concentrated. She reached out.

After a minute, another hand rested on her shoulder. "I-I'm sorry, I don't know your name, but are you okay?"

It was Officer Gonzalez from the apartment. He'd seen better days. His torn and filthy uniform matched the fresh scars on his face and hands. Alex nodded.

"This was all real?" He looked around. The breeze moved the sand across the street like dunes in a desert. Buildings around them stood open and naked, their innards exposed, but with the ruined fronts no longer polluting the street, there was almost a dreamy quality to what they witnessed.

She nodded again. Around her, people regrouped, searching for those from whom they were separated. They addressed their wounds and found them less severe than they previously observed.

"What were they?"

Alex didn't know how to reply. How could she explain a golem?

"Why do they want to hurt you?"

She wiggled her fingers. "They don't control all the magic anymore. They'll do anything to keep the world from learning it exists."

"Why?"

"Why do you think?"

The truth disgusted him, "The same old reason, I guess: Power."

Alex acknowledged Marta and Rose. "I have to go. There's someone I need to meet."

"You can't stay and help?"

Alex wanted to, more than anything. To heal everyone. But as long as she remained, no one here was safe. It was more of Jeremiah's cruelty that she had to abandon the people around her in their moment of need. She told Officer Gonzales as much. "If I stay, more of his followers will come."

"Who is he?"

"His people call him Jeremiah, but you've called him by another name."

Officer Gonzalez started clearing her a path. "Go," he urged.

As Alex began trudging to the door, she noticed a white digit poking through the blowing sand near an upturned panel of sidewalk. Grasping Charon's claw, she motioned for Rose and Marta to follow.

Chapter One Hundred and Twenty-Eight

Alex anticipated someone trying to stop her or follow her, but the confusion, the sudden realization that the debris had vanished and their injuries were healed, gave them a moment to hastily walk away. Although Officer Gonzalez provided an escape route, Alex half-expected a police officer or camera-phone wielding bystander to accost her, but as she, Rose, and Marta snaked towards the open intersection, the crowd mobilized instead to check on the dead and wounded.

Clearing the crush of the crowds and exiting onto the avenue, Alex paused at the intersection to check her bearings.

"Where are we going?" Rose demanded.

Alex stared at Rose. Blood smeared her forehead and matted her hair above her bloodshot right eye. Her shirt was a collection of burns and tears. Alex was no better. People stared as they marched past, oblivious to what happened just yards away. Of the three of them, Marta, the adult of the bunch, looked comparably fine. A fine dust grayed her hair and dulled her darker skin.

How many people just died because of me? The stakes were higher than ever, and each casualty was a rusty chain locked about her heart, weighing on her spirit. And yet, there was Rose, her only concern, killing someone who had gravely wronged her. As though nothing mattered beyond spilling Matthew's blood.

At Rose's impatient expression, Alex answered, "We're going to the door. Matthew is waiting for us there."

Rose huffed. "And you don't think it's a trap?"

Marta squinted at Alex, who said, "I don't. I know he's there."

Before Alex could add anything more, Rose blurted, "You're an idiot. You go wherever he tells you to go. What is wrong with you?"

"I don't expect you to understand, Rose. He fought with us. He protected me."

"He needs to beat a Book out of you."

Marta interjected, "She has a point, Alex. How can you trust him?"

Alex put her hands on her hips. "Matthew went to the door. I feel him there. What do you suggest? Are we ready to go home?"

Rose fought to hide her grin in a scowl. "Don't turn this onto me. He needs to die."

"He knows something," Alex confessed. "I need to know it."

Rose huffed and dramatically turned her back as she walked away. She knocked into a man in a suit who eyeballed her with disgust but didn't slow his step as he wiped down his sleeve.

Marta asked, "You're sure he knows something?"

Alex nodded. "His face went white when he saw Charon's claw."

Marta replied, "Understandable. Where'd you put it?"

Alex turned to show the radius and ulna peeking creepily out from her jeans pocket. "It creeps me out, carrying this around."

"It doesn't look half as bad as you. Look at the two of you. You're bloody messes, burned wretches."

"So?" Rose was back.

"So," Marta replied in kind, pointing a few feet down the street to a rack of white "I♥NY" T-shirts. A handwritten sign above them said "2-4-$10". "Price is right," she added.

While Rose bemoaned having to wear something so kitschy, Alex loved the idea, if only for the practicality of it.

Alex overheard people discussing a steampipe explosion a few blocks away. *The lies are already starting.*

Marta bought two shirts and stood in front of a dark doorway to provide a modicum of cover as the girls changed. Rose pulled on the front of her shirt and groaned, "I do *not* love this place."

Alex pointed down the avenue and westward. "Let's take a walk. It's just a few blocks over."

Rose appeared her Book. "Why don't we just go this way?"

"No Rose. We've drawn enough attention. Besides, I need a few minutes." She squinted up at the sky. "It's a beautiful day. I want to walk. Think about what comes next." She started forward.

Marta and Rose followed at her side.

Marta asked, "What do you think is next?"

Alex shrugged. "I need to know what he knows. That's all he's good for. Then Rose can do whatever she likes. Then, we'll basically be at the Library. Hopefully we're not too late to help Heather and the Book Club find Colette and Lydia."

Rose grinned. "After I kill Matthew, that's a plan I can get behind."

Alex reiterated that Rose must hold until she had Matthew's information.

"As long as I get to kill him," Rose replied, "I'll wait."

Alex scrutinized Rose as they walked. Her anger was troubling. It endangered them if she wouldn't control it. Still, she envied Rose's ability to have such focus on a task. *I'm always reacting. Rose acts and follows through, no matter what.* She appreciated Rose for her single-mindedness. She hoped her aunt and Book Club were safe. Not knowing allowed her mind to devise terrifying scenarios. It had become too easy to conjure ghastly outcomes for her loved ones.

"Marta," Alex said as they turned onto the street with the door, the humming tunnel traffic suddenly audible. "I can send you home."

Rose perked up, "She can go to Susan's." She turned to Marta, "She was Betty's friend. She lived in the apartment that was way high and had a lot of wine."

Ignoring Rose, Marta shook her head. "Alex wants to be with you. He and I, well, he…, what I mean is, our place is at your side."

Alex didn't know how to say it politely, so she just said it, "You hid behind a firetruck."

"Don't worry about us," Marta replied. "Alex and I can take care of ourselves." She nodded when Alex's eyes asked, *Are you sure?*

Alex owed Marta her trust.

"Here it is," Alex stood before the small fenced-in door beneath the staircase. Everything was unchanged from last time. Lurking beneath the stairs, waiting behind two garbage cans, the battered, deep red-brown, six-panel door with its large brass nob waited. Other than someone painting over the green, it hadn't changed since Johnny visited. It didn't look maintained then nor now, yet it was clear someone looked after it.

The gate creaked open at her touch. She looked back at Rose and Marta, "Ready? He's here. He could be peaceful or waiting to pounce."

Rose glanced around, "Or he could be hiding across the street, ready to attack from the shadows."

Alex ignored Rose and grabbed the knob. She gave it a twist and waited.

In Johnny Cortese's memory, she'd just been here. Her father held this knob. How many others stood here before her? Were they more reverential than Johnny and Marco? She recalled the last time she'd stood here. How she struggled to open the door. Each step was a puzzle to solve. How poorly it all turned out. The memory portended bad omens, and butterflies filled Alex's stomach. *This time will be different.* She wasn't sure she could believe herself.

She held the knob for what felt like an eternity, even if it was only a minute or two. The door opened. The dim light in the cavernous room seemed darker today. She stepped in. Marta and Rose followed. Marta was in awe at the rows and rows of men's outerwear, displayed like a museum, demonstrating, like horizontal strata, gradual changes in men's style. She refrained from touching anything, but her hands reached several times as though the little boy inside her kept being admonished for trying to touch.

"Over here, Alexandrea."

Alex confirmed with Rose and Marta before following Matthew's dying echo. Rose hissed, "I know," before Alex repeated even a word of warning. She walked past several racks and turned down an aisle. About two-thirds of the way, Matthew waited, his hand resting on a tan leather jacket. Alex avoided looking at it but was certain this wasn't a ruse. *That's his*....

"Did you know your father came here?" Matthew stepped back to allow Alex to approach her father's jacket. "William—Billy—thought your father would respond best to meeting someone more his own age." Matthew laughed, perhaps seeing new meaning in everything Billy ever told him.

"I know," Alex reluctantly replied. Her concern over how Rose would react to hearing her admit anew that she ate his coin kept her silent. She glanced about for but didn't see Rose. More concerning, she didn't hear her, either. Or Marta. Her stomach felt empty; they might be in trouble. She'd separated from Rose to ensure she'd get what she wanted from Matthew; had Matthew anticipated that? Did Matthew know and set a trap to make their separation permanent?

As Alex touched her father's jacket, Matthew withdrew his hand. Alex freed the jacket from the hook where it had hung for nearly two decades. The light brown leather was thin, more for cool summer nights. She held it close to her face; beyond the dust and mustiness of time, what she smelled reminded her of home. Alex slipped her arms into the jacket and pulled it on.

Though it was stiff with age and only a little large, as Alex wrapped her arms about herself, she felt the long overdue embrace of her father. Not the man she knew as a child, but the one she came to know through Heather and Billy.

The scent of the past and memories of her father wearing this made the time-stiffened jacket feel like armor against her skin.

Chapter One Hundred and Twenty-Nine

"You didn't come here to reminisce," Matthew said. "I fully expect you and your cousin to attempt killing me shortly." He hesitated. "That would be a shame. I have a lot to tell you and show you. I've been planning for a long time. I thought it would be me. But, Alexandrea, if you're to destroy Jeremiah, I must prepare you."

Was this a ruse to distract her while some other henchmen incapacitated Rose and Marta? His earnestness unbalanced her. "We'd thought about putting you down," Alex replied. "But not until you explain your sudden change of heart."

Matthew's expression disarmed her. "I'm not the first person to oppose Jeremiah. I took over from another who took over from another. Our lineage goes back," he hmphed, "nearly as far as Jeremiah. The movement has futilely existed for millennia. I sometimes wonder if rather than working to undermine Jeremiah, we do his bidding. Giving his followers a movement to detest, purpose to rally behind, an enemy to focus on to distract them from his true intent."

"I've thought about that, too," Alex replied. Not necessarily with those words, but it was as though he uncoiled the knotted feelings in her brain. "Jeremiah sent someone to kill whichever one of us was still alive," she told him about Johnny. "When I ate his coin, Jeremiah spoke about *Laurent Robaleaux.*"

At the mention, a smile warmed on Matthew's face. "He was a good man. Tough as, well, as they come. He said he saw potential in me. At first, I thought we were witch hunters, scouring Europe to rid the Continent of them." He addressed Alex's disapproving scowl. "I was invited to the Library through customary channels. When a man hands you a Book and shows you that you can do magic, you will believe whatever mythology he spews. Laurent showed me a greater truth. This was a new idea borne of the Renaissance. That the way to take Jeremiah's power was to use a woman. There wasn't much irony in the Middle Ages, so I'm told, which made the novelty crazy enough for them to believe it'd work. How they tried. It always ended with a witch being burned alive. I believe no one has come as close as Jeanne d'Arc. You probably read about her in your history books. Each generation believed it more and offered it to the next with even more conviction."

"And your point is?"

Matthew fixed the collar on Peter's jacket. "I went further than any of them. My plan made you. Create a single from a twin, put a real witch's power into you, and when you were ready, when you'd taken your fill of his magic, take it from you. Until William, there was always failure. He made it possible. He showed me how, helped me and Peter put all the pieces into place. He proved to me I could, by showing me the times when I already had." He studied her, "But of course, you already know that."

Alex didn't nod. She was caught in the idea that Billy hadn't protected her but served her up. More even than Matthew or her father, Billy was responsible for putting her in danger, time and again. Yet, the more she tried to find his blame, the more his memories prevented her. Billy never intended to create Alex. For him, she already existed. To maintain that one fact, he sacrificed everything to ensure her father succeeded. He never chased his own desire; his every act was to ensure the safety of the girl he knew. *What would have happened if he failed? If he and Peter didn't become friends that day in the Library? What would have happened to me?* It at once seemed trivial and cosmic in scope. Time was confusing that way.

"It's always been the plan. Until now."

Alex was about to respond when his words struck her. He was dismantling his plan before her.

He rubbed his crooked neck. "William knew. When you showed me death's hand…." He seemed out of breath, almost overwhelmed. "That's when I knew, too. That's when everything changed."

"Don't be so dramatic."

"You took Death's hand."

"And still have it," she wished her tone had less braggadocio.

Gritting his teeth, Matthew said, "It's not the hand that matters. You defeated death. Don't you understand? Not even Jeremiah can claim that victory."

Alex was speechless. "He's been alive for eternity."

"If Jeremiah had done anything of the sort, he'd be the one bragging; not you."

Now she really regretted her tone.

"It's worthy of your boasting."

"I used it to take a man's coin. It has Death's power in it."

"When you almost took mine, I figured you'd used it before." A sound piqued his interest. "But I question where exactly the power comes from." He scanned the aisles. "You'll learn more with each use." He put a finger to his lips and cupped the other hand over an ear to listen.

"Why bring me here? Why play these games?"

Distracted again, Matthew craned his crooked neck around. "Your cousin lurks. She really wants to kill me."

"Can you blame her? She doesn't trust you. And neither do I."

"Come," he pointed back towards the door.

Alex didn't budge. "Tell me why."

Matthew leered about. Rose was close. Probably exploding with anger, waiting for him to divulge his secret so she could obliterate him.

"What I need to show you isn't in New York." He pointed at the door. "When you open it from this side—"

"I know what it does," she told him. She tried to find the trap behind his every word. "Can't we just," she wiggled her fingers.

"Cast a spell and he knows. The door isn't magical in that sense. Open it, and it's like any other door."

"Where?"

He pointed to the door with some urgency.

"Where?" Alex asked with irritation.

Matthew sensed her distrust. He pointed at the door. "Through there, third open," he gestured opening the door three times, "quaint little Parisian street."

Alex was reminded of the Book Club's fanciful dreams of using the door as a travel portal to see the world. Now she was going to Paris. And not just Paris, but a *quaint little Parisian street* in Paris. Alex longed for a moment when she didn't have to worry about Jeremiah or Matthew or the fact that Heather was in danger. The longer this took, the more likely her aunt was dead.

"This movement. It's not just me and George. There are others."

"In Paris."

Matthew nodded, urging her towards the door. "You don't understand, do you?" For a change his tone wasn't condescending but instructional. He was trying to get her to see a fundamental fact that would open her understanding. She might have grasped it if not for the monumental blockage of her distrust. He continued, "The moment you took that hand—defeated death—you changed everything. Now I need you to come with me so I can—"

Three red sparks flamed across the aisle, striking the wooden coatracks, blackening and setting them aflame. Rose closed in quickly, repeating the guttural words. Sometimes her sparks didn't leap from her burned fingertips. She'd push the Book back together as though misfires were normal. Following the abbreviated shower of sparks, Matthew tucked between two racks, nursing his wounds.

Matthew appeared his Book. Alex leapt into the fray; she wasn't yet done with Matthew but feared the harm he'd cause Rose in countering her attack, especially if her Book failed.

Rose growled, "Outta my way, Alex!" She charged forward, striking Alex first with a shockingly strong spark, singling her tan leather jacket, and then with her shoulder as they collided.

"Hold her off or I will kill her," Matthew warned, his words slippery and eager. "You matter. She does not."

The two seemed to dance about Alex, who desired harming neither. Matthew murdered Billy, but he had to. Knowing he had no choice wasn't the same as forgiving.

Bolts shot from Matthew's fingertips, narrowly missing—intentionally, Alex believed—Rose. The coatracks upended and tipped backwards, shattering and splintering and collapsing around her. Rose returned fire in kind, completely non-plussed by the devastation around her. Matthew was swift for a man of his age and handicap, his bent neck twisting, snake-like, as he flipped pages with one hand, casting counterspells.

Rose fumbled her Book, trying to reacquaint the pages so her spells would work again. Matthew took the opportunity to strike her in the center of the red NY heart, knocking her to the floor, her Book spilling. Rose groaned as she reached for the discarded pages and saw Matthew looming over her, preparing his next spell.

"Stop it," Alex screamed. The energy of her impatience fled her raised hands and swelled through the cavernous cloak room. Row after row of coatrack skidded away, shattering as they piled atop one another, crashing and crushing against the distant walls, leaving the four of them standing in the center of the suddenly open room. "Heather could be dying and we're wasting time." Alex breathed heavily, impatience exhausting her. The exposed floor was striped, aisles of footworn paths surrounded dust-covered rough-hewn stone. What had stood for hundreds of years was cast to splinters in an instant. "Enough!"

Rose turned, the fire and fury in her eyes momentarily blotted out by the rising tears that angrily flooded her vengeful eyes. Alex swung back to Matthew, who hadn't yet lowered his Book, but in three swift steps had put himself between Rose and the doorway.

"Why do you care about him?" Rose's voice, raspy with anger, was weighted with despair. "He killed—"

"I know what he did," Alex shouted back. "I was there. I nearly died trying to save him." Her mouth was suddenly dry. "There's so much more at stake, Rose." She pointed at Matthew, the thrust of her accusation met with a flinch, "He knows something I need to know. Something I need you to let him…," she hesitated, "or *make* him tell me."

Matthew took small backwards steps. "At least we're on the same page."

"Don't let him do this, Alex," Rose warned. "He's lying."

Alex knew this could be true. Why had Billy trusted him, worked with him, sacrificed himself, if only to prove she could trust him? "Rose, I know you're hurting. We all are, and he was your twin. I can't imagine how that hurts." She glanced at Marta as she spoke, wondering how her words resonated with her own twin. "I'm asking—begging—lower your Book and come with me."

Emotions played out across Rose's face. The conflict between what Alex asked and what she wanted rose and fell in her eyes like a rapid tide.

Matthew spoke to Alex, but projected to Rose, "I'm putting my Book away. If she tries anything, I will not hold back."

Alex tried to quell Rose's reaction before she had a chance to respond. "Don't play his game, Rose. What he needs is easier if I'm alone."

"The three of you," Marta interjected, her hands in the air like a traffic cop entering a freeway. "Listen to yourselves. You," she pointed at Matthew, "need something from her but your only leverage is not telling her." She pointed at Alex, "You are curious enough to follow him even though you know he's probably lying."

"I'm not lying." Matthew protested.

Rose shouted at him, "Shut up! She didn't ask for your—"

"And you," Marta said to Rose, "you want to destroy him, no matter the cost. Even if it kills you. Even if it prevents Alex from learning something profound."

"I haven't killed him yet. I'm not some unhinged maniac."

"That's debatable," Matthew hissed under his breath.

"What?" Rose stretched onto her tiptoes, pushing against Alex as though this were the start of a schoolyard brawl.

"Settle down, Rose," Alex demanded. For a change, she was confident her tone matched how she felt, her words echoing thunderously, as though enhanced magically.

Rose pulled back, whining like a smacked toddler, "Why are you taking his side?"

Alex warned Rose, "Don't."

Marta intervened, "You're the one with the power here, Matthew. You're the one with knowledge that no one else has. Share that and let Alex decide if it's worth following you."

"And give up the only reason the girl has let me live?" Matthew's tone dripped with mockery.

"Yes," Alex and Marta said together. Marta added, "Alex can decide if the information is worth your life."

Matthew pondered the offer momentarily. "Third open," he again gestured as though opening a door thrice, "and we step out onto a cozy Parisian street." He held up three fingers, starting with his pinky, "Three blocks we walk through a quaint neighborhood." Raising the fingers again, he added, "Climb three flights of stairs to a small attic apartment where several of my colleagues are in hiding." To Alex he added, "They are awaiting my return. Waiting for my word."

Marta stifled Alex and Rose with a parental glance. "And what is so important about them?"

"They have the last key to my puzzle, the last coin to swallow. Meant for me, but I'm giving him to Alex."

"Who is it?" The words came out before Alex's disgust could choke her throat closed. *Another coin?* The prospect both thrilled and chilled her. A sacrifice. It disgusted her that Matthew had someone locked away. Someone who he would murder—or worse, make into a zombie—as a part of his cause.

Matthew looked at her sympathetically.

Alex shivered with chills. She didn't know why.

"The boy's name is William."

Alex questioned him, "You say that like I know who he is."

"You should," Matthew said, grim-faced. "He's your cousin."

Chapter One Hundred and Thirty

he air left Alex's lungs. She couldn't breathe. Did the black hole in Billy's memory suddenly have an explanation? Was the one memory—seeing Alex's face—about to happen? *How?*

"What game are you playing?" Rose complained, "Do you think we're that stupid?"

It almost made sense to Alex, the parts and pieces coming together in her head, the random bits of temporal memories settling into their least confusing states thus far. It was as though someone had completed two adjacent lengths of a jigsaw puzzle. She didn't know what was in the middle yet, but she generally knew how large it was. She asked Matthew, "He's sixteen?"

Matthew nodded.

"Rose chided, "You believe this bullshit? Are you an idiot?" She wiped her wet eyes.

Alex didn't know how else to explain it to Rose. "He slips through time, Rose." She moved her hands about, grabbing spaces in front of her as she explained, "He's twenty here and sixteen there and twenty-five there. He remembers all the times all at once. He has no idea what came first."

"Why are you talking like you know?"

Alex knew Rose knew why. "He was older, in my house when Matthew murdered my parents. That was years before he jumped off Picnic Rock." When Rose didn't seem to grasp her meaning, Alex rephrased, "Just because he's older now doesn't mean he can't also be young now." She looked at Matthew for confirmation, "He thinks he leapt off Picnic Rock yesterday. The night you burned me." Matthew nodded.

Marta stepped closer. "He's alive?"

Matthew nodded.

"We can save him? I can have my brother back?" Rose sounded desperate.

Matthew remained silent, working diligently to keep his mouth a neutral slice across his face. *He called Billy a sacrifice. Billy feels that moment is the end. He was grateful for it.* "I don't think so," Alex replied.

Before Rose could respond, Matthew somberly explained. "The boy is gone. He's been travelling through time for over a decade. But this was the first place he went. I learned of his arrival this morning. Time is confusing. But it makes sense, finally. You, inside Sara, a hundred years ago. Returning to the moment we met at your parents' house, saving yourself. You moved through time. Now we slay the ouroboros and close the loop forever."

Alex was only half-paying attention to Matthew. She had questions she didn't want to ask, because in her memory—in Billy's memory—she knew the answers. Billy was alive. He'd just leapt off Picnic Rock a few hours ago. Now he was in some room, blindfolded: the last memory he hadn't lived through. For his journey—his life—to be complete, she would remove his blindfold. How his coin played into things, she had no idea. Could she take his coin, again; for the first time?

She couldn't think of those things. Billy was alive. Her heart sang with hope that the man she saw die could be the boy she saves. She trembled with anticipation.

"I thought it would be me," Matthew told her. "But it's been you this whole time." He grinned. "We are on the same side, Alexandrea."

"Are we? I'm about to try to save my cousin. Will you stop me?" Matthew's face remained as stone. Alex faced Rose, "I didn't know he was still alive."

Rose huffed at her. To Matthew, she ordered, "Open the damn door. Take me to my brother."

Matthew paused and watched the three women. "I can't stop you, Alex. But before you make up your mind, speak with him."

Alex didn't answer. Saying *No, I won't,* sounded childish. He was partly right; she would speak to Billy and figure out how to save him from this fate.

Rose looked on the verge of madness. Her eyes were red with grief, but she was grinning. She shook with nervous energy, her wide eyes daring anyone to cross her now. "To think my brother's been here all along!" She spoke like she'd already forgotten what she saw in Matthew's apartment. "What are we waiting for? Let's save him."

Alex didn't know how else to express her trepidation, "I ate his coin. He's here. It's the same coin."

"What?" Rose pointed at the door. "Are you insane? You're talking gibberish. Let's go get him and make sure he's okay."

He's not okay. I ate his coin.

Marta looked at them both. "Rose is right."

Alex snapped, "You accuse me of falling for Matthew's traps and the moment he offers what you want, you accuse me of stalling?"

Matthew interjected, "This isn't a trap, Alexandrea."

Rose gestured to Matthew in agreement.

Alex shook her head. "Sure, Rose. He gives his word and that's enough for you?"

Rose pleaded with her hands, "It's Billy, Alex. My twin. You owe it to him. And me."

Alex couldn't stop thinking about Matthew's use of the word sacrifice: *One last coin to swallow.* She wouldn't. *Rose will never forgive me.* She said to Matthew, "I have to do this?"

Matthew nodded. "You took Charon's hand. That moment I knew it couldn't be anyone else."

Alex nodded. She glanced back at Rose. *She's not going to like what comes next.* "Are you sure, Rose? If we don't go, nothing happens, and he'll be fine for a few years."

Matthew interjected again. "Everything unravels if we don't."

Rose crossed her arms. "You both talk like you know what happens next."

Marta touched Rose's shoulder. "Let's make sure he's okay."

I owe this to both Rose and Billy. If nothing else, they deserve to say goodbye to each other. Alex started for the door. "Let's go."

Matthew grasped the knob and opened and closed the door. On the third open, he held it. The doorway vignetted a narrow street. Evening shadows cut across the road at a sharp angle, drawing out textures from the large limestone brick building across the way.

"Ladies first," Matthew grinned.

Alex paused at the threshold. "All the doors around the world are the same door?"

"You could say that," Matthew replied. "The Library is a real place, secreted away into the afterlife. The only way to reach it besides these doorways is magic."

Alex stepped through. The air felt different, but that might have been her. She thought stepping out from a door a third of the way around the world would feel strange, as though she'd be half turned upside down, but it felt no different.

"Rose," Marta cooed, "you will see him again."

Rose pulled away from Marta and forged forward. She glared at Alex as she crossed the threshold into the street. Standing beside Alex, she muttered, "We're in Paris, huh?"

One end of the street narrowed forbiddingly. The other widened to an even wider boulevard. An eclectic mix of restaurant storefronts, intentionally graffitied displays, hotels, and private doorways perfectly camouflaged the door they had just exited. Matthew didn't need to point the way, everything about this street pushed her to the bustling throughway. Butterflies infested her stomach; she anticipated Matthew's inevitable double-cross, Jeremiah's followers finding them, some disaster she hadn't anticipated keeping them from reaching Billy....

Chapter One Hundred and Thirty-One

Alex had just left New York City. She had just battled there and in an instant was in another city, another country, another continent, thousands of miles away. It wasn't far enough to be free of the looming danger. Despite the threat that Jeremiah could find them and send another army of golems, Alex remained hopeful: Billy was alive. As much as she craved seeing him—seeing her sixteen-year-old cousin, not yet burdened by his life—she feared seeing him. Feared what she had to do. She felt like she was being brought to the gallows to serve as executioner. Like Matthew would absolve himself of Billy's murder by staining her hands. *How is he alive?* She wanted to believe he was. She wanted to believe he wasn't. Neither was any less painful.

The only memory that haunted Billy more than Matthew's knife was waiting in darkness. It was a memory and their shared future. Alex was about to enter that memory, to experience it from both perspectives, and that made her queasy. It was like living that thought experiment, Schrödinger's Cat. He was both alive and dead, both old and young, and how she would remember him would depend upon what she saw once she opened that last door.

But this wasn't a thought experiment. He *was* alive and dead, *was* old and young. His memories, a flurry of moments across time was—by itself—confusing. Add to that his arrival, on the same day, at two different times in his life; the twists and turns necessary to accomplish that made her head ache.

Marta exited the doorway, Matthew close behind. Alex half-expected Matthew to slam the door shut before him, to make his escape, but he didn't. He stood beside the three of them like a tour guide, waiting for his group to pay enough attention that they would see his extended arm and know the way. She kept watch over Rose for signs that her control was weakening but it seemed the expectation of seeing Billy had—at least temporarily—quenched it. Rose wasn't the same person she knew three-odd weeks ago, none of them were. But Rose's anger took Alex by surprise. The culmination of unspoken frustration and anger was a stew Rose freely and eagerly engorged herself on.

She also worried that Matthew was merely stringing them along. She saw no reason why he wasn't; the old man possessed no hidden nobility. He was self-serving. He did nothing that didn't directly benefit his cause. And yet that was exactly why Alex followed. The expression on his face upon seeing Charon's claw spoke volumes. The widening of his eyes, the gaping of his mouth—too involuntary to be faked—was the singular reason she held Rose back now. If his cause was truly defeating Jeremiah, and that claw was the proof he needed to finally know she was the one to do it, then perhaps his cause—and not glory—was all that mattered to him. Was it possible for a true believer to realize their mistake? *Maybe he thinks that Charon's claw is the way to defeat Jeremiah.*

She thought to Heather—brought back by a cat. She recalled Heather, just a few weeks ago, sitting, reading the newspaper, with Dolly laying down on a section every chance she could. Did Dolly know what was coming? Or was the instinct so ingrained in the species that they couldn't help but sit on everything, unable to tell a newspaper apart from a spellbook?

She believed she knew everything Heather knew. Was there a way to obscure a memory? To bury it deep enough that it's forever hidden? Did Heather know something she didn't? Her father made her an only child to give her the ability to have magic, but the idea came from Billy. In attempting to do the same for her children, Heather broke Billy's hold on time, allowing him to help Peter in the first place. Billy's fingerprints were on everything. Everything he did was supported by circular logic without beginning or end. No matter how innocent he believed he was, Alex feared his motive might have been driven—or perhaps influenced—by some greater malice. The paths Billy forged—meeting Peter, pushing Peter to Matthew, to Holly, creating Alex—all influenced Heather's motivation to give Rose the same opportunity Alex had. It seemed crazy, but no matter how twisted the path, it always led back. It was absurd. Billy's involvement was the motivation for his own creation.

Alex followed Matthew to the end of the street, past restaurants and businesses, and out into the crowded road.

"Rue Christine," Alex whispered, reading the blue plaque on the side of the last building on the road. It seemed delightful that the road was named for a woman. She wondered who Christine was and secretly reveled that the door to the Library was hidden there. Each time a man needed to find his way to that accursed place, the instructions secretly proved where the magic they were seeking actually came from.

They travelled south a few blocks, past hotels and restaurants and cafes; it wasn't just the strangeness of the language spoken around her that made this place seem so delightfully foreign, but the way everything that was similar—pharmacies, cafés, bakeries—were also different enough as to be only faintly related to the counterparts with which she was only tangentially familiar.

"Turn here," Matthew directed. They came to a red awning and a crowd of outward facing diners sipping from ridiculously small coffee cups and glasses of wine, as though to them, the street was some sort of show for which they'd paid admission. No one sat facing one another; couples cozied up, side-by-side. Everyone facing the street, delighting in the movement of the world going past, as though tucked together for a group photograph.

"Rue Saint Andre des Arts," Alex read off the blue plaque on the building side as they turned. She wondered what art Andre was known for.

Marta looked around like her head was loose from her neck. "Where are we going?"

Matthew twisted his head towards Marta. He pointed down the road. "Not too much farther. There's a fountain on the front of our building. *Saint Michael Slays the Dragon*." As he said it, they turned their second corner, the fountain coming into view on their right-hand side. Pink columns and a striped stone façade stood around the weathered green sculpture of a man, one hand pointed to the sky, the other wielding a sword that threatened a winged man underfoot.

"He doesn't look like a dragon," Rose muttered, trying poorly to hide her awe at the scale of the scene before them.

"Neither does Jeremiah," Matthew explained. "That's been our symbol for centuries. Jeremiah looks like a man, but that's just another deception."

Alex noted the four green woman across the roofline. Then the two women on the top center crest. Almost hidden in the designs of the limestone were dragons and cherubs. Alex wondered if they represented Charon. Two green lions with serpent bodies flanked the pool.

"This is beautiful," Alex said to herself. "It reminds me of a fountain I saw in a market on The Between."

"Now you're getting it," Matthew grinned.

Rounding the side of the fountain, Matthew came to the first door that didn't let into a business, a very ornate entry that looked like it led to expensive apartments. Pulling a small, dark-patinaed skeleton key from his pocket, he unlocked the door and brought them in.

The narrow stairwell had a mustiness to it, a historic scent suggesting that while the apartments had all been modernized, the entryway remained unchanged. Alex counted as they walked up four creaking flights of stairs, one more than Matthew said. He knocked on a nondescript wood door; aged, oiled glossy and black from use in the places most touched: around the knob and beside the jam.

The creaking floor announced their approach. "Oui?" An accented male voice. Expectant, yet on edge.

"Change of plans, Jacque. I've brought the women with me. Three. She's done it. The boy waits for her, not me."

"Just a second, Paillasson."

"It's a nickname," Matthew told Alex, his cheeks reddened. "Thinks he's being funny."

Two locks and a latch turned and clicked and slid into place before the door silently opened. Jacque wasn't as tall as Alex. The color of his shirt pleasantly offset his darker skin. Alex thought he looked French. There wasn't any other way for her to describe the subtle sophisticated difference in the way he dressed, the cut of his shirt or the match of his colors that set him apart from any other man she'd seen before. "Ahh," his words dripped with his accent. "The girl from Manhattan. I worried when I saw the disruption on ze news." With a nod, he addressed Alex, "It pleases me you are on our team."

Matthew grunted as he ushered everyone into the foyer. The vaulted ceiling of the attic apartment following the mansard roofline they saw from the street. "Jeremiah was quick. Sent Alex to finish me just like William warned." He looked around the room. "Dany isn't out, is he?"

"No, no, no," Jacque countered. "He is keeping ze boy company." He turned to Alex and Rose and Marta, "Please excuse my English. Is not very good."

Marta giggled. They were probably close in age. "You speak better than most people I know."

Alex thought she was blushing.

"Where's Billy?" Rose looked about the room, her words curt and demanding.

Jacque waited for Matthew's approval. Matthew nodded. Jacque closed the door and threw the three locks, tugging to make sure it was secure.

"'E is right through 'ere," Jacque gestured to a delicate six-pained glass door. The white paint was thick and old and cracked, but not peeling. The glass panes were intricately etched such that whatever was beyond the door looked like an impressionist's study of a room.

Alex stared at the door. In Billy's memory, she heard it open. She recalled the way it stuck, the glass panes rattling.

"Before you go, be warned," Matthew paused at the glass door. "I never lied to you about William. This is a delicate moment, and he—William the older—warned us to keep him blindfolded until, *The time was right.*"

Alex stepped between Rose and the door. "I'm going in first," she said in a tone that dared Rose to contradict. Her eyes ordered Matthew not to delay her any further.

Without hesitation, Matthew opened the door. It stuck slightly. Alex had chills when it opened, rattling and shaking as she'd heard it do hundreds of times.

She looked down at Rose, her glare piercing. *I know she wants to see her brother, but he sees me first.* At first Rose glared back, halving the distance between them, but when Alex didn't budge, Rose relented, her eyes welling.

Matthew stepped aside. Alex waited in the doorway for a long moment.

In the far corner of the room, an older man—dark thinning hair, thick eyebrows above dark, square-framed glasses, a push-broom moustache curled over his upper lip, sat in a dark gray folding chair, one hand in his lap, the other hand holding a young man's hands.

Even with the black blindfold around his head, Alex couldn't be more certain this was her cousin. Her hands trembled. She wanted to race across the room but feared them both exploding into oblivion like in bad time travel movies.

When Rose stepped beside her, Alex placed her hand on Rose's shoulder, and for the first time in a while, Rose didn't shake it off. She felt small and fragile. It reminded Alex of the time she hugged Heather and her aunt felt bird-like in the embrace.

Rose gestured to Billy's blindfold.

Billy's memory centered in Alex's mind as though recalled for the first time.

She sees Billy sitting. He is sitting, the blindfold obscuring his vision, aware someone new is in the room. The air feels warm and close. Her heart is racing. The boy's head gestures his panic, attempting to look around the room, unable to see through the black blindfold. He stops. He stills. Alex is standing in Billy's memory, the sounds her feet make on the floor. He waits in breathless anticipation as Alex crosses the room.

Alex purposefully grasps the dark blindfold and begins rolling it back. Billy takes a breath that might be misconstrued as either anticipation or fear. Alex knows it is rest. His journey is complete. All his work is done. He is sitting there, knowing whoever he sees first will be his executioner, and as Alex uncovers his eyes, she sees herself in his memory just at the moment she sees him seeing her. It is like being the mirror and looking into it.

Alex drops the blindfold and their eyes lock. The memories are over. The time travel completed. From this moment forward, Billy's remaining life is in the present.

Chapter One Hundred and Thirty-Two

ilently, Alex embraced him. He leaned against her. She hasn't seen him in weeks, but he still smells of smoke from Picnic Rock. "Hey," she whispered, "you're finally back."

Rose crept up behind Alex and upon seeing him, rushed towards her brother, nearly pushing Alex aside.

Dany tensed, but Matthew's hand made a sweeping gesture that calmed him. He slipped his hand from Billy's, patting the boy's wrists when his fingers stretched to prolong the contact.

"Here," Dany offered his seat. He then left the room and joined Jacque.

"Rose?"

Rose nearly cried, falling against her brother who still hadn't embraced her.

"I need to speak privately with Alex."

Rose ignored him, "What did they do to you?"

His head tilted. He looked at Alex, "It's so strange to not be living within my memories. I feel lost. They're finally all in the past."

"But you're found." Then Rose started to say, "Why don't you tell them—"

"Rose, it'll never make sense to you. What I will do. What I have done. Today, there's no difference between them."

Alex nodded. "Time gets impossibly confusing."

Rose wasn't leaving. Billy told her, "I'm glad you came, Rose. I wanted to see you one more time." He studied her like he was preparing to sketch her likeness. "I wanted to say goodbye."

She froze. "You've been all over the place. You saw Mom and Alex. Why didn't you ever come to see me?" Tears crested her eyelids, like a storm surge threatening to breach a flood barrier. "You saw everyone but me. I've missed you so much and you never thought about me once."

Billy seemed hurt or annoyed. "You're my twin sister, Rose. I missed you most of all. If I stopped to see you, how could I go on?"

Tears breached her eyelids, cascading down her cheeks, leaving dark spots on her shirt. She couldn't look up at Billy when she mumbled, "You never even said goodbye."

Billy said to Rose, "I waited until it really was goodbye, Rose."

Billy struggled to his feet, his legs trembled, and Rose helped steady him.

Alex watched their reunion, her heart aching for them. She had a fair suspicion of what was supposed to come next, and she feared it. If she thought on it too deeply, she was sure she'd throw up.

Billy calmly said to Alex, "We don't have much time to get this done."

Alex and Rose started asking *What* at the same time. For a change Rose conceded and allowed Alex to finish, "What exactly are we doing?"

Billy looked to Matthew who nodded. He hadn't entered the room more than a step or two. Jacque and Dany remained out of sight in the other room.

Billy touched his throat. "I died this morning. I remember. You were something, Alex." He stared at her in awe. "What you did. What you were willing to sacrifice for me. What your love for me accomplished." He looked down, then back. "But I'm young. The last thing that happened to me is leaping off Picnic Rock with that guy," he said, referring to Matthew. "None of the things I remember doing have happened. Yet they're done."

"I almost didn't recognize you." Rose wiped her face. "You were a lot older. Like thirty." She hesitated, "But that couldn't be you. You're not old." Billy shook his head regretfully. Rose seemed to be bargaining, "You've got years to live. Mom will be so happy to see you."

Alex knew what he was going to say before he said it, "Mom's known for a long time."

Rose's face reddened. "You could *tell her* but not me?"

Alex couldn't tell if she was hurt or infuriated.

Billy continued, ignoring her. "We need to finish this today," he told Alex.

Now she was the one bargaining. "Isn't there another way?"

"I'm still a child. When I die today, I haven't done anything yet, and I won't. Except they've already happened. All those things are in my future. All those things are in your past. That creates a…," he looked to Matthew. "What'd you say that was?"

"A paradox," Jacque called out from the other room.

"Right, a paradox. If I die today, I can't grow older. I can't do all those things. But they're done. If I die now, there's no way to change them." He drew a circle in the air, "We create a time loop and cut it out from time."

Alex scratched her head. "Wouldn't that do something, you know, reset the timeline or something, like in the movies?"

Rose disagreed with Alex. "That's not how time travel works."

Billy grinned, "You have experience with time travel?"

Rose glared at him.

To Alex, Billy said, "You know. You've experienced my whole life. What's done is done. What it means is when I die today—"

"Stop saying that," Rose demanded. "That's not happening."

"*When*," Billy was emphatic, "those things can't happen—even though they did. My loop becomes permanent. No one can change it. Not even Jeremiah."

A mass of thoughts and memories not quite her own floated near the murky surface of her recollection. "Tell me something, Billy," Alex started to say. Fear of the answer knotted the back of her throat and flooded her eyes. She pushed the words out, "Is what happened…, what happened to Sara and me; is all that because of you?"

Billy stared at her as though he was waiting for her to accept the answer without his admission. He nodded. "Everywhere you've been, I've been." He looked away. "I'm sorry, Alex."

Alex was beginning to understand why this was so important to Billy. To all of them. "And if Jeremiah got his hands on you today…."

Billy finished Alex's sentence, "He could follow me everywhere and stop all those things from happening." He paused a beat. "But maybe he'd learn how it works and then he'd know how to move through time, too. He could go back to the very beginning. He'd change everything."

Alex whipped around to Matthew. "I know in some stupid logic it has to happen, but I will not be the one to take his life."

Matthew leaned against the doorframe. He looked exhausted; his neck uncomfortably crooked. "Use Charon's hand to take his coin." He looked away from Alex. "Once you've done that," he looked pained as he fought to get the words out. "Once his coin is gone and he's like Peter, I'll finish things for you."

Alex looked back at Billy. Rose glared at her. If Rose's eyes could, they would have sliced her apart. Billy returned her gaze: smiling.

"I can't," Alex said to Billy. "You knew all this time."

"We share the same memories now, Alex. Search your thought and you'll understand."

"I know. It's haunted you. It hurts trying to remember your memories."

Billy nodded. "It does."

Rose interjected, "What are you talking about?"

Billy explained, "You know Alex ate older me's coin, right?" Rose nodded. "That gave her all my memories: The things that make me… me."

Rose asked, "All your thoughts and memories?" Billy nodded. Rose took a second. Alex could almost see the gears turn in the way her expression shifted. She asked Alex, "All Mom's, too?"

Alex nodded.

Rose grabbed Billy's sleeve. "Come on. Let's get out of here." She tugged, but he wouldn't budge.

Behind Matthew, Jacque and Dany blocked the doorway from the other room.

Matthew centered himself in the doorframe. "He *won't* leave."

Billy agreed. "It has to be this way."

Marta, who kept herself off to the side this whole time, finally spoke, "There has to be an alternative."

Billy stamped his foot. "It has to be this way, and soon." He took a moment, his tone falling as he softly spoke to Alex, "I remember the next several years. As confusing as they've been, I have certainty at each turn. My effects all came before my causes. Right here, right now, I don't know what comes next, Alex. I know you shouldn't understand how scary that is for me, but you do. If we don't do this, everything I've done will be undone." He stared at her. "It was so hard, Alex. Being away from everyone I loved. Seeing how the things I did caused you so much pain." He reached out to touch her cheek. "Those experiences don't go away if I live. They'll always haunt me, even if they're made to never happen. Please don't do that to me. Don't leave me that way."

Rose appeared her Book. A page fell from its sprawling untidiness. "No one is harming a hair on my brother's head." She juggled dismembered pages and tried, unsuccessfully, to keep the Book from separating into two.

Billy placed his hand flat on the open pages and pressed the Book down, away from Rose's face. "You have to help Alex. She needs you, Rose."

"No," Rose cried. Tears and snot ran down her face. "They made you say that. They convinced you. Matthew and those other two. It's that stock-stockaid—"

Jacque called from the other room, "Stockholm Syndrome."

Rose pointed at his answer. "You don't know what you're saying, Billy. They convinced you that you're special and you travel around in time, and they messed up your head. It's all lies. It has to be. Tell him, Marta. Tell him it's all bullshit."

Marta was silent.

"Tell him, Marta!"

"Rose," Marta was in nurse mode, telling her patient the bad news. "I met your brother at the hospital. Before you were born. It was him, the man who died in the apartment. That was Billy."

"That wasn't Billy," Rose cried. "How could it be? He's right here. That was someone else."

Marta wrung her hands. "You know that's not true," she told Rose. "He says it has to be this way. We can't let everything he's done, all his sacrifices, be unmade by Jeremiah."

"Thank you, Marta," Billy whispered. "Please, Rose." He reached for Rose, who refused to come close enough, leaving his extended hand grasping air.

Marta approached Rose and wrapped her arms around her. "Sweetheart, I know. No one wants this." Rose sobbed uncontrollably.

Billy approached Alex; his legs still shaky. His silence spoke more than any words he might have uttered.

Alex couldn't hold her tears back. She felt her insides being ripped out and stomped on. "Don't make me. It almost killed me last time."

Billy consoled her, "For the first time, the future is unknown."

"Isn't that scary?"

Billy shrugged. "Everything unknown seems scary. At first."

Rose and Marta retreated across the room.

"Paillasson, they're coming." It was Dany. He pointed at the window; his words weighed with concern.

"Alex," Matthew's tone was soft and focused. "Jeremiah's people are nearing the square."

"I can't."

Billy hissed, "You know what they'll do to me. You know what they'll do to Rose." His voice dropped to a whisper. "I am so tired, Alex. Let me rest."

"This can't be the only way to stop Jeremiah."

"This won't stop him, Alex," Billy replied, tears welling in his eyes. "The Library was torn out of this world and hidden in the next. Every time you see that mist, that's the agitation caused by an open rip between the two. He's powerful enough to put something real over there."

"What does that have to do with you?"

Billy grabbed Alex by the shoulders. He leaned forward, close enough that Alex felt his breath on her earlobe. "They will come up here and slaughter everyone but me. Jeremiah wants me. Don't allow your breaking heart to make him more powerful."

"Who said my heart is breaking?" Alex tried to joke, but she choked on her tears. She coughed and swallowed to speak again. "How did you escape?"

"What do you mean?"

"I remember. You were here before, when you leapt off Picnic Rock. Then you met Matthew and you were there when I was with Sara. That means you escaped from this room. You went back and you got older and did all the things we remember."

Alex felt Billy's smile against her cheek. "I didn't escape," he told her. "I've been waiting for you this whole time."

He pushed Alex back just enough that they were face to face, his hands reminding her of the moment Matthew murdered him. "Do it now," he begged.

Alex froze. Her whole body trembled. She'd just unwillingly took his coin hours ago. That was horrific, her body broken after battling the Reaper.

"Paillasson," Jacque called out from the window. "They've got our scent for sure. They're scouring the square."

Chapter One Hundred and Thirty-Three

Alex wanted more time to think this through. What she was being asked to do—to kill someone she loved hours after witnessing their death—was cruel and horrible, and more difficult than anything she'd been made to do before. She could smell Billy's desperation. The longer she waited, the more certain it became that the end he'd meet was not the one he accepted when he took on this mantle. Could they hold off Jeremiah's men? What about Rose and her Book? It was falling apart. At what point would it fail her? She didn't care about Matthew or Jacque or Dany. With each moment, Billy's fate became clearer. If she chose to fight, she couldn't protect Rose *and* Marta *and* Billy, and Jeremiah's people would see that. Their wanton cruelty spoke to that knowledge. Fighting for him meant losing them all.

"Alex," Billy pled, "please."

Alex froze, as though not doing anything was a valid choice.

Billy placed a hand on her shoulder. "It's okay," he told her. "I know it must be impossibly hard for you, but you're not killing me. You're giving me life as a part of you."

Tears streaming down her face, Alex pulled the claw from her back pocket.

Alex's heart felt wrenched from her chest. She stared at Billy. Her whole quest was intended to save him and twice on the same day it was left to her to watch him die. Matthew killed him the first time, and then she took his coin. This wasn't just not fair, it was horrifically cruel.

"Thank you," he whispered.

Marta held Rose against her chest, the other bawling unconsolably.

"It's okay," Billy told his sister. "I love you, Rose."

Rose would not look up at him, like it was too painful to see him.

The claw clacked to life, the bony fingers reaching avariciously. The hand wriggled in Alex's, as it sought to claim Billy's coin. The glowing form lifted from his chest, drawn towards the clasping, covetous appendage.

Billy's face glowed from his coin. He grinned at the sight of it spinning on its thread. "There's only one thread."

As the claw closed, encasing the coin, Alex held steady. She didn't want his thread to break. Not until she had no choice.

"I know why I have to do this," she whimpered to Billy. "You've always protected me. You always kept me safe," she said, echoing the words he prepared for her in Heather's hospital room. She hated herself for her willingness to do it. If she didn't want this, wouldn't she find it impossible? All she had left to do was to relieve the claw of its coin and swallow it.

"I know," Billy comforted her. "It's okay." He stepped back, his elongated thread sparking violently against the skeletal fingers. "I've tried to keep you safe, but I can't do everything they want me to do."

Once again, Alex found herself on both sides of the memory. *He means me and Rose, right now. He can't do everything* we *want him to do. Because we want him to live.*

As the sparkling thread fell to sparkling dust and disappeared, Billy's expression deadened. Alex hoped for some sign of life, but Billy was gone. He just stood there, eyes focused on nothing, breathing.

Alex fished his coin from between the bony fingers, which relinquished it at her will. She held it.

I could give it right back to him. Her own memories mingled with Billy's, drawing recollections of Peter. It was unfair of everyone to expect so much from her. *Why do I have to do the hardest things?*

"Alex!" Matthew edged forward, his words waded with concern, "Quick, before Charon comes to claim it."

Alex couldn't take her eyes off the glowing disk pinched in her fingers. She spoke as though not paying attention to her own words, "I don't think I can." Part of her hesitation came from hope that she could still save Billy and was therefore guilt-ridden at robbing him of any chance at life, but also, because she feared what eating his coin *again* would do to her. The first time didn't possess any of the vitality of Heather's or Johnny's.

Rose pulled from Marta's embrace, throwing the woman to the ground. She lunged for the coin, crying out, "Give it to ME!"

Rose missed the coin but entangled her arms in Alex's. The coin was about to spill from her fingers. Alex pushed it with her fingertips, slipping it between her lips. She and Rose tumbled to the ground, Rose's hands pawing at Alex's face and mouth, desperate for her brother's coin.

Alex didn't defend herself; Rose pried open her lips to no avail, screaming and raging savagely when she discovered her brother's coin swallowed.

Alex prepared for the sensation, the onrush of memories, but the coin was gone. Like it had dissolved away. She tried desperately not to give life to the thought, but she found the experience disappointing.

Atop her, Rose heaved. She fell aside Alex, sobbing.

They sobbed together. Alex touched Rose, desiring contact, but Rose pushed her away. Rose sat up, her face mottled and red, and she pushed at Alex, punched at her, moved her away from Billy, so she alone could cry over the loss.

"Alex," Matthew said softly.

"Leave me alone," she replied. She wanted nothing but to be like Billy, devoid of feelings and emotions and pain.

"This isn't over."

Alex looked up and froze.

Rose followed her gaze to the small cherubic child. It entered the room from a small puff of mist. "Oh," she uttered.

Matthew cursed, "Fuck me."

The child looked lost, scanning the room but not seeing what it had come for. Its face was decorated with bruises faded brown and splattered with scabs of former cuts and scrapes. It reached out—palm down—its left hand; its right arm hung loose at its side, ending in a red, angry stump just past its elbow.

The wound on Alex's abdomen burned, a deep, throbbing ache that made breathing difficult.

"I'm sorry you came. The coin is gone," Alex soothed, hesitant to get too close.

The child saw her and froze, withdrawing, as though it were possible for the toddler-sized creature to become smaller.

Rose seemed aghast. She confidently ordered the child—as though expecting her direction was inexorable, "You aren't welcome here."

As Billy wandered from them, Alex took a half step towards the child, her knees bending to reduce her stature. "I didn't mean to hurt you," she said softly. "I can try to help you. Will you let me?"

Charon's eyes widened, like the child had been slapped for experiencing joy and couldn't comprehend what it had done. Its bottom lip plumped as it raised its right arm, pointing at the garish stump.

Matthew's tone changed considerably, "Fuck me."

"It's okay," Alex said, approaching the child. Disinterested in her platitudes, the child crept backwards. It looked frantically around the room. "I'm not going to hurt you," she said as though talking to an injured puppy.

"Don't do it," Matthew warned too late as Alex had already withdrawn the claw from her pocket and presented it to the child.

Charon made a face, its jutting lower lip quivering.

You did that to yourself. She wouldn't soon forget the sensation of the reaper's claw in her abdomen. She touched her stomach, where the intense burning still sizzled; it felt as hot as she expected, as though there was still something of the child yet within her. She presented the claw again. The child looked at it with disgust, pushing it away.

"Please do something, Alex," Jacque whisper-shouted. "Quickly. They're coming."

The child startled when Rose tried to stop Billy's mindless wandering. She glared at the child as though it had threatened her. "Go away," Rose screeched. "Shoo!"

"Don't, Rose."

Matthew told Alex, "Make it go away before we're trapped here."

She'd forgotten about Jeremiah's men in the square. Were they almost at the door? Climbing the steps? Would they soon find themselves backed into a corner, stuck between golems and the child that was death?

Charon's eyes scornfully bore into Rose, returning her glare.

Why is it so afraid? Alex quickly read the room. She, Rose, and Matthew were between the child and the door, where Dany and Jacque lingered. All the while, Billy stumbled about the room, constantly stealing the child's attention. Of course, it felt trapped.

"Move," Alex urged everyone. "Make a path to the door. Give Charon a clear path."

Jacque and Dany disappeared into the other room and Rose and Matthew withdrew to opposing sides of the room. Only then did Alex step aside. The child saw the doorway, its face softening.

Billy's shambling walk abruptly turned as he came upon a wall; he was heading straight for Charon.

Rose leapt to the center of the room and turned Billy from the child. As Billy wandered away, he left a clear path between Charon and Rose. They stood no further apart than each of their arms could reach.

"Oh shit oh shit oh shit," Rose cried as the child's robes and flesh tore and split, the skeletal Reaper shredding through the child as it grew and rose, dwarfing Rose in an instant.

"Fuck me," Matthew cried out.

Rose held her hands up as the Reaper slashed at her with its one claw.

Before the Reaper could lash at Rose again or claim her glowing coin, the far wall and the two chairs exploded as the Reaper was thrown into them.

Alex cried out, "Leave my cousin alone!"

"Fuck me," Matthew uttered yet another way.

"What is wrong with you," Alex screamed as the skeletal mass thrashed about, trying to untangle itself from the chair legs and wall and its own ragged bones. "I'm only trying to help you!"

"Alex, are you okay?"

It sounded like Rose. She felt so distant. Alex squared her shoulders to the broken form of the Reaper. It reminded her of the pile of bones they discovered in the Library just before the labyrinth. The bones clinked as they found their partners, snapping into jointed configurations, the shreds of fabric and ancient flesh swaying and dangling. It stared at her with empty, hollow eyes. Alex glared back. She was no longer afraid of this thing. Watching it shrink against the wall, she understood that wasn't mutual.

Alex threatened a step closer. The Reaper crossed its arms defensively under its chin. One arm ended at a cleanly broken forearm. For a skeletal form, a creature lacking muscle and skin and therefore expression, its fear was palatable. It squirmed. It sought escape. Alex could only think of the pathetic child, nursing its severed wrist—and wondered if helping it might forge an alliance, or at least an understanding.

She again offered it its claw. The skeletal form was a fury of ticks and adjustments as it pondered its own severed hand in hers. Reaching with tremendous hesitation, it touched it. Alex saw the razor talons up close for the first time, fine, nearly macroscopic designs rendered into the bone. The severed claw was dull and ordinary. It tapped bone to bone, nervously drawing the severed claw from her hands. All this time, the skeletal face never shrank from her, it kept its hollowed-out eyes on her, as though fearing her reprisal. It placed the claw against its own arm, aligning the severed ends. It pressed them together and held it pensively. Nothing happened. The bones remained severed from each other. It held the bone a moment longer, studying it, studying Alex, until finally it opened its claw and presented its severed appendage back to Alex.

"I don't want it," Alex told the Reaper, but it was deaf to her pleas. Reluctantly, Alex reclaimed the claw and gently returned it to her back pocket.

Alex eased back a step. It never stopped looking at her, even as bone and flesh shrank and reknit, reforming the cherubic child with deep skin and light hair and impossibly dark eyes. Barely more than a toddler.

Alex reached, slowly, like she was trying to pet an injured puppy. Charon winced at her hand. She touched the child, and although loathe to embrace it, she slowly did.

A moment passed. The child made a sound, but there was no discernable meaning to the breathy utterance. A moment more and she released the child. Its face appeared as it did before their last encounter. There was no healing its hand, but the stump was fleshy and no longer red and angry. It reached up to her; its hand gingerly inspected her charm. It fondled the glass hanging from her neck with a single, gentle hand, its eyes wide with wonder. It looked up at her, mouth agape, and stared as though in awe.

Releasing the charm, it backed from her slowly, disappearing as it receded into mist and was gone.

Chapter One Hundred and Thirty-Four

veryone was so silent Alex expected to find herself alone. Primarily to Matthew, she said, "Don't you dare say a word." In the moment it seemed the right thing to do, but she didn't want to get her hopes up that Charon had gifted her a potent weapon against Jeremiah.

Rose held her shoulder, where the claw marks cut her most jaggedly. There was more damage to her new shirt than the flesh under it, her blood leaving a slash through the I♥NY. Almost before Alex edged forward to embrace her, Rose withdrew.

Alex expected something, anything. Billy's coin disappeared down her throat and was gone. She had been too busy with Charon to fully appreciate that there was no revelation, no lost memory. It just disappeared. As did he. Only his living body remained. Her disappointment felt guiltily. She wanted to feel something, a surge of energy, a memory—anything to suggest Billy's death had been something more than a sacrifice. She hated herself for what she'd done.

"Paillasson," from the other room, Dany pointed out the window. "They've found us."

Marta asked, "What do we do?"

With a sob, Rose wrapped her arms dramatically around Billy's body as though claiming him for herself. Alex was unable to grieve. In some ways, she already had, but having him back for those few moments was crueler in some ways than losing him the first time. Being the one to kill him made it unspeakably more so. Alex believed Billy would have seen it as a just punishment for the things he'd done in the name of protecting Alex.

Matthew simply stared at her. He had no words to offer.

Alex asked him, "What?"

The question couldn't deflect his gaze.

Alex wiped her face. To Matthew, she asked, "What will they do now that he's gone?"

Matthew started his reply when Rose accused, "He's not gone. You killed him!"

The cry shook Matthew back to reality. Words fell slowly from his mouth, his eyes continuously coming back to Alex. "I promised I'd take care of this part." He approached Rose and Billy.

"Don't touch my brother," Rose screamed as Matthew pulled Billy from her. Her cry withered and she relinquished Billy to Matthew.

He covered Billy's mouth with one palm and pinched his nose with his other. Then he drew Billy against his own body, so his jutting neck rested his head on Billy's shoulder. "Close your eyes and sleep old friend," Matthew said in a tone Alex hadn't heard him use before. His soothing words carried the threat of tears. He addressed Rose's accusing look, "He's been my friend and confidant for nearly two-hundred years." As Billy's body jerked purposelessly, he explained, "Just because it's the right thing, doesn't make it any less difficult."

Rose shrieked. "Stop-stop-stop," she begged. She fell to her knees, watching Billy twitch; his vacant eyes exhibiting no expression. "He can have a coin. We can bring him back, just like Mommy. Please stop!"

Matthew hesitated but didn't release.

"Where's his Book? We'll find a cat and he'll have a coin," Rose cried.

Matthew answered as though announcing a revelation, "He never read a Book. He always refused."

Billy stilled, his body falling limp in Matthew's arms, and the two collapsed slowly to the ground. Matthew didn't uncover Billy's mouth until he was certain the boy was dead.

Rose sobbed, falling in a heap on her brother's crumpled body. Matthew pushed himself to his feet. Alex couldn't take her eyes from her cousins. She was empty. The hollowed-out parts ached and were raw from exposure. But she'd already cried for Billy. This was Rose's final goodbye and Alex let her have it without interference.

From the other room, Jacque urged, "Paillasson!"

Matthew rubbed his ruddy face, rubbing tears from his eyes. He snorted and cleared his throat. "We need to go now. Billy cut his loop out of time. There's nothing that bastard can do to change what he's accomplished. But now," Matthew pointed at Alex, "You're the only prize."

Pain was all too easily transformed into rage. All this suffering because of Jeremiah. Alex hissed, "I am ready."

"No one defeats death," Matthew said. "And here you are. Conquering it twice." He rubbed his bent neck. A hint of a smile crept to the corners of his mouth. "We could all go out there. Like in New York. Bring magic to the public. Let the news tell their conspiracy theories. We'll face them together." He looked at Alex. "I bet the public would love to meet you."

Alex nodded. She wondered if this was where she and Rose parted ways.

"Why should any of us trust you?" Rose was kneeling, a hand still resting on Billy.

Alex was sick to her stomach, waiting for Rose's accusation. Rose had every reason to hate her, now more than ever. Alex hadn't wanted to eat

Billy's coin, but that excuse was harder to believe now that she'd done it twice.

Marta knelt by Rose's side. "Sweetheart," she whispered, "they were coming for your brother. It's because of them…. Had Alex…," she hesitated, "They would take—"

Rose's face was a twist of anger and tears. "I'm gonna kill them," she cried. "I'm gonna take their coins and I'm gonna give one back to him." She looked around the room for a reaction of shock she didn't get. "I'll eat the rest."

"We're done hiding. Jacque," Matthew called out at Alex's approval, "get the door, lead the way, Books in hand!"

"Oui, Paillasson," Jacque affirmed. He unlocked the three locks and latches with steady and deliberate care. He pulled his Book from a momentary roiling of mist and opened the door. "Viens avec moi," he said to Dany, and the two disappeared into the hallway.

Matthew appeared his Book. Pausing at the door, he watched Rose charge forward, the mess of her Book in her hands. "Long as I live, I don't think I'll ever get used to women using Books," he said to no one but the room.

Alex told Marta, "You should hide."

Marta told her as she strode forward, "We go where you go."

Alex grabbed her. "Please, Marta, it's my fault if you get hurt."

Marta explained, "Alex and I have figured out how to work together. You don't have to worry about us anymore."

Matthew watched Marta go and turned to Alex as they departed the room together.

Before he could speak, Alex turned back. Through the two doorways, she saw Billy's body. He looked so small, so alone. She knew that was no longer him, but it still felt like they were abandoning him.

"Assuming we're all still here when this is over," Matthew told her, huffing as they trampled down the four flights of stairs, "There's one more coin you must consume."

Alex paused at a turn and looked down the spiraling pit between the staircase railings at Rose, her hand sliding on the banister as she—perhaps too eagerly—raced downstairs.

"Not hers," Matthew said breathlessly. "Mine."

Alex almost tripped. How was it the moment they became allies, he gave up the whole game? "You ate Laurent's?"

"It's how we pass on our knowledge," he explained as they came to the last turn before the last flight. "I did it to my mentor. He to his. The knowledge goes back to the beginning, and you will have access to it all."

Alex was aghast. Heather's memories were difficult enough. Matthew was hundreds of years old. What would his memories do to her, much less all the others before him? Would she have to experience Sara's torture again? Only this time as Matthew. How many others would she—through those memories—torture and murder? She paused at the door. There was no sense starting the argument now.

Matthew seemed to sense her concern. "It's a unique suffering to experience a person's life like that. You must understand, we couldn't see through our own arrogance. We were certain of our purpose: Find the right woman and once she had the magic, only a man could wield it. When your father told me he'd done it, I assumed it would be me because I never expected—I never even thought to dream—it could be you. You will take my coin and you will suffer through all our lives and you will have everything you need to face Jeremiah." He grinned. "Between your magic and the Reaper's claw, he won't stand a chance."

Before she needed respond, they stepped into the street, the fountain to their left, the square—the *place*—just beyond it. The square was filled with people milling about, tourists taking photographs, wanna-be models stretching and twisting seductively before the stepped waterfalls. It was abuzz with activity. Alex could feel her rising anxiety as she saw all these people, completely unaware they were about to be in the midst of a war.

What had happened in New York could not happen again. She couldn't let these innocents suffer because of her.

Nearly two dozen Books appeared, emerging from random spots where the crowds obscured their presence. They all walked toward the center of the square to form their phalanx. Here and there around the square, handfuls of ordinary men appeared their Books.

Alex glared about, her rage boiling with the ferocity of pressure cooker about to rupture. "Not again," she said through gritted teeth.

Rose cast the first spell, practically spitting the guttural words. The snaps of her red, irritated lightning were punctuated by her yelp of pain. The crowd immediately took notice. People screamed. Started running. Crashing into one another. Fell in the crush. In the fountain. One man leapt into the splashing pool to escape the crowd and flee to safety. Some seemed too shocked to move. They stared as though what they were witnessing was so unfathomable they had no reaction, as though they saw what happened in New York City on the news and knew that war had come to their city.

Almost immediately, sparks were returned. Jacque and Dany joined the fray as they ran to the opposite side of the fountain to flank the first group of Books.

Matthew was next. The bolts leaving his fingertips were more than sparks: lightning struck their attackers. They were outnumbered, and everyone—friend and foe—recognized that.

People fled the square, retreating to the periphery and beyond, their phones held like tiny shields, leaving only them and their enemies to stand before Saint Michel and his dragon.

Alex looked towards the sculpture. It really was like the fountain in the market at Yeswhere: people were going to die here, too, because of her. Somewhere behind it, they left Billy. She looked at the fountain, at the women lined across the top. At the man with angel wings—he looked shockingly effeminate in spite of his muscular arms; his face was pretty, his waist cinched, a skirt flitted about his thighs. His foot holding down a man with bat wings. One hand thrust a wavy sword above his head, his free hand pointing to the sky. No blow had been struck. Defeat appeared eminent, but never guaranteed.

Alex looked up to the sky through tear-filled eyes. Behind her she heard the cries of onlookers as they saw one person or another fire their sparks. She heard the static crack-crack-crack as sparks fired and struck. The march of the Books coming within reach of one another. The grunts and cries of wounded friends and enemies.

"Not again," Alex cried out.

The sky moved through the depth of her tears. The deep blue swirled in her salty pain. She hurt for Rose and Billy and Heather and Marta and Colette and Betty and Donna and George. She hurt for the men whose lives she'd taken. None of it had ever been her will. She didn't choose this fight; it was thrust upon her. This battle started long before she was born; before the conceiver of her conception. For the first time, however, she understood: It was hers to finish.

Jeremiah's golems fired indiscriminately into the crowd as they drifted closer and closer to one another. People screamed and fled the spectacle, but too many lingered, thinking they were safe, thinking that war happened to other people.

Men read from their Books, exchanging fire with Rose and Matthew and his men. While Jacque and Dany sheltered behind gigantic flowerpots containing trees, returning fire like cowboys in Hollywood westerns, Rose stood in the open.

People were struck, crying out as the electrical strikes injured them, or fell silently and didn't move.

Grumbling thunder rolled through the air on a hot, wet wave of static-laden, humid wind. The pit in Alex's stomach—the place where her contempt lived—became bottomless. Pain and anger swirled inside this limitless pit of revulsion. She glared at these men who, because they could no longer have Billy, came for her, and she pitied them.

She asked the rising crescendo of voices in her head for help. For strength. Then… she unleashed them.

The sky released a storm into the square, a squall of wind, swirling huge, hot, pregnant drops of blinding, cutting rain. She hollered at the sensation of her draining emotion, the hairs along her neck and on her forearms standing upright as the charged air raced around her like a stalking tiger.

Electricity pulsed around her entire body, racing around her with a buzzing hum that snapped as the raindrops sizzled away to vapor, barely touching her.

As though the sky itself read from a Book, the thunder sounded like a long, rolling, deep, guttural emission. Gusting wind threw people to the ground, cast them off with bits of debris and trash. Spray spat from chimeric mouths across the square and darkened the green metal forms like splashes of sculptural blood.

And then the electricity leapt from Alex, hurtling into the air like several dozen pouncing jaguars, following the direction of her will as though she were its conductor.

Stone shattered throughout the square as the crack of lightning pushed through it, toppling people and shattering windows and setting off car alarms. The echoing buzz of her electricity seemed to dance endlessly around the square before slowly reverberating back from more distant places.

The wind fled and the driving rain stopped falling like an overturned bucket had finally emptied. A long rumble of deafening thunder, like the entire planet grinding against the gears that it rotated on, took an eternity to slowly wander off; waves of grumbling clatter growing quieter and distant.

Alex felt exhausted of her anguish.

Then came stillness.

Waterlogged, Rose and Matthew and Marta and Dany and Jacque slowly, choking and drowned, climbed to their feet. Rose collected her soaked pages that had scattered in the wind.

Matthew surveyed the burned wreckage. "I've never seen anything like that."

Smoldering in the center of the square, charred concrete glowed with heat around the handful of men she spared. Four-odd dozen smoldering shoes scattered amidst piles of ash, the only remnant of the Books.

"I don't want to hurt any of you," Alex shouted to the remaining men. "Please don't make me."

Not one of them moved. Not one of them spoke. Their witnesses climbed to their feet with the gentle shuffling of wet fabric and continued to watch and stream their videos.

Alex took a solitary step backwards. She was stripped of the anger necessary for another spell, but as she prepared to continue fighting, she felt it rebuilding.

Jacque shouted something incomprehensible. At Alex's curious expression, he replied, "Translating you."

"What are you waiting for? Drop your Books and leave," Alex demanded. Jacque shouted again.

Without looking at any of their compatriots, three of the six placed their Books at their feet. The others, watching the first three hastily walking away without repercussion, jitterily followed suit.

Watching them leave, Alex was swamped with relief. She'd averted another New York. People were injured—a few dead—but most everyone was free to return home, unharmed.

When Alex was done—the six Books consumed, their pain now her pain, their voices now her voices, her fire disappeared—she joined her friends.

Jacque pointed something out to Matthew, who came to Alex, "We must get you out of here." Then she saw the crowd, too. Awed by the sudden storm, they continued filming her.

Alex turned to the crowd. "My name is Alexandrea Hawthorn," she shouted as Matthew asked, "What are you doing?"

Alex continued, "And I'm a witch. These men came to destroy me because they're trying to keep magic a secret." Jacque translated as she spoke. "They've been murdering witches for thousands of years to keep that truth from you and it needs to stop!"

Dany asked, "Where to, Paillasson?"

"We need someplace private." Matthew touched his chest.

"We're going to the Library," Alex ordered. "That's where Heather went this morning. She needs our help."

Matthew began, "Not before—"

"I'm not eating your fucking coin," Alex cursed at him. She turned to Rose, "I know, Rose. But he's gone." She pointed off to the left of the square, in the general direction from where they'd come. "You mother went to the Library this morning. If she dies, it will be *all your fault.*"

Rose glared but held her tongue. She glanced back at the fountain and the apartment behind it. "Fine," she said at last.

Alex said to Marta, "I know, you're coming. You sure you and my brother can hold your own in the Library?" She had yet to see Marta protect herself.

Marta grimly nodded.

To Matthew, Alex asked, "Are you coming?"

Matthew touched his chest. "It's the way it's always been done. There are memories and knowledge you can't imagine. You need to—"

"I don't want your memories," she countered. "I don't want your knowledge. I've lived through too many of the things you've done and," Matthew tried to defend himself, but Alex talked over him, "I am not going to give it any further life after yours. Yours is the old way and when your time comes, I will let it die."

Matthew looked hurt. He looked ashamed. His face reddened as Jacque and Dany watched him, but he said nothing.

"Are you coming with me?"

"Oui," Jacque nodded, disappearing his Book, even though Alex hadn't asked him.

"Me, too," Dany said.

Matthew hesitated. He looked around the square, at all the people still filming. Most were wandering away, the show over. Many were hesitantly holding their ground, terrified of getting too close, but a few were slowly coming over, perhaps to see if they could touch the woman who was made of fire, who could control lightning and thunder.

"I'll go with you if you hear me out along the way."

"I will not change my mind."

Matthew pointed the way back to the door. "Just hear me out as we walk."

Alex followed his gesture and the others followed her.

Chapter One Hundred and Thirty-Five

s they returned to the door, Alex listened politely as Matthew explained his case: His coin contained multitudes of memories, some lives lived thousands of years ago, men long since forgotten, all united by one common goal: defeating Jeremiah. He tried, briefly, to appeal to her sympathy, telling her he was tired of living, tired of causing pain. His harm, he explained, was a cruel means to a necessary end. She didn't care.

"Think about it like this," he explained, "one of them, from some unforgotten time, knows one little thing. This meaningless factoid has context only because it relates to something Jeremiah said to you—something equally insignificant. But together they are important. If you don't take my coin, all that knowledge is lost." He paused, disgruntled by Rose's smirk. "Worse, if Jeremiah seizes it; he'll fix his vulnerability. I mustn't be the first one to break tradition. You'll be letting down all those men who proceed me." He turned to Alex, stopping. "Don't you see? I'm offering the knowledge of the eons."

"I don't want it," Alex walked away. Matthew raced after her.

"Tell me why."

This time Alex stopped. She pointed an accusing finger at Matthew, "You all want to take Jeremiah's magic, but you all want to keep it."

"What's your point?"

"Maybe you'd stop making golems. Maybe even close the Farm." She'd never been so disgusted by that word and it came through in her delivery. "But you all covet the power."

"But women are—"

"Don't you dare say we're too emotional."

Matthew backed away. The others stood around them on the slender sidewalk, separated from the road by metal posts.

"Jeremiah won't have magic, but you haven't changed anything," she told him.

"It's what we've always believed," Matthew whimpered. "Now it's up to you."

"Matthew," she said after a moment, "we're barely allies. We're not friends. Not after all you've done to me and to Abby, Billy and Rose, and even to Sara. Every Book I've taken has become a woman's voice I hear in my head. My magic is their magic. You see how strong I'm becoming; I'm just beginning to understand what I'm capable of." Her speech grew louder, "Why would I take your coin? To know what all those men thought," she explained, "when my mind is already full of women?" She touched her temple. "They're alive in here. Not memories, Matthew. Thousands and thousands of women."

Matthew's head lowered in a sulk, but he didn't reply. When Alex began walking again, he waited a single step before following.

Alex found it strange the way people stared and tried to subtly point at her. Especially the younger people, those just a few years older than her. They'd stare and point their phones and whisper. Some were brazen enough to editorialize as they videoed.

When they turned onto Rue Dauphine a short while later, Matthew still hadn't said anything despite clearly wanting to. His head jutting straight from his shoulders just added to his sulking appearance. Jacque nudged Dany and showed him his phone. "I got an alert," he explained.

"We're all over the news, Paillasson," Jacque said. They encircled Jacque and watched the video. In it, Alex self-immolated in Place Saint-Michel and walked along, collecting Books, burning them up in a roiling, tumultuous blaze.

"Is that what I look like?"

Everyone stared incredulously at Alex.

"What? I'm always doing it, never looking at it."

Rose pointed at the phone, "Only the video doesn't capture the heat."

Matthew nodded. "You're something to see."

Marta added, "Really, Alex. I almost shit the first time back at the old Witch's Shack and it seriously never gets old. Every time you… what do you call it, light up? Catch fire? Whatever superhero catchphrase you use to describe it, every time totally freaks me out."

Jacque agreed, "It's crazy. You taking ze Books that way. But important."

Alex pointed at the phone. "What does this mean to us?"

Jacque started speaking French to Dany. Then Dany told Jacque, "You don't know that. You're making all kinds of assumptions."

Several of them asked, "What?"

Jacque pushed Dany to answer. "You're on video in Paris. Just before you arrived, Jacque saw coverage of you in New York. Not even an hour apart. The media is going to freak out." His voice mocked a news anchor with an accent, "How did this young woman get from New York to Paris in forty-five minutes? Can she fly? What horrible dangers are we in with this female terrorist in our cities? Can we survive the afternoon? News at ten."

Matthew placed a hand on Dany's shoulder. "You're about to see Jeremiah's reach. At first, she'll be the big news. They'll label her a terrorist. Maybe they'll talk about movie special effects. In the end, they'll find a way to unravel the hoax, how she's not the same woman in both places. Experts will analyze the videos. You've heard the lies. How it was faked with paid actors and crisis performers. Some company will come forward and take credit for a marketing blitz." He hesitated. "Anyone who so much as tries to contradict the official story will be dealt with until everyone is willingly silent. You've heard this story too many times. *My neighbor knows a guy who says he saw….* They sound crazy, but they're not lying. He'd rather take out a plane over a public beach than let one person betray his secret."

Alex shook her head. "Those are great lengths to silence magic."

Matthew waggled his finger around Jacque's phone. "With this out there, we have to reconsider our plan. He knows. That's the only certainty. He knows we were in New York City and then in Paris and he didn't sense us using magic to make the trip." He pointed up the road, towards Rue Christine. "He knows we used the door. It's not safe to go back that way."

Alex put her hands on her hips. "We're going to the Library." She eyeballed Rose, "Guns blazing."

Matthew groaned.

"Heather and the Book Club went to the Library this morning."

At *Book Club*, Matthew, Jacque, and Dany all exchanged a curious glance.

"My Coven," Alex clarified. "Heather thought I was dead, so she and the rest of the Coven went. They're going to need our help." She checked with Marta who agreed.

Matthew was perspiring. "Why would Heather think she can do this? Is she out of her mind?"

Alex nudged Marta. "Tell him."

"Heather figured out how to get magic out of a Book and into her."

Matthew was confused. "How is that again?"

Rose appeared her Book. "Magic," she banged her knuckles into the cover like a neanderthal. "In person," she touched her chest repeatedly. "No longer need Book," she shook her head and waved her hand over the cover.

Matthew was flabbergasted. "What? Really?" He looked for Alex to clear up his confusion. He gestured at Rose, "But she still uses her Book and she," he pointed at Marta, "doesn't have any magic."

Before Rose could answer, Alex explained, "Rose is still going through puberty and the crazy emotions would make a mess out of the emotional magic." Rose was about to argue when she realized Alex lied to hide the truth from Matthew. Alex added, "And Marta, well, she's got her own things going on."

Rose muttered something about puberty and hormones under her breath. Marta nodded. "Not a story you want to hear, trust me. Suffice to say, there's no magic here."

Dany pointed at Jacque as though he represented the phone. "Do we call things off?"

"If you don't think going to the Library is a good idea," Alex said, "then don't go. Just don't try to stop me."

Jacque didn't wait for Matthew, "It's you we follow."

Alex asked, "You've never met Jeremiah, have you?"

Dany shook his head.

Alex asked Matthew, "Aren't all your henchmen like a hundred years old?"

Dany took offence, "Hey, I'm thirty-seven. He," he pointed at Jacque, "is forty-four." He looked at Matthew, but still spoke to Alex, "We've never been to the Library. Matthew raised us and gave us our Books." He hesitated, "If he's going to be ready for us, how do we not die stupidly?"

Alex wished she had a better answer. "We hope that all this trouble I'm causing distracts him so he doesn't notice Heather and the Book Club. If he can tell when we do magic, then we don't do it. All that matters is making sure they get out safe."

Marta agreed, her tone a little too dramatic, "They believe Alex is dead, so they're on a suicide mission to avenge her."

Matthew digested her words. "This as an opportunity: They're buying you time with their sacrifice. Use that time to get ready. All you have to do is—"

Alex pushed Matthew against the storefront. "I'm not eating your coin and I'm not letting Heather and the others sacrifice themselves." She walked abruptly away. "I'm going to the Library, with or without you. You're welcome to do whatever you want, but I'm making sure my Coven is safe." Rose and Marta pushed past the men to follow her.

Jacque spoke French again. He paused, turned to Alex and shouted, "Attendez! We go with you. Please, wait."

Matthew looked at Dany, who said, "He's right, Paillasson. You told me if you fail that I eat your coin. Jacque and I followed you because when our parents died, you told us who did it and how if we helped you, it would avenge them. Now you tell us it is her. We follow her now."

Matthew touched his chest. "She can't defeat him without—"

"Paillasson," Dany urged, "stop trying to be in charge. If it is her, then she is in charge. When we thought you were in charge we never questioned you." Once Matthew acquiesced, Dany added, "Come. She needs us to help."

Alex allowed the others to catch up. "I'm not going there to fight him, Matthew," Alex spoke softly. "My family and friends are my greatest weakness. Once they're safe, we get out." She remembered what happened the last time she faced Jeremiah. That wasn't the sort of pain a person forgot. Her eyes welled just thinking about it. "Besides, how can I defeat the dark heart of the universe. He *is* magic."

"Who told you such things?"

Alex looked her answer at him.

Matthew rubbed his neck. "Why would he tell you that?"

"Is it not true?"

"I don't understand why he'd brag like that. Unless to frighten you."

"He did a good job."

Matthew squinted at her. "What else did he tell you about himself?"

"Nothing," was her reply. "We touched and I saw this vision of him strangling a goddess. He ate her coin and stole her magic. More lies."

Matthew leaned closer. "This is why you need my coin. Maybe in some memory—"

"Then why don't you know?"

"You know damn well it's not like that. They hit you at first, like you live a whole life in an instant. By the next day, it's like recalling what your mother said to you on the third Tuesday of December at ten-fifteen in the morning when you were eight. You can't. That's why we carry it, so the next ma—I mean—next person can make the connection."

Alex was done arguing with Matthew. She spoke to the group. "Jeremiah is a liar. Nothing he says has any truth to it. He gives you only enough to make you think things might turn out okay, but again and again he messes with the truth. He keeps it circling and circling around you."

Matthew nodded. "That's the Jeremiah I know. Ugly old bastard."

"About that," Rose interjected. "I think he was trying to hit on miss magic-fingers. He's like some hotty now."

Matthew squinted at Alex. "He changed his appearance for you?"

Alex deflected, "He was trying to get under my skin. I think he thought it would turn me on."

"That," Rose explained, "and she totally burned the old version of him to a crispy nugget."

"Wait, what?" Matthew looked between them both, then to Marta for confirmation.

Marta explained, "I wasn't there, remember, you sucked me into your Oblivion."

Matthew seemed stunned. "One day you'll have to tell me how you all got out of there. Do you know where it went?"

Marta shook her head, her grin straightened by pursed lips.

Matthew pointed at Alex, "You fought him?"

Alex nodded.

"And you hurt him?"

"I wouldn't say I hurt him."

"But he changed his appearance? You damaged him enough he had to change?"

Alex shrugged. "For a second, he let me believe I could beat him. Then he came back. Different appearance, same Jeremiah."

"Fuck me," Matthew said, differently from all the previous times. "All this time and you've really been the answer." He was grinning. "This time really is different."

"I thought you already knew that."

Matthew held his hand out, tipping his flattened palm from side to side, "Levels of certainty, of uncertainty. What I'm getting at is that you've already done more than all those before you ever have." He looked at Jacque and Dany, grinning foolishly, "She might actually do it."

Jacque's eyes went wide. "You are doubtful?"

"Doubtful? I think we have, what, one chance in a hundred billion."

Jacque groaned, "Those aren't odds to wage a war on."

Matthew waved Jacque's words off. "It doesn't matter that there are a hundred billion chances we'll fail. For the first time, there's one chance we'll succeed. For all eternity, we've never actually fought to win. All this time, we've been fighting for this one chance."

Chapter One Hundred and Thirty-Six

he door on Rue Christine was an ornate wooden door near identical to the others along the road. Even having come to Paris through this door, Alex struggled to find it. It wasn't hidden or obscured except by its extraordinary similitude. The oil-stained wood patinated nearly black from touches over the years. Alex looked up and down the street, her small retinue gathered about her, waiting for her to open the door.

The large brass knob was awkwardly positioned in the center of the door instead of to one side. She gestured at it and asked Matthew, "Just like the other one?" Matthew nodded.

Alex took hold and twisted, feeling slightly idiotic for holding a knob that wouldn't turn. Neither Dany nor Jacque had been through this door and they watched with anticipation. The door finally clicked open, just as Jacque offered, "Do you need a hand?"

Matthew blocked the others. "Just one moment," he began. "What's your plan?"

Alex rolled her eyes. "My aunt is in there, somewhere."

"Did you try finding her?" Matthew rubbed his neck again.

Alex was so focused on saving her aunt she hadn't thought to verify the few facts she believed she knew. She concentrated all her thoughts on Heather. As opposed to when she searched for Matthew, Heather returned a blinding beacon: She wasn't seeing Heather. "It's not working," she said after a minute. "I think of her but only see us, here."

Matthew drummed his fingertips on the doorframe, his unruly fingernails making a fine succession of taps. "That makes sense. You are as much Heather now as she ever was."

Rose made a face and shuddered. Alex hoped it was for dramatic effect. Although she'd been quiet since leaving Saint Michel, Rose was brooding, perhaps until the right trigger came along to unleash her venom.

Alex crossed the threshold into the cloakroom. As the others followed, Alex was unsure if the state of the room surprised her or not. She half-expected it to be clean and tidy. It was as they left it, coatracks upended and shattered, pushed to this side or that. The floor was strewn with cloaks and hats and all manner of outer garments. No one else had been through here in the last few hours. Alex was grateful she wore her father's tan windbreaker rather than abandoning it to this mess.

"What is this place?" Jacque looked around in awe, unaware the disorder wasn't intentional.

To a first timer, the room was confusing in its disorder: Neglected things knocked asunder, painting the cloakroom with a veneer of abandonment. Had this been any other place, Alex might have paused to describe the wonder of discovering four-hundred-year-old artefacts.

"That is the door," Matthew narrated, pointing back from where they entered, "I've told you about. For us, it's a single door, the outside in Paris and the inside in a cloak room. But there are others. Hundreds of doors. Manhattan, Istanbul, Moscow. All different on the outside, but this door," he dramatically touched the inside door. "This inside door is the same for them all." He paused while Jacque and Dany venerated the door as though it were a museum artefact and Matthew was their docent. "What to you was a journey of a single step was in fact a crossing of unimaginable distances. You are following in the footsteps of great men." He motioned to the room. "A young man, prior to gaining magic, comes to walk the path on which we are currently engaged. Stopping here, he would shed his overcoat or cloak and hat and proceed through that archway. Take a moment to imagine the giants upon whose shoulders we now stand. Though now in a state of gross disrepair thanks to our dear Alexandrea, the coats you see here account for perhaps a thousand years of garments that hadn't yet rotted or disintegrated away over time."

Rose chimed, "Will you be such a dick in every room?" She turned to Jacque and Dany with dramatic flourish, "This is the coat closet. The Library, where they store all the Books stolen from all the women they raped and murdered, is further along."

Alex laughed into her hand; it didn't feel like what Rose said should be funny.

Walking onward sobered Alex quickly. Among those who followed the path on which they were *currently engaged*, was Alex and her Coven. It didn't seem long enough ago to be considering a return. Especially not after such a devastating outcome. And yet, Heather was alive again. Not all of Jeremiah's destruction had been permanent. And if Heather were to stay alive, they had to go, danger be damned.

That there was no indication anyone had been here since they exited, was no guarantee. If Matthew was correct, then Jeremiah knew they would come this way. At any step they could run into an army of Books or men— or Jeremiah himself. Alex recalled the helplessness she felt when Jeremiah nullified her magic. It was like suddenly being underwater, all sound muted. How could she protect anyone if she couldn't protect herself? Her rising voices reminded her that he could stop her magic, but not theirs. That was one truth she didn't have before. Perhaps he underestimated what she possessed. Perhaps he purposely allowed her to see how none of her magic had any effect on him. Either way, Alex took each step with anticipation of surprise.

They entered the narrowing hallway. There was a chokepoint at the end of the tunnel, just before the pile of bones. They would have to pass single-file, and that seemed as good a location as any for an ambush. Alex's chest clenched like a fist as she slipped into the chokepoint. The last time she'd been through this way, she had so much excited anticipation. Now all she anticipated was death, hiding at every turn. Emerging through the chokepoint to an empty hall surprised her more than had she been set upon by an army of golems.

She ambled down the hallway, her eyes ahead. She listened for the slightest sound, the smallest hint of another person lying in wait; a breath, the scrape of a shoe, the friction of clothing. Whispers between Dany and Jacque drew her startled attention. They didn't need to be told—seeing Alex's expression—the way ahead was dangerous.

Each step was like a screw tightening in her chest. The constant anticipation grew as each step went unchallenged. It was as though the expectation that it would happen compressed each time it didn't, until the weight of it was like a neutron star crushing her.

Where the hallway widened, the toppled pile of bones at the dead end ahead, Alex turned about. Rose followed suit immediately, Matthew a moment after. Marta, Jacque, and Dany skirted them wide, walking around them as though diverting a collision. The trio gasped. "That's not… Where did… How did that…," they each stammered at the disappearance of the way they came.

Jacque pointed back to the bones at the end of the hallway and asked, "Does anyone want to explain that?"

"It's a diversion," Alex replied. Matthew looked amused. "It serves no purpose," Alex explained. "It's there to distract people from the labyrinth."

Matthew's smug smile slipped from his face moments before Alex might have resigned herself to slap it off. He gestured to the bones. "The bones have been here, I'm told, over six thousand years. You see, long ago, that served as the entrance to the Library. You entered right into this room right there." He pointed at the entrance to the maze, "And that's where one entered the Library."

Matthew wandered closer to the bones. "The details are sketchy because it happened so long ago. There was some attack. Enemies of Jeremiah. They fought their way in. Some stories suggest they even made it to the Library." His tone changed as he switched from telling to explaining. "Jeremiah loves to allow people their successes to better understand their strengths and weaknesses. When you're immortal, simply outliving your enemy guarantees their defeat." His tone returned to being didactic. "Jeremiah brutally ended the insurrection. He ensured that no one would dare threaten him again, wiping out thousands of people until there was only one left alive to tell the tale. To prevent the Library from ever being breached again, he created the labyrinth and moved the entrance. He took the leaders and put their bones there as a warning. That's the story, anyway. It explains why we must now go through this."

Rose groaned, her head and mouth mocking Matthew's lesson.

Marta, Dany, and Jacque followed Matthew and stood in awe of the vast maze before them.

Jacque said something in French. Alex didn't know what he'd said but was becoming familiar with some of his expressions. She'd uttered a few expletives the first time she saw it, too.

"You believe that story?" Alex asked.

Matthew replied, "Sure, why not? It explains the inspiration of so much mythology. The pharaonic obsessions with their tunnels and booby-trapped graves. The idea of a tomb being the place where they set voyage to the afterlife."

Alex was taken aback; Matthew made sense. She paused on the descending ramp to the labyrinth entrance. "Why don't you lead the way," she told Matthew.

The pregnancy in his pause suggested he would counter her request. Instead, Matthew turned to Jacque and Dany. "As terrifying as this looks, the solution to the maze is remarkably simple."

"Oh, sure," Jacque joked, "as soon as I laid my eyes upon ze puzzle, I knew ze way through would be simple." He traced a jagged line in the air as though mapping out the route.

"There's two secrets for getting through," Matthew explained. "One, just walk: Directions don't matter."

"I knew it," Rose blurted out. She looked at Alex, "I knew you didn't actually know—"

"And the second secret is confidence: No matter how desperately lost you may feel, you must be confident that you *will* get through."

Alex fumed that Matthew hadn't told her that. But she got through. She had been motivated; certain, even. What other madness allowed her to push into the maze alone, visions of her father or not?

Dany said, "How does that stop anyone from getting through?"

"Let me demonstrate," Matthew said. They followed him into the maze. A dozen turns and they came upon the four doors to the Library. He said to Alex, "Tell them what stops most people."

Alex originally walked for significantly longer. She remembered Peter and Billy's conversation. Even her own deduction, that directions had to be simple and easy to remember. "Uncertainty. The more you doubt yourself, the more twists and turns the Labyrinth takes." A palpable fear shivered across her shoulders and she gave it voice, "You literally could get lost in here forever."

"Precisely." Matthew peeked through the doorways, as concerned about being taken by surprise as Alex was. Gasping at so much of the Library in ruins, "You did a number here, Alexandrea."

"You told me to burn it." Much of the wreckage had already been cleared away. The scorched and upended granite floors were reset and mortared. Charred bookcases were disassembled and stacked. In the distance, there was evidence of restorations. New bookcases occupied otherwise vacant aisles. A Book or two relieving each shelf of its emptiness. Were these new Books or the result of some superstition about empty shelves?

"I don't see anyone." Alex hoped finding Heather would be a simple proposition. She'd arrive and, *Oh look, there's Heather and the Book Club*.

Matthew and Rose, alike, awaited Alex's instruction. The wrong choice doomed them to Jeremiah, and there was no guarantee a correct one existed. All eyes were upon her. She had no plan but Heather's. *Heather was coming to save Collette and Lydia. Following that gives us the best possibility of running into them.*

"Matthew, how do we get to the Farm?" Alex turned to the others. "The Farms are where they take and imprison women. They turn them into golems." At their expressions, she added, "Golems? You know, the men with Books tattooed on their skin? They used to be women."

Matthew recoiled. "You do not want to go there," he hissed. "Why would you want to go to the very place Jeremiah would keep you?"

Rose fondled her Book. She'd neatened the catastrophe, her tucked finger holding her place. "Guns blazing," she cheered.

Marta leaned forward. "Did I even hear that correctly? He farms women? Makes golems out of them?" Matthew nodded somberly, taking Marta's breath away. She replied, "What the fuck is wrong with you people?"

Rose tilted her head towards Alex, "You're sure Mom's there?"

Alex wouldn't fall into the *I don't know* trap with Rose. "If we move towards the same goal, we stand a chance of running into each other."

Jacque confirmed, "That holds merit."

Dany looked around. "What are we waiting for?"

Marta asked, "What if she's not there?" Matthew nodded in agreement.

"We do what she came to do," Alex replied. "And free as many women as we can while we're at it."

"I know how to get there," Matthew said sheepishly. "I've never been inside. It's not a place men go willingly."

Alex, Rose, and Marta looked among one another, confused by Matthew's tone; his exasperation suggested he was regurgitating *common knowledge*.

Dany asked, "If only men are allowed in the Library, why don't men want to go to the Farm?"

"That's not what I said," Matthew explained. "Some men disappear there. I've never even heard of rumors of any who escaped."

Marta asked, "What happens to them?"

"No one knows," Matthew dismissed her. "They're, how would you call it, like political prisoners."

Jacque chimed in, "Dissidents?"

Matthew explained, "It's where Jeremiah punishes men who turn against him. Rumors abound about what happens to them, from torture to being turned to food." He turned to Alex, "Many of us assumed *they* were who were turned into the golems."

Alex laughed sarcastically. "Figures. You're all so narrow-minded you never thought golems were made from women."

Matthew's bent neck twisted as though the words he swallowed back down were catching in his gullet.

After an awkward pause, Alex asked, "It's time for you to take us there."

Matthew gestured towards the fourth door. "This way."

Alex and Matthew stepped hesitantly into the Library, eagle-eyed. Matthew waved the others forward.

Following Matthew down a long aisle, Alex kept her eye on the bookcases and their precious Books. They called out to her, begging to be saved. Bearing the pain weighed heavily on her, but ignoring their cries was another kind of agony. Walking past them, she could almost see the women, reaching out for her aid, seeing small glimmers of hope fade from their faces as she passed. *I'll be back. I promise.*

They turned down an aisle slicing through a long run of unrepaired bookcases. There were gaps here and there, the outer reaches of Alex's fire. Like clearings in an impenetrable forest, some of the partially collapsed, charred bookcases lead to huge pockets of utter destruction.

Matthew crept cautiously, his head snapping back and forth at each intersection, expecting someone lurking at every aisle. The Library, however, was proving to be abandoned.

He paused.

"What's the matter?"

He whispered back to Alex, "There's no one here."

She gestured with her fist and extended thumb, "Maybe they've all gone to New York and Paris."

"That might actually be true," he replied. "I'm concerned about what he's planning for us. Why send everyone?" It may have been a rhetorical question, but he paused as though awaiting a reply. His face registered the shock of his epiphany. "Unless he knows what you're capable of; you destroyed legions of his soldiers. He could know you have Charon's hand." He swallowed. "Is he absent because he's hunting you or because he's afraid?"

Alex wanted to believe that their uninterrupted walk was proof Jeremiah was none the wiser. That he might be afraid seemed too gross an underestimation to be anything but jest. "Maybe he's waiting to see what we do."

"A disturbing thought," Marta added, looking around as though expecting to discover a surrounding troop of soldiers camouflaged in ghillie suits made of ruined bookcases and stacks of salvaged Books.

Matthew agreed, "He does like to study our behavior." He, too, looked about.

Alex felt like she was wading deeper into a pit of uncertainty that had long been over her head, but the bottom had disappeared. A creeping fear lingered like cold air against her back, warning her to abandon this quest. *I can't stop now.* "We shouldn't disappoint him then." Alex tried convincing herself. "If there's any chance to help Heather or anyone else, we must try."

Matthew gulped. He touched his chest. "You need to reconsider." He looked down the aisle. "Something's wrong. It's too easy and this," he waggled his finger, "isn't a plan."

Alex replied sternly. "If we turn back now, Heather will almost definitely die."

"Almost definitely," Jacque laughed. "I love ze English language." At Alex's stern look, he said, "Sorry."

Matthew added, "Your aunt chose her own fate. Abandoning her guarantees you live."

Rose snapped, "Are you sure it's Alex's life you're worried about?"

Alex didn't mean to glare at Rose, but it was becoming a reflex. Matthew's desire to sacrifice his coin suggested he was prepared to die. *Maybe he really is worried about me. Maybe he's saying I'm not ready to face Jeremiah again. Even with Charon's claw.* She feared she wouldn't recognize she'd gone too far until arriving there. The bookcases suddenly no longer felt like cover for them. They obscured the evil, horrible things that might creep or ooze or skittle on a hundred feet and devour them alive. *If Heather came, so did Abby. So did Carrie. June and Rachel. This isn't just about saving Heather. None of them deserve to die if I can help it.* In her mind she could see Jeremiah laughing as he callously dismembered them, one at a time, forcing each to watch so they knew exactly what fate had in store for them. She could hear them begging and screaming, pleading and crying out in pain. This wasn't just her imagination, but voices in her head feeding her their own demises. What cost was she willing to pay to prevent that? Would it ever be too high?

"No," she flatly ordered, "we're going. Stop trying to convince me otherwise."

"I said no," she interrupted his preparatory breath. "We're here to do whatever we can. In and out, quick. If we find Heather, great. If we're the diversion that saves her, great." She took a breath. "If you argue with me now, I swear I will go alone and the next time we meet I promise, we will *not be on the same side.*"

She waited for her mocking tone to sink in. He only said, "Consider yourself warned," and proceeded.

Chapter One Hundred and Thirty-Seven

lex didn't know what to expect. The Library was an enigmatic thing, a grandiose building of ornate pretense. A human farm was dungeonesque. Caleb, the young man who gave her the ancient Book when she last burned the Library, blindly pursued scholarly knowledge. Until Jeremiah sent him away, was he aware the Farm existed, or was that another fact he'd convinced himself not to believe in?

None of her whispers knew what to expect; it must be true no one escaped. Ignorance of the Farm allowed her an island of confidence amidst an ocean of fear. She was leaping blindly, anticipating a soft landing, while the drop may very well be endless.

Matthew led them onward. Her ability to accept they were allies was a constant battle of Billy's memories and her own recollection: seen through Sara's eyes as Matthew shattered her fingers with his hammer. In some ways, he wasn't the same as Sara's murderer. He was a broken man now. His bent neck in constant agony, as evidenced by him constantly rubbing it. His change of heart was so dramatic that it stunk of patronization. Was it a disguise for the original plan? A means to get her trust until he had what he wanted? She wanted to trust the information Billy gave her to trust Matthew, but experience was a strong deterrent.

At the distant end of their aisle, Matthew led them to an archway. Was this the exit through which Book escorted Colette and Lydia—and maybe Caleb—to the Farm?

The doorway loomed closer; this was no ordinary exit, but an ancient, colossal archway; weather-worn stones held in place with one immense keystone. Imposing balustrades, like intricate serpents, corralled and led them to the descending stairs carved into the floor and polished smooth with use. Beyond the opening, a passageway disappeared into darkness.

Matthew hissed, pointing around, "There's no one here. He's made our journey easy to take us off our guard."

Trying not to sound too sarcastic, Alex asked, "Doesn't Jeremiah have better things to do than hang around the Library? Doesn't he rule the world? Maybe he has a government to overthrow or a dictator or two to depose." Alex considered what she learned when she ate Johnny's coin—although she didn't want to think upon his memories—he'd done horrible things to many people. Several of whom she'd seen on television. Either through government or industry, they were the men who appeared to rule the world. They had all promised fealty to Jeremiah. They didn't discover him once they achieved their status. Many were rewarded with said status for their unyielding loyalty.

"We made it this far. If he wants to stop us," Alex reminded Matthew, "does it matter if we're here or at home?" She didn't understand his sudden timidity. For a man hellbent on destroying Jeremiah, he lived in terror of encountering his nemesis.

Matthew continued when Alex's body language urged him forward. He pointed at each of them, his lips counting. "We're too many," he told Alex. "We're stepping onto—what did you call it, the Between? There are things here that hunt travelers with coins. A single presence rarely arouses them. Six will be irresistible."

"What are they?"

"Things you don't want to meet in real life. Things that haunt your dreams."

Was Matthew using fear to avoid going to the Farm? Banhi and Khowla spoke of such things, but Alex assumed they were old wife's tales. "Tell me where to go. You and the boys can wait here."

"That's just as unappealing." He considered his options. "Perhaps in smaller groups, if we're quick…."

"Lead the way, Matthew." His nervousness made her wonder if instead of raising unnecessary alarm he was understating the danger.

Passing beneath the stone archway, the character of the air changed. Alex's prior experience entering the Between was through a rift of mist, an agitation created by magic. Here, it was like she'd stepped through a wound that was held open, the edges damp and festering, struggling eternally to close. She felt the difference in her breath, she felt it in her gut. She felt it in the tingle on her skin. The whispers sensed it. It was like her magic sensed it. The passageway was like crossing between life to death. It felt haunted, as though memories and dreams lingered in hidden and forgotten places, attempting to warm their cold bodies by being close to the reality they yearned returning to. It wasn't as though this narrow tunnel was fearsome; passing through the stone gullet felt like walking through a cold breath. What they felt was the unhealing scar made when Jeremiah incised the Between and grafted his Library here.

The uneasiness evoked by the passageway muted their fears of their destination. Where they were going was a place of bondage. Before steeling herself with thoughts of Heather and Abby, the haunted place almost tempted Alex to belatedly accepted Matthew's offer of turning back. She caught herself thinking that no reasonable person would go through with this, yet here she was.

They emerged from the edifice of stone onto a walkway of hard dirt and trampled grass. The stone ceiling gave way to a tepid blue sky.

Alex looked back at the Library. She anticipated some monument worthy of housing Jeremiah's treasure. What she saw instead was a modest cave yawning from a hillside. Even if she had been looking for it, she'd never believe this was the entrance to the Library.

As they walked, the sky brightened. The spindly grasses and wildflowers and weeds growing in the hard-packed dirt underfoot seemed cheerful, however out of place.

"Look," Rose gasped. The path they followed snaked between gently undulating hills, fields of stunted weeds and bright, tiny flowers. It was as though they were walking through a hilly meadow placed high on a plateau overlooking a barely verdant world. As far as Alex could see, swift-moving shadows of unseen clouds raved along the sweeping patchworks of fields and meadows and forests. It was reminiscent of standing at the edge of Picnic Rock.

Rounding a bend, they came upon a monstrous spiral stone tower, an ancient construction. Alex squinted up, spying the top, where it seemed to scrape the sky that drifted past.

It was a stone cylinder with a spiraling, external staircase, like a giant phallic screw penetrating the ground. It looked endlessly gigantic. It cast a bleak, imposing shadow as though it stood in bright sunlight, the origin of which they couldn't see.

Matthew asked, "I bet you want to know what that is."

Alex scanned the vicinity. Although they were clearly alone, she'd thought they were alone in a field before.

"No one comes here who doesn't have to," Matthew said. "We're safer right here than anywhere else." He pointed up at the gigantic tower. "It's said to be an anchor." He gestured back the way they'd come. "Jeremiah put the Library and the Farm here. He put this here like some giant screw to hold it all together." He shrugged. "Or it's utter bullshit. Jeremiah never told anyone himself. But it's thought to contain some tremendous power or magic. Something powerful enough to affix everything."

Beyond the tower, past the sloping hillside, were rows and rows of long, coarse wooden structures, bristling with splinters. Alex followed a step behind Matthew, Rose and Marta distanced behind her, Dany and Jacque not far behind them. There was something sinister about the rowhouses, nightmarish and forbidding. They reminded Alex of photos she saw when they studied the Second World War.

They entered the chilling shadow cast by the tower. It revealed their breath and brought shivers to their bones.

They approached the sharp edge of the shadow. Radiating warmth didn't penetrate deep. Matthew stopped them within the shadow, eager to feel the warmth of the bright sunlight and blue sky inches away.

Ahead, Alex counted twenty buildings, all identical, all grim and low and long, looking like giant arks that came to rest flat and perpendicular on the hard soil.

"We cannot all go any further," he warned. "Stepping past this point," he gestured to the line of shadow cutting the ground, cast by the tower. "We are no longer under the tower's protection."

Alex asked, "Protection from what?"

"How do we know which building they're in?" Rose stabbed a finger in the air as she counted them.

"I don't think it matters," Matthew told the group, ignoring Alex's question.

Alex seethed. Although she had no proof, Billy's memory shed enough light to imagine Matthew standing in this very spot with George as he sent Sara's son to the Farm to make a Book of his own sister.

Matthew continued, "You see many buildings, but there's only one."

Alex squinted at him; she had a reckoning she understood. "It's like the doorways into the Library, isn't it? Those buildings are the conjured exterior, right?"

Matthew nodded. "That's it, exactly."

Dany edged forward; his hand slightly raised as though waiting to be picked to speak. "That place you told me about, where we dream; that's here?"

Matthew nodded. "She calls it the Between. As good a term as any, I guess."

"Between," Dany whispered to himself. "I've wished to come here since the day you told me about it." He knelt to touch the grass and stood, rubbing dirt from his hands. "Seems normal."

"Of course it does," Matthew said.

Alex considered the importance of being here. She recalled her first real experience on the Between, following Banhi to the market, learning that the emotions she was trying to elicit were generating magic differently than intended. She almost gave voice to her recollection.

Matthew grinned. "Do you know why it seems normal but is actually different?"

Alex didn't want Matthew to feel he had all the answers, "Magic doesn't work here. It's imagination."

Matthew made eye contact with his students, who had crowded around him and Alex. "Normally you dream yourself here," he mimed a trailing thread. "You can lucidly impact your surroundings. However, the way we came is the only way in or out you can take, intact."

Jacque asked, "Otherwise you have to die or dreamwalk, oui?"

"You know the myths." Matthew pointed back to the opening in the hillside, now a distant speck. "Persephone may well have been allowed to leave the Farm once each year. This place is where you dream. It's where you die. The things that occupy our minds in life haunt us here in death. Heaven or hell is what you bring."

Alex had seen both. "And those?" She pointed at the buildings. "What's inside those doors?"

Matthew hesitated. "Jeremiah is a deceiver. Where he is concerned, there is only what he needs you to believe."

Rose spat, "He's a fucking liar, all right."

Matthew explained, "Lies can become prisons."

Alex had to go there for the sake of Colette and Lydia, but she feared being unable to ever forget what horrors she discovered there. "What's in there?"

"Nothing I've been told came from reliable mouths." He instructed Jacque and Dany they would all wait for them inside the shadow. He gestured to the break in the shadow. "Don't dawdle. Your presence on the Between will draw unwanted attention."

Alex steeled herself. She wasn't feeling overly confident. Before her was Jeremiah's greatest nightmare, and she wasn't sure she was ready to face it.

Emerging into the light, the slap of warmth on Alex's face relieved her of the bone-deep chill. She shielded her eyes with her hands as though the sun on this side of the tower was fiercer to make up for its absence on the other side.

Leaving the others, Alex, Rose, and Marta raced to the Farm. They hurried down the path, scanning their surroundings as though anything they encountered could be more terrifying than the place they were going to. Everything about this place was repulsive—literally and figuratively. It wasn't just horrible in its garish design and the knowledge of what it contained. It felt so horrifically evil that approaching it was like walking into the wind. As though it warned them, *turn back*.

As they reached the compound, the sky rapidly darkening at the horizon. These were not clouds. They moved with urgency, approaching rapidly, a giant mass of undulating darkness obliterating the sky.

Matthew said it didn't matter which door they chose, but there were so many. Alex chose the first they'd come to. The large wooden door was just several horizontal slats of wood held together by a single diagonal. It looked hastily assembled, nail heads weren't flush and the wood was marred with poorly aimed hammer blows. The wood was dry and aged, soft from rot and fuzzing with splinters. There didn't appear to be a lock—a fact that surprised Alex; she expected some sort of fortification to prevent the women inside from escaping.

Alex grabbed the rust-flaked black iron handle and looked to Rose and Marta. Rose signaled she was ready. Marta said, "Abandon all hope ye who enters here." Alex stared at her. "Sorry," Marta apologized. "I've never been someplace where that statement was more appropriate.

Alex was terrified of what lay behind these doors. She'd seen enough horrors and they were becoming harder to forget. In her quieter moments—however rare—her mind insisted on replaying snapshots. No matter how she tried, she couldn't stop her brain from recalling them. The more she tried not to dwell, the more clarity they came with. She was reluctant to add more fodder to the slideshow. *I'm here for Heather. For Colette and Lydia. Whatever is in here, they're living it.*

Alex pulled the creaking door open.

Chapter One Hundred and Thirty-Eight

erfumed air, smelling of lavender and citrus, bellowed from the brightly lit interior. Alex knew she shouldn't be surprised that the internal dimensions vastly belied their exterior, bothering her eyes and gently aching her head. Although this wooden building was no more than twelve feet across, it seemed possible the space within accounted for every building, the gaps between them, and then some. What surprised her wasn't the size of the interior, but the luxuriousness of it.

This grand foyer was modest by comparison to what lay beyond. The scale rivaled the Library. Multitudinous doorways on the circumference suggested countless other rooms beyond. This cavernous room was a cathedral to elegant decadence. Crystal chandeliers sparkled throughout, supplementing the perfectly rosy glow oozing from the ceiling. Seating and dining vignettes were scattered casually about. Tables with varying capacity, from deuces to grand dining tables to seat fifty or more, dotted the room. Huge feasts already garnished some. Multiple Books—Butler, this woman called them—raced between them, carrying dishes and beverages or served behind innumerable counters and bars, preparing dishes or mixing drinks or any number of other things. Music flowed through the space, its source unavailable to her ears, a perfect complement to drown any echo or hint of the crowds she saw.

"Did someone open the door?" "I think the door opened." "Is someone new coming?"

Several women spoke or called out at once. Just beyond the vaulting, white polished foyer, a group of twelve mulling women—dressed in various ensembles, from silk pajamas, to yoga pants, to casual outfits, to flowy summer dresses, to one woman clad in a white suit—looked up from their white, tufted, leather couches. One among them, wearing a bright butter and blue floral, backless sundress, put down her clear drink down—a tall glass filled with slices of cucumber, dotted with raspberries—and approached the door. Her head tipped to see past Alex. "Where's Butler?"

"Butler?"

The woman peered, still in search. "Yes. Obedient fellows, bald, tattooed. About yea tall," she raised her hand.

"He's, um, not here," Alex stuttered.

Before she could add anything, this woman, who looked slightly older than Heather, her hair in a ponytail, asked, "Then who brought you?"

Alex explained, "We came to find our friends. Jeremiah sent them here recently."

Hands up as though in a sudden panic, the woman's expression was glib and superficial. "Wait, wait, wait," she repeated with an intonation leading to the punchline of a joke, "are you a *rescue* party?"

Alex was uncertain how to respond. This was nothing like she expected. The woman's tone suggested that rescuing her friends was a frivolous attempt, adorable even. She anticipated them wanting, nay, desiring rescue. Peering beyond the immediate setting of women, Alex understood why that wasn't the case. She expected a farm; a gritty place of torture and humiliation. She understood why Matthew was hesitant to believe rumors of what was really behind these doors.

This is how Jeremiah uses lies to create prisons. Call it a farm and it sounds horrific. Give women the opportunity to live in the lap of luxury, and they would forget to escape.

"Oh," the woman giggled. She held out her hand. "Tiffany Mayfield."

Alex shook her hand and introduced herself. "Alex Hawthorne. This is Marta and my cousin, Rose."

Tiffany Mayfield waved her hand. "Never mind why you're here, dear. Come on in. Make yourself at home." She tisked at Alex's jacket, then again at Rose's shirt. "You should change into something clean. I bet you're the ath-leisure type." She waved at the couch. "Make yourself comfortable. I can find you a place to stay or, if you're hungry, tell me what sort of cuisine you prefer."

Rose stared about at the sight, her eyes glistening with stars.

Alex saw Rose's enthusiasm for exploration and dreaded the conflict that would arise from dampening it. "Rose, would you and Marta mind waiting here?"

Rose's reply came so fast it felt rehearsed. "Fuck you, Alex. You want to see this place all by yourself so you can rub my nose in how amazing it was after you save Colette and Lydia and my mom thinks you're her savior. I'm sick and tired of you trying to be the hero."

"Rose," Marta interrupted, "she asked if we'd mind. Don't jump down her throat. She's not your mother—"

"Damn right she's not." Rose continued looking at Marta, "Just because she ate her coin doesn't mean she gets to tell me what to do."

Marta looked pleadingly at Alex.

Alex saw the bemused look on Tiffany's face. Guiltily, she fantasized that Rose would like this place enough to stay. Alex sighed. "Six eyes *are better* than two."

Rose shook her head again. Alex was ready to slap her. "We're here to find your mother," she hissed at Rose. "Remember that." She turned back to Tiffany. "We're here for our friends. Colette and Lydia."

"Colette Enlydia? That name doesn't ring a bell."

"No," Alex corrected, emphasizing the conjunction, "Colette *and* Lydia. Two women. Came together."

"Let me see what I can do." Tiffany escorted them to the couches where she previously sat with eleven others. "Ladies," Tiffany announced, "this is Alex. She's come of her own accord to rescue two of her friends."

The women giggled and tittered. One of them said, "Good luck. You'll stay, too."

Another one piped in, "Tiff, give her a tour. Start with an activity. She looks like she exercises."

The group began debating, rock climbing walls versus yoga versus a cacophony of voiced opinions. One turned to Alex from amidst the debate, "Oh, you'll love it here. There's so much to do. There's arts and gardening. Even science stuff, if that's your thing. You'll always keep busy. Best of all, no responsibility. You'll never get a job and work. There's no rent to pay. Here, you can do whatever makes you happy."

Rose piped up, "Anything?"

"Well," another woman snorted into her hand, "*almost* anything. Men aren't allowed, and Butlers are useless eunuchs."

"Lord knows I've tried," another boasted.

Alex didn't feel like laughing. "What about.... Doesn't Jeremiah make you do things? Doesn't he turn you into… Butlers?"

Tiffany waved her hand. "Oh, that's nonsense. Don't worry your pretty head about that."

One of the women who hadn't thus far been particularly conversive, said, "We've all heard the rumors. It supposedly happens from time to time, don't let them fool you—"

"Stop being a killjoy, Dominique."

"—but even if you believe it, the chances of being picked are like," she blew out her breath.

Alex couldn't believe what she was hearing. "You're okay with what happens?"

Dominique grinned. "Okay? Honey, we want for *nothing*."

"They don't force you to do things? Like heal men?" Isn't that what George said to her, Jeremiah sent him to the Farm to be healed? If men weren't allowed, how did that happen?

"You sound smart. Do you like books?" Tiffany offered. "You won't believe the collection we have here. Probably every book ever written, in any language you prefer. The library itself is probably more beautiful than any cathedral you've ever seen. Whatever your interest, Alex, we've got it here."

Alex leaned closer. "I'd really like for someone to take me to my friends."

Tiffany looked at the tittering group and shrugged. "Suit yourself, Alex. I'll help you find them." And what are their names again? Colette…?"

Alex answered, "And Lydia."

Tiffany grinned. "Dear," she rubbed her eye, "what's Colette's last name? There's bound to be a half dozen women with that name."

Alex's mouth opened but nothing came out. Colette? She couldn't recall anyone ever offering Colette's last name. She didn't know any of their last names. The entire Book Club was on a first name basis and she suddenly recognized she'd been cheated of the information, as though she wasn't good enough or trustworthy enough to actually know their most basic facts. She didn't know Marta's last name, either—and asked her wordlessly for an assist.

"Colette DuChance," Marta offered. She explained to Tiffany, "Beautiful woman, almost six feet tall; eight feet of leg."

Tiffany's eyes went wide, and she wiggled her fingers in the air. "Blue nail-polish," she squealed. "I remember when she arrived with Butler." She pointed at Marta to make her point, "That woman *was* stunning."

Marta nodded, "That's her alright."

While Tiffany consulted with the other women as to where they might find Colette, Alex contemplated Betty and Donna's fate. Betty died rather than come here. At the moment, they believed it was a death sentence and she was bravely defying destiny. How foolish it now seemed. Had she acquiesced, they both would be alive, probably thriving in the lap of luxury. Unless some magic had these women convinced life was so much better here—and Alex hadn't ruled that out—being forced to the Farm was merciful compared to what happened to the rest of them.

Tiffany turned back to them. "Maybe your other friend, Lydia Whatsername, is with Colette. Either way, once we find Colette, I'm sure she can help you find her." She turned her body abruptly. "This way," Tiffany started forward.

Chapter One Hundred and Thirty-Nine

ose was a series of increasingly annoying *Oohs* and *Aahs*. There was something seductive about the glamor of the Farm, but Alex felt there was something more. Something so subtle its insidiousness was barely noticeable. Alex felt it; the voices in her head screamed about it. Maybe some of them—like Abigail—had been here, seduced by the pleasures available, recognizing betrayal only once someone began breaking their fingers to make their Book.

Thoughts of Billy, that lingered in Alex's active memory, seemed to duck inside. With them, the gaping hole of loss seemed suddenly shallow. The anger and sadness that previously consumed her felt muted. Until their absence became so complete, she hadn't noticed they had gone.

Tiffany brought them through what appeared to be the main room, passing several smaller rooms. Some pumped thudding dance music, populated by scantily clad, sweaty dancers. Others were tremendous gyms— some for exercise with weights and machines or mats and balance beams and uneven bars for gymnasts to twirl and flip and spin—while others were smaller, private art studios where women painted or sketched or photographed or sculpted their still life's or nudes or modeled for those artists. They passed libraries, with stacks of normal books, through labs where some women experimented with chemical solutions or peered through microscopes at the cells from their dissected samples.

Like an arm on her shoulder or a hand on her wrist, each room whispered to her: *Climb the rock wall. Dance. Exercise. Study. Be creative. Eat.* In each room, she desired to tell Tiffany to wait just a moment while she picked up a piece of charcoal and some watercolor paper to draw a perfect bouquet of sunflowers scattered about a tree stump and jutting from a rusted watering can. Rose's disappointment, too, grew with each passing room.

Even Marta looked about with gaping eyes, not immune from the wiles of the Farm. Yet, following each came a dismissive expression, as though each room had about it an imperceptible stench that wrinkled Marta's nose.

In one room, a half-dozen women in one-piece bathing suits swam long laps. They raced, their strokes elegant, kicking off the side as they turned. They passed through a doorway; the warm humid air of the pool unable to cross the threshold to mingle with the cool, fan-driven air of the next. Following Tiffany into that cool air, they encountered thumping music lingering at the door. Lights swirled and spun in a dizzying psychedelic show. Fifteen or so women danced in flirty skirts and little black dresses, their bodies drenched with sweat. One approached them. Alex tried to avoid eye contact as the woman danced, swaying from foot to foot, her hips and arms pumping to the beat. She clasped Rose's hands. That was all it took. Initially Rose jumped up and down, eventually finding the beat. Slowly she found her hips and gradually drifted into the crowd. Even Alex found it difficult to ignore the pressure of the music. She wasn't sure what the singer was chanting, but it felt infectious and triumphant. Tiffany took her hands and she and Alex danced.

Alex twirled and the lights sparkled in her eyes, making her pleasantly dizzy, as though the room gently spun. Tiffany's wide grin infected her own expression. It wasn't that she didn't want to dance, but that for a little while, she wanted nothing else.

There was no more pressure, no more danger. Jeremiah would wait, and men weren't allowed here. For as long as she remained, she'd be safe. She could dance or draw and have fun, learn again to be herself. And forget. Forget the pain, forget the loss. She closed her eyes. The lights spinning across her closed eyelids made her feel like she gently floated through space. It was as if the weight of the world had drifted from her shoulders, and she was finally free to be at peace. The lightness in her chest was intoxicating. It was like she'd taken a can of shaken soda and opened it slowly enough that instead of gushing everywhere, it just fizzed and hissed as the immense pressure gradually escaped. Her shoulders eased. As she spun and danced, she felt joyful for the first time she could remember. She'd rescue Colette and the other one eventually. If they were having the same experience, who was she to be the killjoy?

Rose grabbed her hands and pulled Alex close. "I've never had so much fun before," Rose declared. Then without a hint of accusation, said, "No wonder you wanted to keep it all for yourself." Concern narrowed her eyes. "Are you crying?"

Alex wiped her face. "I don't think I've ever felt so good." She could barely remember what troubled her so, to cause her tears when it vanished.

"Alex, come on," Marta grabbed at Alex's shoulder. Alex fought against Marta.

"I'm not ready to go," Alex said firmly.

Marta stilled Alex, holding her by the shoulders. She leaned close enough their noses nearly touched. "Alex, listen to me." Marta's voice was firm. "Think about all the people depending on you right now. I know you want to stay and dance, but Heather is in danger. If you don't stop and something happens to her, what will you tell yourself?"

Alex had a half-dozen snarky responses lined up and ready to go, but as the first one emerged, she stopped after the first few words, "Heather can...."

Her dancing stilled and she returned Marta's stare. It was like stepping outside on a hot, muggy day. One moment she was comfortable and cool, the next she felt smothered responsibility. *Heather is in danger. What am I doing? Why am I dancing?* She gulped air, her hair sticking to the sides of her face. The desire to dance evaporated, replaced with shame.

Alex had read about places like this. But, eventually, in those fictional places—or so the stories went—everyone realized they were trapped. And that was part of the horror. Perhaps this was where such stories came from. Had the writers ventured here themselves or were they just sensitive enough that they dreamed of the place that had a room where every day was Christmas morning?

Together, she and Marta tried collecting Rose. "Come on, Rose, let's go," Alex shouted over the music, which now seemed intrusively loud, but Rose spun away, ignoring them. "We need to help your mother!" Nothing she shouted at Rose seemed capable of penetrating her thrall.

Marta and Alex pulled at Rose, but Rose wasn't to be torn from the mass of bodies. As she pulled on Rose, Alex found her rhythm, her feet taking small steps. She released Rose and swayed on her own, the music willing her to dance. Tiffany took her hand and began swaying their arms together.

"Alex, we need to get out of here," Marta's voice nearly drowned in the sea of music. She tugged at Alex, who refused to be moved.

"Are you okay?" Alex noticed the concern on Marta's face. Marta looked as though she'd drunk poison and although was sure she knew where the antidote should be, she suddenly couldn't find it.

"I need you to come with me, Alex. Right now. It's so important you do."

"What's the matter?" Alex asked, wondering if it needed to be addressed this moment or if it could wait some time longer.

"Let me show you," Marta pointed to the doorway opposite the one they entered through. She took Alex by the arm and guided her. "It's right there, can you see it yet?"

As Alex leaned forward, the pull on her back to retreat from the door would have overcome her had Marta not heaved her through the doorway.

Tripping through, the desire to dance, the joy it gave her, felt ripped from her as though she'd snagged it on a protruding nail. One moment the music filled her ears so she heard nothing else, the next, only the slightest tinnitus buzzing in utter silence. She felt slapped and stunned. Realization returned, and its prickliness filled in all the places abandoned by happiness.

She stood in silence, looking back at the dancing room. The women looked ridiculous, swaying and gyrating to only the sounds of their shoes scraping the floor. Reaching back across the threshold, the bass buzzed on her skin, working its way to her ears through only her bones.

Marta came a moment later with Tiffany. She thrust Tiffany at Alex. "Wait here," she ordered them. "Rose is being a stubborn bitch." She turned and disappeared.

Tiffany looked grimly at Alex. "I'm sorry your mom's such a bitch."

Alex rolled her eyes. "Not my mom."

Tiffany made a perplexed expression. Then realization set in. "You're both so tall I figured…, but you do look nothing alike." She looked back through the doorway at Marta tugging Rose and Rose practically putting her feet on the doorway. "Why do you hang out with her? She buy you booze or something?"

As obstinate as Rose was about leaving the room, Marta's will was stronger. She didn't care if she had to fight dirty to get Rose to leave. It was the *pinch and twist* that caused Rose to lose purchase on the doorframe and fall through. As soon as she landed in the next room, Rose's thrashing ceased.

Rose looked about, one hand cupping her bruised breast. "Where'd…. What just happened?"

"This place makes you want to stay," Alex speculated.

Tiffany nodded. "Isn't it awesome?" She looked at Marta, "Why are you such a killjoy?"

Marta replied, "I don't feel it." She shrugged. "Maybe it's like with the Book."

Alex was grateful Marta didn't feel it. *Otherwise, I'd still be in there. But why'd it affect me and Rose but not her?* Marta wasn't like them: Marta had her brother inside. *It's like she's both male and female. Maybe that's why men weren't allowed in. Maybe it doesn't affect men, and that's why it doesn't infect Marta.*

Alex shook off the last desires from the room, mere scraps of want. "I know we all want to stay," Alex tried to concede, "but we really have to find Colette."

"Go without me," Rose huffed.

"No, Rose. There'll be time for dancing after we find Colette," Alex made up her response as she spoke.

"Colette loves to dance," Marta added, clearly doing the same. "We'll come back once we find her, okay?"

Rose's shoulders slumped. "Whatever."

Alex turned and after minimal cajoling, Tiffany led them onward.

"Not through there!" Alex stopped outside another doorway. She was explicit in her demands to avoid all activity rooms. Demanding Tiffany stick exclusively to hallways and corridors.

At every step, Alex could feel her concern for Heather's safety evaporating. As hard as she concentrated, her mind was quick to wander to something else. She told Marta to continuously remind her why they'd come.

Every time Tiffany complained, Alex interrupted her. "I don't care how long you think it'll take. We're not going through any more rooms."

"Fine," Tiffany exasperated, her hands up in a stop gesture. "You looked like you'd be fun." With a huff, they were off.

The Farm was labyrinthine, far more dangerous than the maze leading to the Library. Even avoiding the rooms, their draw and appeal was immense. Just seeing women enjoying themselves through open doorways induced longing.

This is ridiculous. I don't like math but want to spend the day doing it. Alex watched two women deliberating over a chalkboard covered in symbols and numerals, desperately wanting to join them and inquire what their formula represented. It felt *important*. It felt *accessible*. Each time she felt drawn, her whispers roused to warn and dissuade her. But it was Marta who kept her moving. It was Marta who kept Tiffany focused, for without Marta's constant nagging, they all certainly would have succumbed to the allure of some room and split up and disappeared into the illusion of desire.

"Alex? Rosemary? Oh, oh, Marta? You—you're all alive? What are you doing here?"

Turning a corner, they found Colette. Tall and elegant as always; however, she looked bedraggled. Her hair was unkempt. Her blue fingernails were showing over a weeks' outgrowth. The fit and design of her stylish outfit was exquisite, and yet the care to place her slacks at the right place on her hips or her collar to be square on her long neck, or her sleeves to be scrunched or rolled just so, was evident in its absence.

Alex rushed to embrace Colette. The last she saw her, Jeremiah marched her off to an expectation of doom. By comparison, this place was a country club.

"He didn't send you here, too?" Colette's voice dragged with disappointment. There was no solidarity with the notion they were finally together.

"Not at all," Marta explained, hugging Colette. "I can't wait to get the fuck out of here."

"Weren't you dead? You've got to tell me what happened." Colette's eyes widened dramatically, "It's a spell, isn't it? This place? It makes women go gaga over bullshit."

"I wouldn't say it's bullshit," Tiffany defended.

"And who are you?" Colette eyed her, hairclip to heels.

"Tiffany's helping us," Alex interjected over Tiffany's offended pout.

Colette nodded with urgency. "Helping you, how?"

Alex had heard the line in a movie and tried to find the same enthusiasm the actor had, but fell short, "I'm here to rescue you."

Colette clasped her hands. "Rescue away, darlin'."

"Where's Lydia?"

Colette closed her eyes in disappointment. "You've been to the rooms. You felt that draw, that—that magic—that made you want to stay?"

Alex nodded.

"Lydia didn't last two minutes." She waved her long blue fingernails, "She's off somewhere, thinking she's living her best life. I tried to keep her focused, but it got really ugly. I just couldn't anymore. It was hard enough for me, just being in this place. I tried, but I wasn't strong enough for her, too."

How'd Colette resist for so long? Alex asked.

"I thought I was done mourning Marcus," Colette whispered. "It's been eight months. I've tried dating, but I miss him. He was my soulmate." Colette rubbed her eye. "We did everything together. Since he's gone, my life has been low key and boring. All this," she waved her hand, "it was amazing. The way it called to me, the things it made me think I wanted to do, except it also made me wish Marcus were here. It's like, when the place tells me I can do whatever my heart desires, it's to be with him. Each time, feeling that, it was like losing him all over again."

"When can we go dancing?" Rose, tugging on Alex's shoulder, narrated with a hip-wiggle. "That'll make everyone feel better."

Colette made a face. "You're gonna lose her, soon."

"I really want to find Lydia," Alex urged. She feared she wasn't strong enough to remain here much longer.

Colette warned her, "She won't go with you. And you'll lose Rose in the process."

"Call this a win, Alex." Marta gestured at Rose, "Getting this one to leave is going to be like dealing with an addict." She pointed right at Alex's nose, "I can see the way you're twitching; you're barely holding on yourself."

It was a desire that overrode all other functions. She couldn't stop wanting. As much as she knew they must leave, she was so curious: What hadn't she seen? What would she miss if they left? Was there a room tailored just for her?

Alex saw it in Rose, too. Rose danced to silence, rotating her shoulders and grinding her hips to an absent rhythm. Alex, too, couldn't help but ogle her surroundings, constantly searching for that fix. It was as though they'd been inoculated with the desire and it kept growing inside them.

"Let's go," Alex said, feeling sweaty at just the thought of leaving.

"Oh, you can't leave," Tiffany cooed. "You just got here. There's so much more to show you."

Marta grabbed Tiffany's collar, "Show us the way out of here, right now."

Tiffany's expression of Zen joy was replaced with fear of Marta. Colette couldn't help but laugh, as though it was the first time she had reason to in days.

Tiffany pointed in a new direction.

"And don't take us through any rooms. Straight to the exit."

Tiffany nodded, but Rose complained, "Come on, you said we were going dancing!" She spun around as though putting on a show. She turned back, "Just drop me off at that club and I'll see myself out in the morning."

"I left my dancing shoes outside, Rose," Colette said gently. "I can't dance in these heels and dancing barefoot is dangerous."

Nothing would change Rose's mind. Alex didn't know how much longer she could withstand it. Tiffany might slow-walk them to the exit; she'd be lost before reaching it. If Tiffany was even leading them to the exit.

Marta told Rose, "We need to get the others. Think of how much Carrie and June will love this place." She offered a saccharine smile, "We'll be back. The whole Book Club, and you can show them around, Rose." She forced her gaze around the room, "Think of how much more fun it'll be if everyone is here."

"Can we leave my mom at home?" Rose glared at Alex.

"Sure, Rose," Marta soothed, "Heather doesn't have to come if you don't want her to."

"I think Jennifer would love this place. My dad's wife." Rose continued her dance. "She strikes me as a woman who used to move."

Colette agreed when Marta said, "So we'll definitely get her. Come on Rose, think of the fun we'll all have."

Marta pinched Tiffany's arm in her fist and thrust her forward. Colette embraced Alex and Marta grabbed Rose, practically scruffing her neck as they followed Tiffany. Alex knew all it would take was one wrong turn and all would be lost: Abandon all hope, indeed.

Tiffany led them through the winding central spine of the building. Alex felt desire pulling like a constant undertow. Most women they passed were exquisitely dressed. Even their gym gear looked custom made. It perhaps was. Colors matched hair and skin tone; fit was perfect. Too perfect. The more she saw everything these women had access to, the more she thought there had to be some dark underbelly where these things were made.

Was it all magic? Were there slaves? Were there other women, the truly unfortunate ones who didn't wind up thinking they were having the times of their lives? Or worse, were those women slaving away, happy and contented, certain their endless toil was the most perfect way to spend eternity?

Chapter One Hundred and Forty

"There," Tiffany pointed. The couches where Tiffany previously enjoyed a cocktail were now empty, the table strewn with empty stemware and glasses, crumped cocktail napkins, stirrers, and bowls dusted with crumbs, waiting for some Butler to clean. Just beyond the couches was the closed door they entered through.

Alex thanked Tiffany for guiding them through the Farm, for helping them find Colette, when Colette gave voice to her very thoughts, "We can't leave her here."

Marta added, "If you're going to do something, do it now. We need to get out of here." Marta grabbed Rose, the way a parent secures a child about to run into a busy road. In her clasp, Rose thrashed.

Rose's free hand kept snapping in the air beside her, fishing repeatedly in a tight circle. It looked like her hand was having a fit: she was trying to appear her Book.

Alex asked, "Colette, do you still have your Book?"

"Not since I got here."

Marta, slowly dragging Rose to the door, asked, "Is Tiffany coming or staying?"

Tiffany made a self-satisfied face, pursing her lips like only she knew the answer, "Of course I'm staying. You must have a defect if you can't see it's amazing."

With a nod, Colette sprung and bear-hugged Tiffany about the chest. Alex grabbed Tiffany's ankles and found herself thrust back and forth as Tiffany kicked. Alex did her best to avoid the business end of Tiffany's heels as she walked backwards towards the door.

Tiffany squealed, "Let me go!"

Rose was no less challenging for Marta. While Marta dragged Rose, one hand clasping Rose's wrist, the other wrapped around her neck like a headlock, Rose begged, "Can't you go without me? I'll wait here. You get the Book Club."

They crossed the distance an inch at a time. Rose's begging became cursing. Tiffany's cries for freedom became screams for help. Marta was dripping with perspiration less than halfway to the exit. Rose struggled like she believed Marta was sacrificing her into a volcano. They reached the door. Marta pushed it with her shoulder but didn't have the leverage. She tightened her headlock on Rose with one arm and pushed the door open with the other. Rose dropped like deadweight, slipping out from Marta's grip. The moment she was free, she ran.

Alex dropped Tiffany's legs and tackled Rose. Hearing Rose's head clunk to the ground was more satisfying than Alex would ever admit.

Her legs free, Tiffany dug in her heels and twisted her body, and she and Colette tumbled to the ground. Both women squirmed and fought for control. When Colette's forearm was near enough, Tiffany bit hard enough to make Colette squeal.

Alex struggled with Rose, who kicked and punched and clawed. Alex's longer reach allowed her control, pinning Rose's shoulders with her knees as she sat on her cousin's chest. Rose tried to knee and kick her in the back, thrashing violently, trying to hurt Alex enough to escape. In frustration, Alex threaded her fingers into Rose's hair and banged her head into the ground to knock the fight out of her. Alex didn't want to hurt Rose; the sickly thud of her head hitting the floor ricocheted nauseatingly through her hands and arms. It only further infuriated Rose. But she was blinded with pain long enough for Marta to relieve Alex and drag her across the threshold, tossing her into Matthew's waiting grasp.

Tiffany ran to the safety of the growing crowd forming near the bar. Drying his hands with a rag, a Butler came out from behind it. Alex realized how thirsty she was. She could grab a club soda or… *I bet they make margaritas like Abby. No one will ask for identification.* Colette was styling her hair while Tiffany, still holding fistfuls of it, was telling the others about her new-found friends. Nothing seemed as pressing as the dry patch in her throat that needed quenching.

She took three steps before the ground leapt up and smacked her face. A knee pressed into her back and hands held her ankles. Before she could say anything coherent, Marta yelled, "No you don't."

Alex complained, "I promise I won't ask for anything boozy."

Her ankles and armpits chafed as Colette and Marta dragged her out the door.

Chapter One Hundred and Forty-One

tanding outside amidst the wood huts, in the bright sun, beneath the imposing weight of the stone tower, Alex felt suddenly cold.

It wasn't the temperature, but an emptiness that left her chilled. She felt bereft, desolate, as though she'd lost her greatest love. Beside her, climbing to her feet, Rose shivered. The spell broken, their desire to remain inside the Farm vanished. It was like the tip of an icicle run through her chest. It melted slowly, and as it did, warmth gradually returned.

"What's he doing here?" Colette panicked at the sight of Matthew.

Alex touched her arm and explained, briefly, that Matthew was on their side and could—mostly—be trusted.

Dany and Jacque were waiting in the tower's shadow. Matthew pointed at the sky. Enormous black clouds, like thunderheads, had grown nearer. Alex noticed them before they entered the Farm. From here, they were clearly not clouds.

Matthew looked at Alex grievously. "Understand now?"

"You could have warned me, you bastard," Alex screamed. It was a prison of desire. All the bars and restraints were self-induced. "It's horrible."

Rose flashed a look at her. "What are you talking about? That place was amazing. I was having so much fun until you killjoys made me leave."

Flatly, Marta deadpanned, "You want to go back?"

Rose softened. "I don't think so."

Matthew gestured at Colette. "I see you found someone. No Heather?"

Alex could only surmise, "I don't think she came through here."

Matthew warned, "This was too easy. That means only one thing."

Alex countered, "He wanted me to see it."

Matthew agreed. "Or trapped in it."

Alex wanted to scream at Matthew again for not preparing her. Would any warning have sufficed? "And now that I got out?"

Alex didn't like that he didn't have a reply. Perhaps Jeremiah thought the Farm would trap her. Perhaps he wanted to prove—in his perverted way—that he was kind: Women lived in luxury and wanted for nothing. If he'd only intended that she experienced it for herself, what was his intention now that she had? The thought filled her with dread: Jeremiah could be anywhere, ready to appear at any moment like the bogeyman he was.

Alex found herself staring at Colette. *Was she wearing that inside?* Colette was wearing the outfit she wore to the Library. *Maybe the lighting made everything look so much more beautiful.* "Colette," Alex inquired, "do you have your Book?"

Colette waggled her hand and produced it. She showed it to Alex.

Marta grabbed Rose's already-waggling arm. "Keep your Book safe until we need it."

Matthew cleared his throat. "We need it."

Rose appeared her Book. Tattier than ever, the cover slumped ungainly to one side, slipping to and fro as Rose cradled it. She stuck her tongue out at Marta.

The precautions concerned Marta. "Can we just leave from here?"

Matthew glanced at the clouds. "No magic. Those things are getting closer." He departed rapidly and they followed. He explained, "We're on the *Between*. Our bodies aren't meant to be here. You leave your body when you dream and abandon it when you die. There's no way to come or leave whole without paying Charon." Matthew stared at Alex as he spoke. Maybe he referred to the price her father paid untwinning her. They started towards the tower, undulating clouds in rapid pursuit. They looked like dark fabric floating in water. However curious she was for a better view, her desire wasn't strong enough to wait for them to get closer.

Alex said, "Once in the Library, we'll pop back home."

Matthew nodded. "If by some miracle he still doesn't realize we're here, he'll know then. Taking the door is safer. We should go together. Safety in numbers." He looked at Alex, "You still have it?"

"Have what?" She asked and watched Matthew blanch. When she reached for her pocket and didn't feel it, she could feel the blood leaving her face. She stopped, patting herself down. "Where is it? Where's the claw?"

Marta held it up. "It fell out of your pocket," she said, coughing politely, "when you were fighting to save Tiffany. *Remember*?"

Alex gratefully took the claw and stuffed it in her back pocket. Before she could thank Marta, Marta patted her back and mouthed, *Don't mention it.*

"Come on." Matthew watched the clouds and pointed at the shadow cast by the tower. "Quickly, into the shade."

The cold shadow washed over Alex as she crossed over. Once they were all in shade, the black clouds sheepishly retreated.

Jacque and Dany, already in the tower's shadow, joined them.

Almost out. Somewhere ahead was the entrance to the Library, and once there, a little magic would send them all home. She hoped that was where she'd find Heather. It felt close enough to touch. She couldn't wait to see her aunt again.

"As soon as we enter the Library, we cast our spells," Alex explained. "If he senses the magic, he can't follow everyone if we go our separate ways."

"You and I have unfinished business," Matthew tapped his chest. "Where you go, we follow."

Alex took a deep breath, but Matthew preempted her, "Now isn't the time to discuss your objections. Once we're safely away from the Library, I will gladly listen to why you think it's a bad idea."

"We are glad you're all safe. 'E told us," Jacque explained. "It's crazy."

Dany and Jacque introduced themselves to Colette, who eyed them with suspicion even as she graciously shook their hands.

Matthew had a point. The longer they took the greater their danger. She could refuse his coin at home. It was time they were on their way.

She looked up at the tower. Deep in her chest, she felt energy vibrating from it. Curiosity would ferment to disappointment, however; she would not waste time to discover what was hidden there.

They made for the Library. Expectation raced her heart like a crop-crazed jockey. Desire to be home was enthralling. She tried to smile at Rose, but couldn't get the corners of her mouth to move. She had such desire for home to be synonymous with normal. Going home—be that Heather's or Abby's—only delayed the inevitable collision that would conclude her story.

And Abby—Alex hadn't thought of her former Familiar in hours. *What do I do about her?* Another impossible choice waiting at home. Alex remained focused on the potential for danger. The fields and hills were mostly clear ground, but Alex knew not to take what she saw for granted. Her heart leapt at every snapped twig.

She thought briefly to fly, to survey their path from the air. However, she hadn't mastered landing; crashing in front of Rose and Matthew kept Alex grounded. Thinking about flight, she recalled being blown through the window, tossed into the air outside Matthew's apartment. It was so abrupt and terrifying and fantastical that she doubted her own recollection. *Maybe Matthew was watching and stopped me from falling.*

It seemed a logical conclusion. She could fly on the Between. She could do many things on the Between she couldn't do in the waking world. How else did that happen without assistance? Still, she distinctly remembered having some control of her flight. Was that reality or was her mind embellishing trauma? There was only one way to know.

Pausing at the cave entrance, Matthew asked, "Only from the Library can we leave with magic. Where will you go, Alex?"

Alex's initial desire was Abby's trailer: Her fortress of solitude. Then she thought of the collapsed barn. Abby begging to be her Familiar. She felt too guilty to be annoyed. *I need to see that Heather's safe.* She was determined to believe Heather and the Book Club never left the house. "We're all going to Heather's." Alex speculated, "If Heather and everyone is there, they all have magic. We have the numbers to defend ourselves." *I can't wait to see everyone react when I show up with Matthew.*

"The way you say that," Colette said, "have magic…. You're not talking about Books, are you?"

Rose was about to tell Colette all about how they got Books and then used her cat when Alex interrupted her. "I'm not the only witch anymore. Once we're back, you'll be a real one, too."

Colette's expression suggested the idea was both exciting and unsettling.

"Now hurry," Matthew said as he disappeared into darkness.

Chapter One Hundred and Forty-Two

ncertain, Alex feared she would miss discovering—and saving—Heather here by minutes. If she got home and they had gone, what would she do? That was a greater unknown than Alex was comfortable bearing, but she had no alternative but to allow her hope to buoy her.

The wide-open sky of the Between dimmed the closer they came to the cave, until they entered the black, narrow throat that now loomed heavily over their heads. Their footfalls echoed, racing them forwards and back, betraying them down the shaft.

Soon they'd be in the Library, passing under the impressive keystone and climbing the ramp with the ornate serpentine rails. Then they would cast their spells and return to Heather's home. Alex's chest pounded from the anticipation they'd emerge into the Library and find themselves surrounded by an army, led by Jeremiah. All she wanted was a moment of freedom to escape, but she dreaded it wouldn't happen. She tasted absolute freedom—freedom from care at the Farm—and found it bitter. The illusion made freedom absolute, and it enslaved her. And while she told herself that wasn't what she wanted, the peace she felt in the moment haunted her. That very thing she sought was there. Could she be happy in a fog of forgetfulness? All regret magically transformed into a fog of saccharine happiness. But what a happiness it was. She wouldn't look back; the very act proved she desired losing herself.

Instead, she headed towards the certainty Jeremiah was waiting. Perhaps he'd return Rose to the Farms, where at least she'd have peace. Or he'd prove his cruelty by displaying the Book Club's bodies. *It was stupid to come here. Yes, we saved Colette from the Farm, but what will that sacrifice be worth if she dies now? I should have let Rose stay. Then she wouldn't be in danger now.* Each step increased the likelihood they'd encounter Jeremiah, yet each step mocked their fear when they hadn't.

As they approached the bright end of the tunnel, the opening to the Library, Matthew ran with his tremendous Book held open, keeping his position in the front. He told Dany to join him and while Dany squeezed past the line, Jacque slowed to guard their rear.

Dany asked, "Shouldn't Alex be in the middle?"

Matthew slowed his pace, allowing their line to tighten rank. "She stays up front with us."

"Shouldn't we protect her from Jeremiah?"

Matthew glanced back at her. "She's a formidable witch. She'll be the one doing the protecting. We must give her the chance to use Charon's claw."

Alex didn't like that the responsibility of everyone's safety yet again fell to her, but he spoke truth. Part of her hated Matthew, another trusted him. She rested her hand over the claw, like a gunslinger resting her hand on the grip of their six-shooter.

Emerging from the tunnel, passing under the gigantic keystone, their footfalls echoing up the ramp into the empty Library, Alex worried that if Jeremiah wasn't here, she had her answer why Heather also wasn't. She again feared for Heather and the others, wondering if they were now suffering so she might escape. The unknown was her second most frightful advisory.

Matthew stopped short, nearly tripping as his shoes scraped the granite floor and then again as Dany careened into him. No one said a word. They stood, silent and frozen, their bowels twisting. Alex took a sudden breath. She believed she'd be unsettled as long as she was uncertain. Now uncertainty was the luxury she wished she had. Uncertainty meant that she and her loved ones might yet live. Uncertainty meant she didn't know where Jeremiah was.

His tan face resplendent with a cocky smile, Jeremiah was leaning against a Bookcase like a parent waiting up late for their truant child. In spite of his muscular form, which was visible—for a change—under his clothes—his ensemble still seemed as much a contrivance for his appearance as the tweed jacket and tan trousers had been.

Shattering the silence like it was fragile glass, he directed his words to Alex, "You were gone so long, I figured either ole' crook-neck killed you or you took my warning to heart and disappeared." He grinned. "Where have you been?"

"You knew where I was." No sooner had the words come out did Alex realize he hadn't. She and Abby were trapped in Oblivion for the better part of a week, all but disappearing from the world, making it impossible for Jeremiah to know where she was.

Something caught his attention, and he addressed Colette, "Nails! How lovely to see you? How did they convince you to leave? Kicking and screaming I imagine."

"That place was terrifying," Colette remarked. "I hated every minute of it."

"I can always send you back, but if it was that awful—"

"Don't hurt her," Alex shouted. She thought she'd be begging, but what she blurted was a demand. "Don't hurt anyone. Your issue is with me and him," she nodded to Matthew. Her heart galloped. Adrenaline spilled into her bloodstream like a storm surge. Her fight-or-flight mechanisms pushed her to leap claw-first at Jeremiah and run as fast as she could. As a consequence, she just stood.

"True," Jeremiah said. He looked at Rose, "You remember Caleb, don't you? He could use a plaything."

"You're disgusting," Alex retorted.

"I know," he laughed. "It's hard to know what's acceptable these days. Times are a'changing."

Alex had her hand on the claw. She had to wait for the right moment. She had to be closer. Too far and he might escape its grasp. She had one shot. Alex looked for any way around him. Everything had to be perfect. When the claw activated, the others would have one chance. They shouldn't fight Jeremiah in a line, they needed to encircle him. Bookcases and walls blocked their way except for the aisle where he now stood.

He pointed at Dany. "I don't know you. Have we met before?"

Dany waited for Matthew's nod as permission to reply.

Before Matthew could give it, Jeremiah roared, "If you can't speak for yourself, you're of no use to me." With one swift jerk of his arms, without touching him, Dany's skin ripped from his body, from under his clothes, like a magician pulling a tablecloth from a set table, spilling to the ground in a glistening puddle.

Dany trembled, his clothes saturating crimson. His exposed tissue twitched. It was raw, bubbling with yellow fat and striated red muscle. His nerve endings must have sent too much for his brain to process because it took nearly a minute before his gruesome face recognized his affliction and shrieked, his arms out to his sides, clearly in agony as even the air was torment.

Dry heaves wracked Alex's frame. Rose and Colette both brought up copious yellow fluid. Marta's hands shook as she both tried to touch him and knew she couldn't, the salt on her skin would be like acid to his exposed nerves. She looked at Alex, tears welling in her eyes. Then, she composed herself. Her expression widened and her whole form—clothes, skin, body— exploded into an impossibly dark cloud which enveloped Dany before imploding back to Marta's form. Not even a moment passed between her reformation and her collapse.

Jeremiah slapped his knee. "I've never seen that before." He turned to Matthew, "Tell me where you got that, or I'll take yours."

Alex shot back, "You're not taking anyone." She knelt by Marta's side. *I didn't know she still had Oblivion inside her. That's what she meant, that she could take care of herself. Was that Alex, coming out for a moment? Is Dany still alive, floating inside her somewhere? Why isn't she coming to?*

She'd waited long enough. Alex pulled the claw from her pocket and thrust it at Jeremiah. The skeletal fingers clunk to life, wiggling in the air.

"What's that?" Jeremiah stared at it, taken aback, his eyes wide. "That looks so familiar." He examined his own hand, mimicking the motion of the claw with his own fingers.

Alex and Matthew looked at one another. It was working! Jeremiah's glowing coin stood from his chest, drawn to the claw.

The clawed hand opened wider, Jeremiah's thread sparking angrily as his coin bridged the gap between chest and expectant claw.

Jeremiah snatched at the claw, but Alex wouldn't let it go. They both held it a moment, until it transformed in her grasp, decaying to sand and falling through her fingers until she clutched nothing at all.

Shock painting Jeremiah's face as he waved about his dusty hand as though soothing a burn.

Alex struggled not to look at her hands in disbelief. Not to wallow in disappointment or surprise. Not to waste a single moment while he was distracted by whatever touching that claw had done to him.

She turned to Colette and Rose. She widened her eyes comedically so they would pay her attention. *Go home*, she mouthed. *Use your Book. Take Marta. Jacque if you can.*

Rose and Colette looked down at the Books in their hands. Alex encouraged them with a nod. *Three*, she mouthed. *Two. One.*

Leaping to her feet, Alex felt the energy depart her body like a train. She thought of nothing but protecting her cousin and Colette and Marta. She thought of Billy and how she failed to save him; yet succeeded. Jeremiah was no more or less terrifying than Charon turned to the Reaper. She faced the young man with his wavy blond hair and her body reverberated. Her desperation rose, fearful they wouldn't escape. Terrified Jeremiah would shake off her attack and slaughter them. He was the only threat between them and safety.

The floor upheaved in a cascade of gigantic fracturing panels of black stone tipping and turning. Wind howled and swirled. Bookcases splintered and collapsed. Books slid like trains from their shelves. But instead of littering the ground, the whole collapsing mass fell inward, towards Jeremiah, as though he had become the center of the universe, a black hole attracting everything towards himself.

His hands rose in defiance of the impending collision of stone and wood and paper. From above, the bright glowing, unseeable ceiling snapped like thunder as dark snaking cracks raced across it.

Inside, Alex's desire to protect her friends transmuted to anger at Jeremiah. It was impossible to hold an emotion for too long; once it reached its peak, it permeated out in the form of magic, evaporating from her. Only by changing how and what she felt could she continue the barrage, but she also knew—she could hear Billy's advice—anger was never as powerful a magic as love—and love was nearly infinite. Yet, as her focus shifted, as she hoped her distraction was sufficient for their escape, it was her anger that powered her attack and provoked her voices to scream in solidarity.

Beside her, Matthew joined in, his voice singing out guttural words, crying them into the buffeting wind, shooting bolts of lightning at Jeremiah.

This wasn't like before. Her magic was stronger. Before, Jeremiah survived her burning his body to a crisp. She had to do more. As her extended hand contacted a Book fluttering past in the wind, they both exploded into flame.

She held her flame and she held her anger, letting it grow as the women inside her, and the new women who joined them, were unleashed. The intensity of her flames multiplied. She roared, like a smelting furnace, her flames concentrating, her footsteps leaving brittle charred marks on the floor.

She seized Jeremiah. His flesh bloomed into sizzling blisters in her flaming hands. She bore down, intensifying her heat. Had he been steel, she would have evaporated him instantly.

She pulled him close, pulling him into her form, engulfing him, his screaming breath inside her own face. Her disgust upended more stones and slabs of wood and hurled them spinning through her flame, battering him. Lightning sparked upwards, leaping not from her hands but from all of her flaming form, and the mass of the Library and its stone walls and ceiling cried out as they cracked.

Her fire engorged on Jeremiah. She felt him inside her, writhing, fighting, trying to grasp anything of flesh or substance, his scorched, withering hands snatching through her flames.

She clutched his glowing coin.

She felt the weight of it, the glow of it; so much brighter than her flame, it radiated through her. She drew it from him, the sparking thread taut and vibrating. She tried to consume it in flame, to melt it down. Just like she didn't want to know the pain contained in all the Library's Books but took that pain, she'd take his memories. If only to take them from him. She placed the coin on her fiery tongue and swallowed.

Jeremiah stepped from her flames, his skull bald and blackened, his remaining flesh moved like carbonized scales. He cackled. He snatched his coin back from her and in one instant, her fire extinguished, her magic stifled, the remaining debris battered her, the wind suddenly disappearing as everything fell to the ground.

Rose and Colette were vanished. Marta and Jacque with them. Hopefully to safety.

Matthew read desperately from his Book, unable to make the Book perform. He flipped a page and stared, as though suddenly the shapes and symbols were as alien to him as that first time he looked upon any Book.

Wiping his charred skin away as one might sweat, Jeremiah straightened himself. In an instant, he appeared as he had before. He even covered his nudity, as though for Matthew, he possessed a modicum of modesty. He tisked as he scanned the Library. "You know how to make a mess, Alexandrea."

Wrenching Matthew's Book from his hands, Jeremiah cast it to the floor. "You took my gift of magic too far." He turned his back on her and walked away, like a disappointed parent considering what punishment to dole out to a grossly belligerent child. "Look what you've done. This girl nearly destroyed my beautiful Library. Tens of thousands of years of work vanished in minutes. But of course, all things must come to an end. So, Matthew, it's time I unmade what you've done."

"Heel," Jeremiah ordered Alex, pointing to his feet.

However she resisted, Jeremiah's attraction drew her towards him, skidding and scraping across the littered floor. "I warned you." He grinned with pity. "Now I take my magic back!"

She kicked and clawed, snatched grasps of the battering cracked granite floor only to have her fingertips ripped bloodily from her purchase. No matter how she tried, her body could not be slowed. It was like skidding to the edge of a cliff with no way to save herself from going over.

Matthew screamed the whole time, protesting and threatening and offering himself in her place. He hunted for other Books to read. He hurled stones at Jeremiah.

Her heart thudded hard enough to gag her. It was over. In another moment, despite her clawing, kicking refusal, Jeremiah would end her. Maybe he'd flay her skin or eat her coin. Maybe he'd cause her inscrutable pain as he extracted her magic, tearing the women from her one by one like pulling out ten thousand fingernails. She squeamishly wondered if there might come a time when her threshold would be crossed, when her body would mercifully stop experiencing his torture, but she doubted he would allow her such relief.

She was drawn upright against her will, raised to her feet before him. She tried to buckle her knees, but he wouldn't allow her to drop.

She couldn't breathe, unable to inhale a squeak of air.

Her head was a whirlwind of screaming fear, of cries of despair as the voices begged her to save them. She tried to conjure her emotions, to find her anger, but the pain was too great and deprived her of all other thoughts.

All these cries converged in her center, her chest. Had she the ability, she would have screamed out the pressure. She felt about to explode. Just when she couldn't bear it any longer, a hot rush of vomit brought up a mass of symbols and shapes spilling down her shirt and splashing to the floor with excruciating violence.

She gasped. He was allowing her one breath. Then he immediately resumed. She whimpered; the pain was inelegant. The cries of the women witnessing their inevitable return to paper bondage tore her spirit and broke her will. A moment ago, she feared what Jeremiah would do, but as she vomited a second and a third time, any one of those deaths was a preferable alternative to the suffering she—they—now endured.

At some moment, she wasn't sure how many times she vomited, her dripping clothing overrun with clinging symbols, Jeremiah faltered. Her body, never intending to stand on its own, crumpled to the floor, splashing the vomited symbols, drowning in her own mess.

Jeremiah yelped, twisting from her. His hands wrenched into the air. Matthew, apparently in the distraction, claimed another Book, and used it as his hammer to drive a generous shard of granite into Jeremiah's back.

Jeremiah spun, trying to reach the jutting piece of Library that was always just beyond his grasp. Matthew examined the hammering damage to the cover of his new Book before picking up another shard of stone.

From the ruin, Book emerged, concern dementing his tattooed face, and as Matthew, his neck bent like his threatening arm that clutched the fragment, charged at Jeremiah, Book came to his master's aid.

Jeremiah batted Matthew with a swipe of his hand, the sound of contact less a slap and more like someone stomping a pile of acorns. The ghastly sound echoed throughout the Library, far louder than any slap had the right to. Matthew crumpled beside Alex, his moving body squeegeeing a trough through the vomited symbols. His form was wretched; twisted and jutting with broken bits. Jeremiah had crushed him.

Matthew lay, the bow wave of mess sloping up against him, his head distorted, his body twisted unnaturally. He twitched but was otherwise still.

"Get it out," Jeremiah ordered Book. The golem took hold of the stone and pulled, but it was either in too deep, placed there magically, or it was the suction of Jeremiah's insides refusing to let it go.

The voices in her head cried and begged her to save them. Her hands slipped and slopped in her mess and she looked at the shapes as they wiggled and dangled from her. Could she put them back in? She sucked the symbols from her fingers, tasting the bitter acid bile that coated them, the earthy dust of pulverized stone, and the sharp tang of Matthew's blood. She swallowed, her throat scratched as though she'd swallowed a fistful of pins. She choked and gagged it down, heaving even as she stuffed fistfuls more in her mouth.

"Take it. Swallow it."

Beside her, Matthew sat upright from his broken form, holding his glowing coin before her. "Hurry, Alexandrea."

Matthew's neck was bent, even in death. She didn't want his memories. She didn't want to be forced to experience Sara's death from his point of view. She would not subject herself to wielding the hammer, knowing all too well she also suffered inside.

Matthew looked back at Jeremiah. Book had nearly budged the shard. Other golems emerged throughout the Library. "Please, Alexandrea," Matthew begged. "It's either you or it's him." He shook his coin in the air.

She had nothing left. Nothing to fight for, nothing to lose. All was already lost. If she could avoid losing another woman, maybe it was worth experiencing Sara's plight again. To defeat Jeremiah, maybe it was worth murdering Sara herself.

She reached for the coin.

Chapter One Hundred and Forty-Three

atthew's relief was palpable as he relinquished his coin to her. Alex waited for his expression to shift, to complete the journey from concern to relief to self-satisfaction to I *told you you'd do it*. His relief began to fade, however, at Alexandrea's growing reluctance, as her hand repulsively distanced the coin from her face.

"What are you waiting for?"

Alex didn't answer. As long as Jeremiah was occupied, she could reconsider. Her insides wouldn't cease quivering, as still under threat of further insult.

Matthew urged her attention to Book and Jeremiah's dance, to the ongoing assembly of other Books, Jeremiah's army arriving. Jeremiah's shard was painfully slipping from his body, his blood spilling, his body twisting in his agony. Something about the Library caused him greater injury than anything else. "Hurry, you have only a moment more."

Alex had a third option, a choice that didn't involve either her or Jeremiah. She was incapable of defending the coin from Jeremiah.

Matthew understood. "You're wasting it?" His eyes flashed to Jeremiah. "Charon isn't coming. M-m-maybe the child is afraid of you. Or it's afraid of coming here, afraid of Jeremiah."

That was certainly a possibility. She didn't possess the stamina taking Matthew's coin would require. If she had to see Sara again, murdering her was not how she wished that to happen. However, she was willing to take that risk. She could always swallow the coin in the last possible moment; what difference would that make—now versus a moment from now?

Jeremiah's back arched, his left shoulder raised as he limped towards them, his blood slicking down his legs, trailing footprints behind him as a golem pursued him like a puppy after a stick, trying to attend to his master.

"You're going to regret that, Matthew."

He grew closer, closer, reaching out for the glowing coin in Alex's hand. She held it like bait, poised until the last possible moment, until she realized she had no options left. She was thrusting the coin into her mouth when Jeremiah froze, his eyes wide in exclamation.

Following his stare to the child, its folds of fabric wrapped about its form, its faded bruises and nearly healed scars gave the once cherubic child a ghastlier visage.

"How did you get in here?" The question was more a threatening statement, shouted loudly enough that no reply would suffice. Then Jeremiah noticed the child's missing hand. "What happened to you?" He froze in his tracks in a fit of confusion. Slowly, he turned to Alex. Then to the seasoning of bone dust that hadn't yet dispersed on the floor. Then to Alex. "Huh," he uttered, as though finding the answer to his question holding a switchblade at the end of a dark alley. To Charon, his voice a deep whisper, he said, "She brought your hand in." To Alex, he asked, "How did you plan this?"

Now Alex was confused. Jeremiah accused her of something as absurd as coordinating with Charon to smuggle in the claw; he couldn't comprehend how she had taken it. That was information she preferred remained unspoken, but his expression demanded something in return.

Before she could answer, the child hissed like a feral cat, and lurched awkwardly forward, swiping at the air.

Flesh twisted from its striking hand as the claw emerged, slashing at Jeremiah, tearing ribbons into him. The Reaper shuddered, knocked by a tremendous blast, the casting golem of the group evaporating. It was enough of a distraction for Jeremiah to extricate himself from the monster's skeletal reach.

The golems reordered themselves and another Book exploded into a fit of dust. The Reaper's skeletal form clunked like wooden wind chimes in a hurricane. It turned its full attention to the tattooed creatures as another and then another exploded in a flurry of spells. Its mandible nearly unhinged in rage. The unholy wail it made pulled goosebumps from Alex's flesh. It was a lament unlike any she imagined it might make, like the wailing, snarling yowl of some gigantic, prehistoric cat, but powered by a hulking steam locomotive.

Jeremiah examined the strips of flesh dangling from his chest, his pale face sour with disdain.

Their number dwindling in rapid explosions of dust, more golems scrambled to connect to the group. Two other groups formed, surrounding the Reaper. Battered by all sides, the skeletal horror didn't seem to know where to attack. Shards of bone exploded from its form. It howled and spun, as all around it Books exploded in fits of dust as the groups cast their spell.

Alex watched in horror—what would happen if the Reaper were destroyed? Although she witnessed the torment of the Reaper, she pitied the child and its hidden suffering. What would become of that?

All the while Matthew chided her for waiting. "Eat my coin, Alex. Please, don't let me die in vain. I'm sure there's something hidden in my knowledge that is the clue to defeat him. Look how close we've come! We hurt him today!"

The Reaper frantically turned and twisted in a circle, like a baited bear.

But then it turned once more, nearly falling to its knees from the impact of a blinding bolt of energy. Reaching out, its claw caught the flesh of one golem, shredding it in two swift blows, rendering him to ribbons of quivering flesh.

It's claw, dripping with gore, quickly dismembered the remaining group, even as the other two continued their spells. It was efficient and merciless. When it turned to the second and the third group, its skull charred and cracking, the Reaper began pulling one and then another apart, like a wrathful child dismembering stuffed animals. Its untemperamental rage spread apart those not yet wounded, preventing another spell being cast.

With a single finger thrusting at it repeatedly, Jeremiah shouted, "Remember why I let you live. Remember why I never took your life, Charon. The world would be overrun with the dead. I left you to collect their coins!"

Four remaining Books collapsed in wrecked heaps—their twitching corpses upright only by the violence of the Reaper's onslaught—as it paused its assault. It turned as Jeremiah continued addressing it, "Do not tempt me. You know what I'll do!"

The Reaper stood amidst the carnage and glared at Jeremiah. It looked exhausted—if that were possible—as though the weight of its own bones had grown too much.

Jeremiah leaned forward. He threatened, "Don't make me do it!" He held his hands up as though preparing to cast a spell, but he waited.

Charon knitted back together. The battle had taken a tremendous toll. The child looked brutalized. It did not relinquish its ground, however, but leaned slightly forward, threatening, edging ever more into Jeremiah's space. That the toddler might consider itself more dangerous than the hulking Reaper seemed a comical miscalculation. It hissed and growled like a feral child, chattering its teeth like a cat hunting birds through a window. And then it saw Matthew's coin, re-poised at Alex's lips. It blurred with the suddenness of its redirected attention.

As though Jeremiah never existed, it stared hypnotically at the coin, which reflected like the moon in the child's dark eyes. It hungered at the glowing disk the way a starving man might a morsel of food. It reached covetously but didn't dare touch; Alex hadn't yet offered it.

"Fine," Jeremiah spat, "take the bastards' coin." He pointed a finger at Alex, "The moment the baby is gone, the game ends." Glaring at the child, he retreated into an aisle, a few newly arrived Books at his heels.

Alex's sigh of relief came like she'd been holding her breath. "He's afraid of Charon?"

Matthew stared at the child hungering for his coin. "It may seem counterintuitive, but the longer I've lived the less frequently I've considered my mortality. Jeremiah's immortal." His voice fell to a whisper. "Having to stare death in the face is terrifying to a man who forgot what death is."

Alex wondered if Charon's appearance could facilitate her escape.

Then Matthew hissed, "Swallow it already."

Her presence held the child at bay and in turn kept Jeremiah at a distance. As though just seeing the child discomforted him.

Alex studied the coin. It wouldn't be difficult to swallow. It shouldn't be—except for its memories. She couldn't bear more pain. Consuming Books at least allowed her solace in comforting the victims. Becoming their executioner, even just in memory felt too great a sacrifice. And yet, if it could help her... was it not worth whatever suffering she'd endure? She drew it to her mouth, until it nearly touched her lips.

"Yes, yes," Matthew whispered. "Quickly now."

Taking a deep breath, Alex said, "I'm sorry Matthew." She abruptly offered Charon his coin.

Chapter One Hundred and Forty-Four

atthew cried out as the brightly glowing coin disappeared in Charon's pudgy fist.

Without further acknowledgement, Matthew stood and followed the child. He passed through the mist and was gone, but the child stayed.

It approached Alex and knelt before her. Its plump hand was hesitant, reaching to Alex as though afraid of setting off some snapping trap.

"Is this what you want?" Alex held out her coin. She wasn't sure she was ready to give it up, but how could she defeat Jeremiah? It was only a matter of time before he returned and squeezed out the rest of her magic, guts and all. Perhaps by giving herself over to the child, she could deny Jeremiah his prize after all.

"What are you doing? Do not give the child your coin," Jeremiah roared.

Alex glanced at him. He suffered no wounds. Not from the granite, not from the Reaper. Yet, he kept his distance from the child. His insistence was all she needed.

The child looked from her coin to her and back, then at her charm. Reaching past her coin, with great reluctance it took hold of her charm and admired it, twirling it in its pudgy fingers. Releasing the charm to drop against her chest, it eyed her offered coin. Its eyes widening as its head trembled side to side, a terrified and final reply to her offer. It pushed her hand aside.

"Why won't you take this?"

Charon thrust its stump into her face. *This was why*, its face told her. This was why it would never take her coin. The child backed away. Jeremiah kept his distance from the child, edging closer to Alex as the child retreated.

The pull of Jeremiah's spell jerked Alex even closer. She stilled, as though he was testing to see if either would react. Charon only watched. Screaming as she twirled across the floor, raking across the broken stone as Jeremiah drew her closer.

She struggled and fought, trying to find the anger and the emotion to unleash her magic—the magic of those within her—but fearful anticipation consumed them all. With magic failing her, Alex grabbed the largest stone she could manage and threw it with all her strength, cracking Jeremiah's head.

"You've got too much fight in you," he told her, blood spilling from the gash above his right eye. Her body spun into the air and slammed down, smashing the ground in an explosion of sheer white pain that ricocheted through her skull. Her body rose up and slammed down again. Alex cried as blood spilled from her mouth and nose. The third time, her charm jabbed her throat, wedged between her neck and the ground. With only a pop, the charm shattered.

He raised her up, onto her feet again. Dangling her from his spell. Her legs, unwilling to hold her weight, drew skittering semi-circles through her muck. Her vision blurred and her skin grew hot.

He stepped closer, a self-satisfied grin on his face. "Not much fight now."

With a wave of his hand, her ribs cracked, and a wave of vomit filled into her mouth and spilled out in a gurgling flood, turning her inside out.

Her filthy hands deposited wet symbols on his forehead as her fingers twisted into his hair and pulled out tufts.

He slapped her hands away. "When will you learn?"

As she always did, Alex felt for her charm. The broken bobble was jagged and sharp. *It's not that kind of charm.*

Snapping the silver necklace, freeing her charm, she raked the jagged glass across his eyes.

She dropped again, her body crumpling, splashing: his spell broken. Her charm, still in her hand, was opaque white with fine cracks.

Jeremiah, his face a bloody mess, cried to his Books, "Help me, you useless fools!"

Struggling for air, her chest in fiery agony with every breath, her throat blooming in a bruise from her charm, her eyes begged Charon. She crawled towards the child, towards the safety the child afforded her from Jeremiah. She could barely see through her pain, each movement offered an exquisite demonstration of the extent of her injuries. The child offered no sympathy to her plight. It stared at her; its eyes fixed on her charm.

The charm's rough edge cut her fingers as she waggled it in the air at Charon, like teasing a puppy with a treat.

Charon didn't reach for the charm. Its fingers moved in the air as though it willed it closer. Whatever kind of charm it was, it may yet prove useful slitting Jeremiah's throat.

Two Books attended to Jeremiah, who swatted his servant's meddlesome hands from his bloody face, his seething breaths filtered through clenched teeth as he pushed his skin back together and struggled to see.

Charon stood over her. The child's large head looked even more disproportionate from below. She again offered Charon her charm, but however mesmerizing, the child was hesitant to claim it. *Does Charon think I'm trying to trick it?* The jagged and broken edges hid the universe it contained; the burned herbs twisted in glass. The dark center sphere was lost to the opaque white cross-hatched cracks.

The wrecked glass bauble brought Abby to mind. Destroying this piece felt like her final betrayal. Everything Abby did selflessly for her was now in ruins.

The charm's center sphere once belonged to her father. It was all that remained of his coin. When he paid Charon twice for passage, he cheated, stealing this piece. If Charon wouldn't take her coin, perhaps the child would accept his. Was that why it coveted the charm? Did it know Peter cheated it? Perhaps with it, she could pass over, accept Charon's protection just as Matthew had, and disappear into the afterlife.

"You are going to regret that," Jeremiah grunted, his shredded face beginning to mend. Flaps of skin still seating in place.

Taking it in two hands, the charm flexed in her grip; the glass remained together only by interlocking shards that grated free. She looked Charon in the face as she hurriedly tore the charm in two.

The impossibly dark sphere slipped out and she managed to catch it, fearful of what might happen if it slipped to the floor. Might it become contaminated? Disappear? Shatter?

The small black pea rolled in her filthy palm, among soaked symbols that clung to her. It was an impossibly black dot, that like Oblivion, looked more like a hole than an object, a hole right through her palm.

She offered it to the child.

With careful curiosity, the child gingerly plucked the bauble from Alex's palm. It held it to its face as though scoring a diamond.

Its hand closed around the dot and disappeared into its folds of fabric.

"Please. Can I pass now?"

The child looked at her incomprehensibly. *No* was the answer in its confused expression.

Tears spilled from her eyes. Crying never hurt so much. "Please," she begged. "I'm sorry. I didn't mean to hurt you. I...," she looked back to see whether Jeremiah had healed himself or lost his eye or was bearing down on her for the final kill.

Charon opened its palm before her. The bauble was no longer alone, joined by two dully glowing halves of a coin.

She'd seen them before: Her father handed each of these two halves to the child. She remembered watching Charon unsuccessfully attempt to return the coins whole: They kept falling apart.

"My father's?"

Charon nodded. Its fingers deftly drew the coin halves together, trapping the black bauble between them. This time, as the two halves touched, their glow blossomed, the crack sealed, the dark, missing piece became part of the glowing whole.

"Take it," Alex pled. "Take it and take me."

The child made no remark and with movement of its head, leaned closer, its hand open and extended. Alex felt its little panting breath on her face. Had Charon ever offered a coin back before?

Alex didn't dare acknowledge the movement closing in from behind her, anticipating his hand grabbing her shoulder at any moment.

Alex tempted her hand forward, judging Charon's reaction, as the child usually reacted poorly to those who attempted to steal its coins. It thrust its hand, forcing her fingers into contact with Peter's coin.

Charon's hand empty, it stepped back.

Alex crawled forward. "Take me," she begged. "Please."

Charon shook its head somberly. It stepped further from her.

As it backed away, Jeremiah came closer. She closed her eyes, lost, as Charon enfolded itself into a sudden swelling of mist and was gone. She wanted to curl up and cry. To tighten into the smallest ball her body would allow in hopes the universe would swallow her up and she'd disappear forever. But none of that would happen. Jeremiah would assault her. With no strength to fight, he would take his anger out on her, denying her death. Charon was gone and would not return. Not that it mattered; when he was done removing her magic and torturing her body, he'd eat her coin.

She considered the coin in her hand. Her father could have saved himself. He could have used that bauble at any time, but instead, he sacrificed himself a second time so she might have it. Alex finally understood the full scope of her father's sacrifice. Abby told her to never take her charm off: It's not that kind of charm. Her father always wanted her to have the last piece of his soul.

"One last coin to eat," Jeremiah's taunting voice startled fear into her. "Go on then, swallow and regain your strength. It may *crush* you to learn your father's true motive."

Jeremiah had fixed his face, sealed his wounds. The Books huddled around him protectively.

Tears burned her eyes, blurring Jeremiah.

She hurt so, her ribs on fire; every breath stabbed her lungs. Her fingers trembled in pain; her head throbbed. The frightened whispers begged her to find safety. How she hated Jeremiah. How she hated what he had done to her now; before. What he had done to Heather, to Donna, to Betty. To Lydia. To all the women thinking it was their own will that kept them at the Farm. But in truth, she hated Jeremiah most of all for what he'd done—what he threatened to do—to her.

She hadn't the strength for the fight. She'd slam him with bookcases, shatter the walls and upend the floor, and with a wave of his hand, he'd put order to her disorder, and then he'd crush the life out of her.

She wished she hadn't underestimated him when they first met on the fallow farm field. Why did George summon her there, then, that day? Her mother had just turned her coins, giving her magic, but hadn't yet shown her how to turn them back.

Did her father know something? Had he come across something he believed was the key to stopping Jeremiah? Would his memories re-order Billy's and give them a coherence they currently lacked, that might betray some secret she needed for defeating him?

She held it by her lips.

"Do it," he smugly dared her.

She knew wishful thoughts weren't the answer. This coin would not rescue her.

This was the end.

Alexandrea was dying. But death would not be coming for her.

Jeremiah had won.

What if her father had nothing to help her? Why else leave her his coin? It seemed the only solution, but even if she gained such knowledge, would she have the strength to use it?

She drew the coin towards her face as though to swallow it, but instead felt the satisfying snap as it came together with her own.

Alex struggled to her feet. Jeremiah watched in utter confusion as she took a solitary step towards him. She lowered her head, as though signaling her defeat, and with one final glance at him—she hoped she wouldn't look the fool—she used all her strength to leap into the air.

She soared high into the Library. Above the towering bookcases, nearly disappearing into the ceiling's diffuse glow. Jeremiah looked for her everywhere as though he'd lost sight of her.

"You can't hide from me! I'll hunt you down! I'll destroy everything precious to you!"

Alex held her hiding place, hoping to remain obscured from him until her injury-clouded head could think through a plan.

She had one option: Escape.

She wiped at her bloody face. She'd swallowed so much blood, her stomach was queasy.

Her blurry eyes watched the remaining Books congregate at Jeremiah's order. One exploded, the burst of energy fired haphazardly at the ceiling. They fired again, reducing their number to two.

"Come out and meet your fate," Jeremiah ordered. "You have one chance! I will never be this merciful again!"

The labyrinth and the door were too far. That left one route of escape.

"You will be hunted, Alexandrea! You will never rest! You've sealed the fate of everyone who's heard your name!" He screamed; he sounded unhinged. The calm façade he'd so long portrayed scraped away to expose irrational rage.

The two remaining golems fought with each other. Each swiping the others hand to replace their own, fighting to be the one sacrificed to dust. Infuriated, Jeremiah obliterated one himself.

With that distraction, she careened towards the exit. As she disappeared below the heavy keystone, Jeremiah called after her, "How are you doing that?"

She rocketed through the tunnel, bursting like a missile from the hillside cave. If Matthew was right, she was on the Between. From here, she could return to the world, but first she had to be lost to Jeremiah.

She flew past the spiral tower. Even at this height, it appeared taller still, its apex unknowable, even from her altitude. Her curiosity couldn't overcome her desire to be as far from Jeremiah as possible. Even if Matthew was right and the tower contained some tremendous power, she couldn't risk it if Jeremiah were to follow her.

She flew past its shadow and into the sun, the rows of Farm buildings below her. She scanned for the tunnel door to see if Jeremiah emerged.

On the distant hillside, a solitary Book stepped from the tunnel.

She kept watching as the exit receded. No longer able to make out Jeremiah's cries, his fuming rage was evidenced as the last remaining Book disappeared into a vapor of dust.

Alex flew further. Her pain was lessoned only by the satisfaction of her escape. The grip of impending death slowly slipped from her heart. She thought of the one place she wanted to retreat to. There was something unsettling about leaving the Between too close to the Library or the Farm. She flew onward, until she could no longer see the tower, until she could no longer recognize Jeremiah's influence on the landscape. She flipped her coins dark, making her invisible to magic. Now Jeremiah had to see her to know where she was.

Alex heard Jeremiah's distant voice, carried on the air. "Where'd she go? She can't just disappear!" She didn't, however, see him: He did not emerge from the tunnel.

Even at this distance, his frustration shook the air.

All she had left to do was pass through the mist and disappear.

Chapter One Hundred and Forty-Five

Alex collapsed face-first onto the dirt driveway, the grit and the pebbles indenting her cheek. She lay at the crest of the hill, beside the corn fields. Further along this driveway, down the hill and around the bend, past the remains of a barn, a simple white trailer awaited her.

Abby wouldn't be home, which was probably for the best. Alex was in no condition to hear her petition. She would open the door, collapse, as Quest and Marty, Abby's cats, walked on her. She'd rest. Recuperate. Clean herself up. She had clothes here. Instead, she just lay face down in the dirt, pain consuming her like a hungry carnivore. Relief at her escape couldn't compete with her agony, and although her sobs caused her cracked and broken ribs to squeal in pain, she cried.

How could I have been so dumb? Save Heather? Jeremiah is too powerful. He's, he's—she remembered her mother's words—*the dark heart at the center of the universe.*

She cursed her own hubris. She feared a grand misstep, giving away Matthew's coin. Each success made her more vulnerable to failure as she wrongly believed each success brought her closer to another. She saw now the inevitable end was a dark one. Charon would not have her. Did that mean she couldn't die? Had she not escaped, would Jeremiah have squeezed her until she resembled wrung-out toothpaste?

She believed she deserved her pain, a proper punishment for her overreach. Until her agony abated, she was incapable of reaching the trailer. The scorching late morning sun wouldn't take long before blistering the back of her neck and the side of her face. How long did she have until Jeremiah started his hunt? If he couldn't find her, would he start with those she loved? She concentrated, feeling the wet twists as ribs reknit. She yelped at the pain of healing; it was nearly as severe as the injurious moment.

The grinding crunch of the gravel driveway announced someone's approach. The car engine groaned from being driven too slowly. Braking hard, the car skid in the dirt; rubble washing over Alex like a rain of grit and dust.

She sobbed with relief. For Abby's comfort, she'd offer her anything. Even ask her to be her Familiar again.

A car door opened. Footsteps crunched on the driveway, a hurried worry in the step. A hand gently pressed her shoulder and warm breath washed across her face, carrying a woman's voice, "Where are you hurt?"

Alex's lungs were too tender to suffer speech.

"Did you say something?"

She tried again, "Ab-by."

"You're looking for Abby?" The woman made sounds like she was suffering pain just from looking at Alex. "What happened to you? Were you assaulted? Are they gone?"

With a groan punctuated by a pained squeal, Alex looked at this stranger. "I'm trying to get to…," she had to hesitate, the effort making her lightheaded. "Trailer."

"Alexandrea?"

Alex didn't recognize the woman looking down at her.

"Alexandrea Hawthorne?"

Alex nodded.

"Holy shit. I never thought I'd see you again. Did you escape?"

Alex was hurt but not too hurt to question why this woman knew where she'd come from. "What'd you say?"

"Your parents," the woman clarified. "What happened to your parents?"

"Dead. Both," the relief that this woman wasn't Jeremiah's agent— as unlikely as that seemed—washed over her.

"You killed them to get away? Holy shit. I'll call an ambulance."

The moment the woman pulled her phone from her pocket and stabbed at it with her finger, Alex recognized her. "Charissa, please, no."

Charissa's hair was short, shaved on the left temple. She lowered her phone, knelt, and rested her hands on Alex's back. "Right. Killed your parents. No ambulance."

"Thanks," Alex mouthed.

"I don't think Abby is home. I didn't see her truck." Charissa thought a moment. "I can't leave you here. Let's get you to Abby's. I'll help you up. Are you badly hurt? Is anything going to spill or pop out of you if I try to move you?"

Alex's laugh degraded into a choking groan. "No," she grunted.

"Good," Charissa exclaimed. "I have a really hard time with injuries. Post-traumatic stress, my therapist says, from that day your parents kidnapped you.

Charissa slipped her hands around Alex's shoulders and under her arms. "You've got to help me." Charissa pulled and tugged, and while Alex didn't believe she had any strength, she soon had her feet under herself. "Come on, five steps," when they were close, Charissa opened the passenger door and helped Alex slide into the seat, the vent blowing refreshing cool air. The inside of the car stunk of cigarettes. Charissa smelled her hands. "Is that vomit? Ugh, my car's gonna reek."

Charissa came around and drove to Abby's trailer.

"You sure you want to go to the trailer? You're welcome to come to our house. Dad'll be happy to see you. He'll want to hear all about how you escaped. Are you sure they're dead and not looking for you? I could take better care of you there."

It sounded nice. Charissa was her cousin on Holly's side, the same as Rose was her cousin on Peter's side. She'd be with family. Charissa was clearly misinformed. The only thing Alex wanted was to feel caring hands. However, going to their house endangered them. Abby's trailer was small and remote and if Jeremiah showed up, all she needed to worry about was the cats escaping. Sitting up made it easier to breathe. "Thanks but no," Alex wheezed. "Abby's is best."

"Okay," Charissa said. Alex tried to concentrate, to heal her wounds. Charissa added, "You know, I'm so glad you're here. I mean, I wish you weren't so fucked up. The last time I saw you I got so sick and had a real shit-show nightmare. I thought I watched you die. I thought I was dead." She took a breath to slow herself down. "My therapist says I created a fantasy to explain away your parent's cruelty. When they kidnapped you." She took another breath. "I know this happened to *you*, but it was *really traumatic* for me. I don't actually remember anything until Abby comes and takes me home and my dad tells me about how your mom and dad kidnapped you and I was lucky to be alive...." She looked at Alex. "Did you fall asleep?"

Alex shook her head.

"Okay, we're here," Charissa stopped the car and unlocked the doors. "Let me help you out."

Charissa came around and pulled Alex's arm over her shoulder. Together they walked to the door.

Charissa spoke slowly, "Do you have a key? Alexandrea, you're just staring at it." She pushed and the door eased open. "I guess it was unlocked."

Alex looked up, surprised to see the door open.

Charissa helped her up the step and into the trailer.

One of Abby's cats slept on the couch, curled up in a claw-tattered blanket. That was Marty, she realized, when Quest, her tail curled like a question, rubbed against her leg.

"What a mess. Was Abby always such a slob? Gross."

Alex couldn't disagree. Charissa pushed piles of crumpled and damp newspaper aside and eased Alex to the couch beside Marty. Dirty pots remained where they were placed after cooking, unscraped plates sat in and around the sink. Cartons and packaging curled on counters and scattered about the floor with the random pile of hard vomited hairball and roaming tumbleweed of fur. A pile of dry cat food spilled from the bowl, as Abby had overfilled it, perhaps in expectation of not being back for a few days.

"What happened to Abby?" Charisa asked. "First the barn, now this. My father was always worried about those gas tanks." She surveyed the disaster. "He's going to flip out, but I've got to tell him what this looks like."

What happened to Abby? Alex knew, of course. She was no longer a Familiar. Her desire, her addiction to serve Alex broken, she was like a junkie in the throes of withdrawal. Alex worried that this was more than headaches and shakes and sweats. She worried that this was the real Abby, suddenly freed after nearly two decades. Alex wanted to say something to Charissa in Abby's defense, but the explanation had too many rabbit holes. She collapsed into the couch.

Charissa finished her disappointed survey of Abby's mess and turned to Alex. "Look at you. You're a mess. Come on, cousin. I'm not going to leave you like this. We need to get you changed and showered and…," she trailed off, plucking something off Alex's shirt. "What is this?"

Alex looked at the tiny dark symbol dangling from Charissa's fingertips. Wet and limp, it trembled with Charissa's disgust.

"And there's another. And another. Oh wow, you're covered in them." She made a face, "They're probably all over my car."

They *were* Books. They *were* women. When Jeremiah squeezed them out of her, what had they become? Were they dead? Forever ruined? The ultimate insult to a life spent in servitude? Alex wept for them.

"I'm sorry. I didn't mean to bring up something. If it's too painful for you. We can just get you cleaned up and you don't ever have to talk about it. I'm sorry, Alexandrea."

Alex looked up from her tears. Charissa didn't know, did she? Perhaps it was time. "Charissa, those are parts of magic spells."

Charissa's growing confusion altered her expression. With a count of three and a calming breath, Charissa said, "I said you don't have to tell me."

"You know the stories, like the Salem Witch Trials or the Inquisition; men burned and tortured women who they thought were witches."

"Your parents did a mess on you. I don't know how else to help you see reality. You should see my therapist. But, okay, tell me. Yes, of course I know."

Alex dismissed Charissa's subtle mockery. "It wasn't like the history books tell us. They didn't kill the women just because they were witches. They killed them by beating the magic out of them. They put it into Books. Spellbooks, so that men could have magic."

Charissa was not even trying to look serious. "I'm sure they did. Magic books. Right."

"That day you were at my house and those men came? That wasn't a dream. My parents didn't kidnap me. They died protecting me. Those men came because I can take the magic back. Only it isn't actually magic, it's the women. The two are never separated. I take her in and then I have her magic."

"There's someone else in there? Is that what you're saying? You're not Alexandrea Hawthorne now? You're someone else? An old witch from Massachusetts?" Charissa looked pityingly on Alex. "Did you become someone else to let Alex hide from the real pain? Where's Alexandrea? I want to speak to her."

"Listen to me, Charissa. I am a witch."

"Where's your broom?"

Alex would get no further without showing Charissa, but she'd have to flip her coins, and that was too dangerous. If she could, she'd step outside and fly, but she was in no shape to walk, much less crash land again.

She closed her eyes.

"I'm sorry, Alexandrea, I didn't mean to make fun of you. You're delirious. I don't know what you've been through and," she squeaked, "what's that thing on your chest?"

Alex held it forward, a perfectly black disk that looked more like a hole in her hand than an object resting upon it. "It's my coin," she explained. "It's dark because that allows me to hide when they're looking for me. It also makes it impossible for me to do any magic."

Charissa asked, "So that takes your magic away?"

Alex plucked Charissa's coin from her chest, holding it before her, the silver thread sparkling and dancing. "You have one, too. This is what they normally look like."

Charissa gently reclaimed it from Alex. Awe washed her face. "How long have I had this?"

"All your life. You've never had the need to summon it. Most people go through life without ever knowing."

Charissa asked, "What's it for?"

"For dreaming. While your body sleeps, your spirit walks with it. That thread connects them. When you die, Charon comes. That's the coin you pay to cross over. That's probably when most people discover they have one."

"Get out of dodge," Charissa exclaimed. "You almost had me going there. How'd you do this? Where'd you get it? I bet you stuck it to me when we were walking from the car." She dangled her coin by its thread, swinging it like a yoyo.

Maybe it was best that Charissa remained ignorant. She thought about Rose and how the past weeks damaged her. What would the truth do to Charissa? She was almost willing to give up convincing Charissa, except it was that same ignorance that allowed men like Matthew and Jeremiah the freedom to operate in the world. No one believed what they could do unless they were shown. Or unless they were men, granted power, and allowed to operate without consequence. Their actions couldn't be condemned if no one believed. "Remember the last time you saw me, when I disappeared?"

Charissa grinned maniacally. "I was waiting for you to go there. That was probably an allergic reaction to whatever your mom fed me or mold growing in that house. If I hadn't gotten sick, she probably would have kidnapped me too. At least that's what my dad thinks."

Alex nodded. "Just keep telling yourself that."

Charissa's phone binged. She pulled it from her pocket with Pavlovian hunger. She jabbed the screen, typed a few words. She looked up from her phone as it clicked away. "Mom saw me pull in and wants to know what's taking so long. I'm telling her I found you and you're here."

Before Charissa could replace her phone in her pocket, it bleated again. With a sigh, she repeated the process. "Yes, *my cousin*, Alexandrea," she auto-dictated. For commentary, she added, "Because I know so many Alexandrea's." She looked back at her phone. "At Abby's. She's been assaulted. I'm going to help her get cleaned up."

This time, Charissa cursed, "What the fuck, Mom?" The phone beeped before she even had it halfway to her pocket. She read the message her mother sent and repeated, "What the fuck, Mom?" She looked at Alex. "She's telling me to get home right now." Charissa lowered the phone. "You escaped, right? They're definitely dead? Your parents didn't follow you here?"

Alex wanted to tell her that going back to her house wasn't a bad idea when she tapped into her phone, "I'm not leaving her, Mom. What's the big deal?"

This time she held the phone out, waiting for the reply. "What? What's that supposed to mean?"

"What did she say?"

Charissa read, "Turn on the TV. Look at the news. Then come right home."

Charissa shrugged and headed to the television. "I muted my alerts yesterday. My phone was blowing up. Sheesh, news. Who cares? They hit New York again. I can't even. Don't wanna know. Another nine-eleven? Fucking terrorists. Why can't they leave us alone?" She clicked Abby's television and watched.

They heard the reporter speaking as the picture resolved. "I know it appears to be the same woman in both videos, but experts analyzing every pixel of both videos undeniably and unequivocally claim this is a hoax. A fake. New York and Paris both suffered simultaneous, coordinated terrorist attacks yesterday and a yet unnamed hacker collective manipulated the videos in real time to look like a movie. It's gone viral, but there's nothing to fear. There is no magical flying girl. It's just a movie, folks; special effects."

Charissa gaped, the picture clear. Alex could see, too; buildings collapsed and people screaming, and there was tiny Alexandrea Hawthorne, lightning shooting from her fingers as the road heaved up around her.

"What have you gotten yourself involved in, Alexandrea?" Charissa couldn't take her eyes off the screen. She turned the channel to more of the same. Then again. And again. Alex was on every channel. Charissa backed into the counter, as though needing support to stand.

Alex watched as the news cycled through multiple videos and dozens of angles to demonstrate the tenacity of the hackers. It was just as Matthew warned. The explanations were ridiculous. Multiple simultaneous phone hacks over free public Wi-Fi, using the same VR technology as those games that put creatures in the frame of the camera: they imprinted this girl over the live video people took of actual terrorist attacks to obscure the identity of true terrorists. What people believed they saw existed on their phone. Had they only watched with their eyes! Trauma and dangerous toxic chemicals in the air left them confused and delirious. The terrorists' trick was successful. How many more attacks like this might happen before the terrorists were brought to justice? For the first time, Alex believed magic was the simpler explanation.

At the part in the video where Alex burst into flames, Charissa shrieked and slammed the power button, silencing the television. Visibly shaken, Charissa's hands trembled, tears welling in her eyes.

"They got *New York and Paris*. Holy shit." Charissa pulled out her phone, she clicked open her camera and used it to scan the trailer. "My phone's not hacked. There's no magic Alexandrea here." She looked up. "Just the normal you." She stuffed her phone in her pocket. "Wow. They got New York *and* Paris yesterday." She looked at Alex. "Does this have to do with your parents? Are they involved with the terrorists? Are they the terrorists? Are you a terrorist?" Charissa gasped. "Shit. I'm harboring a terrorist!"

Alex rubbed her head. "Dammit, Charissa. Think. What is the likelihood that actually happened? You heard them; thousands of phones hacked at the same time to make it look like I used magic to destroy the city? I told you. I have magic. I was trying to save people. That is real. Look at me. What you see on the television really happened."

Charissa's tone changed. "That's not funny, Alex. Look at what you're messed up in. They convinced you it was real. That's some serious trauma to put a person through to get them to believe they can shoot lightning and burst into flames."

Charissa leapt into the air at the sound of staccato banging on the trailer door. "Charissa, you in there?"

"Mom, fuck, you scared the shit out of me," Charissa pulled the door open.

Alex didn't know if she'd ever met the woman who entered the trailer. Short and stout, brown hair cropped straight across her forehead at the eyebrows. She came in and glanced disappointedly around the trailer. She stared right at Alex as though afraid if she got too close, she'd suffer a bite that would require stitches and shots.

"You look like shit, Alexandrea," the woman said stiffly. "Abby will be relieved to know you came here. I'm still on the fence."

"Hi Aunt Pat," Alex greeted cheerfully. "It's time you told your daughter the truth."

Pat's mouth drew to a fine line across her face, her eyes squinting with displeasure. "We had to keep her safe after what happened to you."

"None of you are safe anymore." She stroked Marty on his blanket beside her. "Cat's out of the bag, Pat, and it's only a matter of time before Jeremiah figures out where I'm hiding."

"I know," Pat said bleakly. "That's why you need to get out of here, as soon as possible."

"Mom," Charissa protested. "Look at her. She's hurt. What did her parents do to her—"

"It's all true, Charry. I wasn't even in the trailer and I can tell you whatever Alexandrea had to say is true. Every word."

"But the...," Charissa pointed at the television. "What about?"

"All bullshit." Pat shook her head. "Come back to the house. Your father will confirm everything." She nodded at the trailer. "It's why Abby lives here. She's Alexandrea's Familiar. You know that word, like an imp or something. She serves Alexandrea."

"Not anymore," Alex said.

Pat gasped, "What happened to sweet Abby?"

Alex replied, "I released her from her oath. She's not my Familiar anymore."

"You can do that?" Pat rubbed her temple. "I thought that was for life."

"I don't think Abby's taking it well." She groaned as she repositioned herself on the couch.

"You were her everything. What's she got if she's not serving you?" Charissa asked, "Mom? What are you talking about?"

Alex ignored her. "I thought she'd be happy to be free."

"Of course, she *should* be happy," Pat laughed bitterly. "No one wants to live a life of servitude, but that was the choice Abby made. She knew what Peter was asking."

"Mom, you're freaking me out." Charissa breathed dramatically.

Pat told Charissa, "Let's get back to the house. We're not safe out here."

"You were serious, though? It's real? Magic?" Charissa waivered, her arms flailing.

Pat started out the door. She paused to nod. "All of it."

"Shit." Charissa started to the door. "You coming, Alexandrea?"

"No," Pat blurted. "She stays here." She asked Alex, "You look pretty banged up. Do you need a doctor or something?" Alex shook her head. "Clean yourself up. You need clothes?" Alex shook her head again. "When we're done getting Charry up to speed, the three of us'll come back here to discuss next steps."

Alex nodded. "'kay."

"Come-on Charry," Pat ordered.

Charissa paused at the door and stared back at Alex. She wiggled her fingers. "Can you do something? Show me a little magic?"

Before Alex could reply, *No*, Pat shouted, "Now, Charry!"

Chapter One Hundred and Forty-Six

Alex wasn't sure what to do with her dirty clothes. Her father's jacket, once her armor, was abraded and caked with grit and dust. Her "I♥NY" t-shirt was ruined. Bile and blood stained them both, twisted, jangly symbols dangled wherever she looked, caught on fibers inside and out. Could the symbols be reclaimed? Washing them down the drain felt the epitome of disrespect. She placed the jacket on a section of counter she cleared with her arm, shoving everything into a pile.

After picking her clothes clean, she took them off. She winced at the sight of her body. It looked like a map, the topography made from shades of bruising from yellow to dark purple complete with hardened, swollen lumps.

In the bright bathroom light, she attempted to find every last symbol clinging to her. She unknotted them from her hair, discovering them in her creases and cervices. She collected a surprisingly significant pile. As though when she threw them up, they chose to cling to her. She filled the sink with hot water and soap and drowned the jacket in an attempt to save it. Then, she shook out the jacket and hung it reverentially.

She took a shower, careful to pull any symbols that washed from her before they spun down the drain. Once clean and mostly dry, she went into the bedroom and fished some clothes from the drawers and dressed. Her ribcage was a motley of purple and brown, yellow-outlined bruises. She lay on the bed, wanting desperately to doze off, to fall into a week-long, dreamless slumber. But something nagged at her. She rolled to the end of the bed and pushed herself upright; sitting up was still too painful.

In the bathroom, the leather jacket waited on a hanger for her. It was still, formed, as though the previous wearer—her father—had vanished from within it. Although still damp, she slipped her arms into it, feeling the wet leathery embrace through her shirt. With it on, she felt secure, as though it possessed some property that could keep her safe. The holes, burned by magic, suggested that sense of security was false, but Alex didn't care.

Claiming the symbols from the bathroom, she wandered into the kitchen where she discovered Marty and Quest playfully clawing at her clothes, pulling and nibbling on the symbols. She shooed the cats and examined them. Aside from some ragged edges, the cats had done no harm that she could tell, assuming they hadn't swallowed any. *That'll make for a crazy hairball.*

"What do I do with these?" She picked one shape from her collection and examined it. It looked like nothing she'd seen before. A piece of ink, textured from a page, and yet there was an iridescence about it, a shimmering depth. The more she stared, the deeper the rainbow seemed to go.

The first time she read a Book—Sara—the experience was so novel she had no expectation, no anticipation. Each moment was an exploration of what possibility would come next. She saw in each symbol the same depths she saw now. It felt—while she stood there holding Sara's Book—like she grew small enough to fit into that one shape and discover within that dark illegible scrawl on the yellow page an entire other Book. And on, and on, through seemingly endless Books until arriving at the final letters; the true symbols. Perhaps she was so uncomprehendingly microscopic within that symbol within those symbols on that page, that the pressures of her energy compressing into so finite a space, she burst into flames and consumed them all.

She wondered if the essence of the woman and all her magic could fit into a single symbol. If that were true, then why were there so many in each Book? It was as though to be a Book the symbols were multiplied to forge individual spells. Each spell was the woman. This meant the Books weren't what she had been told—they weren't perfect representations of magic—they were the diminution of the woman to make her comprehensible to the reader.

Examining the jiggly little shape that was curling and cracking as it dried on her fingertip, she wondered if it was the first or the last of those symbols. Was this the shape that launched the journey or the one concluding it? Did she need all the others, or did this individual contain multitudes? Were these the original symbols from each Book or were these her own—a recombination of all those she contained?

She peered closely, seeing past the flaking ink surface and into the colorful refractions. Deeper within that tiny shape on her fingertip, she saw there were others and in that exhilarating discovery, she fell down her own rabbit-hole, her whole self, slipping into a design on her own fingertip. Here she was, here they were, a woman she'd known before, women she'd known before, a woman she'd met before and befriended before and saved before. And here she was, they were, waiting patiently—almost in a death-sleep—for Alex to return and save her, save them, again. *I'm so sorry. I won't ever let you go again.*

Everywhere she looked, she saw more symbols, on her clothes, lost across the counter, and she went to each of them, reclaiming all she saw, bringing those lost women home. Realizing too late that her hands had become flames.

"Alex! Holy crap, Dad, do something! Don't let her die in there!"

She scoured the entirety of the trailer, seeking symbols that might have been lost until she was certain she had claimed them all.

The trailer door banged open and the flames, fed oxygen, erupted. Marty and Quest raced out and Pat corralled them, holding their squirming, furry bodies as Steven fought the heat to check if Alex was even still alive.

Her flames, finding copious fuel piled close by, snatched the wrappers and the boxes and the pan of bacon grease, then the drapes and the cabinets, before instantly filling the trailer.

Alex tried to save the trailer by making for the exit, her heat driving Steven back. Spreading away from her body, her flames consumed indiscriminately; the trailer burned. She was a ball of fire birthed from the trailer, flame like fingers holding the doorframe as she stepped into sunlight and Charissa shrieked at the sight of her.

Her flames snatched out, leaving her untouched, her hair settling its dance as the hot air left it to come to rest on her jacketed shoulders. Heat radiated behind her. As fire consumed Abby's home, guilt consumed Alex. She truly had taken everything from Abby now. Even once she realized what was happening, it was too late to stop it. There was too much fuel, as though Abby anticipated Alex's arrival and set out kindling.

The residual pain of her injuries felt like an echo following the flames. They were more her body's recollection of it than the pain itself. *It's like eating a coin each time, only I'm not taking their memories, I'm taking them.*

"Y-y-you're okay?" Charissa wiped her panicked tears. Her blanched face regained color, realizing she wasn't going to see an immolated corpse this day. Alex nodded. "How? I mean, I know how, but how?"

With a theatrical-grade sigh of relief, Steven pulled Alex into a bear hug. "I haven't seen you in ages, kiddo. I mean, we saw you at a distance, running, a week or so ago, but you were a kid last time I saw you up close and held you."

Alex blushed. "I'm sorry. I don't remember." She looked at Pat. "Either of you."

Steven shrugged. "Come on back to the house. We'll let this sucker burn. No sense letting the fire brigade come and risk someone seeing you." As though on cue, the roof buckled in and with a ball of sparks and the groaning of plywood and plastic and shattering glass, the trailer collapsed into itself.

They watched the pile of scrap burn for another minute. Further collapse stifled the fire. Alex felt miserable. She didn't care about the clothes she had lost; everything Abby had left was in there.

Alex took Marty from Pat and they started for the house. Pat stared at her. "Is it possible you look better now?"

"Yeah, the fire heals me." Alex started off unsure if the word fit the man as she said, "Uncle Steven, you should know you're all in horrible danger."

Steven stopped and looked at Alex. "You're here. I assumed as such." When he saw that she took it as an insult, he backpedaled, "What I mean is why else would you be here if you didn't need help." She relaxed. "I don't care what it is. I don't need to know. All I need is to be told what my niece needs me to do."

Pat took Alex's arm, "Do we have time for dinner?"

Would the few minutes it took to eat make the difference of life and death at this point? Alex nodded, "I'm starving."

As they walked, Charissa said, "You were on fire. That was really fire?"

Alex wasn't sure if Charissa was asking or telling.

"What did it feel like? Did it burn your skin? Did it hurt? I bet it didn't even feel hot to you!"

Alex rubbed Marty's head as he clung to her, his claws fearfully extended through her shirt and into her skin. Alex replied, "It's not like I'm on fire. My skin isn't burning. I *am* the fire. I'm transformed into it." *That may not be the most accurate explanation, but it's the best I can describe with words.*

"I can't believe you're really a witch." Charissa's tone changed. "I can't believe my parents never told me. You guys lied to me all these years."

Steven replied, but not to Charissa, "Like I was saying, my sister—Holly—your mom—and I realized it would be safer for all parties if we kept our distance. Peter came back from that thing he did and he was, well, you know. We came by now and again. Once you were old enough, we thought it might be good if you cousins got to know one another, even if you never knew the truth."

Charissa laughed. "I wish I had known. I thought you were so strange and cool. You didn't go to school and your mom left you alone at home all day to do whatever you wanted. I used to tell all my school friends about you and most of them wouldn't believe me."

Alex laughed. She remembered Charissa and her phone and all the photos of her friends. She would never have believed that her life interested anyone. "Imagine what they'd think now."

Charissa cackled.

Pat said, "I called Heather and let her know you were safe. I hope you don't mind."

"You spoke to her? She's okay?"

"Heather? Yes. Relieved, mostly. After the news, she feared the worst." Pat fell silent. "We always knew this about you, Alexandrea."

"Alex," she corrected.

Pat smiled. "Alex. We always knew you were a witch. What that meant, well, that's something entirely different. It was always a word that didn't mean much; until recently."

Charissa stopped. "You knew *before* then?" She waited for an answer that never came. "Why did you tell me her parents kidnapped her? You told me—"

"That day was the last time I used a Book to cast a spell," Steven interrupted. He looked at his daughter with pity. "After what you had seen. I had to do something."

"You…." Charissa struggled to find the words. "Used magic to make me forget the truth?"

Pat attempted to hug her daughter, who squeezed away. "Your father used magic to make you better. You don't remember, Charry, but you saw horrific things. Things no child should ever have to see. We didn't know what else to do."

"I'm sorry," Steven said. "I knew one day you'd find out and you'd never forgive me."

Before Charissa could speak, Alex embraced her. "It's okay, Charissa. Your parents did what they did because they love you and were protecting you. I know you want to hate them right now, but you've got to see past that. There isn't time."

When Alex released Charissa, she looked at her parents. "It's okay," she soothed. "I know you did what you believed was best for me. At least you told me the truth when it mattered."

Steven and Pat looked at Alex, their question screaming silently through their expression. Alex merely nodded.

"How about it Alex?" Charissa sang as she bounded up the walk, "Show me some magic."

"I can't," Alex confessed. She touched her chest. "Remember the black coin? As long as I keep it dark, they can't find me. I also can't do any magic."

"You were on fire! How's that not magic?"

"I don't know what that is. It's something that happens whenever I touch…," Alex wasn't sure how to quickly explain a Book, "symbols like the ones you saw."

Charissa groaned, "Bummer! You're so lame!"

"Charry," Pat chided her daughter. "You saw the video. You saw what those men were doing. If they even thought Alex were here, well, it's too horrible to even consider."

Alex looked at her feet, "I'm sorry I'm putting you in danger."

Steven grabbed Alex's shoulder with a reassuring squeeze. "Nonsense. Your mom and I always knew that one day you'd call on me for help of some sort. To be fair, I always hoped you'd come asking for money." He paused. Alex guessed he meant it as a joke and smiled. "You're here now. Let's get you fed and back with your Aunt Heather." He turned to Pat, "What's that Heather told you?"

"She has magic. All the women do," Pat confirmed.

He looked at his wife and daughter. "I guess it's only a matter of time before that'll include the two of you." He rubbed his eyes. "To think I'll be watching my wife and daughter go to off to war."

Alex wasn't sure she liked where this was going. "They don't have to—"

"Nonsense," Steven chided. "Your parents didn't make their sacrifices for you. They made them for everyone. Don't think I won't let my ladies be part of your glory."

"What about you, Daddy?" Charissa asked.

Steven shook his head. "Men don't have magic, not naturally. They read it out of Books, but that's exactly what you're fighting against. It's wrong. I'd be happy to join the fight, but I swore I wouldn't read another Book after what I had to do to you. I don't think I should—"

Alex interrupted. "If magic has taught me anything it's that fighting for a cause is messy. What matters is the cause you're defending. The goal is to never have any Books left to read. Until we return magic, we must use it however we can." She looked at her uncle. "You'll pick up a Book and you'll cast spells if only to put an end to people doing that." It made her a little sick to already be talking about facing Jeremiah again. But she knew the truth: her opportunity to remain hidden was short. If she didn't take the fight back to him, he'd take it to everyone she loved.

Steven stared at her introspectively. Finally, he smirked, "Yes sir."

Charissa asked, "When do I get a Book?"

Pat groaned. "Soon enough. Don't rush it, Charry. Once you do it, you can't undo it."

Charissa was excited. She opened the side porch door and held it for everyone.

"Whatever you did to Charry back there," Steven whispered with a wink to Alex, "was a wee bit strong."

"Let's get you fed, Alex," Pat said. "Then when you're ready, we'll all drive over to Heather's."

Chapter One Hundred and Forty-Seven

fter dinner, they climbed into Steven's extended cab pickup. It was an older, beat-up maroon truck. Mud and dirt caked the long bed while rusting holes gaped along the sides. Inside, the truck had remarkably clean cloth seats. Alex sat in the back, behind Pat, beside Charissa.

Dinner had been pleasant. After initial awkwardness, Steven spoke mostly about Holly and their childhood. Alex was still putting the pieces together in the truck. Billy met Peter. Then Billy met Steven. Steven introduced Holly to Peter; he was friendly with Peter through their relationship with Matthew. It was all chicken and egg to Alex. She wasn't sure what came first, Billy connecting the friendships that built her parents' relationship or his knowing them that way from his childhood. Did he put them together because he knew that's what happened or did he make it happen?

News of Matthew's death shocked Steven but left him not entirely heartbroken. "I didn't think the old crap-bag capable of dying. Good riddance," he had said. Alex thought people only spoke like that on television and in books.

Steven explained that when Peter came to him with the plan, he was skeptical that it was possible. "I mean Peter had access to the same information as me," he said. "But Peter didn't just have information. He had William." Steven went on to say however distrustful he was of William's motives, the young man always came through on every promise. "I don't know who he was, but nothing Peter accomplished was possible without him."

Alex wasn't sure if there'd ever be a better time to explain who William really was. "Have you met my Aunt Heather's kids?"

Steven looked at Pat, as though waiting for her to tell him it was okay to answer. "No," Pat replied for them both. "We only met Heather a few times, and only before you were born." She wrung her hands in her lap. "Holly was very cautious to keep everyone apart. It might have seemed like paranoia, but she kept everyone distant and apart for our own safety. It's hard to find yourself pushed away from family and not resent it."

Steven nodded. "Heather seemed like a great girl. I'm sure she has great kids."

Alex nodded, running her hands along the tablecloth. Dinner felt formal with linens instead of placemats and paper napkins. "She had two kids, twins of course; Rosemary, who you'll meet tonight. Her son's name was Billy."

Again, Steven looked to Pat. He mouthed something, and she shrugged. Turning to Alex, Pat said, "It sounds like we won't be meeting Billy tonight."

Alex shook her head. It was still so recent; just thinking about him brought tears to her eyes. She wished there had been some way to save him. "No. He died, just a day or two ago."

"Oh, crap, I'm so sorry," Steven blurted out. "Too young, too young."

"About that," Alex explained. "He had a different relationship with time than you and me."

No one said anything. Steven had exposure to magic. He understood that not all things were simple, cut, and dry.

"We—Rose, Billy, and me—were out on a hike in June and Billy flung himself off this rock in the state park. Picnic Rock."

"I know it," Steven said. He turned to Pat, "Remember that big stone I told you about? Matthew took me there once. It's where he told me about the Library and Books and magic."

Pat nodded.

Matthew took him *to Picnic Rock?* She couldn't recall anything that Billy knew that made Picnic Rock special. Was there something about Picnic Rock that she'd know if she ate Matthew's coin? Alex continued, "Well, a week later he did it again, only this time he was saving me from Matthew."

Pat nodded, "That's some coincidence."

"No," Alex said flatly, "it's not. For Billy, it was the same. Billy leapt once."

Pat looked chilled. "How is that possible?"

"Time is… really confusing," Alex mused how jumbled Billy's memories still were. They were connected weakly at odd angles and points like a knot of branches. "He disappeared. Heather never saw him again."

Pat's hand covered her mouth. "I never heard. My heart goes out to Heather. To lose a child so young."

Alex wobbled her head back and forth, visually saying *Sort of*. "For us it was a month ago. For Billy, it was almost twelve years before I saw him again, just the other day. Right before he…, before Matthew murdered him."

Pat lowered her glass, nearly choking on her seltzer. "Did you say twelve years? Murder?" She looked at Steven.

"Hear her out," Steven said. "Go on, Alex."

"Like I said, he had a different relationship with time. He moved through it. To him, things that hadn't happened yet could be like half-forgotten memories." She held out her arms, pointing left then right, as she said, "The past," and then, "the future." She received nodding confirmation from all three that they followed. "To him, the direction, whether I go this way or that way, it's the same. A little this way," she got up from her chair and walked to the doorway to the kitchen, following her left hand, the past. "Now I'm here. To you, I've traveled a little way into the past. To me, to Billy, where I am, is always *now*."

Steven squinted in thought, scratching at his head. "How far into the past and the future did he travel?"

"The future? He never made it past this week. He died two days ago."

"And the past?"

Alex answered with silence.

Steven understood the connection that led to this conversation. "Billy was William?"

Alex nodded.

Steven looked at Pat, his face twisted in concern. "What did we do?" He turned to Alex. "William helped your father," he pointed at her, nearly flicking his finger, "do the thing to your mother. To make you, ya know, not a twin." He looked at his hands, as though they'd held the tool responsible.

"Is that why I'm an only child?" Until now Charissa had been respectfully silent.

"Naw," Steven unsuccessfully tried to chuckle. "When you came out you were so perfect we didn't dare try again. No sense screwing with fate."

Charissa made an angelic face with her hands under her chin. Alex was sure she'd been doing that her whole life.

"He helped my dad figure it all out," Alex offered. "He helped Matthew find out who the witch was whose Book they needed."

Steven nodded. "That old foundation in the woods. Matthew showed me. He said he should have known it was special, being so close to Picnic Rock, but before he made the connection it had already been explained to him."

For the first time Alex regretted handing Matthew's coin to Charon. "What was the connection?"

Steven shrugged. "If I had to guess, I'd say it's something about that valley. It's a magic place."

Alex stared at him. "How's that?"

Steven looked at Pat, who said, "Why do you keep looking at me like I know?"

Steven shrugged. "I don't know. I got the impression when we were standing atop Picnic Rock, looking out over that valley and seeing how it stretched for miles." He grinned, "You know, I read some time ago that back in the days before the dinosaurs, the Appalachian Mountains were the flat seafloor. By the time the dinosaurs came around, they were like the Rocky Mountains, only bigger. Time ground them down and that rounded the peaks and filled in the valleys. That means that valley was filled in and then excavated when a river flowing through it cut it wider and deeper, like the Grand Canyon but a whole lot less majestic."

Pat tapped on the table to get his attention. "What are you talking about and what the hell does it have to do with anything we're talking about?"

Steven's hands rose defensively. "She was askin' about Picnic Rock and that. I was just fillin' in details."

Pat rolled her eyes. "Now I know why you keep checking with me."

Steven explained, "I'm trying to make a point."

Pat smiled politely at Alex but didn't reply to Steven's statement. Her pinched expression made it clear she would have, had there not been a guest present.

Steven continued, "What I'm trying to say is that place is special. Everything you see out there was something else once. Mountains that were ocean bottom, valleys that were mountain peaks. That sort of thing."

After they finished eating, Charissa and Pat cleaned up. They refused Alex's help, and Steven disappeared downstairs. Almost ten minutes later, Steven stomped up the basement stairs, cobwebs in his hair and sticking to his back, and he placed a bundle down on the table. Peeling back the yellowed handkerchief, Steven revealed his Book.

It was smaller than Peter's Book, both in size and thickness. It looked old, the leather cover dry and flaking. Unlike some of the other Books she'd seen, this was ordinary, lacking the traditional embellishments that proclaimed the secrets it held were special.

"Alex, do you want to inspect it?"

Alex shook her head. "I don't think that's a good idea." Her fingers pantomimed an explosion. Alex was sure she was about to overstay her welcome. "You should give it to Pat or Charissa."

Steven's face drew long and serious. "I know what you said, how women read from them now. All my life women were forbidden, like it would harm them. It feels like I'm endangering them. You know? Like the first person who ate a tomato. People thought they were poisonous for centuries because they're in the deadly nightshade family and eating the plant'll make you deathly ill. Imagine handing a shiny red tomato to a loved one and hoping you're not alive just because the one you ate was that one in a million that wasn't poisonous."

"Wow," Alex wasn't sure how to respond to his digression. "I'm not going to lie to you, Uncle Steven, the moment they read from that Book, they will be in danger. Jeremiah will know. But not giving it to them won't keep them safe, either. Eventually he'll come for every woman who knew me."

Steven strode over to Alex and quickly embraced her. "You remind me so much of my sister."

Alex wasn't sure how she felt about his embrace. Steven was her uncle but still a stranger.

He added, "Your mother was very pragmatic. She made sense of things. She had *opinions*. She was a strong cookie."

Pat walked in and pointed at the clock. It was nearing four in the afternoon. "Are we going to Heather's today or waiting for the morning?"

It was nearing five when they pulled into Heather's driveway.

Chapter One Hundred and Forty-Eight

lex had spent the ride considering the eventuality that she'd have to face Jeremiah again. It weighed on her heavily. She wouldn't wait for him to find her. The only way forward was to hit him first. There seemed no way to defeat him. Each moment of triumph ended with him rising in defiance, seemingly unharmed. She was so tired. Tired of fighting, tired of hurting, tired of being hurt. She wasn't without hope, however. Despite her injuries, she prepared for their next encounter. She healed her wounds. She grew stronger. It was too easy to see her failures, but she had faced Jeremiah three times now, and each time lived. Had anyone ever achieved such a feat before? It was tempting to wonder if she was as indestructible as he was.

If that were the case, then perhaps the only way to defeat him was sacrifice. Perhaps the only way to defeat such a force as Jeremiah was by mutual destruction.

The notion didn't set well with her. She had life yet to live. And yet, that life weighed on her. Her exhaustion. Echoes of pain endured. Endless, maddening babble of multitudes in her head. Perhaps she and Jeremiah would continue their fight for eternity. The thought convinced her that if she could end this—no matter the sacrifice—she would. Her death would be a sacrifice to those women who trusted her to keep them safe. To those women who had never heard of her.

She wasn't sure how she'd explain this to the Book Club. It seemed likely that each one of them would try to talk her out of it, try to concoct an alternative, offer their undying allegiance and promise to stand with her to the bitter end if only she'd keep trying. They would argue that a stalemate was preferrable. But could she live her life with the Damoclesian Sword of Jeremiah's threat always over her head?

She liked that even less.

It'd been nearly a full day since she'd last seen Rose, Marta, and Colette. Even longer since she'd seen Abby. Nearly two weeks since she'd seen Heather. So much had changed since then.

Steven pulled his truck into the driveway, pulling up on the lawn beside a motorcycle. He idled a moment and turned back to Alex. "We're here. We're all here for you. You need anything, you ask for it. Demand it. But don't you worry about us. We'll make our introductions to those who need it. You do your thing." He turned to Carissa, "Charry, your best behavior. Things are going to start happening soon. This isn't a game, this is life and death. If I'm going to let you and your mom do your things, I need to know that you've been listening and paying attention."

"I know, Dad," she huffed.

"I'm serious, Charry. People are gonna die. I need to know that if I'm watching your back, you're not going to do anything stupid."

"I know." Her tone was darker, more serious this time. "You could have just told me the truth."

"You would have kept that secret? No one would'a believed you, but when word got to the wrong people, you would have put your cousin in mortal danger before she was ready." He took a breath and blew it out to calm his rising agitation. "What I mean, Charry, I didn't lie to you to protect you. I lied to protect Alex." He reached to his side and handed her his Book. "I'm giving this to you. I'm trusting you to do what's right with it. Don't open it, don't look at it, don't even peek until we get inside and they're ready to show you how it all works."

"I won't. Promise."

"There was this experiment years ago when they left kids in a room with a marshmallow and told them if they didn't eat it, they could have two more when the instructor came back. You know what happened?"

"Most kids ate the marshmallow?"

"That's right, Charry. Rather than wait to get two, they took the sure thing. You've got that Book now. Don't eat that marshmallow."

"I won't, Daddy," she replied. "I won't eat the marshmallow or read the Book." She looked sheepishly at Alex, and whispered, "He'll probably still see me as a kid when I have kids and his grandchildren are older than I am now."

Alex saw Charissa's concern: that Alex judged her for the way her father spoke to her. "You're so lucky," she touched Charissa's wrist, "that you have someone to guide you through this. It's been really hard."

Alex slipped out of the truck as soon as Steven unlocked the doors. She made her way to the house.

The house looked like it had been through a war. Scorches marred the front, especially where the door should have been. Hinged plywood panels framed by two-by-fours made for a makeshift door. As she approached, she thought about the women inside and imagined what it might be like if one of them caught sight of her out a window and came running. Before she got to the door, Carrie seemingly popped into existence. She jumped into Alex's arms and stretched on her tip-toes and holding Alex's face, kissed her multiple times on the forehead.

"I didn't think I'd ever see you again. Holy motherfudger, Alex. I grieved your death. And here you are. Back from your world tour, tearing the shit out of New York and Paris. Holy wow."

Alex adored the tattooed chef. She was lanky and muscular. Carrie grabbed Alex in a bearhug. It felt like being wrapped in steel cable. "I never gave up hope. It's so amazing it is to see you again." She released Alex and stepped back, fanning her face as her eyes teared. "I really thought we lost you," she said, her face twisted as she fought valiantly not to cry. "Don't you dare scare us like that. I don't think I can go through that again." She snorted and wiped the tears away with her wrist. "I just made a mess of myself. Didn't I?"

"No," Alex said, her heart warmed by how important her return was, saddened her absence hurt those she loved. "You're still amazing."

Carrie just stared at her, a grin growing across her face. "Come on," she turned for the door. "Everyone's dying to see you."

As the *door* opened, Carrie shouted, "Hey, look who trolled in here!"

Colette appeared at the entry. She'd shed her Farm fashion for a bright yellow sundress adorned with yellow flowers that matched her fingernails. Her smile was wide as she said, "I feared I'd never get the chance to thank you for saving me from that place." She wrapped Alex in her arms and rocked her gently. She whispered to Alex, "I'm sorry I doubted you. When Rose and I left, we were sure he was going to…. I mean I thought we wouldn't see you again. I won't doubt you again."

As the others clustered around the battered doorway, Nancy came out. Her face looked undressed without a loop or a stud jiggling through her lip. She leaned on the doorframe. "If you looked like hell, it'd be an improvement. Come here, girl!" She gave Alex a long, rocking hug and kissed her cheek twice. "You're back. Back and, wow, Alex. Amazing." Nancy whispered, "I thought we lost you kid. Abby saw you dying." She sniffled. "We keep thinking this is it, and you keep coming back. It's like you have nine lives, girl. What are you on, number twelve?" As they stepped apart, Nancy wiped her eyes. "Please try to stop with the close calls. My heart can't handle the drama."

Alex nodded, trying not to allow her emotions to belie her thoughts. *I'm here but only for a little while.* "I'm back," she took Nancy's hands.

June and Rachel were next, lingering just inside as Alex made her way through the procession. Behind her, she heard Pat making introductions.

She said hello to June and Rachel, hugging each of them. They each expressed similar emotions.

June said, "The next time anyone tells me you're dead, I won't believe it without a body." She paused and laughed, "That sounds horrible. I mean to say I will always believe in you, no matter what anyone says." She added, "A lot has happened since we last saw you."

"I heard," Alex replied. "No more Books."

Rachel grinned like she was about to reveal a glorious secret, "And Heather."

Behind them, rising from the couch, Heather waited. She didn't come closer but leaned on the arm of the couch. She looked tired and tattered, worn thin. Seeing Heather, thoughts and memories surfaced. It felt not unlike looking in a mirror.

Alex had a lifetime of memories that belonged to Heather and seeing her stirred them up. Seeing Heather, given the circumstances, would normally have choked her up. This was different. Seeing Heather was like seeing the embodiment of a most cherished part of herself. It was such a deeply ingrained connection that it caused Alex to rake her fingers through her hair over her right ear when it was Heather's hair that fell forward there.

She didn't want to run, but crossed the room in four long strides and pulled Heather into her arms. Her aunt was fragile and fine-boned, almost skeletal under her clothes. "You're wasting away, Heather," Alex whispered. "Are you okay?"

Heather looked Alex over and with a pinch of her fingertips, touched the collar of Alex's leather jacket. "That's just like his," she said with a glint in her eyes before she clutched at Alex, practically digging her fingernails into her shoulders. "No," Heather whispered back, touching her own forehead. "But I know you understand why. There's so little of me left."

"Are you going to be okay?"

Heather replied forcefully, "Never you mind. Every moment is gifted time. I'll figure out how to see you to the end."

"I know, Aunt Heather."

Heather stared at her. Alex asked, "What?"

Heather played with Alex's hair at her forehead. "I saw you on the news. You're so strong. I know it must have been hard, but you've come so far from that girl who cried and held her head if she heard someone talk about magic."

"That wasn't so long ago…," Alex said. In some ways the past several weeks were like living several lifetimes. Sara's, yours, Billy's…, the others. "…and yet, I haven't been that girl in a very long time."

Heather stepped back, wiping tears from her lashes. She didn't have the strength to cry. "However long or short it's been, I couldn't be prouder. I am certain your parents would agree." She looked at Alex a moment longer and said, "But you have important things to do and we shouldn't hold you up with our flattery."

Alex craned her head over Heather to scan the room. Abby and Rose were conspicuously absent. "Where is everyone else?"

"Abby is in your room with Marta, who's in and out of consciousness," Heather looked up at the ceiling. "Abby's having a really rough time of it."

"Of Marta or the oath."

"I'm sure she'd be worried about Marta if she could worry about anything else. She's in utter misery."

"I know. Last time I saw her, she begged me to be my Familiar again."

Heather nodded grimly. "Have you thought about it? We sent George up there to keep her company. No one thinks she can be trusted to be alone."

"George is here?" Her tone sounded a little too excited for her liking.

Heather nodded. She eased herself into the couch, holding Alex's arm for leverage. She moved like her joints were ancient. She patted the seat for Alex to join her as the others mulled about or meandered into other rooms, trying to give Alex and Heather privacy for their reunion. Alex could see from the concerned faces that everyone worried about Heather's fragility. "He's been a good edition to the Book Club," Heather laughed. "You should be forewarned that Eric is here, too."

Alex nodded. That news didn't thrill her, but the more people she had at her side the better. "Marta and Rose thought you went to the Library to rescue Colette and Lydia. That's why we went."

Heather closed her eyes. "We were all set to go. I guess we got lucky Carrie caught the alert about the attack in New York. Rose couldn't be bothered to wait and left. Once we knew you were alive, all plans changed. When they got back, Colette filled us in."

Alex nodded. "Then you know. Billy, I mean."

"Rose told me." Heather rubbed her eyes. "I've known for years it was coming. I've been trying to put myself at peace with it since the day he was born. I always fantasized you'd…," she hesitated to catch her breath, "…be there and save him."

Alex couldn't look at her. "I'm so sorry, I had no—"

"I know," Heather put a hand on her shoulder. "Better you than someone he didn't love so much." She wiped her eyes. "Please tell me what he showed you."

"When I, you know, your coin? The memories were fluid and linear. Start to finish; your whole life but the major highlights lingered."

"I don't know how to feel knowing I'll never have any secrets from you. Part of me wants to feel ashamed. But part of me feels happy that you can know me so well." Heather didn't say anything more, just gestured for Alex to continue.

"With Billy, it was different. He died when he jumped off Picnic Rock. That's when it all started and ended for him. It was like he lived his whole life in the time it took him to hit the ground. He never knew if he was remembering or anticipating. He had memories of the future and the past, but never knew which was which. Time is so confusing. It was exhausting. It drained me."

"It drained him," Heather replied. "When he visited me in the hospital, he told me he was my son and my first thought was," she and Alex both answered, "not this junky." This gave them something to laugh about. "I can't believe he's gone."

I know. Alex touched her forehead. "For what it's worth, Aunt Heather, you're both in here, together."

Heather managed a weak smile. "Oh, Rose," she announced as she changed the subject. "She's locked in her room. I'm worried about her. Here I was worried she hadn't been the same since getting her Book. It's gotten so much worse, especially once she couldn't do that thing with Dolly. I worry where her head is going, Alex. She's not right. She's so angry. I know she loves you, but it's like she hates you, too."

Alex understood all too well. "I didn't give her the satisfaction of killing Matthew."

"Yes," Heather groaned. "Matthew. Where is the bent-neck asshole these days? I heard he helped you, but that doesn't absolve him of everything else he did. Rose and Colette mentioned that, too, when they came back with Marta and that other guy, Jacque."

Alex told her about Matthew's final moments. How he sacrificed himself for her. How she refused his coin and gave him up to Charon.

"That's more than he deserved," Heather sounded disappointed. "I wonder if I'd feel different if you swallowed it. It's too late now. After what he's done to our family, he didn't deserve to be treated like a human being."

Alex said, "The memories are too vivid, Aunt Heather. To be there when he murdered Sara. Knowing I was in her. It's not like watching. I'd pick up the hammer and beat her to death. Not him, me, because I'd be him and think what he thought. I'd kill her with my hands. I couldn't do that. How could I live with that?"

Heather patted Alex's shoulder. "I sometimes forget you've been through so much."

"The point is, he's dead, and he didn't die the way he wanted. His life ended believing he failed."

Heather asked, "I told you about Rose?" Alex nodded. "My memories are like a fog, they're thin and lack substance. They dissipate with the smallest thought." She looked at Alex a moment, her eyes welling up again. "I know I'm going to lose you. I just do. I feel it."

Alex couldn't help but lie. "You're not going to lose me, Aunt Heather. I promise."

Heather shook her head, "That's a promise you can't keep."

Alex wasn't going to lie twice.

"I'm glad you didn't try to comfort me," Heather said. "I saw what you were up against in New York and Paris. This is different now. We're at war, aren't we?"

Alex nodded.

"You've struggled being in charge," Heather said, "but tell us what you need us to do. No one will question you." A grin came to Heather's lips, "Except Rose."

Alex pretended to be deep in thought. She knew what she wanted to do, she wasn't sure if it was worth telling Heather and the others until her plan was underway. Heather watched her expectantly. Heather would eventually force the information from her.

"It can't be just us," Alex said finally. "I need to get word to Banhi and Khowla. They need to know what's happening. He's mad. Angry and crazy. It's not just me he wants anymore. He's prepared to end the very idea of me. There are a lot of women all over the world who need to know what's happening."

Heather looked away. "What is happening, Alex?"

Alex stared at Heather for the longest time. "My coin is dark, Aunt Heather. Jeremiah doesn't know where I am. I don't know how long we have. He's going to kill everyone who knows me. I can't always be on the defensive. Matthew hurt him. That's something. I still have so much magic inside me, and I think I know of a way to keep it from him for good." She lowered her voice for only Heather to hear. She touched her chest. "I don't think there's any version of my story where I walk away from this. I think the only way to destroy him means I also have to die."

She saw Heather's growing discomfort at where this was going. "I've noticed, Aunt Heather, that Jeremiah never goes on the Between. He stays in the waking world. The Library is special. It's what hurt him." She hesitated. "Also, he didn't like seeing Charon. They're enemies, but it's more like they're afraid of and hate each other. I brought Charon's claw to the Library, and I think that's how it was able to come. Jeremiah was shocked to see the child. I don't think Jeremiah realizes Charon won't take my coin, but it's like he doesn't want that to happen. If dying got him his magic back, why not just kill me? I think if I die, he can't get his magic back." *Or am I just convincing myself that this'll work?* Alex patted her aunt's hands. "That's what I think, anyway. I think he's afraid of that. It's the only thing I have over him."

Heather studied her. "Are you saying your plan is to kill yourself?"

Alex shook her head. "No. I want to destroy him. But I don't know if that's even possible. If destroying him means we both have to die, then I need all of you to help me do it."

Heather threw her head back. It was the first motion that didn't seem weighed by fatigue. "You can't ask me that, Alex. I won't kill you."

"You'd rather watch me suffer? Or lose?"

"No, of course not, but—"

"Then you'll do it. There can't be any doubt in my mind that you or Rose or any of the others will do whatever it takes to put an end to this." She touched Heather's cheek. "He's a horrible creature, and I don't know how much longer I can keep up this game."

Heather wanted to continue to debate Alex but didn't. "It's hard to pretend I have enough energy to have a conversation. It's been a long day. I'm all out of steam."

Alex just got here, so she hated saying, "After breakfast tomorrow, I have to leave."

"Why?"

"You don't know?"

"I'm making sure you do."

"You're a pain in the ass, Aunt Heather." They both laughed. "No one is safe as long as I'm here. First, I need Banhi and Khowla. Then I need to figure out what I can do. My magic is so blunt. You've experienced both using a Book and having it. I have to rev up my emotions every time. Sara told me that witches used recipes to make real magic." Alex explained the pneumonic devices. "If I had more time, I'd experiment, but I don't have the luxury. Blunt magic's got to do. I need my emotions in high gear. It's hard keeping all my pain as raw and fresh as possible, but it won't serve me otherwise."

Heather understood. "I meant to ask you how you did magic when you weren't upset or angry. I didn't know."

"That's what I mean. I stay angry and hurt—emotionally raw—all the time."

Heather pulled Alex into a hug. "My poor kid. I'm so sorry everything is so difficult." She caressed Alex's cheeks. "You're going away to find your friends. Then what?"

"When I come back, I need Marta. I think she's the key to everything."

"Marta's eyes open and roll once in a while. It's absolutely horrifying to watch."

She's not just Marta, anymore, is she? She's Marta and Alex, and now Dany. Only he's in there whole. Inside her in an entire growing universe. No wonder it's killing her. "It must be Dany that's hurting her."

"Dany? I didn't meet him, did I?"

"No. Dany is one of Matthew's. Jeremiah was killing him. Marta… she absorbed him. I think she's keeping him alive and it's hurting her."

"How do you help her? How do you help her and not harm him?"

Alex shook her head. "I don't know. I may not be able to do one without the other. Hopefully I can do both." *And if I do, how will she react when I ask her to do it again?*

Heather brushed Alex's hair with her hand. "I'm so sorry you have to make these choices and suffer these consequences. If I could trade—"

"Why would that be fair, Aunt Heather? We were set on a path by things we can't control. There's always a way off the path, but I believe the cost is higher than continuing. No one wants to be in my shoes, but that doesn't mean anyone else should have to be. Who's to say someone else would do any better? Or worse."

Heather nodded and leaned forward, embracing her.

"I can't stay too long," Alex apologized. "I need to check on Marta and I'd like to pop in on Rose, if she'll let me."

Chapter One Hundred and Forty-Nine

Alex headed up the stairs. She paused outside Rose's bedroom, contemplating all the potential alternatives before her. Knocking, not knocking; it didn't matter. Even in her fantasies, Alex couldn't escape Rose's ire.

It saddened her that she couldn't go to her cousin, her closest friend. Here she was, preparing to meet her end, and she had to keep her personal wants and needs bottled up because she couldn't part Rose from her resentment. It wasn't a large hallway, just three doorways, Heather's bedroom, Rose's bedroom, the bathroom, and yet, standing there, it was vast and empty for how she felt in it.

Just calling it Rose's bedroom belied how hurtful to the sole occupant that designation could be. No matter how much time passed, Rose would forever associate loneliness in her childhood bedroom with Alex's failure.

Alex watched the door a moment. Everything she thought she might do for her cousin, she realized, was a self-centered act, something done for herself. No matter how selfless the act seemed, no matter how desperate she wanted to take Rose's hatred away, it was never purely for Rose's sake. That, Alex realized, was perhaps why it would never work.

She abandoned Rose's bedroom door and climbed the ladder to her attic bedroom. Stepping up, hearing the whirring attic fan, and feeling the heaviness of the air, this was home to someone she used to be.

"Hi, Abby," Alex tried to be cheerful, even as she prepared for an onslaught of requests.

Abby looked up from Marta and tugged at her pink polo shirt. Alex barely recognized her without a sleeveless shirt. She looked like she applied makeup, too. Maybe used gel or hairspray to style her short hair.

Abby was the mirror opposite of Rose. Although they both pointed to the origin of their pain and suffering as Alex, Abby's claim came with a trigger for forgiveness. All Alex needed to fix every one of Abby's perceived slights was to request her servitude again. She wondered how far she was willing to go to achieve reconciliation. How different was making Abby her Familiar from sending her to the Farm? Both were veils over reality that offered a perception of happiness. Did saving Abby from her pain bring Alex closer to becoming like Jeremiah? What did it say about Jeremiah and his Farm if making Abby her Familiar was the right decision for Abby? What did it say about Alex?

And if she did, where would that leave her? Would she see through Abby's kindness and fawning? Could Abby do anything that wouldn't leave Alex feeling guilty? She realized that what Abby was asking her wasn't simply to give her something she wanted back, but to take her pain away and keep it for herself in return.

"Hey," Abby said, her tone dropping through the word as though sadness absorbed the warmth from it.

"I'm so sorry, Abby."

Abby nodded.

"I feel like we finally have a quiet moment." They both looked at Marta, who was clearly not about to interfere with their conversation. "You deserve to have the pain I've caused you acknowledged."

"I appreciate that," Abby said in a hushed way. "But you don't need to apologize. Not if you ask and let me have my happiness back."

Alex found her resentment abandoned her. She saw Abby for all her sadness and wayward purpose. Alex sat beside Abby and embraced her friend. Was Abby her friend? Or was there something transactional about their relationship? All this time Alex believed Abby loved her. Was it all her oath? "Abby, please let me explain. Will you allow me?"

"I'll let you indulge yourself."

Did she just accuse me of being selfish? Am I? "Abby, I understand that you willingly took the oath to be my Familiar, and I appreciated everything more than you can possibly imagine. You were my best friend; I could always count on you for anything."

Abby smiled sadly. "And you want to lose that?"

"No, I don't," Alex replied earnestly. "But it's not that simple. I don't want it if it's not real."

"It is real," Abby urged. "It's the most real thing I've ever had. The desire that motivates me is so strong. I never had emotions so big before I said my oath. I didn't just feel happiness or joy when I was around you, I was uplifted. I was jubilant. When you were in danger, I could take any pain if it meant keeping you safe."

"Please explain to me how those things are real." Alex waited to see if Abby understood. Abby's eyes narrowed slightly and Alex worried her meaning was misunderstood. "What I mean is that I used to be certain you loved me. Now I'm not so sure. I know you felt love for me, but did you feel it or did the oath give it to you to feel?"

Abby seethed; Alex never saw her look so angry, "Don't you dare tell me what is real. Those feelings were more real than anything I've felt before or since. I felt like a superhero. I felt my purpose in every breath. All I did was feel." She looked at her hands, "I feel now. Insignificant. I might as well not feel at all. I used to feel so big. Everything I felt was grand. I loved that. I miss that." Alex turned to Marta and rubbed her arm. Marta moaned. Abby continued, "Maybe you feel some sort of guilt, and maybe you believe that by explaining this to me you can unburden yourself of it. The old Abby would tell you there's no need to apologize, because she loved you without condition. I'll tell you this: Keep your worthless apology. You deserve to wallow in your guilt. Guilt is what you feel because deep inside you know you're wrong. Deep inside you're afraid because giving that back means you are responsible for me. You worry I won't be able to control myself and I'll step in front of some spell Jeremiah casts to kill you. What you'll never understand is that I am fully in control. I make my own decisions. So they're influenced. Who are you to take away the one thing I had that made me special and made me feel good about myself? That wasn't some good deed, Alex, that was cruel."

Alex didn't know what to say.

"I know it must be hard to realize you're wrong, Alex. Please, please, please, don't die on this hill. It helps you; it helps me. What can be wrong with that? We're two consenting adults. Believe me, I know what I'm asking. I'm asking to wear those atrocious muscle-shirts because that's what you expect when you think of me. I'm asking to want to keep you fed and a roof over your head. I'm asking you to be in charge of my life in a way that's probably really uncomfortable now that you understand it." Abby took a breath, "Tell me you didn't like it before you knew." Abby watched her. "You weren't born yet, and I loved you more than life itself. That hasn't changed. That's why I swore myself to you and not to your father. I wanted to serve you and your purpose, and I still do."

Alex rubbed her forehead. Part of her felt like she didn't have time for this debate, the whole world slowly closing in on her, Jeremiah leading the charge. Yet, if she didn't have Abby on her side, where would she be? That felt like the cheap, easy answer to her conundrum and it left her unsatisfied. "Abby, just because something's acceptable, doesn't make it less wrong." She huffed. "I don't know that you can give me what I'm asking from you, Abby."

"What's that?"

"To prove to me that when I ask you for something you don't give it to me because you're compelled to do it. You give it to me because you want to. Think of how I'll feel if I always wonder if there's a small part of you that would never, ever do it."

Tears welled in Abby's eyes. "Look at me, Alex. I've spent my life serving you. When Holly asked me to stop spoiling you so you wouldn't grow up a miserable spoiled monster, I did it. It was the hardest—the second hardest—thing I've ever had to do. It wasn't what you wanted. You wanted

Abby and you wanted toys and dresses and fun. But there was a difference. I chose the right thing over what you wanted. Can't you see that?"

The strength Alex needed for what was to come fled from her. She collapsed against Abby and felt a slight recoil that she—intellectually—expected. It still hurt, even when Abby folded her in her arms and whispered hushes. If in a day or two Alex faced Jeremiah and he killed her, would any of this matter? Alex wondered if she was being selfish or unreasonable. *What would be so bad about just asking her? In a few days, she'd be free, wouldn't she?* Alex didn't know. She'd read about women in India climbing on their husband's funeral pyres and wondered if Abby would seek to be buried with her like one of Pharaoh's servants.

"I've never been asked to do something so hard, Abby. Now that I know, you're asking me to enslave you. You're asking me to take away your freedom and replace it with some good feelings. As much as I want old Abby back, is it fair of me to ask you? Knowing that, is it fair of you to ask me?"

"It is. Yes."

"I have one question, Abby. Only one. If I call on you, beg you, demand even, that you end my life because the only way to defeat Jeremiah is for us both to die, or something is happening or about to happen that will be the most catastrophic thing that could possibly ever happen to me, I mean, if you left me to suffer it would be unforgivable. If I asked you, as my Familiar, would you kill me?"

Abby was almost too quick to answer, "Yes," but then she leaned back, ashamed of how swiftly she'd come to it. "I don't know," her tone fell grave. "I don't know if I could either way."

"But as my Familiar, what do you think you'd do?"

Abby looked about the room for anything else to stare at. "I'd try to protect you. Barring that, if I couldn't—protect you, that is—I don't know what I would do. The pain of watching you suffer would be unfathomable. Not doing what you asked would split me in two. Maybe doing what you ask, in that situation, would be like when you told me to read the Book. I didn't want to, but in the end, following your will was the only way."

"Know this, Abby," now it was Alex's turn for grave words, "I love you. I love the Abby who cared for me and made me a charm and let me have her bedroom when I stayed at her home. I don't want this for you. Seeing you like this, hurting all the time, it tears me apart. I want old Abby and I want to know you're will is your own. I worry I'll resent you every time you do something I ask."

Abby nodded. "It's worth it to me."

Alex sat for a moment in silence. She'd said her piece. She felt spent. There was nothing else she could say to Abby to convey her apprehension.

She placed her hands atop Abby's and rested her head on her friend's thick shoulder. She smelled perfume.

"Speaking of, where is the charm?" Abby's eyes looked panicked. "You didn't take it off, did you?"

Alex explained that—in some ways—she still wore the charm around her neck.

"Your father's coin." Abby smiled for the first time in a long time. "So cool."

Alex sighed and looked away. She knew what she had to do but still couldn't find the certainty.

"How do we do this, Abby? Do I just ask you, like a marriage proposal? Would you be my Familiar?" Alex rubbed tears from her cheeks.

Abby laughed. When her coin appeared, she held it out for Alex. "Take this."

Alex took it. The fine thread sparked and vibrated excitedly.

"Take your coin and place it against mine."

"Does it matter that my coin is dark?"

Abby shrugged. "It didn't the first time."

Alex took her dark coin and held the two, one in each hand. She gently brought them together, and just as they touched, Alex heard and felt the satisfying snap of them coming together. Her thread, and Abby's thread, sparked like a fuse lit along its entire length. They vibrated violently, throwing sparks. In her chest, where her cord disappeared, Alex felt tremendous ache. It wasn't pain, per se, but the most intense heartbreak she could imagine. It staggeringly faded in reverse, slowly filling her, until her heart brimmed with joy.

Teary-eyed, she and Abby exchanged knowing glances. Abby clearly felt it, too.

"Now take them apart," Abby instructed her after several minutes had passed and their joyful tears eased.

Alex pried the two coins apart, her dark and Abby's bright. She let go of her own and stared at Abby's bright coin in her palm. How many times had she held it? This small disk of light was the difference between life and death, of being alive and being a zombie. Yet Abby hadn't thought twice about giving it to her, sending her back to see Sara. She had to die so her thread was severed. Had Alex not returned the moment she left, Charon would have come. The immensity of the risk overwhelmed Alex. This wasn't something she'd asked Abby to do, it was what Abby did for her. That couldn't have been the oath: without it, Abby had done the same for Peter.

Now she could hand it back to Abby. Abby claimed it and returned it to her chest, and the glow faded.

"How do we know it worked?"

Abby shrugged. "I don't know. Maybe it takes a while. Maybe it's immediate. Ask me to do something."

"Like what?" Alex couldn't think of anything. "Don't you just feel, I don't know, different? Shouldn't you just feel good now?"

"I don't know if I feel good or relief. I feel like coming home after a horrible trip, but that could just be, you know, placebo effect."

"Try your magic. Familiars can't do magic, right?"

Abby thought a minute. She opened Alex's desk drawer and pulled out a small notepaper with a pen-check scribble in one corner. She pinched it in her hand and stared at it, grumbling, driving her anger. A wisp of smoke danced off the surface a moment before the sheet disappeared, curling black, in yellow flame. "Fuck," Abby cursed, her fingers singed. She dropped the burning paper and stomped on the floor, all the while repeating, "Fuck, fuck," until it was out.

Alex worried what this meant. "Am I wrong? Familiars can't do magic, right?"

Abby looked at her fingers. "That's what I was told."

"Maybe it didn't work because it was a second time? Maybe you can only be a Familiar once?"

"You felt it, though, right, Alex? It filled you up when our coins were together, didn't it?"

"Yes."

"Then it had to work." Abby mused, "Familiars aren't allowed to read Books. But, Alex, I didn't read a Book. The magic is in me. Maybe this is different now."

"Maybe," Alex replied hopefully.

"Wow," she looked at the singed floor. "I almost burned Heather's house down."

Alex felt an immense pang of guilt. "About that, Abby."

"Well wait, wait," Abby said. "Let's think this through first."

"Abby, I need you to listen to me." Abby looked up. "Marty and Quest are fine. I burned down your trailer. It was an accident. I'm so sorry."

"I know you didn't mean to do it."

Alex stared at Abby. She was certain her blinking eyelids made noise. "Wait, what? You aren't upset? I destroyed your home."

"I heard you. I am kind of bent out of shape about it, but I know you didn't mean it. You're probably really upset yourself. There's no sense adding to how miserable you feel."

Alex kept staring. "I think we can be pretty sure it worked."

"Why do you say that?"

"Come on, Abby. A minute ago, you were begging me to make you take the oath and now you're all, *Burned down my house? No biggie.* Honestly, it's a little disconcerting."

"Would you rather I was upset at you?"

"Um, yeah."

Abby growled, "I can't believe you burned down my house you incompetent fool. What were you thinking? Don't you understand how important those ghastly muscle shirts are to me? What about…. What about," Abby seemed to be struggling with more to say. "It was a mess, wasn't it? I've been a bit untidy as of late." Alex nodded. "Well, at least I don't have to clean up. That's a bonus." Abby howled with laughter. "The poor roaches. You killed my houseguests."

"At least you're not angry with me anymore."

Abby wiped tears from her eyes. "I was never angry with you. It hurt is all." She hugged Alex. "Let's get on with things. What's the story? Tell me what happens next."

The transformation shocked Alex. Abby had her fix and was back to her old self.

"I need Marta to wake up."

Abby looked over at Marta, her slender form lying across the bed. She looked more dead than asleep; her eyes ever so slightly open. "I have my doubts that's going to happen."

"Help me sit her up a little. I've got to try."

Abby wrestled Marta into a partially seated position so Alex could embrace her. Holding Marta, Alex thought about her love for Marta, her feelings for Alex, her twin brother. Alex felt the waves of energy leaving her, but even after a few minutes, Marta still hadn't stirred. After several more, Alex rest Marta across the bed. "I need to get help." She pointed to a darkened corner of her bedroom, where an old photograph of her with her parents had been until George broke it. "I need to see if I can get her to the Between. Otherwise, I'll leave her here and bring them to me."

"Bring who?"

Alex almost said Lesedi but caught herself. "Banhi and Khowla. They brought me out after Rose killed Sara. I hope they know how to bring her out, too."

After a moment of concentration, the mist appeared. She anticipated Charon's arrival; the child never came when her coin was dark, but it would for Marta.

She pulled Marta closer and closer to the portal. The child never came.

Chapter One Hundred and Fifty

Alex passed through the mist with Marta and stepped into the center of the market square. She expected to be alone, but found herself lost in the hustle and bustle of the many women who already were bringing a sense of normalcy to the market.

Lesedi's fountain reigned overhead, a sparkling beacon that in so few days drew and inspired myriad women to return and rebuild. Alex had to stop and absorb it all. The ambition to create a new market meant that their designs, however inspired by the old market, were more creative and grander than what had previously been here. The colorful onslaught of design stole her breath. She'd already gawked at buildings made of bubbles and feathers, but now she wondered at one building that appeared to be made of nothing but gently blowing fabric. It's ochre and rust patters swayed, but there didn't seem to be anything holding the sheath of fabric above the multiple levitating floors.

Her guilt over the destruction of this place was replaced by an air of self-satisfaction. It wasn't the fountain—that many women were just watching and discussing—or the fact that she'd taken that destruction and erased it to allow for the rebirth she now saw. She was nearly leaping with excitement because she arrived in the market square without travelling across the Between. *I willed myself here!*

She settled Marta down beside the fountain. Alex wiped Marta's forehead and called to one of many passing women. They all attempted to look busy so as not to see the only two women on the Between not tethered to the waking world with a thin thread. *Do they think we're dead?* She wondered if the women avoided looking at ghosts the same as people refused to look at the homeless in the cities.

"Excuse me," Alex called to one. "Um, hey, could you please help me?" Several women hurried past, their quickening pace giving away that they heard Alex's plea. Her wonder was quicky replaced with annoyance. She stood upright and grabbed a woman by her arm. "Please, I need your help." The woman pulled free and frantically raced away from her.

Alex stopped herself, even as her sense of desperation was escalating. She considered Banhi, focusing on everything she recalled of the older woman. Her voice, which sounded like she smoked since she was a child. Her joyfully wrinkled face, her long, gray, wavy hair. How Alex's magic thrilled her.

Concentrating, from behind closed lids, amidst a sea of pinpricks, a single coin glowed brightly. Relatively nearby, Alex turned in the direction of the coin, opened her eyes, and charged forward, calling Banhi's name.

Banhi's face alit at the sight of her, then soured momentarily as she read Alex's expression. Before greeting Alex with an embrace, she called out, "Khowla, the girl has come to us again!"

"Alex? She is back!" Kholwa shouted as she made her way through the traffic. She pointed at Alex's dark coins. "Still dead, I see," she said with a laugh as she embraced Alex.

"I am," Alex replied. "My friend needs your help."

As Kholwa peered at Marta's unconscious form, she said, "Did Jeremiah cause her to be like this?"

Alex explained what had happened.

Banhi nodded. "With you, Jeremiah is never far away."

Khowla patted her body only to realize what she wanted wasn't there. She explained, "Apparently, I do not dream my phone." She turned to the Banhi, "Have you seen the news? New York and Paris?"

Banhi dismissed Khowla's enthusiasm. "That was all fake. They said so."

As Khowla defended, "That was Alex," Banhi bent over laughing, unable to keep a serious expression any longer.

Once Banhi caught her breath, she asked, "What have we missed?"

Alex explained why she needed their help with Marta.

Banhi shook her head at the news. "And you come to us to help her? How can we do what you cannot?"

"I don't know or I'd have done it," Alex replied. "I thought maybe you would know something I don't." She was grateful her words didn't sound sarcastic. "Please do whatever you can think of to save her. I need her to wake up." Once the words carried her desperation out, she realized that Banhi was right. She didn't know what to do so she tried nothing. Alex was surrounded by dozens of women who believed in her power. She felt ashamed.

Banhi looked at Khowla, both their faces fell grave. "It is not safe to venture into a person, but that is what has to be done." Banhi continued, "One of us should remain out here."

Khowla looked at Banhi. "How do you know what to do? When have you ever seen such a thing?" She paused a moment and joked, "The internet?"

Banhi answered, "When you sat on the knee of your grandmother and she told you those nonsense stories, myths and legends and bedtime riddles, were you not listening?"

"To childish stories?"

"When who you are must stay hidden to the world, you make up secret ways to say what you really mean. Such stories pass down generation to generation, easy to remember even when their meaning is lost." Banhi watched Khowla for acknowledgement. "Why do you think it is so important we listen and save such stories? Do you think such silly things came from nowhere?"

Khowla took hold of Banhi's arm. "I am sorry, Banhi. I did not understand how you are so certain, and I wonder where the knowledge comes."

Banhi made a face, dipping her head slightly. "Now you know." She turned to Alex, "Girl who is not dead. How is your friend on the Between?" Banhi wiggled her fingers, giggling, "No strings attached."

Alex retold her battle with Charon. She told them about facing Jeremiah again and what he did to Dany, and how Marta briefly turned into Oblivion to save him.

Banhi nodded as Alex spoke. When she was finished, Khowla sighed. "How do you live? You have kicked the bogey man where it hurts. I wonder, do you think he fears you now?"

"I don't think he's afraid of anything." Alex explained what happened when Charon arrived in the Library. Finishing with how the child refused to take her.

Banhi raised a knowing finger. "This is also a tale my grandmother told me. A man with a magic bag." She turned to Khowla, "Do you know it? The bag can capture anything the man wishes."

Khowla nodded, "Yes, yes, I remember. To save some princess, he catches death."

Banhi nodded. Turning back to Alex, "The man holds death to save the princess and everything is wonderful for a while. But then everyone lives to be too old. So old they now want to die. So the man releases death. It claims them all. But it forever is fearful of the man. He is cursed to grow old-old-old and live forever."

"What does that have to do with me?"

Banhi's eyebrows raised. "Who is to say?" She walked towards Marta. As she examined the unconscious woman, she added, "Such a story has perhaps one toe in truth. Death avoids you, fears you. Perhaps you will never die. Perhaps." She grinned, "Or I just liked the way my grandmother made me jump when the man in the story," she paused, then blurted, "*snatched death* with his magic bag."

After a minute, Banhi turned to the others. "There is no story for this woman. These are no dybbuks. But maybe we say they are and remove them the same way. We," she addressed herself and Khowla, "are like ghosts as we dream. If they can enter her, then maybe so can we."

Alex explained how she and Abby fell into Oblivion and now Oblivion was inside Marta.

"You," Banhi touched Alex's arm, "are like the dead. Even with your body, you may also go, just like them."

Alex asked "How do we get into her?"

Khowla crossed her arms, watching skeptically for Banhi's reply.

Banhi shrugged. "I think one among us should wait out here while the other two try. Like mountain climbers, someone anchors the rope."

Alex nodded. "Both of you will hold my rope?"

Banhi countered, "I will go. Khowla can stand the watch." Banhi didn't expect an argument from either of them. "Protect this Marta. If she should die while we are still inside…."

After a long moment, Khowla asked, "What would happen?"

"I do not know," Banhi said. "My grandmother had only so many stories."

Alex approached Marta. Banhi trailed a step behind. Above them, the fountain burbled. Alex glanced up to the distant figure of Lesedi on the top. The mythologic menagerie circling the tower beneath her. Alex hoped Lesedi would watch over her. She recalled her father reaching into Holly's abdomen, as well as Heather reaching into her own. In both those instances the sensation was that of viscera. They touched tissue. Alex had already been inside Oblivion, which now existed within Marta. Could she reach into Marta and go there? Could she without Marta transforming, like she did when she saved Dany?

Alex hesitated. Once inside Marta, they were obscenely vulnerable. Marta was unconscious and defenseless. A complete body on the Between with no way to return on her own. If anything happened, if anyone came, if someone killed her, what would become of them? She looked at Banhi and her trailing thread. If Banhi's analogy were correct, she had a safety line, whereas Alex would be free climbing. She caught Khowla's attention. Khowla acknowledged her silent plea. For what it was worth, Khowla would do whatever she could to protect Marta.

Khowla asked Banhi, "Are you sure you want to go? I think Alex can manage on her own.

Banhi grinned wildly, "And miss the opportunity to do this?"

Alex's hands pressed Marta's abdomen, pushing inward. First, the force of skin on skin was all she felt, but as she remembered coming straight from her bedroom to the market, she also thought about the green hillside and the child's rendition of a house perched upon it. *How different is this?* From behind, Banhi grabbed her elbow, not to hold her back but to follow her forward. Alex pushed against Marta as firmly as she could. Suddenly transforming to a black cloud, Marta's physical gave way to her. Alex felt like she had tumbled forward, half expecting the splash as she fell into the fountain.

Chapter One Hundred and Fifty-One

"This was not what I expected. What sort of house is that? Where are we?" Banhi's thread trailed off to a portal of mist. They were on Marta's Between, in Oblivion, on the Between: A universe within a universe within a universe.

"It's complicated," Alex replied. "We're inside Marta, but also inside my twin brother."

"Brother? What? Inside Marta?"

Alex pointed at the house. She briefly explained how Marta fell into Oblivion. That Oblivion was somehow her brother, Alex. How when she met Matthew here, he created the lawn and that made Marta realize she could teach the brother how to be a child and helped him draw a house. She summarized their encounter with Jeremiah and Marta's brief transformation into Oblivion. "She's been like this ever since. I hope if we take Dany out, she'll wake up." *And then I'll know my plan can work.*

Banhi pointed, "Into that crazy house then?"

Together, they walked towards it; Alex pointed Banhi around the grass, warning, "It's sharp like broken glass."

Banhi walked warily beside the grass. "Crazy wonders never cease. Not when Alex is nearby." She caught Alex's eye and winked.

Arriving at the front door, Marta greeted them. Alex introduced Banhi.

"Hey," Marta said softly. "Seems I'm stuck here again."

"Is Dany with you? I think he's the reason you're stuck here."

Marta nodded somberly. "We bandaged him up as best we could." She shook her head. "It's not good."

"Let me see him."

Marta led them around the staircase to one of the secluded bedrooms. Banhi's eyes were wide with wonder at all the toys and playthings. Her lip curled in disgust at the sandpits and the pools inside the house. She gently elbowed Alex and whispered, "These things… are they normal in American homes?"

As they stopped beside a bedroom door, Alex replied, "Nothing here is normal".

Marta sounded out of breath as she reached for the doorknob. "I'm sorry," she panted, "but seeing Dany like that, without his skin and his screams and everything…." She looked between each of them. "Steel yourself. We've done our best, but what is inside this room," she hesitated, "will be difficult to forget."

"This must be traumatic for you," Banhi apologized. "I'm so sorry you experienced something so horrible."

Marta forced a grin. She touched her forehead. "I'm not sure what Alex told you. Her twin brother, also named Alex, is here."

"She told me."

"He's in my head. I feel his emotions." Marta rubbed her temple. "He's making me anxious. I don't know how to calm him. Don't get me wrong, Dany was in horrific shape. Worst thing I've ever seen, and I've seen a lot of horrible shit." She demonstrated her still shaking hands. "But it's not just something he saw. It's inside him now." She pressed her palm on the door. "What's in there frightens him."

Alex embraced Marta. "You've been so brave, my brother." She kissed Marta's cheek. "Maybe Banhi and I should go in ourselves."

Marta regarded her trembling hands. "I tried to teach Alex to be human. Look what he's done to me."

Alex asked, "Maybe you want to wait somewhere else?" Marta nodded and retreated toward the front door.

Alex waited for Marta to be far enough away that she—they—wouldn't see. She took hold of the knob. *Do I want to do this? I know I have to help get Dany out so Marta can wake up, but can I do this?* Dany was without his skin so briefly before Marta pulled him in, her recollection of what she saw was as much a re-creation as it was a memory.

As the door slowly creaked open, her hands trembled at the uncertainty of what lay hidden in the darkness within.

"Dany? I'm going to throw the switch. It's Alex."

A weak, "Okay," followed.

She swallowed and took a deep breath. Banhi crowded behind her. "I don't see anything," she whispered. "Turn on the light."

In the moment her eyes adjusted, the room appeared empty. Some toys lay scattered about the room in clustered piles as though kicked to random corners. The room was otherwise empty. There was a dresser with an open drawer. An unmade bed. And a giant teddy bear, seated awkwardly on the edge of the bed, staring blankly at them. Alex was about to check under the bed, when the bear waved. "Hello, Alex," it whimpered with the slightest hint of a French accent.

Alex nearly screamed. She was certain she was mistaken and rubbed her eyes. The bear slid off the bed and waddled towards them. The effect was so disconcerting, Alex had to catch herself from jumping back and slamming the door.

"I expected bandages," Banhi spoke flatly behind her.

"You and me both," Alex hissed as she approached the giant bear, only now realizing that its button-eyes were the color of Dany's brown eyes. No wonder her brother was terrified.

Banhi whispered to her, "This is not something you expected, is it?"

"No. Not even a little."

Banhi sighed. "That is such a relief."

The bear shook its head, its whole body joining in the motion. "No bandages here. This," it gestured to itself with thick paws with stitching to differentiate individual toes and fingers, "is my new skin. I guess it's what the kid imagined for me. Marta said it'll probably only work while I'm here."

Alex couldn't help but stare. Dany wasn't wearing a bear-suit, somehow, the same way a child builds a house out of crayon, Marta and Alex made him new skin from a teddy bear. "Are you in pain?"

"Not anymore. It feels very different." The bear rubbed its arm with its other paw. "It's sort of numb in here. It's like I don't feel anything. Although," the bear hushed, "just the thought of how much it hurt makes it hurt. You know?"

"I'm sorry," Alex told him.

"We came to help you," Banhi said from behind Alex, apparently wanting to get past the awkward *talking to a teddy-bear* stage.

The teddy bear looked at its paws. "I've been trying to consider why Marta would do this. Why not let me die?" It looked up at them. "I'm hurting her, aren't I?"

Alex didn't want to, but she nodded. "She's been unconscious for two days."

The teddy bear padded closer. "You'll forgive me, I lost my glasses." Once closer, it held its paw out to Banhi. "Nice to meet you," Dany said to her. "I'm Dany. At least I was before I wasn't this silly bear."

Banhi took the paw in both hands and shook it. Regarding the paw in her hands, "I expected to feel you inside, like a costume."

The bear answered, "No, but I'm not about to pop a seam to see if it's guts or stuffing that comes out."

"Should we try to take him back to the Between?" Alex asked.

Banhi pursed her lips and took a pensive breath. "I advise against it. There are things—I've been warned—that live in black shadows. They haunt our dreams. They give us nightmares. They are guardians of the underworld; they keep the living out. He," she pointed at his chest, "like Marta, is not hidden like you. That would make two waking lives, and that may be too much."

That's what Matthew said. Alex recalled the darkening sky outside the Farm. Would she understand Banhi's warning if she'd eaten Matthew's coin.

The bear's paw raised like it was making a point, but without separate fingers at the end of its blunt paw, it reminded Alex of Charon, waving its stump. "Matthew said the tower kept many things away. Are we near there?" The bear leaned to peek through the doorway. "Did Matthew come?"

Alex told him.

The bear moped. Then it looked at her. "Did you take his coin?" In his voice was the expectation of an affirmative answer. This was the next step in the plan Matthew had groomed him and Jacque for.

The more she had to answer for her decision the less conviction it held. "I couldn't." Before the giant bear could challenge her decision—which irritated her because it was too late to do anything about it—she said, "But let's figure out how to get you out of here. I think whatever is out there is worth facing if it makes Marta better."

Banhi said, "Maybe it is a myth, just another silly story. I know no one who has seen such things. I have many questions to answer if we are to do this. If we take him out, where will he go? He cannot stay on the Between. If he goes back to the living, what will become of him? This skin is part of this universe, like this house. Can it exist in any others? He can't go back, not like that."

Dany laughed, his thick paws holding his lighter-colored belly, "That's a mouthful."

"We have to figure something out. He can't stay here. He's hurting Marta." Alex confirmed.

"You don't know that," Banhi said. "Correlation does not make causation. She's unconscious. What can be other reasons for that? Unconscious does not mean hurt. Look how you were when we found you."

Alex was lost in thought. Was there another reason why Marta was unconscious? It seemed cruel to save her only to ask her to do it again.

Dany interrupted, "I understand. I can't stay. I can't go. I died at the Library." The bear looked at them once each. It straightened, as though trying to look taller or show it could be brave. "It's time. Everyone must sacrifice to defeat Jeremiah." It put its soft paw on Alex's shoulder. "Could you make it easier for me like you did for William? I know it's a lot to ask."

Alex knew what he was asking as the words came out of his little red-felt mouth. It was her responsibility, wasn't it? She didn't need long to mull over what that meant. "I'll do my best," she told him. "But not here. We need to take you out of here and onto the Between."

It rubbed his fur against the knap, "Will this stay as my skin?"

Alex looked to Banhi for an answer.

"Why do you look at me? My grandmother told me no stories like this." She turned around, "She wasn't crazy."

Alex pursed her lips and considered her options. They all had to get out of Marta. Alex had no certainty, but allowing him to die within Marta could do her even more harm. If she brought him to the market and the fur sloughed off leaving his flayed flesh exposed, could she heal him—or barring that, could she temper his pain and bring his end rapidly enough? *I have no idea.* Alex hated that she was probably lying to him, "If I can't heal you, I'll make quick."

Dany embraced Alex, his fat, fluffy arms barely reaching around her back.

He wadded after them, as Alex and Banhi followed Banhi's thread out the bedroom and towards the front door.

Marta was cackling. "I'm sorry," she said, wiping her eyes. "Your brother's an asshole, isn't he? Typical boy. It was his idea not to warn you." She couldn't stop laughing. "He was only disappointed he couldn't see your faces."

Alex found the buildup of tension inside her released and she let out a long, hearty laugh. Banhi held a finger under her nose as she giggled. Only Dany stood silently, looking at the three laughing women, asking, "What's so funny? Besides the obvious, I mean."

Alex explained the plan to Marta. "Ultimately, it's up to you. I won't do anything if you're not willing to try."

"You've saved my life twice now. I'd say whatever sacrifice you ask is fair," Marta said somberly.

"Because I need to ask a lot of you once you're—"

Marta interrupted her, "We are willing to do anything you need."

Alex embraced her.

Marta patted her back before pushing Alex away. "Come now, Alexandrea. It's time we see what happens next."

Alex and Banhi followed Banhi's thread, Dany plodding right behind them.

As soon as their feet landed in the market, Dany's heart-star almost throbbed, beacon-like. A quick glance confirmed Marta's did the same. The air felt hollow and charged, like the sudden lowering pressure of a fast approaching, violent storm; the wind so ferocious, she couldn't breathe.

She asked Dany, "Are you okay?"

Around them, dozens of women stopped whatever they were doing to marvel at the walking, talking teddy bear. Dany urged, "I'm starting to feel. I don't like this. Please, Alex. Please."

Alex couldn't be certain, but inside Marta, inside the bear, he was removed from his actual body. The bear was from Marta and her brother's universe. Stepping to the Between, the bear skin remained like a dream within a dream; it wouldn't last forever.

Banhi pulled on Alex's sleeve, "You sense it, do you not?"

Alex was too distracted by Dany's distress, until Banhi mentioned it. She pointed at Banhi and Khowla, "You two, guard us. You remember how to cast your spells, right?"

"Alex," the bear called out in a warbling voice. "My skin, Alex!" It touched its fur and winced as though touching cactus spines.

Banhi and Khowla nodded; standing on opposing sides of Alex and Dany. Alex wrapped her arms around Dany, concentrating to heal him as rapidly as possible.

Banhi turned her back to them and put her hands on her hips, standing watch.

Dany began screaming. "I can't Alex, it's hurting worse. Oh please make it stop!"

Alex realized healing him would take too agonizingly long. Her concentration shifted. In the moment, although it was muted, every nerve in her body screamed as she took as much of Dany's agony as she could bear. She gingerly helped Dany to lie down, each movement and touch eliciting a yelp from each of them. Khowla went white with terror at the suggestion of killing a teddy bear. Alex wasn't any less thrilled with the responsibilities placed upon her. When she once considered the casualties of those she cared about, she assumed Jeremiah would be the one doing the killing.

Alex eased the giant bear to the sandy ground. It was difficult enough bearing the memories of harming people who fought her, but Dany was her friend. Still, there was no turning back. She told herself it'd be harder to watch him suffer to death than to ease him to it.

The bear looked up at the fountain, its red felt mouth open in awe. A large paw reached up, trembling, "That is the most amazingly wondrous thing I have ever seen." The fur beside its eyes darkened as it cried. Its eyes flitted to Alex, and it spoke as though through clenched felt, "Not a bad view." It watched Alex a moment, and as though sensing what she was waiting for, said, "I'm ready Alex."

Alex placed her hand on the bear's chest. It took her some time to feel the rapid thumping of its heart through thick fur and stuffing. Her body was on fire. Sweat dampened her forehead and dripped down her back as the pain made her nauseous. She wasn't sure how much longer she could keep this up.

Around them, the sky was shifting. The constant blue sky, mottled with decorative puffy clouds, threatened to deep peacock. The wind shifted and raced around them, chilling them as it poked beneath their clothes, darting between their legs, and lingering as it curled around their backs to chill their spines. The air seemed to groan, like a world-weary old man acknowledging he was finally succumbing to the pain.

"I'm sorry, Dany," Alex whispered, wiping its fur as though petting a cat. She realized that while a cat enjoyed being pet, doing the same to Dany was really, really weird. She wouldn't have touched him that way had he not been wearing synthetic skin.

"I know. It's okay. I just feel, I don't know, like I've been torn apart and put back together." Its eyes studied her, "I can feel how you're holding my pain at bay." He paused and asked, "Do you know what it's like? Death?"

Alex swallowed and struggled to speak. She soothed, "I used to be scared of it, but I think it's a lot like this." Around the square, women sensed the change in the weather as wind blew the spray off the fountain in sheets. They began taking cover in the stalls.

"I believe death follows each of us closely," Dany grunted. "It's right here," his padded paw touched the back of Alex's head. "You can't see behind you. But it's not dark like when you close your eyes. It's like there's nothing there. Death is that nothing."

Alex wanted to humor Dany his last confession, wherever it might lead, but as Lesedi's form swayed back and forth atop the spire, Alex dreaded what was coming. Perhaps Banhi was right and there are things that safeguard the Between against the living. Something Alex might know had she taken Matthew's coin. It was becoming an easier decision to regret, but she didn't, not entirely, not yet. Alex squinted into the wind. Perhaps it was Jeremiah making his approach. Recalling him chasing her as she fled the Library, she had been certain he avoided the Between. In fact, she had been counting on it. His appearance now would throw a wrench into her plans, but better to know now. Or it wasn't him. Whatever was coming, Alex could not risk putting this off any longer. Coming to terms with it wasn't easy. Her hand disobeyed her will. It broke her heart how difficult it was; it was hard enough already without having to think on it. She pressed against the furry chest until her hand disappeared through the fur.

Dany gasped, its paws floundering in the air at the newfound tightness in its chest as Alex squeezed. Her hand felt the strength of his heart expanding against her enclosing fingers, pushing them apart a little less each time.

Banhi shouted, "Hurry, Alex. I am growing afraid."

Alex barely heard her.

The wind groaned again. It came from all around them, as though they already were inside whatever made the plaintive cry.

Alex tried to picture the human face Dany once had, his brown button eyes darting about. Its gaze settled on her and its felt mouth smiled, puffing its cheeks.

"Alex? Alex!"

Alex didn't want to take her gaze from Dany. It felt only fair that if he looked at her as he died, she would be looking at him as she took his life.

The groaning was closer, and loud enough that it reverberated through her body. She could feel it inside her stomach, in her chest. Waves of deep, intrusive noise passing through her.

The vibrations were growing stronger. She felt like they boiled her bowels, percolating the digested matter in her colon and driving her to the queasiness that precedes diarrhea. What sounded like fabric flapping in the wind raced around her as the sky darkened even more, their shadows dissolving into the growing gloom.

Around her the remaining women screamed.

With a chill, Dany's pain vanished from her skin. She gasped, sickened by her own sense of relief. She checked Dany; he was gone. Alex bolted to her feet.

Three giant masses, each like a multitudinous layered black sheet, like a man-o-war jellyfish constructed of black fabric, flailed high into the air. They twisted and flapped despite the stillness. They began releasing streamers, like giant coils of black gauze unrolling like cloth lightning bolts. Dozens of them streamed into the air, upwards, downward, outwards, all taking twisting, jerking courses, all targeting Alex and her friends.

Alex concentrated her anger and her pain; the sensation of Dany's heartbeat hadn't left her hand. These—things—couldn't give her the moment's reprieve to grieve for the life she took. She manifested her confidence; whatever these things were, if Jeremiah's tower kept them at bay so could she. She thrust out her hands and... nothing.

"Fuck," she cried out, realizing her coins were dark and she would be unable to cast a spell unless she turned them, alerting Jeremiah.

The innumerable streamers violently twisted on the wind. As they lurched in their expanding reach, they undulated together, as though driven by the rapid ebb and flow of a tide.

Banhi was the first one to let off a mustard-colored fireball. It shot straight through the air and struck a flapping sheet, and the billowing shroud burned.

The thing, the creature, the entirety of it, didn't seem to react like a living creature would under the same circumstances, even as the heat from the flames twisted and jerked the higher sheet. The fabric withered, shriveling closer to the mass of others that formed the body, transferring flame to them, until in little time, the entire mass of fabric and streamer burned.

Khowla conjured a fireball. The creature hadn't moved out of the fireball's path with what appeared to be intention, the flapping fabric seemed to randomly move at the right moments, as though it was luck and not intelligence or skill that allowed it to remain unscathed.

"Alex, do something," Banhi cried.

Alex touched her dark coin. "I can't," she cried. "He'll know and come for us."

Before she could say anything more, Khowla cried out. She screamed not in pain, but an insane, maddening cry that changed pitch and tenor throughout. One of the ribbons touched her face and all she could do was wrench and scream.

Alex rushed forward to pull the ribbon from Khowla's cheek. She heard someone cry, "Don't touch that," but it was too late. Her fingers closed on the black fabric.

Chapter One Hundred and Fifty-Two

lex had been transported back to Matthew's wrecked apartment, the walls smoldering and in varying degrees of collapse. Billy's body lay where she left it, bloated and swarming inside and out with insects.

"You killed him. You disgust me. I hate you, Alex."

Alex turned to Rose. Her cousin's chest heaved as she continued her condemnation. "You didn't even try to save him. All you thought about was taking his coin."

Alex tried to tell Rose that wasn't so, that she had tried, that she wanted nothing more than to save Billy, but she could not compete with Rose's never-ending accusations.

"You don't deserve the magic you have. You don't deserve the Book Club's loyalty. If they knew you like I do they'd be disgusted. They'd hate you, Alex. Look at my brother. Look at what you've done to him."

"I loved your brother, Rose," Alex got a few words in.

"You loved him?" Rose shooed some flies away. "This is love? This is what love does?"

Alex didn't have an answer. In her case, this was the result of her love.

Rose came closer. "This is what's left of him, Alex. You took his coin, all that he was, and you digested it. He became a part of you like a steak becomes a part of you, digested and assimilated."

Alex's hands trembled. "That's not true, Rose." Her heart ached with the desire for Rose to feel her pain, but she knew that Rose's anger was nothing more than her pain dressed in fighting clothes.

"No? Then show it to me." She held out her palm. "Barf it up. Prove he's still here."

"I can't do that, Rose—"

"Of course, you can't, because you digested him. You cannibalized my brother. You evil, disgusting, vile," she seemed in possession of a thesaurus as she continued, unabated.

Alex had never been so angry. Not when she'd fought Matthew. Not when she'd fought Jeremiah. Rose continued the insulting tirade, hurling foul words as she walked tight circles around Alex.

Alex loved Rose; at least she did once. Rose was her best friend, her sister, if only in spirit, and now Alex was approaching the precipice where, if Rose didn't stop, she'd plunge over the edge.

Alex's entire body clenched as though she steadily turned to stone. She felt feverish. Her stomach roiled, acidic and sour. Her heart ached. Rose was the one person she could share her feelings with, the only one who knew what Billy meant. Yet Rose was disinterested in hearing such things. The last bit of Alex's heart shriveled and bruised. She lurched at Rose to still her mouth, her rage-trembling hands intending to clamp on the girl, her own jaw clenched so tight, that when she grabbed Rose, she didn't just hold her, but released her emotions as a spell. In her hands, Alex tore Rose in two.

Alex leapt back in horror. Rose collapsed to the floor, her body bisected diagonally, from left shoulder to right hip. All sorts of glossy viscera bulged from the gaping wound.

Alex cried out. *What did I do? I didn't mean to hurt her. I only wanted to make her stop.* She was sick with regret and fear and too many emotions to feel. Her trembling hands smeared her tears. Alex lurched as she dry-heaved, a wave that brought with it a flood of tears. "I never wanted to hurt you, Rose. I love you so much, you and Billy. But all this," she motioned as though referring to the apartment, "all this makes it so hard. Everyone I love. Everyone I hurt. All I want is to protect you and look what I do. Look what happens to everyone who comes near me." Alex collapsed in a heap and sobbed.

"You never loved me. You were jealous of me. Your parents died. Your father murdered your twin brother. You were jealous because I still had all those things."

"I thought I had them too: you and Billy were like my twins." Alex couldn't look up but anticipated Rose, with her glowing coin, awaiting Charon. "I was never jealous because I was part of your family."

"You were never family. You were a burden. An extra mouth for a single mother. You made everything harder. We had to protect you. You took our freedom away. You made us have to hide to keep you safe. You ruined our lives."

Alex had no argument. Although Heather always treated her as family, when she found Heather stressing over bills, she always dreaded that her extra mouth to feed and body to clothe caused those problems. Heather always dismissed her concern, but what else could she have said? "You're right. I did. I am sorry, Rose. Tell me what I can do for you to forgive me."

Alex looked up and shrieked as Rose awkwardly raced towards her. Her bisected bodies hinged at the shoulder, her gaping wound a viscera-filled mouth. Intestines curled and pulled her along the floor like an octopus; the gigantic wound open like a broken rib-toothed jaw.

Alex tripped on debris when she tried to run. Hot, wet breath from the gaping maw dampened her back. She felt herself slipping into it, the jaws ferociously clamping down. Rose's exposed ribs, like fangs, speared holes in her flesh, perforating her. She screamed, or tried to, her chest squeezing her lungs like a stoppered bottle. The sweaty, slimy, wretched creature that was Rose thrashed about like a shark trying to tear its prey apart, its jaws trembling as the clenching muscles drove the flesh-clotted ribs deeper into Alex until they pierced through. Alex tried to punch at Rose, her fists thrusting through the air as though unable to move fast enough to strike with any force.

Spasming esophageal muscles in Rose's middle began swallowing her.

How am I not dead? The creature thrashed, trying to position her for a clean gulp. *How is this not hurting?* She could feel the pressure of the bite but not the pain. It was difficult in the panic of the moment to even have these thoughts, to not scream in panic and cry in anguish, to not be hysterical in terror, but Alex realized as soon as she questioned her state that she likely hadn't left the Between: the ribbon's touch inducing this nightmare.

She thought of trying to wake up, opening her eyes as wide as she could, but the mechanism inducing the dream disconnected her unconscious from her physical self. All that was left to do was see the nightmare to its end.

Alex? Alex! She took a single step forward, daring, threatening the Rose-monster. "I get it, Rose," Alex shouted at her bifurcated cousin. "You're not angry, you're not even here. Those are *my* fears. The things *I* worry about. That I was a burden on your family. That behind every hug was resentment because there was less to go around. Whenever Heather worried about money, I secretly believed she meant me."

The Rose-monster spoke again, a second, gurgling-wet, growling voice coming from her abdominal mouth, "She was talking about you, she—"

"Shut up, Rose. This is my dream." Rose looked shocked, hurt even. "I know I was forced on Heather. I wasn't wanted, I just showed up one day, along with all the responsibility that went with me. Heather never once made me feel like an outsider. I did that all by myself." She approached Rose, the giant wet mouth quivering and slobbering down her jeans. "But you, Rose, you fed on that. Your jealousy fed on that. You were the older sister until I showed up. You were Heather's star until I showed up. You were the center of the world until I showed up. But you could hear when people talked about magic. You knew, and that made you special. Then one day, not only could I hear it, I could do it. I could and you couldn't. But then one day you could, too, and you should have been Heather's star again, but you weren't."

Rose-monster babbled a few words.

"You could have been at my side, Rose. You could have been my equal, but instead, you allowed your jealousy to rule your emotions. And that's fine, you're entitled to your feelings, but I allowed my insecurities to let you, because I believed I deserved your anger. But you know what, Rose,

I see the truth now. I never deserved that, and it's because I wasn't strong enough to put you in your place that you've become a monster. It's my fault that I never told you the truth because I was always afraid of it. I *was* a burden. I *did* take away from your lives. These were sacrifices you weren't asked if you wanted, just like I wasn't asked if I wanted this."

The Rose-monster bawled, its wagging tongue of entrails rising and falling in its sobs.

Alex held out her hand. "This is peace, Rose. This is me finally understanding and accepting that I've been afraid that I've hurt your family."

Monster Rose took Alex's hand and held it against her chest.

This wasn't Rose-monster forgiving her, this was Alex coming to peace with it herself. "But this is so much more than that, Rose," Alex explained, the words straightening her back as she spoke. "I faced my greatest fears and there's no Jeremiah in sight."

Rose-monster sobbed; she started slapping Alex's palm. She started shaking Alex's hand in such a jerking saw-like motion Alex's whole body felt pushed back and forth. Blinking, as her eyes opened, Alex found herself again in the square, surrounded by her friends who took turns trying to shake her awake once the ribbon fled her.

Khowla, no longer touched by the ribbon, shivered, weary of the others hovering nearby. Banhi continued to throw balls of colorful flames at the undulating masses of dark sheets. They burned the sheets, but the nightmares loomed closer, their tendrils unfurling into the market by the hundreds.

Alex had to do something—and feeling retribution was due—she leapt into the air, flying closer to the creatures to draw their tentacular ribbons away from her friends, allowing them to fight back without reprisal.

If only I had magic. She touched her dark coin. *Is it worth the chance?* She didn't think so. *And yet.... I'm flying without my coin. My magic doesn't work, but they don't have magic, either.* She built the fountain; was that built with magic or imagination? *This is the place of dreams....*

Alex imagined her counterattack. Instead of trying to cast a spell, she thought about what it would be like as the heat of a bright blue fireball grew in her hand. She focused on her bare palm, swooping and climbing to avoid the straining ribbons as they chased after her in a winding, spiraling dance. Each moment one of the three creatures drew near enough to touch her, she evaded it only by breaking her concentration. She told herself the imagined power didn't disappear with her broken concentration, but lingered, waiting for her to continue.

Finally, taking one last opportunity, she imagined energy traveling down the length of her arm. She imagined the tingling in her skin, the dull ache in her flesh, the way her bones crackled with energy. She imagined it pooling in her hand, imagined the weight. She imagined the rising heat searing her palm, feeling it radiating against her face like she stood too close to Abby's kiln. She imagined the glare in her eyes and shaded them even though nothing shone. It was most difficult believing it could happen, but she cocked her arm for the launch. Had she not been two hundred-odd feet in the air, pretending to throw an imaginary fireball would have made her feel like a complete idiot.

Wanting desperately to believe something was where she saw nothing, Alex followed through. Nothing left her hand, even as she clung to her desire to see something. Watching along the imagined trajectory, she thought she saw the faintest smudge of blue. It was all too easy to dismiss it as a fizzled attempt at magic, but as in her nightmare, she told herself it wasn't a smudge or a flaw in her eyes, but her fireball.

The air around the smudge suddenly rippled with heat and a long blue tail sprouted from seemingly nowhere, the fireball coming into existence—finally—from her thought. It exploded against one of the creatures, just as she told herself it would. With a splash of napalm, the flapping black sheets were all but consumed in the flames. In her concentration, they grew exponentially hotter, the flames roaring like a blowtorch tip, charring and decomposing the nightmare. The ribbons convulsed, disintegrating to ashes. The sheets shriveled and tore like tissue paper. As her imagined flames carbonized it, the nightmare stiffened until it dropped firmly to the ground, striking and turning into a billowing explosion of ash.

Turning her attention to the other two, Alex threw a second fireball. Then the third.

The two burning creatures withdrew, their ribbons and sheets burning to rags. The withering nightmares twitched and swatted at the dwindling flames as they fled in desiccated tatters.

Alex crash-landed by the women. Khowla embraced her. "I have never been so frightened."

She held Khowla, her own heart punching the inside of her ribs. For a while, neither had she. And yet, in spite of how frightened she had been under the thrall of the nightmare, she knew something about herself she hadn't before.

Banhi shouted, "That was not the magic of before. What was that?"

"What you told me," Alex replied. "Like in a dream, I imagined them."

Khowla asked, "How were your fireballs so powerful?"

"I imagined them that way," Alex said. *It was like a lucid dream.* "I willed them to burn like that."

Distracted, Banhi groaned, "These horrors never end." Following Banhi's fearful gaze, Alex saw Charon had arrived.

Chapter One Hundred and Fifty-Three

howla leaned forward. "I have heard of the child, the Ferryman, Charon. Is this?"

Alex nodded. She looked back at the teddy bear, nearly forgotten during her nightmare.

Dany stood silently, his skin, his push-broom moustache and thick eyebrows all returned. Only the lack of square-framed glasses made him look any different than Alex remembered when they met. "I go with the child?"

"Give your coin to," she fumbled, "it."

Banhi squinted. "What happened to you, Child?" She turned to Alex, "The child is missing a hand?"

Pursing her lips, Alex nodded. "The child *is* the Reaper."

Banhi eyeballed the child suspiciously. "This adorable thing? No." Still, she took a healthy step backwards.

Charon eyed Alex carefully as it approached Dany, clearly suspicious of her.

Beyond them, out in the square, few women remained. Most fled during the nightmares, the recollection of other attacks fresh enough to parch any curiosity.

With a hand on his shoulder, Alex brought Dany to the child. "Here," she told it. "He's my friend. Please take care of him."

Dany smiled as the child held out its hand. "Thank you, Alex."

"For killing you?"

"When you put it that way." He placed his coin in the child's upturned palm and watched the tiny fingers close around it.

The child held its clenched fist before its face, its mouth pinched as though deep in concentration. It closed its eyes, as though afraid to watch as slowly it opened its palm. Peeking, the child's tantrum struck immediately, shaking its fist and dancing in a stomping circle: The coin had vanished. It closed its fist and opened it again and again, each time in a more desperate attempt, as though willing the coins return. It looked at Alex, showing her its empty palm, shaking it with great concern. The child was bereft, its eyes welling with tears.

Dany asked, "Is something wrong? Is that supposed to happen?"

As she approached the child, Alex replied, "The coin always disappears, but I've never seen it on the Between before. I think it expected the coin might stay." She knelt before the child and as gently as she could, placed her fingertips in its palm. "You can't keep the coins? They don't stay?"

The child looked at her uncomprehendingly. It shook its palm again, swaying side to side as it sniffled and moaned.

"It never stays, does it? Only my father's because he didn't give it all to you." She touched her dark coin as she spoke, and this sparked some comprehension in the child's eyes. It reached for her chest.

"Look-out, Alex!" everyone around her cried out simultaneously.

Charon gently touched her breastbone where her dark coin rested. It petted the spot. Instead of looking at the coin, however, the child's eyes fixed on Alex's.

"Do you want this?"

The child petted the dark spot one final time before its shoulders slumped in defeat. It looked at Dany and jerked its head in the direction from which it came. The child turned and walked away. Dany followed. Alex watched; this was unlike any time she'd witnessed before. Dany died in the place the dead go. Where might Charon lead him?

Alex wondered about the implications of what she'd actually seen. *Is that why Charon is so covetous for our coins? Because they vanish and it's always hoping to find that one that won't?*

Charon walked a short distance. Glancing back, it reached for Dany's hand. Together they continued until like the heat of a mirage, they were gone.

Khowla's hands found her hips. "Why is he so fortunate to get an afterlife but no women were so fortunate?" Her anger came out in her words; another slight to her sex.

The only difference is he had his coin and *body with him.* "I don't know," Alex answered. "Same thing would probably happen to Marta." Turning, she saw Marta stirring. *That took a long time. We took Dany out and she didn't come to for several minutes.*

Banhi shuddered. "Look, she awakens."

Marta looked about. Although clearly dazed, their outlandish surroundings only led her to further confusion. Twice, she shook her head and rubbed her eyes. To Alex she asked, "You see all this, too?"

Alex nodded. "It's quite a thing they've made here. Like the house you and Alex made."

Marta scanned the square. "This is nothing like that house." She took a deep breath. "This is amazing." She saw Khowla and Banhi and weakly waved. "Hi. You must be Alex's friends."

Shaking her head, Marta told Alex that she was okay.

Alex turned to Khowla and Banhi. "I need your help."

Alex felt the weight of their stare. She could feel, just by cutting through the false neutrality of their expressions, that they were feeling put upon. "Nearly every time we meet, it's because I'm asking for help," she said. "I need it now, more than ever."

Khowla looked back the length of her thread. "Morning is nearly come. We must be going back." Banhi nodded in agreement.

"Please hear me out. I need you. I once asked you how many people would have to die for this to be over. Do you remember that?"

Banhi wet her lips. "I do not like where this is going. Tell us; we will hear you."

Hear me? "Jeremiah has hundreds, maybe thousands of women, trapped in his Farm."

Banhi nodded. "This we heard in rumors."

Khowla nodded. "Horrible places, women treated like farm animals, living in muck."

"It's nothing like you can imagine." Alex explained the imprisoning desire.

The notion awed Banhi. "They want to stay? Even though they know what he does?"

"They believe they're having such a good time they don't care they're prisoners." She explained Jeremiah's army of Books, the tattooed golems he makes from women.

"That is horrible," Banhi muttered.

"That's why we have to stop it," Alex pleaded. "And I need your help to do it."

Khowla shook her head. "We do not have magic like you. Haven't you learned: What are we to do that you cannot?"

"That's the thing. The Farm is here, on the Between. When you're there, outside, you'll have your magic."

Khowla shook her head. "I cannot." Looking back her thread again, she said, "Morning comes and I must wake. There are many who rely on me." With a sigh, she added, "My family must be fed and cared for. Women need me to help them. I am sorry, Alex. Maybe another day when it is not so late."

Alex didn't feel disappointment as she expected. "You have families and responsibilities. But some things are more important." Alex was drawing attention from the handful of remaining women around them. "He won't stop. He's always behind the scenes, twisting things and making things chaotic. He'd rather destroy us than let us interfere. He's immortal." She took a breath. "And I'm a witch. I'm fighting for every one of you. I'm terrified. Help me save all those women. I need you to do something that will make a greater difference than whatever you have to do today."

Khowla looked to Banhi, as though begging Banhi to find some story her grandmother told her to answer for them both.

"What you propose is important," Banhi began. "I cannot stay here when the house around me awakes. They will wake and pull me from this place. Our threads are stretched long, and we will be pulled all that way to awaken. We must go, and soon."

"I know," Alex said through gritted teeth. "And once you're home, I can bring you back, just like I did with Marta."

"You propose to take our bodies to the Between?" Khowla gestured at the sky. "Did you not see what happens to the living here? I cannot survive another nightmare like that."

"We won't be here long enough—"

Banhi asked, "Why us? What happened to your people?"

Alex answered, "They're all coming. But you know things no one else knows. I—my people—don't have that knowledge. We need you."

"They are children's stories," Banhi said. "Nonsense." She looked at her thread. "We must go. Now. Someone is bound to wake us. Do you know how hard that bounce is when the waking flings you this far?"

Why won't they help? What are they afraid of? As soon as Alex had the thought, she understood. *Why didn't I realize it sooner? Heather said it about the Book Club, but I thought she was excusing them.*

Alex arrived at her point so quickly she almost stuttered, "I understand. You're scared. I'm asking you to go to war. That's it, isn't it?"

"What do you think?" Khowla looked too ashamed to admit the truth.

"I think Lesedi is dead *and you're terrified*. You've seen what he can do, and you're scared, which is exactly why he does those things."

Khowla's face reddened; Banhi placed a soothing hand on her shoulder. To Alex, Banhi explained, "We live dangerous lives already. To say we are afraid is to insult us for living. We are never too afraid. Tell us how we can help when you are here and we are half a world away and about to awaken."

"I'm sorry, I...," Alex didn't know how to finish. She suddenly grabbed Khowla's thread in a loose fist.

It buzzed and vibrated, convulsing like an injured snake. Through her hand Alex sensed the full length of the thread, each zig and zag through the market, its winding path through the desert beyond, to where it exited through a pulse of mist. She understood power now: Khowla's entire existence vibrated against her palm. She could squeeze it, twist it, sever it, and there was nothing Khowla could do to stop her. But touching it, she also could see Khowla, in a white linen bedgown, asleep in her bed. The vision was clear, as though Alex stood in her bedroom.

Khowla stood fearfully before her, perhaps afraid Alex wordlessly threatened to snap her string. On the far end of the thread, Khowla slept fitfully, dreaming herself threatened by Alex in a market, beneath a fountain.

Alex explained, "If you'll let me, I can bring you here."

Khowla looked at Alex sternly. "Tell me child. Is this a thing that you cannot do without us?"

Alex fought the urge to blanketly reply. "I don't know. But I need all the help I can get." She paused. "I will end this, but I need to know I have everyone helping me."

Khowla nodded. "Then bring me here."

The thread was like a conduit, and touching it, both ends were suddenly within reach. Alex reached to touch both Khowla's gently on her cheek.

The thread disintegrated in a shower of dimming sparks. Khowla screamed: Her thread was gone.

"What have you done?" Banhi raced around Khowla—who was gasping in panic—looking for a sparking remnant of the broken thread, but there was none.

Khowla hyperventilated, "Am I dead? Will my family awaken to my body?" She wasn't aware she was in her bedgown.

Banhi stepped closer before poking Khowla's chest, "Your heart-star glows. Your yarn is gone. That can only mean…."

Khowla was reduced to laughter as she realized she was in her pajamas.

"What is so funny?" Banhi went to her, "Are you well?"

Khowla's hair bobbed atop her head as she cackled, pointing at Alex. "The girl brought me here. I am on the Between!" She stomped her foot. "I'm actually here, not asleep in my home. Imagine everyone's surprise in the morning when I am just gone. Vanished." She shrieked with laughter and pantomimed looking under the bed, "Where do you suppose Mother has run to? She's always threatened to sell the home and run away if we did not behave!"

Alex, realizing she hadn't thought through all she asked of her friends, asked, "They won't be worried?"

"Yes, they'll be worried," Khowla nearly shouted. "But *look at me*! *On the Between*!" She leaned closer to Alex, "Can you bring me clothes? I'll tell you what I want to wear."

"I think we can get a change of clothes for you."

Banhi demanded Alex allow her to choose her own clothes. "I'll go back. Wake up. Change. Lie down. And come right back," she panted; not breathing between sentences. "I am very fortunate you didn't ask me first. How embarrassed I'd be to be standing here!"

Khowla tried to ask but Banhi wouldn't give her more than a wink. The moment Alex acquiesced; Banhi was off like a spark.

A few minutes later, when Banhi returned, Alex drew her onto the Between as well. "I left a note and asked that someone call your family," she told Khowla. "I told them to say, *She's gone off to save the world.*"

Khowla scowled for as long as she could hold back her laughter. She reached out and took Banhi's hand. "Dear friend, we've never actually met before."

While Banhi and Khowla acquainted their corporeal forms, Alex saw to Marta. They hadn't much time. Perhaps the nightmares had enough intelligence to reconsider returning, but Alex couldn't count on that. While she was no longer fearful of the things, she knew not everyone would have the same epiphanies.

The sights of the market still managed to elicit oohs from Marta at every glance. The fountain, the stalls with their impossible façades; Marta could not stop swooning in wonder at every sight. As Alex prepared them for leaving, Marta said, "I know you won't, but please lie to me and promise I will come back one day to take this all in."

Alex tried to, but Marta was right. The unwritten future possessed too many possibilities where things went wrong. Was it fair of her to bring these women into such danger, knowing that many of them would not return? That she had to die to succeed, she accepted. She was tired, worn ragged in a matter of weeks. She felt as fragile as a wet tissue, apt to come apart at any moment, and yet, she held. *As many as it takes. Everyone who knows you.* The words haunted her, and yet, here she was, fulfilling them.

Bahni asked, "Where do we go? Is it far?"

Alex grinned at her. "No, not far at all." With little in the way of concentration, a swirl of mist appeared. With it, as Alex expected: Charon.

The child held out its hand, it addressed each of them with its demand.

Khowla asked, "We have to pay to leave, too?"

Alex stepped before her friends. She held her arms out. Charon's hand reluctantly fell to its side. The child's normally neutral expression turned to frustration. It shook its one fist and scrunched its reddening face as though falling into a tantrum. Alex took a step towards the child. Immediately, it flinched, seeking to turn and flee, clearly terrified of what Alex had done to it previously.

Alex knelt by the child. "You will have these," she whispered, touching her dark coin. The child looked past her to the others. "Not today, but soon." Alex told it. "Please, let us pass."

The child leaned closer, looking upon her with a hunger she'd not seen before. Staring in its dark eyes, she noticed the shifting reflection sparkling in them. Not unlike the writing in a Book, she saw in the child's eyes a multitude of others. As people died all around the world, Charon was there, simultaneously, taking their coins. Coveting their coins. Wracked with furious disappointment when the coins it rightfully claimed vanished within its very grasp. It was like watching a person parched with thirst, only the waterfall they intended to gorge themselves evaporated as it passed their lips.

Alex touched the dark disk on her chest. "When it's time, maybe my coins won't disappear."

The child looked at her and then at its feet, its toes curling in the dust. She touched the child's damaged arm; it flinched at first but then acknowledged her with a subtle nod.

She urged her friends to pass.

Once the others were through, Alex addressed Charon, "I know I hurt you. I'm sorry."

The child's regard for her melted.

Alex gently stroked the child's cheek. "If I could take it back, I would," she whispered. The child looked at her as though finally understanding. Then she stood and left.

Chapter One Hundred and Fifty-Four

Alex entered into her attic bedroom. Abby sat upright on the bed, apparently startled by Khowla and Banhi's sudden appearance. The two women talked at a stunned Abby, who was reeling from the barrage of two foreign tongues spoken at her simultaneously. Marta stood back from the threesome.

Alex tried her best to calm them, but their inability to speak anything close to fluent English brought their anxious chatter to a peak, the words and phrases they did know lost to their accent-thickening nerves.

"We're not on the Between anymore," Alex said loud and slow, "we," she motioned to Abby and herself, "don't understand you."

"I am foreign," Banhi managed, the words twisted by her accent, "not deaf."

Banhi said a few words to Khowla. Khowla shook her head. With a sigh, Banhi said to them, "She speaks no English. No Hindi. I speak not her Zulu."

Alex's chest was tight and stifled, like she was trying to breathe underwater. She hadn't taken languages into account and wondered what twists this would throw into her already convoluted plan. *What am I doing?* She thought of the women waiting downstairs. *Are they ready for this? Do I have the right to bring them on this journey? They could all die. And for what?*

She thought about Billy; the difference between when he was missing and knowing he was dead was the complete absence of hope in her heart. It was as though she was aware that his passing left the universe changed.

That was because of Jeremiah. Everything is because of him. My parents, Sara, everything that's happened has its root with him. If I don't do this, he'll always be a threat. If I do, she looked at the four women in her bedroom, *will they forgive me for what I am asking of them?*

"Are you okay?" Abby touched Alex's cheek; it was wet. "Why are you crying?"

Alex found it difficult to look Abby in the eye. She felt she was betraying her. *Not Abby. Not after everything….* "I need to talk to everyone. What I am going to ask…. What I need you to do…. What I…," she couldn't find a way to say it that didn't diminish the gravity she felt. "I need to know they're ready."

Abby tried not to grin at Alex's hesitations, "They're ready, but if you need to hear it for yourself, by all means." She gestured at the dark opening to the lower level. "Everyone's asleep."

Alex's shoulders fell, time pressuring on her shoulders. Suddenly, it didn't feel so preciously limited. "How are you?"

"Fine."

"Did it stick? I mean, you know," Alex insinuated without saying.

"I guess. It feels different," she shrugged. "I don't feel empty anymore, if that's what you mean."

Alex sat beside Abby, the impression in the mattress tipping them together. Alex leaned against Abby and Abby let her. Marta took the desk chair and turned it around to sit and keep her eye on Alex. Banhi approached the bed and pressed it; disagreeing with how soft it was, she kneeled on the floor. Khowla joined her.

After a few minutes, Abby said, "Spill it, kiddo. What's troubling you?"

Before she could find the words, Alex fought her tears. She couldn't keep herself from thinking about everyone who was so eager to come with her. They didn't realize the certain death they would face. In the news, war was always about heroes and villains. When the heroes would be her friends it felt like she was betraying them. As though because she failed to find a peaceful solution, the only alternative was to destroy it all.

"It's that bad?"

Alex nodded. She tipped her head into her hands, her long hair spilling around, insulating her from everyone's view. She sobbed and couldn't seem to stop.

Abby rubbed her back. Movement on the bed proved to be Marta sitting opposite Abby. Hands on her knees were Banhi and Khowla. Surrounded by people who cared for her, Alex still felt alone. Even Abby felt like a stranger today. Was her comfort genuine or a result of her oath? Just the thought diminished the perceived sincerity and left Alex with doubt.

Eventually, her emotions ran their course, leaving her dry on the inside, her face wet from tears, her shirt dotted where they'd fallen. She was more aware of the weight responsibility placed upon her. This too, she would endure. She pulled her hair back and sat up. Her eyes raw and red; her whole head clear as though the flood of tears washed everything out.

"The things I've seen these few weeks," Alex began; "the things I've done—had to do—or had done to me...." She shook her head. "They're mine and they shouldn't be a burden for others."

Marta tried to speak, "Alex, we're all here—"

"Let me finish," Alex interrupted. "But I'm not the only one who's suffered. You, Abby. You, Marta. And Banhi and Khowla. And it's not over…. What I mean is…. I need to ask you and you and them," she went around the room, "and everyone downstairs, to do something because it's something I believe in." She looked Abby in the eye and refused to flinch. "What I'm asking…. It's not unlikely…. To go along with me means you're going to be in tremendous danger and might die. Could die. Probably…." She looked around the room again, "I'm going to ask each of you. Because asking you if you'll die for me is the only way I can be honest about the danger."

"We're all with you," Abby replied.

"Shut up, Abby," Abby winced at Alex's words. "How can I believe what you say? Are you with me or is the oath making you want to be?" Before Abby could answer, Alex continued, "Don't you see, Abby, I can't trust you. How can I ask anything knowing you'll always say yes?"

Abby bobbed her head in understanding. "Your father told me that becoming your Familiar meant more than being your servant. It meant accepting the responsibility for your life, even if it meant my own."

"I was a baby. You were, what, a few years older than I am now? Just last month my biggest problem was Heather not letting me go to college. What could you have known?"

"I know it seems that way to you. Look at me, Alex. I was the fat kid. The queer girl. I grew up in a stupid small town where a boy once made fun of me so bad, I peed myself. If I didn't have the responsibility of your life, I'd have nothing. I was miserable and depressed and your father gave me purpose. He put me in charge of protecting the first real witch. So maybe you ask me to do something and I die doing it. The thing that scares me more than dying, Alex, is failing to save you."

"That's just it, Abby. How can I know you'll do what's best for the situation and not for me?"

"Have faith in me the same way I had faith in you. When I took this oath, I had no idea if *you'd* be worthy of *my* sacrifice."

"I was a baby."

"Exactly! Look at you. What you've done. What you've had to do and what's been done to you. Each time you keep getting up. You sit here and instead of weeping about *Oh woes me*, you're worried for *us*. Don't you see what that means to all of us?"

"I didn't take an oath, Alex," Marta's words seemed to slow down as they passed. "The person Abby describes—the person you are—that person is a leader I would follow anywhere."

"Me too," Banhi whispered, rubbing tears from her eyes. Khowla looked between the four of them, uncertain what was said, but crying and nodding the same.

Alex put her arms around Abby and Marta. She looked at Banhi and Khowla before closing her eyes. "Thank you," she sighed. She didn't know if it made her feel better. Part of her wished her friends were cowards who would flee to someplace safe.

Banhi patted her knee. "One hour behind, I am sleeping on the bed on the other part of the world. You take me to America. What is it, the pail list? That was top on my pail list. You make that, um, poof," her hand flourished to the air. "You tell us to do. To go. Wars make people dead. People die every day but do not a thing important. Will we? Because you, we will."

Alex nodded. She offered them her thanks. She wished she felt as worthy as they made her out to be. "I'm exhausted," she said at last. "Everything hurts."

They made room on the bed. Abby took the chair and allowed Marta to sleep beside Alex. Although offered a place on the bed, Banhi eagerly took the floor. Khowla agreed, whether or not she understood what she was agreeing to.

Alex closed her eyes. Thoughts swirled. She took a few deep breaths, trying to dispel them. How long did she—did any of them have before facing Jeremiah's wrath? *Tomorrow I make sure he can't hurt anyone else, ever again.* Making the first move seemed the only logical path forward. Accepting that there were no other options, she allowed slumber to enfold her in a dark, dreamless night. For the first time in a long while, Alex rested.

Chapter One Hundred and Fifty-Five

Morning crept silently into Alex's attic. Beams softly creaked and groaned as the roof warmed. The house spoke its popping, creaking greeting. Alex opened her eyes and saw daylight streaming through the cupola above her bed. She stared into the cupola and let her focus go blurry. She wished she had the luxury to pretend the sounds downstairs were Heather and Rose and Billy. But those mornings would never return: Billy was gone. Although Heather was downstairs, cooking, she seemed an incomplete facsimile of her former self. And Rose…. Rose was so different. So angry. Alex couldn't help but feel Rose always condescended to her, expressing disappointment in her, and targeting anger at her. Much deserved: Learning to innately use magic wasn't the same as reading spells from a Book. Was this the same Rose? Alex wasn't so sure. Or it was that Book? Billy did warn Heather of the consequences of Rose taking that Book. Was this what he meant?

She closed her eyes and rubbed the crust from them. She never knew how much she'd miss those mornings. Was it a sign of how difficult things had become that moments once ordinary had become her fondest memories?

Alex sat up. Abby, Marta, and Banhi were gone. Khowla snored softly in the chair beside her desk, swimming in Abby's clothes: a sleeveless shirt and jeans, a belt cinched tight around her waist. As Alex pushed the sheets off, Khowla peeked from under her heavy lids. Seeing Alex, she sprang into action.

A series of gestures and a constant barrage of sounds and clicks Alex couldn't make any sense of, Khowla managed to explain that everyone was downstairs waiting for her and that she—Khowla—remained by her side, to protect her until she woke.

"Thank you, Khowla," Alex said, collecting some clothes. She held her clothes a little higher and motioned to the ladder and downstairs, pantomiming as she said, "I'll meet you downstairs after I change."

Khowla made a face, chattered and gesticulating.

Khowla followed her to the ladder. It was then Alex understood: Khowla was guarding her. It was the older woman's intent to not leave her side. Alex sighed and ushered Khowla back to her seat. When Alex began to change, Khowla turned the seat away, and with a flourish, likely told Alex to proceed.

Heading downstairs after Alex dressed, Khowla went on for an unseemly long time, obviously complaining about the ladder. While Alex washed, Khowla graciously waited in the hall. Then they made their way downstairs.

Alex paused at the bottom of the stairs. The lower level of the house was a flurry of activity. Heather held her coffee mug in two hands and watched as Carrie cooked for the masses. She used every burner and inch of counter space but had meal after meal hot and ready. People took their plates and mugs of coffee and found places to sit and eat and chat and then clean up or request seconds. She surveyed the crowd, all her friends.

It didn't feel that long ago when Heather first introduced her to the Book Club. They seemed so much older, and Alex a child by comparison. They were so worldly and elegant and smart and maybe a little crazy. Now Alex saw them without façades. Or perhaps it was her veneer that was missing. Even Heather, her father's twin sister, didn't seem old anymore. Their ages, for the first time, felt within reach. Carrie and Nancy especially, no longer seemed much older than she was.

Abby's face lit up at the sight of Alex and waved her over. She held a plate smeared with yolk. Even Abby, Alex now saw, wasn't the person she thought she was. She held them all up on some sort of pedestal, an artifice of childhood, which complicated her vision of adults by transforming them into something greater than the sum of their parts. But for the first time she could see that these were just people. These were children in bodies that had mellowed and matured. They were haunted by the same fears and doubts and insecurities, perhaps even more so, Alex reasoned, because they were no longer children and should know better.

Alex ate her breakfast, mingling with the group, chatting with everyone. Conversations mimicked one another. They never felt so afraid as they were when they heard—erroneously—that Alex lost her life battling Charon. They were so sorry about Billy. They were worried about Rose. They were concerned for Heather. When they saw Alex on the news, using magic in New York City and in Paris and realized not only wasn't she dead but she hadn't stopped fighting that whole time. They couldn't wait to be at her side again, especially now they all had magic. Whatever was coming, however afraid they were, they knew everything would change today, and they wanted nothing more than to be at her side. Not one of them had any expectation of one day basking in some heroic St. Crispin's moment. They all sensed their heroics might only be recalled by others.

"I want to say it'll be different this time," June said, sipping on a mimosa. "That because we all have magic, we're going to kick his ass. But that's not the way it's going down, is it?" June studied Alex. "What's happening in there? How are you so calm? So brave?" She held up her flute. "I wanted a screwdriver, but Heather wouldn't let me have anything stronger than bubbly. But I'm coming apart inside. I'm pretending to be brave, you know, faking it until I crap my pants."

Alex didn't know what to say to June. They were all so scared, pretending not to be because of her. Then June graciously excused herself. She poured a full glass of sparkling wine, clinking the flute with the orange juice carton.

As others sat beside her, Alex was gracious and managed to say little, somehow coaxing whoever engaged her to do most of the talking. It was strange how different she felt. Instead of a small boat, tossed down a swift-flowing stream, she was the island, the river flowing around her. Whether she spoke to Carrie or June or Rachel, she felt their equal instead of a child. Yet she also perceived their reverence and wondered if they were now the ones who craved her attention and recognition.

"Can I speak to you? In private?" It was George. His clothes looked pressed. *Maybe Eric's work clothes?* His hair was militantly combed, parted at the side. Flustered with nerves, he looked about to ask her to the prom.

Alex looked around. "There isn't much privacy here. You want to step outside?"

George nodded and followed Alex out the temporary front door.

The air outside was already warm and humid. The sun felt close to generate such heat. "What's up?"

George wrung his hands. "I haven't seen you since Matthew's," his voice crackled with nerves. "I heard he's gone." He looked around as though recognizing someone from a distance.

"He was like a father to you, wasn't he?"

"I guess. Yeah. He was."

"It's okay to miss him," she said.

"He wasn't a good person."

"No," Alex replied. "But that doesn't mean you shouldn't miss him. He said we were on the same side. I didn't believe him because his approach to the problem was so different than mine ever could be."

"He made me do horrible things."

Alex wanted to be delicate. "You did those horrible things yourself. He encouraged you, but they're yours to own."

He didn't seem capable of looking up at her. "I wish I could tell them how sorry I am. Abigail. My mom. The others. You." He looked up. "I'm so sorry, Alex. I know I hurt you."

Alex wanted his apology to take away the way his words made her feel. Abigail was somewhere inside her, one of the multitudes whispering in her head. Would his apology make her feel better? Alex doubted with certainty. His apology only served one person: George. He flinched as she spoke, "Don't apologize, George. Apologies are meaningless without action backing them up. You can't change what you've done, but you can make sure they're not the actions you're remembered for."

"I intend to," he said, stiffening his shoulders. "Whatever happens today, I'll be at your side."

"I appreciate that," she began.

"Because it's my intention to make sure nothing ever happens to you again."

"I am sure you'll try your best."

He reached out to touch her cheek. It was all Alex could do to stifle the reflex to recoil.

"Know I will do anything to protect you." He took a deep breath. "I love you, Alex."

Alex's words failed her. She knew exactly what he meant. This wasn't friendship he spoke about. This was adult love of a one-hundred-fifty-year-old man. Someone who was old enough to know the difference.

She didn't know how to respond. The first time she saw him, when he was lurking in her bedroom, she half found him cute, in a teen-crush sort of way. She'd nearly killed him that day, and the next time they met she nearly burned him alive. She could still feel that part of him, now forever a part of her. She felt something for him, too. She couldn't help it, at each stage, he had been there. He was Sara's baby. Matthew's sidekick. Now he was her... what?

She took his hand from her cheek and pressed it to her chest. "Do you feel my heart?"

He nodded, "Yes."

"For a while, your mother and I shared a heartbeat. I with her and later her with me. Your sister shares it now. I share it with thousands and thousands of other women, too. So many that it doesn't even feel like it belongs to me. Not anymore, anyway." She held his hand there. "You love *them*. You love the woman who came to you and healed you when I was unconscious. You think you love me because those people you love share this beating heart. You love *them*, George. I'm the woman who burned you alive. You maybe love the *idea* of me, but you don't love me, and you know how I know that, George?" She didn't wait for an answer. "I know that because when I think about you, my heart swells with love, too. But that love for you isn't mine. It's them. Your mother. Your sister. Not mine."

She released his hand and he took it in his other as though nursing an injury. His eyes sparkled with tears he blinked away. "I, um; sorry, Alex. I don't know why I said that."

"Because you felt something."

He nodded; for a man of nearly one-hundred and fifty years, he looked so young and sheepishly small.

"I need to get back inside," she told him. "I understand if you don't want to stay now."

"I'm not going anywhere," he told her. "You can say what you want, but you can't know what I feel."

"Maybe not."

"Whatever you need me to do, just tell me."

Alex leaned forward and kissed his cheek. "Thank you, George," she said as she stepped past him. She held the door open before recognizing he wasn't following, at least not yet.

Chapter One Hundred and Fifty Six

nside, Alex found Rose, stalking through the house. She'd apparently gotten Alex's scent or heard she was about. Rose saw her across the room of chattering smiles and pushed her way forward. She paused to stare at Charissa and Pat, uncertain who these strangers were.

"My mom's inviting everyone these days," Rose joked, gesturing to them.

"Remember the girl I told you about who was with me when Matthew came? I never knew what happened to her?"

"Is that?" Rose turned abruptly around, her hair whipping Alex in the face. "How'd you find her?"

Alex explained how Abby lived on her parents' farm and Charissa's father, Steven, was Holly's twin brother.

"That's in-sane." She looked back again before returning to Alex with her purpose restored. "At the Library, I didn't have to go back. I could have fought with you."

Alex stifled her grin. Rose was acting like Alex telling her to do something was now enough for her to do it. Had Rose really wanted to stay and fight, she could have. Still, she wouldn't rub that in Rose's face. "I needed someone to look after Marta, Colette, and Jacque. No one's better with a Book than you."

"It's fixed, you know. I was up half the night sorting it out, taping the pages back together. It's like twice the size now, but it won't fall apart."

"That's great."

Rose looked awkwardly about like she was looking for something to do with her hands that didn't involve Alex. It became clear she was biding her time to find the right words. "You were pretty amazing at the Library. When I saw that kid become that monster; well, you were fearless." She looked away. "What's the plan?"

That's why she's being nice: She wants information.

"Everyone's going to the Farm. Bring that place down. Free those women."

"What about Jeremiah?"

"What about him?"

"Do you think he's just going to let you destroy it?

"I said everyone's going to the Farm, Rose. I never said I was."

"I'm not going back to the Farm. I go where you go. You'll need help."

Alex couldn't tell Rose it was too dangerous or that she believed she was on a suicide mission. Both were expressions of weakness.

"You can't defeat him without me," Rose protested. Alex wanted to slap the smug expression off her face. "You'll manage to screw something up." This was Rose-monster talking, and her words couldn't hurt Alex anymore. This was jealousy and anger talking.

"I'm done talking about this with you, Rose," Alex's tone was cold and dismissive. More of each than she intended but she didn't care.

"You know my mom knew Billy was going to die since before he was born? Can you believe that? I mean, what can you do with information like that? She didn't even try to save him. I mean," her tone showed she was exaggerating, "she could've taken out an insurance policy."

"What's your point, Rose?"

"My point is this was never about Billy. No one ever showed me the big picture. I had to put the pieces together. If it weren't for Jeremiah, I'd have a normal life. Live in a normal town, go to a normal school."

Alex bated her hook, "And I'd have a twin brother and my parents would be alive and I never would have come to live with Heather."

"Exactly," Rose said. "That's what I mean. He ruined both our lives. I have just as much against him as you do."

"Do you, Rose? Really?" Rose didn't seem to grasp Alex's accusatory tone.

"Absolutely. He made my parents split up. He's what really killed Billy. He's the reason I have to read magic from a stupid Book. If you're going to face him, then so am I. Both barrels, guns a' blazing, remember?"

"I don't think that's a good idea," Alex said when Rose paused.

"I don't care." Rose poked Alex in the shoulder. "We're doing this together."

Does she have a score to settle with Jeremiah... or with me? For Alex it was becoming more difficult not to conflate the two. She felt like she couldn't exist without Jeremiah. "Rose, fighting Jeremiah is a suicide mission. Your mother already lost one child."

Rose gestured to the other room. "That's not my mother. That's a ghost. She's barely even here."

Alex looked to Heather to refer to her in retort, but the way Heather's frame leaned on the couch as she walked past, the way her supporting arm trembled, Alex had to agree with Rose. In her head, she could hear Heather; the same way she heard Heather say her name no matter who else was talking. If the real Heather was in her head, Alex wasn't sure she knew this one she saw.

"If you're coming with me," she told Rose, "you have to do as I say. I need to know you'll do things you maybe don't agree with."

Rose bristled but didn't argue. "Just make sure your plan is clear," Rose poked Alex's shoulder. "That way I don't have to wait for instructions."

"Alex, Rosemary, come here." Heather called to them as she headed into the kitchen, her hands holding each surface as she passed.

"I thought you should know," Heather said once they'd arrived and they had a moment of privacy, "I'm not going with you today."

"You can barely stand," Alex said, relieved she wouldn't have to argue the point.

Heather eased herself against the counter. "I'm too weak to go, but I can be useful here."

Rose huffed, "In case we're hungry when we get back?"

Heather ignored her. To Alex, she said, "You have too much to worry about me, too."

Heather groaned as she pushed off the counter and approached Alex, wrapping one arm over Alex's shoulders and her other about Rose's. "I love you both," she whispered. "Always know that."

Rose ducked under her mother's arm. Alex could feel Heather's body straining to keep her daughter there a moment longer. With Rose gone, Alex bore Heather's weight. There was barely anything there. She took her aunt by the waist. "We need to get things started," she told Heather. "Let's get you out to the couch."

Heather accepted her charity for a moment. "I'll manage the rest of the way. No one needs to see you carrying me. They all suspect I'm weak, but no one needs to know how I'm struggling but you."

With Heather seated, Alex watched the group. They sensed she was waiting, and one by one they offered her their attention.

"Thank you all for coming," Alex said and then repeated a little louder to bring lingering conversations to a close. All faces turned expectantly to her. A few weeks ago, being the target of such anticipation was excruciating. Today, she was grateful for it, fearful this was her last. "We're going to leave soon," she said. "We're going back to the Library today. There are a few of you who need a Book."

Eric asked, "What's going to happen at the Library?"

Several others, Carrie and June among them, hissed, "Let her speak," and, "She'll tell us."

Alex tried to hide her distain for Eric. Rose, however, glared at her father. *If only Eric knew how lucky he was; if she could, Rose would be firing lasers from her eyes.* "By now you're all up to date on what happens at the Farm." She watched the faces following her; several people adjusted their seats. "The Farm must be destroyed. Free those women. And Lydia. End that place."

Rose's petty tone told everyone she had inside information, "And what will you be doing?"

Alex shot her a look that Rose either missed or ignored. "I'll begin destroying the rest of the Library. I'm your diversion."

Rose snorted, "Then what?"

Alex frowned at her. *Then I'll probably be dead.* She lied, "We'll meet back here." She could hear the strain in her voice to articulate something she didn't believe. No one seemed to pick up on it.

Eric accused, "You don't actually think Jeremiah won't come after us for attacking him?"

"Oh, he'll hit us," Steven gruffly shot back. "We'll be in danger the rest of our lives. Those of us who survive, that is." He caught his tone and lowered his voice. "If we chicken out now," he gestured at Alex, "it's just a matter of time before he comes after her and us."

"I never suggested chickening out," Eric corrected.

"This is ze point," Jacque countered in his accented voice. "We have to hit 'eem 'ard enough 'e does not. Nossing can be half-the-ass. Zen maybe we have time to scatter like ze winds. Be gone before 'e knows ze thing zat hit him."

"Maybe more others? To help fight," Banhi offered. "Many more others." She scanned the room for a clock. "They sleep now. Time is good."

"Sleep?" Rachel didn't understand how that would be helpful.

"We've forgotten *here*, but elsewhere in the world, women purposely visit the Between in their sleep," Alex explained. "The Farm is on the Between." She thought about how and when Banhi or Khowla should get reinforcements. *Will anyone come knowing the danger? Can I afford to have people I trust go searching for more?* "Once we're there, one of you will go to the Market. Ask anyone willing to fight to come."

"There are other markets," Heather offered.

Banhi pointed at Heather. "One go to market. We send," she thought a moment, "five people from market to other market. Again the same."

Alex worried a relay race could dilute the message. "That's good. As long as you can be quick about it." She noticed Rose rolling her eyes.

Nancy asked, "Are we driving to the door again?"

Pat asked, "What door?"

While Carrie explained, Alex spoke over her, "We're not using the door."

Alex looked at Marta. "I'm sorry. I know this will hurt you. But I need you to do it again."

Marta stared back gravely. "I'm smuggling everyone in?"

Alex nodded. "I don't know what he's aware of. But if it's only me and you." *And it's easier to protect one person.*

"I told you we'd do whatever you asked." Marta announced.

Abby pointed, "We're going inside her?"

The others didn't understand. Carrie asked, "How's that gonna work?"

Alex explained how Jeremiah would know the moment they used magic. Not everyone had magic to travel to the Between. "This isn't like dreamwalking, when you leave your body and travel to the Between at the end of your thread. We're going whole, bodies and all. If I open the mist and Charon is there demanding coins, we can't pass. Marta and I got through before." She explained how they would all hide inside the entire universe that existed inside Marta.

What she didn't explain was that it might kill Marta. Trapping them all. It was a risk worth taking. Driving to the door took too much time. Magic alerted Jeremiah. Would Charon allow all of them to pass? There were no guarantees, but this offered the best chances Alex could consider.

"I'll get you all to the Farms," Alex said. "Heather will wait here for when we return. In case someone needs help. Rose and I go to the Library."

Colette interjected, "Lydia would rather die than leave. Everyone there is more than happy to stay. The same thing'll happen to every one of them. How are we going to do anything but get stuck there ourselves?"

For a change, Rose wasn't so quick to add her opinion.

Alex continued, "That's why you're all going. Force your way in. They don't allow men because it doesn't work on them." Marta was her proof; a test group of one. She hoped it was a valid assessment. "They'll keep everyone focused. Colette, you saw how it works. You know how."

"I sure do," Colette looked at the group as though fretting who would be most troublesome. When someone asked if they really wanted to stay, she said, "You won't believe until you see."

Abby stepped forward, "I'm going with you, too."

Alex hadn't planned on this. "Abby, I need you to go with them."

"I'm going with you."

Alex stared at her. "It didn't stick?"

Abby shook her head. "I think it did. I will do whatever you need, and that's that."

Which is more important, that Abby does what I say or shows she has free will? Suddenly everything about her Familiar seemed more complicated.

Alex looked around the room at all her friends. *Jeremiah obliterates insurrections to show he's still in charge.* How would she remain in charge with everyone giving their opinions? Her concern was that Abby's outburst would change the dynamic in the room.

"If anyone should go with you," Carrie said, "it should be Abby. I get it, Rose kicks ass. Every one of us would rather be at your side, but the Farm needs to be destroyed."

Several others agreed. *I wonder if Jeremiah ever feels this kind of comradery.* To Abby, Alex said, "It's settled, then. You'll come with us."

To the group, Alex said, "Get yourselves ready."

Carrie grinned, "Should we bring Dolly? If anyone else gets a Book she can do her thing and, you know, make them a real witch."

Rose adamantly replied, "Dolly is definitely *not* going. She's *my* cat. Don't any of you even think about smuggling her. I will not be kind to whoever puts Dolly in danger."

Carrie's tone suggested she was kidding, but Rose didn't think so or care. The air prickled with tension under Rose's glare. Hoping to break the hostility, to Marta, Alex said, "Once everyone is ready to go, I need you to gobble everyone up."

June looked startled, as though of all she'd heard today this concerned her most. "Wait, what? She's eating us?"

Marta touched her forehead. "He's ready. He understands what you're asking." Her eyes got glassy. "He wants you to be proud of him."

Alex couldn't help but smile. "I am, Marta. So proud of my brother."

Chapter One Hundred and Fifty-Seven

veryone nervously awaited the details about how Alex was going to smuggle them inside Marta. Abby wasn't talking, just like Alex wanted. The whole Familiar thing left her baffled.

Alex approached Marta and took the others' hands, bringing her into the kitchen. "Tell me what you're thinking."

"I'm a little scared, Alex. It was hard coming out last time, and that was one person."

Alex understood her concern. She'd been justifying reasons as to why Dany was different: his hideous injuries; his new skin, which was part of Marta's universe. "We'll find another way."

Marta's face softened, "Give me an alternative that's half as good and I'll consider it. Barring that, I'll play my part."

"We could, um," Alex tried to think. "There's always the door. Getting to the Library is easy now. We just drive to the city."

Marta shook her head. "We both know that's not good enough, Alex." She held Alex's hands and pulled them to her chest. "The drive will take hours and we need time and surprise on our side." She looked Alex in the eyes, "I know what you're asking of me—of everyone. We're going to war. There will be sacrifices." Before Alex could interject, Marta over-spoke her, "Who are we to shy from sacrifice?"

"It's only a six hour drive. We'd be there by dinner."

"Or five minutes. Don't forget, you're a terrorist now. Don't you think the FBI or the CIA, or whoever, is hunting down the internet star of the moment? The girl who shoots lightning and can go from New York to Paris in no time. The whole world's probably looking for you. It's a wonder they haven't found you already. Your parents did a good job hiding you away. Maybe you don't even have a birth certificate. Or Jeremiah has his plan and is letting you get away with things for now. He'd expect you to use the door. Don't do things his way."

"Okay." They returned to the living room. Alex asked if everyone was ready, and much as she expected, she got a few head-nods and voiced confirmations, but aside from the weak affirmation, no objections or questions. She looked to Marta. "Whenever you're ready."

"Stand back," Marta held out her arm like a crossing guard and pushed Alex back.

Rachel asked, "What's going to happen?" A few others seconded her concern.

Much like before, there was no intermediate step. Marta was there and in the next startling moment, she was a swirling patch of infinite darkness.

"Let's be quick about this." Alex pulled at Abby's arm and guided her towards the event horizon. "You know where to take them. Bring them into the house." She couldn't help but add, "Remember not to walk on the lawn."

Colette's tone was incredulous, "What kind of place is, um, inside her? Don't walk on the grass. Sounds fancy."

They formed a pyramidal line behind Abby and one by one, Alex guided them in. When it was Eric's turn, he held up the rest. "How do I know it's safe?"

"Eric, I will not argue with you now or once we're over there. If you're having second thoughts, you know where the door is."

"Just promise you're planning on letting me out."

Alex caught her affirmative reply and instead told him, "If I wanted to make an example of you, I'd have done it already. This is the least of the risk we're about to face. If you're not up for that, go to your family."

Eric didn't argue, but his expression showed he took offence at her accusation of cowardice, whether or not that's what she said.

Rose was last and she, like her father, paused. "I don't have to go in, do I?"

"I'd prefer you did." Alex winced at her middling words. They were all Rose needed.

"Then it's settled. I'll stay with you."

It wasn't fair to expect Marta to stay like this and arguing with Rose burned valuable time. For a moment, Alex almost resolved to let things stand for the sake of expediency. Then she said, "I misspoke. There's too much at stake and my relationship with Charon is questionable at best. I need you to go in."

Rose's posture changed. "Why did you say it was okay if it wasn't?"

"That's not what I said. It's what you heard. Now either stop arguing and get in or tell me you're too scared so I can tell you to stay behind with Heather."

"I never said I was scared, Alex. That's what you heard."

Alex thrust her arm to the Marta cloud.

"Fine. Don't be testy." Rose took two steps and disappeared.

The blackness swirled, agitated.

"That's it, Marta," Alex nearly shouted, uncertain if the cloud could hear or if Marta was somehow controlling it. She half-pictured Marta with a hand-counter, clicking as each person crossed her threshold. *Click-click-click. Sixteen. All present.*

The cloud slapped back to Marta, again, too quick to perceive, but like an unfolded Marta formed around the mist. If she had any concern of the difficulties Marta had through the transformation, there was no confusing Marta's expression as she collapsed to the floor. The transformation had been agony for her.

Alex fell to Marta's side to make sure she was alive. Marta trembled at her touch, gesturing at the couch. Alex eased Marta to a seat on the couch beside Heather.

"Water," Marta barely whispered.

After she'd finished the third glassful Alex had fetched from the kitchen, Marta closed her eyes and eased back against the couch. "It's okay," she whispered, repeatedly, her voice louder each time. Alex wasn't sure who she was telling.

"Talk to me, Marta."

Marta took a slow breath. "I'm okay," she began. "It feels strange. I'm okay. I'll be ready in a few minutes. But I'm okay." She looked up at Alex. "Give me a few minutes and I'll be good."

Alex started to say, "If I asked too much," but Marta spoke over her, "Let's wait until I feel ready; it'll be better for everyone."

Heather privately asked if Marta was okay. "She says she is," Alex said aloud. There was no sense hiding her concern from Marta. "But I'm not so sure. I have to take her word for it.

Marta didn't respond from her meditative rest.

Heather asked, "You have everything you need?"

"I think so." Alex touched her chest, like she had done since Abby gave her the charm. Its absence left her feeling unprotected, even though the very thing it contained, her father's coin, was now paired with hers.

She took her father's jacket from where she'd draped it over the arm of the couch and pulled it on. The stiff leather, the familial scent, made it again feel like she wore armor. The leather crunched as her arms positioned the jacket into place, holding onto her firmly like an embrace transmitted across time.

Heather smiled at the tan leather jacket. "He lost that going to that place. It's right that you found it and brought it back." Heather struggled to stand. It took her a second attempt and Alex's help. She looked like an accordion; her body not yet straightened from the seat. Heather barely resembled her aunt. Her movements were stiff and arthritic. Her hands trembled, her fingers, unable to straighten, were claw-like. Her heavy eyelids gave her a sleepy appearance and her mouth strained against gravity, pulled down at the corners. Her once youthful aunt appeared old and diminished. Alex half-expected to see through her skin.

Heather placed her hands on Alex's shoulders and looked up at her, her eyes widening and sparkling like Alex remembered they used to. She smoothed a wrinkle out of Alex's shirt and finding her bra strap twisted underneath, flipped it back. She played with the collar of the jacket, as though folding it properly into place. She pushed the hair off Alex's face and tucked it behind her ears.

"Dear, sweet girl. They don't know, not yet, but I do. Oh, I do. Your mother was right. Sara was right. You told me how the universe whispers to them. He's waiting for you. To put this uprising to an end, like he's done many times before."

Alex understood what Heather was really trying to say, but she chose to respond to the words. "You don't need to hear it from the universe, Aunt Heather. It's obvious," she glanced back at Marta, "to anyone not blinded by hope."

Heather nodded. Her hands trembled. "There wasn't much of me in that Book," she said after a moment, her hands still fussing over Alex. "And I think I've used it all up."

"This is goodbye, isn't it?" Alex could have said it as a reply to Heather, but it was as much a statement about herself. "Did you say goodbye to Rose?"

Heather shook her head, the strain of overwhelming guilt shrank her form, as though it crushed her a little more. "I have my reasons, and you may not understand them now, but if you have a daughter, maybe one day…."

"You don't need to justify yourself to me, Heather. I think I understand." There were many reasons Alex could think of: Rose's reaction might be worse than leaving it unsaid.

"Please understand, I'm not staying because I'm weak or dying." She looked away and then back at Alex. "I believe I can be more useful here. I hear the universe whispering. I don't understand it. But the closer to the end, the clearer it becomes. It'll help me know what to do."

Alex told her aunt, "I understand your reasons better than anyone else. When I look at you, Aunt Heather, it's like looking at a familiar reflection." She hesitated, uncertain she wanted to say more. Realizing there may never be another opportunity, she tried her best to express what she was feeling. "It was horrible, what Jeremiah did to you. But forcing me to swallow your coin wasn't the punishment he thought it would be. I got to know you so well, Aunt Heather. I don't think, even if we'd had a hundred years to talk, that I'd ever get to know you as well as I do." She wiped a tear from her aunt's eye. "I would give it all back in a second for us to have more time, but Jeremiah doesn't realize what a gift he's given me: To know how much you've loved me."

"Did you ever doubt that I did?"

"What's important is I don't anymore."

Heather momentarily looked rejuvenated. Her smile became too much to maintain and exhaustion returned.

A lump rose in Alex's throat. Heather wasn't just her aunt, but her parent these last several years. Her coin notwithstanding, Alex knew Heather better than she ever knew her own parents. It tore at her heart knowing their time together was through. Heather wouldn't be here when—if—she returned.

"Whatever you can do, Heather." Alex helped her back to her seat. "Some of us would like to believe you'll greet us when we come home."

Heather managed to touch Alex's cheek. "I know you well enough. You don't plan on coming back."

Alex couldn't answer. It was like they were both lying to one another about their intentions out of some silly fear that admitting this was the end would make it so. Alex couldn't understand why saying it aloud hurt so much more than keeping it inside.

Heather continued, "I've thought about death. Being a Hawthorne, it's hard not to. It stalks the family. Until recently, I never thought of it as a thing that would happen to me."

Alex nodded; her eyes misty. "Me too." She knew if she just held her aunt like it was the last time, and told her the two or three things that mattered most, she'd be able to go. "Aunt Heather," she started to say.

"We're among the lucky ones, you know? You and me. We've been there. We've crossed over and wandered among the spirits. Not like everyone else. For them it's a dream. We go and we come back. We know what's waiting for us. *Who* is waiting for us."

It was a reassuring thought. Alex hadn't before considered if she'd get there or wind up like so many others, her coin swallowed or destroyed. She expected this to be a quick goodbye, but neither one wanted the other to go. It was like leaving required pulling out her own heart. Saying goodbye was admitting they would perish, and Alex didn't know how she'd ever be ready to let Heather go.

"But we've never had to experience it before. We've never had our thread severed and our body left to rot. What do you suppose it's like?" Heather asked.

"I don't know," Alex lied. She'd died in Sara. Admitting aloud that the end was a relief after such suffering was like telling Heather it was okay to die. It wasn't. Heather was still young, and Alex still needed her.

"Tell me anything," Heather begged. As though receiving Alex's thoughts, she said, "Lie if you have to. You've been there. As Sara. If I'm going to be honest, I'm a little scared."

"It isn't much different than dream-walking. You imagine the world you want to live in. Like my mom, you can make this house just as you wanted it to be." She grew quiet a moment. "When I was in Sara and we died, sensations grew numb, like they do in dreams. But that was okay."

"It's interesting," Heather said wistfully. "That we have here and there. And we dream ourselves there every night. Do you suppose it's the same once we're there? Do you suppose I'll dream of coming here? Is that what ghosts are, dreams of the dead?"

"I don't see why not." Alex hoped Heather was right, that once she died, she could dream of seeing all her friends and family. She imagined visiting the Book Club and Rose. It made the notion a little easier to bear.

She wanted to thank her aunt for taking her in and caring for her. She hoped Heather would say it wasn't any trouble, that it gave her purpose. She wanted to say meaningful things, but they felt too corny and sentimental. Her heart felt hollowed out. She wanted to hold her aunt, the closest person she had to a parent, but part of her was hoping Heather would tell her it was okay to go.

Heather forced a smile. The longer she held it, the more genuine it became. "I'm proud of you, Alexandrea. You need to go. Don't look back." She let her tears fall. "Make him regret ever messing with you." She took a shuddering breath, her smile brightening her crying, red eyes. "You're a witch, Alex. Don't ever forget that. My brother and I spent our entire lives getting ready for you. I wish your path were easier, but barring that, I wouldn't want anything to change."

Alex held Heather close. As she helped her aunt back to the couch, she said, "I love you, Aunt Heather. Thank you for everything you did for me. You took me in and made me part of your family. That couldn't have been easy for you."

"Love makes everything easier," Heather said as Alex lowered her to the couch.

Alex gave Marta's thigh a gentle squeeze. She regretted leaving everyone inside of her so long, but this moment with Heather couldn't have happened with anyone—especially Rose—in the house. To her aunt, she said, "Rest."

Heather sunk into the couch. "I will. I don't want to burn the last of the fuel in my tank just yet."

"I'll see you, Aunt Heather." Alex knew her words were false, but she said them because they implied she wanted to, because goodbye meant something different this time.

Heather leaned between the couch back and the arm, as though sitting upright was laborious. She was looking more and more like her brother. Heather finally found comfort, or else gave up on seeking it. She didn't look at Alex but focused on whatever she saw in front of her and regarded it with her utmost attention.

"Give me a hand," Marta said at last. She took Alex's extended hand, but it was mostly on her own that she stood. "Bye Heather," Marta whispered. Heather seemed too drained to even respond. "Come on," she told Alex. "Let's get these witches to the Between."

Alex concentrated. Marta's coin glowed brightly. Heather's was obviously diminished. The mist appeared, but the opening was unguarded. Alex waited, but Charon did not appear.

As much as she wanted one last look at her aunt, Alex couldn't turn back. They'd said their goodbyes. She already knew wherever she went, Heather was with her.

Alex thought about that place on the Between, the sloping hillside with the tunnel carved into it. The tunnel that led to the Library.

She took Marta's hand and together they stepped through the portal.

Chapter One Hundred and Fifty-Eight

Alex and Marta stepped into bright sunlight and a disobediently blue sky.

Marta grinned at Alex. "I never thought I'd get back here." She took a deep breath and closed her eyes to soak in the sunlight. "It's amazing." Before Alex could course-correct Marta, she straightened her own keel, "Where do you want me to do my thing?"

Alex gestured in the direction of the tower. "Let me know—"

Marta interrupted. "Don't do that. We're not some fragile flower. Your brother and I are holding things together quite well. In fact, he's really enjoying the company." She grinned at her own humor. "I told you, I'm good. Now you can tell me what you want me to do."

Alex understood how weak it made her sound to defer to Marta like that, but they were on the Between, between the Library and the Farm. If anything happened to Marta, no one was left to ask for help. "We should get as close to the Farm as possible. The closer we are, the better our chances of not attracting one of those nightmare floating thingies."

Marta concurred. With a hesitant step, Alex brought their journey to a beginning. They walked through the hillside and made their way towards the shadow of the tower. For now, they were still protected, until they crossed its shadow. That didn't mean she wasn't thinking about what happened once they did. Her concern was preoccupied not with Jeremiah but with nightmares. It felt like leaving their backs exposed, as though by not constantly worrying about Jeremiah, she allowed him to sneak closer. What had moments ago seemed like the best plan now felt flimsy at best: Everything rested with Marta. *All my eggs in one basket.*

Perhaps understanding her significance, Marta kept unusually close.

Alex hesitated to enter the shadow of the tower. She could recall the chill and how it seeped into her bones. Even feet from it, the cool air radiated into the heat like dry ice sublimating in the sun. But it wasn't the cold that gave her pause: It was another step closer to the nightmares, to the Farm, to Jeremiah.

"It's okay," Marta said, resting a hand on Alex's shoulder.

Alex was grateful Marta thought her hesitation was a sign of concern for her and not outright fear. Alex stepped into the chill.

With no sign of anyone in the surrounding hills, their step was only quickened by the possibilities that pricked their fear. In the shade, Alex stared—without squinting in the glare of daylight—at the distant top of the immense spiraling structure.

"You should go," Marta said, like she was daring Alex. "You want to know what's in there as badly as I do."

Pointing to the Farms, Alex started to speak, but Marta interrupted her with strange sounds like she was shushing her. "No one is here but us." She pointed up. "Matthew said it was important. Once we start everything in motion, there won't be time."

Alex disagreed, but Marta had stoked her smoldering curiosity. She started to ask Marta if she was okay and Marta interrupted, "I want to see you fly."

Alex couldn't help but grin. "It is really cool," she said. She trained her eye to the tower and with a small push, launched into the air.

She soared, her elongated body rocketing into the sky. Her speed revealed the true scope of the tower; for some while, the distant top never became any closer. Wind whistled past her; the spiraling structure was a blur. Below, Marta was so small her location was easy to lose. From this height, Alex could see forever. Behind her was the cave to the Library—oddly enough, she saw no building. Was the Library here? Subterranean? Invisible? Beyond the tower, the Farm. From this distance, the long, wooden buildings looked even bleaker.

The tower's terminus neared. Whereas the entire structure resembled a screw, the peak looked more like a point that had pierced through the ground from some other place, rather than being driven down, into it. Staying within the shadow, she discovered a solitary arched opening nearly at the point.

Slowing as she reached the opening, she meant to float closer, succeeding instead in bashing against the stone structure. She frantically grabbed at the sill. Stabilized, pressed against the wall, she peered into darkness.

Her eyes gradually adjusted to the minimal light that dared enter this gloomy rotunda. The air tasted of dust, stone, and time. The expansive room was choked by a forest of fine threads as though it had been stuffed with spun sugar. Pushing the fibers apart, Alex swung her legs over the sill and found the floor. Inhaling, the scent was familiar, but in such an unsettling way the shiver it gave her made her consider leaping back out. It was her curiosity that kept her feet on the floor as she pushed through the fibrous forest. She'd have no other opportunity to solve the mystery; to prove to herself that for all his knowledge, Matthew had not known as much as he professed.

Wading through the fibers—weeds—hair…. The realization sunk in her gut like a stone, settling in her pelvis. The room wasn't overgrown with plant-life, but time-silvered hair.

As she pushed toward the center of the room, the minimal light faded as though it feared illuminating the secrets hidden there for so long. The resistance of the tresses pushed against her body as though wading against a current. As she pushed, it matted, thickening as it piled and bunched upon itself.

And there, at the center—as evidenced by the circular stonework— lay a pile of dull stones. As she ventured deeper into the room, before she was even aware of the stones, they made their presence known. Some power radiated from them, like a rumble too deep to be heard, but that radiated in the bowl of her gut, in her pelvis. Were these the source of Jeremiah's power? Were these some relics that possessed the answers Alex sought?

She knelt—pushing and moving the hair out of the way. Touching the stones broke their cocoon of dust, revealing their true design. The mummified flesh reminded her of the dry cover of an ancient Book. She identified a petite, fragile ribcage. Then hips. The legs drawn to the chest and the arms holding them. Pushing the hair, she exposed first the shoulders and then the head.

Alex froze, unable to breathe. Unable to think. Unable to see anything outside beyond this nest of hair growing off the head of the desiccated body gracing the center of the room. Unhidden from beneath its unruly locks, empty sockets welcomed her, a mouth—its lips drawn tight around perfect teeth—poised to speak once it knew whose name to use in address. Even so disgraced, time-ravaged, spoiled by death, she was still beautiful.

"He imprisoned you here," Alex whispered to the woman. She considered the moment she and Jeremiah touched, during their first encounter in the Library, and she saw his vision of the woman whose power he stole. Here was the truth to Jeremiah's lie.

Judging by the copious hair, she was alive for centuries before time or starvation or despair claimed her. It reminded her of Rapunzel. But without hope. *This is the truth of Jeremiah's vision. Whatever power she had, he trapped it here. In a place she was unable to ever escape.*

However she pitied the prisoner, the lesson wasn't lost on Alex. Whether it was her discovering the corpse or the corpse discovering her, the energy washing through her seemed to be growing. Her vision blurred as it vibrated through her, chattering her teeth. It threatened her somehow if she remained any longer, as though she would take the corpses place and become forever imprisoned. She immediately retreated to the window. It felt impolite to leave without acknowledging her, so Alex whispered, "If justice is what you want, I will do my best to avenge you." She leapt into the air.

No matter how she tried, Alex's landing resulted in her lying on her back.

Marta helped her to her feet, an amused expression cover for whatever snark she wasn't uttering.

"I know," Alex answered the expression. "I can't land for shit." She dusted herself off, examining the new wear beaten into her father's jacket.

"You can fly," Marta gushed. "Who cares how you finish." She eyed Alex a moment before asking, "So? What did we learn?"

Alex explained what she called the goddess's corpse. "I don't know why it's up there, what's significant about it, or if it even matters anymore. It's been so long, it's no surprise that not even Matthew knew." She paused, wanting to hear what Marta thought about it, but she said nothing. "Maybe Jeremiah used her to put everything here, to bring the Library to the Between." They both looked up, as though bearing witness one final time before they continued through the deep chill of the tower's shadow.

"We're not safe past the shadow." Alex pointed to the distant Farm. "That means while you're doing your thing, you're unprotected." Alex took a deep breath. "I wish I had thought this through better." She had a nagging thought her tactics were flawed.

"You're doing fine," Marta told her, patting her shoulder.

They hurried towards the Farm.

They hadn't even covered half the distance when the first nightmare appeared in the sky.

"Hurry," Alex cried as Marta fell behind, panting for air. Even if they made it to the Farm before the nightmare caught up to them, Marta still had to let everyone out. It's not like they could first duck into the Farm for safety.

"Go, Alex," Marta huffed as Alex slowed to allow her to catch up. "Don't wait for me. I'll get there." She was barely walking, trying desperately to catch her breath.

With one look to the sky, Alex said, "Hold onto me." She grabbed Marta about the waist and leapt into the air.

Marta howled wildly for the entire flight to the Farm. Alex tried desperately not to botch the landing, and listened to Marta shouting out a litany of *oof's* and *ouch's* as they tumbled to a stop.

Alex jumped to her feet. Marta wasn't moving. As she asked Marta if she was okay, Marta said, "Stay back," and exploded into turbulent darkness.

Alex kicked against inertia, nearly falling in. She watched the violently active darkness, eager to see her Coven. She called out names at random, "Do you hear my voice? Come to the sound of my voice!"

The sky darkened. Flight had bought them time, but if people didn't start emerging soon, none of that would matter.

Someone appeared, swiping at the strands of darkness like they cleared spider webs from their face. When enough of her was out to fall to the ground, Carrie clawed at the gravel to extract her lower half.

She eagerly accepted Alex's assistance. Alex pulled as Carrie struggled, anxious to break free as the dark seemingly pulled her back.

"Pull," Carrie begged, her muscular arms straining, her hands clamped on Alex's with enough strength it felt like she might pull the skin off Alex's forearms.

Alex pulled, groaning, her heels digging into the ground, kicking up chalky divots.

"Don't let go," Carrie cried. She looked back, where her legs disappeared into darkness just below the knee. She uttered, "Abby."

Alex understood immediately. Without letting go, Alex made her way down Carrie's body, grabbing her waistband, her thigh, before plunging her hand into darkness and feeling Carrie's leg for Abby's hands. When her hand found purchase, she pulled.

Freed from Abby's grip, Carrie rolled out. She jumped back to assist, wrenching Abby from the darkness; Khowla and Colette each clutching at an ankle. As each emerged, there was an extra set of hands to make the extraction faster. Alex called out their names as they emerged.

Eric emerged last. "Marta," Alex called, "come back, Marta!" She reached to the edge of the mist, waiting—hoping—Marta would pop back into existence.

As the others pointed to the skies and asked things like, "What are those floaty things?" and "What's that tower for?" and "Where are the farms?" June called out, "Anyone see Rachel?" Everyone looked about. Rachel wasn't among them.

Eric raised his hands defensively, "She was right behind me. She must have slipped off as I was coming out."

Rose screamed at her father, "And you didn't say anything when you came out alone?"

Alex dove to the edge of Oblivion, plunging her hands into darkness.

"Alex," Khowla said stiffly, "the nightmares are too close."

Eric struggled to respond. "It's not my fault she didn't hold on tight enough."

Rose screamed at her father, calling him incompetent and irresponsible among other, less kind things. Khowla and Banhi repeatedly warned Alex of the closing nightmares, but she had to get Rachel first, so Marta could snap back. Alex searched blindly, edging forward into the flat blackness. The ground was firm beneath her hips, the solidity then giving way as she stretched deeper into the void. Abby grabbed her by the waist and heaved her out.

"Stop, Abby! Rachel's still in there!"

"Alex. Look!"

The nightmares were nearly on top of them. Calling on Banhi and Khowla, Alex screamed, "Do whatever it takes to keep them away!"

Without waiting to see if they understood her request, Alex told Abby to secure her ankles as she dove blindly into Oblivion. She reached, calling for Rachel, the words falling into a vast, echoless world. She was blind to what was happening outside; dread parasitically attached to her shoulders, feeding on her hope, poisoning her with thoughts that the nightmares were too close, the Farm was too far, Jeremiah knew exactly where they were.

Panicking her, Rachel grabbed her hand, appearing as they touched. As though reading her thoughts, Abby hauled her out like she was a sack of potatoes; Rachel following. Leaving the utter darkness for the bright Between, hot magenta and cobalt fireballs roared into the sky, one after another as Banhi and Khowla attempted to keep the nightmares at bay.

"Who was that boy?" Rachel asked, only her torso free from darkness. "I never would have found you without him guiding me." As she emerged, she became suddenly aware of everything and turned from Alex in panicked wonder.

"How are you doing that without magic?" Rose's question to Banhi and Khowla sounded accusatory. "Are those fireballs?"

Behind Rachel, Oblivion snapped into Marta, as though each of the billion motes of darkness were simultaneously forged into human purpose. Marta wobbled, weary and dazed.

Pat waved her hand across her view of the Farm, "It reminds me of photographs of the holocaust camps." She shivered and pulled Charissa close.

Steven agreed. "Probably where the Nazi's got the idea," he grunted. "Sick fucks."

"Fucking magic," Eric complained. "Nothing good ever came out of it." He watched Steven's face, as though expecting the other man to agree with him on a matter of shared anatomy.

"Nothing good because it is stolen magic," Jacque argued, his accent thickening with his anger. "We don't come here to fight because we want magic. We fight to put it away where it always belongs. As men, we should not want it most of all!"

Steven eyed Eric with suspicion. "Jack here's right. Magic is sacred and we've forgotten that."

"Imagination," Khowla answered Rose. "Imagine the flame and," she walked through the motions as she explained her actions, "throw them."

Banhi grunted in disappointment as yet another fireball punched through the gossamer creature as though it were smoke. "We are not having success," she warned Alex.

Rachel gestured at the clouds. "They look like thunderstorms. That's what nightmares are? Storms?"

June accused Khowla, "Since when do you speak perfect English?"

Khowla responded, "I'm speaking English?" When Carrie and Colette also nodded, she replied, "Here. On the Between we all speak the same language."

As Alex fired her own crimson fireball, she did her best to remind them they were on the Between. "Like in mythology when the living go to Hades."

"Wait just a second," Carrie said, her eyes filled with wonder. She paused to touch the ground. "This is the stuff dreams are made on?"

"Alex?" Khowla called out, "Should I go to the market?"

Alex needed a moment to think. Her plan was to leave the others at the Farm to go after Jeremiah. Her growing discomfort disappeared the moment she considered staying with her Coven.

"Child, there might not be a better time," Khowla said, already distancing herself from the group.

"Be careful," Alex told Khowla. To the others, she gestured and shouted, "Get to that door!"

Khowla grabbed Banhi's hands. "Goodbye friend."

Banhi was taken aback. "Goodbye? You're coming back!"

Khowla looked at all of them. "We all plan. I say goodbye because plans change, and I am preparing for all possibilities."

"Everyone else is going to the Farm," Alex announced as she threw another fireball. "The Library can wait."

Although flames devastated some nightmares, their sooty embers crashing to the ground, the sky was filling with them.

Rose failed to hide her panic from her face. "Why not the Library?"

"It's too dangerous to split up now." She thought a moment, devilishly realizing the truth behind Rose's questioning. "If you're frightened to go—"

Rose blurted, "I'm going. If you are."

Alex told the others, "The women inside won't let the men in willingly. We'll have to force our way in, and magic doesn't work."

George gasped, "You want us to fight? Women?"

Alex shot him a glare. How much of a stretch was this for him? Alex rested a hand on his shoulder and offered a reassuring squeeze. "Whatever you have to do. Jeremiah won't be a threat if we can't get out of there." She looked to the sky. Their fireballs had at best slowed the nightmares.

Imagining the heat of flame in her hands, Alex launched a massive burst of heat into the air. It struck the nearest nightmare like it was wet tissue. It singed at the edges, smoking.

The things reacted with agitation, elongating their sheets as though trying to appear larger. Others were crowding behind it and dozens more dotting the sky above the horizon.

Alex kept her gaze on the rough wooden door, not looking at any of them as she warned, "Remember what I told you. This place will make you forget everything important. Colette and Marta should still be able to resist it."

The closest nightmare seemed to shiver. The air vibrated like a snare drum as dozens of streamers erupted from it, like snakes from Medusa's head. They unfurled in random directions. Then, as though guided by scent, they all at once drooped to the ground, heading towards them.

Alex stared at the door, aware of how easily she was lost to the Farm last time. *Which side is worse?* Her emotions were like a pendulum that had reached the peak of its arc and was returning. What had moments ago seemed so important now left Alex questioning her plan. *Was this stupid?*

June called out, "Those things are getting really close." Nancy seconded.

"Don't let them touch you," Banhi warned.

While they spoke, Abby tugged on Alex's sleeve. "Give me an order. Tell me exactly what you need me to do." Struck by Alex's blank expression, Abby clarified, "Say something that'll over-ride whatever's going to control me in there."

"What are those dangly things? They look like party streamers," Charissa was asking, holding her phone to take a picture.

Pat slapped her forehead. "Seriously, you brought your phone?"

"Geeze, don't act so surprised," Charissa stuffed it in her back pocket. "It's not like I have a signal."

Alex held Abby's face in her hands, drawing it to her own. "Keep everyone focused, Abby. Say anything—do anything—to keep everyone safe. Use any means necessary. Don't let anything have any power over you. Don't lose yourself to its allure. Get us all out. I'm not kidding, Abby. By whatever means necessary, do whatever it takes to get the job done."

Abby nodded. "Okey-doke, kiddo."

Alex put her hands on the door. All she had left to do was open it. "These women don't deserve what's happened to them, but they'll fight every attempt to free them. That makes them dangerous. We're here to save them, but if they make you choose between us and them, do not hesitate to take a life."

Pat gasped. "You said nothing about killing anyone."

"No?" Alex's eyes bore into hers. "What did you think this was about?" Alex lurched the door open, unleashing the warm scent of lavender.

Pat stuttered her reply, "I-I thought. I don't know what I thought." She looked at Charissa, clearly regretting giving her daughter Steven's Book, but now that she'd read from it and had Dolly sit on it, there was no going back.

The nightmare ribbons thrashed in the dark skies all around them, slashing the air like whips. Alex withdrew to let everyone go before her. She would remain outside to ensure the nightmare tendrils didn't capture anyone.

"Go, Abby," Alex called out. "Go, go, go!" The tendrils spilled around them. She and Banhi fired fireballs at them. They reacted to the flames like toddlers touching a stove. Nothing was enough to quell their hunger as they snaked the ground, blindly searching for prey, sweeping closer and closer, curling and twisting like tentacles.

Abby weaved her way through the suddenly reluctant crowd and disappeared through the door.

"Protect them, Rose," Alex called out. *They're not going to make it.* Her imagined fire launched into the air again and again, but each time she forced the nightmares back, they lurched forward more aggressively, always gaining ground.

Rose panicked at the sight of the army of ribbons scraping the ground and twisting in the air, heading right for them and pushed the others through the doorway.

Alex watched the last of them make their way through. She followed right behind Nancy. Steven guided Pat and Charissa, followed by Eric.

Before Nancy crossed the threshold, their progress stalled. *Probably Tiffany Mayfield, telling them they weren't tall enough to ride this ride.*

Before she could think to ask what was holding them up, Alex knew she had to protect her Coven at all costs. *I beat them before.* She slammed the door into Nancy's back, pushing them into the Farm just as a dozen ribbons struck.

Chapter One Hundred and Fifty-Nine

Exhausted from battling the nightmares, Alex stumbled through the doorway into the Farm. Outside, black, burning fabric littered the fields, the devastation like wrecked dirigibles.

How long ago were the others here? Battling the monsters had been difficult. That she survived mostly unharmed now felt a triumph, but it had been arduous. Recalling aspects of their battle, the memories slipped from her mind as though made of sand. How long ago had she parted from her Coven? Had it been minutes or hours? Now, standing in the bright foyer of the Farm, she searched for signs that might tell her what happened. The Farm looked like a war-torn city after the soldiers and civilians abandoned it.

The shattered remains of colorful glasses littered a marble-topped table. The shards sat in puddles of spilled beverages congealing across the tabletop. An overturned stool; a chair hobbled by a broken leg. A table, the top cracked in upon itself. Cradled in the buckled surface a collection of broken plates and glasses, littered with forks and knives and bits of food. As she ventured through, only the sound of her feet broke the silence, crunching on the sparkling of glass, dispersed across the floor. A silver bucket bent out of round, unable to roll. *Where is everyone? What happened?* There was no sense of what caused the destruction, of one event leading to another; everywhere was in ruins.

Overhead, the smooth vaulted ceiling looked like skin stretched over the gracefully arching rib-like struts connected along a long central spine. Trompe l'oeil ivy climbed the walls, a network of veins snaking over and around the beams.

Beside one bar, a collection of broken bottles was held together only by the adhesion of their labels. Green and blue glass cast shadows of aquamarine and sea green, dazzling the light. Glassware overturned. Bowl-less stems hung from racks; the shattered wine glasses collected below like piles of unmeltable ice.

Her every movement projected back to her, echoing off the multiple facets of this grand hall. Just inside a doorway, laying in a puddle of what she thought was spilled wine, a Book—named Butler by the residents—stared at her with surprised, cloudy eyes. His skin was a sickly pale blue beneath greenish tattoos, eviscerated by a broken wine bottle.

Alex pressed further, disturbing the emptiness. Half-opened doorways in every direction. Dizzying lights, the gearing whine of their motors, projected dancing, grotesque shadows. A torn dress, snagged on a broken doorframe, ruby sequins littered the floor like scales. She was chilled to think of her friends, racing through this place in a mad slaughter. *Where is everyone?* Even as her mind conjectured worse-cases, the destruction and their absence suggested a story too bleak to tell.

Moving to another, to a third, to a fourth room. Exercise equipment, pottery, science labs, sleeping quarters: everything wrecked. Stacks of chairs, a confusion of chrome legs, heaved against and broke through the wall of another room. The last time she was here, it teemed with women. *What happened? Did they free everyone and escape? Did I come in just as they left?* She imagined her Coven finding the battlefield littered with nightmare remains and wondering, *Where had Alex gone?*

Alex passed into another grand ballroom. Eight enormous crystal chandeliers, like the tattered remains of dew-covered spider webs. The floor sparkled with their shattered cousins.

Something is wrong. How long have I been here? In retrospect, her battle with the nightmares seemed longer now than she initially remembered. She had defeated them, though. She distinctly recalled them, their torched sails unfurled in the wind, looking like torn laundry burning to the ground. She wanted so desperately to find a chink in her memory, but she could not.

The tinkling sound of rain. Bouncing, spinning crystals threw hypnotic flashes of rainbow hued light. One of the chandeliers just dropped, silently falling. Alex jumped; the explosive crash slapping away her daze at the desolation. Exploding shards spun like a scattering of glistening buckshot pelting her.

Debris spun like coins as the room stilled. Beside the crystal behemoth's mangled skeleton of pipes and wires, a body. Even at this distance, Alex knew. Abby was seriously hurt.

Alex raced, her legs like pinwheels, striking her off balance and throwing her headlong to the ground where she crashed into Abby.

She grabbed her friend, struggling with the dead weight. Trying to grab the right part of her to fish her face around. Abby seemed to be made only of arms. Alex twisted her one wrong way and then another until Abby's face came around.

"Talk to me, Abby! What happened?" Alex trembled. "You're going to be okay, Abby. I'll heal you. You'll be fine."

"Why'd you abandon us, Alex?"

Alex started to answer, "I didn't," but realized she'd battled the nightmares longer than she realized. Recollections surfaced of the waving ribbons wrapping around her body like tentacles. She fought with desperation, her heart pounding in remembrance; she barely escaped with her life. "I'm sorry," Alex said instead. "I meant to be here."

"Not one of them would leave."

Before Alex could ask what happened, Abby held up her hands, "Lydia kept squirming to get away. I held her tight. Until she was still. I crushed her." Abby's face fell into her hands as she sobbed. "What did you make me do?"

"I thought…." She stopped. *Can anything I say give Abby peace?* "I'm sorry, Abby. I didn't mean for this—"

"You never mean for it. It just keeps happening." Abby was raising her face from her hands. "Nothing you do ever goes right. Why do we keep listening to you?"

This wasn't Abby's voice alone. Alex spun to confront the other voice and just as she anticipated, discovered Rose. Rose's body was decorated with bruises, barely covered by an elegant, long black sheath dress. It glittered here and there with randomly stitched sequins. Its low cut inappropriately suited her shape, and as she stomped closer to Alex, her thigh peeked from the long slit in the skirt.

"I don't think you know how to succeed."

Alex expected the verbal onslaught, but Rose's march promised a physical one.

"You keep sending us to die. You finally got your wish. We've been here for days. Lost to the spells. Abby and Colette were the only ones not affected. They fought to bring us to our senses. I killed Colette before I knew what I was doing." She produced her Book. "He sensed the magic immediately. He came and, well," she looked around. "It's all gone now, Alex. They're all gone."

The news hollowed her out. *All?* "I didn't mean…."

Rose's opened Book and guttural outburst was the only preparation Alex had for the lightning strike that felt like it ripped her in two. Her hands clenched in pain as the electricity worked through her nerves, like ticklish thorns convulsing through her.

"Do it again, Rose," Abby cried out. "Show her what it was like."

Bolts fired from Rose's hands striking Alex again. Her head felt like it was exploding, her insides heating up as though coming to a rapid boil. Alex tried to scream out the pain, but her clenched throat only let out the meekest of hisses.

"Stop, Rose, please," Alex begged.

"Do it again, Rose," Abby screamed.

Alex turned to Abby. "Why?"

Abby cackled. "I begged to be your Familiar, but you had to be all holier than thou. *Oh, Abby, I don't want you to be my slave*." Abby's mocking tone stung. "Rose fixed me. She had me pretend I still needed you."

"You were Rose's Familiar? And kept asking me?"

Abby nodded. "That's why it wasn't sticking."

Abby's lightning hit Alex and the bright flashes played off Abby's face. Her grin maniacally joyful as Alex twisted into contortions of pain.

"Not you, Abby. Anyone but you. Please stop," Alex begged, dropping to the floor, the cold marble her only comfort; sharp pieces of broken chandelier jabbing into her face.

Lightning struck repeatedly. Alex had little left to live for. The pain her heart felt at Abby's betrayal was greater than anything Rose could do to her. Why was Rose doing this? Alex thought she understood, but as moments between blasts grew longer, instead of feeling betrayed, she became infuriated.

Jumping to her feet, Alex caught Rose's next blast in her hand. Rose's eyes widened with surprise as molten light dripped from Alex's palm. "Put your Book down, Rose. I won't say it again. Don't blame me. I wasn't here. This is your failure."

This time the lightning came from behind, striking her in the back, twisting her spine, her head pounding. In her fury, Alex turned and fired back at Abby. The immense cascade of lightning from her fingertips cast a single stark shadow against every wall, jumping and shifting the same vignette in all directions. The light grew as strong as Abby's betrayal, and when it stopped, Abby was gone.

"What have you done?" Rose cried. "You murdered my Familiar!"

Alex was stunned. She couldn't believe what she had done. *What did I do? I didn't mean…. I never mean to, yet somehow, I always do*. Alex was sick with grief.

Rose glared though her tears. "You're a horrible monster, Alex. That's all you've ever been, a monster! You destroy everything. Killed everything good and ruined everyone's lives. We were all happy before you came to us. But you helped me see the truth. It's not you I should follow, you and your stupid, *I don't know the answer* excuses. It's Jeremiah. You thought you were doing the right thing, giving magic back to women, but look where it's gotten you. He was right to take it away." Rose's chest heaved. She looked beautiful. Glamorous. Standing nearly as tall as Alex, the black dress clinging to her, suddenly more mature than her sixteen years should allow. "Jeremiah promised he would rebuild the Farm and grant me my perfect fantasy if I kept you here long enough."

"What have you done, Rose?"

Rose grinned, her lips red and glossy. Her makeup dramatically accentuated her cheekbones, smoky eyeshadow brought out her eyes. "He promised me even more if you were dead before he arrived."

She raised her Book.

In her wrathful consternation, energy surged through Alex like an overtaking wave. It stung her fingers as it pulsed through. Before she realized how much power she'd unleashed, her cousin obliterated into a thousand dancing particles.

Alex collapsed to the ground, holding her face in her hands, sobbing. She'd failed them all. She'd killed all the people she loved. She ate Heather's coin. She ate Billy's twice. She'd killed so many, and now the two people she cared about more than any others. She wanted nothing more than to curl up and die. *What have I done? What's the point of anything?*

Chapter One Hundred and Sixty

"I knew you had it in you. To be a god, you must be capable of sacrificing anyone unworthy of your love. Be capable of detestable things. Especially to those you most love. The people must first be fearful. Only once they worship you do you grant them your love. Only then, trapped between fear and love will they shower you with overwhelming devotion."

Alex shivered at Jeremiah's voice.

She had no protection, no safety, her back facing the sound of his approach, the hairs on her neck at attention in alarm. Her stomach twisted to face him even before she could crawl to her feet.

"You don't understand where you are."

Alex didn't respond as she seethed. He took everything from her. Worse, he made her do it.

"You think this place is real? You think the Library is real? Why, because they told you? Why would I hide this in the dreamworld when I could just imagine it? Who are any of them to say they know?"

Matthew and all the others failed. Why had she trusted him? His every belief was based on the information that doomed them all.

Jeremiah approached, all bouncing blond curls and grinning youthful face.

"You failed because you're not in dreamland, Alex. You're in *me*. It's my body, my mind, my imagination. Like you saw the universe inside your Marta, here, you are in my universe. Here, you can never defeat me. Not without destroying yourself and everything you cherish."

The vaulted ceiling, the beams and central spine did look like a ribcage. *How didn't I see that before?* The trompe l'oeil wasn't ivy, but pulsing veins, throbbing in the moist, bloody cavity somewhere inside of Jeremiah.

"What should become of you, Alex? What should remain when I'm through with you? You satisfied my purpose. An entire Coven destroyed by the one they followed."

Alex had visions of her body, spent and used, exhausted and squeezed thoroughly, as though not even having bones to support her structure.

He pressed closer. "It's okay, Alex." She felt his warmth, his hands coming onto her, pressing her closer to him. His mouth opening like he might devour her, the heat of his breath as his lips pressed hers. She thought she might be sick as he kissed her.

He said a god must be willing to destroy even the things they love. I have done that. Is that what he is telling me? Then there is one final sacrifice to be made: mine.

She pulled from him and ran.

"What are you doing, Alex? Come back here, right now. We are only beginning!"

The distance growing between them made her ache, as though she longed to become a part of him. She could return to him and became a god, become another face he showed the world. Or she could be her own: a destroyer of worlds.

The walls around her throbbed and were wet and hot and pliable. Her fingertips snagged the wet velvet flesh. It convulsed at the scratch of her fingernails.

Jeremiah groaned, doubling over.

Realizing it was harming him, her fingers pierced the walls and tore them.

This was no elaborate country club gone to ruin, but a colon or a gullet. She tore into the wall, ripping it wide, her hands dripped with hot mucus. He groaned, his cries coming both from within and far away, distant.

Abby was gone. Rose was gone. But she was defeating him. Wasn't she? She looked for him, but even he was gone, leaving her in glistening darkness. Alone.

It's over. He's gone. He's really gone. She thought of Heather, waiting at home, and realized not all was lost. *How did I get here?*

She'd brought everyone. Marta. The great spiraling stone tower. The Farm. They climbed out from Marta. The door.

The nightmares. Ribbons swirling above her. Then she destroyed them. But how? She recalled an ending, but her recollection was poisoned with glimpses of Banhi and Khowla at her side. *That was before, not now.*

She stood beside the grand fountain sputtering and burbling, Lesedi's form commanding the peak, overlooking the grandeur of the market, the buildings made of iridescent bubbles, lit by rainbows.

Women shuffled past, hordes of them, bumping and ignoring her, pausing to engage one another with a cheerful greeting in some gibberish Alex could not comprehend.

"It is strange to be so unimportant, no?"

Lesedi placed a hand on Alex's shoulder. "It is okay to be forgotten."

"What happened? I thought I was…," She had been at the Farm. She had a vague sense of sorrow, an ache in her heart from a missing piece. *No, I dreamed that. The Farm wasn't real. It was so scary.* She had come here and created the fountain after seeing her mother. She must have dozed. Dreamed the whole thing. She was grateful for finally being awake.

As though hearing her, Lesedi said, "You feel it, no? Your heart aches and you know not why."

Tears brimmed Alex's eyes but held there. "What's happening to me? I feel so sad, and the more I stop to feel it," she grabbed a fistful of her shirt, "the more it hurts."

Lesedi looked upon her with pity. "Sweet girl. I only wanted joy for you and here you are with so much pain. Come, be happy." Lesedi laughed, as though suggesting how Alex feel.

Alex looked to the towering fountain.

Lesedi nodded pridefully. "A wonderful likeness."

Alex stared at it a moment. Absently, she said, "I imagined all of that, didn't I?"

"You did not go to the Farm. You did not battle Jeremiah. Who fights him and lives?" Lesedi laughed. "Such a silly dream." She pointed at the fountain. "What sort of beasts are those?" She wiggled her finger at the tower. "What were you thinking when you conjured those?"

"I don't know," she replied disappointedly. One looked like a pig. Another an earthworm. Beside it was a chicken.

Lesedi accused, "Why make such a thing? Why put me on top of something so ugly?"

"I don't know." She laughed at the preposterousness of it. "It's like a joke."

Lesedi wasn't laughing. "Think, Alex. Tell me, why did you put me on such an ugly pile of shit?"

"What's the matter with you, Lesedi?"

"Alex, think."

"I don't know."

"Think, Alex."

"I made that," Alex said if only to shut Lesedi's repetitive question down, "because...." She couldn't recall. She concentrated. She remembered her fists pounding the dirt, an odd pile of rocks and rubble to one side of her. "I made that," she said with sudden recollection, "because you died. Because I couldn't save you and you died because of me."

"That is right, Alex."

"You died," Alex reiterated, "and I buried you. Then I made the fountain. I imagined it into being."

"Then how are you here?"

"I'm not here, am I?" Alex told Lesedi, "You're not here." *Where was I?* She struggled to remember, her mind presenting the remembrance of a journey through the Between, with vast experiences trekking through mountains and valleys. One valley reminded her of the overlook at Picnic Rock. *I've been there.*

She walked back from the edge of Picnic Rock. *Didn't that break in two halves?* She remembered it clearly in both states. *Where'd Lesedi go?* The forest was impenetrable. *Maybe I dreamed that.*

She took a few steps, exhausted. *How long have I been walking?* She stood before the old stone foundation. *I walked so far in the summer heat.* Wiping sweat from her brow, she climbed atop.

I was here with Rose, wasn't I? We slept under the stars. Only Rose was nowhere to be seen. This was Sara's house, aged, timeworn, gone to ruin. She remembered the walls; she remembered the furniture. She shuffled through the overgrowing vines and dead leaves and found the broken remains of a crib, wet, rotting blankets coddled the rusting remains of a hammer. She picked the rotted metal husk and aided by decomposition, crumpled it to dust.

"That's not what you fear anymore."

Alex knew it was Sara before seeing her. "I've missed you, Sara."

Sara approached, more beautiful than ever, more stunning than Alex remembered, wearing shorts and a tank top. She pointed at the rust staining Alex's hands. "Remember when that was a hammer? Remember what horrible things it did to us. Look at it now. Who would ever imagine that streak of red powder could do such things?"

Alex rubbed her hands, wiping the grit from them.

"Sometimes we fear things in one moment of our lives that in another could never do us any harm. Because we've become stronger. Perhaps we always were. We must ask, why did we fear it in the first place?"

"Just because it's not a hammer anymore doesn't mean it couldn't ever have been a hammer."

"Think about it. Would you fear that hammer now?"

"Of course not."

"Yet you did. Hear me. You're not listening to what I'm saying."

"I'm trying."

Sara pressed closer to Alex. She smiled. Alex felt such warmth for her. She was so stunning, Alex almost thought to lean forward to kiss her. Sara noticed and with a blush, drew Alex into an embrace. Alex held her, finding her scent so familiar, her warmth, everything about Sara was comforting. Then the feeling departed, revealing an aching chasm. "You're dead, Sara."

Sara withdrew. "It's a fate I suffer, dying. How many times did Matthew beat me to death until you saved me? Then Rose killed me. How many times do I have to die, Alex? What did I do to deserve my fate? Was it my fault I had the last magic?"

"I didn't ask for it, either," Alex replied.

"You and I," Sara whispered. "We've shared the same fate all along. I am the victim; you, my avenger."

"Matthew's dead."

"And his coin? Did you gobble it up? Take it as greedily as they wrote my magic into that Book?"

"I couldn't. I didn't want to live through what he did to you."

"What *he* did to me? Alex, *you* did that to me. Had you taken the coin you could have stopped it. You could have saved me."

Alex knew it couldn't be, yet the logic was sound. "I didn't know." She hated herself for letting Matthew's coin go. It was the secret to everything. Had she swallowed it all of this would be over. She'd be free. She would have spared Sara the hammer. She followed the line of events through her parents, through Billy and Heather. Everything would be as it should have been.

Sara told her, "It's probably time you got home to Heather. She's worried about you."

Alex looked to the path that would take her to the farm field, to the dead end, to the road, to home. The woods were unfamiliar. The path no longer obvious. *Am I heading in the right direction?* She was lost. She was frightened and alone. She tried to call out, to scream for help, but all that came from her was a hissing whisper.

The trees creaked and cracked, the branches swaying as something gigantic rushed through the dark, forested recesses. Alex ran from the path, away from the approaching horror.

Branches and leaves and vines and thorns swept by her, slapping and scratching. The weight of the creature bore on her, its gravity slowed her, drawing her towards it. Behind her, trees shattered and splintered and were matted into the ground. Nothing was there. Nothing but a hint of a shadow. A mere trick of light. She knew shades: The empty husk of a forgotten soul, sold for an empty promise, and filled with another's wrath.

There's a place I go when I have a nightmare.

Comforted by Rose's voice recalled in memory, Alex knew the place Rose would go, where Billy could find her. Maybe one of them would be there. Billy—wasn't he dead?

She ran with desperation, the creature's icy breath on her neck, its thunderous chase tearing trees at the roots when at last she came upon the door and struggled with the locked handle.

The weathered wood door was not the entrance to Rose's house. *Where am I?* Desperately, she tugged at the door, pulled and tried to wrest it open. The door was familiar. *I've been here before.* She held onto the large brass knob, her sweaty hands squeaking as she fought to maintain her grip for long enough to open it. The frosted panes of glass that she knew would rattle when it became unstuck.

Confusion spun her head. She tugged and fumbled with the door, trying to get into Heather's house, not sure why the door Heather never locked wouldn't open. She tugged and pulled, her heart pounding. She yelped at the sudden drop in temperature as the shade came closer. The chill like being in the shadow of the spiral tower.

The door. The streak of terror trembling her shaking hands as she shook the door. The simple, rustic door with rusting hardware.

She knew this door. One hand touched the weathered wood. The other protected her face.

"I'm still dreaming."

Alex's vision of the forest become folds of torn, rotting fabric undulating in the breeze. There were dozens of them. Each reaching out their crêpe-like tentacles. They undulated, attaching to her wrist, to her throat, to her face. Attaching her to the gigantic mass of faceless, formless, nightmares. Pulling her hand down from the sky, the ribbons stretched, snagging tighter around her hand and her arm.

The door opened without effort; the blast of tempered, perfumed air wafted over her in a powdery wave. The ribbons straining, their fabric stretching and creaking like an old, brittle shirt; it swelled and knotted to pull her from the opening.

The doorway was inches away. The doorway bridging the Between and the waking world. With one step, she'd cross the threshold. These two places touched here, without fog or mist, the tension palatable, like one splinter of a world stabbing another. The last time she crossed that threshold, she lost herself. Did she murder Rose and Abby and the others by sending them here? How could she parse the real from the nightmare when both were equally absurd. She resolved to cross it, damn the outcome, and close the door on her nightmare.

The nightmares resisted her desire. Reaching, the unemotional things pulled from her rather than be drawn in, as though they feared entering a world not designed for their existence. The mass of nightmares were knotted about her, wrapped over and under themselves. If the things could feel or think, their panic was clear.

Her muscles strained, trembling with effort as she edged forward. The more the nightmares attempted to free themselves, the tighter they knotted about her, twisting among themselves. She bunched together all the ribbons around herself and pulled. One hand clasped the doorframe. It was like hauling a boulder. In their panic, ribbons cut her circulation, tightening like tourniquets, biting into her flesh. Her face crossed from the Between and into the brightly lit, glossy world of promises and lies. Across the threshold, desire wrapped her in its covetous grasp and pulled.

In one final thrust, she forced herself across. The sheets fluttered, straining against the strips of crêpe wrapped around her. As though they could no longer withstand the inevitability of the Farm, or perhaps because the spell infected the nightmares too, they at once lost their resistance and rushed forward. The giant creatures rocketed through a doorway too small to accommodate their mass. One after another pushed forward with the inertia of a freight train. Outside, their remaining counterparts squealed as though they had mouths and cried horrified laments. A few managed to sever their own ribbons, becoming even more ragged and threadbare in their escape, but most weren't so lucky.

Crossing the threshold, the nightmares were like sandcastles unmade by a single wave. The ribbons degraded and disintegrated about her, as though static alone held the fibers together. Within the Farm, the filthy, undulating sheets billowed past her in great clouds of fibrous dust, choking the room.

As the dust dirtied the polished walls and sparkling fixtures of the Farm, however, the varnish of elegance evaporated. Slatted walls oiled and fetid with filth was revealed as the nightmare envisioned a new reality.

Chapter One Hundred and Sixty-One

bby was half a dozen steps inside the door; she felt like she was fifteen, walking into class wearing her underwear on the outside. Her stomach churned; she felt grossly out of place. It wasn't simply that the swanky elegance surrounding her was off-putting. Nor that she had simpler tastes and found herself judged by the décor. Or how beautiful the women were who enjoyed it. The rare parts of her unreserved for Alex still suffered adolescent insecurities. The room and women around her oozed an effortless, sophisticated elegance that gave those insecurities endless fodder for feasting. But it felt more than that. An urge pulled at a place in the center of her chest, like a hook captured a hunk of flesh around her heart. The pull irresistible. And yet, Alex's words were like prison bars she couldn't squeeze through. No matter how she desired the glistening surfaces, no matter how hard desire tugged her will, she found herself torn between the two. Although initially they threatened to shred her will in two, her need to please Alex was stronger than her own desire.

The others filed in behind her, with Alex at the rear. Then Alex turned towards the growing darkness. *What is she doing?* Abby wanted certainty Alex was okay, but that was not among her instructions. Instead, she surveyed Alex's Coven, and saw them captured by the same sights and sensations that caused the conflict in Abby's gut.

Rose stopped in her tracks, jamming others who couldn't push past. She ogled the luxury. Then the door behind them closed, Alex still outside. Abby couldn't take her eyes from Alex's younger cousin. The expressions on the girl's face swirled like mixing paint, from bright green when she silently condemned Alex for remaining outside, to wide-eyed pink, agog at their surroundings, as though she stumbled upon them for the first time. Part of Abby didn't blame Rose for her jealousy towards Alex. *She needed to go to the Library alone.*

"What are you doing here?" The voice was argumentative and panicked. "Your kind isn't allowed here." The speaker wore a leopard-print jumpsuit, complete with green-tinted fluid in the martini glass perched on her extended fingertips as she sauntered up to them.

Rose lit up like she'd discovered an old friend. "Hi Tiffany!"

"You know her?" Eric pushed through the group, purring, "Who's your friend?"

Behind them, Colette whispered to the others, "That's the woman we told you about, Tiffany. We tried to save her."

"I met Tiffany last time. We told you, remember?" Rose explained to her father.

Tiffany didn't seem in agreement, "You tried to kidnap me." Shifting her weight on her hips, she pointed at Eric. "You're not allowed here." She pointed at George and Steven and Jacque. "You, you, and you, leave. Right away. Or Butler will deal with you."

Steven edged closer to Charissa and Pat. He raised his hand, "Who's not surprised this place has a butler?"

"Where's the butler?" Charissa strained to see past the others.

Abby pointed to the bartender across the room. "That's Butler. There are dozens of them. Golems. Jeremiah makes them."

Steven nodded, Charissa straining against his grip on her shoulder, stretching to her tippy-toes as she pulled away from him.

"I think there's been a misunderstanding," June stepped forward, her tone practiced and confident. Her smile had no joy, it was only for show. "We're all welcomed here. This place is too grand to be exclusionary. I'm all for empowerment, but isn't this swinging the pendulum back a little too far?"

"We're not leaving," Colette said. "And they're staying."

Carrie pushed through to stand between Colette and June. Marta hadn't stopped watching them.

Rose absent-mindedly fished her hand in the air as though stirring an imaginary pot. She glanced down, troubled. "I can't get my Book."

"It's okay," Colette said. "She's not going to hurt us. It's the men we need to protect."

Carrie surveyed the room. "We're outnumbered; like a hundred to one."

Tiffany repeated her warning, stressing the urgency with which they needed to comply.

"It's them we need to watch," Abby gestured to a Butler, who paused serving drinks, scowling from the bar.

George looked around. "Part of me wants to wait outside, but Alex said—"

"And where's Alex now?" Rose's hands were on her hips. "As usual, she's off on her own adventures."

Butler the bartender stepped out from behind his bar. "You can't be here," he shouted, balling his bar-rag in a clear warning.

Banhi warned, her words thick with accent, "The thing comes."

Other women crowded into the foyer, followed eventually by another Butler and then another.

Jacque motioned at them. "Does anyone else find the jumeaux... twin thing creepy?"

Butler the bartender paused behind Tiffany. "They need to leave," he said, fingering the air towards the four men.

"I think there's been a misunderstanding," Eric said. "We were told to come here, but if we're not welcome—"

Abby hissed at him. *The tough guy's a coward.*

Butler yanked open his tuxedo shirt, spraying the floor with pearl buttons, to read from his chest. Tiffany reflexively knelt to collect the opalescent baubles.

"Do something," George pleaded.

Rose complained, "Why does their magic work? So not fair!"

The Butler's sparks showered the group. Without magic to counterstrike, they threw themselves in random directions, escaping for cover.

Abby pushed a clearing around her. Beside her, Eric fell to his knees, his teeth chattering from the electrical convulsions. Pat and Charissa attempted to shield Steven, but when Pat collapsed, Steven pulled Charissa behind him. George skittered towards the exit, yelping like a hurt puppy when hit square in his back. Carrie, Marta, Rachel, and Nancy stood in front of Jacque, and when she had a moment, Carrie yanked Tiffany's cocktail from her fingers and threw the glass at Butler.

Abby couldn't hold back any longer. Hesitation only increased her will, like red-lining an engine and then releasing the brakes. She tackled Butler, his body crunching against the floor. With all her strength, she punched his ink-stained throat, gagging the spells in his esophagus.

Tiffany screamed at the violence. Two more Butlers raced towards them, rending their shirts. Abby backed from the incapacitated third, turning her side to them, her arm covering her face in anticipation of their strike. She cried out at the intensity of the stings. Looking for anything to use as a weapon, she growled as she clean-and-jerked Eric's unconscious body. She threw him like a ragdoll, and he and the two Butlers collapsed in a heap.

"He was unconscious," Abby defended as she turned to the shocked faces of the others. She knew she had seconds to act before there were more to contend with. "Come on," she ordered the others, knowing there'd be some safety among the crowds.

Everyone followed her, except Rose, who stared idly at the ceiling, swaying gently as though some unheard melody brought her back to some romantic dance....

Abby didn't know what to do. Perhaps Rose was already lost. Carrie commented on one woman's dress and said she'd love one just like it. Rachel and June had already wandered to the bar and were mixing drinks. Nancy kept exclaiming how beautiful everyone looked. Pat asked another woman if the bar had virgin drinks for her daughter, who was furious with embarrassment. "Mom," she elongated the word, "why do you have to use that word?"

Colette screamed, "Why won't anyone do something?"

Abby was losing the group; they were wandering apart, the danger forgotten.

Abby called to Colette, "What's happening to them?"

"We're losing them," Marta explained. "We can't help them until we figure out how to stop it."

Steven pulled on his wife, trying to return his family to Abby's protection, but Pat pulled free and callously told her husband, "If it's too fancy for your *simple tastes*, you didn't have to come." She held a willing Charissa as proof that it was Steven who was at issue.

Two more Butlers pushed their way through the crowd, a glamorous crush of curious women, many of whom were compelled to look and hiss and catcall the first un-identical men they'd seen in sometime.

Abby wasn't sure drawing the men to her was a wise idea. They were an easy target for the angry Butlers, but they were waiting for her to show initiative. She shouted, "Run!"

Abby grabbed Tiffany, who cried out a series of progressively louder yelps, using her as a shield between the men and the Butlers.

"What are you doing? Let me go," Tiffany struggled, unaware of what was coming as the Butlers prepared their spells. When hit, Tiffany's eyes went wide and she immediately fell to hysterics, hissing at every attempt to stand under her own weight, as though Abby wasn't already carrying her.

Preoccupied as she was, Abby didn't notice the additional Butlers. Tall shadows flashed on the ceiling. Before she turned around, it was over. The Butlers shoved Colette and Marta aside. They collected a barely conscious George; his short-lived struggle ended with burns covering his chest. Others grabbed Eric and Steven and Jacque. Once the men were taken from the room, the remaining Butlers disbanded, but not before collecting abandoned beverages and the broken martini glass.

Abby let Tiffany slip from her bearhug. As though nothing happened, Tiffany touched Abby's sleeveless shirt and rubbed her fingers as though testing for grease. With a crinkled nose, a non-plussed Tiffany said, "Oh, darlin', I bet you can't wait to put yourself in something nice."

Colette and Marta came to Abby's side. Colette asked Abby, "You okay?"

"I like your fingernails," Tiffany exclaimed, examining her own. "I've thought of going a bold color, too, but I don't know that mustard would look good on me. It's perfect with your complexion. What do you think?"

She smiled and held up her hands beside her face, splayed fingers nail-forward.

Abby answered Colette, "Killer headache. I'll live." She rubbed the burn on her hip. With a gesture, she, Marta, and Colette started walking.

"You don't feel the pull?" Colette patted her chest, "It's strong, but Markus is keeping me safe."

Marta shrugged. "Alex's brother keeps me from feeling it at all."

Abby explained, "It's so strong, but so is Alex's command. I feel split in two."

The others already disappeared into the crowd. Rose grabbed Carrie and Nancy, and the three wandered off like Musketeers. Banhi disappeared through a doorway. June, Rachel, Charissa and Pat were at the bar, Butler shaking their cocktails.

Other women approached. "You're new," one of them said. She was older and heavyset, her casual gray slacks and emerald blouse fit her as though custom. "I'd be happy to show you around. Get you new clothes to wear."

"Now what do we do?" Colette looked about, ignoring the eager strangers. "What's Alex up to?"

Abby shook her head. "I don't know." Marta agreed.

They all looked to the exit. Finally, Abby said, "We can't leave. Alex warned us this would happen." Abby looked like she suffered a cramp or gas. At Colette's concern, she explained, "We've got to find the men. Waiting around hurts a little." They followed in the direction the Butlers dragged the men.

Marta said, "It wasn't like this last time." She turned to Abby and Colette, "I saw it on Rose's face the second she came in. I saw it on everyone. It's like even once you leave, you're still tied to this place."

"What about the others? Even the foreign lady," Abby said, "Alex's friend. Even she was all too happy to go."

Marta's voice dropped. She motioned to Colette as she said, "It's like we carried something back and infected all the others. Made it easier for them to get stuck, too."

"There's lots of activities," Tiffany explained, still following a step behind. One of the other women started naming a few, "Dancing, archery, sculpting, chess, bodybuilding, art...."

Colette rolled her eyes.

Abby asked, "Do they ever shut up?"

Colette replied, "I had to pretend I was enjoying myself before they left me alone."

Marta said, "Should we pretend we're having too much fun?"

"That's not going to happen," Abby proclaimed. "We're good," she told Tiffany and her two friends. "You can leave us alone now."

Tiffany demurred, "It's okay. We don't mind."

Abby froze in her tracks. To the third woman, she said, "Can you get a napkin?" To the second, she said, "Tiffany needs your help." Before Tiffany could object, Abby dropped her with a punch to the face.

Leaving, Marta and Colette stared at Abby. Abby knew the nature of their shock. "Don't look at me like that. I punched her softly."

Chapter One Hundred and Sixty-Two

Abby, Colette, and Marta wandered the large, elegant chasms and intimate activity rooms that formed unending mazes. Everywhere they went, women wanted to help them. Help them find things to do. Help them find new clothes—especially Abby. Help them enjoy themselves.

"Look who it is," Colette pointed at Carrie in a boxing ring. Her hands were wrapped in tape, she took a few punches but was quick to give back in kind, driving her opponent back as she swung and kicked.

"We should do something." Abby wanted to help Carrie; the urge to manhandle her from the ring was nearly overwhelming, but Carrie would never accept her intervention. Besides, her opponent was already sprawled on the canvas.

Two rooms later, Colette groaned, "I'm so confused. There's no rhyme or reason."

"Everything looks the same," Abby complained as she walked past a room where two women were definitely not doing arts and crafts. She stared as her view shifted through the opened door until she couldn't see anymore. "Well, almost everything."

Marta asked, "What are we expecting to accomplish by wandering?"

Abby told them to hold up. "Alex is counting on us. If we don't get this right, the whole Coven is lost."

Colette gulped at Abby's words. They rattled Marta, too.

Colette asked, "What do you have in mind?"

Abby hesitated. "We need to find ourselves a *Butler*."

Abby saw Rose at one point, wearing an impossibly cut red sequined dress, glistening with sweat as she danced. *Where'd she get the dress* so quickly? Abby was grateful Heather was spared having to see her daughter dressed like that.

Colette pointed to a Butler. "Look, *Custodial* Butler." He was collecting dishes and dumping food in a mobile trash bin. "What now?"

"Follow my lead." Abby approached him. "Excuse me," Abby sounded lost, looking around for effect. "I need your help."

Custodial Butler looked up as he scraped a dish into his trash-pail. He returned the dish to the table and afforded Abby his attention. "What do you need?"

Abby crossed her legs. "I'm so embarrassed. I'm new. We," she motioned to Colette and Marta, "just arrived…, was that today?"

"I think so," Colette replied, uncertainly.

"Might have even been yesterday," Marta exaggerated.

Abby continued, "We've been eating and drinking. As you might imagine, I'm a thirsty girl. Colette here, don't let her fool you, she puts them away, too."

"Abby!"

"Now I need to have a, you know, a siss."

Custodial Butler strained to understand, "Who do you need to find?"

"Not who. A bathroom. A toilet. I need a *siss*, you know? To *pee*?"

Custodial Butler stared at her. "They're everywhere. Just pick one."

Colette explained, "Last time, someone helped me find it. Afterwards, I didn't stray too far. I have no idea how to get back there."

Abby pulled Custodial Butler closer with his shirt collar. "If I don't find a bathroom, I'm going to piss myself. You'll have to clean it up."

Custodial Butler replied, "I'm happy to clean up after you. It's why I'm here."

Abby felt like she was pushing against a barrier. The urge to push through was overwhelming. She growled, "Bring me to a damn bathroom or another one of you will clean up your brains after I bash them all over the walls."

Collette scolded, "Abby!"

"No," Abby snapped back. She didn't know where her outburst was coming from, but as soon as she set her mind to the plan, her aggression surged to the surface. "I need a bathroom and this shit-for-brains needs to bring me to one. I'm exploding!"

"Maybe there's another way," Marta started to say.

"Oh, I understand." Custodial Butler's cheeks blushed under the tattooed symbols. "This way." They followed him to a wall. It was perfectly smooth. He pressed it and a door gently swung open.

Abby complained, "How was I supposed to find that?"

Custodial Butler raised an eyebrow. "You don't just know?"

"My head's all wubbly," she plucked the word out of the ether, "maybe it hasn't all settled yet."

Custodial Butler stared as though secretly subjecting her to a lie detector test.

"Well, go on," she ushered him. "What are the chances I'll figure how the toilet works?" She pushed him onward.

Reluctantly, Custodial Butler stepped through the doorway. "I-I'm not allowed in here," he told them. "It's right through here."

They stepped into a lounge. At its center was a large velvet, circular couch, not unlike a purple tufted hat sprouting white lilies and purple gladiolas out its top. Hexagonal white tiles glistened across the floor, the purple grout like spider-webs. Bold eggplant and gold diagonal stripes patterned the walls. Gigantic floor-to-ceiling mirrors looked casually propped against the wall here and there.

Abby caught sight of her reflection. "Why didn't you tell me I was such a mess? My shirt is burned, and I mean, I look like a slob." Abby was enraged at how much of a mess it was, but the anger came from somewhere deeper.

Custodial Butler desired to inflict satisfaction. "I don't see what you—"

Abby roared, "Look here!"

Custodial Butler, cowed, looked in the mirror for a hint of the horrors Abby spoke of.

Grabbing him by the back of his neck and waist of his slacks, Abby threw him face first into the mirror. She startled, as though the sparkling reflections cascading to the floor, splashing like water made of infinite razors was unexpected. Even before the raining silver was at rest, Abby snatched a large fragment. As Custodial Butler struggled to extricate himself from the lacerating waterfall, she sliced his face.

While Marta stood, frozen, Colette squealed, "Abby, stop! What are you doing?" she repeated when Abby plunged the sliver into his face.

Abby couldn't answer. What was she doing? She felt like a puppet, her strings being pulled to embarrassing and horrific ends. But the moment her eyes fell upon Custodial Butler, it was like a switch was turned from *confused* to *enraged*.

"Don't confuse him for a man," Abby screamed at them. "Butler isn't human." Her own facial expressions were in conflict; anger let through glimpses of shock. In the remaining mirrors, she stared back at herself. As she shifted her gaze around the room, the expression that greeted her differed in each mirror. Was she so maniacally confused or were there a half-dozen look-alikes in the room staring back at her? Rather than contemplate the chilling vision, Abby guarded her eyes from the reflections with her hand.

Custodial Butler finger-painted the floor red as he squirmed away. Two gashes on his face opened like bloody gills. He panted, hyperventilating, his eyes wide and white, flashing fear at Abby.

Abby saw the shard still in her hand and threw it away, horrified at what she'd done with it. She wasn't sure whether she was more surprised the mirror lacerated her palm or what she did to earn it. She bunched some paper towels in her bleeding fist. Custodial Butler's eyes begged Colette and Marta to intervene.

"I showed you the bathroom. You made me come in. What do you want?"

"Your kind took four men."

"Men don't belong here," Custodial Butler pantomimed the rules.

"Where are they?"

Custodial Butler shook his head.

Before she had thought through a plan, she found herself charging the bloody man. She had no idea what she was going to do, her hands snatching him and lurching him from where he lay into the cascade of another mirror.

"Abby, stop," Marta said weakly. Her face looked green.

"I can do this all day. I'll cut out a page at a time until all you are is an empty cover and spine."

Custodial Butler comprehended the implication if not the analogy.

"Abby, Abby," Colette chanted, fixed on the blood as though her eyes were magnetized to it. "What are you doing? I'm going to be sick."

As though unable to help himself, Custodial Butler pushed open a door. Lights blinked on. "Stalls and sinks are through there."

Abby let Colette pass. Although Marta stared at her, she was grateful no question was asked, because she had no answers. Her hands trembled; she felt sick. What was she doing? All she wanted was compliance. As the question rose in her throat like queasy bile, the anger followed closely. "Tell me where the men are, and I'll stop."

"Tell her already," Marta pleaded.

This isn't working. She didn't want to hurt him. She felt sick each time she did, but she couldn't help herself. "Last chance," she shouted, grabbing his collar, preparing to heave him through another mirror.

"That's enough, Abby!" Marta screamed at her.

"Tell me where they are, dammit!"

"I can't," he sobbed. "I can't!"

Marta gently pried Abby's hand from him. Lying in the shards of glass, Butler sobbed. "I can't," he kept repeating.

"Enough," Colette cried as she re-entered the room. She knelt and dabbed his face with a towel. "Come on, buddy," she said gently. She looked at Abby. "It sickens me what she's doing. Please help us. Please. Then she won't hurt you anymore."

"I'll show you," he whimpered.

"You'll what?" All three asked.

"I can't tell you where they are. I'll show you."

Abby took another from Colette. "It's okay," Colette whispered to Custodial Butler, pressing a towel to his forehead. He claimed it gratefully and fell against the wall, sobbing.

"I'll show you," Custodial Butler whimpered. He stood right up and tugged the wrinkles from his shirt, tucked them into his belt. He picked a few larger pieces of glass from his hands. He was a bloody mess, smearing blood on himself.

Abby's stomach was suddenly queasy. "I need a second." She retraced Colette's footsteps into the bathroom with the intention of washing some of the heat from her face. Once clear of the room, her vomit splashed onto the floor. Once her stomach was only quivering and not convulsing, she washed her face and rinsed her mouth. Seeing herself in the mirror, she saw the mess she'd become. Sweaty, half possessed with a mad rage, Abby almost didn't recognize herself. *Any means necessary*; Alex's words echoed in her head. She took a deep breath and whispered, "I need to tell her to be more careful with her choice of words."

Abby found Colette, Marta, and Custodial Butler waiting at the door. Although he held a blood-soaked towel to his face, he greeted her with tour-guide enthusiasm. "This way, please," he nodded, leading them into the large vestibule.

A group of women walking by took notice of him. Most of them gasped, one asked, "Are you okay? Do you need a doctor?"

Custodial Butler left a red handprint on her back as he comforted her. "I'm fine. Don't you worry. Once I'm done showing these three ladies around, I'm happy to help with whatever you need."

Placated, they continued on their way.

Abby, Colette, and Marta shared a darkly themed snicker at the handprint as Custodial Butler lead them away.

"What happened to you back there?" Marta hissed at Abby.

"I'm not really sure," Abby lied. Blaming Alex for her murderous rampage didn't feel right.

Marta said, "I never saw anything like that. Remind me never to get on your bad side."

Wandering through a half-dozen rooms, Abby's temperament remained stable, even as she questioned if they were being led astray. "Here," Custodial Butler pointed to a doorway. He pressed the doorframe, smearing blood wherever he touched. He acknowledged the blood. "I'll come back and take care of it. We can't have this place look messy."

The triumvirate regarded one another as they entered the room and passed through a second and then a third doorway. Custodial Butler stumbled, his face ashen, but when Marta and Colette steadied him, he politely shook them off.

"Where are we going?" Colette asked at their overly circuitous route.

"I don't know," Custodial Butler said, matter-of-factly. "I'll show you."

Marta asked for clarification, "You are taking us to where those men are being held, right?"

Custodial Butler's voice didn't sound insulting, "What have I been saying, silly?"

Whereas most of their way had been though large atriums separated by warrens of smaller activity rooms, it was clear their journey was nearing a conclusion when a singularly long hallway ended with a doorway guarded by several more Butlers.

"They need to go inside," Custodial Butler told the others.

"Women aren't allowed," one Butler warned. To them his raised voice advised, "You need to be on your way."

Begging cries of men whimpered through the closed door.

"Let us in this second," Abby protested.

"I'd listen to her," Custodial Butler warned, stepping aside.

All the Butlers began conferring with one another. Speaking in broken sentences as though most of their dialogue remained internal; they said, "Was that? You sure? Do you think? I am confident it was. It is what we should do now. Do we all agree? What about them? Definitely. It's happening. They're here. Not they…. She."

She. They mean Alex.

"Let me pass," Abby thundered. The urge to turn back, to find Alex, to protect her and keep her safe was rising like floodwaters in a cave. The way out was blocked, and the air was growing warm and stale. "I need to get to the men in there."

"Can't do that," one of the Butlers said.

"That was dumb," Custodial Butler commented.

Abby tried to consider what she should do, started when she found herself rushing forward. She threw one of the Butlers into the other two. Fists started flying as they grabbed at her, trying to pull her from the door, but she was unrelenting. They tried opening their shirts, but she kicked their groins, punched their faces, pounded them once they fell, kicking and screaming. One of the Butlers managed to crawl free from the melee and opened his shirt, searing Abby with sparks.

Colette immediately joined the fray, using her gigantic nails to scratch at flesh and gouge eyes, even as she cried out in disgust.

"Step away from him!" Marta cried. As soon as Colette released the Butler, Marta exploded into darkness, her form returning near instantaneously. It happened so fast it looked like Marta opened into a pitch-black mouth and swallowed the butler whole.

Colette awed at Marta, who leaned against the wall. Through clenched teeth said, "That hurts a lot." She exploded once more, and what she expelled only showed signs of its former humanity by the stained clothes amidst the pile of putrescent viscera.

Seemingly not noticing what Marta had done, Custodial Butler urged the others, "They need us." They acknowledged him by scrambling away, their defense ended, taking Abby's final strikes in their scurry. Custodial Butler waited behind. "I can't tell you where they are, but you'll find them in here," he offered them the door. "Before I leave, do you need anything else?"

Abby panted, her face flush, trying to catch her breath. "We're fine," she said between breaths.

Custodial Butler nodded. "It's okay if I go, then?"

"Just a second," Abby called out; Custodial Butler hesitated. "The girl they're sending you after," Abby waited for him to confirm he understood, "stay away from her if you know what's good for you."

"If I could," he told her. He turned and was off.

Colette flicked scraps out from under her fingernails. Two nails broke and she pried them off, cursing each one as she pulled them away. To Marta she said, "You're full of surprises."

Marta belched. "Ugh," she groaned. "Let's hope I don't have to do that again."

"But you can if you need to?" Colette asked.

Marta nodded.

Abby prepared to open the door. She warned, "Ready?"

Colette rolled her shoulders. "Let's go."

Chapter One Hundred and Sixty-Three

The matt of fibers settled around Alex, dissolving the illusion of luxury, of elegance, of stone and glass and crystal and steel. Revealing rough wood, splinters, and layers of grime and filth. The slick skin of magic peeling and dissolving wherever the filaments of dust touched mesmerized Alex. Even the light cast by the grand fixtures, themselves yet untouched by the dust, decomposed to a stark glare as the dust drifted through it.

Crossing the boundary from into the yet pristine, the pull of the Farm was startling. Sudden and intense. Reacting more through sheer shock and reflex, with a retreating step, the sensation dissolved. Had it not been for the nightmare, she was certain she'd be lost to it. Her stomach dropped: Rose. *What happened to her? What about the others?*

The aftereffects of the nightmare still rattled inside her, like a bruise that only hurt to the touch. Her brain wasn't through digesting the fears and the terrors the nightmares bled into her. They haunted her, snippets of visions and memories hung about the back of her shoulders like lice-covered ghouls, breathing rotting, dank breath onto her neck. She couldn't shake the betrayal. The cruelty of her friends had hurt. However unreal it was, it still had claws in her.

The copious piles of nightmare lint continued to stir and blow throughout the room. It never seemed to lose potency; the enchantments couldn't withstand them. Alex wondered what that said about what the nightmares revealed to her: Were they destroying magic or revealing the truth?

She'd been so captured by the rapid disintegration around her that she almost failed to notice that no one was here. The empty foyer held such a foreboding sense of déjà vu, that she anticipated the bar stocked with broken glassware. Her heart skipped a beat at the sight of the bar on the opposing side of the room. It was, fortunately, intact. That it as white and chrome and slick as she remembered released her from a burden of guilt she, until that moment, hadn't realized she carried. Her pounding chest eased a moment: Rose and Abby were still alive. The fibers billowed over it. The glittering stemware became chipped, filthy glassware. The marble bar-top was but a slab of bloated, water-stained wood. The collection of top-shelf liquors was a random collection of jars containing fetid water.

"What have you done?"

Alex startled at the exclamation. Book entered the room, shocked at the erosion of reality. Seeing the degradation, everything about his approach changed: his posture, his pace, his glare. He prowled, positioning himself the apex predator, Alex his prey. She refitted her father's jacket to her shoulders.

She caught his hesitation. Although subtle, she understood she needed to move to her right. Then immobilize and confuse him, before he struck. Her thoughts preparing to fight were vicious, informed—she realized—by Johnny's memories. That sleazebag influencing her actions troubled her. But she felt confident the information would give her an upper hand.

As she skirted to her right, she took hold of her dark coin. "Stop right there," she warned Book, even as two others joined him, calling out the inevitable and cliched, "There she is," and "Get her!"

She swiftly pulled apart and snapped her coins together. The white glow was even stronger. Was this because instead of her infant brother, her coin now paired with her father? Perhaps it was her imagination, but she was certain it had never shone this brilliantly before.

Alex searched for an emotional concoction. Magic on the Between was so much easier; imagination allowed her greater control. She wanted wind, and to shorthand the right mix of anger and fear and joy and anxiety to achieve the conjuring sensation, she recalled from her mother's house when her emotions created a storm. The thought wafted gray whisps of fiber aloft where they further eroded the false reality.

"Stop her!"

Alex wished she had more time to experiment with combining emotions. The apex Book approached with dangerous intention as others still entered the cavernous foyer.

Apex Book's hands curled as though taloned. He tore open his shirt. *They're Books, why do they need to read themselves?*

Her breeze whipped into a frenzy. Apex Book dropped to his knees, clutching his tearing eyes, as the infinitesimally small fibers became a sandstorm of lint. His nostrils blackened and he hacked to clear his throat.

Billowing fiber-clouds expanded through the room, morphing the decorated walls to wood slats. The high-gloss table and chairs where she'd previously met Tiffany Mayfield became a knotty slat table and simple stools. The chandeliers, crystal-by-crystal, evaporated into giant sodium lamps. Fixtures more at home on a highway; the obvious source of the crass light. Interior walls dissolved, opening the great hall even more. One of the many Books entering the hall, his slashed face bloodied and ghastly, froze.

I bet he met my friends.

Apex Book, now blinded, listened for her movement through the growing squall. She grabbed at her shirt, pulling them together. His fear at her touch sent him tumbling backwards. She reached again, struggling each time she grabbed him to maintain contact, but each time, before her fire was actualized, he managed to pull away.

The other Books charged.

Alex noticed too late as one Book fired sparks through her storm.

The first spark stung like a stinging wasp; the swirling wind hesitated; all the fibrous debris in the air stalled as though they might sink to the floor. Then, the wind picked up, howling against the wood-slat walls, the boards straining against the pressure. Conjuring and controlling was becoming easier.

The next sparks sizzled through fibers in the air, leaving smoky paths as the wind quickly swirled away, the stench not unlike burned hair. Alex deflected those that hadn't burned out in the haze of lint.

As she'd been distracted, several other Books reached for one another. Alex had seen the power of their conjoined spell take down buildings. The room deconstructing around her left her little cover, and as much as she tried to thwart them with lightning and wind and bolts of her own, they ignored their stinging eyes and burnt limbs to contact one another.

Alex released the wind to focus on this new threat. The singe on her hip stung. Her anger grew. Her body drew its tension in, her muscles tightening as though her anger boiled, the conviction and certainty that what she would unleash would devastate them.

The fibers fell from the air to settle into rolling piles, revealing two other groups of touching Books. Part of her was impressed by their tactics: However she tried, she could never fend off all three groups.

She thought of her cousin. She thought of the Reaper, its hand deep inside her viscera. Her battle in New York. On the Between. Paris. The indiscriminate destruction and wanton slaughter of innocents became her emotional nourishment.

The blast of lightning surged through her, her skin prickling and sizzling as it leapt from her fingertips. Lighting up the room with a blinding flash, the group of eight golems collapsed in a shuddering, singed heap.

Immediately she turned to the twelve. Her anger depleted, she enraged herself anew with concern for Abby and the others, seasoned with thoughts of Heather, of Donna, of Betty, of Sara. Of Jeremiah awaiting her arrival.

The air became unbreathably hot. The twelve golems cried out, their skin blistering as she bombarded them with heat, driving them apart, pushing them back.

Turning to the six, she realized her misjudgment. The freight-train blast of electricity coincided with the explosion of the casting Book. Alex could barely guard herself with her hands, attempting to catch and control the power.

The blast threw her backwards. Its light was blinding, instantly burning a negative of itself on her retina. Her hands trembled, her skin on fire. Her head screamed, her brain was too panicked to think clearly, as though bits of the electricity still sparked inside her skull, shorting out any coherence.

The intensity of the terrifying blow was still ringing in her head. She was furious at how outnumbered she was. Grateful she didn't have anyone to protect. All these emotions stirred within her. With a scream, recalling Matthew's smug bastard face as he smashed Sara's knuckles, a concussive blast struck the remaining five Books, blowing them into the air, their limbs and bodies twisting and shattering as they landed, crumpled to the floor.

The dozen had rejoined, ignorant of their burns and ghastly wounds. The eight crawled, touching one another ankle to wrist like a chain. Each time she lost the emotion, burned out of her as fuel for her magic. It didn't matter how she tried, there wasn't time to regain it.

One golem disappeared in a swirling explosion of dust as she was struck again.

Consumed by pain, Alex had to reorient herself to the room, having been swept into the surging power and tossed about like a leaf in a tornado.

She scrambled backwards to distance herself from them. Her body felt like it was on fire. An upraised, delicate red pattern ran up and down her arms, like fractal roots covering her skin, tracing the path the lightning burned through her, cooking her skin and her insides.

She hadn't experienced such a literal or figurative shock before. The magnitude startled her. She had to gain her bearings before they struck her again with the same power or—she feared—greater.

Scrambling to her feet, the burn-like welt that striped her flesh throbbed like the worst sunburn she'd ever experienced. Her clothes felt like broken glass against skin, which oozed heat like it glowed.

She fed on the pain. Tears raced from her eyes as her trembling hands shot sparks of electricity like bullets. She wanted to be angrier, to have greater anguish to feed upon, but it swirled into her magic and out of her like an unstoppered drain.

Outnumbered and outgunned, she searched for safe retreat. The entrance was too far and the nightmarish dust had disappeared all the walls that might have given her cover. Ignoring the unconscionable pain, she raced to a nearby table. Filthy dishes explosively crashed to the rough wooded floor as she tipped it on its side to shelter behind it.

Her Coven was still here—she hoped. She wished they'd find her and make the fight fair.

She told herself this was not a time to be afraid. These were golem, not real men, but robots made of flesh, incapable of deviating from their orders. Priming her emotions while she was so rattled didn't come easily, but she tensed, her skin stinging in response to contracting muscles. Reaching aside the table, the energy leaving through her arms felt as though it was too great to fit in her hands, splitting the line of Books split in two. The burst of energy scattered them into the air like insignificant debris.

Indifferent to their fallen comrades, other Books regained their connection, nearly eighteen of them, touching one another, each chanting the words of the spell, passing the power to the next, to the next, to the next.

If I can't beat them, what chance do I have against Jeremiah? There was no further opportunity to forestall the inevitable; she braced herself. Told herself she'd catch this one. She didn't care if she'd never trapped such power before. She'd control it. She'd throw it back to them.

She tried flashing horrors through her imagination. Billy's throat being slit. Sara's devastated, dying body. Betty, burning alive.

The table exploded in a roaring shower of splinters and char. The residual static brought her hair to stand and discharged everywhere with snapping sparks that sounded like packs of firecrackers.

The air snapped blindingly as she reached forward to catch the next strike. Her palms felt like her skin had been grated off. Even through her closed eyes, she could see the bones in her forearms and hands.

She cried out at the agony of her hands. The whirling power and heat ate at her skin. She pushed at it, like trying to move Picnic Rock. She didn't think she had the strength to move it until it whirled across the room. The sparking energy obliterated two Books and debilitated three others as it burned through them.

She reflexively looked at her hands, fearful of the damage she'd see, but her eyes were blurry and spotted with deep purple blobs that raced from her as she tried to focus.

Separated and regrouping, three Books exploded. The roar of power burned into her side, her gut so hot she wished it would spill out to relieve her of the pain as she pinwheeled through the air.

Frantically looking around, she spied the ceiling, the door she'd come in through, the floor, all before discovering the remaining golems—perhaps sixteen—rushing towards her, hands to shoulders in a single mass. Before she could so much as raise her hands in a feeble attempt to defend herself, the leading Book exploded and the room went black.

Alex felt as though she'd been wrenched open. She wished to die, just to make it stop. She writhed and grunted in convulsing pain, fighting for control of her own body as the energy surging through her refused to dissipate.

Her body vibrated with pain. It was like liquid steel burning through her veins, like ten thousand needles piercing her. It was the most intense burning—far worse than any fire she'd been subjected to. She didn't want to breathe. She didn't want to move. She whimpered, only wishing it would end. They fired at her twice more, throwing her body about, before it stopped.

She lay still, unable to whimper. Pain was all she knew, all she had to feel. Like there was nothing left of her but a twitching battery of raw nerves.

Somewhere around her, dozens of feet crunched through debris.

Burning, her eyes flooding with tears. They didn't seem capable of opening, the utter darkness never changing no matter how wide she believed she opened them. Touching her hand to her face to pry her eyes open, she discovered that her world had become a black pool of darkness.

She promised herself it was temporary. Sick with the potential she'd told herself a lie. She'd never before felt so vulnerable; startled at each sound that—without vision giving context—could have been anything.

She twisted about frantically, trying to orient herself to the approaching noises. They had to be preparing another strike and at each brush of fabric, she braced.

Her body suffered more pain than she could remember; and that fed her fear that the next time—which could come at any moment—would be far worse. She cowered, tucking herself to a knee, one hand over her head, the other desperately grasping at the air, hoping to touch anything, maybe even to sacrifice her hand to lessen the next bombardment. The whispers in her head cried to warn her, but they, too, were lamentably blind.

Chapter One Hundred and Sixty-Four

She tried summoning anger. She tried to find her confidence, to feel powerful, to recreate her recipe, perhaps even to fire blindly into the room, but overwhelming fear castrated other emotions. Each time she tried to stand, to elongate her body to allow her emotions to better fill her, her inner ears overcompensated for her lack of vision. It was as though the ground tilted beneath her.

She couldn't narrow the direction of scraping footfalls. She turned rapidly, hoping to pinpoint them, but with each turn the room tipped and wobbled. Her heart fluttered, more a spasm in her chest than a rhythm, as her fear bubbled up and tickled the back of her throat.

Fear was eating through her like caustic acid. She couldn't take another attack like that. Fighting through the fog of pain, the fear and anger and agony burbled out of her in ungraceful, inelegant bursts, fired randomly about the room in the hopes of striking any of them.

Like lances thrust through her body—spasming contortions fitfully throwing her about—spell after spell struck her. They were firing normal sparks now, striking her when she was defenseless. Without respite, all she could do was endure it. She feigned death, collapsing and balling up, hoping it would end, but they were relentlessly cruel: they would stop once she was dead. The thought was infuriating. It was like a spark in infernal darkness. Even a spark, not bright enough to be noticed in daylight, when darkness was deep enough, could be blinding.

Through the unending pain, through the nagging terror that they would never stop, one spark of emotional passion birthed others. That fear, that pain, that anxiety, that anger. Her chest burned. She felt bloated and sickly full. She screamed out her agony, the sparks zapping her this way and that; the swelling energy inside of her spilled as though she'd been split open to allow it to gush torrents. Even her father's jacket—once her armor— couldn't withstand the assault, falling from her body in burned pieces.

She was aware of the rush of power by the creaking timbers and boards splintering as the shockwave crashed through the space. Tables screeched across the floor before flipping into the air and shattering and blowing around the room. The golems screamed and shouted, their bodies crashing into one another, into floors and walls and ceilings with bone crunching results.

Alex cried in anguish as she clawed herself upright, the assault ended—for now. She held the wall for support. The room still wobbled; the structure afforded her an anchor of stillness.

Debris clattered to the ground as things settled and collapsed. Bodies groaned and fabric shuffled. She wished she could see. Could know what she'd done. Recollection allowed her memory to paint a picture for her, to see the deconstructed room and fill in details, but her imagination was no match for the truth.

She took the silence to measure her own injuries. The pain was too distracting to think. Wrapping herself in her arms, Alex concentrated on healing herself.

Her skin burned. It itched so deeply she wanted to cut it open to scratch at the source. Her eyes felt like they were wrapped in sandpaper.

A footstep crunched on debris to her right. She turned towards it, dumbly expecting to see but greeted with the dark. Near to her left, someone pushed a timber over with a grunt and climbed to their feet, dusting themselves off. Alex faced each sound, her mind conjuring visions of one Book after another climbing out from under debris and limping or crawling to join the others before her.

She felt the breath on her face—dry and musty like an old, damp book—as the golem knocked her to the ground.

She cried out, losing her bearings as she painfully crashed on her side.

She wished they'd leave her alone to her pain. Footfalls approached. Rather than wait for what came next, she lunged blindly to the sound and, colliding with one golem, secured her purchase as her hands clamped onto his flesh.

One of them grabbed her ankle to separate her from the other. She would not let go, as she was pulled, so she dragged her prey.

Others grabbed at her, pulling her legs, her arms, trying to pry her individual fingers, rip out her hair, her ears. Fists beat on her. They pulled at her feverishly trying to break her connection, and she would allow them to tear her apart before she let him go. Hands closed around her throat.

Her clothes rapidly soaked in her perspiration. As she asphyxiated, the Books screamed. Her hair matted flat to her scalp and stuck to her face in thick strands as sweat poured out of her.

Alex twisted in the Books' grasp. She clamped onto the wrists holding hers. Their cries grew louder. They were no longer restraining her, but now she wouldn't let go of them. Her body jerked as they thrashed, attempting to shake her free, screaming.

Something dripped on her, wet and slimy. Splatter sounds slapped the floor around her as though it rained. She didn't realize how much she relied on her vision to confirm her other senses: familiar sensations became alien in darkness. It was only once she rationalized what was happening, pictured it, that any of her sensations felt true. Even the moment her flesh sublimated to flames could only be understood through her imagination. She felt their grip slip through her limbs. Her hands wrapping around them. She embraced them, hungrily and angrily consuming them in her flame.

She reached through the room, her screaming roar a mix of angry flame and vengeance. Soon, there was no more flesh on which to feast. She felt at once vast and then aware of her limbs and fingers and feet.

The air cooled. Finally granted a moment of respite, she opened her eyes. She'd been remade from the healing flames, burning over a dozen Books. Yet it wasn't enough. Her skin was burned tender. And darkness continued whispering to her that she was alone. It was not unlike being in Oblivion. Although there—in her brother's universe—new worlds could be imagined, here the world was cruelly hidden from sight.

Feeling her way, the wood-slatted walls were cracked like crocodile skin. Carbonization chalked her hands which she suspected would leave handprints everywhere, including her face.

The silence made her feel safe, but she knew not for long. She continually examined the extent of her blindness hoping to discover a chink in the darkness, a dim spot—anything to prove her vision loss wasn't complete or permanent. She eventually became convinced that her eyes had been scorched blind.

Would Jeremiah come for her now? Defeat her at her most defenseless, or would he not bother now that she was like a rat in his trap?

Rising slowly to her feet, the floor unreliably steady. Only with her palms pressing a wall would her brain accept her surroundings weren't moving.

What do I do now? She'd always been able to heal. Injuries—aside from the psychic kind—never proved permanent before. *How can I face Jeremiah like this?* His cruelty would never allow sympathy. She helplessly clutched the wall like a shipwreck survivor waiting for the last remaining piece of hull to sink, leaving her adrift in a dark sea of uncertainty.

She cried, "Abby? Abby, help me!"

The voices in her head stilled; even they eagerly hoped for a reply.

"Rose? Carrie? Colette? Anyone?" She cried out the names her mind could recall. Blindness, uncertainty, debilitating, sickening fear fogged her brain. The only certainty was her palms trembling against the charred wall.

She rested her head against the slats. She felt broken, unrepairable. Constantly haunted by glimpses, recollections manifesting as faux vision. It was as though her brain was trying to reboot her eyes: psychedelic swirls and designs appeared, like when she was a child in bed and pressed against her closed eyes to see shapes and flashes swirl around her. Except these came unbidden, spinning and swirling like she'd come unglued from reality and swam in a neon universe. As much as her hands and feet told a story of an unmoving world, her head wasn't ready to believe her tactile senses without visual proof.

Her back to the wall, she embraced herself. Closing her eyes, her concentration focused not on the echoes of pain but her eyes. *Help heal me*, she begged her voices. She felt their initial stir, the knitting of flesh, and was hopeful her sight would return. As an added measure, she kept her eyes tightly closed long after they had concluded. Opening her eyes, darkness remained.

She collapsed to the floor. It was far worse than having too much to drink at Abby's trailer; her head swam, and she felt sick from the wobbling ground.

"Make it stop," she cried, her face pressed to the floor, trying to suppress her heaving stomach, wishing the floor could cool her feverish forehead.

She lay still. Without movement, the dizzying rotations of the world slowly came to a grinding halt. She wished herself to sleep, hoping to lose herself to unconsciousness, if only not to be awake in this unending, psychedelic nightmare her brain kept hallucinating. Swirling neon forms. Glimpses of the room. Somehow her mind understood its condition and rather than showing recollections of the slick, polished room, she not only resolved the rough slats but the char she'd put upon them.

It was ridiculous to hope her vision was returning: her eyelids were closed.

The longer she endured the hallucinations, the more fixed they became. Tilting her head, rather than spinning her about like a dizzying tilt-a-whirl, the room shifted appropriately. She allowed this imagined world to give her hope. But when she opened her eyes, all sight vanished.

Chapter One Hundred and Sixty-Five

"What the heck happened here?"

"Oh no. Is that…."

"Alex, you okay? Why aren't you answering us?"

"Say something. Let us know you're alive. What happened?"

"You look hurt. Please say something!"

Three voices.

They entered her head after what sounded like a journey of a thousand miles. Once heard, she travelled to within inches of the speakers.

"Merde, is she dead?" A forth voice—male. Her brain took a moment to find familiarity. A grunt was all she could produce. In response, a palm pressed firmly into her back.

"Talk to me. The Book-people, they came for you? What happened to your skin? What happened to this room?" *Abby*. For the briefest moment, Alex saw her imagined face. Alex experienced both the swell of relief and the withdrawal of hope, like a gushing wave that came in and, with an unfathomable undertow, receded.

A second hand, gentler than the first, cupped her forehead; fingernails against her skin. Colette's name came naturally to mind.

She spoke the names aloud, her voice parched.

"Can you sit up? Can you show me your eyes?" This was Marta.

She lowered her hand from her face. Nothing changed.

"Over here," Abby snapped her fingers. "What happened… to your eyes?"

Alex briefed them about her encounter with the Books. "Everything's black." For a change, she felt deserving of their pity.

"This is just great," a different male voice said.

"Shut up, she's blind, not deaf," threatened another. That sounded like George.

"Like an encyclopedia," Colette blurted.

"What?" Both Abby and Alex asked.

"A collection of Books: Like an encyclopedia."

Alex's laugh emerged as little more than a gurgle. "Like New York. Awful."

Abby touched Alex's arms. "Your burns look like healed scars. Does it hurt?" When Alex said she didn't think so, Abby continued, "The pattern is all over you. I've read about this. When electricity tattoos your body." Alex turned her head as though she could see. Her brain pretended to see her arms before her, reddish patterns of electricity branching out across them disappeared into darkness as swiftly as it emerged.

"I don't understand," Alex whimpered. "When I turn to fire, it usually heals me."

"Maybe this is beyond that," Marta supposed.

"Beyond that," Alex repeated, mouthing the words. She'd all but promised herself this was temporary. The truth deflated her.

"Sorry, Alex," Marta soothed. "I should have kept that to myself."

"What are we standing around for? We're fucked. We failed. I knew it. I fucking knew it, since the beginning I knew it wouldn't work."

Abby growled, "Eric, shut the fuck up or I'll put you back in that room and beat the shit out of you myself."

"Sorry," Eric whimpered.

"You need to try something," Abby said. "Maybe one of us has a spell to cure blindness. You need your sight. Anyone?"

Alex knew if she couldn't heal herself, it was unlikely anyone else could help her. Fearing more danger could be following, she asked, "What happened?"

Colette responded, "The Butlers took the men. Abby, Marta, and I found them. They were being tortured."

"Put to death," a younger man interjected. "Very slowly."

"We found an old friend." Alex could hear Colette's smile. "Jeremiah didn't kill Caleb."

"Maybe we can help you see?" Abby urged, "Let us try."

Colette and Abby put their arms around Alex. She could feel the warmth, feel the energy giving her strength. She shut her eyes, so she wouldn't see if the dark remained dark. After a few minutes, they released her. Abby asked, "Anything?"

Alex's lids fluttered open.

"Can you see?" Marta finished Abby's question.

Alex shook her head, reaching out to them. They took her flailing hands. She refused to cry.

They helped Alex to her feet. She was unhurt aside from the scars. They vibrated, as though still possessing some of the energy that seared them there.

"We need to get you home," Abby said. "Heather will know what to do."

At the mention of her aunt's name, sadness overcame Alex. She wasn't sure why, but she knew when her aunt said goodbye, it was meant as a finality. "I can't go back," Alex warned them. "Not until the Farm is empty." Alex recalled what the dust had done, the fibers from the nightmare eroding the spell that enchanted the Farm. She asked if any of them saw remaining piles.

"It's all over," Colette said. "Piled up in clumps."

"The spell is broken wherever the dust touches. Your magic will work here. Blow it around." Alex waved her arm in the air to demonstrate she meant far and wide, striking one of them in the head. "Sorry," Alex withdrew, embarrassed.

"No harm done," Colette laughed. "You couldn't…."

"That's it? Just blow it around?" Eric sounded doubtful.

Another man asked, "What good will that do?" It sounded like her uncle Steven. "It's just dirt, right?"

Alex described what it actually was.

"Okay," Abby said. For a moment Alex could see her, rubbing her arms as though rolling back invisible sleeves. Abby's breathing slowed in concentration. A Book opened. George spoke the guttural words. She'd never hear a man read a Book aloud and not have her gut tighten in anticipation of a fight.

At first, nothing. Then Colette said, "I think it's working." Something tickled her cheek. All at once it was like someone threw a bucket of air at her. The gust splashed around her in a wild, turbid dance. Her mind clearly pictured the distant walls dissolving as the dust blew against them.

"What the…," Alex heard Colette crouch. "Is it okay if it gets on us? It's dissolving the walls!"

"It's safe," Alex acknowledged. "It's the remains of a particularly nasty nightmare. I don't know why it does this. We're not on the Between, so it couldn't survive when I pulled it in, but the spell that makes this place falls apart when they touch."

"How far should we blow it?" *That sounds like June.*

The next male voice was younger. Maybe this was Caleb, "Blow it everywhere. Ruin this shithole."

Alex agreed, "Everywhere you can." She could nearly see it, like smoke from a fire seeping under doorways, channeling through the warrens of rooms until all the stalls and secrets were revealed.

"They're not walls," Marta gasped. "I wish you could see this, Alex, but walls are disappearing. This is just one giant…," she hesitated, "prison." Others in the group were commenting on what they saw with a stream of expletives. Alex understood; the lint revealed the Farm's truth.

At some distance, a woman screamed. Then another. Followed by more… many, many more. Alex craned her head, as though stretching or tipping it might allow her to see around her blindness. "What's happening?" A flashed vision of disappearing walls revealing women—in mid-activity—

their equipment disappearing—leaving them aware and self-conscious as the veil of the Farm was scoured from around them.

Colette narrated; Alex formed a picture in her mind: As the dust swept through the building, the small rooms were revealed to be an illusion. The decor, the fixtures, also illusions. There were no couches, no cocktail bars, no elegance. Just filth. Women wore the soiled clothes they were captured in, torn and stinking and decaying from time. There were no bathrooms, just moldering buckets. The food they ate were piles of stale and moldy bread and meat, the water feted and brown. The spell forced them to believe they were doing whatever they wished, and as the nightmare's remains blew through and the enchantment dissolved, the women rejected the harsh realities.

"Turn it back," someone cried. "Stop destroying everything," another threatened. They weren't alone; dozens cried out in complaint, more willing to believe the new reality they experienced was the fantasy. They cried that their lives had been destroyed. They demanded their lost paradise returned.

The grumble of a discontented and confused mob grew closer. There were expressions she understood, but more she didn't. Many weren't speaking English; their ability to universally communicate also lost.

"We need to keep her safe," George said gruffly. Then the sounds of movement suggested a line forming between her and the approaching crowd. Alex's heart swelled as her Coven prepared to protect her with their bodies.

"Stay back," Steven shouted to the crowd.

"Daddy!" Charissa cried for him, her voice coming from beyond her Coven. Alex pictured Charissa, among other women from her Coven, now freed from the spell, returning to them, racing ahead of the angry mob. Pat was closer when she said, "Steven, you're hurt."

"Let me through! I can't believe you came for me!" Lydia's polka-dotted jumper stood out from the others as she ran towards them.

Colette lurched forward. "Lydia, I'm so glad you're safe."

"Tell them the truth." Alex struggled to assign the voice to the person; probably June. "Tell them why they've been living in this dump for years."

Abby used her best authority voice, "Magic. Magic let you live here thinking it was different."

Someone from the crowd cried out, "Magic isn't real." Even without her vision, Alex knew everyone around her rolled their eyes.

Other voices from the crowd tried to find fault in the claim, "Wouldn't we know if it were magic?" "Wouldn't magic sparkle or something?" "It didn't feel fake." "I'd know if it weren't real."

"It felt real." Alex's voice trembled with uncertainty. "Because magic made it real to you. Made you think you were happy. It was always a prison. Instead of bars, he made you so happy you never thought to leave. Take away the magic and this is all there ever was."

"It was never like this," someone cried. Others agreed. Murmurs from the crowd gave Alex an indication of the push and pull as truth battled desire.

Alex retorted, "That's his cruelty. He made you believe you liked this."

Some seemed to understand, but there were many others demanding she return it as it was. They accused Alex and her Coven of witchcraft. They suggested she was the source of the magic that hid the old, beautiful rooms from sight. They accused her of wanting to ruin it because it was so wonderful. Alex listened to multitudinous debates taking place. But without magic, the infectious deception also drained away. The pull trapping them disappeared and some missed the feeling, while others recognized what they no longer felt. Those in the crowd who accepted the truth attempted to explain it to the others: they had been deceived for too long.

"What happened to you?" A hand took Alex's arm. Twisting it gently.

Alex recognized the voice. "I got tatts, too, Carrie."

Carrie whistled. "Bitchin'. Looks like they hurt."

"Easy," Abby warned. "She's blind."

"What?" Carrie cried out.

Several others asked, too. "What happened?" "Who did it?" "Did you try healing her?" "Let's try again."

Arms wrapped around her. Alex felt the kindness in the limbs as everyone stretched and strained to touch her once the depth of encircling bodies grew too deep. Her skin prickled and tingled. Her eyes burned. But even after several minutes, her vision hadn't improved. She so desperately wanted their love to fix her that she imagined she could see. Even in the darkness, she saw their faces, all crammed around her in hopeful expectation, waiting to hear that she'd been healed. And then it was gone, swallowed in darkness.

Alex whispered, "I'm too broken to be fixed."

"Don't you dare just give up like that." *That is definitely Rose.* "We're not making some bed to carry you around on." The contact of bodies and push of fabrics announced Rose forcing her way through the crowd. "You've got to see. How else will you fight him? You think you're facing me now? You're not. How will you direct a spell at him?"

Rose wasn't wrong. Alex turned slightly.

"Still not facing me."

Alex turned a little more in the opposite direction. *I don't know what else to do*, was what she wanted to say, but she knew Rose would snap at her. "I'm figuring it out," she said instead. Alex's spirit weakened. *Rose is right. How am I going to fight him like this?*

"Let me look at you," Nancy said. "I'm going to touch your face and shine a light in your eyes, okay?"

Alex tipped her head up in acceptance. Nancy's hand cupped her chin. She could feel something happening close to her face, but not see anything until through the darkness, a gentle brightness appeared, like the sun before it burns through thick fog. Alex imagined Nancy waving her cell phone's flashlight in front of her eyes.

"Pupils react normal," Nancy said. "Can you see the light?"

"The darkness got brighter." She didn't tell Nancy how clear her imagination rendered the scene. How Marta hovered over her shoulder or how upset Abby appeared.

"Maybe it's just temporary." From the concern in Nancy's voice, Alex didn't believe it.

Alex was aware of the surge of women pushing towards them. Their emotional turmoil was palatable. Alex could smell their conflicted feelings. As they accepted the truth, they began longing for home. Some were overcome with guilt that they willingly stayed, forgetting their loved ones and old lives. Some cried for their children, wondering how much time they'd missed. Would their children accuse them of abandonment? Did their loved ones think they were dead? Had their husbands or partners or lovers moved on to someone new? Some had been lost here for years—many for decades—and feared no one would remember them.

Alex stifled the tears these emotions brought her. There was so much hurt. But instead of blaming the man who imprisoned them, these women were all blaming themselves for not being strong enough to see through the deception. They blamed themselves for the pain they knew their disappearance had caused their families.

Alex considered what came next. They couldn't stay here. Unfortunately, leaving was even more dangerous: All these women entering the Between would be fodder for nightmares. Could they get everyone to the tower's shadow in time?

A hand rested on Alex's hand. Someone knelt at her side. "What do you need us to do?" June asked. "These women need someone to lead them."

I don't know how we're going to work out the logistics, was what she wanted to say. But she soured at the expectation of Rose's barbed remark. "We can't stay here," Alex replied. "I'm going to need the whole Coven working together to get them to safety."

"How will you do this?" Alex knew Banhi's gravelly voice.

At every turn, Alex's blindness made everything more difficult. What had been ordinary before now became impossible. Yet at every thought, there was Rose, her snotty face like Alex's conscience, countering each doubt-filled thought. Rose hadn't said a word and Alex wanted to smack her. And yet, Alex realized, her own expectations of Rose were pushing her to better decisions. Why was that so infuriating? Alex was blind. *Blind.* The moment she realized she desired their pity she hated herself for being so weak. She brought them here. They were in danger. Jeremiah had to know they were here. If they were going to get out alive it wouldn't be because anyone pitied her.

"I'll figure it out," she told Banhi. If they escaped, it seemed wishful thinking to hope Jeremiah wouldn't hunt every one of them down.

"When are you planning to do all this figuring?" Rose demonstrated that any statement Alex made was fodder for her obnoxia.

Alex didn't want to respond, but when Carrie did, she was aware of Carrie's glowering expression. "Why are you being so hard on her? Have *a little* sympathy. Look at her."

Now that she'd received her first dose of pity, Alex found it bitter. Before she could interject, Rose's reply was fierce with resentment, "Who do you think you are to tell me?" Before Carrie could reply, Rose continued, "Why don't you look at her, Carrie? She's the most powerful witch, ever. You saw what she can do on television. And at every turn she's a whining baby: *It's too hard.* Or, *I don't know.* None of us know. But we're all here. She's too afraid to do what she knows she needs to do."

As Carrie answered, "She's not afraid," Alex spoke over her, "You know why I'm afraid, Rose. I'm terrified one of you will die for my mistake." She struggled to her feet. "I don't know why you can't see it, Rose. Having you beside me is my greatest strength *and* weakness. If something happened to any of you, how would I live with myself?"

"I can take care of myself, Alex."

"Were you taking care of yourself, enchanted at the Farm?"

"It doesn't matter. You killed his enchantment. Figure out what's next and let's get that done, too." Rose took a deep breath and continued, "My whole life, my mother talked about magic. It ruined my family." Eric groaned. Alex felt dizzy, a sense of déjà vu from her nightmares. "And along comes Alex and suddenly I learn that not only was it all true, but you've got it. You've really got it. You took off the Reaper's arm! You beat Death! But you never want to use it. You're always afraid. You're always worried about everyone else. How many of us do you need to lose before you stop worrying and do what you were destined to do?"

Alex wanted to respond, but this silenced her. She hated Rose and loved her. Like in her nightmares, she wanted to rip Rose apart, but she also wanted to embrace her. Her greatest fear was that Rose resented her, that Rose hated that she'd come into her life and ruined it. Yet here was the truth, right out of Rose's mouth. The explanation for why she was so condescending: Alex hadn't yet lived up to Rose's expectation.

Alex lowered her head in thought and shame. She never expected Rose to be so right. But Rose wasn't the only one looking up to her. How many others was she letting down?

Around her, her Covens' audible silence was louder than the din of the swelling crowd. They silently watched Alex. Alex's imagined vision couldn't tell whether they agreed with Rose. She didn't care: She wanted them to agree for the same reason she wanted to believe Rose was wrong. She wasn't ready to face the difficult truth that she believed in something that wasn't true.

"I'll figure out how to work around this," Alex waved her hand in front of her face. "Then we'll get everyone to the tower."

"If you can't see," Caleb proposed, "could you try magic? I've read of spells to help people see in darkness and even through walls. I've heard about a spell to see ghosts and evil spirits, but I think that was an old-wives' tale." He gulped, "Oops, sorry, poor choice of expressions."

Alex started to respond; Rose interrupted her, "He's right, Alex. You should try."

What emotions will accomplish that magic? She nearly said, *I don't know how to do that.* "Not in here," she offered. "Outside, on the Between. Magic is different there. It's not emotional. It's imagination." She would imagine her ability to see. That sounded ridiculous, but so did thinking a fountain into existence. She hoped it would last outside of the Between, but she had her reservations. Dany's bearskin couldn't cross from Alex's brother's universe to the Between. "We need to get these women to safety, first."

Carrie said, "Or you could give them Books. We'd have an army."

Alex suppressed her natural inclination: Her gut instinct was to keep these innocent women safe. She guessed one, maybe two hundred women had gathered; from both the intensity of their murmur and flashes of experience. She tried to hold the vision long enough to tell, but darkness always flooded back. *Maybe I'm not fantasizing. Could this be magic?* If her visions were the result of magic—and if she could make them last longer—then Carrie's idea had greater merit than even she'd first assumed.

She pictured them swarming the Library, collecting Books, reading. She knew Jeremiah's men, or his Books, or perhaps he, himself, would try stopping them. Dozens could die. Could, would, might. These words were costumes disguising fear. She could imagine them taking their Books and swooning, firing and being struck by sparks. It was like a movie, the final battle as the heroes overtook the villains in a last-ditch effort, a go-for broke attempt, throwing everything they had into the fight, one shot at victory. There'd be death. There'd be heroics. *How many?* Alex knew the dark answer: *As many as it takes*.

For a change, it was Rose who had doubts. "That's crazy. These women can't fight. You expect them to take a Book and become instant warriors?"

"Rose is right," Eric replied. "There's no way it'll work."

When asked if his doubt was based on their sex, Eric stammered unintelligibly.

Carrie defended her remark, "Rose, you didn't know how to cast a spell until you picked up your Book. You did more than a little all right your first time out."

"That was different," Rose defended.

"Carrie's right." That was George. "Alex is the only one who can face Jeremiah. Even if she could see, the odds are shitty. With an army, maybe there's a chance."

Alex listened to her friends' discussion spiral near the fringes of argument. Rose had told her what to do: make a decision. Alex interrupted the debate. "Anyone who wants revenge will stay and fight."

No argument came from any of them.

"Now help me get outside so I can try and see again."

Chapter One Hundred and Sixty-Six

Abby allowed Alex to lean against her, one solid form she trusted. The prisoners of the Farm deserved to have the choice to either go home or join the fight against Jeremiah. Without vision, her brain fixated on each noise or groan or muffled conversation. Had she eyes she might have seen that these women were confused and tired and disgusted. She might have seen that they were unhappy their paradise was lost. That they were ashamed they had been complicit with a lie that took them from their families and friends and everything real that they loved and care for. That they were confused and scared of the implications of returning to that abandoned life. That they were terrified of being rejected by the people they'd left behind.

Abby told her the crowd was splintering. "The larger group wants to leave; I think the other wants the spell back."

How can I convince everyone they can't stay? Alex said to Abby and anyone nearby, "This place needs to be destroyed."

Abby warned, "But Jeremiah can't find you like this."

Alex thought sightlessness would make concentration easier. "That he hasn't already is a miracle." It bolstered her theory that he couldn't go on the Between. *Why? What's stopping him?*

Abby sensed something was troubling her and wrapped Alex in her arms. "You'll figure out a way to get your sight back."

Alex paused and listened. Even the voices in her head remained silent. Maybe they saw the same darkness and didn't know what to make of it.

"Show these women how strong you are, and they'll follow you."

Alex thought of the most dramatic show of her magic: flight. On first blush it was a brilliant idea: Leaping into the air, swooping over the crowd. Followed by blindly crashing into a wall or the ceiling. "I can't, Abby. Not anymore. Maybe someone else, like—"

"Don't you dare say *Rose*. That girl, that *child*, is clueless and dangerous. Impulsive. She thinks only of herself."

"She can't hear you?"

"She's too busy marching around, complaining."

"Sounds like Rose."

"Suck it up, kiddo. They're waiting. They're scared because they gave away their lives for a lie. They don't know what comes next or who will lead them to it."

How is she doing that? Alex wondered if Abby were somehow tapping into her own thoughts. She tried conjuring vision, but the darkness remained unchanged.

Abby continued, "Tell them why you're blind. Tell them the Butlers took your eyes for saving them. It sounds biblical, like Sampson having his eyes ripped out. Puts the fault on them." Abby poked her in the side of the head. "Think about what you want to say. Most people are terrified seeing the audience. You've got that licked. Pretend it's just you and me."

Alex closed her eyes to find her thoughts. *If I can't see, why do I still close my eyes?* As she contemplated what she wanted to say, Abby rubbed her neck and arms with the aggression of a corner coach in a boxing movie.

She needed to pretend she was somewhere comfortable and intimate. The first place to come to mind was Abby's trailer, but that was gone. Rather than dwell on what she'd done, she pictured herself in her attic. In front of her large mirror. Abby behind her, holding her. She felt safe. Secure. They were alone, and when it was just Abby and herself, she could say anything.

She whispered, "Get their attention."

Abby shouted like a truck driver cut off on the highway. Then she said, "Alex here has something she wants to say to you, and she deserves your attention."

Alex whispered her thanks when Abby told her the room was hers. She focused on the mirror. She let her volume carry her voice even though she spoke only to Abby. "Jeremiah is who made this place. He needed a place to store women. But prisoners want to escape their prisons. He used magic to make everyone want to stay. To make everyone believe they were already free. Made them want for nothing more than this horrible place."

Gasping and grumbling.

"It's not the prisoner's fault. Even freed of the spell they feel shame at being tricked. But they weren't tricked. What Jeremiah did was to give them no choice but to believe. No one stayed because they wanted to. They stayed because Jeremiah's magic gave them no alternative."

"Keep going, Alex. Keep telling them it's not their fault."

"Jeremiah's magic didn't hide the truth from them. It took it away from them. It took everything away from them. For no other reason than because they're women." Alex took a breath. "He kept each one of you here because you are women. He used magic to control you. To make you forget. But that's over now. I brought my Coven here to free you. I brought something from outside those doors that broke the spell."

"They're listening. A few maybe don't want to believe you. Keep going."

Alex could imagine the sea of faces staring at her. Their intensity drove the words from her. Alex focused on the mirror. On Abby.

"The Butlers who served you, who cleaned up after you, all lied to you. The illusion didn't affect them. When they discovered me ending the magic, they tried to kill me. They failed. But now I'm blind."

Someone cried, "What happened to them?"

Alex wasn't sure how they would take the truth. It was too complicated to explain they were golems who had once been prisoners, too. They could have been women some of them knew. How would they react to learning she'd murdered their friends?

How could she simply explain the truth? How deadly they were. How they sacrificed themselves to be more powerful. How they wrought destruction in New York and Paris. They wouldn't learn about what happened until they were free in the real world. "They took my sight, so I took their lives."

Gasps. Grumbles. Cries of, "You?" and "Then where are the bodies?" intermixed with dozens of other calls questioning Alex's legitimacy. She felt the rising tide of heated anger. She just saved them, and they doubted her. No, they hadn't the right to tell her she lied; not after she lost everything to emancipate them.

Then, Abby's voice, "Prove it to them, Alex. Take this place apart."

Alex raised her arms. A few snickered at her. Her whispers resumed, like a call chain of comments routing over and over through her head, finally aware Alex wasn't slumbering. Waves passed through her muscles, tensing and drawing back her shoulders. Veins bulged along her forearms. Since the first day her aunt brought her to the clearing by Sara's house, she'd suffered. She'd burned hundreds of thousands of books, millions maybe, and now, the one chance she had to save living, breathing women, they laughed at her.

Agitated, Alex accused, "You'd rather believe the polished lies than the truth."

She felt like she was at the center of a whirlpool, a dangerous wind howling tightly around her. This was her anger, the heat of her emotions boiling her blood as though preparing to explode. She felt like a feral animal, so engrossed in her anger—not at these women—but at the man who so damaged them that they willingly condemned her for saving them.

"Oh boy!" Abby backed away. "Do it, Alex," she shouted.

The concussive force pushed her nearly off her feet. Without sight, she was left uncertain if it was wind or electricity or plasma. Only of its roar. Shockwaves rumbled away from her like thunder during a passing summer storm. Then, just as quickly, her hatred and rage drained from her as though they'd spilled out. Everything she felt a moment before was gone. Some magic left her feeling empty, but not in a cathartic way. She still had reason to be angry, but it took its time to fill back up.

The women began applauding, a voiceless cheer of endless clapping. Her imagined vision flashed. The conflict of vision and sound left her confused.

"What's happening?" Alex was frantic for Abby. "Abby? They're not clapping, are they? What did I do?"

Abby grabbed her. "Come on! We need to get everyone out of here!" To Alex, she hissed, "The whole place is falling to splinters."

Given context, her brain reinterpreted the sounds. Suddenly what she perceived made sense. All around her, timbers cracked and groaned. They didn't snap like logs giving way to weight they could no longer bear but collapsed like toothpicks. Splinters rained in torrents.

Abby grabbed Alex about the chest and began hauling her. Alex couldn't tell where Abby was dragging her, each step thrashed her one way and then another as though Abby merely shook her back and forth. Barely audible over the falling wood, her ears muffled against Abby's bosom, was the stampede. Everywhere, women were racing for the door, screaming. They were running from one slaughter to another: once outside, the nightmares would instantly be on them.

Alex pulled from Abby. "Stop. Leave me."

Abby hesitated, "You're not dying here."

Alex turned away and tipped her head towards the falling detritus. The movement left her spinning, her eyes unable to show her movement had stopped. Alex wobbled, unsure where the floor lay.

Abby grabbed her. "Whatever it is you need to do, we'll do it together." Abby held her upright, prepared to die with her.

Alex's stomach churned. She went too far and instead of freeing everyone, she was burying them alive. She saw flashes of frantic panic. Movement so jarring and chaotic it made little sense. Sawdust and wooden shrapnel cascaded down from everywhere. Her whispers were a muddle of confusion. Calling out in darkness; frantic. Alex had to do something. If it didn't work, she and Abby would be buried alive, crushed by the debris.

Like she had the mirror, she pictured the building as best she remembered it. She conceived wood timbers, and she pictured pieces tumbling through the air as they fell apart, opening slivers of blue sky, streams of sunlight striking through. When flashes of vision stuck her, she tacked her imagined structure onto it, fixing the walls and ceiling around her as though she wasn't pretending she saw. She concentrated until she could look around the inside of the decaying structure. What emotions would stop this? She couldn't hope to know. Instead, her arms upraised, she fantasized her hands could push the ceiling up, like she pushed a cushion of wind. She strained against resistance, real or imagined, trying desperately to keep the ceiling from collapsing. Then everything gave way. Alex's arms strained as the ruins collided with her magic. It was as though her imagination pressed against her palms. Even without her eyes to verify her imagination, she knew she was controlling magic the way she controlled it on the Between.

"You're doing it," Abby cried into her hair.

What she was doing, Alex had no idea. She pushed, her imagination working through the details to keep her emotions going. She pushed and her mind imagined the blue sky and sunlight piercing the ceiling. Timbers and beams crashing into her magic as though it were an invisible dome. It rumbled harmlessly aside.

Deep, reverberating thuds, like dozens of fallen trees hitting the ground, nearly jostled everyone to their knees. The warmth of sunlight struck across her face just as her imaginary view opened to the sky. She pushed the tumbling debris aside, and when the rumbling became no more than a settling of dust, Alex saw that too. The growing breeze cut through the open structure, clearing away a great expanding plume. As she imagined looking into the vast blue sky, tinged and streaked with high, white clouds, she saw the tall spiral tower in the distance.

Everywhere cries roared out. She didn't need Abby to tell her these weren't cries of women dying, but cheers. Alex turned to Abby, imagining her friend—her Familiar—before her. Her recollection of Abby was so clear, so certain, she could see dust graying Abby's hair, a wound where a piece of debris lacerated her forehead, now caked with bloody sawdust.

Alex discovered Abby exactly where she imagined her. Taking her in an embrace, Alex shuddered. "I did it," she said, tearfully.

"You destroyed the shit out of this place, and no one got hurt."

"You got hurt." Alex touched the cut. It was damp and gritty.

"You can see?"

She wasn't facing Abby, only imagining her. When she gave up her concentration, the haze of darkness swallowed everything up. As long as she pretended to see the remains of the building around her, she saw. "It's different," Alex explained. "My eyes are blind. I imagine seeing the building. I imagine seeing you right now." She reached out and brushed the dust from Abby's short hair.

Banhi marveled, "You see by imagination?"

"Yes, Banhi," Alex turned to the old woman, her gray hair even grayer.

Something caught her eye; Khowla approached them.

Alex expressed her concern, "Khowla, you look panicked."

At the sound of her name, Khowla spoke. At first it made no sense. But, as when Alex was quick to ask Heather, "What?" only to have her brain decipher the words, Alex realized Khowla said, "Everyone mutters jibberish and expects me to understand."

"I'm sorry, Khowla," Alex replied. "Once we're back on the Between, you'll understand."

Khowla shrieked with joy and surprise. Banhi leaned closer to Alex, "What did you just say?"

Alex repeated herself.

Banhi stared intensely. "That time you said it in English. You understood what Khowla said?"

Alex replied, "Didn't you?" She motioned at the destruction. Maybe we're on the Between now."

"I don't think so," Abby corrected. "I didn't understand a word from either of you."

Alex's immediate reaction was to think they were gaslighting her. *They wouldn't screw with me.* "Did I imagine that, too?"

Khowla touched Alex's arm. "You *imagine* yourself speaking my language?"

Alex replied, "I'm not doing anything."

"Not to sound *that way*," Abby said, "but could you all speak English?"

"Sorry," Alex said. "I can't help it. I don't know what language I'm speaking. It all sounds the same to me." She looked to the blue sky. "I guess just because the building is gone doesn't mean we're on the Between yet." That was a relief. Once there, the nightmares would come.

"Is she okay?" Alex imagined Rose. "That was quite a show. I'm impressed."

She replied to Rose, "Thanks. Not sure how I pulled that off." She leaned to Abby, "They're starting to leave," she pointed to where people climbed over debris. "Once they get out, the nightmares will come."

"I don't know what you just said," Khowla said, "but I brought women. They're outside; from many markets."

"Don't leave yet," Alex shouted. She snaked through her entourage, toward the crowd clambering over the debris.

Pointing outside, Alex explained the Between. "Out there is where you go when you dream. But you're not asleep. You're awake, and there are things here that sense that. They will come for all of us. They're nightmares. When they touch you, as perfect as the illusion was while you were in the Farm, the horrors they show you will seem just as real."

The crowd lamented, "Then how do we get out of here?" and "We're trapped?" and "So do something!"

Alex walked around the crowd. She tried her best to imagine them, but there were too many. Most resolved as faceless representations. The effect was chilling.

One woman reached out to Alex. Contact resolved her. Her oily lavender shirt stained so yellow it looked brown. The fabric hung, weighed by filth. The woman's long hair was straggly and knotted and peppered with dust and splinters. She pulled Alex into an embrace and Alex tried not to cringe at the odor, which wouldn't lessen no matter how hard she imagined it away. She held the woman, seeing faces around her transforming into people.

"You saved us," she said. Countless others agreed.

"It's not over yet," Alex warned.

She raised her voice again, addressing the crowd. "Before you leave here, you have a choice to make. I can help you get home."

She paused. The crowd restlessly anticipated the second option.

"What will I find?" Another asked, "What year is it?" Another added, "I've been here since twenty-fifteen." "Twenty-ten," said another. "Eighty-eight," cried another, adding, "twenty-fifteen? How long have I been here? Everyone must think I'm dead." Others cried out other years. Many from long before Alex was born. It humbled and broke her heart that the only thing she could offer these women was to return them to a world they wouldn't recognize. Cell phones and the internet and self-driving cars and computerized everything's were unimagined by these women before they'd been snatched. What would life be like returning them now? How would they acclimate to a world so foreign?

"There's a tunnel, it's not far. It leads to *his* Library," Alex said. "You don't realize how lucky you were. You were snatched and brought here. Many other women were tortured to death. He made Books out of them and filled his Library with them."

The crowd gasped.

"That's what they make when they take magic out of you. They murder for power."

Only the sound of bodies standing, breathing, crying.

"You can come with me. I'll show you those Books and how to take the magic back. You'll cast spells. You'll fight. We'll take the Library. Destroy it like this place. Help me end this."

She anticipated a roar, but there wasn't one. She wished she hadn't walked from Abby; she could use Abby telling her what she was missing. She tried to imagine why they were so quiet, but all she saw was women staring back at her.

"Fight with me," she told them.

Someone asked, "Is it dangerous?"

"Very."

"Could we die?" asked several others.

"Tell me now if you want to go home," Alex said, receiving silence. "Then fight with me, we go there now." Alex's uncertainty made her blinder than her lack of vision.

She began climbing over the pile of debris. From the top of the pile, she imagined the rolling hills beyond the tower, and the fields of flowers. She saw a bird making lazy circles in the sky. She saw bees and bugs and butterflies gliding between patches of wildflowers. Just as when she looked at her Coven, it was different than seeing it. It was livelier. It brightened her heart to see how beautiful the hillsides, rolling off into the distance, were. But there were limits. This was the place created by dreams and was only as wide and vast as people dreamt.

For a moment, she wondered what to do. Even from here, she could see the vast distance between the Farm and the tower. Inside that small room at the top of the tower, the ancient, mummified woman hadn't crawled up into a ball and died. She had wrapped her body around something that she protected covetously until her last breath. Alex climbed down the other side of the debris pile and stepped onto the hard-packed soil. After taking a moment to steady herself, she started for the tower to discover what that was.

Chapter One Hundred and Sixty-Seven

Alex worked exhaustively to see the universe of the Between. She could resolve as far away as she dared herself to imagine. She wanted to see it one last time because there could be no more running. Blind or sighted, she would face Jeremiah soon enough.

She considered the others: her Coven, the survivors of the Farm. It didn't seem fair to tempt them with stories of war and glory only to lead them to certain death. And yet, that was how it had always been done. She wondered if she had the stomach for it. To exhaust the enemy's munitions with sacrifice.

She worried for them all. They needed her more than she needed them, and that meant—for better or worse—by not choosing home, they had to accompany her the remainder of the way.

Alex imagined her Book Club clamoring over the debris and trudging towards her. Her ears, however, created an imagined view of a crowd following behind the Coven.

Alex asked, "They're coming?"

Abby's voice was clear, "All of them."

Rose laughed, "They want a piece of whoever took their lives away. Plus, you promised them magic."

The mass exodus materialized. Rose and Abby and her Book Club proudly lead them. There were too many to count, even in her imagination.

Khowla tugged on Alex's shirt pointing to the field beyond the Farm. Alex's initial mental vision returned a blur of sparkling light. As her mind clarified things, she recognized that these were threads, attached to the dozens and dozens of women Khowla brought from the markets.

Alex scanned the imagined skyline. Without disappointment, more than a dozen nightmares raced from the distant horizon. The temperature dropped with the sudden darkening of the atmosphere. They swelled into the sky, rapidly approaching.

Her Coven herded the mass of women to the tower's shadow. Khowla enlisted those from the markets—who were not endangered by the nightmares—to help.

"There are a lot of them." Alex could tell without looking this was Carrie. Just at the thought, Carrie resolved, standing outside Alex's normal field of view. The ink under Carrie's skin pulsed and animated her designs, making the cleavers cut beef and the skulls grin. Speech-bubbles boiled as if they were actively speaking the words. The effect was both hypnotic and nauseating, and Alex could barely keep her eyes off them. She turned to better focus her attention and stared at Carrie, eliciting a grin from the other.

"They look like filthy dinner napkins," Carrie pointed up at the nightmares. "First time I thought pirate ship sails. They remind me of salamander gills. If that makes sense. I saw that once on television."

The group streamed around them. "Keep them going," Alex shouted to Abby. Her Book Club dispersed throughout the crowd to ensure no one fell behind. As each member of her Coven passed, she called to them. "Get to the tower."

Matthew showed her the tower's shadow was safe. So far, he had been right. *If the nightmares can't cross into the shadow, was it put there to protect people or the Library?*

If the nightmares were going to attack anyone, Alex would allow it to be herself. *And maybe Rose.* She regretted that momentary thought but still wondered if her cousin could use a dose of horror to understand what she'd been dealing with. *What would Rose's nightmares be about? Probably me taking her room.*

The nightmares were close. Dangerously so. "Try to keep the women safe," she told Carrie. "Tell everyone that out here, they can use imagination. Magic won't work. It's like when you dream, and your thoughts change things. Don't let them touch you; you won't be able to tell the nightmare from reality."

Carrie nodded, looking back on the immense, looming nightmares. "You're gonna draw them to yourself, aren't you? To protect everyone." When Alex nodded, Carrie touched her again. Looking at Alex, without releasing her touch, Carrie told her, "You're one badass, Alex." She hesitated like she had something more to say. She smiled. "See you by the tower. Be safe." Carrie checked the sky and shivered before leaving Alex to finish getting everyone to safety.

Standing alone once again, Alex reached skyward. She'd read about black holes once. Not even light can escape their gravity. She imagined she was like one. The draw of her gravity was irresistible to everything above her. The first of the black filaments slipped through the air to her hand. It twisted and writhed through the breeze, coiling and uncoiling loops along its length. It sniffed the air like a living appendage, seeking prey. None of them could escape the pull of her gravity and were starting to show their writhing panic as they swam in the atmosphere against increasing currents.

I am fire. Nightmare to the nightmare. I am the bad dream that keeps the bad dream awake. She wasn't sure she believed a word of her encouraging thoughts. Regardless, she repeated them.

With a slap, the first one hit Alex's wrist, instantly latching on. There was no pinch, no discomfort, no sensation at all as it began feeding.

Alex closed her eyes. She released her imagination so everything around her went black.

A swirl of images surfaced and drowned in the deep darkness of her sight. Twisted faces, mangled bodies, people she knew crying for help.

She imagined. Within her arm was a liquid besides blood. A purple so deep, nearly black. It gushed, pressurized, forcing it up the length of the creature's gullet. It reminded her of a soda bottle, the audible, dull thunk as it was squeezed and popped back. That's what Abby drank to die for her to go to Sara.

There was Sara, standing in the doorway of her cottage, leaning against the door with her mutilated hands, the last breath of life leaving her as Matthew skulked away with her twins.

The fluid was strong, a sour tart like an acid, but thick and sticky like a juice concentrate that plops out of the can. Almost immediately, the crêpe twisted to free itself, to regurgitate the foul liquid that surged through it. Alex wrapped its length around her free hand and held it there, imagining the purple liquid, fouler tasting than any poison, slimier and more repugnant that any liquid the creature had ever experienced, pushing through it.

It was but a moment before the purple liquid reached the larger mass, spreading between the dark fabric sheets like a stain bleeding through a napkin. The nightmare stilled. It trembled. It allowed the nightmare to believe a giant, horrific monster held it, force-feeding it, preparing it to be consumed. The entire mass convulsed as every living bit of it fought to be away.

And then, movement stopped. The entire mass careened from the sky, crashing into the field below in a silent explosion that rendered both nightmare and dream to nothingness. Disappearing up its length, even the tendril wrapping her arm vanished.

The other nightmares attempted circumnavigating her in their hunt of her Coven. As though these hellish collections might float past her unnoticed. Lightning crackled from her fingertips. Unlike before, she wasn't coaxing her anger, wasn't transmogrifying emotion into magic: she imagined it.

The massive nightmares seemed to possess awareness. As Alex turned her attention to them, their segmented tendrils froze in the air like observing mouths, agape in horror.

Alex raised her hand, tempting them to feed. None of the nightmares accepted.

Keeping an imagined eye on her Coven and the women from the Farm, the first were just reaching the protective shadow of the tower. She needed to buy them more time. She imagined the draw of her raised hands was irresistible, too great for the creatures, a curiosity of such immense gravity that no matter their exertion, they had to feed.

The immense masses attempted drifting in retreat. Their tendrils fought against the pull as they unrolled and elongated. While the mouths targeted her directly, their lengths pulled futilely, trying to keep away from her. At once, her hands were host to dozens and dozens of black streamers. They strained as their bodies floated away, willing to tear themselves apart to escape her. Alex would not let them go.

Alex remembered the way Charon, the child, cowered in her presence. It feared presenting her with its Reaper visage because she had hurt it in that form. It remained a child because to the child, she had always been kind.

Let's see if I can reason with these things. Rather than feed them her imagined purple poison, she thought of Sara and what Matthew and his hammer did to her. She thought about Jeremiah slaughtering her Coven in the Library. The attacks in New York and Paris. The way the golems blinded her. Her recollections were vivid. Each detail, each sensation she forced into the creatures, hoping these creatures could sympathize with her pain.

The nightmares flinched and twisted rhythmically to the imagined beats of her narrative. They contorted as if trying to avoid the hammer coming down on their hands. They shriveled as Matthew threatened them, as if trying to hide.

Then she pulled them closer. She imagined they could feel her heart swelling as she thought of her family. Of Rose, Holly, Peter, Abby, Heather, Billy, Sara, George, of her entire Coven: her Book Club. This was who she was. She allowed them to feel her love for her friends and family as if it were the very love she had for these creatures. She fed them the emotion with the same intensity as the others, so they'd be overwhelmed by it.

The strain on her arms slackened. The nightmares drifted closer. The remaining tendrils reached for her. Their twisting lengths coiling about her, enveloping her.

And then Alex allowed her sight—her imagination—to return to darkness. She waited for what the nightmares would feed into her mind, but her world remained dark.

Alex mused over what a few nightmares did to the Farm and wondered what it might do to the Library. Could she entice even one of these creatures into the Library to find out? The thought sent to them, darkness flashed with their returned images: A horrific tower, glowering against a bright sky. Its very stones sharp and threatening. The dark shadow cast by the tower was not a contrast of light and dark, but a knife's edge. All she felt was pain cutting through her until she looked away from the tower's shadow.

These creatures would not come with her to the Library, nor would she force them.

She slowly lowered her arms, the coiled tendrils gently releasing and retreating. They hovered around her, almost reverently, as though awaiting her. She understood them, at least a little. And they understood her. She could be a nightmare. A true horror if she needed to be. But her choice was never to harm.

Alex left the nightmares, which slowly made their retreat, to rendezvous with her Coven at the base of the tower. When she'd cut the distance in half, she turned back and from this first hill, surveyed the remains of the Farm. Although she was only beginning to understand her imagined sight, she was surprised when a sudden move enshrouded the world in darkness. She imagined the Farm, the hard mud pathways leading to piles of wooden rubble. From this distance, she saw something more. It looked like a scrape, like when she'd fallen on her knee, before the blood began to flow, the layers of pink skin were abraded, row after row, exposing darker flesh below.

It was no secret that Jeremiah hid the Farm here. That he'd put a real place on the Between, but she now saw the wound he'd created. The Farm was torn from the real world, its edges raw and festering. The Between had been incised to accept the graft, the edges of the wound unhealed and angry as they pressed against one another. Was there some way to heal the wound? She imagined the field swallowing the Farm, its edges crawling and creeping over the other. But nothing happened. No matter how she imagined the Farm sinking into the ground, being buried by the real Between, whatever power put it here wouldn't allow her to alter it.

She was unable to heal the Between. She couldn't erase the Farm.

When Alex met the others at the tower, Abby was the first to greet her. "What now?"

Alex wasn't sure. Her imagined sight worked on the Between, but would it work inside the Library? Her doubts resurfaced. Could she wander down an aisle she hadn't been before and imagine it correctly? Were her imagined visions even real?

"Are you sure you can't see?" her Uncle Steven asked. When she explained how she saw by imagination, he said, "I read about people blinded in accidents who could tell everything about an object they were holding, its color and size. They could see, but the signals never got to the parts of their brain that told them they could." He looked at Pat's disappointed expression and said, "What? Am I not helping?"

"We go to the Library," Alex interjected. "As soon as we get there, give everyone who needs one a Book. Be ready to fight."

Alex turned in the direction of the cavern entrance, still too far away to see, and yet in her imagination, there it was, visible through the multiple folds in the earth, shining through the hillsides. Her whispers seemed enthralled at his, their din rising.

"I've got to face him, Abby," Alex said absently, her attention focused on the distant opening, the throbbing hillside surrounding it, swollen from the vicious wound created to hold the real Library on the Between. "Remember this. I'd rather die than let him take my magic back. Do whatever you can to help me, but it's also possible that I won't ever defeat him, or him me. If that's the case, then maybe the only way we end this is if you all can destroy us both."

"We'll do everything we can to—"

Alex interrupted, "I mean it. Either way, I won't be leaving. We've got one shot at defeating him. Either I take his magic, or we both must be destroyed. If—when—he starts taking the magic back, you've got to kill me. Charon will do the rest. If I can hold him long enough—distract him—everyone must attack us both. We must end him today, no matter the sacrifice." Alex had come here today to put an end to Jeremiah's reign. *How do I destroy the black heart at the center of the universe? What happens if I do?*

"Promise me, Abby."

Abby groaned. "I promise." Her words sounded small. Still, her Familiar made her a promise. Alex didn't care if this was the oath or not.

"What's the plan? We going in both barrels blazing?" Alex knew Rose was making guns of her fingers whether she imagined it or not. Rose was off as soon as Alex replied, "Yes."

She took stock of the army massing around her. Hundreds of women. Thousands. Most here, but others, from disparate parts of the world, dreaming themselves into the war. This was now her Coven. These women would become witches. She hoped they'd be enough.

Chapter One Hundred and Sixty-Eight

lex had one last opportunity to visit with her original Coven: her Book Club. She asked Abby to bring them to her. Although she couldn't see them unimagined, she desired to feel their presence, this one last time.

It seemed so long ago when she met these strange and diverse women and could barely remember their names. She recalled their excitement as they went to the ruins of Sara's house to cast their first ever spell. Now these women had magic. Most had cast spells, had fought. They'd witnessed loss at Jeremiah's hands. They knew what lay ahead or believed they did.

First was Nancy. Alex touched her hands to Nancy's face, imagining Yellow Scrubs as she was when they first met in the emergency room. She wore none of her piercings, even though Alex's imagination put them there. Her hands touched flesh where her mind's eye saw steel. "My healer," Alex whispered.

Nancy's face reddened with blush. "I wish I could fix your eyes," she said to Alex. "I wish I could make everything better, but I know I can't." She sighed, "This is it, huh? It feels like a lifetime ago when we met him in that field."

Alex nodded, recalling her dizzying glimpses of fiery tornadoes, "The odds are slightly better today."

Nancy nodded. "I'm proud to be at your side, you know?" She wiped a tear. She kept moving her mouth like she had something to say.

"I know," she told Nancy.

Alex then found June. "I can't really see you, but whenever I think of you, you have a wineglass in your hand."

June laughed, embracing Alex. "I hope it's filled with something good."

"Always."

"I used to take my career so seriously. After this, what's even real? What matters? I don't know how I'm going to go back to that life."

Alex appreciated June's optimism. It concerned her, too, as perhaps June wasn't grasping the gravity of the situation. Apparently sensing this in Alex's silence, June added, "If, that is, we get out of here. Just know I'm honored to call myself your friend."

This pulled a smile to Alex's face. "So am I," she told June.

"My boy," she embraced George. "My little boy." For some time she wondered why seeing George always pinched a little. At one time she was concerned it was a crush. It took him confessing his love for her to put it all in perspective. He was Sara's son, but Sara had spent enough time inside of her and she inside of Sara that they shared her mothering bond. "I'm so proud you found your way back to us; to me."

George blushed. "Me too." Alex sensed he wanted to say more. He had tried to apologize once; he desired absolution from his sins.

"Today is the day you'll make up for all those regrets. Keep these women safe, George."

He embraced her. "I promise I will. I'll make you proud." As Alex pulled away, he wiped a tear from his eye. "I know you're not her, Alex, but I love you the same. I always will."

She cupped his cheek and kissed his forehead. "So will I."

She came to Khowla and Banhi next. "My fairy godmothers," Alex said with a giggle. "My wise women. You saved me and helped me find my way. You showed me the Between and taught me that magic was emotion *and* imagination. I have learned so much from you both." The two women each touched opposite sides of Alex's face.

"Child," Banhi said, "my gift to you was wisdom. Do not thank an ignorant old woman for telling you stories. You saw the truths and found your own way."

Khowla spoke next. "I am honored here at your side. We all dreamt ourselves at the market, hoping there is more to magic than fancy dreams. You revealed the truth none of us wanted to see. You showed us how to see the things that were always before us. You can never be blind, Alex, because you see greater than all of us."

"Thank you for going back to the market, Khowla," Alex said. "I will do my best to keep everyone safe."

"No Alex. Do not trouble yourself with their safety while you have such dangers facing you." Khowla pursed her lips. "They are here because they understand the danger, Alex. This is a worthy day to die."

"Let's hope it doesn't come to that." Alex didn't understand why she suddenly had words of optimism when they so conflicted with her impending dread.

"We always hope that," Banhi interjected. "Some of us live our lives under the heel of dangerous men. It has always been the curse of being a woman. Today, we can change that." She leaned forward and whispered, "For everyone."

Next, she approached Pat and Steven. Charissa stood between them, each had a hand on her shoulder. For a moment, Alex's mind fixated on the image of an unconscious child sprawled at the foot of her bed. "I always wondered what happened to that girl who came to my house and couldn't stop showing me her phone."

Charissa snorted. "I'm sorry if I ignored you, Alex."

Before Charissa could say anything more, Alex said, "You never ignored me. I'm so glad I got to know my cousin." To Steven, she took his hand in a desperate grasp. "My Uncle Steven. I wish we had more time. I'd show you around the Between. I'm sure Holly would love a visit from her brother."

He stammered. "She's here?"

"They all are," Alex said. "Except Peter." *And Donna. And Betty. I wonder if I'll ever see them again.*

Pat rubbed Alex's shoulder. "I'm glad you got to meet your family. We love you so much, Alex. Your parents would be so proud of you. Always know that."

Alex sensed something was bothering her and asked.

Pat answered, "I'm scared, Alex. I've talked to the others and I know what's coming. The Farm puts it all into perspective. We want to help you, but my priority is to protect my daughter."

"Patty, we discussed this," Steven said.

Charissa added, "Mom, come on."

"It doesn't matter what we said before. Alex should know she can't count on us if Charissa isn't safe."

"She doesn't mean that," Charissa said urgently.

"I can send you three back," Alex offered. "There's no shame in that. You can look after Heather."

"We're coming with you," Charissa said bluntly. She cast glances at each of her parents. "My dad's doing this for his sister and her daughter," she touched Alex. "I'm doing it for my cousin, because what she has to do is too great for one person." She looked at her mother. "I understand, Mom. We're going to war. A lot of bad things are about to happen. We can't run from it. It's too important."

The way Pat asked, "Is it important enough to die for?" suggested she knew the answer.

Charissa fell silent, not because she couldn't reply, but because she didn't need to.

Alex embraced Marta next. Her hands nearly completed the circle back to herself. "The first member of the Book Club." Alex grinned. "And my brother. My twin."

Marta nodded. "I'm ready, Alex. We both are." She touched Alex's shoulder. "When we go in, don't even think of us. Do what you've come to do."

"Don't say that," Alex could barely get the words out. "I can't do that."

"I now know what happens when I die. I'm not afraid. But you need to face Jeremiah and you can't have all of us to worry about."

"Keep my brother safe, okay? We have a lot of catching up to do when this is over."

Marta nodded tearfully. "We look forward to it. Thank you," Marta said, touching her chest.

Alex shook Jacques hand. "It was wonderful to meet you."

He gently kissed her right cheek and then her left. In his accented way, he replied, "Pleasure is all mine. I am your soldier. Send me to danger."

Alex nodded. "I'm so sorry that I will."

"William, your—what is your word for him?" Jacque roughly explained their relationship.

"Cousin," Alex answered.

Jacque's eyes lit up. "Really? Funny, that is our word too. Your cousin was a brave man. He was my friend. I hope to live up to his—what is the word—example."

"You already have. He'd be proud of you."

Rachel hugged Alex. When Alex started to say, "I'm really glad you're here," Rachel interrupted her, saying, "Please don't say anything."

"Okay," Alex worried.

"I know what's next," Rachel said. "A few of my friends enlisted after nine-eleven. I thought they were so brave." Tears fell from her eyes. "I'm so ashamed I'm so scared. I don't know how they were so brave. I wish I could be, too."

Alex wiped her tears. "You are that brave. You're here. They were just as scared as you are."

"You think so? You're not."

Alex forced a smile. "Rachel, I don't believe there's anyone here more frightened than me."

"Really?"

After Alex nodded, Rachel said, "You don't show it." She sniffled and wiped her running nose on her wrist. "Gross," she said. "Thank you for telling me it's okay."

Carrie practically leapt into her arms, hugging and swinging her. She gave Alex a kiss.

"My champion," Alex said, her lips tingling.

"When this is over," Carrie enthused, "assuming I survive, that is, I'm getting my whole back done." She rubbed Alex's arms. "Something that matches yours." She blew air out, not quite whistling. "Magic. Who would ever have imagined? Not in my whole life did I ever think I was special. Now, not only am I a real witch, but I'm here. When the world learns about what we've done every one of us will be heroes. We are living a story of myth." She kissed Alex again, knotting up fistfuls of Alex's shirt. "Thank you for including me in this."

Alex touched her kissed lips, "What was that for?"

Carrie looked fearful. "Was it not okay?"

Alex was more surprised than anything else. "It was."

Relieved, Carrie grinned. "Waiting for the right time is always a bad idea." With a wink, Carrie added, "I told you I like 'em tall."

Alex touched Carrie's face. She had so many things she wanted to say that the words were confusing. "I wish I could see that tattoo when it's done."

At that, Carrie chuffed. "Don't give me that crap, Alex. Of course you'll see it. No one sees it until you do." She grinned, then let go of her grip of Alex's shirt. "We've seen his shit before. Do what you were born to do. Just know I'll be protecting you."

"Thanks," she told Carrie.

Carrie smoothed out a wrinkle on Alex's shirt. "Kick some ass, Alex."

Colette made a point of pretending to be looking at her nails when Alex approached. They took each other's hands.

Colette referenced her hands, "I tore off a couple of fake nails attacking those Book-Butler-men. It looks so tacky but I don't want to give up my talons just yet."

Carrie had jumbled Alex's head a little and she felt lost for words.

Colette filled in the silence, "It's funny, Alex. I joined this crazy group of women because I was trying to blunt the loss of my husband. They gave me purpose and helped me believe in something more important than myself. When I was at the Farm, it tore my heart out that there were these wonders I couldn't share with Marcus." She took a sniffling breath. "He's out here somewhere, isn't he? In this Between. I know it, because he was looking out for me the whole time I thought I was alone at the Farm." She laughed tearfully. "I joined you to get away from his memory, and because of you it's stronger than ever. I know I'm going to see him again, Alex, and I know he's with me now. No matter what happens in there, I am ready to face it. I will be strong like Betty was. Like you are, because I know I can be."

Alex pulled her close. "I wish we had more time. We could go and find him."

"Knowing he's so close is more than I can ask for." Colette made a face that suggested she knew what she was saying might not be realistic, "Maybe when this is over, we will. I'd love for you to meet him, and for him to meet you."

"That'd be very special."

Alex asked Lydia, "How are you holding up?" Lydia had been at the Farm over a week. Alex regretted not trying harder to rescue her when they saved Colette.

Lydia held out her hand and wabbled it side to side. "So-so," she said. "It's like waking up from the most amazing dream. I'm constantly disappointed it's gone." She referred to the others, "Some of them were there so long. I can't imagine what they're going through. I don't know how they're surviving. I wonder how long I'd need to be there before I'd beg Jeremiah to put me back."

The insight twisted Alex's insides. Might they double-cross her? It was an unnerving possibility. It reminded her of Abby's withdrawal. "I hope it gets easier for you, Lydia."

Lydia nodded. "I'm sure it will."

Alex had avoided Eric thus far. She was making her way to Rose and decided she shouldn't pass him. She stepped up to him. He was silent, his eyes avoiding hers. "Things haven't been great between us," she told him. "But you're here now."

Eric finally looked at her. "I didn't want any of this to be this way. Had your father not done what he had done, none of this would have happened."

Alex grinned. "You're wrong, Eric. All of it would have happened. But none of us would be here to stop it."

"It shouldn't be our responsibility. We didn't give Jeremiah his power."

"If it's not our responsibility, then whose is it?"

Eric couldn't answer. With a sigh, he said, "I told you I'd step up when it mattered. I will prove myself to you today."

"Thank you for that, Eric. I expect nothing less from you."

Rose was giggling with Caleb, they were sharing anecdotes and acting like children. The boy was enamored of Rose; Alex saw it when they met at the Library; he couldn't keep his eyes from her. In some ways, the attention made Alex jealous. She wished she had someone to flirt with her like that. She imagined she saw Carrie, and—the way Carrie returned her glance—realized she did. She just didn't have time for it.

"Hey, look who it is," Rose said, her tone cocky and condescending. She looked right at Caleb for his reaction. When he didn't seem to approve of her tone, she returned to Alex, "How are your eyes?" She touched Alex's arm. "These scars look like they hurt like hell. You've been through the ringer today."

"I've been better," Alex replied. "I can sort of see as long as I concentrate. I think it's that imagined magic I told everyone about."

Caleb leaned closer, his voice hushed, "I read about things like that, especially in some of the ancient scrolls. Fascinating. We've been taught women had emotional magic and that made it dangerous, and now you're proving that emotional magic isn't the real magic."

Alex asked, "How do you suppose?"

"Because emotional magic only works with what you're feeling. Imagined magic…, well, I suppose it can do anything you want it to do." He stopped citing examples when Rose elbowed his ribs playfully.

Alex thanked Caleb for his insight and turned to Rose, who had been staring at Caleb as though reading the words as they left his lips. "You've always been my best friend," she told Rose. "The past few weeks have put a strain between us. I want you to know I still love you more than I could love any sister."

Rose looked away, "I'm sorry about Sara. I really though—"

Alex interrupted her with a hug. "I know. You were trying to protect me. When we go in there, I'm counting on you more than anyone else to be the strongest, most badass witch. I'm counting on you to protect me."

Rose cocked an eyebrow, "Guns blazing, right?"

Alex gestured in the direction of the sounds of growing impatience, "Guns blazing. Especially once every one of them has a Book."

Rose nodded, "I'll try to wait. Then what?"

Alex couldn't help but grin, "Then, Rose, do try and keep up."

"Challenge accepted," Rose grinned.

"I understand what you've been trying to tell me, Rose."

Rose put her hands on her hips. "And what's that?"

"That I should be the witch I was always destined to be. No more fear. No more trying. I will go in there and I will destroy Jeremiah."

Rose grinned. "Your problem is that you care too much. Don't worry about us. I can take care of myself. I'm not your responsibility anymore."

Alex wanted to contradict Rose, but Rose's waggling finger forbade it. Instead, Alex hugged her cousin. "I love you, Rose."

"Me too," Rose said. She put her arm around Caleb, who blushed when Alex smiled approvingly.

"That's everybody," Abby told her.

Alex turned to her Familiar, "Almost."

Abby shook her head, "I already know how you feel about me." She touched her chest, "I feel your love all the time."

Alex embraced her, "I don't know what I would do without you, Abby."

Abby laughed, tears falling, "All I know is it would suck." They both laughed. "I've got your back in there, Alex. I know I can't protect you if I get reckless. I'll do what you've asked, but first I'll do anything to keep it from coming to that."

"Everyone's telling me they've got my back. It's nice. I worry about you all, though."

"We've met Jeremiah before. We will see you through to the other end. You and us.

Alex put her arm around Abby. "If we get out of here, Abby, let's do something. Something crazy and fun. Fun for both of us."

Abby grinned. "I like this plan, Alex."

Chapter One Hundred and Sixty-Nine

lex looked back at her Coven one final time, imagining them all. *Can I do this? Can I keep going if they start dying?* She heard what they promised her: words of optimism and bravissimo. Alex understood that bravery wasn't running towards danger—that was stupidity. Bravery was unintentionally encountering danger and still accomplishing what needed to be done.

She hoped to remember them like this. *I have no idea what happens next.* She didn't want to speculate.

As they departed the ancient spiral tower, distance improved the view. Time had eroded its aged stones, softening their edges, widening and deepening the gaps between them. It seemed to serve no purpose except to jut from the landscape like a knife in a wound or a giant screw. Leaving the cold shadow, the warmth was welcoming—to those who didn't know what their destination held.

"What do you suppose?" Carrie asked Alex, pointing back to the tower. Hers was not the only voice to inquire. Countless others in their army made suppositions about its purpose.

Alex offered an abbreviated answer, explaining what she'd discovered in the tower: another prison.

They marched over the undulating hills of grasses and wildflowers. It was a trudging hike, mostly uphill, the weight of their destination bore on their shoulders until they ached.

Reaching the tunnel, Alex stopped at the entrance. She'd been this way last with Matthew. Disturbed to find him in her thoughts, she couldn't help but wonder why. He murdered her parents, he murdered Sara, he tortured her, all in the name of defeating Jeremiah. Her hands weren't so unsoiled that she could judge him. How many had *she* killed? How many would die in her name for the same cause? She recalled him burning her at Picnic Rock, to force her magic awake, and wondered: Had the tables been turned, would she have done the same? It was a convenient lie to say no, but behind her stood an army of rescued strangers. How many was she about to martyr for her cause? How many had to die before the weight of loss was too great? *As many as it takes.* She looked at these women, at her imagined version of them. *I wish I could really see their faces. I should know each of them.* It seemed a responsibility she should shoulder: to know her pawns before sacrificing them.

Once the cavernous Rubicon was crossed, she was as complicit as Jeremiah in the ensuing suffering through her choice to cross it. Would she have it any other way? Could she? She had an army now. She was no longer sending just her closest friends into the mouth of danger. If their action benefitted all women, was it not appropriate? These women were abused, their lives stolen for a false promise, and whether they understood the true breadth and scope of what was to come, they willingly went to face it. *I just think it's all about me. Because I'm the one with magic. I'm the one Jeremiah wants to destroy. But it's not. It's about magic. About who should have it. It shouldn't be him. It shouldn't be me. It belongs to everyone.*

It felt selfish to think of herself when so many others were about to lose their lives, but Alex couldn't tell if she dreaded taking that first step or desiring it. She carried the immense, crushing weight of what was to come. She had just left this place not three days ago. Three days hadn't dulled her pain. It hadn't taken fear from her bones. And yet, knowing this was the final time she was entering the Library made that weight lighter. One way or the other, this was her end. Enduring pain was a negotiation between discomfort and its succession. Any agony was endurable given a short enough duration. The end of her story had finally come, and it was because of that knowledge that Alex eagerly moved onward.

Without looking back, Alex urged everyone to follow. She entered the cave, her coin glowing brightly, a beacon for Jeremiah to know she was near.

"Abby," she called for her Familiar. "If I can't see in the Library, please stay at my side."

Abby was there. "I got you," she said, taking Alex by the wrist as they disappeared into the tunnel that burrowed beneath the hillside and led to the Library.

Emerging into the vast space, Alex expected resistance, but encountered none.

What's his game? Where is he? That Jeremiah wasn't there to greet them was not surprising. That no one was there was a portent of some greater doom.

As though waking and rubbing the sleep from her eyes, her recollection of the handrails and the ramp and the battered bookcases and the fire-stained walls was sufficient to slowly resolve them to her mind. She looked about like a person who misplaced their glasses, struggling to decipher what her eyes perceived until her imagined vision clarified, and she saw.

The Library was abandoned. She brought her women in, urged them past the charred and collapsed bookcases until they came upon a section that was only heat scorched.

No matter where she looked, no matter how far the aisles continued, they were alone. It seemed a great moment of chance, as though they stumbled into the Library moments after it closed. It also felt perilous. Dangerous. Was this not evidence of a trap? Some grand warning that in no time all life within the thick stone walls would be extinguished. Although Alex walked with extreme caution, the possibility gnawed at her. With her first step she had gone too far to turn back. She would not return again.

Pausing beside the end of one bookcase, the wood dried and cracked by heat, her Book Club went to work. They'd done this before, when they claimed their own Books. Now they formed fire-brigade lines and emptied the shelves, passing handfuls at a time, giving out Books.

"Open it; read," they repeated like a mantra. She imagined the wonder crossing their faces upon seeing the illuminations, the confusion over the bizarre text. She imagined them swooning as they fell into the words and discovered the hidden deeper truths. Those who recovered joined the bucket brigade, emptying shelf after shelf until the row was bare and then emptying the next. Wave after wave, the former prisoners claimed their Books, collapsed to the floor, and then stood as witches.

Each sound, each time a removed Book had kept order on the shelf and the remaining Books collapsed like dominoes, Alex's hackles rose. *Something's not right. It's like he wants us to do this.*

"That's everyone, I think," Abby said before calling out to the group, "If you haven't got a Book, raise your hand!"

It was difficult to tell if Alex imagined vision as others saw it or imagined it magically into reality. Was her sight trustworthy or a trick? All she knew was she hadn't knocked into anything. At least, not yet.

Why isn't he here? What's his plan? She feared that with each stride she'd stepped further into his snare. At what point would she find herself too deep to escape?

Now it was Alex's turn. Her hands on Abby's shoulders, she whispered. "I am so tired of this."

Abby told her, "Then make it count, Alex." She reached for a solitary Book askew on an otherwise empty shelf and handed to Alex.

Alex took the Book. She didn't want to open it. She knew what it contained. Just the thought fatigued her. She looked out over these women, hundreds of women who had escaped the fate that befell the woman whose Book she held. This was for them: Her promise that no one else would ever share that fate. Beyond them, were hundreds of other women, their fragile, sparkling threads snaking for an eternity across the Between, bridging the scar into the Library. This was for them, too. And for all those women lucky enough to never know a place like this existed.

She wasn't sure what the Book looked like. She didn't want to imagine it. The leather cover was textured in a fine, intricate design. The spine creaked open, the separating pages gasping at their first breath of air, perhaps in centuries.

Alex imagined the page, the symbols and shapes dissolving into existence. Her whispers roared as she felt her reality slip, but instead of falling, the Book exploded around her. Twists and turns of ink snaked about her and wrapped her with its embellishments. Colorful strokes danced before her eyes as she swam amidst the swirls and illuminations.

Within each shape—each *letter*—was another Book. Swirls of ink danced around her. Like gashes in reality, contained within their wounds was whole realities unto themselves. They wrapped around her, descending with her, carrying her on a wave through their new truth. Like passing through the slit in a curtain, she passed into new realms, the Book revealing itself to her yet again, a special revelation of extraordinary beauty.

Her only reluctance was the expectation of pain, the anticipation that at any moment the shapes around her would transfuse to her the memories of cuts and burns and broken bones, but as she traveled deeper, passing through each layer of the Book, the only sensation that grew near was the warmth of whomever had for so long slumbered, lost at the very bottom of this tumble.

Like Alice through the looking-glass, falling into a new, undiscovered country, Alex became aware as the slumbering giantess flinched awake.

Passing through the final swirl of ink, the world resolved around a woman, dressed not in a stitch. This woman reached for Alex's embrace. She took the woman in her arms and drew her close, feeling the warmth of her soft flesh pressing against her. *You found me*, the woman said, her lips unmoving, her voice spoken directly to Alex's mind.

Alex tightened her embrace to offer comfort and shuddered as her flesh and the woman's slipped together. As though passing through yet another sliver of ink, this woman's body joined her own.

Alex found herself in the Library, Abby at her side, her hands unexpectedly empty.

Abby leaned to her, concerned hands touching Alex's shoulder, "It didn't work?"

Alex showed Abby her empty hands; there were perhaps motes of dust left behind. The sensation Alex experienced was peaceful and joyous. She felt warmth and love and salvation. The lack of pain from not bursting into flames, however, was the trade-off for expediency. How could she empty the remaining shelves one Book at a time? She expressed her concern to Abby. "Everything's different when I imagine it. I don't know how else to make it work."

"Why can't you just do that with every Book at once, like you do when you turn to flame?"

With a breath taken to contradict, Alex realized Abby was right. Her imagined world was different than the one she saw in. If she could imagine taking one Book, why not all of them….

The women around her gushed, showing off their Books; her Book Club culturing their impatience. Her Coven's concern for the abandonment of the Library was equal to Alex's.

Alex imagined every Book in the Library was within view. Each one of them opened, revealing their secrets to her. Tumbling into the symbols, disappearing into thousands of Books at once, Alex felt as if lost in a maze of mirrors. At every turn, she found herself surrounded by symbols and shapes, as though they floated in the air before her. At every step, she passed through layer upon layer. The dizzying rate with which she ventured deeper into meaning made her previous exploration stilted by comparison. Expecting to find the woman at the end, what she found was herself—alone—surrounded by thousands of symbols, as though she'd arrived at the center of every Book to find herself.

"Whoa, where'd they all go?" Abby shrieked. She pointed around the Library. Unless a member of her army held it, all the Books had vanished.

Consumption of the Books was no longer the torturous experience it had just been. She looked about to confirm Abby's outburst, finding that she had in fact removed the last unclaimed Book from the Library.

Her head was abuzz. Multitudinous new voices had joined the countless others.

Abby cheered, "That was amazing! They all vanished." The others in her Book Club came forward. Rose and Nancy and Colette and Carrie patted her arms, her back, congratulating her. The only remaining Books in the Library were theirs.

Caleb hadn't left Rose's side since their reunion. "I've never seen it empty before." He cast a glance around. Each sound they made danced with its echo, the emptiness mocking their every noise.

Marta asked, "Waiting seems stupid, don't you think? You have all the Books. What more do we need?"

Carrie nodded towards the army of Book-bearing women. "They can't decide if they want to be scared or bored." She seemed to regard the air and said, "If we go home now, we'll never have an army like this again. It's an opportunity that won't knock twice."

June agreed, "Maybe that's why he's hiding. He saw our numbers and he's afraid."

"Don't misjudge him," Alex warned.

"I said maybe," June admitted. "Why else isn't he here?"

Alex didn't like the emptiness one bit. She'd done what she came to do; the Books were all hers. Only a small number still existed in the wild, most carried by whatever men were loyal to Jeremiah. Some hidden in musty basements for decades, like Steven's. Was this enough? Had she taken enough of Jeremiah's strength? Would she have had an answer if she'd eaten Matthew's coin?

She came with the intention of facing Jeremiah a final time. Not to be disappointed by this outcome, Alex wondered if it would be worse to return home and worry—for however long he allowed her to—when he would come for her, for each of them.

Yet, something gnawed at Alex. She looked to George, imagining his face. He'd warned her in this very place: Women and Books were dangerous. She trusted her Book Club because they understood the burden a Book represented. What responsibility did the others know of magic? She had armed them out of necessity. If she let these women go, how many would become like Rose, their anger driving them to read? Was it fair that so few were the only possessors of what little magic remained? This was not returning magic to the world, this was repeating what Jeremiah had done.

"Maybe we should start sending people home," Alex started to say when she heard the first screams.

Chapter One Hundred and Seventy

lex spun pointlessly around, imagination failing to capture the frantic rush as hundreds of women surged past, bumping and knocking her about. She feared being trampled until Abby wrested her ribcage and lurched her from the stampede.

Carrie waved Rose and Colette forward, shouting, "We're not alone anymore!"

The golems and a few men were still popping into existence, their fingertips alight with sparks, showering the fleeing women as they chanted their spells from their flesh and Books. *Why are they running? Don't they understand they have Books, too?* Abandoned Books littered the floor, dropped in panic.

Alex's mind remained focused on comprehending the disorder and misdirection as her enemy appeared everywhere she looked.

Sparks flew at her. She stood in the center of the aisle, unmoved. In her mind, she imagined lightning flowing from her fingers: giant, thick bolts that hummed and crackled. Energy shot through her body, a mix of her anger and imagination. Her body vibrated as though she electrocuted herself. Her eyes, through her blindness, registered the eruption as though she looked directly at the sun.

With a thunderclap, the show was done. Ozone charged the swirling air. To her right, Carrie pumped her fist. She imagined Rose nodding at her, impressed at the strike, but that wasn't the expression Rose gave her. Although she'd plowed a path through them, to either side of the electrical carnage a dozen Books grouped into formation. Ahead in the aisle, three dozen men with Books in hand wondered what caused the destruction before them. Every few seconds more appeared behind them.

"There are so many it's like you didn't do anything," Rose complained. She read from her Book, its askew cover and pages thick and glossy with tape.

Carrie fired as well, her magic coming from within. Colette and Nancy, Charissa, Rachel, and June all made their magic without Books, their spells growing in confidence as they experimented with their emotions. Lydia, George, Banhi and Khowla, Pat, Caleb, Eric, Steven, and Jacque all used Books. They randomly fired in whatever direction caught their attention. Their sparks struck golems and men; counter sparks struck them. The next blast from Alex's fingers knocked a group of golems asunder like bowling pins just as they'd connected.

"Better," Rose shouted at her, the sparks from her blackening fingertips looked molten and fiery and red. A bolt hit Rose's shoulder, knocking her like a punch. Wincing, she fired back in rage, her raw spark ripping straight through her attacker, debilitating even the man behind him. Several others nearby witnessed what she had done. While some lost their resolve, for others it was doubled.

Marta exploded into a steam of darkness, swallowing a group of men and golems. As she returned from her cloud to human form, bodies tumbled out of her, broken and mutilated. The wounds looked like they'd been caused by razor claws and devouring teeth. Alex wondered what monsters her brother created in his universe for this purpose. It chilled her that he had to learn so quickly about death. Marta grinned pridefully at her.

A new rise of screams came from behind them. Other men and golem still popping into the Library, blocked the retreat of her fearful army. Instead of panic, this time the men were met with magic as the women—having witnessed magic—read from their Books. Sparks gave confidence to their guttural voices as more and more of them joined in.

Alex worked ferociously to envision the rapidly changing, chaotic battle raging all around her. People were moving fast, sparks and bolts of lightning sizzled through the air as people on both sides fired and dove for cover. Her tightly packed army began to disperse, spreading out as they fired back.

A few golems exploded. Dozens of women were thrown into the air by the blast-wave, which obliterated countless others, leaving a swarth of wounded to pave the gap.

More golems arrived—until they significantly outnumbered the men—as though strategically placed to encircle their army. Some joined together for explosive attacks. Others snatched threads and broke them.

Carrie disappeared after saying, "I've got to help them." She then appeared two dozen feet away, where she scooped several discarded Books from the floor. She disappeared, reappearing in the center of the army, handing those Books out to women who'd lost theirs.

Rose hadn't left Alex's side. Alex told her, "Help them, Rose." She called out as sparks showered them, "Help the others, all of you."

Alex hadn't stopped. Her imagined magic didn't need her to prime her emotions, although she engorged on the carnage. Lightning tore through phalanxes of golems. Fireballs splashed across groups of men, scattering those who survived. Bookcases and debris spun from the floor, caught up in howling wind, machine-gunning her enemies with debris.

From close by, Abby stated, "I'm staying by you no matter what." Followed by, "Right?"

Alex nodded as wind whipped her hair over her head and her fingertips tingled, her imagined lightning indiscriminate and lethal.

Reason haunted the men, driving them to seek safety from the unnerving ferocity of the battle. *They probably don't know who they were fighting or why.* Others, like Johnny, like some from New York and Paris, were true believers. Proving their loyalty through death. They would never be convinced they followed a falsehood. Not even if Jeremiah personally confessed. The reasons that brought most of them here were like towering sandcastles. They seemed solid until the turning tide collapsed their wills. Witnessing death and destruction was enough for many men to throw down their Books or vanish: a glorious death in battle was still death.

Alex imagined ferocious, angry faces. Their mouths moving as their fingers, sticky with sweat, stained the pages containing the spell they read. But also, uncertainty and fear. The nervous choice of casting a spell versus fleeing. More and more, the men used their Books to escape.

Alex reasoned destroying golems was more effective. They would never run, never faulter. By rendering them to wood pulp, she might conjure sufficient fear in the men; doubling the efficacy of her magic.

A roiling ball of hot plasma fell from her fingers and swallowed a dozen golems, leaving the floor glowing red, the granite melted. The floor heaved up, slabs of stone cracking like thunder, swallowing dozens more before the immense plates thudded down atop them.

A blast upended and shattered a bookcase beside her, showering her with splinters. Before she could react, Rachel collided with her, the shockwave of another explosion throwing them to the ground. She rolled Rachel toward her but her friend had taken the brunt of the explosion protecting her. Shrapnel had torn through Rachel, leaving half her body unrecognizable.

Alex fired at the first group of men and golems she saw. She didn't care if they weren't responsible for Rachel's death. Her lightning whipped with her indignation and their convulsing bodies danced on tiptoes, almost leaping into the air like ballerinas before collapsing. Some men noticed they only fired sparks; her lightning tipping the scales of their fear.

"I don't know what you can see, but it's not good," Abby spoke in rapid staccato. "Women are dying everywhere."

Alex was loathe to admit that had been her plan. Her Coven was her real army. These women were distractions to disperse the enemy fire. It wasn't that their deaths didn't pain her, but for all intents and purposes, the prisoners from the Farm had died long ago. She hoped that their numbers made up for inexperience, but these pawns were most useful when they obscured the advance of her more powerful pieces.

Imagining her next strikes, Alex thrust bursts of energy from her hands. They shattered bookcases and cracked the floor as they shot past, the air moaning like an elderly man struggling from his seat. It burst apart a group of golems, showering all those nearby with both energetic and golem shrapnel. She cleared swaths of floor with each attack, drawing fire to herself, her Coven doing what they could to protect the women.

Terror moved the women like a murmuration of starlings. Their collective mass prevented effective counterattacks, their panic protecting the men and golems who tormented and killed them.

Alex passed Banhi and Khowla, both tucked beside a collapsed bookcase. Like cowboys behind a toppled stagecoach, firing and crouching, the wood framing taking the returning fire.

"Go, Alex," Banhi cheered as she passed them, Khowla howled her agreement, raising a thumb.

Her lightning shot through the group of men pinning Banhi and Khowla down.

Ahead, Steven spun in the air, a strike to his head burning his hair to the scalp. Pat huddled over him, protecting him with her body. She was struck twice, while Charissa relentlessly fired her glowing bolts, driving their attackers back.

Alex eased Pat to safety between two immense collapsed bookcases. With a gesture, Abby was there, helping Charissa drag Steven. They were each struck; Charissa cried out, dropped her father and collapsed. Abby fell to her knee when struck, but with a grunt, managed to pull both Steven and Charissa behind debris for Pat to tend to.

Rose was maniacal, cackling joyfully as she fired, her sparks red and flaming, as broken and twisted as her Book. They struck their targets like daggers, spinning men about and dislodging their Books from their hands. Some panicked and ran, leaving their only chance of escape lying sprawled where they dropped it. Others limped and groaned, took up their Books and fired again as even more men appeared around them. Caleb followed her, reading spells, using his knowledge to alter their function. "Look, look," he cried out when he'd made the floor so slippery three men spun and danced as they kicked and climbed over one another trying to gain a footing. Once they were down, Rose took advantage and struck them unconscious.

Abby pointed to June and Lydia. They were among a group of twenty or so women; surrounded and outnumbered. They fired sparks in every direction. Three dozen golems and half a dozen men fired into their circle from all sides. June and Lydia positioned themselves to the front of the group. They fired relentlessly at their attackers. Alex leapt into the air, just as several of the golems joined together. She flew at them, imagined her hands fired bursts of energy, blowing one group of golems apart like an anthill struck with a garden hose. As she fired concussive blasts at the next group, one of the golem exploded. His spell cut a straight line through the circle of women, throwing many of them down, including her friends.

Alex, screaming, crashed to the ground. They were being slaughtered. She screamed and her imagined magic pulled the remaining Books and men into the air and smashed them into the ground at some distant end of the Library. She scrambled to where she'd last seen Lydia and June. Lydia's polka-dotted outfit was shredded and bloody; the only evidence remaining. June looked at Alex, her mouth and teeth bright with blood. As Alex tried to embrace her, June snatched her wrist. She choked out the words, "Finish this first."

Alex couldn't take her eyes from June as she left her until it was clear June needed her to look away. Alex screamed with rage. *Where is Jeremiah? He's letting them do all the work. Could he know my plan? Maybe he knows I'm not willing to die while these women are in danger.*

Ahead, Nancy, her left leg burned nearly to the bone, was trying to stop another woman from bleeding. A third and a fourth and fifth lay lifeless nearby. Nancy said to Alex, "They're being slaughtered."

"You're hurt."

Nancy regarded the charred mess above her knee. "I don't feel a thing."

Alex wanted to heal Nancy. As though reading her mind, Nancy said, "You've got more important things to do."

Alex felt the will to fight leaving her, the electricity of her pain no match for the whizzing bolts that sizzled all around like tracer fire in war movies. The people she cared for most were being hurt and killed. They could tell her a hundred times that they did so willingly for her, that they weren't her responsibility, but she'd never accept that. It was difficult enough watching total strangers die, but her closest friends were an exquisite agony.

"We've got to get everyone out of here," she told whoever would listen. "Get everyone somewhere safe. Take them to Heather's if you can."

The remaining women from the market, still in possession of their threads, were in retreat. Alex was glad to have them gone to safety.

Most of the women from the Farm fled one danger to encounter another. Some used their Books, returning fire, but panic was infectious and the women ran like wild-eyed cattle to slaughter. Others held their Books defensively, shielding against the spells that tore through their Books and their bodies.

Alex reached them, exchanging spells with two groups of golems. Their devastating attacks bisected the group, cutting through the middle and slaying those unfortunate women.

Alex knew she had to save these women. Send them to the fallow farm field; it was the only place large and clear enough that she didn't risk them materializing on a busy roadway or inside a wall. As she built her emotions and imagined the workings of the magic, the golems reconnected. Alex instead cast it on them. She imagined their surprise, materializing high in the air above the valley overlooked by Picnic Rock.

She was struck and knocked into a toppled bookcase. Her ears rang as sparks sizzled past, concussing around her. Her head screamed. Each wound ached, grievous trauma she healed and suffered anew. She cast her spell again, this time—hopefully—sending women to the fallow field. Then again and again, disappearing small groups, one after another. She imagined where they appeared to ensure their safety and could only hope they were safer than here.

With a rolling crack, like the groaning complaint of thunder, a larger group of women disappeared. Alex hadn't done that. The instant they vanished peeled a scab in her brain: they were not sent to safety.

Cries rose as thunder shook the floor like a slowly-rolled boulder, vanishing half the women around her. Sparks came from every direction. Deadly strikes from connected golems. Even from the few men who remained—the truest of true believers. Alex couldn't tell the direction anything was coming from anymore, she stood in a squall of piercing spells blurring the air and exploding around her. It was like standing in a swarm of stinging bees. Her heart pounded; she couldn't catch her breath. It was near impossible to choke down her fear and allow her emotions free reign. She wasn't sure it was best for her to think about what she was doing as she sent a group of men to appear in the clouds over the valley or blew apart a group of golems before they could slaughter more innocents.

What had been an army, a group too large for a casual count, diminished to scattered handfuls. Spread out across the Library, they drew together. Their diminished numbers made it feel like they were preparing for their last stand. The other side also suffered catastrophic casualties. Everywhere she looked, she observed regrettable destruction of life. *How many? As many as it takes.* The realism of these numbers made Alex wonder if she'd even know when she'd gone too far.

She fired spell after spell, lightning, concussive energy, fireballs, blasting the enemy. It never seemed enough to diminish their numbers.

The remains of her Book Club coalesced around her like armor made of flesh and friendship.

A blast hit one group of women, shattering them into unrecognizable forms. A second struck her Book Club. Colette cried out as the spell tore her body apart. She lay on the ground, her last words begging they not stop to help her.

"Who's doing that?" Alex cast her spell again. No matter how many golems she obliterated, there always seemed to be more.

Rose raised her finger. Alex thought she was pointing out her father. Eric raced towards them, Book in hand, casting his spells over his shoulder. He was struck with such force all that remained was crimson aerosol dissipating in the air.

Rose let out a cry of surprise that withered into a sob. Alex's heart shattered; her people were being snatched away. She saw no coins or ghosts left behind, no fodder for Charon to collect. *What's happening to them? Where are they going?* Charon coming was part of her plan: the child came for Matthew. *What's different? Do battlefields have different rules for the dead?* Would Charon claiming a wounded soldiers' coin shift the balance of war? Especially if anyone tried to stop the child. She tried not to let the twists of logic distract her from her defense. Her fear that her plan wouldn't work left her wondering what she had done. She never paused her attack. Another strike, more powerful than the last, hit Jacque and Nancy, tearing them apart. Alex could barely see through her tears of rage.

Alex didn't need her imagined sight to know *he* had arrived.

As soon as her mind accepted his presence, she saw him: flanked by a dozen golem and two men.

She fired at him, a strike of such intensity she hadn't ever imagined its equal before. It tore at her skin as it roared from inside her, moving with such mass and force that it threatened to suck those around her into its wake. It exploded through the remains of the Library, drawing shattered bookcases and debris up into its wake, smashing into Jeremiah and his entourage with enough force it seemed to punch a hole clear through the distant Library wall.

The sparks flying around them stopped.

A handful of survivors from the Farm coalesced around Alex and her Coven. Fewer than three dozen remained. Bruised, burned, bloody, they limped beside her, watching the remaining golems running to aid their master.

There wasn't silence, but the incessant patter of decay and collapse. Taking the moment to breathe, the realities of the horrors they witnessed still not sinking in. They huddled with frightened anticipation that this fight was nowhere close to over.

Chapter One Hundred and Seventy-One

From the pile of collapsed debris at the terminus of Alex's strike, Jeremiah stood, a body in his arms. The men and golems that had surrounded him were gone; he approached alone.

"He's carrying a body," Abby warned in case she couldn't see. "It looks like a woman…." Abby's voice trailed off, her squinting eyes looking away as though she knew something horrible and couldn't share it.

Alex could not recognize the battered form in his arms. This wasn't a woman who died in battle. This woman was tortured to death. She checked those near her. *Who is missing?*

Emerging from more distant aisles, dozens of golems crept out, many nursing grievous wounds that would have felled ordinary men. Stillness surrounded her—a calm she didn't trust to be more than a realignment of forces.

Alex whispered to Abby. Abby immediately spread Alex's message to the others. As much as they intended to protect her to their end, she ordered them to spread apart, to give him multiple targets, rather than a singular mass to strike. She told them to escape once they could; having them end her life—even to also defeat Jeremiah—now felt selfish. Once they were safely gone, she would no longer worry about them. Alex would deal with the consequences herself.

Jeremiah came closer.

Alex tried to picture the old man or the vain blond. However she tried, her mind couldn't compose an image.

Her Book Club spread apart. They found chunks of bookcase to tuck behind. Every one of them kept a line of sight opened to Alex, but no one left, even as she hissed her begging supplication.

Jeremiah stopped. His features resolved in Alex's vision: a forever shifting expression of a man, the whites of his eyes the only constant as the colors and features blurred endlessly. Was this all the men he'd been? The effect disturbed Alex's eyes, his features shifting so rapidly there was a chance he wasn't even there.

Carrie popped into existence beside Alex. "I know what you said," she told Alex. "But my place is beside you."

Jeremiah dumped the body to the ground.

Rose screamed.

It was Heather.

Rose started to taunt, "Stupid asshole, that wasn't my mother," her words losing their strength, anger shifting to agony, "you killed… my mother. Why'd you have to kill her, again?" Rose's fists clenched as tears spilled down her eyes. "What did she do to deserve that?"

Jeremiah pushed at the battered body with his foot. Heather's body was painted by the brutality which ended her life. Also by how furiously she fought. How long she endured.

"Because I thought she was you," Jeremiah answered the unasked question. "You were hidden away. I sensed bursts of powerful magic. I went to destroy you." He sneered. "She wasn't surprised to see me. But I was. Before I ended her suffering, she told me why," he explained plainly. "She vainly sacrificed herself to give you more time."

Alex recalled Heather's exhaustion back at the house. Had that been a deception? It explained where Jeremiah had been all this time, taking his frustration out on her aunt. In that instant, her mind swirled with a thousand recollections and memories. She knew Heather perhaps better than she knew herself, and the woman still surprised her. Looking at her body, however, felt more like looking at her own corpse. The sight broke something inside of her.

Marta stepped out from behind a bookcase, mere feet from Jeremiah. He startled at her exploding into roiling darkness. He backed away from her approaching cloud, fear clearly painting across all his faces. He dared to take his eyes away from Oblivion to look at Alex as if to ask what she had done when the darkness lurched forward, swallowing him.

Marta reformed, the smoke snapping back to flesh, two Book bodies slipping out in the instant.

Silence descended on the Library. The remaining men, the remaining golems all turned to Marta. Lightning crackled from Alex's fingertips as she warned them away.

"It's over, Alex," Marta said softly. "It's finally over." She held out her arms as she marched towards Alex, dropping to a knee like she'd mis-stepped. Her eyes widened in horror as her hand muffled a silent scream. "No," she chanted. Tears tumbled down her face as she screamed, "Alex, no!" She exploded to Oblivion; the dark cloud expanding until it was merely mist, and then it was gone.

Standing in her place, Jeremiah questioned Alex, "You had an entire universe at your disposal and you squandered it?"

Rose cried out. She showered him with her red, fiery sparks. They buzzed and sizzled like overburdened circuit breakers, tumbling through the air.

Immediately, the golems returned fire, drawing together. Rose saw this too, and with one bright red, jagged blast, hit Jeremiah like a truck, throwing him into the air to crumple lifelessly to the floor.

Everywhere, the remaining women cast their spells, either emotionally or reading from their Books. Sparks zipped in every direction, sizzling overhead and percussing all around. As Alex fired at Jeremiah, Carrie stood at her back, firing into the remains of the aisles, protecting Alex from the golem's attacks. The first strike dropped Carrie to her knees. She gasped for air and fought back to her feet. "Be right back." She vanished, the air swirling smoke and dust into the vacuum she left behind.

Down an aisle, Carrie appeared behind the golems, striking them from close range, dropping one and briefly incapacitating another, disappearing again as they turned around, reappearing back behind Alex.

Abby twisted to the ground, quickly rising to her feet. Jeremiah's strike hit her hard. The second time it felled her; she crawled away, grateful for the safety of rubble to hide behind.

Disappearing, Carrie appeared behind a second group of golems, taking out three of the five this time, but was struck twice more before she reappeared beside Alex. Panting, her chest dark and wet with burn, her hands trembling as she leaned against Alex, still shooting her sparks, slowly slipping to the floor as her rubbery legs refused to hold her up.

Alex couldn't help but grab her, hoping she could infuse her with enough strength, enough healing that Carrie might disappear from the Library altogether. *Why won't they go?*

Rose fired again at Jeremiah. Although her spells were read from her Book, her growing rage made her flaming red sparks look like spurts of molten steel. She struck Jeremiah with deadly aim. Alex was certain she saw him explode, yet after the frenzy of fiery dust settled enough, he remained. His ever-changing visage had stumbled back; he grunted and cursed: Rose wounded him.

Alex released Carrie. She fired at Jeremiah. Carrie stayed at her side. Alex's burst of energy twisted Jeremiah's body and shattered the Library wall into a spider's web of cracked debris.

Rose raced towards Jeremiah; she never stopped reading from her Book, preparing another strike. With the wet sound of an egg crunching to the floor, Rose twisted with agony. She disappeared, flung down the length of an aisle. Alex was only beginning to comprehend what she'd seen when the thud of Rose's impact reverberated back.

Alex cried out for her. Had she just watched her cousin die? She tried to strike, mustering her anger, imagining the energy leaving her fingertips, but she couldn't get her concocted vision of Rose, tossed like a ragdoll, thrown with such force that she instantly vanished. She took a breath, trying to focus, trying to concentrate. She never imagined she'd witness Rose's death.

Chapter One Hundred and Seventy-Two

Alex screamed, "Get out of here!"

Carrie crawled beside Abby. They helped one another to their feet. A few aisles down, Khowla and Banhi, Caleb, Charissa and Pat all exchanged fire with three golems. When the three became two, Banhi collapsed from their spell. Khowla tended to her for the moment it took her to realize she was gone. Pat was struck next. Charissa, Caleb, and Khowla concentrated their magic on the remaining golem. His body convulsed with their electric strikes long after it was obvious he was dead.

George found himself surrounded by three golems who all fired at him. He fired back, concentrating his spells on one of them rather than all three, the other two striking him relentlessly. He fell to his knees even as Charissa and Caleb came to his rescue, incapacitating the remaining two. George thanked them. He headed straight for Alex, to stand at her side when a distant one of a distant group of four, exploded. George was looking at Alex when the light left his eyes. He collapsed with his running momentum; his back burned to char.

Alex never imagined it like this, she never stopped casting spells, but they never seemed enough. Carrie and Abby shot at another golem. Once he was closer, they both leapt on and beat him to death.

Alex asked the women in her head what they were waiting for. She thought of her love, the loss of all those she cared for, the chasm in her chest so great she couldn't hope to see the opposing side. She knew they felt it, too. She knew whatever was left of Heather, whatever was left of Abigail, whatever was left of all the women inside her, they all had to be feeling her grief, her rage. She turned to Jeremiah. A torrent of energy bloomed from her body and like a locomotive, it raced for him. Its force threw her back, the ground nearly knocking consciousness from her.

Carrie and Abby, Khowla, Charissa, and Caleb raced to her side. "The Books are all gone," Abby told her, her face streaked with soot and tears, her body covered with burns and wounds.

"Jeremiah's all who's left, Alex," Carrie choked, her voice barely a rasp. She gestured to the flaming pile where Alex's spell turned even the granite floor to magma.

"Go," she told them. "Save yourselves. You're all I've got left. I can't lose you."

Without question, without confirming with the others, each of them—except Caleb—embraced her.

Alex felt the warmth of their energy, the strength of their love for her, surging into her. Her wounds itched as they scabbed and healed. Her trembling muscles were ready for more.

"Take it," Caleb ordered.

Alex looked at the boy, his hand offering his coin. "I know what it'll do, Alex." He told her. "You need all your strength."

Abby slipped from the embrace and collapsed. She had given Alex the last of her strength.

Charissa and Carrie dropped to Abby's side. Carrie sobbed; Alex feared the worst.

Without thinking, she took Caleb's coin and put it between Abby's lips. "That's for you," Caleb cried, his thread sparking in agitation. But Abby was gone. Alex looked at Carrie and Charissa, embarrassed and shocked she thought to sacrifice one of her Coven for another, even if that other were Abby. *How many will it take?* She returned Caleb's coin. "I'm sorry," she said. "I can't take it for myself. I shouldn't have done that. That was wrong of me."

His sacrifice refused, Caleb joined the embrace.

Alex's heart left utterly empty as her Familiar left her. She understood Abby's withdrawal. She didn't have tears left for Abby, even as her whole body trembled at the loss.

The others were still holding her, healing her. She felt their strength pushing through her body. Too much strength. Alex realized too late what they were doing, giving her whatever remained. "No, stop," she cried out, but no one heeded her.

Exhausted, Caleb fell away from her. Khowla collapsed next. "He's there," she said as she slumped away.

Carrie whispered, "Finish this." She held out her coin. "Let me help you."

Charissa held out her coin, too.

"No," Alex cried. "I can't."

"It's what he would do," Carrie said. "Please."

Alex couldn't move. A part of her knew it might be the only way she'd stand a chance against him. But it was too much. She could barely shake her head. Even her imagined sight was blurry with tears. "He might," Alex sobbed, "but I won't."

Carrie lowered her coin to her chest before sinking to her knees. Charissa, who was leaning against Carrie, collapsed, too. They had sacrificed too much of themselves healing her. Alex wanted to give it back.

Alex cried out. "What is the point? How many is too many?"

Jeremiah marched threateningly towards her but offered no reply.

Alex was sick. In the same moment it looked like they might be close to some bastardized version of victory, it became evident Jeremiah was in no way done. They were all dead. Everyone she cared for. Everyone she loved. *How many will it take? All of them.* This sacrifice was too great. Had she vision, her vengeful tears would have blinded her, but in her imagined visionscape, she now saw perfectly. Her swirling emotions brought pristine clarity. She wanted to vomit fiery nails, to rip out her hair and tear clothes and lay waste to everything with bare hands. Her whispers screamed, masses of energy swirling inside of her. She held it in, feeling the pressure surge, hoping it might grow so tremendous it would explode.

How long do we play at this? Alex heard his voice, clear as a whisper in silence, as though spoken within her own skull.

Alex's rage was equal to her anguish. The bodies around her were those she cared about most. All those who fought for Jeremiah were gone, too, but she doubted that mattered to him.

In the corner of her eye, an insignificant motion caught her attention. Carrie rose to her feet. Charissa followed, then Khowla. With hopeful anticipation, Alex waited for Abby.

Alexandrea, I allowed you to have my Books. What good have they done you?

Carrie gurgled, standing like an exclamation point, her posture jutting straight, her face blistering red, tears running down her face. Her eyes bulged as they rolled in their sockets.

Alex tried to pull her close, but Carrie's posture wouldn't relent.

"What's happening, Carrie? What can I do?" Alex begged her to say anything, to explain the source of her excruciation.

As though witnessing their own futures, Charissa and Khowla watched for but a moment, until their bodies, too, were twisted upright.

Recognizing what he was doing to them, Alex begged Jeremiah to stop.

Carrie made as if to speak. When she opened her mouth, what gushed from her were another kind of words. She dripped with symbols and shapes, little dark squiggles. They poured in intermittent gushes from Carrie's gullet as Jeremiah squeezed them from of her.

"Alex, Alex," Charissa reached out and touched her arm just as her eyes went wide.

Alex tried to imagine a way to make it stop. She knew what this felt like. In her mind, she imagined herself prying giant hands from around their bodies, but nothing she did in her imagination eased their retching as Jeremiah squeezed magic and life from their bodies.

"Stop it, please," Alex screamed and begged, loathe to step away from them. She stepped forward. "I'll do anything you ask, please, anything! Just stop hurting them!"

Alex was desperate. Just as she had hope they weren't dead he was killing them. She begged him again, her cries stifled with sobs, but Jeremiah's shifting face was stony with resolve.

"Everyone before you wanted to claim my Books. No one ever succeeded before."

She nearly offered to give them back in exchange for her friends, but they'd never forgive her.

"Killing them is my mercy for the world you'd have them live in. A world with magic. None of you understand: power never motivated me. Equalizing it, minimizing it was all I have done."

"Please," she whimpered once more. "I'll give it back. We'll all give it back. Please."

"I know you will."

Alex looked at what remained of her Coven; her loved ones. What was the point of begging for mercy when there would never be any? She hated Jeremiah. Not just for his actions, but for how helpless he made her feel. He hadn't yet taken away her magic. He was taunting her. Torturing her by making her endure watching everyone she loved die. Whatever plans she had, whatever way she fantasized this would go, they were gone. She had begged her Coven to ensure they would be merciful. How could she not give them the same?

He was torturing them to death. She had no way of stopping him. But there was one thing she could still do to save them. To keep their magic from returning to him. She feared she loved them too much to do it. As soon as the solution presented itself, Alex knew it was because she loved them so much that she could. They had given her strength because they loved her, and now Jeremiah gave her strength because he couldn't comprehend how deeply she loved them.

She picked a squiggle from the floor and looked into it, into its depths, and imagined her body changing to fire.

She swirled around Carrie and Charissa and Khowla. The symbols they vomited sizzled as they passed their lips. Alex imagined her flames growing hotter, stronger. It was like a spear stabbing her heart as their skin blistered. She lied to herself that she was sparing them even as she sizzled away their hair and blackened their skin. When Jeremiah's grip released them, they each took one final deep gasp of Alex's flames and collapsed.

She wailed as she burned up the last of the magic symbols. Her heart felt like a ball of iron in her chest, solid and heavy.

She reached out her flames and found Abby and Banhi and Nancy and June and Colette and Heather. And all the others. Their bodies whole or otherwise. She gave them the only burial she knew, consuming them.

They were gone, and as her flames dissipated and disappeared, for the first time she ever could recall, Alex was alone.

She faced him; her despair grown beyond measure. In the entirety of the planet, everyone she loved was gone. The emotions she felt for him—resentment, rage, wrath, hatred—coupled and danced inside her with what she felt for those she lost, and she prepared herself for the abominable magic these emotions created. She once anticipated perishing in Jeremiah's grasp, but now knew her end would be when the uncontrollable loss inside of her exploded outwards, raising the Library from its foundation on the Between and blasting it into oblivion.

Her chest tightened, her heart, like a leaden ball, clogged her gullet and pressed against the inside of her ribs; she realized only then it was her turn.

Turned to face Jeremiah, the voices inside her head screaming, the magic rising inside her. Alex groaned as her ribs cracked. Her feet stretched to keep her toes on the floor as he raised her from it. Magic bubbled to the base of her tongue. Her heavy heart pressed back. She felt the ache of her ribcage expanding, pushing against his magical grasp.

A bolt of fiery red lightning exploded with sparks around Jeremiah. Then another. His grip released. Several more in quick succession, and Jeremiah's body smoked.

Rose stumbled into view, her hair matted with blood, her eye swollen shut. She limped, crying out with each step, her leg torn and bloody. She carried her lopsided Book, the cover and half the pages in one hand, the remainder of the pages in another, bones protruding from her forearm. Through her grunts and her cries, the only sound she made were screams, the repetition of her spell, firing bolts at Jeremiah. She howled the words, crying them out, tincturing the spell with her own blood as red breath sprayed into the air.

The strikes gained strength and power. Alex fired too, finally releasing the swell of emotion that threatened to burst her. Their spells struck him with enough force that Alex was certain she briefly saw two or three of him, as though he was struck from himself, each time driven back, each time the look of shock and pain increasing on his face, until he disappeared in an explosion, excavating a crater through the granite floor down to dirt.

Rose collapsed against Alex. Alex held to her, but Rose was at the end of her strength. She cried out when Alex eased her to the ground.

"I can't beat him, Rose," Alex whimpered.

Rose's eyes begged as she slumped to the floor, her gritting teeth stained with blood. She cried out. She looked for Abby or Carrie or anyone. Alex followed her gaze. She knew Rose understood: They were all gone.

"Don't say you can't," Rose spoke with panting, agonal breaths. "Try what you haven't yet."

"I've taken every Book, Rose. I have all the magic and he's still stronger."

Rose raised her hands with grunting effort. "There's still one left," she nearly lost consciousness from the effort.

Alex's imagined sight blurred with tears. "No," she started to say.

Rose cut her off, yelping in pain, blood flowing freely from her fractured forearm. She tried to speak, to tell Alex what to do, but the pain was too great. She collapsed, the Book tumbling to the ground, the pages stained and fingerprinted red. She looked up at Alex. Her voice was barely a whisper, her face so pale she looked ice-blue. "Make it hot. Make it fast."

Even crushing her eyes closed to hold the vision away, her mind forced her to see Rose's broken body. Jeremiah emerged from the wreckage, examining his wounded and scorched flesh. He stepped forward, hollering out as raw meat on his leg dropped him to his knees. He contemplated his wounded body with shock, trying to wipe the injuries away. But he also timidly eyed Rose, perhaps trying to determine what threat she still posed.

"I'm sorry, Rose," Alex whispered.

Rose's dilated pupils made her eyes seem deep and dark. "I love you, sister."

Alex's flame spiraled to the ceiling, growing as tall and as hot as her rage. She wrapped Rose's broken book in her fiery hands and drew it into her. She could hear Rose whimper as the pages blackened and curled, the blood sizzling and congealing in the heat.

Rose screamed as her body erupted in flames, "Don't stop!"

Alex's fiery hands trembled as she tried to burn the Book faster, tried to burn hotter.

Rose's screams of pain sounded not unlike the cries of wounded animals. The pages disintegrated in her heat, their faces scorching brown to black to dust, revealing the next and then the next and then the next. She cried and screamed, burning the Book, burning her cousin, until nothing remained of either.

She turned to Jeremiah and with all the energy that she could muster, surrounded him in flame. She was certain that with Rose's Book she would burn him, but she again found it impossible.

Resuming her flesh, Alex shot at him expressions of her anger and grief. The magnitude of her emotions shook the Library, but hardly bothered Jeremiah.

Alex collapsed to the floor, sobbing, her hands striking the hot granite, her skin blistering, as she cried out her rage and pain. Her heart felt absent, a gaping vacuous hole in her chest. She was spent and had no notion of what was left worth fighting for.

Jeremiah staggered to his feet. His face revealed that he still didn't know what to make of his wounds or why they weren't healing.

"No one left to rescue you," he said. "It is time we ended this for good."

Alex didn't care. He had taken everything from her. Abby, Heather, Rose. He would take his magic back. He would end her. But, she would be damned if she would allow him to have it easily.

She hurt. She wanted this to be over. She wanted to be home. She wanted to crawl into her attic bedroom and go to sleep and wake up and find Heather making breakfast and Rose and Billy making fun of her for sleeping late. She wouldn't annoy Heather with repeated requests to go to college. She would just shake off the horrible nightmare and instead of going on her Saturday hike with her cousins, they would sit at home and read normal books.

Alex took a breath and choked on her tears. Lightning sparked from her fingers, forced from her, as though squeezing out the last of herself. She didn't stop, her diminishing attacks, whether lightning or plasma of shockwave, continued until her body was clenched by his distant grip.

His hold returning to her, the crushing grip squeezing withered life from her. Alex closed her eyes. Her fingers buzzed, but the electricity leapt only finger to finger. How easy it would be to let it happen? How easy it would be to regurgitate all the magic, to allow all those women another chance at life when the next champion came to claim Jeremiah's throne. *How many times have these women been certain they'd found their savior, only to find themselves enslaved in Books for another millennia?* Had she claimed Matthew's coin, she might have an answer.

She let out a choking grunt as the squeeze kept her from breathing. The pain was someone else, just like it had always been, with each Book, with each woman. Never hers: theirs. Her body was someone else's. She drifted on a stream, a dark river taking her to some new oblivion. She thought about the child and wondered what Charon would do. Like the story Banhi told her, would the child fear her forever? Or would it finally claim her coin?

Chapter One Hundred and Seventy-Three

Alex was dying.

Never in all her years, the eighteen she lived in her body, or the lifetime trapped in Sara, did she expect it to end like this. She believed she might defeat Jeremiah, but she was certain she'd hurt him, take his magic away, leave him in some lessened state, and that would be her success. Instead, she was the last of her kind, the last witch alive, the only member of her Coven with a beating heart, and that utter failure was too great to fathom.

She drifted on a dark, rushing river of pain. The deeper into herself she traveled, the more the water burbled and flowed around her, the further she was from her body, from Jeremiah, from her agonies.

She thought of those whose faith in her ended with their death. All those people who believed she was the one. She was the first real witch, and she was the last. Although her mind fought the crush, imagined whatever it dared to counteract it, everyone she tried to protect was gone. In a moment or two, Jeremiah would overpower her will and begin forcing magic out of her again. She'd only begun understanding her magic. Everyone was wrong about it. The common knowledge was a deception. They told her magic was emotional. They believed magic was pure and perfect in Books. Emotion might be magic's fuel; it took losing her sight to see truth. The magic she'd seen on the Between was the real magic, fed by emotion but given real strength by creativity and imagination. And now, just as she understood the truth, it would be taken away.

Jeremiah would take her magic, just as he took everything from her. Her loved ones, her friends. Natural disasters and terrorism and wars did that to families all the time. But none of those things had a conscience. None of those was a person or a being or whatever Jeremiah was. The idea that she'd been chosen for this infuriated her. Her parents' sacrifice, their desire to make her special was an overreach of hubris on the grandest scale. How many others found their lives cut dramatically short because they'd been chosen by some manipulation of destiny?

Alex begged her friends to leave, to flee for their lives. Instead, Abby gave her the last of her strength. They all stayed. They all fought and died, sacrificing themselves for her. She believed those she loved were her greatest weakness; she could be hurt by harm done to them. Yet once they were gone, their absence was a greater weakness. Jeremiah gave her the chance to face him unencumbered by them. They could no longer be hurt.

Yet, instead of avenging them, she closed her eyes and fled into her mind to escape the agony.

And she was spending her last moments escaping rather than facing her pain, rather than trying every damn thing before her dying gasps. What had been the point of their sacrifice? She was living on their gifted strength. Didn't that deserve to be spent? If she was dying, why not be at the throttle?

Alex resented her cowardice. They were gone: He couldn't hurt her anymore. She knew she'd tried everything, but that wasn't near enough. He didn't care about his followers, his Books, or the golems he made. If she couldn't harm him, she would die destroying everything that mattered to him.

Finding new strength, her rage burned like glowing steel. Her hatred was a fury. Hurt him—Alex felt bloated with certainty that this one thing she could do.

Her consciousness returned, the strain of his crushing overcoming her resistance to it. She imagined the Library. Long aisles. Enormous proportions. Bookcases. She imagined the walls and pretended fine hair cracks raced along their length. Fine dust danced from those deepening cracks. She recalled the scars on the Between and the Library, like grafts of foreign flesh sown together. She imagined them pulling apart, ripping imaginary stitches. She pictured the land, real and imagined, dismantling, the ground dividing, the Between eager to be freed from the foreign contaminant.

Jeremiah grunted. His ever-changing visage scrunched in concentration; his body tensed as though squeezing harder. He approached Alex as though with proximity he'd have greater power over her.

She strained against his grasp, her breath nary a whistle as her lungs sucked a drop of air down her throat. Breathing was a distraction. The cracks. She visualized fissures elongating in a jagged race. She told them about love, and they longed to touch one another, to touch all the others.

A distant thunk; a small chunk falling from the wall, crumbling to the floor. Then another. A subtle tremble reverberated throughout the Library. More pieces; hunks of stone crashed to the ground. They shattered broken bookcases, exploding balls of soot and dust into the air.

The voices in her head roared approval. Their rising will buoyed her own.

"What are you doing?"

In his curiosity, Jeremiah's grasp eroded slightly. A sweet rush of air inflated her lungs.

Alex screamed. Her hands clenched as though each clutched a stone. She trembled as she attempted to crush them.

The Library rumbled, fragments raining down. Waterfalls of dust obscuring every view. Chunks and slabs of glowing stone collapsed from unperceivable heights, pummeling the floor as the ceiling began to collapse. The building seemed to speak as it groaned.

"You're not strong enough. How are you doing this?"

Alex had been unable to destroy the Farms. Could she destroy the Library? She thought about the spiral tower. *Who put that there? What empire was it stolen from? Did it matter?* It marked the location of the Library and the Farm like a pin through a map. It protected the precious Library. A barrier to keep the nightmares and whatever else away. It was the extended finger of Jeremiah's victory. She imagined it crumbling, imagined it collapsing to the ground, but it wouldn't budge. How was it so strong?

Her mind wandered to the tower, coming to the prison in its peak. There, she found the corpse, lying on the floor in a fetal position. She asked it, *Why did you never leave?*

Her heart stirred. It was flooded with a sense of loneliness. Not the desolation of watching her friends perish, but the isolation of millennia. The corpse turned to her, its desiccated eyes wide and empty. It held out its hands as though offering Alex whatever it had protected for so long, but her palms were empty. Reaching forward, it wrapped her in its embrace. *Here*, it told her in its dry, breathless voice, *Succeed me.* The corpse withered to dust.

She stood alone in the tower, but this was not her prison. The corpse had nothing in its hands, but it had given her something. It raced through her in a way that brought her sense of self outside of her own body. As though beyond her flesh, beyond her touch, she existed everywhere.

Alex had known this feeling. When she read Caleb's Book. She had been the earth. The progress of men churned her flesh. What she felt now was the bloated stiffness of inflammation: A foreign object infecting her flank. Although she stood in the Library, her body felt momentarily vast, expansive. Most of her was waiting to become, as yet unimagined. But in one place, hardened by infection, were three objects festering in her. Three objects she intended to excise.

The tower. A screw. Driven into her, holding everything sickeningly in place. She imagined it auguring from the ground. The soil boiled around its rotating base. The tower turned. Its movement—imperceptible at first—increasing. All at once the foundation uprooted. In the momentum of spin, the tower twirled and twisted before tipping, falling, collapsing—in a billow of debris—into a pile of stones that rolled and tumbled and crashed against one another until finally to rest.

The Library lurched as though suddenly untethered from the ground. It shook as though the tower truly was the artifice that once stabbed through realities like a skewer, but held them together no more. Beams of sunlight burst through the ceiling and the walls, piercing the gloom, stabbing like glowing, fiery swords.

Jeremiah screamed, "Stop! You're too naive to know what you're doing!"

He tightened his grasp; Alex breathed freely.

Like digging her fingers into her own abdomen, she cried out in pain and relief as the Farm tore from her soil, the remains of the long wooden buildings rendering to dust.

The Library trembled as though its footings had collapsed. She felt it in her flesh, a welt in the vastness of her expansive Between. She dug her own fingers into her hot, swollen, infected flesh and found herself in the Library.

She looked about the building as it decayed. Jeremiah had torn some piece of reality and he forced it to remain, like a graft or a parasite, a wound that even after ten millennia—twenty, a forever—wouldn't heal. Whether that woman was a goddess or a metaphor for the Between, she had been the key. Just as Marta had been trapped in her own body, Jeremiah trapped that woman inside his world, inside her world—her universe—imprisoning one within the other. The Between was that woman's universe, and she had given it all to Alex.

She needed to put it back, to return order. Wherever it had come from didn't matter; she wanted to free the Between from its horrible corruption.

It was like attempting to lift a boulder. As hard as she strained, only her hands and feet moved; never the object of her intent. Veins bulged from her arms and neck and temples. She strained against the limits of her body; the building around her becoming a tempest of dust and debris. It seemed impossible, but then the boulder lurched; the entire building groaned like a muttering old man with an unsettling outburst just as death claimed him. The effort exceeded her; Alex's head exploded in pain, the rising cry of her voices momentarily drowning out the din around her.

The wall nearest her exploded. Stones burst inward with unimaginable force, capturing them both in the flow of soil and stone and collapsed wall.

Alex's pain was too great for her to bear, hit by the percussive shock shifting the flow of rubble. It swept them both into its turmoil and threw them like they were hit by a crashing ocean wave of concrete and earth.

Then, the rumble settled. As the din plinked and tinked to stillness, Alex was shocked to observe how thorough the silence, besides stilling rocks and pebbles, was. Even her whispers were silent.

Alex dislodged herself from the overflowing debris, pushing herself upright. As the dust rained out of the air and cleared; she couldn't stifle her laughter.

Her uncle once told her that the valley had once been a mountain top. The mountain top had once been an ocean floor. Tectonic plates pushed it up, creating tremendous mountain spires that time eroded, rounding peaks and filling valleys. Then some trickle of water took an eternity to cut a valley through those stones. This place was timeless, existing as sea floor and mountain top and valley.

Not long ago, a giant stone had rolled down the valley-side. A collision had forced the stone upright, pushing it back up that cliffside, returning it to near its original location, making it nearly whole once again. Among all the names written and carved in its face, the largest and oldest among them read, "Johnathan William Frost, 1826".

Chapter One Hundred and Seventy-Four

Alex took a moment to collect herself. The stone—the broken half of Picnic Rock—seemed out of place until viewed through the shattered ceiling and ruined walls. It wasn't high on some precipice, teetering on the edge of the valley. The Library filled the valley once again.

Alex was home. She couldn't tell if what she felt was atmospheric; the sudden change in pressure and humidity, or something more subtle, more insidious. The sensation settled within her, not the satisfaction of coming home, but of returning to a place she knew intimately, a place that belonged to her so thoroughly it had become a part of her.

Beyond the ruins of the Library, lay the destroyed tower, and the overturned Farm beyond that. This alone was triumph to celebrate, yet; if she survived there was no reason to believe he hadn't. She scanned the rubble. Dust settled in the gentle breeze. If he was alive, Jeremiah was buried deep.

The silence around her was too tempting not to enjoy. It had been so long since she could relish a moment. She found no joy; there was no one to share it with. The blue sky overhead, the two halves of Picnic Rock. The breeze, the insects, the call of an occasional bird, and the animals rooting around the woods; there was noise all around her and yet she experienced a solitude previously unknown to her. Her whispers were silenced, perhaps by the same exhaustion, the same wonder of what this all meant. She looked beyond Picnic Rock and knew in a few miles' walk were the ruins of Sara's house. She wondered if there was some coincidence that found Sara here, so close to the conclusion of Alex's story.

She knew of another house and further questioned coincidence. Where the Library now rested in ruin would have been Rose's dreamed house. Its disappearance likely coincided with Rose's death. She felt buried by the weight of her loss. She might as well have been in the bottom of the valley when the Library appeared. Tons and tons and hundreds of feet of crushing soil and rock weighed on her, not just her heart, but burying her entirely. They were all gone. How had she survived, the one among them so certain that her death could save them all? Alex's mind kept projecting on her imagined vision the last moments of each of her loved ones. Each eschewed salvation to sacrifice themselves for her. Each of them loved her and believed in her so completely that they gave her the last of themselves.

She wiped the muddy tears from her dust-strewn face. If she was going to properly mourn her losses, she was doing herself no favors remaining here, in the house of their murderer. In less than an hour she could be resting on the foundation, imagining the house where she once lived, long ago, within Sara. Maybe there, given how special the place was, she could summon the mist. Disappear onto the Between. Finally have the chance to explore those markets. Maybe even venture to New York City and eat something from those carts. Or Paris....

She climbed over the debris, the stones loose and eager to tumble from underfoot, to scale the remains of the walls and reach Picnic Rock.

"Do you have any idea what you've done? Can you even grasp the immensity of it? I saved this world and you've undone it all."

The startling voice chilled her. Turning slowly, her stomach curdling, a dust and blood-caked man emerged from the rubble. This was not the Jeremiah she had met before. Not the ever-changing visage, not the young, vain man, not the old man. This creature was stained with blood, hidden with dust. His body deformed and contorted, behorned with protruding bones.

"You have no idea the horrors you've unleashed." He choked and spat; the gritty spittle swirled bright with blood. "This Library wasn't hidden away like some dirty secret. It was the only way to separate the two worlds. To save everyone. To make the world safe. I separated them, and like some careless, foolish child, you've returned them together."

He patted giant plumes of dust from his body. Alex's fight was unfinished. As long as he lived, he endangered her. He looked so small from the top of the crumbling wall, barely a speck in the vastness of ruin around him.

Just looking at him, her body tensed. She despised him. He killed them all.

"There's still time," he said after a moment of thought. "To restore everything. It won't all reconcile in a matter of moments or hours or even days. We can put everything back and keep the world in balance."

Alex looked around, more for the drama of the act. The faintest trace of its structure surrounded her again. With her imagined sight, she was perhaps still seeing the Library. She answered him, "If you did it, it should stay undone. I prefer it that way."

"You won't."

"That's not for you to decide."

Jeremiah smeared his face with blood as he tried to wipe it clean, his wounds open and bleeding. He reached. Alex's feet slipped from the stones. Pinwheeling her arms as she fell, bracing against the sharp edges beneath her, Jeremiah's pull dragging her to where he stood.

Struggling against his gravity, she found resilience in her own effort. His pull was no longer absolute. She dug in her heels; her trembling legs held her immobile. His certainty dissolved. She seized the opportunity, bounding into the air.

He took a moment to realize she'd eluded him. He looked desperately around as though she'd vanished. Slowly, reluctantly, he gazed upwards. When he laid eyes upon her in the sky, the shock on his face told Alex that even though he'd seen her fly before, he still didn't believe it.

A quick stretch of her limbs and she soared upwards, the air cooling as she distanced herself from the ruins and climbed into the breeze that no longer found itself winding through a valley. She tried to find her anger, but her grief was so great it bore her tears. Her imagined vision saw beyond the former valley, to the forests, spying roads and farms and glistening lakes and the rolling mountains beyond. From this height, the world was magnificent, and she had no one to share it with. Looking down at the dot of a man amid the ruins, a shadow marking his presence like an exclamation point, she wondered if imagination alone was enough. She was flying. The phantom Library aside, she saw well enough to question whether vision returned to her blind eyes. She felt the change, as though finding it as she neared the clouds. She hadn't just freed the Between from the Library. In its extrication, she'd done something more. Her whispers sensed it, as though this whole world belonged to her now. She didn't know what she'd truly accomplished, but if Jeremiah feared it so, she had indeed triumphed.

She extended her arms and imagining, unleashed a single arcing snap of lightning. It seared the air, sizzling particulate, as it flashed from her fingertips, snapping of thunder. She anticipated his invisible fortress repelling it, but his convulsing form spun a dozen feet away.

She swooped lower, keeping an eye on the black smudge her lightning burned in the ruins, knowing he was nearby. Before she saw him, she saw the bolts shooting from his fingers. She spun to evade them. Like a hole punched through her, one hit and then another. The strikes spun her out of the air and even as she tried to right herself, she hit and rolled across the rocks, as ungainly a landing as ever.

Her world rattled and her head ached, as she tried to judge where she landed in relation to him. With each second she nursed her wounds, she was sure he was upon her. She forced herself to her feet, unsure where he was.

The illusion of the Library reformed around her. It was a shadow, an afterimage. Its solidity becoming harder to disbelieve; as though just as she willed its destruction, he willed it remade. He would undo all her effort, make all sacrifices in vain. She didn't see him until the first bolt of electricity dropped her to her knees.

He leapt through the air—as though flying instead of falling—and their collision entangled their limbs as they crashed to the ground. He reached for her throat. Growling and sneering and cursing at her in his frenzy.

As soon as they made contact, his visions infiltrated her head.

Alex remembered the last time she saw the goddess, the first time Jeremiah touched her in the Library.

The woman struck at the young man, her lips, lush and swollen, silently begged him with her withering strikes to release her. He was tall and handsome. He grit his teeth, his eyes, perfect and sparkling in her presence, dripped iridescent tears as he knelt, and she collapsed, his hands crushing her throat.

He eased her perfect, naked form to the ground. Her beauty was so bewildering Alex could not help but envy her.

He gasped, as though overcome with power. Around him, the fabric of the world tore open, revealing the dark beyond. He trembled. His eyes went wide and white. He cried out, dropping to his knees. About him, the wounds healed.

In the goddess's chest, her glowing coin. Pure and white, it was so bright that Alex, even staring at this memory, shaded her eyes.

The child appeared. It held out its hand, and seeing the beautiful woman, gasped. Its hand recoiled; covering its mouth.

The young man claimed her coin. The child did nothing to stop him.

The vision abruptly disappeared, Jeremiah inches from her face; still holding the coin. The thread sparking all the way back to Alex's chest. He celebrated his theft.

She reached to reclaim it. For a moment they shared it, each holding a precious piece until the bond holding her coins broke and his greedy hands wrenched away her second coin. They each claimed one. He bounded from her, examining it as though he'd never before seen a coin.

"Don't come any closer," he warned, holding her coin between them like a talisman. He grinned at his own self-satisfaction. He tauntingly waved his trophy in the air. Behind him, rows of ghost-bookcases appeared.

At the grinding sound of footsteps on rubble, her heart soared as she thought, *Abby*.

The child, Charon, approached, its fabric wrapping whitened from the dust its feet kicked up. It held out its one hand. Alex looked at the child, its expression ferocious. Her middle twisted with the realization that death finally came for her.

"Not yet," she begged, obscuring her solitary coin with her hand. She remembered her mother telling Charon it had to wait because her daughter wasn't yet safe. It didn't seem to care however she begged.

It stepped closer, its covetous little hand clenching at the air, half demanding *Come here* and half *Give it to me!*

"Please, not yet," she begged, taking a step backwards, falling through the ghostly form of a bookcase. This child was not afraid. This was the end. The moment she finally believed she might defeat Jeremiah; her time was up. Jeremiah held the second coin she would hide with. No options.

If she gave Charon her coin, perhaps she could take Jeremiah's magic with her. If the world lost all its magic, who among those remaining would know?

She didn't need but a heartbeat to consider it. "Please give me this one thing. He must be stopped," she told the child and turned to Jeremiah, to show Charon who she meant.

Behind her, Jeremiah's eyes were wide with fear: He thought Charon had come for him.

"Get away from me. You have no business here. You know you can't hurt me here," Jeremiah screamed at the child, his lips wet with blood speckled spittle. In the places he'd wiped enough dust away, his shifting visage emerged from smeared filth.

One of them misread the child. There was only one way to be sure. She stepped aside; the child's gaze didn't follow her. It closed in on Jeremiah.

Her second coin in one hand, his other fired sparks; the child cringed at the impacts, its flesh blistering and searing black. Its covetous hand opening and closing, regardless.

It snatched her coin from Jeremiah's hands.

Alex gulped; had she misjudged the child's intent?

The child examined its prize, its face softening as it turned the coin over in its fingers. Even Jeremiah was uncertain of the child, until it took three quick steps and offered the coin back to her.

Alex haltingly accepted the gift, the child's dark, wide eyes smiling as compassionately as its cherubic face. Jeremiah resumed his attack on them both, but the child wouldn't release the coin to her. She feared she was mistaken. She stared at the child, it at her, the coin shared between them. And then it opened its fingers. Alex immediately joined it to her own coin.

Then the child turned back to Jeremiah, rage returning to its face.

Jeremiah sneered wrathfully. "You shouldn't have come back," he warned the child. "It hasn't been so long that you've forgotten what I did to you." Even as he threatened the child with his harsh tone, Jeremiah backed away.

He fired anew, first sparks, then flames. The child endured the wounds and continued forward.

Alex fired lightning of her own. "Stay out of this," he warned her.

She flew to his opposite side, landing firmly, the stones beneath her feet grinding and locking together. Jeremiah was trapped between her and

Charon. He had nowhere to retreat, and his actions grew frantic. He extended one arm to each of them; his target chosen by a turn of his head.

Even as she attacked, Alex gritted her teeth at the searing intensity of his spells. Her flesh burned, the electricity searing her skin, convulsing her muscles. Twice she nearly dropped to her knees, but she kept finding the will, as though there were others behind her, helping her to her feet.

He turned to her, "You don't know what you're doing! Charon isn't an innocent child. It's a monster."

It was nothing she didn't already know.

He noticed something and turned to her. "You disfigured the child?"

The accusation hurt, true though it was. She told him, "I took the Reaper's hand."

He grinned at the revelation and turned to the child. "You're not impervious." He showed it his hand. "She took your hand. I *can* defeat you!"

Given reprieve during his destruction, the child leapt onto Jeremiah, and they tumbled to the ground.

The child crawled about him, suffering his slaps and spells; doggedly pursuing his coin. The child grasped it, and Jeremiah clasped his hands over the child's. Charon tugged, and when it couldn't wrest the coin from his grasp, it sunk its teeth into Jeremiah's wrist. Growling like a feral dog, Charon's cherubic face snarled and twisted as it worked off a piece of flesh.

Alex grabbed Jeremiah's filthy, sweaty neck. His moist heat revolted her; she released a barrage of electricity into him. Alex saw her again, the goddess and her beauty.

The child gnawed as Jeremiah's fingers spasmed. He cried out, giving up his coin, and with his unbitten hand seized Alex's wrist.

The child pulled away, Jeremiah's coin in hand. There was no tether, no fine thread holding it to Jeremiah's chest.

The heat of his breath washed across her face once Jeremiah pulled her closer, his teeth snapping dangerously as he threatened, "You'll pay for this, girl."

The young man released the goddess's crushed throat.

Jeremiah's vice of a grip numbed the extremity of Alex's arm, and he tossed her around like her weight was inconsequential. "I am eternal," he shouted. "I am magic. Mine is the dark heart at the center of this universe."

He threw her a distance to the ground; the goddess disappearing at their separation. He showered the child in flames. The child screamed like a wounded animal, tripping backwards, collapsing to the rubble. It squirmed and writhed, but even as its skin blackened, it would not release his coin.

Jeremiah pried his coin from its hands, stomping the child repeatedly even once he'd replaced the coin in his chest. Around them, bookcases resolved. The sky dimmed as a ceiling reformed above them.

Though Alex witnessed the brutality Charon—the Reaper—was capable of, she could not bear the child's suffering. She could not defeat Jeremiah alone, and with the child so brutally incapacitated, she was.

She tried to draw on her emotions, her anger, her pity, her rage, her heartache. Her love. She pictured the landscape around her, the rubble, the ruined Library. She imagined the stones around her. She imagined the sounds she wanted to hear. If Jeremiah could turn Books into men, why couldn't her imaginative magic make something from stone?

Dissolving out of the air, as though Jeremiah conjured the vision, rows of bookcases stretched into the distance, becoming more than apparitions.

She concentrated: Limbs. Tail. Teeth. Wings.

Jeremiah placed his hands on Charon's body.

The floor trembled. Dislodged dust vibrated into the air. The Library resolved. The walls gained clarity; the woods, Picnic Rock becoming vague.

Wooden bookcases became solid; Jeremiah was using the child for his own will.

Scales. Eyes. Talons.

The Library became more substantial, the child shriveling in his grasp. Its eyes fluttered open and it whined.

Its eyes fluttered open and it roared. The creature turned, its tail battering bookcases to splinter, shattering the newly reformed wall.

Jeremiah startled at the deep vibration of the creature's growl, and startled again, staring at the dragon's black iridescent scales. It twisted and slithered, its claws scarring stone.

Without releasing the child, Jeremiah struck the terrible lizard with lightning, a strike of the intensity normally conjured by multiple Books. The lizard reeled and twisted like an earthworm severed by a garden shovel, the scales on its side blackened, decaying to carbonized dust, its insides revealed.

Alex pitied the writhing creature. She'd brought it to life only to watch it suffer and die. As though it sensed her willing it to survive, its great wings hauled it into the air with a few wind-driven flaps, blowing and toppling bookcases.

The dragon gulped like a child forcing a belch. Before the dragon regurgitated fire or acid or whatever dragons did, Jeremiah's next strike—a churning electrocution—dropped it from the sky, its burned scales flaking from its powdery-white skull. Bookcases shattered and smoke from the carcass swirled and pooled at the ceiling. He fired on it again, rendering the creature to dust. Alex feared Jeremiah's next strike: it wouldn't just cover her in scars.

He glared at Alex, "Fool!" He screamed at her. "You stupid, stupid little girl. You have no idea how dangerous you are."

She guarded against his anticipated strike.

"A dragon? What would that have done if I hadn't slain it? How can't you see what you've done?"

She waited for him to continue admonishing her, but he returned to his work.

Around her, they were no longer in the valley. There was no Picnic Rock. Jeremiah was returning them to the Between. The tower, the Farm. All the ground she'd won, he was claiming back.

If the child was giving him the strength to resurrect the Library, she had to stop him. She wrapped her arms around Jeremiah to pry him from the child.

When the dead goddess's coin glowed, and the young man claimed it, Charon appeared. This was not the Charon from Jeremiah's recollection, wearing only a few folds of fabric. This child wore a riot of colorful swatches, its dark eyes wide at the sight of the goddess, one hand reaching for the coin in the young man's hand, the other, a stump.

How are you here, too? The words were spoken by her mind. Although the child didn't answer, she knew: *I grabbed Jeremiah and he's holding the child.*

The child shook its head at the scene. As Charon took Alex's hand, completing the circle, the young man's hands wrapped around Alex's throat. For a moment, she was shock-frozen and unable to resist. Then she took the young man's wrists and pried them apart. She rested her palm on his forehead and with an imagined bolt of power, rendered him to ash.

The child grinned at her revelation: She had freed the goddess. Replaced her. What she had done—what she had undone—removing Jeremiah from the Between reminded her of what Marta had said about each one of them having their own universe. They were like soap bubbles, sticking to one another, touching, loving, but never becoming one, never knowing the universe inside another's bubble. The goddess had surrendered to Alex her own bubble, her own universe: the Between. And now she had burst Jeremiah's bubble, his universe. That was why the valley felt different: The goddess was returned to life; the Between and the waking world were becoming one again.

Jeremiah was trying to use Charon's energies to jam them back. He had shown her in this vision the derivation of his power. It came from tension—the energy—created by keeping the worlds separated. If the separation of these two worlds was the source of his power, reconciling them was its conclusion. He was once the dark heart at the center of the universe. She was claiming that center from him.

The Library was collapsed and whole, like two ghosts of the same structure, like two realities slowly forced together. Preventing it from being remade was her only chance. She feared she wouldn't have the strength to bring it down a second time.

The child sobbed, its withering body desiccated and sickly. She tried to pull the child from Jeremiah, reaching around from behind him. His jaws clenched into her arm. She recalled the nightmare and the disgusting fluid in her bloodstream, and at once his jaws released. He spat and dry-heaved.

"What did you…," he hadn't the means to ask what he couldn't understand had happened.

In his momentary distraction, Alex ripped the child from his hands.

Jeremiah wiped his bloody mouth and tongue with the back of his hand and forearm, trying to wipe the taste away. His face contorted into a ball of rage: without the child's strength, the Library vanished. Only rubble remained.

Alex pitied Charon, recalling the way it kicked at the floor in fear of her. She held the child close to help it regain some strength. Alex rested the child on a slab. It was weak. The effects of Jeremiah's grasp wearing off as rapidly as Picnic Rock appeared.

"Your Library is gone, Jeremiah. It's not coming back."

Jeremiah's ever-changing eyes snapped about, rabid and ferocious.

Jeremiah crackled with electricity. As he fired, Alex returned a strike, their lightning like high-voltage cables brought together, bursting into a deafening snap, washing them both with the remaining charge.

Jeremiah fired the faster bolt, but Alex caught it. The molten light dripped between her fingers; her palm raw from its heat. She imagined the flames of a fireball born of the heat. He hadn't expected her to catch his strike, and as she threw the rotating cobalt flame, he expected this less. He roared, the flames contorting him in heat and pain. Even before his cry subsided, he resumed firing lightning at her.

Alex's heart felt like she was in a car driving over the rumble-strip. Jeremiah cast everything, fire, lightning, ice, and she had an instant to react, to counter the spell and create her own attack. It wasn't unlike battling the shades, constantly reconfiguring her magic to keep ahead of him. Theirs was a dance of magic, a constant barrage or sparking incendiaries. It was exhausting. It seemed inevitable that this would continue until one of them slipped up or grew too exhausted, handing the other victory because of the slightest mistake.

With his concentration focused solely on her, the Library remained its ruins. He didn't show any signs of weakening. The energy he stole from

Charon still sustained him. Alex was beginning to sense that magic couldn't end their conflict in her favor. Even as her weariness weighed on her shoulders and strained her neck, Jeremiah seemed as fresh as ever. Magic was no effort for him, as though he was the source of its energy. As though she drew hers through him, fighting his resistance to make it. She didn't know how much longer she could go on.

Finding the timing, she deflected his burning energy and leapt into the air as she imagined a glowing orb of lightning and threw it. She raced in the air behind it. Her landings were never graceful, and she expected this to be the least of them. Jeremiah recognized the trick as he deflected her spell, raising his arms defensively, casting, as they collided.

The impact was jarring, her head ringing from the prematurely cast spell exploding in a flash of energy at their contact, but before she even had her bearings, she scrambled for his coin.

He slithered out from under her, throwing her aside and raising his hand triumphantly. A thread snaked back to her chest, sparking wildly, her twin coins blazing like a miniature sun, spinning in his hand.

Chapter One Hundred and Seventy-Five

Alex answered Jeremiah with her own raised hand. A thread attached the coin in her palm to his chest.

"You won't do it," he sneered. "You didn't eat Matthew's coin because you feared pain. I've exterminated millions. My pain will destroy you."

Alex looked at the coin, momentarily curious of its secrets. This coin was the truth of truths. Buried at the base of an unfathomable tower of pain were all the answers of this universe. Alex said to him, "What makes you think I have to eat it?" She tossed the coin into Charon's waiting hand.

Instantly, Charon violently shred its flesh, the Reaper emerging, growing monstrous.

Jeremiah fired frantically at the Reaper. The hulking monster lumbered towards him. It seemed unfazed by his efforts. It towered over him. Jeremiah offered the towering behemoth her coin.

The creature stared lustfully at the spinning, glowing disk.

Jeremiah grinned in triumph. His smile faltered when the monster took his arm at the wrist; his hand and her coin thumping to the ground.

Before Jeremiah could react to his severed limb, the Reaper ripped him apart.

Jeremiah screamed as the single claw rendered hunks of flesh. His lightning, his fire, his concussive blasts had no effect as the skeletal nightmare flayed him alive.

Jeremiah begged Alex, "Help me."

Alex staggered backwards, her thread still in his severed hand. She could not avert her eyes from the scene. If Jeremiah would escape the attack, she would be ready. The claw tore into him, thrusting deep. Alex cringed, remembering her own pain. It pushed and dug, violently thrusting as the skeletal horror forced its way into Jeremiah.

Alex couldn't watch but couldn't divert her eyes. As the Reaper tore deeper and deeper into Jeremiah, shaking him about like a ragdoll, she needed to witness his suffering. She needed to know the second when the dark heart of the universe was silenced.

The Reaper lowered Jeremiah's limp body to the ground. It huddled over him as though preparing to feed. And then it forced itself deeper inside of him until all its gargantuan structure disappeared within Jeremiah's corpse.

It writhed in the rubble, as though the Reaper were carving him out from the inside, as though it were finding places to fit its claw.

The monster pushed into Jeremiah's head, breaking apart his skull, distorting the proportions. His eyes scanned for her as his new jaws snapped opened and closed. It was horrifying. Jeremiah's face, stretched over the Reaper's skull, studded with his shattered bones like horns and flesh-piercing scales. Viscera spilled from Jeremiah's abdomen. Its one claw filled out Jeremiah's hand, talons tearing through his fingers. The other still ended as a stump. Climbing to its feet, its voice emerged.

At its feet, the spilled viscera broke like an amniotic sack, and Charon, the child, crawled from the afterbirth.

The monster's language was a guttural flood of gibberish. It wasn't unfamiliar to Alex. It was the language of magic. However she imagined she might, she could not translate. Lightning and flames sparked from its clawed hand, a range of attack dwarfing even what a dozen golems in an encyclopedic attack were capable of. The attack took her by surprise, slamming her to the ground. She examined her abdomen and found it charred and raw. Touching the wound, it smeared away, as though not even real.

The monster glowered at the child, who crawled towards Alex. Its face white with panic, stumbling because of its missing hand. It looked at her as its salvation, as though she were "base". Alex refused to lose another life to either Jeremiah or the Reaper.

Alex roared, "Don't you dare touch the child!" She stepped between the monster and Charon.

The creature turned to her. Bloody and reborn. Jeremiah's skin stretched over the Reaper's bones, pulled too thin and ghastly to be recognizable. But it was more than that. She felt it in her heart and her gut. The creature oozed terror. It belonged with the nightmares. But this was the real boogeyman, the original fear. This was death reborn without the child's empathy.

Alex squared her shoulders as the creature lumbered towards her, its claws gnashing air in preparation of ripping her flesh.

Alex held her ground. She'd defeated the Reaper before.

She thought of everyone she loved. They were all gone, but that no longer mattered. Every one. Sacrificing themselves for her. Abby and Carrie embracing her, giving her their remaining strength. Rose, handing Alex her Book. Heather, remaining home, her dying act to give Alex more time.

Alex grieved every one of her friends and family. In her blind concentration, the light around her turned the purest white. She focused on how each person loved her. Billy, his entire life devoted to ensuring each moment of hers. Her parents, sacrificing their lives to hide her from Matthew. Even Matthew, offering her his coin.

She saw them all. Shadowy figures stepping into her light. She was imagining them, but they each appeared as though she had summoned them.

As though she returned each of them to life. One by one, they came to her. Rose and Abby, Carrie and Heather. Banhi and Khowla and even Lesedi. Donna and June and Betty. George, Steven, Caleb, and Peter, Matthew, Dany, and Jacque. Even her brother Alex, beside Marta. And there were others, at first dozens, but then so many more, tens of thousands: all her whispers, all the women whose Books she'd read. They all stood at her side. Alex never felt more loved. Sara reached out and took Alex's hand. Rose reached out and took Alex's hand. Heather reached out and took Alex's hand. Abby reached out and took Alex's hand.

In each of her hands, Alex clasped the hand of innumerable women, women she knew, women whose Book she'd read. She felt vast, the body politic of her grasp transcending her physical form. Each person gave her their love. Each person gave her their will. Each person told her, in their own way, how much she mattered.

She knew what she had to do, but in this moment, surrounded by such love, Alex wanted to spend the rest of her life. It warmed her, filling her, satisfying her. It was as though each one of them had her ear, whispering to her, "Alex, I love you."

Alex knew this was not hers to keep. This was for her to use. Their love swelled within her. Filled her. She had wasted so much energy nurturing her anger to feed her magic. But their love multiplied within her on its own. When she could no longer contain its warmth, when she felt swollen from its growing power, she allowed it to pass through her.

It opened around her, like glowing white petals peeling away from her, filling the air around her as the bloom grew and expanded.

The light exploded from her, the radiation exceeding a thousand suns. Its bloom marched steadily across the landscape, obliterating shadows. The world beneath her feet hummed, a vibration so deep, the Library rubble collapsed to dust.

The light swaddled the Reaper. It struggled against it, its claw cutting lines of darkness as it slashed at the warmth and love. She could feel the creature. Sense it. In her love, she reached out to it, and in her embrace, turned it to dust.

The power expanded like an explosion, no longer under Alex's control. It grew like a sphere consuming everything.

Then, the light dimmed. Daylight returned. The breeze began to blow the remnants of the Library, of Jeremiah, of the Reaper away. She still had the warmth and love inside of her. She listened to the breeze as it captured the leaves and grasses. The birds, the buzzing insects. Yet she stood in silence. She hunted for her whispers. Her mind was silent: the whispers were gone.

When Alex fell into Oblivion, she saw that universe as an enormous emptiness, with herself as a speck at its center. Now that Jeremiah was gone, his dark heart no longer beating, she felt vast. In the silence the whispers left behind, she sensed so much more than herself.

She felt the blades of grass in her hands and sensed her hands on them. A dragonfly buzzed stalk to stalk and she knew the grasp of twig in its claws. The wind rolling beneath their extended wings as the birds overhead glided on the breeze. She allowed her mind to wander beyond the field. She began to feel them: all of them.

The sensation was bewildering. Marta had described it like a soap bubble surrounding each person, keeping them all separate. For Alex, there were no longer barriers separating each person's heart from hers. She felt them all.

There were too many, a flood of emotions that could have crushed her had she not known how to silence the whispers in her head. She breathed the overwhelming sensations out and turned to Charon.

"Hey," she said to the child.

The child raised its hand as though returning her greeting. Its fingers opened to reveal her coin, its gossamer thread sparkling back to her chest.

"I guess it's time," she said peacefully. Although she could have climbed atop Picnic Rock and looked out over the new landscape for hours, she was ready. She never imagined she'd reach the other end of her story. If she'd brought the waking world and the Between together, where would the child take her? The prospect of discovery excited her. "I'm ready," she told the child, "for my next adventure."

Instead of claiming her coin, the child stood before her, its expression wide-eyed and expectant. When she hesitated, it made a face of frustration. With an exaggerated huff, the child waddled over to her. With its stump, it raised her hand and placed her coin into her palm.

When Alex returned it to her chest, the child grinned mischievously and withdrew from the folds of its fabric another coin. It turned it over in its fingers with wonder. Its eyebrows raised joyfully; it showed Alex the coin on its palm. It closed its hand and opened it again: it wasn't disappearing.

Alex took a guess, "You got your coin back?"

The child pointed at its own chest. A coin already glowed there. The child grinned again, an excited expression of a child taking cookies that were supposed to be for later. The coin in its hand, Alex realized, was Jeremiah's. *How long has Charon waited for that coin?*

Alex touched her own chest. She expected Abby's charm, which made her think of her Familiar. If anyone would know, it would be the ferryman of the dead. "Do you know where they are? Are they all gone?"

The child tucked the coin into the riotous folds of its fabric. It looked around as though looking for them with her.

"Is this how it was, before him?" Alex didn't want to say his name, not because she feared it, but because she wanted it to disappear along with him.

The child didn't answer, nor did its serene expression hint at one.

"But things are back the way they're supposed to be, right?"

The child smiled. Alex wanted to believe it grinned in affirmation of her question and told herself it did.

"I don't know how to thank you," Alex whispered.

The child held its palm forward. Opening and closing its fingers: Goodbye.

Chapter One Hundred and Seventy-Six

Alex stood alone, surveying what was no longer a valley. Jeremiah's buildings had been expunged from the landscape leaving only battered and upended ground, a riot of wildflowers delineated the absent foundations. In time, they'd fill in the empty soil and heal these scars.

Alex walked to Picnic Rock. The upheaval pushed the two halves nearly back together. With the valley filled in, Johnathan's carving was at eye level. Alex traced the edges of a few letters with her fingers. She remembered the day he finished carving; it seemed another lifetime ago and yet so close that she felt a connection to him simply by touching the places he had touched.

Alex passed Picnic Rock, looking at the piled stone steps, knowing that on top of this stone she'd find the remains of a bonfire. *How connected everything is*. She walked along the path.

Everything felt new. She held onto the love that helped her defeat Jeremiah. Although she missed her Coven tremendously, that part of them was with her. It always would be. She walked along the trail, full of hope for the future. Where uncertainty used to be, Alex saw only opportunity. There was a world out there. To think that a few weeks ago her only thoughts were to go to college. Now she wanted to explore.

She'd become so used to the constant din of thousands of voices in her head that she couldn't help but hear the leaves fluttering in the breeze, as the trees whispered to her. The insects paid her no mind, flitting all about, a myriad of activity everywhere she looked or listened. All the noises of nature around her; the wind, the birds, even the sunlight sparkling seemed to have a sound of its own, all joining together to create a mélange that was like the universe whispering to her. If only she knew what she wanted to say.

The afternoon sun was high in the sky when Alex came to the old foundation. She entered the clearing and saw Abby's faded tire tracks. She recalled Sara's gardens where now wildflowers poked through felled trees and vines. She hopped onto the foundation to sit and rest a while.

She looked over the foundation, seeing a mix of the present and the past. She wasn't imagining her vision any longer, but she also hadn't regained her sight. It was the paradox of living in her own universe, she guessed, the ability to see everything.

Her mind and her heart were a tumult of thought and emotion. Everyone she loved was gone, but together, they'd defeated Jeremiah. It was difficult to feel any sense of accomplishment, and yet, they'd done what many others had tried and failed. She didn't need Matthew's coin after all.

She was victorious, but she didn't feel like celebrating. She couldn't help but wonder what would come of it. She had lived her entire life within Jeremiah's universe. And now it was hers. How different could it be for that reason alone?

Although she now shared her world with billions, she felt alone. She had no one to share it with, to explore it with. How she longed for Rose and Billy. The walks they could take!

She had feared that having her friends nearby put them in danger and made her responsible for them. Jeremiah warned her what he would do if she crossed him, and he was true to his word. He took away everyone who so much as knew her.

They were dead because of him, but he couldn't take them from her. She saw that now. Their memories were in her heart, and like the whispers that once rattled her head, they were real: a part of them truly forever belonged to her.

Knowing they were with her didn't stop her from missing them; her heart ached. She thought of Sara and of her house. She hopped down and walked to the edge of the clearing. Looking back, she recalled her time here. Her Book Club removing her curse, transporting her back to Sara. It was such a horrific experience, and yet she thought only fondly of Sara; nostalgia overpainted the experience with softer hues. She understood Matthew's actions. She could not undo that trauma without taking away some important part of herself in the process. She had walked a long journey to where she now stood. Had she removed any single step, where would she have ended? Certainly not here.

She pictured Sara's house, the little jewel box Johnathan built for her. Sara's life seemed like a made-up story. Was it real only because she remembered it? She closed her eyes a moment to better see the memory. When she opened her eyes, Sara's house remained. Alex eagerly climbed the stairs and opened the door; hopeful she'd find Sara waiting inside.

Inside, everything was as she remembered it in Sara's day. But vacant. With curious reluctance, she looked at the kitchen table. There was no nail driven into it. The furniture, the décor, was all in place. In the bedroom she found the crib. She didn't bother to check; she knew she'd find no hammer.

She toured the small home, her hands caressing every surface as though if she lost contact it might vanish. This was like her attic or Abby's trailer—before it burned down—this house was her home.

She wished Sara could be here, to see it and share the experience with her. Sara lived and died long ago, and yet to Alex, they were the closest of confidants. "You would have been so proud of your son," she told the house. She couldn't help but think of George as hers, too. Her heart ached when she thought of him.

Alex's wounds were healing. The gnash where Jeremiah bit her was hot and tight and itched ferociously. Still, the lightning marks on her skin hadn't changed or faded. Her tattoo was permanent. It made her smile; she'd earned them. They reminded her of Carrie. Thinking of the tattooed chef made her smile. *I told you I like 'em tall.* She wished she had known Carrie was flirting with her then. She had been so oblivious. *What would I do if she were here right now?* She let her question remain unanswered.

Stepping onto the front porch, she sat to admire the view. *Will everything ever stop reminding me?* She'd sat here before, at the end of Sara's life, looking out over her gardens. Dusty beams of light broke through the forest canopy, like when the Library ceiling opened to the sky. She missed the whispers. She'd become so accustomed to their incessant din they became a form of silence in their own way. As much as she wished for a moment of peace while they pestered her, now that she had it, she felt a need to fill her silence with thoughts.

Abby's trailer was gone. When she reached Heather's house, she would know what Jeremiah did to her aunt—Alex wasn't sure she would ever want to stay there—and while Pat, Steven, and Charissa were technically family, it felt inappropriate to move into their home. They were all gone. As family, maybe they'd want her to have what was theirs, but what Alex wanted was something that was hers. That felt like this place. Sara's. The Witch's Shack. Few places felt as appropriately home as this.

Before it got too late, she decided to visit Heather's house, pack up her clothes and scrounge the refrigerator for leftovers. One last meal made by her aunt before she said her final goodbyes. She didn't relish revisiting Heather's, expecting it to feel more like a mausoleum or a crime scene. But the majority of memories the house contained were joyful. She resolved not to let what happened there spoil what it meant to her. She would take Dolly. Then she'd get to Charissa's and collect Marty and Quest. Then she and her cats would come home.

Chapter One Hundred and Seventy-Seven

"See you later, Sara. I'll be back," she said contentedly to her home as she closed and secured the front door. She crossed the clearing and wandered along the path through the woods.

Alex approached the edge of the forest, bracing herself to be haunted by the ghosts the fire-whipped grasses would conjure, but stepping from the woods to the fallow farm field, her heart soared. The field was footworn and the grasses beaten down. She'd forgotten that in the chaos at the Library, she'd sent many women to the field. Here was proof they arrived safely. From the footsteps and tracks, she couldn't discern how many, but the sight dulled her pain, if only a little: She'd saved them. She'd harbored such guilt that she saved them from the Farm only to have them die in the Library. Because lurking in the darker recesses of her mind was the thought that had she left them at the Farm—maybe—when she defeated Jeremiah, the enchantment would be broken and they all would have been saved, anyway. She could only tell herself their numbers were necessary for her to defeat Jeremiah. That each sacrifice played a pivotal role.

As she walked the snaking animal paths through the field, her mind wandered. The destruction and the hopefulness apparent in this field reminded her of the market. As she approached the guardrail, she paused to look back.

Recalling the creation of the fountain in the market, Alex thought to imagine another. She didn't know who to put on the top, so many friends deserved that honor, but none more than Abby. Yet, every time she started the process of picturing it in her mind, her thoughts were drawn to actual events. *I conjured a dragon!* She wondered how or if it thought or felt in the short moments of its life. It seemed so unfair for something of its like to live so short a life, and yet, Jeremiah had a point: What would she have done had it outlived the fight? What would a dragon do out in the world? She'd seen enough monster movies to imagine.

Jeremiah said it'd take time for things to reconcile. I wonder what that will be like.

She could picture the market on the Between with perfect clarity, the sandy boulevards between buildings of bubble and feather, all roads leading to the central square and the towering fountain with Lesedi at the top.

The late afternoon light streamed through the dust and pollen in the air, the beams dancing across the field. In the glare, the buildings and the fountain sparkled as the light inexplicably bounced off their surfaces; Alex's vision solidified. *Am I doing this?*

She turned away and when she looked back, the markets' solidity was final. She walked through the wide lane to the square. She approached the fountain, entranced at the way the burbling water glistened and sparkled, the sunlight making water appear as flame.

Alex splashed her hand into the pool. She marveled at the buildings, the way the early evening sun glinted off the shapes and materials in ways it never could when the sun was always high in the sky, imagined in place, on the Between. She walked around the fountain, looking up, until she faced Lesedi.

"You and Banhi and Khowla were always there for me," she said aloud. "You warned me what it would take." Lesedi couldn't answer, her arms extended, the multitudinous creatures crawling up the spire around her. "I didn't understand until it was too late," she looked away. "I always took it to mean other people, I never thought it meant those I cared about." She hated herself for her foolishness, her selfishness. Looking up again, she said to Lesedi, "When you told me you were gifting me joy, I didn't believe in fairy godmothers or wishes. I know I should be sad they're all gone. But I feel their love. It's so strong." She smiled and then the smile faded. "It's not fair that they're all gone and I'm the one who gets to live."

She thought of Billy, just before he leapt off Picnic Rock, telling her that people threw coins in the fountain to confuse Charon. Now that Charon had its coin, she wished for a piece of change to toss into the fountain. If she had one, she'd wish for one moment to share the experience with any of them. *What I wouldn't give to be here when they see it for the first time.*

"It's magnificent. Exactly like you described. I've never seen anything so beautiful."

Alex's breath locked in her lungs. It had to be an illusion. Perhaps through her desire she imagined, or it was a voice so similar her brain made her think it was someone she knew. She didn't want to turn around and spoil the illusion. And yet, in her heart, she felt the pull of her Familiar.

As she turned, Abby pulled her into a bear-hug and raised her from the ground, swaying her back and forth. As when their coins touched and Abby said her oath, Alex could feel Abby's love for her, an overwhelming beacon throbbing in her chest like a lighthouse she could see through the thickest fog.

Alex sobbed joyfully into Abby's shoulder. "I thought you were dead. I can't believe you survived. I thought you were gone."

Abby didn't say a word. Gradually, she released Alex. "It's happening all over the world," she nodded at the fountain. "Imagined places, dreamed locations, becoming part of the landscape."

Alex stared at her, trying to understand whether her imagination was being cruel or kind.

"Ow," Abby slapped her hand away, "why would you pinch me?"

Alex laughed through her tears, "I thought I was imagining you."

"And you'd imagine me in these ghastly shirts? I'm disappointed in you." Abby giggled as she draped her arm over Alex's shoulder. Alex could tell she was not resting her full weight. "It was horrible, Alex. We were being slaughtered. You told us to find somewhere safe." Abby leaned her head against Alex's shoulder, this time without restraint. "Last time we thought you died I told you I'd never doubt you again."

"You gave me your strength."

"I didn't have enough to give."

"But you survived. Abby, this time I doubted you!"

"You didn't," Abby said gravely. "I gave you everything I had. I died."

Alex took a deep breath. *Abby's confused.* Alex said so.

"It was like half-waking from a dream, Alex. You brought us in. Like being alive and dead. They were all there, inside you. I saw Carrie and Nancy and June. I think Lydia and Charissa, too. Women we saved from the Farm. Everyone."

"You saw them?"

"Like in a dream. It all faded. Everyone disappeared. And then all of a sudden, I'm not a part of you anymore. Not exactly." She pressed her hand against Alex's chest. "I was a part of you. And then I became a part of you," she gestured at the world surrounding them. "I found myself alone, sitting on a hillside, someplace I'd never been before, and that was it."

"What's it? How'd you find me?"

Abby shrugged. "I'm your *Familiar*. I felt you in my chest. I danced for joy because you were alive and I knew if you were alive, you'd won. I knew if you were alive, I'd find you."

Alex hugged Abby, dripping tears on her shoulder. "You died and you're alive. I can't believe you're really real."

"I'm different," Abby pointed at her coin. "It's just there. No thread." To demonstrate, she collected her fingers around it and attempted to pull it from her chest, but it slipped through her fingers. Alex knew the dead on the Between—like her mother—didn't have coins.

Alex tried the same with hers. She pulled them from her chest and her thread sparkled. Just to be sure, she pried apart the two halves. She returned them as they were.

"I still have magic," Abby said, "but it's much weaker." She demonstrated, her fingertips spurting a small fountain of sparks, like a birthday cake sparkler. "I used to shoot lightning."

Alex knew her magic hadn't weakened, but didn't want to test it if she didn't have to.

"You're still as powerful as ever. I can feel it when I'm close to you." Abby asked about her vision and Alex told her a partial truth, that she could see fine. "Those scars ever going to heal?"

"I'm kinda okay with them," Alex said, examining the intricate patterns running down her arms.

Abby offered a plaintive sigh. "This has been so nice. I never imagined I'd get to see you again. But, I don't want to wait until the end before I say goodbye."

Alex nearly burst into tears. "You just got here. Don't tell me you have somewhere to go."

"I died, Alex. It's only a matter of time before Charon claims my coin."

Abby's statement was like discovering a horrible day could end with a perfect evening. "I don't think Charon will be coming around," Alex told Abby.

"You scared the child that much?"

"I think I saved it. The child saved me, too. I think everything's changing." She looked up at the fountain again. "Like this…."

Abby looked up and just stared. She turned to the buildings and whistled. "So beautiful. If I really am staying, I can't wait to explore."

Alex felt her chest growing warm. All the hope she'd lost was returned, and then some. "You died, but you're alive. You're absolutely sure you saw everyone? So they could be here? They could all be alive, too?"

"Yes. I mean, I was there, in that liminal space, so I don't see why I'd be some special exception." Abby rubbed her arm. "How'd you do it, kiddo? Tell me your story."

Alex laughed.

"No offense, Alex, but you look like shit."

"None taken," Alex said, examining the bite mark Abby eyeballed with disgust.

What did that?

Alex asked, "Did you say something?"

"No offense… but you look like shit," Abby repeated slowly.

Alex rubbed her ear. "I thought I heard something." She thought she felt something, too. A shock of surprise tinged with fear of something unknown and unexpected. Something other than her.

"Is it your whispers?"

Alex told her they were gone.

"You probably need a good meal and some sleep."

Alex agreed.

"You hungry?"

Alex grinned. "I love that we both always think of food."

Abby grabbed her stomach, "A body like this can be yours, too. Little to no effort involved."

They both laughed.

Alex said, "I was heading to Heather's. There's probably a *little* food still in the house."

Abby's laughter stalled as anguish stepped in. "Heather was really brave." Abby looked down like she was taking a moment with her thoughts. "I'd suggest we go back to my place, but it was a total disaster, and that was before some nincompoop burned it down."

"Sorry about that," Alex said. She knew Abby was trying to make light, but she felt too much guilt to laugh.

"I'm sorry. I was hoping to make a joke. Anyway, back to hungry. I think Heather would like that we raid the fridge. She hated when food went to waste."

Did I do that? I did that, didn't I?

"What?" Alex asked.

"I said that Heather hated wasting food." She rolled her eyes. "I'm sorry if my jokes are too soon. I think Heather would prefer we laugh about her than cry."

"I agree," Alex answered. "Shall we?"

As they reached the guardrail, the first of several cars stopped, gently rolling on the grass and broken gravel. People got out, men, women, whole families. They spoke in hushed tones to one another about the bright explosion they saw from this direction, hearing things on the news, stories they saw online. Seeing the market across the field, as though drawn to it all this way. They wandered towards it with cautious reluctance, their mouths wide in wonder, their language twisted to gasps as they saw one bizarre, exotic, fanciful, building after another. Finally reaching the square and seeing the fountain, they all spoke their first coherent words, "I wonder who she was."

Women emerged from the buildings, at first alarmed at the interlopers. Many had been here before, but only in their dreams. Most emerged as surprised as the local visitors, unsure how they arrived half a world away when they had been in bed, asleep. They knew that appearances deceived them; this was no longer the market on the Between, as much as it appeared the same. Friends found one another, shaking hands and meeting in person for the first time, having never seen one another without a thread trailing off into the endless imagined distance. She considered joining the local tourists, who mulled about the market timidly and enthralled with excitement at the discoveries they made. The two groups spoke, their language barriers shattered.

It's like magic.

Alex pulled her ears, unsure if she was hearing ringing or whispers or voices. "It is magic," she half thought, half said.

"What?"

"Nothing," she told Abby.

Who's that? Is someone talking to me?

Alex grinned. It was just like Marta explained, the sensation of hundreds or thousands of little bubbles within hers, the vibrations of feeling and thought seeping through the otherwise impenetrable membrane, allowing her a glimpse of what was happening in someone else's universe. She heard them but she also felt them. She sensed them like a distant memory of a phantom limb, the same way she had hoped she might have teased her whispers apart and learned who each one was.

She sifted through the sensations. There were too many. But they were all there: Billions of them. People everywhere, suddenly aware of the universe and hearing it whisper.

This time she thought, *I returned magic, for everyone.*

There was a moment of silence in her head, followed by a flurry of voices. A barrage of questions and concerns. Alex welcomed the cacophony back. She'd missed it and it made her feel whole again. *In time*, she thought, *you'll all learn what happened.*

"You wanna go there?" Abby sniffed at the air. "I smell tandoori and curries." She wet her lips. "Want to see what they're making?"

Alex recalled her first trip to New York City and how she most wanted to pause and taste the foods being cooked in the small carts on the sidewalks. Part of her desire was an innate sense she wouldn't be returning. The idea appealed to her, but the people deserved to explore and discover it for themselves. If she walked among them, if only one person recognized her, then she'd become the center of fascination. She wanted to go home, to sit reverently and eat something Heather made and Abby reheated. She wanted time alone with Abby, her Familiar, her friend.

"We will have many opportunities to come back and explore," Alex said.

"Sure. Let's go to Heather's."

They passed more people as they started down the road. Cars caravanned down the street and people chatted on their cell phones, talking about the miracles. Alex listened as they walked past, hearing them talk about reports the valley was filled in, that there are other places appearing all around the world, and speculating if *that girl from the news the other day* had anything to do with it.

Yes, she did.

Abby punched her arm.

"Ow, why'd—"

"So you won't let it go to your head."

You brought the magic? That news story was true? Are you that girl? From New York? From Paris?

Yes.

They came to Heather's house. Heather's yellow car out front. It was almost like Heather was home. Alex paused. She couldn't go any further. Not yet. She closed her eyes and just pretended all was as it had been.

I knew it was true! I can't believe it. Do I really have magic?

Yes.

And you gave it to me?

Yes.

And you can teach me how to use it?

I can help. You and all the others.

Others?

I hear them, just like I hear you.

I'm not the only one? Will I meet you some day?

Perhaps.

"It's filled with good memories, Alex," Abby pointed to the old house. The temporary front doors were ripped to splinters and cast across the yard from when Jeremiah had come here. "Don't let him take that from you."

"He can't take anything from me. Not anymore."

"Then why are we waiting out here?"

"I'm taking a moment to miss them. All of them."

Abby wiped her eyes. "Me too."

Alex heard more voices now, whispers in her head. Instead of women she'd saved from Books, these were women who discovered their magic, magic she took back from the Library. Magic she returned to the world.

It gave her pause. George warned her. Jeremiah warned her. Could they be trusted with magic? Realizing the question could result in analytical paralysis, Alex decided that if Jeremiah warned against it, it might not be such a bad thing. Besides, the universe was speaking to her now, and she could understand every voice. *Am I the bright heart at its center now?*

"Before we go in," Abby said, "I just need to ask, you're *certain* he's gone?"

Alex nodded. "Saw him go."

Abby held her chest like her heart hurt, "Because if we're all coming back, I thought maybe he might, too."

"Nope," Alex said, "Not a chance."

Alex saw the damage Jeremiah wrought to the house. It was difficult to look at it and not think of Heather's suffering, not construct the chain of events leading from the shattered makeshift front door to the overturned couch, to the busted kitchen table. It was difficult not to see Heather doing her best to forestall the inevitable, the burn marks on the walls and the broken drywall.

Dolly crawled from beneath the couch. She meowed and arched her back for Alex and Abby to pet. Alex picked her up and cradled her in her arms. "You're a brave kitty." She said to Abby, "We'll go for Marty and Quest after we eat."

Abby grinned. She watched Alex holding Dolly, looking at the wreckage of the place she once called home.

"She did this for you," Abby whispered. "Because she loved you."

Alex thought for a moment. Rose said that wasn't really Heather. Alex had eaten her coin. The real Heather had been with her all along. But that *was* Heather, whatever was left of her, like all the others, using their last little bits to give Alex more strength, more time. She looked out the open door, half-expecting to see Heather coming up the steps, like Abby, but no one was there.

All Heather's memories were still inside her. Alex looked outside with wonder and no small hope that she might find her again one day.

Abby rummaged in the kitchen. "No small surprise, kiddo. We're in luck. Leftovers, galore." Abby reviewed the menu and together they chose a smorgasbord, some of this and some of that. One last meal made by her aunt.

As Abby reheated dinner, Alex turned on the television and listened to news reports that interrupted every channel, including those dedicated to news. There was footage from all over the world. Bizarre buildings appearing on city streets where alleys had been. People returning home when their families thought they had died decades ago. Whole swaths of land or lakes or oceans coming into existence, making maps obsolete as the world became infinitely larger. Wonderous stories of people suddenly understanding foreign tongues. Women described strange phenomena, their surprise that when their child fell, the cut vanished with their kiss. There was such joyful wonder. But there were some things that gave Alex pause, like sightings of distant storms drifting out to sea. Storms that looked like giant billowing sheets.

The people who yesterday adamantly belittled the possibility that the stale news reports of a flying girl were obvious fakes now agreed with the spiritualists and quacks that magic was real, somehow returned to the world. The reports always came back to footage of Alex in New York and Paris. They were calling her the First Witch: the first known sighting of magic.

The more Alex listened, the less concerned she became. Magic was finite. While held by only a few, each woman was powerful. Now, magic was spread across the world. Shared by so many, its strength was diluted. Yet Alex's power was undiminished. She always attributed her ability to the voices in her head, believing they were responsible for the magnitude of her magic, but those voices were gone, and her magic was as strong as ever. Was she now the source of all the magic in the world? Her thoughts returned to the reconciling world. *How long will it take? How else will the known world change?*

Who else is out there? Will I see my mom again? Does the door still work? Is the labyrinth still there? Do the doors still lead all over the world? If the Between is gone, what wonders are out there, waiting to be discovered? Lesedi was right to wish me joy.

Alex's mind was a cacophony of thoughts, her own and so many others. She wanted to answer them all, but that was impractical. Answers for them would come in time. Her fairy godmothers showed her how to control the voices in her head, and she subdued them for now.

Refreshing Heather's leftovers, Abby over-seasoned one. The heat made Alex's lips burn, albeit pleasantly. The sting reminded her of Carrie and their kiss. She put her fork down to touch her lips, unsure she wanted the burning to subside.

She closed her eyes and thought about Carrie. Like the glow of a burning ember on a dark night, she found her. Her hands trembled. She concentrated on Colette. Then on George. Each time she found them. She was afraid if she kept trying, she'd be unable to find someone. That she'd know they hadn't come back. But not knowing was worse than foolish hope. She thought of Rose. Of Heather. Of Billy.

"Let's get up early tomorrow," Alex excitedly said to Abby.

"What do you have in mind?"

Alex gestured at the now black television screen. "They're out there." Her chest swelled with hope and expectation. Alex felt like she was a helium balloon, free and aloft in a friendly breeze. Suddenly anything was possible, anything she could imagine. "Tomorrow, we'll start our search. We'll find them all and bring my Coven home."

Abby smiled. "That sounds like a great plan."

Alex grinned. "I thought you'd like it."

The end

Independent and small press authors need your support.
If you enjoyed this book, please leave a review: https://amzn.to/3q9Wl54

Acknowledgements

The first people I must thank are my readers. I believe a book isn't finished until it is read. Writers may create worlds with words, but readers possess the magic to bringing those worlds alive. Thank you for bringing The Books of Alexandrea to life. You've reached the end of Alex's story. Thank you for having the faith in me to take this journey. I hope it was enjoyable and satisfying. I am eager for your magic to breathe life into my next adventures.

There are many steps that go into making a book, and a writer cannot take them all alone. I am grateful for the comradery and assistance I have had along the way.

My alpha and beta readers: your feedback helped me refine this into the best story I could. The established trust we share allows a level of honesty about my work that I crave, and I appreciate all that you have done for me. My Book Club Beta's: Nicole DiGiose, Tiffany Wesley, Peter Aperlo, Jackie Gallo, Joseph Morris, and of course, Laura, the alpha of alpha readers.

My editor: Julie Perry. Working with you is a joy and a pleasure. I am grateful we are able to work together. I look forward to the time we will spend on future projects.

I used to dream about hosting a book launch. Sparkling Pointe, Peconic Bay, Jamesport. Mike, Evan, Brianna. Thank you all for making reality surpass that fantasy.

My friends and family: I am fortunate to have such a tight group of friends. Your enthusiasm, your excitement, your support means the world to me. You've been to my launches and signing, you've asked about the book, you've been there for me. I can only hope I am thought of with the same fondness with which I hold each of you. I know I can't include everyone. So many of you ask after the books every time we're together at events. This thanks is for you, too. In no particular order: Mike, Tom, Gina, Jackie, Rich, Susan, John, Chris, Laura, Brewster, Gaurav, Leila, Jess, Joe, Jodi, Michael, Leah, Darrin, Melanie, Anita, Albert, Gary, Mom, Marcy, Dad. Apologies for anyone I missed.

One final, special thanks to CJ and Coco, for their inspiration. Before you there was Nicodeamus, Chaos, and Ebony. I'm told you're cats and can't read, but I don't believe a word of it. Thank you for always sitting on my books and trying to make magic.

On Wednesday, June 13th, 2018, I created the document that was supposed to be the single novel entitled, "The Books of Alexandrea". Five years, thirty drafts, half-a-million words, and three books later, Alex's story was finally finished on Friday, August 4th, 2023.

Coming in 2024: Shadows at Dawn

About the Author

JH Nadler

"The Library" is Jason's third novel, completing "The Books of Alexandrea" trilogy.

He lives on the North Fork of Long Island with his wife and two cats, CJ and Coco. When he's not writing, he can often be found at the fantastic North Fork wineries.

Join the Book Club and learn about new releases and upcoming events at jhnadler.com